With Faith and Fury

With Faith and Fury

a novel

by Delos Banning McKown

Prometheus Books

Buffalo, New York

Published 1985 by
Prometheus Books
700 East Amherst Street, Buffalo, New York 14215

Printed in the United States of America

Library of Congress Catalog Card No. 84-43180
ISBN 0-87975-280-7

Chapter One

If the truth were known, the old Nash must have driven itself home that summer night when Manly John Plumwell returned from the Pilsudski County Free Fair. Had he been asked for any details of his homeward journey, he could have supplied none, so deep was his absorption in the singular events of that wondrous night. Even after he had safely parked the car in the barn adjoining his grandmother's house, he was still so giddy he nearly lost his balance slamming the car door behind him. Utterly preoccupied, and unaware of the circular spot by the zipper on his jeans, he climbed the steps to his grandmother's back porch and found himself a moment later staring stupidly at her kitchen door, not having had the presence of mind to take the key from his pocket. Once inside the house, by whatever miracle of behavior habit made possible, Manly tiptoed to his grandmother's door to assure her, if she were still awake, that it was he who had come stealthily down the hallway and not some prowler bent on doing her harm. But she was already asleep, though not peacefully, judging by the anxious moan and the restless stirrings that Manly did not hear, as he made his way to his own room farther down the hall.

Manly probably did whatever he normally did about getting ready for bed, but who knows? Certainly *he* did not and does not. His consuming desire just then was to throw himself on the bed in the hope of reliving again and again those stupendous experiences whose memory he had savored—no, devoured—all the way home. "Dear God," he said fervently, "if there was ever a time for total recall, this is it!" Thus, flat on his back and stretched out straight down the middle of his bed (a testimony to how keyed-up he still was), Manly made ready to see it all, to hear it all, and to feel it all once again.

"Land o' Goshen!" his grandmother had said as he stepped into the kitchen late in the preceding afternoon, "you goin' to the fair in them duds?" That was not an idle question, nor was the quizzical look she turned upon him merely something to do with her face, for in those days and in their hometown of Nickel Plate, he was known by one and all as a spiffy dresser, especially when the occasion was as momentous as the Pilsudski County Free Fair. But there he stood, out of character, in his work shoes, wearing a pair of faded jeans and a nondescript sport shirt open at the collar. "Well," he said, hoping that his face was straight enough to fool her, "I decided to wear these old things, because I expect I'll spend most of my time in the barns looking at the animals, and I sure got messed up last year, if you'll remember." Since that explanation satisfied the old lady, she dismissed him with the reminder that he was to start home no later than 11:00 P.M., fireworks display or no fireworks display. With those words for children ringing in his grown-up ears, Manly bounded lightly out of the kitchen and down the back steps toward the car, his grandmother returning to the sink to scour the spider.

Manly tempered his exuberance by driving out of the yard ever so sedately. His grandmother, whom he called Ma, was given to shuffling around the house talking to herself. As likely as not, she had left the sink and was at that very moment watching him turn out of the driveway onto Rumsey Road—and commenting aloud on every detail of his departure.

Once over the hill to the north of the house, Manly began to talk aloud to himself. "Everything has worked out just right so far, just couldn't be better," he exulted. He was sure he had allayed his grandmother's mild suspicions, because at the fair the previous year he really had been splattered with watery cow manure. But that wasn't the reason he was wearing old clothes; the real reason was to remain as inconspicuous as possible. To guard further against being noticed, to say nothing of being recognized, he planned to wear dark glasses, something he had seldom done before, and to part his hair differently, something he had never done before, willingly at least. Best of all, Ma had decided not to visit the fair that year.

Previously she had always tagged along, putting the kibosh on his freedom at the fair by her mere presence if not by her direct superintendence of his every act. That year (Praise the Lord!) she was beginning to feel her seventy-six years. She had in fact felt poorly of late, was much too fleshy as she liked to put it, and was given to recurring attacks of the only two ailments she had ever admitted to having, gas and nerves. When attacked by those two banes of her declining years, she would simply bear the discomforts stoically. She had never taken aspirin, no matter what, for fear of becoming a drug addict (something she feared almost as much as alcohol) and was not about to take anything stronger. Moreover, she avoided doctors like the plague. One could hardly submit to their ministrations and retain one's modesty. So, Marynell Plumwell, Manly's grandmother and surrogate mother, remained behind, moping more than a little, while he drove off to the unannounced adventures that her absence had suddenly made possible.

Free at last of a great moral restraint, Manly could simply not contain himself. As he turned off Rumsey Road onto the state highway leading west to Pilsudski, he whistled merrily, slapped one thigh again and again, and, finally, sang a certain obscene song, something he had never ever done

2

before. Oh, he had heard it plenty of times, had rehearsed the words in his head, and knew them as well as his name, but until that very moment he had not actually sung that dirty ditty out loud. In a little child's sing-song fashion the forbidden words came tumbling out:

> Roly-poly
> Finger my holey
> Feel of my slimey slew.
> Rub your nuts
> Across my guts,
> I'm one of the whorey crew.

Thus began a young rake's progress.

Manly had been right about Ma. Even before he had started the car, she had left the spider to soak a little longer and had shuffled to her bedroom window to watch him leave. Her failure to visit the fair had certainly not decreed that he should go alone. She would have been a "whole lot more satisfied," as she had said, if he had offered to take a couple of nice boys along for company. He needed more friends than he had. She had lectured him repeatedly on that and had clinched the point by remarking on how her own revered grandmother used to express the same view of various loners, and in no uncertain terms. Marynell had made this point in private on many occasions, too, when she had thought that Manly was off and gone. Over and again, she would say aloud to herself, "Manly's kind of funny, a good boy I know, but kind of funny; what he needs is to be more sociable."

Also, there were several deserving boys, the grandchildren of friends, who would have given their eyeteeth to get a ride to the fair with Manly, and possibly, just possibly, there might have been some really nice deserving girls as well. It was getting time for him to start thinking about them too, and it was certainly time that he stopped being so aloof. He walled himself off too much to suit Marynell Plumwell. She began to fear that he might turn out to be an "old bach," as she called bachelors. It wasn't that she favored all aspects of marriage—in fact she felt deep distaste for its carnal aspects—but old baches were looked on with some suspicion in her day as being a little undependable, "if you know what I mean," she would say to herself. Furthermore, a lot of old baches did not keep themselves up and got "kind of nasty." "An old fogy like me ain't going to live forever to look after that boy," she would add.

The fair-bound Manly, however, would never have dreamed at that point of asking a girl to go anywhere with him, or, to put it more accurately, he would only have dreamed of asking a girl. He certainly could never have come right out and asked a real girl to make an actual trip with him, and as for boys, nice or not, well, he didn't want any boys along for fear they would "leech onto him" once they were at the fair and would then be able to tattle on him. Manly had planned to do certain unprecedented things for him, things that a young rake might do, things that absolutely had to be kept from Ma. To accomplish his bold mission, privacy was essential. Since all the pieces were falling into place, is it any wonder that he smiled, laughed, whistled, slapped his thigh, tapped his unoccupied foot, and sang an obscene song while driving out of Nickel Plate?

The young rake's progress was not smooth, however, nor did it turn out to be altogether enjoyable. Anybody who could have gotten within gunshot of Manly that afternoon would probably have noticed how jerky his journey was. For the first five miles or so the old Nash purred along smoothly through rolling farmland and apple orchards. Then the car slowed perceptibly and began to weave. Close observation would have revealed that Manly was groping for something under the driver's side of the front seat. Alternating each hand between the steering wheel and the floor beneath the seat, he seemed to be straining to reach some elusive object. After a mile of erratic progress, the car abruptly turned off the highway onto a gravel-mouthed farm road. An exasperated Manly flung open the door, jumped out of the car, thrust his hand under the front seat from the outside, and seized a small, dark, tubular object. One within earshot would have heard him say, "Come here, goddam you," as he grasped whatever it was.

The "goddamn" was an expletive the full benefits of which he had discovered only recently and enjoyed rolling off his tongue when nobody could hear him say it. With the elusive object safely in hand, he slid back into the driver's seat, fiddled around for a minute or two, and then sent the car lurching forward onto the highway, leaving a spray of gravel and a cloud of dust to mark his departure. Thus began the third segment of his journey, a segment during which wisps of smoke could be seen streaming through the left front window.

The object of Manly's search and the source of the smoke were one and the same, a large cigar that he had acquired unexpectedly and had hidden under the front seat for smoking at that very time, should his grandmother remain at home. It might hardly seem noteworthy that a boy of eighteen should smoke a cigar, but for Manly it was an event. Everything in his life was fraught with significance, and nothing was easy. In fact, he had borne, and was still bearing, so many of the world's burdens that he looked a full two years older than he really was.

At the tender age of two and a half or thereabouts, he took to noticing where his grandfather was likely to discard cigar butts. No sooner had the old man crushed one out in an ashtray and turned his back than Manly would, surreptitiously, stuff it in his mouth and begin to suck air as best he could through the masticated end in order to savor the taste of burned-out tobacco. Nobody knows why or when he gave up that practice. He doesn't know, nor does he recall ever being caught at it or punished for it. Nevertheless, he quit and in quitting made a virtue of it, becoming insufferably self-righteous.

As a child of nine or ten he would scowl in the presence of cigar smokers, pinch his long nose in evident disgust, fan the smoke away furiously, and stare censoriously at the oblivious offenders. His grandmother took all this as evidence of the high moral integrity and spiritual purity that, to hear her tell it, had always characterized her maternal ancestors, particularly her sainted grandmother. Herbert Plumwell, Manly's grandfather, had other ideas about the young moralist in the family, fearing that he was raising a sissy and a prig. But he wisely kept those views to himself.

Manly's purity in relation to tobacco gained so much applause from his grandmother, from other nice ladies, and from God (as was supposed) that he became a paragon of virtue, an achievement he relished for a time at least. "There goes that Manly Plumwell," mothers would say to their chastened and resentful sons. "He is such a nice boy; why can't you be more like him?" they would ask. Everyone knows, of course, that paragons are watched not only for purposes of applause and emulation but also for reasons of envy and spite. Perhaps that was why Manly always had the feeling that he was being watched, that he must always posture and pose, even before total strangers, as befitted one of his reputed goodness. Perhaps that was why he preferred his own company.

Though Manly had long enjoyed the role of public paragon of juvenile virtue, privately he found his rectitude increasingly burdensome. Despite his shining image, both sartorially and spiritually, the inner Manly was becoming increasingly corrupt. For some inexplicable reason, his taste buds had begun to crave the flavor of burned-out tobacco again, and a spirit of iniquity had recently been enticing him, or, better yet, driving him to sample alcohol at the earliest opportunity. Worst of all, perhaps, impure thoughts had been monopolizing his conscious hours progressively and were driving him to indulge in the secret vice with alarming abandon.

As if the chemical machinations of his maturing body were not enough, Manly had, two years earlier, come upon external stimuli so alluring that he could not free his mind of them. Quite innocently he had come upon the centerfold of an old *Esquire* magazine. There before his startled eyes appeared a ravishing girl, as naked as a jaybird, displaying her charms for "every rogue to see" as the caption had it. Manly had never thought of himself as a rogue, but see he did, caressing every bulge and curve and indentation with his eyes. That singular picture gave so much form and substance to his fantasies that they were never again the same.

Glorious though the image was, a time came when Manly felt the need for more than icons, the need to cast his eyes beyond the two-dimensional, to behold life in the round, as it were. That posed a problem, because he had had nothing to do with girls; yet it was they who possessed just those features that he yearned most desperately to see and perchance one day to feel, to fondle, and to probe. Reeling under the temptations of tobacco, alcohol, and sex, his fertile mind, its vaunted virtue fading fast, devised a plan that had been suggested to him by his visit to the fair the previous year.

The smoke that billowed and swirled from the old Nash as it bore down on Pilsudski was eloquent testimony to the fact that he had embarked boldly upon one aspect, at least, of his plan, but that aspect was not an unqualified success. Manly's previous experience with tobacco had been limited to discarded cigar butts, more or less soggy on one end and burned-out on the other. Such experiences failed to prepare him for his first encounter with a fresh cigar, dry at one end and alight at the other. Thus, when he took his first drag, his mouth was assaulted by hot smoke. It bit his tongue, pinched his nose, took his breath away, and watered his eyes. Moreover, his ineptitude caused him to dump hot ashes on his pants and on the car seat beneath his crotch. As if that were not enough, he also began to feel light-headed.

So, Manly decided to extinguish the cigar, the quicker to taste the burned-out flavor of tobacco, but the cigar stoutly resisted being put out. For the second time that day, in what might be thought of as the fourth segment of his westward journey, the Nash could have been seen slowing down and weaving slightly. Close inspection would have shown Manly screwing his cigar into the dashboard ashtray. For what seemed to him an eon, the wretched thing continued to blaze, despite his best efforts, emitting smoke first from one side and then from the other, and all the while filling the car with acrid fumes. In the end, Manly prevailed over the "goddamned thing," and it lay dead and cooling in the ashtray. Reminding himself that he must empty the ashtray before returning home, he said aloud, "All hell would break loose if Ma found ashes in that damned ashtray and traced them to me." He was right.

On the road once again, Manly retrieved his cigar and drew repeatedly on its cold remains, oscillating his tongue from side to side and up and down and rolling the cigar around and around in his mouth, sucking every atom of flavor from its charred end. Occupied thusly, he drove without incident for nearly ten miles, completing the fifth and final segment of his trip to Pilsudski. When the cigar lost the last of its flavor, he carefully replaced it in the ashtray, because it had a potentially important role to play in initiating phase two of his plan, a phase that was to occur in Pilsudski, close to the fairgrounds, if all went well.

Tense with excitement, Manly drove straight through Pilsudski, rarely looking right or left, until he reached the vicinity of the fairgrounds. Once there he drove straight to a shoddy liquor store he had remembered seeing. Parking the car out of sight, he braced himself for the ordeal ahead. Whatever his new-found sins, he was not yet brazen; but that very characteristic might be needed if he were to buy a bottle of beer successfully, thus effecting the next phase of his progress as a rake.

Silently rehearsing his lines and trying to foresee various contingencies, Manly put on his colored glasses, even though the sun was already dipping below the tops of the tallest trees to the west; shoved the cold cigar into the left side of his mouth, where it seemed to fit best; and strode into the liquor store with what he hoped was disdain. His strategy was to act enough like a veteran drinker to forestall any question as to whether or not he was old enough to buy beer.

After rummaging around in a cooler for what seemed an age, all the time trying to assess his performance, he dredged up a bottle of something called Czerney's Bohemian Beer. Taking it to the clerk behind the cash register, Manly said in a tone both dubious and critical, just as though he were an important taster come to sample the local brew, "I believe I'll try this product today; I don't believe I ever have before." Had he been questioned about his age, he would have turned tail and fled without a squeak. As it was, the character on duty sold him the beer without a glance and with only a grunt.

Manly was enormously relieved at having succeeded but really peeved that his efforts at deception had been lost on that sub-cerebral creature. He had, after all, gone to considerable trouble and would have liked some applause for his performance in the form of a sceptical look at least. He had not shaved closely that morning so as to darken his four-o'clock shadow, making him look older, and had effected disdain rather well he thought; but not once had the clod at the cash register paid him the slightest attention, let alone challenged him.

Manly locked his beer in the trunk lest a parking lot attendant or cop on the prowl might see it and deprive him of it on some pretext or other. That done, he drove off. Moments later the old Nash crept, bumper to bumper, through the great gaudy gates of the Pilsudski County Free Fair, so-called because no admission was charged for parking. After driving all the way to what he told himself was "hell and gone" beyond the midway, Manly was finally flagged into an empty space by a feisty attendant. It was 6:45 P.M. The first order of business was food to go with his rapidly warming beer. A quarter of a mile away at a concession stand, he bought an immense bag of overly salty potato chips and two long inferior hot dogs smothered with mustard and horseradish. Five minutes later, he dug the beer out of the trunk and crawled into the back seat to enjoy his licit food and illicit drink.

If Manly's infantile encounters with burned-out cigar butts had prepared him poorly for his first drag on a freshly lighted cigar, imagine how much more poorly his complete innocence of alcohol had prepared him for his first drink of warm beer. Good Lord! he thought, wondering whether to spit or swallow, Ma was right; this stuff tastes like swill with liquid soap slopped in. Impetuously, he began to pour the vile stuff on the ground, then thought better of it, realizing that he would need something to drink with his meal.

For the next few minutes, a chance passerby, interested in young rakes, might have seen a string bean of a boy engaged in what looked like a high-speed ritual. First a bite of cheap spicy hot dog, swimming in mustard and horseradish, then a quick sip of beer, then a grimace, then a mumbled oath, then a mouthful of super-salty potato chips, then a quick sip of beer, then a really bad face, and, finally, something said that was better left unsaid.

Finished in short order with his repulsive meal, Manly stepped out of the car disgruntled. His first angry act was to fling the beer bottle to the ground. Then, wadding up the waste paper he had accumulated, he threw it down with all his might and ground it under his heel. Still feeling truculent, he stamped off toward the fairgrounds. Thus ended another phase of the rake's progress, no part of which had been thoroughly satisfying. But better things were to come, so much better that for a while he counted part of that night as the happiest time of his life.

A charade in three acts began when Manly set foot on the fairgrounds. The first act consisted in visiting several livestock barns, the second in appearing at the automobile pavilion, the third in taking one of the wilder rides along the midway. Manly wanted to be seen of men, as it were, but not to meet anybody, above all not to encounter any old buddy who would invite himself to tag along. Should any of his doings that night get back to Nickel Plate, he wanted it to be something like, "Hey, Manly, we seen you droolin' over them new cars," or "Whadja think of that Super Cat O' Nine Tails?" That kind of report would help keep his deceit from Ma.

Manly did not visit the livestock barns simply to posture and pose, although he did plenty of that. He really wanted to see some animals. So, braving the nose-puckering odors of mingled manure and human sweat, he plunged into the throngs of people milling around and immersed himself in the pandemonium of their happy banalities. Although he glanced around furtively and frequently to see if he were being watched, he spent the better part of half an hour looking fairly intently at various animals. He gazed with renewed amazement at the huge Clydesdales and with a vestige of awe at the sweeping horns of the Ayrshire bulls. He peered affectionately into the soulful eyes of some Jersey heifers, chuckled at the curiosity of a Nubian nanny goat, poked his fingers into the deep fleece of a Hampshire ram, and slapped the rump of a grossly fat Chester White sow, raising a cloud of dust and chaff.

Next, he picked his way along the northern perimeter of the fairgrounds until he reached the automobile pavilion, which was situated close to the main gates where cars were still arriving in droves, their horns blaring, their occupants whooping it up in antiphonal response to the midway's din.

The new cars were a cross for Manly to bear. Everything that was male about him, everything addictable to power and speed, magnetized him to the Cadillacs, Lincolns, Chryslers, Buicks, and Packards. But everything that was loyal about him, everything that smacked of the devotee, drew him to the Nashes, especially to the Ambassadors, which were certainly a cut above the cheapest, weakest, and slowest Nashes his grandfather always owned.

Manly lived in Ford and GM country; yet, throughout his whole life and for years before, his grandfather had driven nothing but Nashes and was usually the only soul for miles around to own one. "They make a right good machine," the parsimonious old codger would say, extolling their good gas mileage and other virtues. When, at the tender age of fourteen, Manly learned how to drive, some of the other boys, rowdies in his eyes, dared and double-dared him to race them, but he always declined (on some principle or other, of course), and, so, they teased him for having to drive a turtle and taunted him, saying, "Nashes have sewin' machine motors in 'em." One smart-alec asked him repeatedly, "Where are the pedals you push to make that dumb thing go?" Smarting under their taunts, yet feeding on every word of praise his grandfather lavished on the people who made the "right good machines," Manly became defensive about Nashes, a champion on their behalf. Still and all, as he postured and posed in the pavilion, he knew the seductions of power, speed, size, and opulence.

Wearied in short order by his ambivalence, Manly turned away from the ravishing new cars and left the pavilion, having duly put in his appearance for any prying eye. Up to that point he had not penetrated the vitals of the great Pilsudski County Free Fair but had merely knocked around its periphery. At last he was moving straight into its maw, surrounded by thousands of fellow fairgoers, yet alone, and becoming nearly as anxious as he was eager for what lay ahead.

As darkness fell, the midway became a place where light and sound were strangely one. The screams of girls plummeting earthward on heart-stopping rides pierced the night. So too did the million-candlepower searchlights that advertised the fair to people far and wide. A mighty din seemed to well up from the earth, as palpable as a mushroom, against the silence of newly fallen night, and the myriad dots and rays of colored lights from unnumbered rides, side shows, and concession stands blossomed dustily against the dark. For every watt of garish light there was a decibel of raucous sound. For every sight bathed in lurid light there was a cacophony of con men hawking their wares. Moreover, for every quantum of light and every wave of sound there was a particle of scent emanating from cheap perfume trailed by poor women and girls, plus the scent of manure wafted from nearby animal rides, plus the smell of sweaty bodies, tightly packed, plus the odors of food and drink and candy, of things being eaten, being dropped, being smeared on clothes. With his senses under heavy assault, but excited by it all, Manly marched up to a new and fearsome ride he had heard about. He would try it, would let himself be seen, before moving unseen, he hoped, to his ultimate objective.

The Super Cat O' Nine Tails was more than Manly had bargained on. Alternately and repeatedly, it flipped him upside down and spinned him around and around with awesome force. Moreover, it kept changing his altitude abruptly, precipitately, in a sickening way. As if that were not enough, and in spite of the safety bar that was supposed to lock him in place, the several simultaneous motions of the confounded contraption sent him careening from side to side and from top to bottom of the metal capsule in which he rode alone. When the malevolent monster finally came to rest, it was a shaken and slightly bruised Manly who staggered out with blood drained from his head and his stomach churning. Though he did not stagger for long, he could not forestall a belch that burned his gullet. Along with the uncouth noise, to which nobody took offense, there came the vile taste of partly digested beer to which Manly most definitely did take offense. Hoping

9

to settle his stomach and sweeten his mouth, he made a beeline to a nearby concession stand where he bought a bottle of ginger ale. While sipping his drink, he began to look for a men's room where he could relieve himself and from which he would emerge a new man in appearance, or so he hoped.

It was not Manly Plumwell the spiffy dresser who stepped out of the men's room; it was just an ordinary unknown farm boy in old duds. It was not a person of spit and polish and well-combed hair who emerged; indeed not, it was a fluffy-headed young lout, not worthy of any particular attention. It was certainly not the moral paragon of Nickel Plate's young who strode down the midway; it was, rather, a hot-blooded young rake who marched purposively down its sawdust trail looking for a certain sensuous entertainment he had yearned for a year to behold.

If an acquaintance were to penetrate his disguise, Manly was prepared to be preoccupied, to hear no greeting because of the din, to look over the offender's head, to rush off toward some object of intense interest, to lose himself in a gaggle of fairgoers. He had even toyed with the idea of putting on his dark glasses (the midway was, after all, plenty light), but it would have made him look a fool, something he could never do to himself knowingly.

Because he had a reputation for being able to wall himself off from others, he felt reasonably confident that he could elude any acquaintances using his various ploys. No one who knew him would really have been surprised to have met him only to have him march right by a proffered hand, unseeing and unhearing. Made redoubtable by his reputation and indiscernible (he hoped) by his disguise, Manly marched straight to the tempting titillating object of his intentions. The object of those intentions, and of a year's yearning and scheming, was a large gaudy tent that housed what the men and boys at that time and place used to call a burleque show. Rumor was already rampant that it was no ordinary show that year, but was a real humdinger. It was called "Schweitzer's *New* Bourbon Street Revue," and it went a whole lot farther than the law had previously allowed, or so said everybody who knew anything about such matters. The proprietor, Mr. Emil Schweitzer, taking advantage of the new permissiveness following World War II, decided to export to the rest of the country a good deal more of the real Bourbon Street than he had ever dared to do before. Elsewhere in America the success of his bold new show had been instantaneous and overwhelming. Pilsudski County was to prove to be no exception.

When Manly had come to the fair the preceding year, his grandmother had kept him on a very tight leash. She had led him straight to the home and garden pavilion where he fumed in silence among prize winning preserves and blue-ribboned flowers. Actually, he had ample cause for resentment, since he was the only boy in the pavilion past puberty and was imprisoned there for nearly an hour. Whatever his grandmother's reasons may have been for his servitude, it seemed to him as though she were using him to win the grand prize for the strongest apron strings. Unmoved by her tyranny and only half-conscious of his increasing rage, she finally turned to him in her own good time and said, "I expect you'd like to go off by yourself and see the livestock and motor cars."

"Yes," he snarled, "if you think you can look at these fruits and vegetables without me."

Ignoring the sarcasm, she went on, "Now, Manly, I don't want you on any of them dangerous rides like the roller coaster and such as that. You know the ones I think are all right for you, don't you?"

"Yes," he seethed between clenched teeth, "the merry-go-round and the kiddie kars and the . . ."

But she shut him up with the reminder that he was to be back in about an hour and a half. "I don't want to have to worry none about you," she said.

With her admonition about safe rides clanging loudest in his ears, he stalked off clenching and unclenching his fists and cursing fiercely to himself.

After visiting the automobile pavilion and the livestock barns where, as it turned out, he was conveniently splattered with manure, he began to feel better. By the time he had smashed his electric car broadside into as many other cars as possible, he felt almost as good as new.

It was while riding the Ferris wheel that Manly was tempted to do something not explicitly covered by his grandmother's injunctions for the day, but something that would have taken priority even over dangerous rides had she dreamed he would consider so shameful a thing. The source of his temptation made part of his anatomy rise and swell even as he was borne aloft. In the melee below and some 200 feet off to the left stood a tent on the sides of which were huge placards in full color of lusciously busty young women, nearly naked and anything but demure. It was the tent housing the Bourbon Street Revue. The barkers who announced its delights said that it was a sensation in more ways than one. Profoundly aware of one of its sensations, at least, Manly would have scrambled off the Ferris wheel that very moment, had it been possible.

The moral paragon of Nickel Plate knew in an abstract way that there were such things as striptease shows, but around home he could not let on that he had even heard the term *burleque show,* let alone show any interest. Previously, when he had attended the fair, he had not dared to acknowledge their presence and had glimpsed them only out of the corners of his eyes as he marched down the midway, intent on going elsewhere to all appearances. Moreover, he had to pretend that he had never heard the siren song of the barkers, that no hint of sensuality had ever tickled his ears. In fact, whenever sensuality was at issue, Manly had to play the deaf-mute.

As he circled up and down and around and around, he could not visualize himself actually standing in front of a burleque show ogling the girls who were brought out to entice customers nor daring to concentrate on what the barkers had to say about the delights inside the tent when the girls showed their stuff. But from the top of the Ferris wheel he had noticed something that cried out for further investigation.

11

The burleque tent was oblong. He could see part of what looked like a circus wagon standing at right angles to the back of the tent. Undoubtedly it was a dressing room for the girls in the show. Somehow or other they would have to move to and fro between the wagon and the stage inside the tent. "I just wonder," Manly murmured to himself, "if perchance they could be seen coming and going?" With uncommon daring he resolved to find out.

Trying to look nonchalant and posing as a young man who entertained only the most elevated thoughts, he sidled unseen, or at least unstopped, behind a canvas flap that linked the Revue tent to the one housing freaks to its left. Hidden from the midway, he stepped gingerly past tent pegs and ropes, around guy wires, and over heavy power lines coiled ominously on the ground. He was right in thinking that the circus wagon served as a dressing room and that there would be a way for the strippers to move from it to the stage and back again. A wooden ramp beginning at what looked like double doors in the side of the wagon extended for about six feet out from it and then disappeared past a flap into the back of the tent. The trouble was that canvas blinds shielded the girls on both sides as they moved to and fro. But if the ramp was not made of solid planking, if there were gaps between the floorboards, or cracks in them, perhaps, just perhaps, he could lie flat on his back on the ground under the ramp and see a dandy show overhead.

"Hey, you fuckin' little prick, you," said an unseen voice, "get the hell outa here or I'll knock the shit out of ya."

Manly fled, careening into guy wires and stumbling headlong over tent pegs.

A full fifteen minutes before he was due back at the home and garden pavilion, a chastened young man, trying hard not to limp, rejoined his grandmother. "Let's go home, Ma," he said, "that is, if you're ready." Surprised at seeing him so soon, and in such a decent mood too, but pleased that he had come, she turned her back on him and said softly, "Manly is such a good boy." How little the old lady knew of the plans he was already nurturing for the fair the following year!

"Things are sure different this year," he told himself with satisfaction as he stood bravely before the *New* Bourbon Street Revue, and they were. For one thing he did not have to fret over bluffing his way into the girlie show, because he had come of age for that. He was bolder, too, in spite of his need for a disguise, so much bolder that he had even been prepared to break away from his grandmother and go to the fair on his own, "no matter what," or so he had told himself. It was, of course, fortunate that in addition to being under the weather she had not objected to his attending the fair alone, because if he had come right out and told her that he was going whether she liked it or not, there would have been an awful row. Moreover, her suspicions would have been aroused, and she would have tried to find out what in tarnation had gotten him so "het up," as she would have put it.

Often he had felt like saying, "What's it to you, Ma, what I do anyway?" but though he might have said it, he was not yet quite ready to act on it.

Perhaps the old lady had finally accepted the idea that he was old enough to do a few things on his own. After all, he was eighteen and was about to be a senior in high school. In any case, she hadn't made a fuss when he had driven off and, wonder of wonders! hadn't even cautioned him against dangerous rides. That happy turn of events had left Manly's psychological reserves intact and had heartened him to face whatever perils of shame and disgrace might be involved in his unprecedented attendance at a burleque show.

As he stood gazing lustfully at the gaudy pictures of Mr. Schweitzer's luscious wares and listening to the barker exhort people to take moral responsibility into their own hands and be their own judges as to whether or not the show was immoral, he rehearsed his plan of action. It was, after all, not simply a matter of buying a ticket and walking in when the next show began. Nothing was that simple for Manly. He wanted a seat squarely in the middle of the front row, first, because he would abide nothing between him and what he had come to see, and, second, because he wanted nobody in front of him who might turn around and penetrate his disguise. Furthermore, when the performance was over he wanted to be among the first to leave if there was a side exit near the front of the tent, or, failing that, to follow the bulk of the patrons out the way they had all come in.

Satisfied with his plan, Manly joined a knot of hot-eyed men, some with their wives or girl friends, waiting to buy tickets. Although he had expected no trouble doing that, and experienced none, he breathed an audible sigh of relief when he pocketed his ticket. Then he took his place uneasily in the line awaiting the beginning of the next performance. The wait was a short one, for in just a few moments, 200 or more enthusiastic patrons came streaming out exulting in what they had seen. Within ten minutes, Manly's group began to funnel into the tent. When he came to the ticket taker, he held back and said repeatedly to those coming up from behind, "Go on ahead, I'm waiting for someone farther back." Thus he remained at the front of the line without going in. Finally, when the tent could hold no more, a chain was stretched across the entrance, and Manly settled in for a twenty-five-minute wait.

During that time he became excruciatingly tired, because he stood stiff with tension throughout. Not once did he relax; not once did he turn his head; not once did he engage in the small talk that makes time fly. If the ticket taker had not been absorbed in doing her nails and chewing her gum, she might have thought Manly was doing eye exercises, for there he stood, straight as a ramrod, swinging his eyes from left to right and right to left. He was not, of course, exercising his eyes the better to see the stripping girls but was, rather, surveying those about him as best he could for potential spies and tattlers. As far as he could tell, he had not been discovered, yet at least.

In addition to the physical and emotional stress he felt, standing at the head of a lengthening line of lustful males bent on ogling nearly naked women, Manly was increasingly irritated by the constant harangue of the barkers who challenged all comers on the midway to come, to see, and to judge for themselves whether or not the Revue was immoral, as some of Pilsudski's preachers had said. His only support during the eternity he waited came from within the tent. Above the raucous, saucy music he heard periodic whoops, yells, whistles, and foot-stampings that fired his imagination; and on more than one occasion he caught such titillating refrains as, "Take it off, all off!" or "Come on, show a little more, won't ya?" or "How about another piece of that, huh?"

In due time a thunderous outburst of clapping, hooting, and whistling notified Manly's reddening ears that his eon of preparation was drawing to an end. But his time of tension was by no means over. As departing patrons came streaming past him, he set his jaws against the blows of embarrassment he knew would fall should anybody recognize him, or, worse, taunt him with, "Why, Manly, what's a nice boy like you doing in a place like this?"

When the tent was empty, the ticket taker languidly unchained the gate and took his ticket. He was tempted to run down the aisle, but that would have attracted attention. So, compromising on long, quick strides, he made a beeline toward the front row and would have gained a front-row center-aisle seat had he not been contending with men less concerned than he with decorum and anonymity. In fact, he was elbowed out of his two favorite seats but was, nevertheless, on the front row with an excellent view of center stage. Frozen in posture, staring straight ahead, he sensed that the tent was filling fast, that the show would soon be under way. Even so, he was startled when a brassy fanfare erupted.

Without further ado, the stage lights went up, the curtains opened, and twelve statuesque beauties came bounding into view. Each wore a black top hat, each wore a black cape apparently made of very fine netting that was bound together at the neck and breast levels with golden chains, and each wore a short, black, wrap-around skirt fastened with a golden ornament.

Acknowledging the audience's applause, the girls tipped their hats and bowed in unison. Then they formed a circle that nearly filled the stage, and each began to follow the other in a circular motion. At a prearranged signal, the girl who at that time was prancing from the back of the circle straight toward the audience removed her hat with a flourish and flung it into the wings to Manly's right. When all twelve had removed their hats in that manner, they broke into pairs and did a brief dance, then reformed the circle.

After that, each girl gave a teasing shrug of her shoulders and threw away her cape at the point of turning toward the audience. When that was done by all, twelve girls stood before the onlookers completely naked from the waist up except for the minutest of pink pasties behind which their nipples coyly hid. Manly had never seen anything like it, and he could not see enough.

Then, after pairing off for a mincing step or two, the girls again reformed their circle and, with a mischievous wink, tossed their skirts away to reveal the most gossamer of G-strings to which the smallest imaginable deltas of

14

diaphanous cloth were attached fore and aft. About to explode, Manly, trying to appear casual, folded one hand over the other on his lap lest someone (who, pray tell?) might see his erection.

The girls then went into what Manly presumed to be a bump and grind routine. How little the local clergy, who had criticized the Revue, knew of real debauchery! Those girls were not merely displaying their jiggling breasts, they were thrusting themselves forward at every man as though pleading to be sucked. Nor were they merely swiveling their hips. They showed off their bare bottoms in such an unabashed way that every delightful curve, every provocative undulation, could be seen and savored to the full, and when they turned to face the audience, they thrust their pelvises forward and outward as if inviting penetration by every fiery arrow there. Manly was already orgasmic.

Blotting out faces and arms and feet, which he could see any time, he drank in every pert curve of every uplifted breast, fastened his attention on every rippling buttock, caressed with his eyes the lovely soft skin of every inner thigh, and tried to probe the dark mysterious grottoes that beckoned now and again for fleeting moments from between the legs of each girl.

The second routine of the show, unlike the first, was not designed to stimulate prurience through the simple and brazen display of as much bare skin as possible. It was, quite the contrary, meant to excite male sexuality through what appeared to be a kind of progressive, even demonic, frenzy that had unexpectedly possessed twelve modest girls as unaware of their nakedness as they were of the lust of unseen viewers. It was a routine that fused the talents of ballerina and acrobat. Physically, it demanded immense energy and skill. Theatrically, it required a projection of mounting tension and abandonment unbesmirched by any sordid desire to fan the flames of masculine carnality.

That second routine, ever accelerating in tempo, was about half over when the unexpected happened. Nobody, including Manly, knew precisely what caused it. Perhaps it was a tiny pebble or a splinter on the floor near the edge of the stage, or maybe a heel gave way just enough to throw the dancer off balance. Anyway, one of the girls turned her ankle sharply. In the painful attempt to recover her place and direction in the maelstrom of movement, a second girl bumped into her, pitching her off the stage in a crouching position straight into Manly. Her head and shoulder struck his lower chest, her torso lay on his lap, her thighs dangled against his shins, and one of her knees came to rest between his feet.

The sensations he suffered were as varied as they were keen. Since he had been trying to absorb all the erotic frenzy being displayed, he had not been focusing on any individual performer at the moment. Moreover, he was not aware that anything was amiss until the girl, a looming black object against the gaily lit stage, crashed into him. So rapidly did the unexpected happen that his hands had just begun to leave his lap to ward off the blow when he was sent rocketing backward by the impact. His first sensation was of falling helplessly and foolishly in front of the whole audience. Actually he did not fall over, because his chair was anchored to several others. But he did teeter for an eternal instant before their combined weight pulled him back with a thud.

His second sensation was of difficulty in breathing, and he heard himself cough several times as if barking. Then the nausea came, followed by pain surging outward from his wishbone. But worse than all that was the fierce humiliation he felt irradiating him with fire and setting his face ablaze. It was as if he were a glowing cherry-red object set at the very navel of attention for all to ridicule. For an awful instant he knew that his sins had found him out. At any moment he expected flash bulbs to pop, for he knew that his picture would be emblazoned across the front page of every paper in the state. Mockingly, they would announce, "Manly Plumwell, the moral standard of Nickel Plate, the nicest boy in town, was caught last night at a striptease show with a naked girl on his lap." How his enemies would crow, how they would exult, how utterly undone he would be!

But Manly did not writhe for long in the excruciating fires of shame. He was quickly brought back to the real world by low moans that turned his attention from himself to the girl who until then had lain limply and silently on his lap. One glance told him that her face was contorted with pain, and he could feel her body stiffening in the attempt to resist it. "Mister," she said through clenched teeth, "could you please help me out and around to the back?" Those few words, sweeter than any Manly had ever heard, flooded his being with a strange new emotion and galvanized him into action. Gone, all gone, were his suspicions that the whole episode had been engineered for the sole purpose of humiliating him.

The girl needed help, and she would receive it too. Let any other men so much as raise their little fingers, and he would fight them off for the privilege of giving aid and comfort to that sweet, sweet creature who lay against him. But Manly had no need for aggressiveness. Despite the shocks and confusions heaped upon him, he reacted far more quickly than any of the clods sitting nearby.

Before they had fully collected their wits, he had already begun to act. Besides, the show went on as though nothing had happened, and who among them wanted to miss that matchless routine, especially as it neared its orgiastic apex, just to help a broad with a sprained ankle out of the tent? In a flush of new-found joy and excitement, Manly found wells of energy hitherto unknown to him. In a trice he lifted the girl from her strange bed of pain and cradled her in his arms, his left arm under her knees, his right arm compassionately curved about her shoulders, her left arm lying limply around his neck.

As he gained his feet, she said in a voice thickened with mucous, "If you'll move over to your right, I'll show you a way out." The way out proved to be a tent flap that could either be tied down against wind and weather or raised to provide patrons an extra exit after the show. Since the flap was

16

dangling loosely, Manly simply turned and backed through it into the sobering air of night. Reviving, the girl said in a stronger voice, "If you think you can carry me that far, there's a dressing room right behind the tent, and I could get help there and not be a bother any more." As Manly reassured his precious cargo that she was no bother, that he could certainly carry her there, his bedazzled mind tried to take stock of what it was, really, that was happening to him. It was no time, however, for reflection, because the girl, muscular and not small to begin with, was getting dauntingly heavy. Moreover, in the uncertain light, Manly had to be very careful not to blunder into guy wires or stumble over tent pegs or ropes or whatnot. With his muscles pleading for relief, his energy ebbing fast, and his heart beating anxiously lest they should both fall, he circled the end of the circus wagon behind the tent and headed straight toward the only door in sight. Putting his right foot on the lowest of three steps leading to the threshold of that door and supporting the girl's back against the inside of his right thigh, he pounded desperately on the bottom of the door.

The circus car's occupants were at first annoyed by the urgent banging on their door, then greatly surprised at what they found upon opening it. So skilled were the performers and so routine their acts that no one expected such an event to occur as the one Manly described breathlessly as he and the girl were hauled aboard. Since Schweitzer was away, his second in command, a choreographer named Stoddard, took charge. Together, he and Manly laid the girl gently on a folding cot hastily set up by two Egyptian belly dancers. Before removing her arm from his neck, she murmured heartfelt thanks in Manly's ear and, to his intense delight, burnished his cheek with her lips.

Stoddard and several girls, including the belly dancers, began hovering over her. Even the Star of the "Revue," LaBelle Irvine, the queen of all strippers according to the placards in front of the tent, bent in lithe nakedness over her lesser but fallen sister. With all attention focused on the suffering girl, Manly felt awkward and badly out of place (to say nothing of being ignored), so he slipped unseen out of the door and dropped to the ground where for a time he merely tried to keep his balance while various ideas churned their turbulent way through his mind.

Perhaps he had been a fool to have missed half the show. In time someone else would surely have helped the girl if he had stayed in place. But if he asked, maybe they would let him back in, even give him a free pass for his services. But what the hell! Why did he care? He had just had the most exalting experience of his whole life. Suffused with that wonderful realization and touching his burnished cheek as though it were newly sacred, he ran toward the parking lot.

Anyone noting him as he careened through the crowds might have thought him propelled by some dire emergency, so fast did he go, except that now and again he skipped and leaped and bounded as he went. The smile that wreathed his face announced to all that he ran not from fear but with elation. Some breathless moments later, still euphoric, he reached the old Nash.

17

No sooner had he slipped into the old heap than he became aware of a cold slimy spot spreading over his underpants, next to his skin. The fastidious Manly would normally have found such an occurrence irritating to say the least, but not that night. So great was his good cheer that he laughed aloud, wildly, uproariously, exuberantly. In that state of mind, he left the fair and somehow made his way absently but safely home to Nickel Plate under the robust light of an August moon.

As he lay naked on his bed in the dark protection of night, his mind churned on and on as though it were a kind of perpetual motion motion picture projector showing over and over and over, in living color, a film of endless variations. It was quite magical, that machinery of his mind, for in less than the twinkling of an eye, he could stop the reel and start the sequence of images over again at any point he liked. He could speed up or abolish those images that were boring or painful and could slow down or expand those over which he would linger. He could even see footage of events that had not really happened. No power could prevent him from splicing together factual memories with unrestrained fantasies, nor could anyone forbid him to do so.

In that way, he saw her again cradled in his arms. How unself-conscious she was with him. Maybe it was because of the pain she bore, or maybe it was just that after displaying herself to anonymous men, she liked having a particular man with a particular name hold her close and treat her tenderly. Whatever the case, she had not made him self-conscious, had not reproached him in any way for staring at her doubled up and pressed against him. Holding her with arms that could not tire, her head resting lightly on his shoulder, he dwelt on the sweet curve of her right breast rounding away from him. The pasty was gone, and her nipple stood free, bathed in air and yearning. The joy of Manly's desiring, however, lay concealed in a secret valley made by his left arm as he held her thighs tightly together. But that valley could be opened, its mysteries brought to light, thought he; and so it was in fraudulent footage.

Again the girl was pressed against him, yet he did not hold her and expended no effort. He had returned to the fair to see her, to learn of her recovery. Miraculously, she was whole again, as sound as could be. No pain contorted her face, no twisted ankle disfigured her stance, no bruise blemished her skin. She was delighted to see her benefactor and insisted on his just reward. With the impediments of time and space and gravity abolished, she floated before him recumbently. This time he saw both breasts to the full and sampled their confections. The joy of his desiring was no longer hidden, no longer forbidden, for as she levitated to him, her pelvis arched upward to receive him, and her thighs parted in loving invitation. The sailor came home from the sea and slipped into safe haven, the sojourner satisfied at last.

As drained of emotion as he was of semen, Manly arose to clean himself, and in so doing managed to shut down the perpetual motion motion picture projector in his head. Exhausted at long last, he stepped slowly into his pajama bottoms and fell languidly into bed. Sleep was not long in coming and announced its arrival by unhinging his ideas and melting the logical links that bound his waking thoughts together.

A scream rent the silence, a scream compounded equally of pain and dread. Manly leaped to his feet, grasping at the darkness for support, and found himself teetering in the middle of his bedroom floor without knowing how or why he had arrived there. Hearing nothing further and feeling faint, he returned to bed assuring himself that it must have been a nightmare. But then, it came again, and it was no mere cry extorted by a fleeting pain; it was a prolonged howl of anguish coming from his grandmother's room. Something was wrong with Ma, something terribly wrong. With his mind clearing fast, Manly lurched out of his room and down the hall pell-mell.

Without pausing to knock, he flung open the door and burst into her room. "Ma, what's wrong," he yelled, "are you all right, Ma? What is it?" Getting no answer, he fumbled for her bedside lamp and jerked on its chain. The lamp contained only a 40-watt bulb, but in its faint glow he saw his grandmother as never before. Her face was the color of dying gardenia blossoms, and it glistened sickly with beads of sweat that stood out in sharp detail, especially on her forehead.

Wave upon wave of excruciating pain, beginning at some remote point within, ravaged her abdomen. If only she could have writhed or in some other way responded to the pounding surf within, she might have gained a moment's release, but she could not, for, simultaneously, she was overwhelmed with nausea so oppressive she dared not move, could not move even to throw up that which sickened her so profoundly. Manly searched for the pot under her bed, but when he placed it where she might have vomited into it, she could only moan between clenched teeth and roll her eyes in mute futility.

When the full realization of her desperate illness dawned on him, Manly wheeled from her bed and darted into the kitchen where, in groping for the phone, he managed to knock its receiver to the floor. Giving the phone a mighty crank, he ordered the operator to get Dr. Oesterly right away. An eternity later, a woman's voice made cross by interrupted sleep said, "Dr. Oesterly's residence."

"Send the doctor," Manly yelled without preamble, "as quick as you can up to Plumwells'. Ma's awful sick."

"I hate to awaken him," said Mrs. Oesterly, "because he delivered two babies last night, and had a busy day at the office all day, and is quite tired. Couldn't your grandmother take some of the medicine he gave her last time? It's probably just indigestion, something she ate that made gas, you know."

"No, no, I don't think so. It's worse than that."

"Well, you take my advice first, and if she doesn't get better, Doc'll see her in the morning. Bye."

Stunned, undone, stupified by the response he had just received, Manly returned to his grandmother's side hoping that the worst had passed. But that had not happened. In his absence, the old lady had exploded, soiling herself and the bed gaggingly. How ashamed she must feel! thought Manly. But not so, for Ma Plumwell had neither time nor energy nor intentionality to give to such trifles as shame. She was sick unto death and was even then, before his eyes, drowning in the pain and nausea that engulfed her.

Staring helplessly at her through tear-drenched eyes, he suddenly remembered something (was it in real life or in a movie?) about a person who had called the sheriff to force a doctor to come to a dying loved one. Back to the phone he flew, and when Mrs. Oesterly answered again, he screamed at her, *"Ma's dying!* Get Dr. Oesterly up here fast, and if you don't, I'll call the sheriff, and he'll make him come and keep his oath."

"All right, but do calm down," said Mrs. Oesterly, "he'll be right along."

"Doc's coming," yelled Manly as he raced back to his grandmother's room, "just hang on a little while longer." But that was precisely what Marynell Plumwell could not do. Then and there she released her hold on life and died without so much as a word of farewell, or a gesture of parting, to the one person who, in her crotchety way, she had always loved best of all.

Revulsion over the dreadful mess his grandmother had left overcame him. He bolted from the room, slamming the door behind him, without so much as covering her dead face. Then, waiting for that doddering old fool of a doctor to come, Manly, still clad only in his pajama bottoms, paced to and fro like a caged animal snarling at its bars. Fifteen minutes later, and in the dead of night, he saw from the south parlor window two headlights winking along Main Street, moving eastward. With infinite patience the car whose headlights they were came to a full and complete stop at the empty intersection of Main with Rumsey Road. After an interminable pause, the car turned left toward the Plumwells'. But no sooner were the lights pointed in the right direction than the car stopped again, that time for a railway crossing. Everybody in Nickel Plate knew that no train was due until the morning flyer at 6:04, but Dr. Benny Oesterly would have to stop and look both ways, not once but twice, before proceeding. The snail's pace at which he drove and the crazy illegal things he did when "motoring," as he called it, had already caused a half-dozen normally alert people to crash into him or into objects close to him with the result that he became alarmed at the slaughter that accompanied him on the highways. To compensate, he determined to drive even more slowly and to do even crazier things than before. Without doubt, in one way or another, he had caused as much pain in his lifetime as he had ever palliated, but he was the only physician for miles around, and that was that.

Benny's progress up the Rumsey Road hill was so agonizingly slow that Manly felt like running out to push. During the eon it took for him to pull nearly to the top of the hill, then turn right onto the dirt road that bounded the Plumwells' place on the north, and finally turn right again into the driveway leading to their barn, Manly reviewed everything he had ever heard about Nickel Plate's medical institution.

Rumor had it that Benny had come from Canada and that he was not a real medical doctor but something called a mill doctor. Some said that mill doctors knew nothing about diseases, medicines, or such as that, but were merely trained to set bones and treat wounds of the kind liable to happen around logging camps and sawmills. Whatever his origins, Benny had taken Nickel Plate by storm thirty years earlier when he hung up his shingle. During all that time, he had dosed everybody, no matter what the ailment, with his own product, something thick and brown and puckering called "Dr. Benny Oesterly's Remedy." Some swore by it as a cure-all. Moderate detractors called it "Oesterly's Urp Syrup," and enemies, mostly people who had lost loved ones following his ministrations, called it "Benny's Bowel Bomb."

Even as Manly listed the various rumors about Dr. Oesterly, that illustrious developer, producer, and sole distributor of the aforementioned nostrum was backing ever so cautiously out of his car. With great care, he adjusted his hat, hoisted his medical bag from the floor of the car, and waddled prissily toward the back door. Meeting him there, Manly said flatly, "Ma's dead; I'd have called you back and told you not to come, but I suppose you'll have to pronounce her dead anyway."

"Well, if she is indeed deceased, I would have, eventually, so to certify, unless you want the coroner," said Benny in measured terms, squeakily, as he and Manly advanced on the death chamber. When Manly saw the old woman's body again, he broke into a petulant lecture: "I called you, I mean I called your wife, and she said you were all tired out and wouldn't come, but Ma was dying, and I told her I would call the sheriff, and he would have made you come whether you liked it or not. Why didn't you come the first time? Why did your wife make me have to threaten her? Isn't a doctor supposed to come when there's an emergency?"

"There is no occasion for blame," said Benny evenly, surveying the room. "If you will observe the nightstand there, you will perceive a bottle of my remedy. I don't recall prescribing it, as you could hardly say she was a regular patient of mine, but there it is; bootlegged, perhaps. I could have done no more had I been here. No man could have done more. Medical science has yet to supersede my remedy."

"But how do you know that?" Manly exploded. "Because you don't even know what Ma had."

"From the looks of her," said Benny, "she had acute indigestion which in turn caused gas to crowd her heart, and I shall so state as the cause of death on the appropriate form. If my remedy won't handle gas, nothing will; you can be assured of that. Well, good night to you, son, that'll be five dollars—a night call, you know—but you can bring it by in the morning, no need to fish it out now. And, oh yes, you would be well advised to get Harrison Bane up here right away to remove the body for preparation as soon as possible. There's liable to be rapid deterioration in cases like this, and you'll want her to look nice at the funeral. Also, don't forget to notify the relatives first thing in the morning. There aren't many, I should guess, not around here any more, but they'll want to know wherever they are, so don't forget."

Manly lost no time in calling Harrison Bane, Nickel Plate's one and only undertaker and sole furniture dealer. Since Harrison was an insomniac bachelor who usually skittered, wraith-like, about his establishment at night, it took him but moments to respond. In fact, Dr. Oesterly had scarcely reached the midpoint in his perilous journey down the Rumsey Road hill when Bane's ambulance, hearse, and carry-all (he had even transported extension ladders in it) rumbled across the tracks at the foot of the hill.

When Harry emerged from his all-purpose conveyance and made his way toward the Plumwell house, he cast such a pall about him that even the night was darkened. As a youth, Harry had envisioned a life of fame as an operatic performer, but he had not reckoned on his father, Jonathan Bane, a tyrant by nature, a carpenter by trade, and a Calvinist by grace. The old man, a superb craftsman, had developed a flourishing business as a coffin maker, and it seemed only reasonable to him to consolidate the family fortune by having Harrison, his only surviving son, learn the undertaking trade. Despite Harry's pitiable and long-term pleading, together with the good wishes of many who had heard his splendid, if untrained, voice, the old man turned down every screw he could find to make the boy do his bidding. So, Harry, never a very resolute character in the face of despotism, became a mortician, hated every minute of it, ceased singing altogether, and took to drink.

During his long years of durance vile, he had removed so many of his boyhood friends and sweethearts from their homes, had anointed so many of their bodies with his tears, and had conveyed so many of them to their silent homes beneath the sod that the corners of his mouth were turned downward in perpetual grief. He had said, "Till we meet again," so often that he had forgotten how to greet people in happy encounter, merely grunting instead.

Professionally hardened to death though he was, Harry's mission to remove Marynell Plumwell's body was especially poignant for him, for once upon a time he had been her swain, she his sweetheart. But then came the bitterness that led him to drink, and she, a lifelong member of the W.C.T.U., had spurned him without a word and denied him all chance for repentance. He could still see the opening sentence of her wedding report in the paper. It said, "Herbert Plumwell stole a march on all the other young gentlemen of the Nickel Plate area by leading Marynell Bronson, one of its finest young women, to the altar." Stole a march, indeed, thought Harry, despising the memory of his father, as he trudged toward the house with his shoulders hunched, his face to the ground. Just before knocking on the kitchen door, he lifted his eyes to the house and said, "So, it's you this time, Marynell! Well, good-bye, dear dear girl, good-bye. Tell them all 'hello' for me until I can do it myself."

Manly was slow to answer Harry's midnight knock, because as the hearse turned off Rumsey Road, he realized that he had nothing on but his pajama bottoms. As he opened the door some moments later to admit a misty-eyed

Harry, left alone too long with his memories, a sporty coupe swerved into the driveway showering the yard with gravel. Thus arrived Bochieh DeBoer, whistling a nondescript but very merry tune. Seldom have master and factotum been more different than Harrison Bane and "Bokie," as his assistant was universally known. Bokie loved to sell furniture, adored the mortician's lot, and rejoiced in being able to organize and direct people, if only at funerals. Where Harry was doom and gloom, Bokie was sweetness and light.

Wise judges of character might have foreseen Bokie's predilection for pathology, morbidity, and embalming, for, as a youth, he always seemed most elated when others shrank in revulsion. One of his prized possessions had been a bottle containing the pickled remains of two tonsils and a badly disintegrated adenoid. Thinking him a clever lad, Dr. Oesterly whetted his appetite for the pathological by conferring upon him, after their excision, his own diseased organs. Bokie's indulgent parents allowed him to leave his pickled organs on a mantel in their parlor where they served as a centerpiece and a conversational ice-breaker among unsuspecting guests. Bokie took them to school once and in that way helped an arthritic janitor set a record for speed in clearing the building during a fire drill. For a limited time, he also possessed a sheep's eyeball, which he took to class and revealed to selected victims covertly. Several teachers knew something was afoot but could never pinpoint the cause of the pandemic gagging and giggling that convulsed recitations.

Of dead bodies Bokie had a photographic memory. He could recall what each corpse he fetched looked like, where it was at the end, its attitude, its condition, and what the circumstances were when he had engineered its removal. Those with an appetite for such details found him a walking treasure trove, the premier necro-historian of the area, and, for that reason, one of its most valued members. He could be depended on to recount just what it had been like the night Marynell Plumwell died. "How well I can see her lying there on that bed," he would say animatedly, "with excrement at one end and vomitus at the other. She died in awful agony and made quite a sight, just between you and me. Acute indigestion and gas, you know, just about blew her apart. One of the worst cases I ever saw, and I've seen aplenty."

By the time Harrison Bane and Bokie had completed their work's initial stage, Manly was so deep in shock and exhaustion that he could hardly comprehend the unlikely procession that left the house. First went his grandmother, zipped up and lying in a canvas bag on wheels. How incredibly small she looked! But she went with good speed, if not with grace and reverence, for Bokie literally sashayed out to the back of the hearse where he had the doors open so fast he had to wait for a hand while Harry shuffled along, still blackening the night.

With death omnipresent in the house and sleep elusive, Manly remembered his grandfather's passing. He had been only ten at the time and had marked the old man's departure with his own secret ritual. He had taken his air rifle and climbed a box elder tree. There, roosting on a favorite branch and looking into the golden clouds of sunset on the day of burial, he had wept and wept. Finally, lowering the flag in his heart to half-mast, he had taken aim at a point far beyond the clouds and had fired bebe after bebe at it in a solemn, sacred memorial to Herbert Plumwell, his matchless but fallen grandfather. In reliving those mournful moments, the tears came profusely, and he wept for the first time that night for his grandmother, and as he cried, he vowed that somehow or other, no matter what, he would find a splendid way to mark her passing.

Then came the pain. It was as though a hemisphere of hot lead were being jacked up inside his head and pressing inexorably at its top. Shocked, spent, torn asunder by crosscurrents of powerful emotion, he stumbled from room to room for a long time before reeling into the parlor and falling asleep on the davenport.

When Manly awoke to find the sun riding high, it was as though he were drugged and not merely for that day but for countless days to come. It seemed to him that he was forced to see the world from inside a barrel, dark and deep, and that his eyes, under heavy pressure, were being constricted so that he could no longer look about him at the big round earth. But it wasn't merely his eyes that were affected. Every perception of self and world seemed to be narrowly circumscribed, and his head felt strange. The normal sights and sounds of a summer's day were beyond his ken, and the characteristic anticipations with which he met most mornings were denied him.

Some things, however, were painfully clear. Sleep had by no means allowed him to forget what had happened in the dark of night, to think death but a dream; nor did diminished consciousness relieve him of the crushing responsibilities that lay ahead. With little or no recollection of whom he talked to or of what he said (except in one case), of what he wore, of what he ate (if he ate), or of how he got through the day, he forged ahead like a well-programmed robot and did what people must do when there has been a death in the family.

Manly was the only child of the only child (a son) of Herbert and Marynell Plumwell. His parents died while vacationing when he was but three. They had taken flight at Marquette, Michigan, in a Ford Tri-Motor to see the pictured rocks along the southern shore of Lake Superior. No one knew what went wrong, for no part of the plane was recovered, and the cold waters of that great maw regurgitated none of the bodies it swallowed on that ill-fated day. Since Manly's parents had been living with the elder Plumwells at the time, he suffered no great disruption in living arrangements and after a short time ceased to grieve for them or even to remember them very plainly.

Without hesitation or self-pity, his grandparents assumed full responsibility for him. That was more than satisfactory to his mother's people, for they lived half a continent away and did not relish the thought of acquiring an orphan. Manly notified them of his grandmother's death, of course, but perfunctorily, expecting neither attendance at her funeral nor much in the way of sympathy.

Herbert Plumwell came from a family of four boys but, although the eldest, survived them all. Marynell Bronson was the youngest of six, only two of whom outlived her. Of those, one was hospitalized in a state mental hospital, and the other was immobilized by a painful illness in a remote part of the state. Thus, the task of notifying relatives was easy. It consisted mostly of calling a dozen or so cousins in surrounding counties. As for friends and neighbors, well, there was no need to notify them in a town of 925 souls, like Nickel Plate. Dr. Benny Oesterly, Mr. Harrison Bane, and, above all, the loquacious Bokie DeBoer saw to it that the news was spread widely, rapidly, and quite accurately.

Harrison Bane, who knew Manly's economic situation better than Manly did, selected a casket and a coffin in the right price range, and Bokie made all other funeral arrangements, save one; and that was Manly's secret and master stroke. Despite being only half conscious, he knew by mid-morning how he could make his grandmother's departure moving and memorable.

Except for tangential efforts as janitor at the "church house" (as he called it), Ikey (for Ichabod) Strubble (pronounced Strooble) was said to be retired (even he said so, and proudly!), but nobody was sure what it was from which he had retired. He owned forty acres on the northern fringe of Nickel Plate, but he had never seemed to work it when young and out of retirement, nor did he appear to do anything with it when old and in retirement. Like the lilies of the field, he toiled not, neither did he spin, yet he flourished, and on a diet largely of goat's milk, corn meal, honey, apples, apple cider, greens, vinegar, and sauerkraut. Throughout the years he had retained his boyish mien and had invariably ministered to his wife, Liz, with a tenderness born of perpetual puppy love.

It was easy for everyone else to forget Liz. She had been bedridden and out of sight for so long, it was natural to think of Ikey as a widower. Moreover, Liz was simple and had been shunted aside socially even when ambulatory. When able to do so, she told over and again to all comers the story of a forgetful woman who kept telling the same story to everyone on every occasion. The irony of that soon wore thin on most people, but Ikey always rejoiced to hear Liz tell the tale and had innumerable opportunities to savor it.

The Strubbles lived in a shanty once removed from a log cabin. The front of their abode, facing the county road that meandered past, was whitewashed and fairly presentable. The other sides had never known decoration and were unbelievably weatherbeaten. The kitchen, whose floor was hardpacked, well-swept earth, was housed in a lean-to added to the main structure at a later date, but still at a time so remote that living memory could not recall when it had first enhanced the building. When not tending to Liz, Ikey spent a great part of each day, weather permitting, rocking on his "piazza," as he liked to call his front porch. It was there that Manly surprised him with a visit. Ever wary of reproach over his janitorial efforts, Ikey yelled, "I'll have the church house in apple-pie order for your ma's funeral," even before

Manly had shuffled halfway from the car to the piazza.

Seventy-five feet above the ground and just below the steeple of the church whose apple-pie order Ikey had pledged hung a magnificent bell. It had been cast in Pennsylvania well before the Civil War by a family of immigrant masters from Bavaria who, on that occasion, had even exceeded themselves. The result was an instrument of extraordinary power and timbre together with sonorous charm. In point of fact, it was worth far more than the modest price it had brought and was much too good for a town like Nickel Plate.

"Ikey," said Manly, "I remember several times hearing Ma tell that when she was young they sometimes used to toll the bell when bodies were being brought from home to the church or taken from church to the cemetery."

"Oh, yes, indeedee they did," Ikey agreed, his sky blue eyes fixed on the distance as though to visualize the past more clearly, "why, I can still see Cap'n Wheelock when he was buried like it was yesterday. He liked me, he did; used to pat my head 'n' say, 'Why, bless his little heart.' Of course, he was talkin' to my daddy about me, you understand. Yes, it was some day. His Civil War mates that was still alive, especially the ones that was with him down about Chickamunga, or Chickamauga, whatever they call that place, come up, 'n' while they was makin' ready to fire over his grave, the bell tolled every few seconds. I don't have no idee who done it. I was just a little tyke in them days, but it did happen more'n once. Yes, I reckon, now that you got me to thinkin' about it, that it was tolled when they taken Elmo Andrews to the graveyard."

"Ikey, can it still be done?"

"Why, lord have mercy, Manly, I don't rightly know but don't see no reason why not. But you couldn't do it from down below where the bell is usually rung with the rope—no way— 'cause a body couldn't control it right; it'd be too loud for one thing, 'n' then too, they ain't no way from there to see a procession comin' 'r goin'. No, a body'd have to climb way up in the tower where they could see good and manage the clapper by hand."

"I really want you to do it, Ikey, and I'll pay you well for your trouble. Hearing that bell at funerals made a grand impression on Ma. I don't know whether or not she could hear it from where she is now, but I'd like to give her the chance anyway."

"I'd sure be proud 'n' all to do it for you, Manly, if I could, 'n' it wouldn't cost you nothin'," said Ikey speculatively, "but it ain't gonna be a'tall easy to git these old bones up in there. I ain't a kid no more! You got to git a ladder up in that second floor Sunday school room in the back at the head of the stairs, 'n' then you gotta go through a trap door in the ceilin', 'n' once you're up in there, they ain't no light. Course you could take a flashlight. Well, then you gotta walk back the full length of the church house on just narrow planks that's laid down loose across the rafters. Then, if you ain't fell through by that time, you've got to climb straight up in the bell tower twenty feet 'r more on a ladder that's nailed right into the studs, 'n' then you go

26

through another trap door, 'n' there's the bell, big as life."

"Could you see our house from up there, and also the cemetery?"

"I ain't got no way of knowin', Manly, them trees around the church house have growed a lot since I was prowlin' around up in there the last time, whenever that was. I 'spect you could see parts of the cemetery, it bein' down hill 'n' all from the church house. But I don't know about your place, unless a body might spot that big Norwegian spruce in the front yard. Even then, I wouldn't want to say you could see a funeral procession 'r anything like that start out, 'cause I don't believe you could."

"I'd always be in your debt," Manly pleaded, "if you'd toll the bell when they take Ma's body from the house to the church and then when we leave the church for the cemetery. It would mean an awful lot to her."

"It ain't that I don't want to do it for your ma. It's jist that I don't know it's possible. Course, I'd be the best person to do it 'n' all. Let's jist leave it this way: If I can, I will. If you hear that old bell tollin' day after tomorrow (it is then, ain't it?), you'll know I made it, 'n' if you don't, you'll know that I broke my fool neck or got hung up in them rafters some'rs."

"That would be just wonderful of you, Ikey," said Manly, turning to go. "Oh, say, could we just keep it between the two of us, let it be kind of a secret and all?"

"Lord have mercy, Manly, I'd never tell nobody," protested Ikey. Then, after a thoughtful pause, he asked of Manly's departing back, "But it wouldn't do no harm, would it, if I's to tell Liz? She don't have much to keep her interest in life up, and I guarantee she won't tell nobody."

For the first and only time during that traumatic episode in his life, Manly smiled, and said, "By all means, tell Liz, and tell her that I hope she hears the bell when you toll it."

Wreathed in smiles, Ikey could hardly wait for Manly to drive off before bounding into the house with exciting news for the simple old crone who languished therein.

It was shortly after 2:00 A.M. when Marynell Plumwell died. By evening of the same day she returned home, in a manner of speaking, looking as though nothing had happened (except that she slept profoundly), a tribute to the reluctant art of Harrison Bane. With her came a multitude of people, close friends, relatives, neighbors, mere (but necrotropic) acquaintances, and several complete strangers, to Manly at least. As they came, for whatever reasons, food piled up in fat hills, and the house was awash with such nonalcoholic drinks as coffee, tea, and Kool-Aid.

Since Manly was the sole close relative and, therefore, the principal mourner, he was not expected to do anything useful once the body came home again. Moreover, it might have been bothersome to have let him do much anyway, as his behavior was not conspicuously rational. Finally, since he was only a man, even if young and still educable, it was agreed that he would be all thumbs at a time like that. Thus, for practical purposes, he was simply dispensed with and allowed to roam about distractedly. By early afternoon, experienced matrons had descended on the house to clean it, to prepare, receive, and distribute food as the need arose, and to make plans for tidying up after the house was vacated of the deceased and her mourners.

In the rural areas of the state, such as Pilsudski County, funeral chapels had not yet caught on. So, bodies prepared for burial were customarily brought back home to lie in state prior to the funeral service, which might take place there if the person were not known to have been a strong church member, or which might take place at a local church of preference, or at the graveside.

Marynell's body was to lie in state a night, a day, a night, and a morning. Shortly after noon on the day of burial, it was taken to her church for the customary 2:00 P.M. funeral service and thence to the Nickel Plate cemetery for burial beside the remains of her husband. While her body remained at home, she was never left alone, one or more persons hovering about the casket at all hours of the day and night. It did not matter where Manly was, whether he even existed or not, or had any wishes. Experienced matrons understood such things and needed only a corpse to activate their routines.

Manly did, however, come alive briefly when Harrison Bane and Bokie arrived to convey the corpse, its casket, and surrounding mountain of flowers to the church. He was not surprised that the bell had not tolled exactly when the hearse moved out of the yard, but as it gained momentum and disappeared to the north on Rumsey Road prior to turning left toward the church, he was bitterly disappointed. Ikey had either not been able to see a thing from the bell tower or else had not been able to get up into it, but was stranded somewhere, God alone knowing where, and might not be able to toll the bell at all. Restraining himself against a wild urge to dash to the church to see what was wrong, he paced about the house anxiously, refusing the food and drink with which insistent matrons tried to stuff him.

At the funeral Manly sat in a pew, reserved for family, with some old and little-known great-aunts and -uncles and a distant cousin or two. Keenly aware of how men were supposed to act on sad occasions, he strove to remain dry-eyed, thus showing his relatives the stern stuff of which he was made. But just beneath the stoic exterior, he was wallowing in sentimentality and was at any moment ready to burst forth in torrential weeping.

At best, his thoughts were focused only episodically on what was being said and done at the funeral. When those thoughts were unfocused, reason whispered to him that Ikey had simply not been able to see the hearse as it delivered his grandmother's body to the church and had wisely refrained from tolling the bell, lest he do it amiss. Unreason insisted that the bell would not ring at all, that Ikey had failed to make it into the tower, that at that very moment the good old fellow was trapped in the rafters above the ceiling, hurt and perhaps dying as well.

In such pendulum swings of mood as those, he heard with no more than half an ear what the Reverend Elmer Titus Pearl said about the death of his grandmother and about her prospects of endless life when the Lord Jesus returned, at the trumpet's call, to claim his own. Only phrases caught Manly's attention, no connectives binding them into intelligible wholes; yet, somehow, it helped to hear "the valley of the shadow of death," "going down the valley one by one," "will fear no evil," "the everlasting arms underneath," "the redeemer liveth," "the many mansions of the Father's house," "will wipe away every tear," and "death shall be no more."

The next thing Manly knew, Bokie, his eyes glittering with excitement, was at his side pulling him briskly from the pew so as to conduct him and the family, and anyone else who cared to follow, past the open casket for a final look at the body. Once outside the church, Bokie hustled the family into the first three cars lined up behind the hearse, dispatched the flowers to the cemetery by pickup truck, and transformed the hitherto leaderless pallbearers into an organized troop bearing the casket smartly out of the vestibule and down the front steps past people lined up three-deep on both sides.

Then, like an unexpected thunderclap, a single throaty peal descended, engulfing them all in wonder. Some thought a terrible accident had happened, or, perhaps, a miracle, for plainly nobody stood by the bell rope. Bokie was dumbfounded, since ringing the bell had played no part in his game plan for the day's exercises. One pallbearer stumbled under the shock; another let go altogether for an instant. After five seconds or so, the sound came again, magnificent and not nearly so frightening, and then, after another five seconds, it came again and continued to do so metronomically.

As mellifluous sound settled upon them, bathing them all in its beauty, it became obvious that somebody, somehow, had laid careful plans to honor the dead with a splendor unprecedented in recent years. Those who had never heard a bell tolled for the dead thought it a marvelous idea, and those who remembered Captain Wheelock and Elmo Andrews felt lumps of sweet association rising in their throats as the dear dead days beyond recall were remembered anew. Many an unexpected tear was shed that day as the burial cortege wound its way to the cemetery suffused by the sweet melancholy of the great bell tolling, tolling, tolling.

Amidst tears (first of mourning and then of joy) and many a nose blowing and hard gulping, Manly said under his breath, "Good old Ikey, good old Ikey!" Good old Manly too! for Ikey and he won many a new friend that day and enriched many an existing friendship.

Until the unforgettable night when he "entertained the angels unawares," Manly continued to live at the bottom of a barrel, dark and deep. He was forgetful of the past, inattentive to the present, and oblivious of the future. His mind played the nomad and wandered far and wide from wherever his body was. Some thought him prematurely deaf, so truant was his awareness of any topic of conversation in which others might have thought him a participant.

At home he had to learn to do for himself, for with each passing day the death-inspired largess of friends and neighbors diminished. In the process, he did many things "bass-ackwards," as his grandmother would have put it. Many a sauce pan boiled over; many a stew burned black on the bottom; many an ingredient was left out; many a load of wash was done without soap; many a button was tangled on with thumbs.

But, worse than that, things that began sensibly ended foolishly. Once he went to the bathroom to put on a necktie, saw his toothbrush, dropped the tie, brushed his teeth (even though he had done so moments earlier), put on his jacket, and hurried out of the house for an engagement only to discover hours later that he was tieless in his best suit with his collar gaping open at the neck. Many other things happened witlessly while he dithered about the house. Somehow or other he lost his hair tonic only to find it in the refrigerator. Imagine his surprise to find the filthy rag with which he applied shoe polish lying on top of some freshly laundered T-shirts in the bureau where he kept his underwear! Perhaps the prize should have been given for the time when he went to the bathroom with a large pair of scissors to clip some offending hairs. Wearing only his jockey shorts, he dropped the scissors, when finished, where his right front pants' pocket would have been had he been wearing pants. He had a sore foot for several days thereafter and managed to keep his mind on his business a bit better than before.

At work at the end of each school day, Manly could never make the amount of money in the cash register jibe with the total for that day indicated by the bills of sale. But Josh Tharp, the proprietor of Tharp's Hardware and Herbert Plumwell's lifelong friend, remained indulgent, fearing no larceny. He had given Manly a short-term part-time job to help him keep body and soul together—as he announced to all and sundry—until such time as the Probate Court might rule on Manly's inheritance of the Plumwell property. Throughout the months involved, Manly took no apparent interest in keeping body and soul together and seemed to care less than the proverbial fig about being defrauded by the State or by his attorney, lest others defraud him by exerting claims against what everybody agreed was rightfully his.

At school, his senior year passed not so much as a dream as a night of dreamless sleep. He must have gone to classes, must have read his assignments, must have done his written work, for he not only passed his courses but was graduated as the valedictorian, the first in a class of thirty-three. He memorized his valedictory speech and delivered it in what appeared to be an extemporaneous manner but, keeping no record of its contents, forgot what he had said as soon as the saying was done. The striking way in which that speech was delivered, however, together with the splendid manner in which he had conveyed his grandmother's body to the grave, lingered long in the minds of Nickel Platers and enabled Manly to one day return to his own country as a prophet with honor.

It would be impossible to recapitulate precisely the ontogeny of his dark preoccupations in the weeks and months that followed his grandmother's passing. At different times, in varying ways, in changing sequences, shock, grief, self-pity, and remorse came and went, merged and parted, predominated and subsided. At some point in early fall, shock disappeared and bouts of weeping became rare, but self-pity persisted, depression deepened, and remorse mounted on high. Perhaps it was in the depths of winter when the ominous realization could no longer be denied: He had killed his grandmother! It was his disgusting lark at the fair, together with the degradations preceding it, that had done her to death. Bad as that was, her death was not, could not be, the end of his punishment. Foreseeing the worst, dreading the pain and humiliation to come, but not knowing when or how the axe would fall from God's hand, sovereign anxiety dominated his life. Moreover, it paralyzed him and made all thought of expiation impossible. He had had his chance and muffed it.

When, at long last, Manly had clambered down from the box elder tree, having peppered the sky with unnumbered bebes to mark his grandfather's earthly exodus, he knew what he must do. With tear-stained cheeks and bits of bark in his hair, he dashed into the kitchen to tell Ma about his momentous decision. She was not there but was not far away either, judging from the audible conversation she was having with herself. "Of course he was a man," she said, "and men have their ways." "But," she answered herself, "he could have been a lot worse. Grandmother used to say, 'Be thankful for what you've got and leave well enough alone.'"

"I 'spect you want your supper," she said as Manly came into view.

"Ma, I want to join the church."

"You what?"

"I want to join the church and be a Christian."

"Well, not just now," she said absently.

"Why not?"

"I'll fix a bite of supper pretty soon," she said, and she did, and shortly thereafter sent him to bed. "Funerals tire a body out," she announced, "and you need your sleep."

Variations on the same theme were played several times during the following weeks, even after Manly had ceased to be tearful at the mere mention of his grandfather's death.

"Ma, I still want to join the church," he announced gravely at breakfast one morning.

"Whatever for?" she asked, somewhat puzzled as to why such a "little tyke" would persist in a notion like that.

"I just do."

"Ain't you kind of young to know what it's all about?"

"No, I go to Sunday school and church every week, and I've read the Bible a lot."

"You have?"

"Yes, I have; I really have, lots of times when you weren't even around and didn't even know about it, and the Bible says you should."

"Should what?"

"Join the church."

"Oh, I see, said the blind man."

"Can I, Ma?"

"Well, we'll have to think about it some other time," she said, "but right now, you finish your breakfast and skedaddle out to play. I want to get these dishes done up, and it don't help none to have you under foot."

No sooner had the screen door slammed behind him than she said, "He really is a caution sometimes."

The Plumwells had been Campbellites right back to the Kentucky days of Alexander Campbell himself. Following family tradition, Herbert (and Marynell Bronson too) had been members of the Nickel Plate Christian Church (Disciples of Christ) since their early teens. The Campbellites, or Disciples as they preferred to be called, practiced what was, and still is, known as adult baptism by total immersion following the repentance of sins and confession of faith. They did not then, and still do not, put much stress on the ideas of original sin and total depravity. So, there never seemed to them to be much reason for children under the age of accountability to confess sins and seek divine forgiveness. To be washed whiter than snow in the waters of baptism before one had even become tattle-tale gray seemed to them to be rushing things. As for the outlandish idea that unbaptized children would go straight to hell if they died, well, hadn't the Lord himself said, "Suffer the little children to come unto me, for of such is the Kingdom of Heaven"? Indeed, he had, but he hadn't said one word about their having to be baptized first, no sirree.

Marynell knew that Manly was naughty sometimes, but he wasn't wicked and hardly needed to join the church to keep from going to hell if he died. It was just that his grandfather's death had frightened him and had gotten his poor little mind to dwelling on death. "He'll get over it pretty soon," she told herself while finishing the dishes. But she was wrong about that.

Looking like the quintessential Dutch lady in bonnet and apron, minus only the wooden shoes, she stood one day shortly thereafter watering the peonies she raised for sale and carrying on a spirited conversation with herself. She hadn't heard him come up beside her and was, quite frankly, scared out of her wits when he yelled, *"Ma, I want to be a Christian and join the church! You've got to let me! It's wrong of you not to help me!"*

Pursing her lips, she said, "When you get a bee in your bonnet, you really get one, don't you, young man? I presume the only way I'm going to get any peace and quiet is to do your bidding. Well, all right, all right, I'll speak to Reverend Pearl about it come Sunday. Now, get along with you, you little scamp, and let me be."

Hardly anybody, including Marynell, liked Reverend Pearl very well. For one thing, he was as dead as last year's hay and, for another, seemed to like books about Jesus better than Jesus. But the Nickel Plate congregation was small (and getting smaller) and too parsimonious to get anybody really good. Furthermore, Reverend Pearl was a Disciple and cheap and available on a part-time basis provided that the congregation would hold its Sunday worship services in the afternoon to accommodate him.

The Reverend Elmer Titus Pearl, B.D., YDS (for Yale Divinity School), as he always signed his name, was Professor of Religion and Dean of the Chapel at the Alderson-Stokes Military Academy and Preparatory School in the McIntosh community of Cumberland County twenty-five miles east of Nickel Plate. The inmates of the school likened it (and McIntosh) to Siberia but made no fine distinction as to whether they meant pre- or post-revolutionary Siberia.

Built like a fortress, Alderson-Stokes specialized in boys who specialized in undisciplined behavior, not a few of whom had run afoul of the law and some of whom had served time as delinquents. It was often said that when a young hood was graduated form the State Reform School at Limestone Wells he went straight to Alderson-Stokes (or "ass maps," as its acronym was pronounced) for postgraduate work, provided, of course, that his old man had enough dough.

Reverend Pearl perceived the boys' principal problem to be one of values. To that problem he brought all the Law and the Prophets and the Savior and St. Paul, over and again. Since his Sunday afternoon sermons were largely built around his boys and were profusely illustrated with references to them, and since he spoke only of values, or of priorities of values, and never came right out and spoke of sex, drink, deceit, theft, assault, bushwhacking, back-biting, or of anything recognizable as sin in Nickel Plate, folks could only shake their heads in wonderment, trying to figure out what he had in mind. But he was inoffensive personally and a damned sight better than what the Presbyterians had. That he had attended Yale Divinity School was as lost on them as it would have been on a gaggle of geese, but he did not know that and, like St. Paul and his insufferable boasting, adverted whenever possible to his "halcyonian seasons at Yale," as he liked to put it.

Marynell put on her "best bib and tucker" for church the following Sunday, but without enthusiasm. After the sermon, entitled "The Value of the Master," which was much like the one two weeks earlier called "The Master's Priorities," she dithered around the sanctuary waiting for the other folks to say their "howdy-do's" to Reverend Pearl and be gone. By the time she reached his pastoral hand outstretched in greeting, she was deeply preoccupied with how she was going to put what she had to say. For his part, Reverend Pearl was as deeply preoccupied, but with a quick getaway to ASMAPS.

"It's about Manly," she said.

"Thank you," he responded, thinking he had heard a compliment, something about a manly sermon, perhaps.

"What?" she said.

"What?" he said.

"It's about Manly."

"What's manly? Oh . . . your . . . your grandson, Manly."

"That's what I said."

"Well?"

"He keeps plaguin' me about joinin' the church."

Reverend Pearl winced as the terms "plaguing" and "joining the church" breezed by in rapid succession.

"I don't think I understand."

"I don't think he does either."

"I seem to be having some trouble in getting the point."

Thinking him duller than she had realized, Marynell said, "He's got this bee in his bonnet, don't you see, about joinin' the church. I think it's just that his grandfather dying and all has got him scared good and proper. I presumed he'd get over it, but he just keeps at me all the time, and finally I said I'd take it up with you."

"You were quite right to do so, Mrs. Plumwell."

"I think he's too young, if you want my opinion; of course, I'm no authority, but he claims he's been reading the Bible a lot."

"He is quite young, but fairly mature for his age, wouldn't you agree?"

Glancing around and lowering her voice, she said, "You know, just between me and thee, he's kind of a scamp sometimes, but he ain't what you'd call a bad boy, just a boy, I guess, like my grandmother used to say."

"He seems a bright lad, quite alert for his age, don't you think?"

"Oh, he's good with his letters and all, but he's kind of funny in some ways, if you know what I mean. Seems like he don't always have good sense."

"Of course, he is still quite young and inexperienced."

"That's what I told him, but he won't take 'no' for an answer. He's a lot like his grandfather in that way."

"I see," said Reverend Pearl, stalling in order to get straight about the value priorities involved in the situation.

"I guess it comes right down to this: Would you turn him away if he was to answer the call and come forward next Sunday to confess and all that?"

"No, no, I don't think I could, in good conscience, refuse him even at his tender age. I feel sure that his values are developing in the right way."

"Could we get the baptizin' done the same day?"

"Yes, I suppose I could bring my baptismal vestments with me, but someone would have to notify the sextant, Mr. Strubble."

"Who?"

"Mr. Strubble."

"Oh, you mean Ikey. Don't let that worry you none. I'll get him crackin' with the baptistry and all that. You just have to be firm with him."

"Perhaps, if Manly were to confess his faith next Sunday and were to defer the baptism until the following Sunday, we might be able to notify people so as to have a goodly number present."

"No, that won't do. The rest of you don't have to put up with him like I do. I can't take two more weeks of him plaguin' me all the livelong day."

"I see. No, of course not."

With that, Marynell retrieved Manly, whom she had told to go outside and play, and set off for home.

Nickel Platers knew something out of the ordinary was afoot when, on the following Friday afternoon, Ikey arrived at the horse watering trough opposite the lumber yard, driving Josh Tharp's pickup with half a dozen empty clattering milk cans in it, each of which he filled in the artesian-fed trough and then hoisted back into the truck. That done, he would rumble off to the Christian Church only to return for another load of the tooth-numbing water. Making trip after trip between trough and church, it was obvious that he was filling its 500-odd-gallon baptistry. The grapevine crackled into action with the news that there was going to be a baptizing. A simple process of elimination identified the convert, and several people who had said they would scream if they ever heard the word "values" again resolved to see Manly baptized.

Late on Saturday afternoon, a sore and stiff-backed Ikey descended into the cellar beneath the church and set a match to the old kerosene water heater to take the edge off the baptistry's cold, cold water. On the rare occasions when anyone was baptized in Nickel Plate (what the Presbyterians called baptism was more like dry cleaning and didn't count) Reverend Pearl always insisted on comfort. Ikey and other old-timers could remember baptisms in the rivers and creeks nearby, sometimes even in the winter with snow on the ground. Those who had had their sins washed away in ice water always seemed to remember the event more vividly than did other folks. It was a treat for the onlookers too as they, bundled up to the gills, watched pastor and convert force themselves down through a big hole in the ice into the green waters of winter.

"That preacher-fella we got now," said Ikey aloud as he emerged laboriously from the cellar, "ain't even content to be warm. He's got to be dry too, in that rubber suit of his'n. Ah, well, I reckon that's what they teach 'em up at that fancy school he's all the time carryin' on about."

The day of Manly's second birth dawned placidly except for him. Anxiety about getting to heaven to see his grandfather again had turned into anxiety about getting up in church in front of all those people and answering questions and submitting to baptism in full view. The chances for humiliation were legion. Already too sick at his stomach to eat much of the "nice breakfast" his grandmother had prepared, to say nothing of the abundant lunch to come, he kept saying such things as, "How will I know when to go down in front?" and "What am I supposed to say?" and "Will I get water in my nose?"

"Land o' Goshen, Manly, you been to church before, ain't you? You've seen baptizin's before; I know you have. There ain't nothin' to it. You just go down front when Reverend Pearl finishes his sermon and comes down from the pulpit and asks if there's anybody there that wants to join the church."

Even though he knew better, he could not resist asking, "Do I have to make a speech or anything like that?"

"What in tarnation would there be to make a speech about? He just asks you if you're sorry about all your sins and if you believe in Jesus."

Not really feeling sinful and not having a solid grip on theological niceties, Manly asked for the tenth time that week, "Yeah, but what about Jesus? What is it I'm supposed to believe in exactly?"

"Sakes alive, everybody knows that, about him bein' the Son of God, and dyin' on the cross to forgive folks their sins, and savin' them. It's just common knowledge, that is."

"I sure hope I won't get scared in that baptistry and get water in my nose or drink any of it."

"Oh, he'll pinch your nose with a hankie over it when he puts you under."

"I hope he won't pinch too hard."

"*Stop it, Manly!* Nobody's ever got hurt gettin' baptized, and nobody's ever got drownded up in that baptistry that I ever heard tell of."

"Ma, I feel sick."

Quite out of sorts over Manly's conversion, she said, "There ain't nothin' wrong with you. It's just nerves. It's all in your head. Now, you eat them cinnamon rolls that I made special for you and run along. Time's a'flyin'. We'll have to go before you know it."

Baptisms were as rare as hen's teeth in the chapel at ASMAPS, and among the boys who had been baptized a fair number must have been baptized in rusty water, as the saying goes, judging from the amount of larceny that occurred there. With something out of the ordinary to look forward to, Reverend Pearl, B.D., YDS, arrived in Nickel Plate in high spirits bearing his baptismal vestments, a pair of black hip boots and a rubber robe to match. After protracted thought, he had elected to speak on "Forming Values in Youth." Even those who had sworn to scream upon hearing the word "values" again kept their peace and thereby contributed to the air of happy expectancy that possessed all comers that day except two: Marynell, who was quite put out over the whole thing, and the ashen-faced Manly, who, more antsy than usual, made the entire pew he sat in throb with his perpetual motion.

"Amen," said Reverend Pearl as though to endorse his own sermonic product, "and now let us rise to sing the first, second, and last verses of hymn 147, 'Almost Persuaded.' If there is anyone here today who would forsake a life of sin, who would take upon himself or herself the yoke of values taught by the Master, let that person come forward during the singing of the hymn, 'Almost Persuaded.' Let us stand to sing."

Manly couldn't believe it when the first verse was finished, so fast did it speed by, and, if anything, the second verse seemed to be accelerating. A jabbing push or two to the ribs unmesmerized him as his grandmother whispered loudly, "Well, go on, Manly; what are you waiting for?" So, a lad of eleven slipped out of his pew and set foot on the heavenward path leading

36

not to God, but to Herbert Plumwell.

With his hand grasped in Christian acceptance and his gaze fixed upon the orbs of Reverend Pearl, made large like new blue moons by tinted magnifying lenses, Manly affirmed (but none too convincingly) that he wished most fervently to repent of his manifold sins and to forsake his former life. His voice was stronger and more assured when he piped, "Yes," to the questions "Do you believe that Jesus Christ is the Son of God, and do you accept him as your personal savior and take him as your Lord?" He had no inkling of the metaphysical issues involved in celestial sonship, had no notion of what a personal savior did apart from assuring trips to heaven to see one's grandfather and the like, and had only the foggiest idea of what it would be like to have a lord. But he could find out what he believed later. There was no need to know at the moment. He could ask around. It was, after all, common knowledge. Even Ikey would probably know. The important thing was that what he was doing at that very moment was what one had to go through to get one's ticket.

When Manly emerged from the watery grave of baptism, he felt no stirrings of new life, nor did flesh nor feather of the Holy Spirit appear to anyone that day; but he did feel relieved, for he had acquired the priceless ticket, to be used at life's end, that guaranteed him joyful reunion with his grandfather, who at that very moment, no doubt, was awaiting him contentedly up beyond the sky somewhere.

Upon changing clothes and reappearing in the sanctuary, he was the center of attention for quite a while, a real, but ephemeral, celebrity.

"May God grant his richest blessings to you, my son," said Reverend Pearl.

"I was right proud to get to fetch the water for your baptizin', old feller," said Ikey, "I'll tell you that much."

"We're certainly glad to have you as a brand new Christian and a member of our church," said several ladies, beaming on him.

"Congratulations to you, young fellow," said several men, proffering their hands, but with something less than enthusiasm in their voices.

"Gee, Manly, how could you do it?" asked a cute girl with sky blue eyes, a turned up nose, and long lion-colored hair, who had a tendency to crash into people. "I mean, I'd never be brave enough to stand up in front of a church full of people—no way—and walk right down the center aisle like you did. How could you stand to be baptized in front of all of us? I'd be so scared I'd have to do it all alone when the church was empty," the very thoughts of which made her shudder and giggle simultaneously.

Swelling with pride over his confessional accomplishments and baptismal bravery, but not brave enough to look squarely into her bold blue eyes, he glanced at the floor and said, "Shucks, being baptized is nothing; I wouldn't even mind doing it again."

"Well, Manly, I hope you're satisfied with yourself now," said his grandmother with evident relief as they strolled homeward at peace with each other for the first time in what seemed like a coon's age to her.

In the months and early years after his baptism, Manly found the Lord's yoke easy, its burden light; and, like St. Paul, advanced beyond many of his own age, so zealous was he for Christ. He never missed Sunday school or church, commenced to say grace at table, memorized many a Bible verse, and when his grandmother began to dole out a regular allowance gave 40 percent of it to Christ's work, to her displeasure. Whether or not he was "kind of funny," whether or not he lacked good sense, being too withdrawn, he was a good boy when measured by the meter stick of morality accepted in Nickel Plate—perhaps too good for his own good.

Then, by his mid-teens, it became unmistakably clear to him, in secret discovery, that the old Adam, despite being buried in baptism, had not really died, but had only been playing 'possum. That which had been as moribund pre-pubescently was resurrected in direct proportion to his mounting virility.

At school, he always tried to sit across from girls, hoping to see up their skirts. In the hallways, he feigned collisions (rather adeptly by putting the blame on them) with several of the bustier girls. He stole furtive glances at bits of bare breasts revealed by clothing fleetingly parted. He relished, but furtively, the sight of certain girls being goosed now and then by any one of several unsaved classmates. During the summers, he yearned to go to Sapphire Lake, not to swim, but to try to get to a certain spot in the men's dressing room from which, it was boasted, one could look into the women's dressing room through a natural crack (improved by the hand of man) in the wooden planking that separated the two. Failing that, he settled on climbing a tree, verging on Plumstone Creek, from which he tried, unsuccessfully, to peer into a clump of bushes where one of the adepts at goosing schoolgirls had said some of the finest local "pieces of ass" changed into and out of their swimsuits.

Frustrated in such endeavors, Manly would lock the door to his room, take out his magnifying glass and some of his more lurid comic books, and examine the pubic areas of scantily clad females in the absurd hope of seeing something his naked eye had missed. In private, of course, by day and in the dark of night, he sought the semi-satisfactions of the solitary, milked his dingus repeatedly, and scattered his semen with abandon.

Meanwhile, the Old Adam took lively interest in certain other ways of this world. Manly lost his enthusiasm for saying grace, and his prayers in general became perfunctory. Ravished by desire for the glittering goods of this world, his charity decreased, falling from 40 percent to a mere tithe of his meager income. His taste for tobacco was whetted anew; curiosity about demon rum got the better of him; profanity invaded his vocabulary, and something less than candor entered his speech. In witness thereto, remember the fair.

Then Almighty God, justly enraged by such treatment from one unto whom he had been so gracious, struck. With imperious authority he revoked Manly's ticket to heaven and denied him his grandmother in one fell blow. The Scriptures were assuredly correct. It was, indeed, a fearful thing to fall into the hands of an angry God. Such, anyway, were Manly's thoughts as unmitigated remorse plunged him deeper and deeper into depression and despair.

Two aimless weeks had passed since his graduation. High school had prepared him for nothing, nor did he raise a hand with which to seize the future. Moreover, his recent past had been nothing but a reproach, his present a pitiless misery. In the gloaming of a day in early June, as useless, as worthless a day as all the rest had been, he sat rocking apathetically on his screened-in front porch. His awareness of life was so curtailed that he scarcely noticed an old but good-looking car roll up Rumsey Road hill, hesitate momentarily, and then park directly in front of the house. Two well-dressed, clean-cut young men, looking much like today's Mormon elders, stepped out and walked purposefully toward him.

Prior to the time when God had laid him low, shredding his ticket, Manly would likely have retreated unseen into the house, leaving his grandmother to answer the unexpected knock. But his current mood was so flat that he simply sat and watched the strangers, letting them knock a while before moving a muscle. He did not want to see anyone or talk to anybody, having no zest for familiar company let alone that of total strangers.

"Are you Manly Plumwell?" they said as though on cue and almost in unison, with smiles on their faces and hands outstretched.

"Yes," he said aloud, but listlessly to himself, "Who cares?"

"I am Scott Truesdale," said one.

"I am Emory Plunkett," said the other.

"We are royal priests of the Holy Nation Association," said one or the other. "Ours is the Church of the Chosen; we are of the New Israel," said first one, then the other.

Before the astonished Manly could respond, one of them said, "Be of good cheer and rejoice, for we come to you from God the Father (as directed) to announce that your iniquity is pardoned. We address you through the matchless grace and mercy of God's Son, the Savior Jesus Christ, who calls you even now out of your darkness into his marvelous light. We also greet you in the revered name of Miss Alice McAlister, the Handmaiden of the Lord."

Manly was struck dumb and rooted to the spot, still not knowing exactly who the two young men were, how they had found him, nor what they knew of his secrets and his suffering. If they had spoken to him as ordinary strangers might have, he would probably have kept them cooling their heels on the doorstep. But he opened the porch door to them spontaneously, for they were obviously extraordinary, speaking as they did with a certitude the like of which he had never heard. The best intentioned words of others who had tried to console him at the time of his grandmother's death and to en-

39

courage him onward in its aftermath had merely ricocheted off the walls of his solitary cell and left him imprisoned. But the words of those amazing young men had breached the walls of his cell with ease and set him free, not yet knowing what to do nor where to go, but free nonetheless.

They announced that they had come to him from God as directed—*as directed* no less!—and verily it did seem, as he peered at them long and hard, that they must have stood only lately in the presence of the Most High. Even the porch seemed alight with more than the dim afterglow of departing day, yet no electric light was there, no switch was on, no current flowed.

Firmly, compassionately, serenely, they spoke to him of Christ the Redeemer and of his sacrificial love, love so efficacious that not even the chief of sinners could exceed its seeking, sanctifying grasp. Then, as the mysterious light paled, it was succeeded in Manly's consciousness by a warm ocean of peace washing over him therapeutically. He was not only free, but clean and well!

The young men did not speak to him of values, but of the Sovereign Majesty of God; they did not speak of books about Jesus, but of Christ the Commander; they did not speak of the Social Gospel, but of a wicked world speeding toward cosmic catastrophe; they did not speak favorably of Christendom, but exalted a single Holy Nation, the New Israel; they did not read the Bible as though it merely contained an eternal abstract morality, but as though each word had been uttered by God expressly for delivery to Manly John Plumwell, at that moment. Thus, they fueled him with the nutrients of meaning for which he had hungered most (without knowing it), and thus he was filled.

They spoke to him of fields white for the harvest and of reapers few and of time fast fleeting; they spoke of work so critical that no moment could be lost; they spoke of a royal priesthood so small in numbers that each chosen member had to do the work of many; they spoke of Spirit-filled lives that mounted up with wings as eagles and knew not fatigue; they spoke of God's plan for his life (ordained before the foundation of the world), of wondrous deeds to be declared, of missions for Christ to be undertaken. Not only was he free, not only was he clean and well, not only was he filled, he was also energized and uplifted. Depression was no more, despair but a fading memory.

In the platinum light of an overcast morning, the alarm clock on the floor by Manly's bed jangled angrily. He lunged down to turn the accursed thing off. It was 5:00 A.M., and it seemed as though he had slept but a few moments. Lying down again flat on his back to recover from the shock of the clock's racket and to collect his wits, it seemed to him that he must have dreamed it all—the unexpected visit from two strangers, the certitude of their message, its blessed aftermath. But, no, it had been no dream! Once fully conscious of that fact, Manly bounded from bed, bathed quickly, shaved, put on a white shirt and a red tie and the pants to his gray summer suit, and went to the kitchen to make a quick breakfast. No, no indeed, it had been no dream, and what was more, they who had come to him would come again for him, "no later than 6:00 A.M.," they had said, for on that very day they were taking him to Big Bend to meet the Handmaiden of the Lord.

With breakfast over, with his hair combed a final time, his teeth brushed, his shoes polished, and his suit jacket ready for a quick departure, he had time to spare. Whistling a sprightly hymn, something he had not done in ages, and feeling wondrously alert, despite only four hours sleep, he went to the family Bible in search of a passage, something about entertaining angels. He rummaged through Genesis for a while and came to chapter 19. Therein he found the story of the two angels who visited Lot and his family just before the destruction of Sodom and Gomorrah. But that was not quite the passage he had in mind, so he took down *Cruden's Concordance* and looked up "unawares," and thus came to Hebrews 13:2, which says, "Be not forgetful to entertain strangers; for thereby some have entertained angels unawares." Although he had not really entertained them (unless being dumbfounded, weeping, kneeling, and praying are entertainment), the strangers who had come had certainly been angels to him, for no mere mortals, thought Manly, smiling, could have wrought so great a change in a person's life as he had experienced in the hours following their unexpected arrival at his front porch.

At 5:55 A.M., the same old but good-looking car came over the crest of the Rumsey Road hill. Before it stopped, Manly was out of the house walking briskly toward it, excited by the prospects that lay ahead.

"Good morning, Brother Manly," said Scott Truesdale.

"Good morning," added Emory Plunkett.

"Top of the morning to you both," said Manly Plumwell, something he had never said to anyone before in his life. Then he said something equally unprecedented, "I now know what it's like to have entertained angels unawares!"

Each smiled, but neither looked self-conscious at so great an elevation in status, for God had wrought the same effect on others through their ministry before, or so they believed.

"Praise the Lord," said one.

"Give God the glory," said the other.

"Oh, yes, yes," said Manly, still in disbelief that so momentous a change could occur in a human life so quickly.

By 6:00 A.M., as the angels had promised the previous night, all three were on their way from Nickel Plate, heading south for the Big Bend country of the Kinross River. On and on they went through the southern reaches of Pilsudski County, then on into Andaman County, up and across the Andaman Plateau, and on toward the great hill called "Rimrock" that overlooks the big bend of the Kinross and the Shadrach Plains below. As they drove on, at a stately rate, the angels took turns telling Manly about the one they were to see that day, the one known as the Handmaiden of the Lord, and how she came to Big Bend.

41

Chapter Two

Alice Woodmancey McAlister was born in the family farmhouse on the tree-carpeted hills northeast of Nashville in a crook of the Cumberland River. She arrived pink and white and plump all over and remained that way except that her platinum blond hair became prematurely gray and, by the time she was thirty, snowy white. It grew in ringlets and always rested upon her head as though it were a cloud of gossamer threads. Her eyes were the blue of the sky at dawn on a wintry day. Yet, despite irises ever so pale, her pupils were always wide, it seemed, as though in perpetual wonder. So inviting were those windows of her soul that people habitually seemed to be trying to look through them at what was inside. As a small child it often frightened her when perfect strangers would bend over, staring her in the eye, but with time she grew accustomed to it, giving it no mind.

Two brothers preceded her, leaving her the only surviving child of Silas and Myrtle McAlister, forty-three and thirty-nine years old respectively at her birth. They were a hard-working couple and fairly prosperous for those parts, stoic in outlook, puritanical in morals, and conventionally Christian in the Methodist way. Content with each other and with the work of their hands, they displayed little feeling at home and even less at church. One thing was crystal clear: They were not going to love her too much only to have her taken from them as had been the case with her much loved brothers.

There was nothing noteworthy about her girlhood except that she was more isolated than most, being simultaneously an only child and the youngest inhabitant, by far, in her neighborhood. If she was lonely, she did not seem to know it, preferring her own company to that of other children, especially the rowdy ones whom she encountered at the one-room schoolhouse where she was sent at six years of age. For the most part, she was what was called "feminine, real feminine, and domestic," quite content to be housebound, at first to play with her dollies, hour upon hour, and then by the tender age of eight to become mama's little helper in a big and genuine way. In the years that preceded adolescence, she had already become a competent cook, an enthusiastic housekeeper, and a promising apprentice in handwork. Never a tomboy, not much interested in animals, and totally uninterested in the boys she knew, she left the great out of doors and its masculine ways to her father and his kind. Sometimes, the elder McAlisters had a hard time maintaining their stoic reserve, a hard time not loving her too much. But their sense of foreboding persisted.

As a youngster of twelve or thirteen, her happiest moments were spent alone on the widow's walk atop her parents' imposing frame house. Excited by the height and bouyed up by breezes that spurned the ground below, she could, by looking all around, see more than her fair share of the wonderful hills of central Tennessee and off to the west a silvery swatch of the Cumberland as it curved toward Nashville, disappearing under trees made fat by the waters at their feet. It was on that widow's walk, so far from the sea and really out of place on the banks of the Cumberland, that she identified herself most closely with Jesus.

Of all the Bible stories she knew about God's Son, the one that struck her fancy most was the one about his temptation in the wilderness—not so much about temptation nor about wilderness per se, neither of which she understood—but the part about how Satan made Jesus go up on the pinnacle of the temple. Thinking of how much the pinnacle of the temple must have been like a widow's walk, she would stand on her tiptoes on the walk, holding tightly to its balustrade, and look as straight down at the ground as she could over the sloping roofs below. What fun for Jesus to have jumped off, she thought, knowing that he would land softly on angels' wings at the very last moment and then be ministered to by angels, whatever that meant. Perhaps the angels gave him lemonade, or iced tea with sugar in it, or something fit for a king that she did not even know about. She also liked the part about how Satan took Jesus to a high mountain and showed him all the kingdoms of the world. How like central Tennessee, when seen from a widow's walk, that must have been!

It never occurred to her then, nor later in life, to question how it came to pass that the devil could order the Son of God around like that, could simply set him up on the pinnacle of the temple whether he wanted to be there or not, or take him up a high mountain without even asking first. Just how God the Son, for whom and through whom everything was made that was made, could be tempted by anything so paltry as the kingdoms of this world remained beyond her ken. But she loved the pinnacle of her temple, and maybe Jesus liked high places too. It had not, however, been very nice of the Spirit, in her view, to lead him out into the wilderness to be tempted by the devil and certainly not nice of the devil to make Jesus do things he did not want to do or to tantalize him with thoughts of things of which he ought not to have thoughts at all.

Except for the worst of all that happened to her, which also turned out (as she saw it later) to have been the best thing that could have happened to anybody, the worst thing that happened to her took place in the spring of the year when she turned fourteen.

It was late on a Saturday morning. She was helping her mother lay the table for the midday meal. Her father, who was not expected for another half-hour, stuck his head in the kitchen door, looking tense, and said, "Myrtle, drop everything you're doin' and come down to the cow barn. I need your he'p right bad."

Without a word of protest about dinner's being nearly ready, she said to Alice, "You tend to fixin' the rest of the food, but hold things up a little. We'll be back directly, but maybe not directly at noon." Then she hurried out of the kitchen, almost as though she had half expected an emergency.

Slightly mystified, Alice turned down the heat to hold things up as long as possible without overcooking them or drying them out. When she could wait no longer without ruining everything, she took the food up and put it on the table, arranging everything nicely. It was already 12:20. Five long minutes passed, and, though she looked repeatedly out of the east kitchen window, she could see no movement around the cow barn and no sign that her parents were about to come in to eat. After five longer minutes, she went out into the back yard and rang the dinner bell quite assertively for her, but, still, no response. Curious and beginning to imagine dire happenings, she made one of her rare trips toward the cow barn, pinching her nose as she went against the foulest odors.

What she saw upon rounding the far corner of the cow barn was as fascinating as it was disgusting. A cow had given birth to twins, one of which appeared to be all right, but the other one (stillborn and dead for who knows how long) lay in a disgusting blob on the ground, covered with flies. The cow, swaying with fatigue from its hard delivery, dragged some ugly thing, still attached to its rear end, through the dirt, also blackened with flies. Her parents, just then recovering from their exertions, were dirty, bespattered with blood, and looking sorely vexed.

"*Alice!*" shrieked her mother without warning or explanation, "you bad naughty girl; you ain't supposed to be down here. I told you to fix dinner. You git back to the house and be quick about it. Silas, make her mind."

"*Alice!*" roared her father, waving his arms as though to push her out of their sight forever, "you mind your maw. I've got a mind to get me a switch and give you a hard whippin'."

Alice fled to the house, gasping for breath between sobs and barely able to see for the tears in her eyes. Never before had her mother looked at her in that terrible way, nor spoken to her so stridently, and never, never had her father threatened to whip her with a switch. And for what? She did not know, could not know, because she could not ask them, either then or later. For their part, her parents, refusing to advert to the episode, offered no word of comfort, of explanation, or of sorrow. The remainder of the day, needless to say, was spent in an agony of silent tension.

Left in the outer darkness of ignorance and guilt, she experienced the kind of hell that night in which there is weeping and wailing and gnashing of teeth. With the new day, a Sunday, her parents treated her as though nothing

44

had happened, and to all appearances she returned to sweet normalcy. But, unable to expunge the horrid episode from memory, she entered a period during which she had nightmares and, unknown to anyone, began to walk in her sleep.

Summer came, followed by fall, winter, spring, and, then, another summer. Life for the McAlisters went on as usual, leaving them largely untouched. Alice, very much the homebody, remained the busiest of busy bees with her perpetual handwork, her daily cooking, weekly cleaning, occasional canning, and other seasonal activities, always of a domestic variety. Although she was, at fifteen, slowly advancing upon young womanhood, her emotions seemed to have ceased developing, leaving her a kind of eternal twelve-year-old. Perhaps she was growing secretly in wisdom, in stature, and in favor with God; but with man, she grew only in stature and remained shy, childish, and fragile.

The occasion for the worst (but also the best) experience in Alice's life began as did almost any other night when bedtime beckoned. With "good-nights" all around and wishes for sweet dreams, she retired to her room earlier than usual, wearied by a hard day of canning. Within the hour, the elder McAlisters followed suit. Once undressed and then dressed again, and the light put out, they customarily raised their window shades to admit any natural light there might be and opened their windows, weather permitting, for the night air. It was late September and still oppressively warm during the daytime, but at night the faintest hint of fall could be discerned in the air, especially when it was wafted to them from across the river. The light of the moon, riding high at the moment above their south bedroom window, fell upon them in all its reflected glory.

At peace with themselves and with their world, bathed in mellow light, and caressed by gentle breezes from across the Cumberland, along whose banks they had courted on many another moonlit night, what began as a perfunctory kiss became a warm wedge that opened Myrtle's lips and her legs simultaneously. Surprised but quick to sense her potential acceptance if not her outright invitation, Silas, made young by unexpected opportunity, brought into play their own private and well-remembered, but seldom used, rituals of love-making. With his nightshirt on the floor, the sheet thrown off her bare and parted legs, and her nightgown nestling under her chin, Myrtle drew him to her.

While giving to each other and enjoying the giving, neither having yet received the supreme gift, Myrtle sensed a ghostly presence at the foot of the bed. Screaming hysterically and shoving Silas from her as though he were a rapist, she rocketed upward into her nightgown, letting it fall about her nakedness. Shocked as never in his life, but not knowing what was wrong, Silas scrambled under the sheet at the foot of the bed, looking much like a great white crayfish zooming backward into its redoubt. Torn from the arms of her somnambulism and aghast at what she saw of her parents in the relentless light of the moon, the ghostly presence, also commencing to scream, plunged from the room.

Never very demonstrative either in grief or in joy, Myrtle nevertheless howled and sobbed interminably that night, or so it seemed to Silas, who had witnessed nothing like it in his married life. In a voice made hoarse with strain and thick with tears, she hurled question after aggrieved question at him, such as, "What are we goin' to do with that child? What can have possessed her? What in God's name did she think she was doin'? Has she lost all respect for her parents; what about her own self-respect? Did anybody ever hear tell of such a shameful thing? Ain't we always done right by her? What could have gone wrong?"

Shaking with shame and befuddled, Silas could only mumble, "I dunno, Myrtle, I jus' don't know. Whatever you say; you're her mother. I don't guess we've done as good by her as we might've, but I don't know wher' we went wrong. Children are jus' different—seems like—these days, I reckon."

Life in the McAlister family never returned to what it had been before that shattering night. During the following two years, until Alice went forth into the world alone, to return thereafter but briefly and infrequently, no kiss Silas could bestow upon his wife and no physical contact had the power to become a wedge to amorous acceptance, even though the bedroom door was securely bolted each night. The parental bedchamber was invaded by an ice age so benumbing to all sensuality that husband and wife were crystalized into brother and sister. Moreover, whenever Alice was around them, gestures and signs of affection between the two, rare even in the best of earlier days, became nonexistent. Then, too, when she was up and about, easy conversation between husband and wife disappeared, communications becoming curt. It should surprise no one that Silas and Myrtle spoke no further word to each other about the mortifications of that horrendous night, that neither ever mentioned it to Alice, that no questions were asked of her concerning it , and that she, too, remained forever mute on the topic, in the company of her parents. What is surprising is that, eventually, she found she could speak of it freely to others and often.

Enormous changes occurred in Alice. As though by prior agreement, she remained in her room for several days after the sleepwalking episode, laying no eye upon her parents nor being seen by them. When it became blessedly clear to all that she would not appear at such appointed hours as mealtimes (nor be sought out), Myrtle began to leave food and drink by her bedroom door. Alice drank the drink, picked at the food, and returned the dishes to the hallway outside her room unseen. By devious means (mostly after dark) she went to the privy in the back yard to relieve herself. During the days of self-imposed exile she neither washed nor did she bathe beyond dampening her hands on the washcloth Myrtle began to include with the food and drink left by her door.

When Alice reappeared, it was with eyes downcast and tongue tied. Slowly she resumed the rituals of essential work about the house but without zest, her exquisite handwork languishing. Never again, as far as the elder

46

McAlisters knew, did she do anything merely decorative. Turning her back on the space inside the house much as she had always spurned the great out of doors, she withdrew in spaces within herself, spaces that were known, if at all, only as a result of her own explorations. Although she and her parents lived and moved in one and the same physical space when they were at home together, it was increasingly clear that she and they inhabited different realms, scarcely sharing a common tongue. Uncharacteristically, she began reading a great deal of the time. Judging from its omnipresence by her favorite chair or in her room by the bed, the Bible was what she was reading, and judging by the progression of the bookmark in it (the one with the purple tassel), she was reading the Scriptures from beginning to end.

On the first Saturday in October, as was their long-standing custom, the elder McAlisters went into nearby Hartsville to the famous syrup soppin', a festive occasion at which cane syrup was freshly pressed, boiled, and sold and at which people from far and wide indulged in a mammoth pancake feed that lasted from late morning until early evening. Before leaving, Silas and Myrtle urged, even implored, Alice to accompany them in a vain attempt at restoring a semblance, at least, of the old happy times.

"You need to get out and see some other young folks," said Myrtle.

"I b'lieve you'd have a right smart good time, if you'd care to come," Silas opined.

"No, thank you," Alice murmured, dashing their hopes to the ground, "I really wouldn't care to go. I would much prefer to stay here by myself."

Not about to beg her on bended knees, the elder McAlisters rattled off in their truck, shaking their heads simultaneously in silent communion over what on earth to do with the child. Meanwhile, the slow implosion that was Alice went her inward way, skulking from one empty room to another, haunting the house with her inwardness and isolation.

Around mid-afternoon, she went into the parlor and sat down in a favorite chair, hands folded primly on her lap. Having sat there no more than a few minutes, she had the first of three paranormal experiences. Without warning, she seemed to be afire, yet neither suffering nor fearful. It was not that she felt feverish, nor did she feel sweaty or overheated as one often did while cooking or canning on a hot, humid, summer day in central Tennessee. On the contrary, it was a bone-baking heat she felt. It seemed to be everywhere—in her, over her, and all around and about her. Her skin served neither as a barrier to it nor a container of it, for it surrounded and pervaded her whole being and the locus of that being. No part of her, neither past, nor present, nor future, could escape it. At the height of the experience, if it had height and depth and median and if it could properly be called an experience—as though it were just one more conscious episode among myriads in her life—she heard a sound, or what she took to be a sound. Shortly after the sound disappeared, the heat also vanished, but more slowly. Once it had passed completely (if "it" is the proper word to use in referring to so stupendous an event in a person's life) and all seemed to her to have returned to normal, she tried to formulate the voiceless sound with her own voice.

"Izwollwithee" was as close as she could come to it. But, having approximated it, what, if anything, did the sound mean, or did it matter?

For reasons unknown to them, Silas and Myrtle came to look back on the day of the syrup soppin' as the date that marked the beginning of new but subtle changes in Alice's behavior. Whether or not the changes were for the better or the worse, they could not decide.

"Seems like she's got a little more git up 'n' go lately, don't it?" Silas asked, bolting the bedroom door preparatory to sleep.

"And a little more talkative too," agreed Myrtle, "not quite so hangdog all the time. 'Course she ought to be good and ashamed, bargin' in here like she done, but, still, it's right nice to see her hold up her head now 'n' then."

"I don't b'lieve the cat's got 'er tongue quite so much neither," Silas observed, sitting on the bed and easing off his heavy work shoes.

"Funny thing is," mused Myrtle, "she's taken to settin' in the parlor ever' chance she gits, but she don't read the Good Book nowhere near as much as she done there for a while; jist sets 'n' looks off into space."

"I heerd 'er say a funny word two, three times the other day," Silas volunteered. " 'Course she clammed up 'n' wouldn't tell me what it was, and I never heerd it plain enough to call it right off."

"I ain't mentioned this to a soul before," Myrtle said, a bit apologetically, "but I swear she's got me kindly spooked up. It jist seems like she's got her ear cocked all the time lately, listenin' for somethin'. It jist ain't right, her carryin' on that way all the time."

"But, things're a mite easier between me 'n' her, jist the same," said Silas, " I'm grateful for that much."

"I reckon you may be right about things easin' up a bit," said Myrtle as she turned her back to him on the far side of the bed and tucked the sheet and the quilt carefully under her backside, walling him off.

Alice was, indeed, sitting in the parlor every chance she had and while there doing everything she could think of, as well as dredging up every possible association, that might summon back the bone-baking heat of last syrup soppin' day. Moreover, she did have her ear cocked whenever she could manage it. She yearned to hear that intriguing word again (if that was what it was) and to understand it, if it were intelligible. Although she had repeated it to herself over and over as best she could, it still made no sense, yet the memory of it tantalized her waiting, hoping ear.

She had just about given up ever experiencing either of those amazing happenings again when (almost six months to the day, in mid-March) she was baked to a "fare-thee-well," as her mother would have put it. Despite the absence of the strange word or of any sound, she was enormously more elated by the second experience than by the first, although she remained secretive about it, lest parental questions be asked, questions that she could in no way answer.

In the afterglow of the second baking, the search for the missing sound or meaningless word, whichever, became an obsession with her. Not content to cock her ear in idle moments, she began searching for any place where even the slightest whisper of it might be vouchsafed to her. Back and forth she paced, day by day, when not otherwise occupied with daily duties, personal responsibilities, or sleep. Into used rooms and out she paced. Into seldom used or unused rooms she went and out again. Into closets and into the kitchen pantry. Up to the widow's walk and down again. Down into the cellar and, of course, up again. Out and around the house. Outdoors around the house, mind you!

Even Silas, who was off and gone most of the time, noticed Alice's bizarre new behavior. "What is it now?" he asked, bolting the bedroom door.

"Well, sakes alive, you tell me, mister," Myrtle answered, double checking to be sure that the bolt was properly in place.

"Seems like her mind's jist adwellin' on somethin' don't it?"

"I don't pretend to know what her mind's adoin', but I do know what her feet're adoin'. They're cuttin' paths through my carpets, that's what they're adoin', even in the comp'ny bedroom!"

"I reckon we could buy new carpets, if it comes to that."

"Oh, that ain't the point; the point is she's drivin' me to drink, her 'n' pacin' around ever' blessed spare minute."

"That cain't be!" said Silas, knowing that his wife never touched a drop of anything, not even of the homemade elderberry wine that was usually exempted in local thought from Protestant strictures against strong drink.

"Confound it, Silas, I don't mean that kind of drink; I mean Nervine. I'm keepin' the Miles Nervine people in business these days single-handed; that's what I mean an' don't you dare breath a word of what I jist said."

"Well, I don't guess we kin do nothin' about it the rest of the night," Silas said between yawns.

"No, but I wished we could," avowed Myrtle, rolling up tightly in her cocoon of covers, the bottom of her long flannel nightgown pulled up tightly between her legs and bunched behind her.

The pacing phase of Alice's quest for the Holy Grail of sound ended abruptly on the second Sunday in May. It was in the middle of the afternoon. Her father was in the back yard talking to some men about whatever fellow farmers talked about. Myrtle, drenched in Nervine, had taken to her bed, hoping to sleep off a sick headache, something she had commenced recently to suffer a good bit. Alice, alone, had just sat down in the parlor to rest from her arduous pacing. In a twinkling, the heat was upon her, within her, and all about her. It seemed to her to be colliding with itself fiercely, welling up from within only to be inundated from without. As surging tides met head-on, as it were, she saw dots of light, much like fireflies at night, spangle every inch of her body exposed to the air. Baked to the bone and aglow with twinkling lights, she heard the sound she had sought so earnestly and so long. "Izwollwithee, izwollwithee." But then a change began to occur in its enun-

49

ciation. It was as though the sound were being pulled apart, spaced out, and slowed down. When she heard it clearly for the first time, she understood it immediately, and knew that it was meant just for her. "It is well with thee," said the sound, "It is well with thee." Then, growing faint and speeding up simultaneously, it sounded like "izwollwithee" again and quickly disappeared. On the heels of its departure, the heat subsided, too, neither to return ever again. She would have welcomed one or both, but sought neither of them after that, having no need of them. On the following Saturday, after a week of devouring the Bible, she too disappeared, not permanently, but long enough at first to frighten her parents badly and then to anger them thoroughly.

Around 11 A.M., on the Saturday in question, Myrtle called, "Alice, it's about time to think about gittin' a bite to eat."

But there was no answer.

"Alice, I need your he'p, honey."

Again, no answer.

"Alice, wher' you at?"

Silence.

For the next several minutes, Myrtle called down into the cellar, trudged all the way up to the widow's walk, and looked into every room of the house. Outdoors she went, "yoo-hooing" at places where Alice might conceivably be. Finally, she hurried down to the barns.

"Silas, have you seen hide'r hair of Alice?"

"What'd she be doin' down here?"

"Well, I don't know, I'm sure, but have you laid eyes on 'er?"

"Why, no, 'course not. She don't come thisaway."

"Kin you tell me wher' she's at?"

"No, I cain't."

"I'm afeerd somethin's bad wrong; she ain't around the house nowher's."

"She wouldn't've gone to the woods fer to pick wildflowers, would she?"

"She might could've, but she ain't never before."

"Let me take a look-see down around ther 'n' you search the house agin'. I'll be up directly."

Ten minutes later, two concerned parents met on the back porch to compare notes.

"Silas, I'm afeerd somethin's happened to that child."

"You stay here, Myrtle, 'n' try to keep calm, 'n' call out 'er name ever' now 'n' then, 'n' I'll go up 'n' down the pike a piece in both directions. Like as not, she's gone to one of the neighbors."

Disbelieving it, Myrtle agreed, nevertheless, that it was a reasonable thing to do. She was vindicated half an hour later when Silas returned, shaking his head. "Ain't nobody seen 'er," he reported. "You don't reckon she'd go into town with somebody without tellin' us, do ya?"

"I don't know what she might do no more," said Myrtle, alarmed.

"Well," said Silas, getting anxious himself, "I reckon I'd better git on into Gallatin 'n' tell the sheriff."

"I sure wished you would," she agreed, urging him to get a move on.

Twenty tense minutes later, he parked the overheated truck a block and a half away from the Sumner County courthouse and strode toward the sheriff's office within. As he bore down on his destination, he couldn't help noticing a large group of folks standing in a ragged milling circle, or semi-circle, facing inward at somebody or something presumed to be in the middle. Then he heard some words that had a "preachy quality to 'em," as he was to tell Myrtle later. "Ah, it's just some jackleg preacher," he said to himself. He had witnessed a "right smart" of that kind of thing on Saturdays in the mountain towns to the east, but it was a little out of the ordinary in Gallatin, though by no means unheard of. Getting the better of his curiosity, he pushed past the crowd to tend to his business. As he was taking the courthouse steps two at a time, he froze in his tracks.

Alice! That was Alice's voice!

"What in God's name?" he said to nobody.

Disbelief turned to blessed relief, for at least the lost was found, alive and well, not kidnapped or murdered; but the relief was short-lived and passed abruptly into emotions so confused and distressing that he seemed to be paralyzed. He did not know whether to hold his ground or to run headlong from the place, whether to let himself be seen standing there or just to melt into the sidewalk, to keep his peace or to yell out at her to shut up and get herself home and be quick about it.

With eyes that transfixed every person upon whom they fell and with a self-confidence so surpassing that it stamped "certified" on every word she uttered, Alice was describing the night when she had intruded upon Myrtle and him, naked and in bed making love. As if that were not far too much to be telling in public, he, Silas McAlister, was known by a full quarter, if not a third, of all the folks who stood there, mouths agape, drinking it all in and thinking God alone knew what about him, and Myrtle, and Alice, and common decency.

Instinct, or something like it, eventually took charge and delivered him to the other side of the street where he hid, as best he could, standing sideways behind a utility pole. There he waited, there he endured it, until the viper he had nurtured in his bosom finished her homily. As folks broke up and began to wander off to savor the other sights and sounds of Gallatin, he walked quickly across the street, looking neither left nor right, and, coming up on her blind side and speaking no word, clamped his right hand on her upper left arm, and, jerking her neck sharply, marched her off to the truck.

Unable to speak or to describe any of his feelings, except for the rage with which he seethed, he drove home, like Jehu, furiously. Barely able to see, he jerked Alice out of the truck and dragged her into the house.

"Hey, Myrtle," he yelled, "here's y'all's daughter."

"Wher've you been, young lady?" Myrtle asked, angry as a wet hen but relieved as she looked Alice up one side and down the other.

"To Gallatin," said Alice sweetly with aggravating composure.

51

"To Gallatin? What was you doin' ther'?"

"Preaching the gospel."

"You was what?"

"Preaching the gospel of the Lord Jesus."

"You ain't no preacher."

"I am now."

"Why didn't you tell us?"

"You wouldn't have let me go."

"Well," sputtered Myrtle, "be that as it may, you might've at least had the courtesy to have given us the chance to think about it."

"No, for then I would have had to lie," said Alice, "and lying is a sin; besides, the Lord Jesus did not tell his parents when he disappeared to preach in the temple as a boy."

"You know good and well that you ain't Jesus," said Myrtle, fearing that Alice might have blasphemed, thereby endangering the whole household.

"I hope you won't take it into your head to pull that trick ag'in," said Silas, trying to get a word in edgewise.

"I must preach untold numbers of times yet," Alice assured them, eyes on the entire length of her life to be lived in God's service.

"Well, we'll just see about that, young lady," Myrtle announced without thinking, " 'cause here and now, I'm puttin' you on notice that I don't intend that no daughter of mine is goin' to do any such thing, at least not until you are growed up; even then, it ain't no business for a woman."

Then and there, Alice put her parents into a dilemma whose horns were more than two and all of which pointed straight at them.

"Whether it be right in the sight of God to hearken unto you more than unto God, judge ye," she intoned. Then she paraphrased Acts 4:20: "For I cannot but speak the things which I have seen and heard."

It was not and still is not in the blood of Tennessee farm folks to say to a child, "Child, get your nose out'n the Bible; you read it a heap too much." Nor could Silas and Myrtle really say, "No, Alice, you may not do God's will; you may not testify to your faith in the Lord Jesus; you may not speak for the Holy Spirit in season or out." If they had said anything remotely like that, and if it had gotten out, it would have been better for them for all their bedroom activities to have been performed in public. Accordingly, they caved in, and Myrtle passed into a state of mind that Nervine could not touch.

"Silas," she said, "ever'thin's kindly black-like and swimmin' around. Could you he'p me to the bedroom?"

None too steady himself, he steered her to the bedroom, helped her onto the bed gently, and then sped back to the door, bolting it with a bang too loud for such a small device. Pacing around the room like a caged tiger, he said explosively, "While you're layin' there 'n' cain't git no lower, jist let me tell you what happened today when I found 'er."

"Do," she sighed, thinking things could get no worse.

"Oh, she put it nice enough, all right. She says to all them people, 'The

52

spirit of the Lord drove me from my bed and delivered me into my parents' bedchamber wher' I beheld their carnality, in nekedness, knowing each other lustfully.' S'help me God, Myrtle, them were her very words. Then, holdin' the Bible kinda prim-like, she worked in that stuff about Ham comin' in 'n' seein' his father, Noah, drunker'n a lord 'n' layin' bare neked in his tent. Then she says, 'Jist like the Lord put a turrible curse on Canaan for what his father, Ham, done when he seen Noah neked, so the Lord put a turrible curse of sin and guilt on me for witnessin' my parents, stripped of all garments, immodestly engaged in an act o' passion.' Finally, she says, 'n' this beats anythin' I ever heered tell of, she says, 'The Lord come unto me and into me in heat three times, 'n' baked me clean 'n' made me pure, 'n' said, "It is well with thee." ' She knowed then and there, she told 'em, that she was a chosen vessel of God's to be used in preachin' the gospel and in doin' the work of the Lord Jesus."

Knowing that she would be a prisoner in her own home from that time on and that she would never again dare show herself in public in Sumner County, Myrtle began her imprisonment by covering her face with her pillow and wailing, thinly to be sure, but for a very long time.

It was not in their nature to want "to be shed" of their own flesh and blood, but Silas and Myrtle knew, from that moment on, that it was only a matter of time until Alice went forth into the world, forsaking mother and father for Jesus, never to return, perhaps. They felt powerless in the matter and resigned, making no attempt either to hasten her departure nor to stay her foot from the path she was bound and determined to tread.

When her parents closed ranks against her and said almost in unison, "No, sirree, we ain't gonna cart you hither, thither, and yon jist so you kin preach whatever comes into your head all over hell's half-acre," Alice was not surprised, for the Lord Jesus had said that a man's foes shall be they of his own household. She was, however, relieved and pleased that Silas and Myrtle steadfastly refrained from laying straws in her path. "Judas Priest!" her father said, choosing his words with uncommon care, "go along with any old Tom, Dick, 'r Harry that'll take ya." So, on weekends and holidays, she bummed rides off folks up and down the pike and, like the Holy Spirit, blew where she listed, turning up in small towns here, there, and everywhere, preaching.

Alice did not mean to be egocentric nor selfish, but she was so super-abundantly full of herself, having received "the Lord in heat three times," as she put it, that the word she preached was largely autobiographical. Her unconscious involuntary transportation (courtesy of the Spirit) to her parents' bedroom proved to be an indispensable boon, for until that time she had not really known sin and could, therefore, neither receive nor understand grace.

As a child, Alice had neither comprehended nor tried to believe in the Pauline doctrine of original sin. The idea that her very being, as a natural creature, was fallen and depraved never clouded her little-lady's mind. As for individual sins, well, she had committed so few of those that they really didn't matter, no, they really didn't matter. But upon invading her parents' bed-

53

room, beholding their nakedness, witnessing their intimacy, and sensing their shame, she found herself vying with St. Paul for membership in the "chief of sinners" club.

Then (that she might know grace) came the terrible time of alienation from her loved ones and the hell of outer darkness, God having absented himself from her life. Finally (that she might know saving grace to the full) came the experiences of bone-baking purification and the blessed message that all was well with her. Alice, the eternal twelve-year-old, could only interpret the heat as heaven sent, the message as divine, simple soul that she was. So, when she preached the word in those early days of her ministry, it was largely about herself. Had anyone accused her of wallowing in egotism, she would have insisted (assuming that she could have understood the point) that she was merely glorifying God as that Supreme Egotist would have her do.

It was not that Alice had no feeling for her parents. It was just that they had failed to understand that her unexpected observation of their sexual intimacy was an essential part of the Father's plan for her life and his greater glory. Seeing them in naked union on that fateful night had simply been one of the more mysterious ways in which he had worked, his wonders to perform. Alice could only hope that her parents would get over being distraught by her vivid and oft' repeated descriptions of the event and come to a humble acceptance of it as but one more instance of God's sometimes incomprehensible, sometimes hard-to-accept, will for mankind. Meanwhile, the best she could do was to pray for them; and she did. That their teeth remained set on edge was hardly her fault. She had accepted God's plan for her life; it remained for them to do the same.

Alice lingered at home, but always on the verge of departure, until the following spring, nearly a year later. While there she did the minimum amount of work acceptable to her parents, but did it dutifully and well, dropped out of high school, and divided her free time between prayer and Bible reading. She spent no time on sermon preparation but waited upon the Spirit to tell her where, when, and of what to speak.

Away from home, usually on Saturdays and Sundays, she was either preaching the word or traveling to and fro and, in season and out, gathering her strength against the unknown day when the Spirit would send her into wider fields of service. Both she and her parents knew that that day would come; the question was whether or not it would come as a thief in the night. It did. Early one fine morning in April, they found a note on the kitchen table by her place. It said:

Dear Mother and Father,
    The time has come for me to go. I do not yet know where, but I shall in good time. If God wills it, I shall see you again. If not, farewell. I pray that he may send his Spirit to you even as he has to me and that you will be born again as surely as I have. I also pray that you, and your baby boys,

54

and I may all be reunited one eternal day in the Father's house up yonder.

In the love of Christ, Amen.
Alice

"I know'd it was bound and determined to happen," said Myrtle, choking back sobs and sitting down for fear she might fall.

"I reckon she done what she had to do," said Silas, excusing himself hurriedly and speeding toward the barnyard, lest he seem unmanly.

Alice made a beeline toward the mountains to the east, hitherto unknown to her personally, to the Cumberlands, the Alleghenies, and the Blue Ridge from which the preponderance of her help was always to come. Unto the holy hills and hollers (hollows) of the Appalachian heartland she went, led, as always, by the Spirit and waiting upon him to tell her whether or where to go next; to Kentucky, or to the Virginias, or to the Carolinas, or to Georgia, or to remain in the eastern fastness of her native Tennessee.

She had no personal plans, no program, no discernible theology, no organization, no money, and, like the Lord Jesus, nowhere to lay her head. She simply went where and when she felt she was supposed to go and preached about, witnessed to, and testified to the majesty of God, the love of his Son, the power of his Spirit, and the miracle of divine grace performed in her, and for her, and for those beloved listeners unto whom she had come in childlike faith.

If people made contributions to the itinerant, she ate; if not, she went hungry. If they offered rides, she rode; if not, she walked. If they took her in, she slept in a bed with a roof overhead; if not, she slept where she dropped. If they opened their buildings to her, she preached indoors; if not, she preached outdoors. Even her detractors agreed that she was plucky, that she had lots of grit.

Her pluck, or grit, call it what you will, together with her tenacity came from a variety of sources. First and foremost was the insuperable self-certification of her mystic experiences. She never wavered in believing that she had been purified by holy heat sent from God (not once but thrice) and never doubted that she had received a divine message assuring her not only that all was well with her in the present but that it always would be in the future. Secure in such knowledge, she could never be afraid.

Second, she was completely at one with herself and contented beyond belief, even during the dismal days and lean years of her early full-time ministry. She never suffered from second thoughts, never asked, "What might have been, if?" never looked back from the plow she had seized, nor returned to bury the dead, and never agonized over decisions. Indeed, she was never conscious of making decisions. The Spirit did that for her. So, she simply waited and listened for his decisive word. Upon hearing it, she went where bidden and did as directed.

Third, she had a cast of mind that made her immune to such feeble opposition as the world provided. No high monkey-monk of a professor could correct her reading of the sacred text, because the Spirit told her, on demand, what a particular passage meant, no matter what it might seem to say to the contrary. No hoity-toity historian could inform her of changes and developments in Christian thought, because God's word was eternal, not historical. No holier-than-thou theologian could teach her systematic theology, because, since God spoke directly and most fully to chosen vessels such as herself, his message was utterly personal, particular, and individual; not universal, rationalizable, and public in an abstract way. No know-it-all philosopher could point out contradictions in her logic, because, quite literally, she did not think logically and could recognize no validity in ideas not her own. No uppity-uppity scholar could daunt or dissuade her, for she was profoundly ignorant and, therefore, supremely free to feel, to intuit, to hear, and to believe whatever convinced her. Neither great learning nor small could restrain her with disagreeable facts or unpleasant alternatives, for she had no learning at all. No high panjandrum of a wise man could teach her anything, because God had chosen the foolish things of the world with which to confound and shame the wise. She gloried in her folly for Christ, and could even be silly in good conscience, for her heart told her that it was the wisdom of God. No wise guy could set her straight about the ways of this world, for she was not of this world, nor could it tempt her in any way. No ideas ever clouded her vision or muffled her inner ear; no hint of critical thought ever furrowed her brow; no threat of intelligence ever disturbed her faith.

Fourth, and perhaps finally, she was strangely prepossessing both personally and physically. She looked like everybody's grandmother, yet was young. Because of that, her life seemed to span all ages of life, thus, putting her in touch with the whole of it. She looked like a girl budding into young womanhood, yet she was old somehow. She was, therefore, taken to be wise beyond her years, in the deep things of the Spirit at least. While appearing to be selfless and fragile, she exercised enormous self-possession. Not appearing forceful, she could, nonetheless, and did (without ceasing) exert tremendous forces of will power on others. Her eyes, always amazing to see, could immobilize people; her demeanor could put them simultaneously at ease; and the well-nigh omnipotent certitude with which she spoke of herself and of God could fill to the brim those who hungered for the kind of prodigious fare she had to offer.

It is written of Jesus that if all the things he did had been recorded in books, the world itself might be unable to contain them. On a lesser scale (as befits her modesty), much the same can be said of his servant, Alice Mc-Alister. Just as the few recorded signs and deeds that Jesus did were recorded that the reader might believe, so the following is presented that you might know how she became the unquestioned leader of an important, if not the

56

most important, sect in American Christianity.

One night, while conducting a revival in a rented tent in Smoke Hole, West Virginia, the Spirit gave her a gift as dramatic as unexpected. In a moment of ecstasy, her tongue seemed to roll upon itself and twitch uncontrollably, scrambling her words. But instead of stopping to reorganize her thoughts and beginning anew, she continued to scramble her words, but effortlessly, fluently, electrifyingly. She was speaking in an unknown tongue. The gift of the glossalalia was hers.

"Praise the Lord," wailed a thin voice from the center left of the tent.

"Thank God," boomed a male voice antiphonally.

"Thank you, sweet Jesus, thank you," chorused several voices scattered throughout the tent.

With head thrown back and eyes glassy, unseeing, but with ears open and hearing every word of encouragement, Alice gave herself to the Spirit.

A graduate student in anthropology from the University of Pittsburgh happened to be in the tent that night. Home on vacation, he had attended the revival out of one part curiosity and one part professional interest in experiences of group ecstasy. Having witnessed the spectacle, he could scarcely wait for the vacation to end to share his observations with his fellow students. In part, here is what he said.

"It didn't sound like French, or German, or any foreign language as we would think of it. It sounded like English, but English words with their syllables out of place, all screwed up, if you know what I mean, and it had a kind of biblical . . . ah . . . King James Bible cadence to it. You couldn't tell one part of speech from another, yet it sort of came out in sentences, and part of the time it was as fast as anything in Gilbert and Sullivan."

"Couldn't it have been planned?" asked a sceptical city girl. "You know, a little showmanship to dazzle the natives?"

"I really don't think it could have been. No, it was spontaneous, and if you want my opinion, I think it surprised the evangelist as much as the crowd. Of course, she was already high as a kite and had the crowd as taut as a fiddle string when it happened."

"So, you don't think it was memorized?" asked another sceptical student.

"No way, and if it had been, it would have been almost as amazing, because she kept at it at top speed for over five minutes, and, like I said, it was delivered like something out of Gilbert and Sullivan."

"The words weren't slurred?" asked the professor.

"I really can't talk about words, because I couldn't recognize words as such, but the syllables were distinct, even though they made no sense."

"How did the people in the audience take it?"

"Well, there were quite a few 'hallelujahs' and things like that, but for the most part they seemed to sense that they were in the presence of a mysterious power and that it was doing something meaningful—and probably good—for them, even though they couldn't say exactly what it meant."

"Sort of a spiritual fireworks display, you might say," observed another student.

"Yes, and that they were getting a message at that level even though it couldn't be verbalized."

"Well, thanks for working off duty and sharing your vacation experiences with us," said the professor.

Long before that academic episode occurred, the folks around Smoke Hole had spoken their minds on what had happened.

"I've heerd it, man and boy, for fifty-five years, but never anythin' like that," said one man in admiration.

"Me neither," said another, " 'n' I'm like you; I've heerd it most of my life now 'n' then."

"And she didn't have no interpreter neither," said a third, "but I still feel like I got a good message out'n it."

"The Spirit was on her the likes of which I've never seen in all my born days," said one lady.

"Oh, yes, she was truly filled," said a second lady.

"I don't reckon I was ever so uplifted in my life," said a third.

"I'm jist sorry she's gone," said a fourth, "but I'm right proud it happened here in Smoke Hole."

"And I hope she comes back real soon," said a fifth, " 'cause she's got real religion, none of this educated stuff you get so much of these days."

For her part, Alice was modesty incarnate. She had not sought the gift of tongues and scarcely knew when it was upon her, nor did she enjoy it particularly. She did not seek it actively, but whenever the gift was hers, she shared it fully. And many, praising her both for the gift and for her modesty about it, sought her presence in their midst.

For his part, the Spirit was apparently so pleased with the pure and empty vessel that was Alice that he decided to fill her to overflowing occasionally and, thus, to share himself with certain others in close proximity to her. At least, that is how she looked upon it after what happened at the Pentecostal Church of the Holy Flame, which clung to a ridge to the east of Brasstown Bald, the highest mountain in Georgia.

Brother Fugate Pierce, the minister of the Holy Flame Church, first heard Alice at a revival in Ducktown, Tennessee, where he was working by day as a stone mason. Clearly impressed, he humbly besought her "to come on down to Brasstown Bald and preach at the folks there." Eager to comply but unwilling to do so without the Spirit's consent, she said she would have to pray about it first, and did. Several weeks later, in early September, she arrived to preach for a week beginning with two sermons on Sunday and then one a night through the following Friday. Since her fame had preceded her and since her Sunday morning sermon was a "regular stemwinder," as some put it, no one was surprised to see the house packed that night.

The church was a simple rectangular affair with a raised platform about eighteen inches high that ran across the entire front end of the building, the pulpit being situated in the front midsection of the raised area. To its right, left, and rear were chairs lining the bare walls where pickers, singers, and the "chief mourners," as their detractors called them, sat. Other folks had to content themselves with sitting on the floor or on pews made of rough-hewn timbers, many of which had been hammered together such that people could not sit up straight on them but were forced to bend forward like supplicants.

The service had no formal beginning but just sort of got under way when the pickers (two men on guitars and one a banjo) began to pick. Two ladies sitting on the platform arose holding castanets and began to enhance the picking with their rhythmic arts. Many people scattered throughout the building then began to clap, thus falling into the spirit of the music. Quite at random, to all appearances, somebody began to sing, others joining in rapidly until nearly every voice was lifted in song.

Without prior agreement, as far as an outsider could tell, and with no clear sense of what was supposed to happen next, the pickers began to pick out the tune of "Barb'ry Allen" for which religious lyrics had been written locally. That done, everyone had a go at "The Blasted Fig Tree," an old English hymn. Following that, pickers, platform singers, and most everybody else re-grouped and belted out all the verses of the most singular hymn of the evening, "There Ain't No Flies On Jesus."

Intuiting that it was high time to address the Lord in prayer, Bro. Pierce elbowed his way to the pulpit and, grasping at the ceiling with both hands, bellowed in the general direction of heaven. "Amens" from the crowd punctuated his phrases, and, every now and again, a picker would underscore a particular message to, or request of, God with a resounding chord. Even a castanet jiggled into life a time or two in endorsement of what Fugate had to say. After his five-minute prayer was over, there was a kind of calm before the storm, so to speak, during which Alice was introduced as a heaven-sent woman with God's message to a perishing world on its last legs. Bro. Pierce ended his introduction by saying, "I thank the Lord that I ain't never been to a theological semithary wher' they teach folks this here modernism and evolution and what the world calls learnin' but is nothin' but how to blaspheme, and I know that this won'erful woman that God has seen fit to send us, that the Spirit has delivered to us at Brasstown Bald tonight, ain't never studied in no such school neither, but preaches the gospel as the Lord gives it to 'er heart. And, so, brothers and sisters, I'm right proud to turn this meetin' over to Miss Alice McAlister."

Chords, castanets, hand-clappings, "amens," and "hallelujahs" greeted Alice as she arose, in all her purity and innocence, to speak. Since no sermon can get off to a more attention-getting start than one that begins with sex and sensuality, with nakedness and passion, with sin and shame, Alice began as usual, with the heaven-sent episode in her parents' bedroom. Beyond that and her subsequent descriptions of holy heat, twinkling lights, and revelations, she did not know what she would say nor whether she would say it all in the known tongue or in part, at least, in an unknown tongue.

Since the Spirit enraptured her quickly that night, Alice gave vent to an unknown tongue within a few minutes after beginning, titillatingly, in the known tongue. When she was disenraptured, five or six minutes later, she found herself in the middle of a melee. Bodies were swirling about her so fast and colors were so blurred that she had to grasp the pulpit to keep from pitching to the floor, so dizzy was she for a time. It was all quite confusing, because she did not know what was happening, where she was, nor how she had gotten there. She had, of course, been oblivious to the Spirit's handiwork while enraptured.

Alice had no sooner begun to discourse in an unknown tongue than castanets rattled, chords resounded, "amens" erupted, hands clapped, feet stomped, and Bro. Pierce began to say "Thank the Lord," repeatedly, dropping his voice to its lowest pitch on "Lord" each time he said it. Although he did not get the Spirit himself, he had an uncanny knack of accelerating into the holy vortex those who did, simply, it seemed, by saying "Thank the Lord" in his own special way with his own special timing. One after another, the women on the platform stood up, their heads bobbing like so many biddies taking walks in a chicken yard. Then, with arms raised, they began to spin faster and faster (mostly counterclockwise), their heads falling backward pointing glassy eyes to the sky. This was followed by a holy din resembling pandemonium, each of the Spirit-possessed women shouting her prayers at the ceiling with utmost volume.

As the possessed went around and around like dervishes, a plump girl fell off the platform onto the floor, a foot and a half below, but bounced up and back again as good as new, unaware that anything jarring had happened. The only man to get the Spirit tended to lose his place and wander in eccentric orbits. At one point, he ricocheted off a bony lady, banged into a wall, and fell back upon the lap of another lady who, newly depossessed, was recovering on a chair. A woman in the congregation also got the Spirit and began to spin between pews, *in situ,* as it were, her hair coming out of its bun into a long pigtail trailing her 180 degrees behind, showering nearby worshippers with hairpins.

It was in the midst of all that that Alice clutched the pulpit to keep from falling. Assessing the situation correctly as Spirit-directed, she did nothing further except to serve the Lord by standing and waiting. The spiritual exercises, continuing for a long time, ended when the younger women and girls, in particular, began jumping up and down until exhausted, finally subsiding onto chairs.

When the Spirit left the Holy Flame Church that night to attend to business elsewhere in the cosmos, it was agreed upon by common consent, but voicelessly, that enough was enough. Alice preached no more at that service, and people began to disperse, but before leaving, they praised her lavishly for her uncommon power "to summon the Spirit and quick." The man who had received the Spirit thanked her profusely and said with unfeigned joy, "The Lord give me a good blessin' and thanks to you for your he'p." Bro. Pierce expressed enormous satisfaction over how well things had gone and bade Alice a good night's rest, wishing for her the sleep of the blest. Long since confident of the Spirit's gifts in her own life and newly aware that he could possess others in her presence through her person, she did sleep the sleep of the blest, and arose the next day strengthened and even more self-confident than before.

What Alice did not know was that the Spirit came often and easily to the Holy Flame congregation. Nor did she know that two buxom lasses were in such a frame of mind when they left the service that they fell easy prey to the blandishments of two boys in the crowd who, later that night, fathered infants upon them. Nor did she know that there were old men in the crowd who came to meetin's and preachin's expressly to see the Spirit take possession of girls and younger women. As they trudged home that night to their respective cabins in the hills, one old reprobate said with a leer, "A body coulda got a good milkshake there tonight, especially toward the end." "Amen to that," said another reprobate, "I don't believe I've ever seen bosoms get churned up any better than that." "It's gonna be a week to remember," said a third, chuckling over his recollection of jumping girls and bobbing breasts.

The sign that sealed Alice's future more than any other was given in Woolwine, Virginia. She went there in response to a Macedonian call to conduct a revival, the proud possessor not only of her own revival tent but of a truck with which to transport it. By the time she reached Woolwine, Alice was seasoned and had coordinated her abilities into evangelistic virtuosity. Make no mistake about it. She could play upon a congregation as though it were a superbly trained symphony orchestra, she its magisterial conductor. She could hold thousands in rapt attention, could call forth groans and lamentations from sinners, and could humble the wicked, making them kneel in contrition at the foot of the cross. She could elicit "hosannas," demand "hallelujahs," and make those who hung on her every word rejoice that they were not such as other men, damned to eternal flames. She could uplift the downtrodden and exalt unto the third heaven those who regarded themselves as the offscourings of the world (even as the world regarded them). She could hearten the disheartened, console the disconsolate, and inflame the lax with righteous indignation against the enemies of the Most High. She could propel sinners down the sawdust trail to repentance and fling wide the pearly gates of redemption. All those things and more she did in Woolwine. Pleased with her stewardship, the Spirit decided to give her a gift she had hitherto not even dared to hope would be hers.

On the next to the last night of the already great Woolwine revival, Alice surpassed herself. After her sermon, a legion of sinners stepped out and stumbled forward to repent and confess their faith in Jesus as Christ. After hearing each confession, blessing each penitent, and adjuring each to seek baptism speedily, she remained, as was her custom, to mingle with those who had come to meet her. As was commonplace, many clustered about her to see her closely, to look into her eyes to see the soul within, and to feed upon her presence. Then above the noisy confusion, a child's piping voice cried,

"Mama, Mama, I can hear!" "Praise the Lord! Little Sophie can hear, and she ain't heard a word in three years. *Oh, praise the Lord, praise the Lord!*" Others took up the refrain at once, and many people departing the tent turned on their heels and hurried forward, some running, to join the electrified tumult orbiting around Alice. Before the tent was cleared that night, a middle-aged woman with chronic appendicitis lost her symptoms and a hyperactive boy of nine who had jerked, jiggled, and jittered his way through life had been cowed into quietude.

Well within twenty-four hours, the child who had recovered her hearing had been deaf from birth; the woman whose symptoms of chronic appendicitis had been allayed had suffered persistent pain from acute appendicitis since early maidenhood; and the jumping, jerking boy had had the prince of all jittering demons cast from him. Such, anyway, was the work of the grapevine.

When Alice arrived at her tent, in the fading light of day, for the final service of the Woolwine revival, she was received as a conquering hero by a throng so great that it overflowed the tent, spilled outside, and swirled around and about. When she was seen attempting to enter, it was as though the Red Sea were parting, leaving her free to walk alone down the center aisle toward the pulpit at the far end of the tent. Thus, in triumph, she made her way. Goose pimples rippled up many an arm; scalps crawled; tiny hairs stood on end; people's voices cracked as they said, "Look, there she is," or choked as they said, "See, here she comes!" Many felt that night as though they were in the presence of a Great One whose long-promised, long-awaited epiphany had just been granted, and, Praise God! in lowly Woolwine.

When she ascended the pulpit and stood before the people, lifted up on a high platform, a mighty tumult of hand-clapping and "hallelujahs" greeted her, and would not be quickly stilled. Without so much as a prayer of invocation or the usual opening hymn, she spoke at once to the multitude directly from the heart. "Dearly beloved," she said, as though addressing each one individually, "I have never asked God for the power to heal, nor did I ask it last night. I have never presumed that the Father would grant me so great a gift, nor did I presume it last night, nor do I presume it now. At no time have I dared to stretch out my hands in healing, because the Holy One of Israel has already graced me with spiritual gifts far exceeding my merit. Yet, as you know, being yourselves witnesses, miracles of healing happened here last night without so much as the laying on of hands. How, then, you ask, could it have happened? By the power of our great God, of course. But why did it happen here? Not to magnify his servant, oh, no, surely not! Why, then, did it please the Father to overshadow us with his mercy, to send his Spirit of healing into our midst? Because of you, dearly beloved, because of you here in this place, for you have found favor with him that made heaven and earth, because you have pleased him surpassingly with your faith in his Son, our Lord, Jesus Christ. So, I say unto you, blessed art thou, Woolwine of Virginia, and exalted am I, through the matchless grace of God, to have

62

been called here and even now to stand in your presence."

"No, no," cried a masculine voice far back in the tent, "blessed are we to be in your presence."

"Yes, yes, oh yes," cried other voices, male and female.

"You are the Handmaiden of the Lord," said a powerful bass voice resonating throughout the tent and calling forth a harmony of many voices, "the Handmaiden of the Lord, the Handmaiden of the Lord, the Handmaiden of the Lord."

"Dear God, I can see!" sobbed a piercing voice almost at Alice's feet.

"And I can throw away my crutches," echoed a distant voice exuberantly.

"My pain is gone; for the first time in forty years, *my pain is gone!"* exulted someone else close at hand.

"The handmaiden who heals without a touch," said an ecstatic voice.

"Oh, yes, yes," chorused others caught up in the spirit, "the Handmaiden who heals without a touch."

"No," whined a high-pitched voice, "far more than that, *The Daughter of Deity;* you are *The Daughter of Deity,* Alice McAlister!"

There are no words to describe what happened after that nor to tell exactly how long it lasted. There was, alas, no chemist of the soul whose presence that night could (at leisure later on) sort out the variables that were present, delineate their architecture, identify the precipitates, and describe the chain reactions that occurred then and there at the feet of Alice McAlister. Perhaps the most astonishing facts were mundane, such as how the tent stood without being rent asunder, how those who swooned rose up unhurt, how the weak and the frail were delivered from trampling feet, and how not even a single little one was crushed by the enraptured multitude.

When with arms outstretched, as though in tireless benediction, Alice restored order, it was not with exaltation that she spoke but with fear and trembling. "May God have mercy upon us," she said imploringly, "upon him who first said the dread words, 'Daughter of Deity,' upon those who thoughtlessly repeated them, and upon me for the unintended sin of hearing them. Such words, beloved, are never to be thought, never to be said, never to be heard. Let it suffice, please God, that I should be known, henceforth, as the Handmaiden of the Lord."

On unnumbered occasions after that the Handmaiden of the Lord prayed for the sick and laid her hands upon them, sometimes with success, sometimes not. Her fame as a healer, however, rested primarily upon the fact that she could cure merely by her presence, and sometimes over great distances. This was amply borne out by grateful responses to her radio ministry and later on to television. Perhaps the most telling evidence of this came from a lady who owned the first television set in her part of the country. She wrote to Alice as follows:

I have been healed many times on radio but never before on TV until the other day when I saw your evangelism program. I was having a lot of the same old pains at the time and I reached out and seized the rabbit ears of my set with both hands and looked at you at the same time and could feel the healing power flow into my arms as you spoke. I am wondering if you know of healing anybody else on TV, and has any other healer that you know of healed anybody on TV before. Please write as I would like to claim it as a record if possible.

Sincerely in Jesus,
Mrs. Inez Boulton
R.F.D. #1
Witcherville, Arkansas

It should go without saying that no man ever breached the portals to the Handmaiden's womb nor did the Holy Spirit—God having sent his Only Begotten Son nearly 2,000 years earlier—yet Alice felt strangely full after the Woolwine revival and could only liken her condition to pregnancy. Something was striving to be born, some great thing to come forth from her. Becalmed by icy roads throughout the mountains and needing confinement until the time for delivery, she retired for several weeks to a house placed at her disposal by well-to-do converts in Hazel Green, Kentucky. There in restful seclusion, she awaited developments, meditating much and beseeching God to facilitate her delivery. But it pleased God to send her forth from Hazel Green still great with child. South to her native Tennessee she went to preach a revival, and only then to give birth.

The Reverend Ardmore Kendall, B.D. (Boston U.) was the shepherd of the Methodist flock in Soddy-Daisy, Tennessee. Although he was a well-intentioned young man and a dazzling pulpiteer, he could never corral his scattering flock let alone lead them anywhere. It was as though his crozier were bent in the wrong way irreparably, due (no doubt) to his mistaken conviction that he could use the Methodist ministry as an instrument with which to undo superstition. The poor man believed vociferously in certain ideas that were anathema to his sheep and disbelieved in almost everything they took to be crucial to Christianity. He was, for example, an advocate of gun control legislation in a region where 57.3 percent of all pickups were outfitted with gun racks across their rear windows. He was a pacifist in a place where folks were famous for volunteering, on the spot, to fight against anything the federal government (any federal government) said ought to be fought against. He was passionately ecumenical (regarding most denominational differences as picayunish) in a land where religious unity often extended no farther than one's own holler. Moreover, he disbelieved volubly in the mystery of the Holy Trinity (thinking it neither mysterious nor holy, just confused), rejected the virgin birth of Jesus as an affront to the beauty of God-given sex, contended that the physical resurrection of Jesus' body was as theologically unnecessary as it was unhistorical, made light of the nature miracles in the New Testament as though they were just tall tales, abolished hell outright and depopulated heaven of cherubim, seraphim, angels, and archangels, alarmingly, leaving God still splendid but in isolation. Needless to say, he was not successful as ministerial success is usually measured. Sensing that and brooding on his uncertain future, he remained edgy most of the time and was no stranger to distress.

The Handmaiden of the Lord arrived at the front door of the Methodist parsonage in Soddy-Daisy early on a Tuesday morning in March. She had come to call upon the minister, presumed to be therein, not because the Spirit had selected him but because she was still a Methodist formally and, to all appearances, merely happened to be in Soddy-Daisy at that fateful moment in religious history. Ardmore had just finished a farmer-sized breakfast, preparatory to grappling with the superstitions of yet another day, when a series of sharp raps rattled his front door. Putting on his jacket to look his ministerial best, he opened the door only to find a perfect stranger standing there, pink and white and plump all over.

Greeting him as though there were not a minute to lose and refusing his invitation to step inside, Alice inquired hurriedly, "What do you do to start a new church?"

"See an architect or get a good contractor, I guess," Ardmore answered, caught somewhat off guard.

"No, no," she said, but with no hint of vexation in her voice, "I mean start a new denomination, sort of." She let it go at "sort of," because she was not quite ready to call her new denomination "the one true church."

Choking back the urge to shout that there were already about 300 denominations in Christendom and refusing, to his great credit, to indulge himself in asking, "Who the hell needs more; won't any one of those do?" he said flatly, guessing as he spoke, "Set up a national headquarters and submit your membership figures to the census bureau."

"Thank you kindly," said Alice, turning on her heel and hurrying off the porch to do so.

"And who was that?" chirped his young wife, Marilyn, sweetly.

"I don't know, but I sure as hell blew it," he answered explosively.

"You blew it, did you?"

"Yeah, I should have told that benighted character, 'Make believe you're Jesus and go find a Peter'."

Not pretending to know what it was all about, nor caring really, but thinking the last part of the suggestion not a bad idea at all, Marilyn nodded coquettishly toward the bedroom with its bed still unmade and inviting.

But Ardmore, distraughtly pacing to and fro in the living room, kept asking himself aloud such questions as "I wonder if the Unitarians would have me?" and saying such things as, "I can't take any more of this Methodist stuff in these Soddy-Daisy places of the world." With the eyes of his mind thus fixed on troubled vistas, he neither saw the sweet signal sent by his luscious wife nor did he recognize that it was he, Ardmore Kendall, ardent ecumenist, who had helped to launch on that very day the divisive new sect called "The Holy Nation Association of Churches of the Chosen."

Before leaving the ministry in favor of hospital administration, the Unitarians having too slender a sheepfold to need more shepherds, Ardmore learned to his chagrin a great deal more about Miss Alice McAlister, the Handmaiden of the Lord. Not only had she started her new denomination with his help, she had also taken his advice about getting a good contractor. Having discovered an abandoned church building in Soddy-Daisy, she bought it for a song, paying little more for it than the price of the land on which it stood. Since it was in desperate need of repair, she sought out a born-again building contractor (if that is not a contradiction in terms) who would comply with her wishes at cost. In that way she not only established a national headquarters building for the Holy Nation but also laid down a novel pattern (of which more later) for extending Churches of the Chosen.

Before leaving Soddy-Daisy, amidst cheers over his departure and mutterings over his apostasy, Ardmore went about saying "good-bye" to a few friends of the cloth, one of whom was Rufus K. Wombak, newly imported by the Presbyterians from a seminary in Louisville. Summarizing his negative views on religion for Rufus, whom he believed to be a bit fatuous, Ardmore said caustically, "The Jews have their Jerusalem, the Moslems their Mecca, the Catholics their Rome, the Anglicans their Canterbury, the Christian Scientists their Boston, the Mormons their Salt Lake City, and the Holy Nation its Soddy-Daisy." Both grimaced, laughed dark laughs, and bade each other farewell.

When Alice awoke to what had happened, saw the child, recognizing it as her own, she was overwhelmed at what she, by the power of God, had been permitted to bring forth. Since in retrospect she was as fascinated by its conception and delivery as she was by the parental bedroom episode and the related events that followed thereupon, a permanent new element entered her sermons. She never tired of telling how the Holy Nation Association came to be born.

Like all creative people who are also modest, Alice was the first to be amazed at what she could do and was always more astonished at her accomplishments than were others. At no time did she plan to perform her prodigies. She never said such things as, "Tonight, I shall speak in tongues," or "I shall share the gifts of the Spirit with multitudes this day," or "I shall heal the sick when next I preach." She was conscious only of waiting upon God's pleasure, of letting him work through her in his own good time. Still and all, when the newly christened "Handmaiden of the Lord" entered her confinement in Hazel Green, Kentucky, she knew that she had been accredited by God extraordinarily with mighty signs and wondrous works. Moreover, she was convinced at that moment (and as close to being smug as she ever came) that greater things lay ahead. But let her tell the story, as excerpted from her sermons.

"Beloved, when I went, as the Spirit directed, to Hazel Green, I wandered around there in a kind of wilderness. Hour upon hour, day by day I walked about the house and grounds, which loving Christian friends had placed at my disposal, looking, looking everywhere, awaiting a sign, but none came. I prayed much, asking God for his guidance, and meditated even more, in hopes of deliverance from my confusion. The Holy Book, always at hand, and so often a portal wide open to spiritual truths, seemed to me to be a closed door, locked against my understanding; oh, yes, it did seem so, it really did. And so, beloved, I knocked upon that door; no, I did more than that, I really did; I beat upon it, pleading as I have never pled before, that it might be opened to my understanding. I recognize now that God did open the door to me, even if only a tiny crack, when he inspired me to begin reading about St. Peter in the Gospel of Matthew, but I did not know that at the time, and I was afraid—oh, yes, I surely was afraid—that I was just reading at random and not under inspiration, and that the door was still bolted hard against me. That is a terrible feeling, brothers and sisters, it really is.

"Well, just as I said, I began to read about St. Peter in Matthew, chapter 16, beginning with verse 18, where our Lord says, 'And I say also unto thee, that thou art Peter, and upon this rock I will build my church; and the gates of hell shall not prevail against it.' Oh, how I wanted to know more about that wonderful rock, and so, brethren, I read all four gospels again, devouring every word about that one who meant so much to Jesus that he chose him to be the rock upon which to build his church. Just think how strong that rock would have to be to resist Satan, to resist this wicked world! But I still hungered to know more about that rock than the gospels told me. 'Let me receive some word from Peter himself,' I prayed to God, 'that I too might be more rock-like.' And then I remembered to my shame, yes, indeed, to my shame, that the Apostle Peter himself wrote two short epistles. I turned to them at once, near the back of the New Testament, with trembling fingers, realizing that I had never done them justice, that I had not read them enough, that I had spent so much time reading the gospels and the letters of Paul that I had neglected the epistles of the Apostle Peter, the great and solid rock of the church.

"So, beloved, I read them eagerly, but fearfully, again and again, praying much as I did so. I was greatly blessed by them, but still confounded as to what God would have me do. Then, Praise his Holy Name, he directed my attention expressly to I Peter 2:9 where I read, 'But ye are a chosen gene-ration, a royal priesthood, an holy nation, a peculiar people; that ye should shew forth the praises of him who hath called you out of darkness into his marvellous light.' My, but aren't those wonderful words? I knew they were when I saw them. I knew that God was blessing me through them, but I did not know that he had already opened to me the very door upon which I had been pounding for so long. He had, but I knew it not. No, it was not until I had left Hazel Green, not until I had headed south to Soddy-Daisy to conduct a revival that the scales fell from my eyes, giving a revelation as plain to see as the sun at noon on a cloudless day. That happened when I was passing through Knoxville.

"When I saw the light, brethren, I was so enraptured that I do not remember how I got out of Knoxville and on to Soddy-Daisy. I am sure I took the road, but maybe I didn't; I suppose I passed through towns, but I don't remember any; I am certain that I went through the lovely countryside of Tennessee, but I can recollect no detail of it, no flower, no tree, no distant mountain, no farm, no person. Whether I was in the body or out, I know not, but God delivered me safely to my destination, and I preached to the people there, telling them what he had shown me. Beloved, would you like to know what he showed me? Of course you would, and I will tell, for he wants me to, and he wants you to accept my message and help me spread it all over creation.

"Dear friends, when I left Hazel Green to carry out God's will in Soddy-Daisy, I traveled many a mile over the pikes of Kentucky and Tennessee, and as I passed, I saw many churches, many of them being of different denominations. I wondered about that; I really did. But God didn't give it to me as a revelation until I reached Knoxville. The road there was torn up, you see, and I had to make a long detour through the city. Never before had I seen so many churches of so many different denominations so close together, one on every other corner, it seemed. It is truly a religious city, I thought to myself, but then, God gave it to me to ask, 'But, is it a Christian city?' Before I had finished asking, he answered, saying, 'No, it is not a Christian city, for all those different churches are the doings of men, of men inspired by Satan. Look about you,' he said, and I did, and what, beloved, do you think I saw?

"I saw something called St. Mary's Catholic Church. There is no St. Mary in Scripture; she didn't found a church; the word 'catholic' is not in the Bible. The head of that church and of all Catholic churches lives in Rome (or Babylon as the Book of Revelation calls it), and he is called the Holy Father, and the priests of that idolatrous church are called Fathers against the express word of God in Matthew 23:9 where Jesus himself says, in red letters, 'And call no man your father upon the earth; for one is your Father, which is in heaven.' And the Pope and the priests of that church teach that the Lord forbade them to take wives. But the Apostle Peter, upon whom they falsely say their church was founded and whom they claim as their first pope, was married; otherwise Jesus could not have healed his mother-in-law (in Mark 1:30-31), could he? And those idolatrous priests teach all manner of things not in Scripture such as that folks should not eat meat on Fridays." (As a child, Alice had heard Catholics referred to as mackerel snappers, but the Spirit forbade her to call them that in her sermons.)

"Well, dear friends, I drove on and came to the Protestant Episcopal Church. 'Episcopal' is a human name; it is the name for a kind of church government. It is not God's name for his church. You may have heard these people called Whiskeypalians, for they consume much strong drink; indeed they do. I have even heard that where three or four of them are gathered together, there there will be a fifth." (This was a witticism Alice felt free to

68

use in Kentucky or in Jack Daniels' Land, but not elsewhere.)

"When I began to think I would never get off that detour in Knoxville, God showed me the Christian Science Meeting House, something else he wanted me to see. Can you find any such name in the New Testament, any such church? No sirree, you cannot, nor can you find the false ideas they teach. The people who go to that meeting house, brethren, are like Grape Nuts, neither grapes nor nuts; they are neither scientists nor are they Christians.

"Then the Spirit showed me other churches. I saw an ugly great thing called the First Baptist Church in big letters and underneath, in small letters, Southern Baptist Convention. Dearly beloved, these are deluded people, deceptive people. Satan has made them cunning. They pretend to be strong in the Spirit, and they make out like they know their Bibles. But if they really did, they would know that they have named their church after a man and not a Christian man either. They have named their church after John the Baptist. Do I need to remind you that he never became a Christian? Our Lord says of him (in Matthew 11:11), 'Verily I say unto you, among them that are born of women there hath not arisen a greater than John the Baptist: notwithstanding he that is least in the kingdom of heaven is greater than he.' And what do you say to that? Does Christ lie? Surely not! God forbid that it should be so, beloved, but there could be a First Alice McAlister Church, and it would be based on a person greater than John the Baptist, not because I am anything except what God makes of all true Christians, but that is something far greater than the greatest of men merely born of women and not born-again in the blood of the Lamb. And, friends, God didn't identify his church by any such direction as 'southern.'

"Brothers and sisters, I could go on and on and speak of the Lutherans named after Luther Martin . . . er . . . ah . . . Martin Luther," (Alice could never get straight on that.) "and the Moravians, and the Abyssinian Baptist Church, and the Methodists—now, there's a human name for you—and the Congregationalists, and the Presbyterians, none of whom have scriptural names."

(Alice did not mention such denominations as the Church of God and the Churches of Christ, which do have biblical names, for fear that she would not be able to make her point as effectively as she wanted to. In any case, those groups did not share the truth that God had revealed to her. If so, she reasoned, she would have been one of them and not the founder of the Holy Nation Association. Clearly, those groups did not have a Handmaiden of the Lord like herself—at least as far as she knew or wanted to know—one who could speak in tongues, could share the Spirit with others almost at will, could heal the sick, and could receive revelations directly from God even while passing through an unchristian city like Knoxville.)

"When God had shown me all those churches, dear Christian friends, and had opened my eyes to see all the divisions in the Body of Christ and all the unbelief and wickedness in those so-called churches, he spoke to me in

69

the very words he had inspired the Apostle Peter to write, the very words I had read in Hazel Green: 'But ye are a chosen generation, a royal priesthood, an holy nation, a peculiar people; that ye should shew forth the praises of him who hath called you out of darkness into his marvellous light.' And God said those words to me over and over. The sound of his voice—oh, I can't even begin to tell you what that was like—just surrounded the car and filled it and surrounded me and filled me with sound. Maybe the car was lifted up by a cloud of sound; I cannot tell. Maybe it flew all the way to Soddy-Daisy on the wings of sound; I do not know, nor do I care about that, though it would have been a great miracle. What I do know, what I do care about, is that God showed me that I was to restore and to lift up anew his true church which has languished so long in the hands of apostates and unbelievers, that I was to rebuild it on the solid rock that is Peter, that I was to give it its proper scriptural name.

"Dear hearts, we are the chosen people of God. Isn't that wonderful? Ours is the Church of the Chosen. We are God's Holy Nation. Our churches are united in the Holy Nation Association that we may serve him as royal priests all across this great country of ours. Think of that, beloved, just think of that, a royal priesthood! We are also a peculiar people, oh, yes, Praise God, we are peculiar that we may shew forth the praises of him that called us out of darkness into his marvellous light. There are many who cannot see that we praise God through our peculiarity. Oh, I weep for such people; I pray for them; I surely do; but if they would harden their hearts and condemn themselves—so be it. God has already destined them to stumble as he said in I Peter 2:8.

"It may amaze you, beloved; it may hurt you; it may even make you just a little bit mad; but I have been called peculiar; oh, yes, I have; I surely have. I have been accused of being simple and uneducated by some of these professors who call themselves theologians. I have been reviled by so-called servants of God and ministers of churches. But if we are to praise God as the Scriptures say, by being peculiar, then we must expect the wicked to scoff and the wise of this world to ridicule us. Such people are really fools, beloved. Of course, Christians are forbidden to call any human being a fool, but God is no fool and knows a fool when he sees one. In any case, beloved, I am peculiar; I admit it; Praise the Lord, I am peculiar, and so are you!"

After the virgin birth of the Holy Nation Association of Churches of the Chosen in Soddy-Daisy, Tennessee, Alice not only continued her revival ministry throughout the southern mountains, but also launched her radio and television ministries and began to travel, at the Spirit's bidding, all over the continental United States. Since it was a rare tent or church building that could contain the crowds clamoring to be in her presence, she began to rent municipal auditoriums and university field houses. It became a trademark for her to conclude her sermons by exulting in her peculiarity. With arms uplifted and head thrown back, eyes upon the heavens, she would say, "I am peculiar, oh, yes, I am; Praise the Lord, I am peculiar." Then she would lower her head and somehow manage with a single glance to look everybody in the eye and say, "And so are you," whereupon 5,000, or 10,000, or however many would take up the refrain. Many an unsuspecting passerby in Anywhere, U.S.A., would go by the largest auditorium in town only to hear it swell and reverberate with the joyful chorus, "We are peculiar people, oh, yes, we are; Praise the Lord, we are peculiar."

Anyone who can bring 10,000 people to their feet to declare their peculiarity in thunderous choruses, exulting all the while in their foolishness, can separate those same people from their money. At first it was hundreds of dollars, then thousands, then hundreds of thousands, and, finally, millions of dollars a year that poured into the Holy Nation's coffers. It came primarily from two sources: from a very small number of people who had it in super-fluity (being able to give generously) and from vast numbers who had scarcely any and could ill afford to give such as they gave, yet gave freely without thought of the morrow. Together with the nickels and dimes of orphans and the mites of widows came a coal mine in Kentucky, an enormous pit of optical-quality sand in West Virginia, several gas wells in Louisiana, a half-dozen oil wells in west Texas, and even a small uranium mine in Colorado, to say nothing of stocks, bonds, and securities of various sorts, farms, orchards, estates, and valuables of exotic variety.

Early on, Alice perceived a causal connection between those gifts and her supplications. As a supplicant she took a shopping list with her to the Lord in prayer and, when successful, thought of the resulting bounty as having been, quite simply, prayed-in. Her associates would say such things as, "Praise the Lord, the Handmaiden prayed-in a sand pit today," or "Give God the glory for that peach orchard the Handmaiden prayed-in." When the One whose ways are past finding out responded affirmatively, he was praised lavishly (in keeping with his desires) and thanked for his goodness; when he did not respond, he was praised lavishly, thanked for his goodness, and feared, his chosen ones looking within themselves for some lurking sin or other which had stayed the Holy Hand. Sometimes, he was praised and thanked merely for withholding what his chosen yearned for most but as-sumed they were not yet strong or wise enough to handle as he would have them handle it.

The Lord, of course, knew what was needed even before Alice had completed her shopping lists and often gave freely before his stewards knew that they were able to use rightly whatever was given. Along those lines, the Lord had never before done so much for his Holy Nation as he did when he inclined the recently hard heart of the eminent American industrialist and financier, Cyrus Dewayne Pritchard, to benefit his chosen with the great estate at Big Bend.

"*Mother of pearl!*" said the Handmaiden, reverting to an almost for-gotten exclamation from girlhood. "Mother of pearl," she said again and then, more characteristically, "Praise the Lord," and "Thank you, Jesus, thank you." That which evoked her outburst lay all about her. Below the sod at her feet, as she stood on the edge of Rimrock Hill, was a sheer cliff of naked limestone, sixty-five feet deep. Below that for nearly 200 vertical feet was a slope as steep as a talus slope can be, and verdantly covered. At the foot of the great curving slope was the big bend of the Kinross River. At 472 miles, the Kinross is the longest river in the continental United States to flow in a northwesterly direction. Geologically young, it flows in a remarkably straight course except for its big bend, a thirty-five-mile stretch along which it angles northeast for a short distance, then turns almost straight north, then surges in vain at the foot of Rimrock Hill, then turns abruptly toward the southwest before resuming its northwestering way some twenty miles downstream. Ahead of her, to the south and about 265 feet below, stretched the bountiful Shadrach Plains, an undulating peninsula delineated as though it were a great arrowhead by the curving Kinross.

It was not the sheer beauty of that sight, however, that wrested the words "Mother of pearl" from Alice's unexpecting lips. It was, rather, what lay at her back, rising slightly above her at its highest point and curving down and away both to her left and her right. It was, in short, the 5,160 acres of the great estate at Big Bend that made her cry out as she did. It was the magnificent chateau behind her, looking as though it (and its formal gardens) had just been plucked from the valley of the Loire in France and transplanted in America, that overwhelmed her. It was the orchards of both fruits and nuts, the meadows, the croplands, the vegetable gardens, the barns, the greenhouses, the dairy, and the excellent breeding stocks in cattle, sheep, and swine that made her feel giddy. It was, after all, *hers,* all hers; well, not hers literally, but the Holy Nation's, or, most precisely, God's. Still and all, as Alice perceived it, the Lord had delivered that priceless possession into her keeping and had done so even without her full realization that it was needed for the next great achievement of her stewardship. So, for all practical purposes, it was hers until such time as the Lord should summon her home to heaven to be with him for eternity. Little wonder, then, that she shook with joy as she gazed upon the Kinross and wobbled as she walked toward the chateau to take upon herself even greater burdens than any she had shouldered before.

To the profane eye, mystery clings to the gift that Cyrus Dewayne Pritchard lavished upon the Holy Nation. Although that exceedingly grasping gentleman had been converted shortly after his retirement and equally shortly before his death, he was not and did not become a royal priest, nor had he met the Handmaiden of the Lord prior to his decision to help underwrite her efforts with the great estate at Big Bend. Perhaps he had a premonition that he was soon to stand in the office of the chief of all chief executives, one who, with no need of board approval, could prevent his promotion to the heavenly host and deny him the ultimate acquisition, namely, eternal life. Or it may be that patriotism motivated him. He was convinced that only in the United States of America could a simple farm girl who hadn't finished high school become a major religious leader and the chief administrator of a multi-million-dollar enterprise. Or, it could be that he was trying, misguidedly, to repay the economic system that had benefited him so preternaturally. It was, after all, well known to him that Alice thought (insofar as she can be said to have thought at all) that capitalism was divinely inspired, that it was, quite simply, Christianity in action, economically. Whatever the case, he had no sooner given Big Bend to the Holy Nation than his soul was required of him, the bigger barns he had so raptorially acquired having been given away, perhaps, in the nick of time.

It is written in Ecclesiastes that the race is not to the swift, nor the battle to the strong. It might equally well have been written that the founding of seminaries is not to the learned, nor teaching in them to the wise. Alice and her cohorts demonstrated those eternal truths beyond all doubt when, having already moved the headquarters of the Holy Nation from Soddy-Daisy north to their great new estate, they also established the Big Bend Bible School on the chateau's second floor to train royal priests to serve the Churches of the Chosen and to minister to the religious needs of "new Jews," as they often referred to themselves. After receiving Big Bend, it was clear to all that God had given it to them not only as a suitable national, if not planetary, head-quarters for his chosen but also as a truly inspirational setting in which to train his royal priests. As Alice perceived it, it wasn't that she had been slow to realize the need for the school, it was just that God had wanted to arrange suitable housing for it before revealing its need to her and, simultaneously, providing the way to meet that need. Once it was clear that God wanted her to found a school, Alice proceeded forthwith, undaunted (nay, emboldened) by her ignorance.

Over the years, the Handmaiden also became an expert fisher of men, of whom five deserve special notice. If she were to have an inner circle, Alice had secretly hoped to have it composed of three, four, seven, or, best of all, twelve intimates. But, for reasons that escaped her, she developed a long-lasting group of five, a number toward which the God of Israels, old and new, had not previously shown any conspicuous favor. Despite the slight unease that went with the number, she took heart in the fact that her inner circle was composed entirely of men, even as Jesus' inner circle had been.

The prodigious Mordecai Montefiori not only blinded his economics professors at Chicago with brilliance, he astounded his fellow graduate students, putting those luminaries-to-be into deep shade with his incandescent abilities. With the Ph.D. in hand at the tender age of nineteen, he went straightaway to teach economics at New York University where by his twenty-seventh birthday he had rocketed up the ranks to a full professorship (his chair being endowed), had gained tenure (NYU having begged him to stay), and had earned an international reputation. Abiding cheek by jowl with great captains of industry and finance as well as with highly placed academics and government officials, he seemed destined to become one of the few dominating figures in his field. Rich, influential, perpetually in demand as a consultant, the author of three important books before he was thirty, and the major professor of swarming Ph.D. candidates, he could never understand why economics had come to be known as the dismal science. Delightful science was more like it, thought the once impoverished lad from Manhatten's lower east side.

Enormously busy, he looked askance, at first, at the letter that came one fine morning from Pueblo, Colorado. Something calling itself the Edgington-Frothingham Fund (if it were not a put-on) wanted him to undertake a definitive investigation of the fund raising and expenditure practices of certain Protestant sectarian groups in the United States. A good deal closer to Mt. Sinai than to Calvary's hill in such fugitive religious thoughts as he entertained, "Mordy," as intimates called him, pushed the letter aside, snickering. But the standard fare contained in the balance of his mail that day was just that, standard fare. A bit jaded, perhaps, by more consultancies of the same old order (offering good money but no challenges), by more opportunities to speak on the same old subjects, more invited participations at professional meetings, and more opportunities to testify before government sub-committees, etc., Mordy's eyes wandered back to the Edgington-Frothingham envelope peeping from beneath the mound of correspondence lying on his desk. In a rare moment of idleness, he fished it out and read it again.

The letter pointed out that the United States was awash in Protestant sectarian activity, that hundreds of millions of dollars were being raised annually by revivalists and faith healers, by radio and television ministries, and by a multitude of burgeoning sects. The Fund wanted to know how the money was raised, whence it came, how much there was, how it was used, and what the economic impact of tax-free sectarian business activities really was. The Fund had chosen Professor Montefiori not only because of his eminence in economics but also because of his broad knowledge of the social sciences and because of the objectivity he would surely bring to the study. It was not expected that he should do the legwork himself but rather that he should organize the research (to be done by underlings), observe its progress periodically, and superintend the writing of the final report, to be published as a book. A two-year study was suggested; the benefits to NYU and its economics department were substantial and Mordy's compensation nothing to be snickered at. After dinner that night, while sucking meditatively on a panatella, he decided to do it.

Mordy's letter of acceptance had no sooner reached Pueblo than he learned by coincidence (to all appearances) that a certain person known as the Handmaiden of the Lord had rented the civic auditorium in Hackensack, New Jersey, for a week so as to conduct a revival. When an agnostic Jewish friend in Columbia's religion department told him that the Handmaiden's group was the fastest growing and one of the richest sects in America and that its members called themselves new Jews and thought of the Church of the Chosen as a kind of New Israel, Mordy bestirred himself in a way uncharacteristic of economists to cross the Hudson to the west, something New Yorkers are loath to do unless California bound.

On the night when he ventured across the Hudson to sample some of the sectarian wares whose financing he was to study, Alice was inspired (the sceptic will say by coincidence) to prove to Jews for the benefit of an exclusively Gentile audience (except for Mordy) that Jesus really was the once and future king of Israels, old and new, that he was foretold by inspired prophets, sent by God in the fullness of time, crucified according to a divine plan for salvation, and that he was, even then, ready to return to fulfill his promises to new Jews of the Holy Nation. There is no doubt that the Handmaiden succeeded, for when her spectacular performance in citing proof-texts was over, the only Jew present that night (together with many Gentile sinners) hastened down the sawdust trail with joyful tears in his eyes to confess his faith in King Jesus.

When Mordy arrived at the Hackensack auditorium that fateful night, hoping that his gnome-like figure would not be recognized by anyone prominent in monied or academic circles, nothing could have been farther from his mind than his own conversion within two hours. Yet, when it happened, nothing, it seemed to him, could have been more inevitable, more right. The problem was how to break the news to Huldah, his acerbic wife, and to his many gimlet-eyed associates. Euphoric but wary, lest his faith of a few hours be tried beyond its infantile endurance, Mordy resolved to wait upon the Spirit to give him voice. Accordingly, upon arriving home, he slipped into his wife's studio and stood meekly and mutely, waiting for her or the Spirit to say something. Clad in silk lounging pajamas, Huldah was poring over some sketches she had done relative to the interior decoration of an office suite. Glancing up at long last, she said, "Oh, it's you, Mordy; where the hell you been?"

"To Hackensack."

"Oh, to Hackensack," Huldah mused aloud, thinking that Mordy was trying to be funny in his typically compressed, not to say constipated, way.

"Huldah."

"Yeah."

"I found the Lord Jesus tonight."

"No easy task in Hackensack, I should think. How come he was over there in the first place?"

"Please, Huldah, try to understand, I have been converted. As soon as I am baptized by the Handmaiden of the Lord, I will become a new Jew, a Christian, and a member of the Holy Nation Association of Churches of the Chosen."

"Jeez, Mordy, come off it, will you?" said Huldah, alternating between mild alarm and vexation.

"I beg of you, Huldah, please do not take the name of my Lord in vain any more or say it in a light or bantering tone."

"*Jesus Christ!* Mordy, what are you talking about?" Huldah demanded in a voice too rasping to be either light or bantering.

"Huldah," said Mordy, wincing at her habitual profanity, "I am trying to tell you, dear, to witness to you that I have repented of my sins; I have given up my former life; I have confessed my faith in Jesus Christ; I have committed myself without reservation to the work of his kingdom."

Knowing that Mordy had never been any more religious than she and that he had been a Jew only out of birth, habit, and pride over the Nobel Prize winning ways of their people, she felt alarm triumph over vexation.

"Mordy," she cooed, twirling a forefinger at her temple, "you're not sick, are you, or overwrought from working too hard, or anything like that?"

"Sick, overwrought, working too hard? Why, I've never felt more fit in my whole life. I'm whole, Huldah; I'm healed; I'm uplifted as never before! The power of Jesus can do all things, can make all things new."

"Jeez, Mordy," said Huldah, fearing that a deranged man might be even more of a drag to live with than an economic man (Mordy's aesthetic tastes were awful), "if you only had a respiratory infection or something gastric, I'd fix you some chicken soup, even at this late hour. But what," (she continued under her breath) "do you fix for someone who's gone to Hackensack and come back bananas?"

"Better run along to bed, Mordy, new Jews need sleep just as much as the older variety," she said, wondering what it would be like for a fallen Jewess like herself to crawl between the sheets with a creature made new by Christ and deprived of his marbles.

So inimitable was Mordy's genius that colleagues and graduate students alike followed his comings and goings and effortless achievements with admiring affection, no tincture of envy souring their observations. Sensing one day that Mordy was soon to depart to tend to something really big, a colleague asked him, "Where to this time? London, Brussels, Zurich?"

"No, Tennessee."

Thinking that there was nothing in Tennessee worthy of Mordy's attentions unless it were a lecture at Vanderbilt, or just possibly something to do with the TVA, the colleague persisted, "You mean you're going to Nashville?"

"No, Soddy-Daisy."

"Soddy-Daisy?" repeated the colleague, trying vainly to think of some economic index on which Soddy-Daisy might appear. "To do what, Mordy?"

"To get baptized, and there's not a moment to lose either."

History does not record what the colleague tried to say as Mordy sped from the room, face turned south and eyes glittering in anticipation of baptism at the Handmaiden's hands.

When it became clear, in all its enormity, that the preeminent Dr. Mordecai Montefiori, Culver Warbingdon Professor of Economics at NYU, would resign his position, renouncing his present life, at the end of the academic year so as to devote himself to full-time Christian work as treasurer, business manager, and investment counselor (and later as bursar at the Big

Bend Bible School and paymaster at the estate) of the Holy Nation Association of Churches of the Chosen, disbelief was rampant, and consternation prevailed. Certain captains of industry who had benefitted enormously from Mordy's almost clairvoyant consultancies were aghast at his folly. Graduate students in mid-dissertation cried piteously at the thought of losing their indispensable mentor and favorite recommender. NYU, steadily building its reputation in economics on Mordy's brilliance, was staggered, and the people at the Edgington-Frothingham Fund felt that a rather dirty trick had been played on them. Those who feast upon correlations will want to know that the New York stock market performed badly during the remainder of that academic year.

An acquaintance in the history department at NYU, trying to explain the bizarre behavior in question, opined that, like St. Paul, Mordy's great learning had made him mad. A professor at Union Theological Seminary, hoping to set the record straight (while remaining anonymous) let it be known that although St. Paul was, indeed, mad, it was not due to excessive learning. Several close Jewish friends, who could not accept the idea that the God of Israel could convert whomsoever he pleased to Christianity, tried to explain Mordy's lamentable decision by blaming Huldah for her acerbic ways and aesthetic preoccupations that could hardly minister to the needs of an economist's economist like Mordy. As for Huldah, well, English has no words with which to describe the derisive quality in her snorting laugh when Mordy implored her for her own sake, if not his, to accompany him to Soddy-Daisy, Tennessee, to embark upon new life in Jesus Christ together.

Let there be no doubt about the genuineness of Mordy's conversion. Next to the love that leads to the supreme sacrifice, greater love hath no academic economist than that which prompts one to rise up from an endowed chair never to sit thereupon again, to spurn the lifelong security of tenure, to reject frequent opportunities for fat consultancies, to wave away government grants, to disregard promises of guaranteed publication, and to give one's book royalties to Jesus. When the definitive history of American spirituality is written, it will record no conversion more unexpected, more dramatic, or more illustrious than that of Dr. Mordecai Montefiori, an old Jew made new.

Thrice married and thrice divorced, Clifton Marsh Cricklet was a misogynist by his early forties and a victim of excruciating irony. His three wives looked back upon life with him as a kind of unholy bedlock rather than the holy wedlock each had hoped marriage to him would be. It might all have been avoided, he thought (reflecting on his marital agonies), if only he had been allowed to marry his schoolgirl sweetheart, Trixie Ann Proffit.

Half Cajun on his father's side and half English Protestant on his mother's, Clifton was raised a Catholic. But, rebellious against all authority, too logical to savor the mysteries of religion, and devoted before puberty to anticlerical literature, he decided at the tender age of thirteen that Voltaire was right in thinking that religion got started when the first rogue met the first fool. Since Clifton was also loquacious and verbally combative, he was notorious, by his mid-teens, as the boy atheist of Opelousas, Louisiana. Shunned by most, openly ostracized by some, and made a scapegoat by not a few, Clifton turned increasingly to the truest of his friends, the adoring and adorable Trixie Ann Proffit.

Conventionally religious in the Protestant ways of her family, toward whom she was most dutiful, Trixie Ann cared not a fig (insofar as she understood them) for the theological trifles separating Catholics and Protestants and never worried her pretty head over whatever it was that divided believers from unbelievers. Furthermore, in addition to loving Clifton madly, she admired him for his lonely heroism, for the courage he displayed in expressing his convictions, whatever they were. His courage, however, was nothing compared to hers upon introducing him to the Proffit clan and announcing that she planned to marry him on her eighteenth birthday, a scant two months away. Aghast and speechless, the clan, behaving like a herd of musk oxen, butted their rumps together, as it were, and pointed their horny heads outward in all directions as though Clifton had single-handedly surrounded them with unspeakable dangers.

The first to find her tongue was Grandmother Proffit, a well-known churchwoman. She announced in no uncertain terms that Clifton would first have to undergo heartfelt conversion and join a Church of Christ, else there would be no wedding. When he refused, undiplomatically, to do any "such preposterous thing as that," she said triumphantly, "All right, mister, have it your way, but if you so much as lay a finger on that sweet thing, I'll blow you to kingdom come with Roderick's blunderbuss," (a shotgun that had belonged to her dead husband) "and, furthermore, if you sneak off and do it, I'll track you down with dogs if need be, and shoot you on the spot, so help me God!"

When it became clear to Clifton that Grandmother Proffit was not being hyperbolic in her threats but meant them literally, that she really did not care what the authorities "done with her afterwards," as she put it, and that the rest of the clan would resort to anything, short of murdering Trixie Ann, to prevent the marriage, he realized not only that he had been bested but also that the way of the transgressor is indeed hard. It should surprise no one that a young chap like Clifton, after tangling with Grandmother Proffit, the gunslinger, would jump to the conclusion that the love so glibly mouthed by Christians is as fraudulent as their beliefs. Utterly undone by the unequal contest in which Trixie Ann had embroiled him and heartbroken as never before nor since, he turned his back on Opelousas (the yam capital of the world), never to return, and stalked off to New Orleans where he sank indiscriminately into fleshly ways to forget Trixie Ann, and immersed himself in strong drink for good measure.

When not actively engaged in forgetting his true love, Clifton worked for a construction company, day after exhausting day, and also put himself through night school in drafting. Elevating his professional sights, he next went to Georgia Tech in civil engineering. But, dropping out one year short of graduation, he lowered those sights and completed the curriculum in building construction at Auburn. Then a modest legacy enabled him to raise his sights again, and off to the University of Pennsylvania he went to study architecture.

It was as an architect that irony overwhelmed Clifton. No sooner had he received his degree than an immensely rich graduate of the Wharton School of Finance and Commerce at Penn retained his services to design a lavish playhouse for his three young daughters. From the moment it began to take shape, Clifton's fabulously imaginative playhouse was the talk of its aristocratic neighborhood, and beyond. Wealthy parents and grandparents of small children came from far and wide to behold it, marveling at what was being wrought. Before it was half finished a motor mogul from Grosse Pointe, Michigan, had engaged him to design another one, provided that it was uniquely different from the one under construction. It was; and then it was off to Charlevoix to design yet a third playhouse (for summer use only) for a Chicago family wallowing in money. And so it went. One dazzling triumph after another made Clifton the darling of certain children of great wealth, especially of little girls who became princesses the moment they stepped into the palaces he had created for them. Within five years after graduation he reigned as the most imaginative and successful designer of children's playhouses.

"Yes," he railed at himself, "the premier architect of playhouses, of playhouses, mind you, for the spoiled brats of the filthy rich!" Prosperous but as distraught over his reputation as a character actor with aspirations, he did everything he could think of, except praying, to escape the luxurious prison he had unwittingly built for himself. Hoping desperately that somebody somewhere somehow might want him to design a hotel or, perchance, a bank or even a courthouse, Clifton (in the throes of his second expensive divorce) succumbed next to the blandishments of certain developers of high-class amusement centers just then springing up across the country. So, he designed more make-believe palaces and castles together with fortresses and pirates' lairs for the delectation of paying customers hoping to immerse themselves in convincing fantasy. Again, his soaring imagination and consummate art propelled him to the forefront. "But the forefront of what?" he asked himself in aggrieved tones and then replied stoically, "Ah, what the hell, at least it pays the alimonies."

Among those who marveled at his handiwork in playhouses and felt themselves transported to different worlds by his castles and other works of make-believe were certain pious people who at different times and in different places concluded that the architect, whoever he was, was the very one who should design the new church buildings or temples for their several congregations. No less antireligious than when he had gained his unsavory reputation as the boy atheist of Opelousas (thus losing his Trixie Ann), Clifton had, nevertheless, matured to the point at which he could keep his mouth shut, in public at least. So, it came to pass that Cricklet, the closet atheist, designed a church. Accepting that first ecclesiastical commission as a welcome change of pace, he awoke one morning shortly thereafter to find himself more a prisoner than ever, for his first church was a transcendent success; yet it was no more than a prelude to a host of sublime religious structures to follow. The tight-lipped but flaming atheist had clearly found his forte.

It has been said of Rouault, the painter, that he hoped to do a painting of the Christ so moving that it would convert the beholder on the spot. History is uncertain of his success. There is little doubt, however, that the unbeliever, Cricklet, was able to achieve what Rouault, the believer, failed to accomplish. A genius in wedding form to function; a magician with line, light, and color; a master of texture, shape, and space; his churches and other sacred structures were crystalline anthems, stone and ceramics poeticized, fabrics and furnishings made lyrical with praise. If a congregation of Jews, for example, wished it, he could put them, through the magic of architecture, in the numinous presence of the burning bush that was not consumed. If they wished to be with Moses as he received the stone tables of the Law, he could put them on Mt. Sinai itself. As for designing a facsimile of the Solomonic temple, well, that was duck soup for Clifton. If a congregation of Christians wished to be abased in the presence of the Most High, he could design a structure so somber and oppressive that they would, naturally it seemed, fall to their knees in contrition. If they wanted to experience this life as a perilous crossing of a tempestuous sea, he could design a nave that seemed to pitch and roll and creak under menacing skies. If they would focus on the safe haven and joyous reunion awaiting the Christian at the end of this vale of tears, he could design an apse as resplendently irresistible as any this side of heaven itself, and at modest cost. If they were Orthodox and wanted to be bathed with the divine effulgence from above, he could shower them with cascades of light, natural, artificial, or mixed, and caress their worshipping heads with Holy Wisdom itself.

Contemptuous of his clients, disgusted with himself, and trying fitfully not to become the nation's premier church architect (having had his fill of fantasy and make-believe), Clifton grudgingly acquiesced to the demands of a large, rich, and pugnacious congregation of Missouri Synod Lutherans in Davenport, Iowa. They wanted to glorify the Heavenly Father with a sanctuary and church complex that would crystallize, insofar as possible, all the sentiments in Luther's great hymn, "A Mighty Fortress Is Our God." The renowned Cricklet, though regrettably not a Lutheran, was the only one in their opinion who could realize the desired vision architecturally. Agreeing with their assessment and already paying alimony to his third wife, he took the job.

Wise to the cunning of contractors and the venality of subcontractors, Clifton paid a surprise visit, one evening, to the site of the massive redoubt for embattled Missouri Synod Lutherans rising, more or less according to his plans, in Davenport. Uncertain of the fidelity of the construction firm of Hansbarger, Himmelwright, and Wedemayer, Clifton poked around suspiciously and unseen in the dim light of evening. Finding the situation worse than he had feared but unable to conclude his investigations due to darkness, he left, resolving to identify the nefarious contractors or subcontractors who were short-changing his clients and weakening their fortress.

Reflecting sourly on the scrofulous types he had to deal with, Cricklet left the construction site for his room in a mid-town motel nearby. To his astonishment, as he ambled by it, the municipal auditorium burst forth exultantly with the words, "We are peculiar people, oh, yes, we are; Praise the Lord, we are peculiar." "What in holy hell is that caterwauling all about?" he asked aloud in wonderment, not having caught the full meaning the first time through. Pausing as if to get its breath, the building burst forth anew with "We are peculiar people, oh, yes, we are; Praise the Lord, we are peculiar," and continued in that vein for some moments. Rooted to the sidewalk during the short time it took to conclude whatever it was that had been going on inside, he couldn't help noticing the people who had been assembled within as they began to stream out into the night. Almost everybody seemed uplifted, and some were clearly ecstatic. No sign of self-contempt marred those faces, neither cynicism, hypocrisy, nor world-weariness. Although he didn't realize it at the time, Clifton must have been profoundly struck by that sight of inspired humanity, for, after a stormy day with Messrs. Hansbarger, Himmelwright, and Wedemayer, he returned to the municipal auditorium almost in spite of himself the following evening. By week's end, the Handmaiden had landed another mighty fish.

Repelled by the idea of diving for sponges for the rest of his life to make a living, Iskander Moutsopoulos of Tarpon Springs, Florida, broke with family tradition and, at the age of nineteen, set off for St. Petersburg where he took a job selling Persian rugs and other orientalia for Jacoby's Eastern Imports, Inc., owned and operated by Mr. Levi Jacoby. The descendant of Greeks except for his maternal grandfather who was, surprisingly, a Turk, there was something of the oriental bazaar about young Isky from the beginning. No mean salesman himself, Levi soon regarded his handsome young persuader with awe. Isky not only became the best salesman in the firm in six short months, he was, quite simply, superlative at the art of separating people from their money in ways delightful to all concerned.

Having trouble importing rugs as fast as Iskander could sell them, Levi said in a jocular mood one day, "I swear, Isky, you could sell tickets to hell and make people look forward to the trip." Intense, possessed almost, and only half joking, Iskander replied that he would not be content until he could sell tickets to hell to those who had already been there and make them look forward to returning. Levi, clenching a cigar in his teeth, held his fat tummy with both hands and chortled. Iskander, allowing himself only the hint of a smile, moved off suavely to captivate a lady who had just come in to browse, she thought, before talking to "that absolutely marvelous Mr. Mout . . . er . . . ah . . . well, whatever he calls himself."

Beginning with one store in St. Petersburg at a time when the climate was right for orientalia, Levi soon saw his business expand into a small empire with new outlets already in Miami and Orlando and with plans for others in Jacksonville and Pensacola on the drawing boards. "Today Florida, tomorrow the whole Southeast," he mused. Hoping to retain Iskander in perpetuity and sensing the need to combine advertising and public relations in one office, Levi arranged a work-study program whereby the young man could attend the University of Florida at Gainesville to study speech and journalism. Within six years Isky had acquired a master's degree in speech and had impressed his professors as the most effective persuader they had ever encountered in the classroom.

For the next seven years, young Moutsopoulos labored brilliantly and indefatigably for Jacoby's Eastern Imports, Inc., enriching his employer enormously and himself as well, but the lure of the classroom had seized him. The master persuader, it seemed, wanted more than anything to develop the persuasive abilities of others. Happy compliance in Gainesville enabled him to return to the University as a lecturer and Ph.D. candidate. Earning his doctorate in two years, he remained there and began a swift ascent through the professorial ranks. Well before he reached the full professorship, students referred to him affectionately as the Professor of Persuasion.

Although the University of Florida was (and is) commonly thought to be an institution of higher learning, its religious affairs committee (like many another) felt no need to mix academic responsibility with spirituality when inviting divines to participate in religious emphasis week. In that manner the Handmaiden arrived in Gainesville. Though nominally Greek Orthodox, Iskander had little interest in religion. Thus, he brushed aside initial student suggestions that he hear Alice. Finally, he agreed to it but only out of professional interest, since she was reputed to be a masterful speaker.

The great persuader left the auditorium dazed. He could not remember what that pink and white and plump little lady had said, could not (to save himself) make a mental outline of her points. Yet, he felt that he must be up and doing; the trouble was that he didn't know what it was he was being persuaded (no, compelled) to do by her lasting influence. Iskander tried thereafter to pick Alice up on radio or TV. When she returned to Florida the next summer to conduct a revival in Jacksonville, he simply went there for the duration to listen to the high school drop-out who could unite thousands and hold them in rapt attention artlessly. Needless to say, the Professor of Persuasion was persuaded by a greater. Thus, the Holy Nation won a spellbinding advocate.

Before leaving Florida to join Alice at Big Bend, Iskander bade his many friends in Gainesville farewell and also drove to St. Petersburg for a parting word with Levi. "Mr. Jacoby," he said, "do you remember when you told me I could sell tickets to hell and make people look forward to the trip?"

"Oh, sure, and you could do it, too," replied Levi, pleased to see Isky again and to relive old times.

"Well, wish me equal success in selling tickets to heaven."

"To heaven?"

"Yes, I have accepted Jesus Christ as my Lord and Savior and have given myself totally to serving his way and doing his work."

"Well, it's a free country," said Levi lamely.

After Iskander had gone, a funereal mood settled over the executive offices of Jacoby's Eastern Imports, Inc., Levi moping for a considerable time as though remembering a dead child of great promise. "God, what a rug salesman he was!" he said to nobody in particular.

The man who could have made a name for himself as a biblical scholar, despite his slow start, was born near Great Saltpeter Cave in Rockcastle County, Kentucky, Emmet Langhorne Van Hook by name. Graduated *summa cum laude* in classics from the University of Cincinnati, but finding no agreeable position, he returned to his farm, turned it over to sharecroppers, and set his hand to woodworking, his favorite occupation next to reading the classics in Latin and Greek.

While visiting a cousin in Lexington, Emmet and his wife chanced to attend a revival meeting, then in full cry, at the Miracle Auditorium. Born and bred a Southern Baptist, he had, nonetheless, become disenchanted with that group, because they did not emphasize sanctification enough in his view nor did they exercise sufficiently such gifts of the Spirit as speaking in tongues and faith healing. In short, though fervent, bombastic really, the Southern Baptists were too rationalistic in a narrow way and too self-satisfied to be Spirit-filled. Feeling thusly, it is not difficult to imagine the delight he experienced as he sat at the Handmaiden's feet throughout the remainder of her crusade in the heart of the Bluegrass. Nor is it hard to imagine the delight she felt in his conversion. What is harder to imagine is the precognition (one might almost say) that she exercised in sending him to Harvard (all expenses paid by the Holy Nation) even before the gift of Big Bend and the revelation that she was to found a Bible school, a school in whose diadem Emmet, with his Harvard degree, was to become a glittering jewel.

No strangers to brilliance, even to genius, the faculty of Harvard's Divinity School were, nevertheless, enormously impressed by Emmet's rapid attainments. Able to translate koine Greek on the spot with extreme accuracy and elegance (never using an English New Testament), he added Hebrew, Aramaic, and German to the Latin and French he already knew. Taking every course in New Testament studies he could work in, he also became well versed in the history and most advanced techniques of biblical interpretation (including form as well as literary and textual criticism). But when it came to

83

writing his dissertation, he chose to do a textual study of certain variants in documents from the early church that were not in the New Testament and thus not scriptural. Since it had become clear in the intervening years that he was being groomed to teach New Testament at a place called Big Bend Bible School, why was he not doing his dissertation in some aspect of the New Testament rather than on post-biblical material—material that would never be touched upon in a place like Big Bend?

Since Emmet had met all the requirements for graduation, had done superior work academically, had had his dissertation topic duly approved, had defended it ably, and had made a genuine, if narrow, contribution to scholarship, his graduation could not be prevented, justly at any rate. But his case did cause a furor. Between Emmet's defense of his dissertation and the awarding of the degree, the Dean of the Divinity School hastily assembled his senior professors and invited the Graduate School to send a representative.

"Gentlemen," said the dean in his flat midwestern accent, "at the risk of boring you, let me say that, generally speaking, there is no degree at any level more coveted in this country than the Harvard degree. I would also note that the one word which appears on the shield of the University is *veritas*. I have always taken this to mean, to use the vernacular, that we are in the knowledge business. Even at the Divinity School, where some might think that the faith business is uppermost, or should be, I still contend that the discovery of and dissemination of knowledge remain paramount. This is particularly true at the doctoral level in purely academic, as opposed to professional, pursuits. So much for my prefatory remarks.

"At present we have with us a certain Emmet Van Hook, a mature man about to receive the doctorate. Those who know his work will agree that within a decade or so of continued development, at his present rate, and presupposing the publications of which he is clearly capable, he is a person whose abilities might well include him, one day, in our own number. Yet, I regret to inform you that he is an egregious example of a kind of parasitism afflicting the Divinity School. Disquieting reports, plus a bit of investigation on my part, indicate that he came here neither to learn, for its own sake, nor to utilize what modern scholarship has to offer relative to the biblical texts, their authorship, history, redaction, and transmission, but, rather, to garner a Harvard degree to use, I should think, as a cloak of utmost respectability in which to wrap himself before the ignorant and as a badge of attainment which he can flaunt before those who, with a modicum of perception, may question what he is about at a place called Big Bend Bible School."

"But, Dean," said a professor of Christian ethics (a gentle old man who always tried to find some good in every situation but who did not know Emmet well), "aren't you, perhaps, being a bit hard on this person? Surely, his intentions are Christian."

"The dean doesn't exaggerate," said the New Testament man who was Emmet's major professor. "Van Hook has mastered nearly everything we can teach about modern rational techniques of textual inquiry, but he won't use what he has learned whenever biblical texts are at issue, which is most of the time, I might add."

Hoping to bait his colleagues, the resident atheist (a renowned professor of the history of Christian doctrines, not one of which he believed in) said in mock seriousness, "But why ever not?"

Taking the bait, another New Testament expert said, "Because he might learn something that would upset his faith."

"Oh, my, we certainly can't allow anything like that to happen around Harvard," said the resident atheist, feigning alarm.

"Surely, he'll come out of it," said the Christian ethics man, exuding confidence, "with some experience and maturity, you know, growth . . ."

"He certainly won't," cut in the professor of philosophical theology. "The man is one of those brilliant asses we get around here. Item one: In private conversations he has said, over and again, that no good at all can come of Christian scholarship, that the wisdom of man, the very thing Harvard specializes in, cannot deal with the eternal truths of the Spirit, that reason, i.e., 'mere human logic' as he likes to call it, can't judge God's revelation. One can only accept it or reject it. Item two: He says that scholarship can't affirm or deny or tell us anything about such sublime miracles as the virgin birth, the incarnation, or the divinity of Jesus. Item three: He says that scholarly solutions to exegetical problems are utterly irrelevant to the Christian faith and useless to redemption and salvation. Item four: He says he believes every word in the gospels just as they are written. . . ."

"But that's a logical impossibility," roared the representative of the Graduate School, who happened to be a philosopher. "Hasn't the miscreant ever read the New Testament? No sane person could believe all of it as it stands."

"Be that as it may," said the theologian, regaining the floor, "Item five: He refuses to have anything to do with theology on the ground that all one has to do is to read the Scriptures, just as they stand."

"Oh, for pity's sake," lamented the biblical theologian in their midst, "doesn't he know that that in itself is a theological position, and the height of naiveté? Doesn't he know that Scripture is often set against Scripture?"

"Maybe he's wiser for avoiding theology as he does than you give him credit for," jibed the atheist, "for as we all know, the New Testament is not sufficiently consistent to support a truly systematic theology acceptable to all informed people. It was not in the beginning, is not now, and never shall be."

"Yes, but don't you see," said the more naive of the two New Testament men, "he thinks he can by-pass all these problems by maintaining that God literally and objectively inspired, or dictated, every word of Scripture."

"What pernicious rot," said the philosopher. "That ploy enables him to escape nothing in reality. Doesn't this Van Hook person realize that claims about divine revelation are based on the subjectivity of those who make the claims, in other words, on faith and faith alone, rather than on any external, public, or testable data that reasonable people could accept?"

"I used to think I could assume something about what our students might understand," said the dean wearily, "but I am not at all sure that I know what the Van Hooks of this world understand or do not understand. The issues as I see them are (*a*) whether or not you all agree that we have a problem, perhaps a growing one, (*b*) whether or not such graduates as Van Hook reflect detrimentally on Harvard, and (*c*) whether or not we should investigate the possibility of initiating preventive or remedial measures."

"And (*d*)," said the philosopher testily, "whether or not you people should get your heads on straight as to what you are about over here. Is this a glorified Sunday school in which students are solidified in the *a priori* infantile beliefs they bring upon entrance, or is it a significant part of an educational enterprise whose aims include the pursuit of testable information, unbiased by fear or faith, and the dissemination of warrantable beliefs? I suspect you're doing both. If so, may your several gods have pity on you; Harvard certainly should not, but should hold you to academic aims exclusively."

"Really now!" protested the professors of the psychology and of the sociology of religion, "from the standpoint of the phenomenology of religion, people like Van Hook are as legitimate as the most main-line Protestant or the most elevated Anglo-Catholic. Just because he's a sectarian, thinks he's a new Jew or whatever, belongs to something called the Holy Nation, and relates himself in a dog-like adoring fashion to a backwoods, high school drop-out, faith healing evangelist doesn't mean that he isn't grist for our mills."

"That is hardly at issue," replied the atheist, "for pigeons are legitimate in their way, and Skinner studies them here together with vermin and many other things, but that does not mean we should matriculate them and then award them degrees. Obviously we must do better in screening applications for admission."

Resolved at the outset to take decisive action by appointing a committee and to wait until the hubbub became unmanageable or until the clock reached 5:30 P.M. (whichever came first), the dean finally broke in to say that he would refer the problem to a new committee to be assembled forthwith.

Whatever the new committee may have recommended, if, indeed, it has acted yet, Dr. Emmet Langhorne Van Hook, wearing the crimson proudly and holding his diploma high, went down from Cambridge to Big Bend, and mighty were the impressions he made there.

Despite his distinguished name, despite his extensive holdings in real estate that enabled him to live opulently without working, and despite attendance at such staid and proper schools as Phillips Academy, Williams College, and Yale Law School, Endicott Peabody Dickinson of Bangor, Maine, was a maverick and, to many, a damned nuisance. Dressing conservatively and looking every inch a member of the establishment, he thought

86

radical thoughts, nevertheless, and blurted them out at the most inopportune times, offending many.

At receptions following weddings or at commencement teas, for example, he would victimize unsuspecting guests with his loudly stated view that nowadays one was either a socialist or a son-of-a-bitch, leaving little doubt in the minds of most as to how he categorized them. At cocktail parties or in bars he would refer to Imhoff's Law. "Do you know how a capitalistic bureaucracy is like a cesspool?" he would ask. "No," his victims would say (some not wanting to know, others hoping to be diverted). "In each case," he would answer, "the larger chunks rise to the top; chunks of shit, that is," he would add for the benefit of those made dense by shock. The family, scandalized but unable to shut him up, endured him as a skeleton that would not stay closeted.

Living lavishly and unapologetically off the profits of his many properties, the better to weaken the capitalistic system, Endicott had ample time in which to express his left-leaning views and to do good works on behalf of the little guys, the downs and outs, the underdogs of this world to whose verbal aid he habitually flew without actually knowing any of them or admitting them into what was left of his social circle. A thoroughgoing environmentalist, he believed passionately that all would be as he, given his wealth and privileges.

It is not altogether clear what it was that prompted the governor to act as he did. Perhaps it was sympathy for the family, perhaps malice; or, perhaps, it was to throw a bone to the liberals yapping at his heels. Whatever the case, he appointed Endicott to the state parole board. Stunned by his choice and none too quick to respond to the opportunity to put some of his most heartfelt ideas into practice, Endicott, nevertheless, accepted the appointment, letting himself be so consumed by it that many teas and receptions thereafter were spared his presence. But, alas, in the process of becoming the most caring parole board member in the country, that brash young man developed a chronic case of the affliction known to sociologists as cognitive dissonance.

An ultra-liberal Congregationalist who believed that God's creation was altogether good and that human beings were bad only when corrupted by society, he out-Flanaganed Father Flanagan. Not only were there no bad boys, there were no bad girls either, and no bad adults at all. Yet, before him, in his new job, there passed in endless procession what looked for all the world like thoroughly bad people, if the words "good" and "bad" are to have any meaning. Before him, seeking parole, stood pitiless rapist-murderers who prolonged their victims' agonies, the better to enjoy the music of their screams; sadistic torturers who thrilled at the prospects of mutilation and relished the snap of bones breaking, the thuds of bodies being pounded; petty-tyrant-muggers who delighted in their power to degrade their victims, forcing them to grovel in terror; arsonists who burned up babies as well as buildings to escape boredom or to collect insurance.

Believing that all human beings were created free but that most had subsequently been enslaved by sinful social institutions and exploitive class structures, he saw before him people who were supposed to be enslaved, in theory, but who, in fact, were astonishingly free in ways he had not dreamed of hitherto. The rapists were supremely free from any concern for the rights of their victims; the stranglers were blissfully free of pity for their dying prey; the arsonists were free of fellow-feeling for those who were choked to death by smoke or consumed by fire; the bunko artists who had swindled widows and orphans out of their last thin dimes were delightfully free of remorse; all were supremely free of any constricting sense of justice that might limit their depredations, free of all nagging demands for fair play, untroubled by conscience, unmoved by compassion.

Taking it to be a sacred truth that all men are created equal in all ways (not just in their possession of certain unalienable rights), Endicott not only encountered those who were clearly deficient in their sense of justice and defective in having no milk of human kindness, he also encountered some major criminals so brilliant they could have done well at Williams College and, of course, a host of morons who might still be preying on their neighbors had it not been for their own ineptitude. Just how sinful social institutions could cause and explain all the criminality that paraded before him baffled Endicott at times, causing him more than one sleepless night.

It was Dickie Eugene McLaughton, however, who, more than anyone or anything else, turned Endicott's case of chronic cognitive dissonance into the kind of acute case that ruptures. He found in Dickie what he thought to be a paradigmatic case confirming his theories. Allegedly born to a broken home, beaten regularly by his drunken father and neglected by his prostitute-mother, Dickie was raised in the crime-ridden streets of a slum. First a truant, then a delinquent, Dickie sped up (or down) through the ranks of depravity. He was, at one time or another, a con man, a thief, a pimp, a trafficker in drugs, a rum runner, a rapist, and a torpedo.

While investigating Dickie's pre-prison career, preparatory to writing what he hoped would be a definitive book on the so-called criminal in capitalistic America, Endicott suffered four experiences that propped open his eyes to realities he had not wanted to see. The first and third experiences were of a kind. He was, in short, mugged viciously on two different occasions, the second time by the same savage who had done it the first time and who was out on bond awaiting the court's disposition of the previous attack.

The second experience involved falling prey to a badger game played by two of Dickie's alleged acquaintances. Refusing to take the bait initially, Endicott had to be drugged by the couple in question before they could take the desired pictures. Of decent enough quality, the pictures were not very convincing even though the female involved managed to smile ecstatically for the camera from under the dead weight of Endicott Peabody Dickinson, the latter obviously drugged or deranged in some way. Still licking his wounds from the first mugging, embarrassed and angered by the badger game, and suffering a horrible headache from the overdose of knock-out drops he had been given, he staggered out into the world only to be mugged the second time.

It was none other than Dickie who provided the fourth and final experience. With blood, sweat, and tears literally invested in his manuscript and with a major publishing house showing interest, Endicott discovered to his dismay at the last moment that Dickie was a consummate liar and that he (Endicott) had been fed an enormous amount of rot. Perhaps Dickie was angling for the notoriety a book about himself would bring; perhaps he was seeking a new trial; perhaps he just couldn't resist the opportunity to stuff a sucker to the gills. In any case, he fed Dickinson the kind of story the latter had wanted to hear to confirm his theories. As imaginative as a major novelist or an ordinary theologian, and a good deal more consistent than the latter, Dickie was so masterful a con artist that he often misled and confused himself as to just what had happened. How easy it had been to lead a bleeding heart down the primrose path of perfidy! And what great fun it had been!

By the age of thirty-three, Endicott was a new man. Gone from his repertoire was Imhoff's Law; gone was the exclusive disjunction between socialists and sons-of-bitches; gone were the vicious jibes at capitalism and class structure. The family, breathing a collective sigh of relief, shunned him no longer, one of its more testy members noting that with the onset of long-delayed puberty, Endicott had finally grown up.

The pendulum that was Dickinson did not, however, come to rest in its mid-position but inched ever more to the right. He stopped doting on the Hebrew prophets in whose passion for social justice he had reveled in his ultra-liberal days and began to study the Mosaic books closely and increasingly. To the chagrin of the family, he left the Congregational Church and joined a local Presbyterian congregation ministered to by a disciple of Dr. Burl McDuffie, arch-fundamentalist. Terms and phrases such as "lex talionis," "let the punishment fit the crime," "an eye for an eye, a tooth for a tooth, a life for a life," began to pepper his speech, and he referred often to original sin and total depravity, all allusion to the basic goodness of man dropping from his conversations.

Nor were the members of his family the only ones to notice the change. Both his peers on the parole board and the miscreants who came before it sensed a dramatic conversion, for Endicott began to speak thusly: "You freely chose a life of crime, did you not? Why should decent people show mercy to one who has never shown it to his victims? In point of fact, you were simply subjecting those in your clutches to the naked exercise of your own brutal power, were you not? You did what you did largely to savor the very exercise of that power, did you not? You realize that you are a social parasite feeding upon the labor of others, do you not? Why should we think that you have changed for the better as a result of being in prison; is there any evidence of reformation in your character? Why should society suffer to live those who have no sense of justice, no fellow-feeling, no compassion, no conscience? Parole denied."

The very same members of the family who had breathed easier a short time earlier began to hold their collective breath again when Endicott turned his ire on government, lambasting the federal and state bureaucracies much as he had once slashed away at capitalistic organizations. But in addition, he began to exhibit a fatalistic attitude toward human life in general and spoke darkly about how everything must first get worse, the only thing really worthwhile being the salvation of the individual soul before it was too late.

It cannot be said that Mercedes, his long-suffering wife, was either surprised or upset when after a long period of brooding, together with several mysterious trips out of state, Endicott announced that he had joined something called the Holy Nation Association of Churches of the Chosen and that he was going off to some place called Big Bend to do legal work and to teach Old Testament to ministerial students at a Bible School there. A social climber early in life, Mercedes was well established in Bangor, thrilled with her married name, and pleased by the family's acceptance of her. Furthermore, she intended to raise Endicott Peabody Dickinson, II in the opulence to which she had grown accustomed. Since she cared little for her husband, it gave her no pain to wish him well in his new endeavors and to invite him, none too enthusiastically, to pay them a visit from time to time, should he be in their neighborhood.

When the roll is called up yonder, the names of Mordecai Montefiori, Clifton Marsh Cricklet, Iskander Moutsopoulos, Emmet Langhorne Van Hook, and Endicott Peabody Dickinson will surely be announced with a quaver of excitement. Never in the annals of discipleship have five such different men so admired, so reinforced, so stimulated, and so supported each other. They agreed completely and observed often that nothing short of the power of God, the grace of Jesus, and the Holy Spirit dwelling in the Handmaiden of the Lord could possibly have called them forth from the wicked world, uniting their hearts in perfect faith; not government, not the army nor the navy, not business, not General Motors nor IBM. Not even a cosmopolitan university could have welded into one an indifferent Jew, a Catholic-born atheist, a nominal Greek Orthodox, a disgruntled Southern Baptist, and an ultra-liberal Congregationalist.

And how they covered the waterfront! Mordecai Montefiori, business manager, treasurer, and investment counselor for a multi-million-dollar enterprise (growing daily), Bible School bursar, and paymaster at the estate; Clifton Marsh Cricklet, draftsman, engineer, construction expert, architect, interior decorator, experimenter with plastic stained-glass windows for low-budget churches, professor of chalk art and flannel graph evangelism, and overseer of all building programs for the Holy Nation; Iskander Moutsopoulos, chief substitute evangelist for the Handmaiden, director of public relations for the peculiar people, director of all radio and TV evangelism, professor of preaching and other forms of Christian persuasion, and choirmaster at the seminary; Emmet Langhorne Van Hook, possessor of a Harvard Ph.D., professor of Bible (New Testament), professor of special insight into the mind of Jesus (since both were carpenters' sons as was supposed), principal radio and TV commentator (of the Holy Nation) on world events from God's point of view, director of all student work programs, and possessor of a Harvard Ph.D.; Endicott Peabody Dickinson, professor of Bible (Old Testament), chief legal counsel for the Holy Nation, administrator of all bequests, trusts, and annuity programs associated with the Churches of the Chosen, director of church extension and of property acquisition (of which there was much), and chief contingency planner for the last days leading up to and including Armageddon.

Brilliant, indefatigable, and omni-competent though they were, the Five, as they were known, regarded themselves individually and collectively merely as servants of the Lord's Handmaiden, divinely accredited to this perishing world in its last hours. Each waited upon Alice, each deferred to her, and, from a merely human point of view, each indulged and humored her, but lovingly. Although she sometimes uttered dark sayings, no one of them ever thought of contradicting her, nor did a single one of them ever disobey her decisions as far as church historians can ascertain.

An expert in southern religion at Atlanta's Emory University (who desires anonymity and will deny that he said it) observed rather merrily at a cocktail party that Alice had been more successful in picking her inner circle than had Jesus. Peter, he observed, simply petered-out in the New Testament, no matter what the Catholics claim for him. The beloved disciple was just that, beloved, but not very effective. Paul, who made up most of Christian doctrine as we know it today, was a Johnny-come-lately who overwhelmed all the other disciples except James, the brother of Jesus, who was also a Johnny-come-lately. But the latter was killed in 62, and the Mother Church in Jerusalem over which he presided was in ruins by 70. The expert (whose identity will not be revealed) thinks that the big difference in achievement lies in the Holy Spirit, who, in his view, was both more active and dependable in the days of the early church than now.

Scott Truesdale and Emory Plunkett did not, of course, know everything about the Handmaiden nor about the Five, nor was there time, even during the long drive from Nickel Plate, to tell Manly everything they did know. But so suffused with wonderment were their narrations, so adoringly, so exultantly did they tell him their stories that he was fallowed for the fast-growing seeds of hero-worship, together with the choking tares of self-doubt. He, Manly Plumwell, a nobody, was about to stand in the presence of greatness. Or should he kneel or abase himself in some way? He really did not know. After all, those who are born and bred in the Nickel Plates of this world do not know how to mind their manners in the presence of greatness, for they seldom, if ever, get to appear even on its periphery and, so, have no chance to learn.

As the car approached the main entrance to the estate, great gates of wrought iron opened as if by magic. With Scott Truesdale at the wheel, the car moved with dignity between massive limestone gateposts and almost at once began a sharp ascent on what Manly could only think of as a boulevard in the middle of nowhere, for beyond the stately trees bordering it thickly, there lay lush meadows and open fields as far as the eye could see. After a quarter of a mile or more, the car crested the hill, and there before Manly's dazzled eyes stood a magnificent chateau (*no, a castle!*) of stone and yellow stucco capped by purple slate. But most exciting of all was the fact that somewhere within its Gothic fastness awaited the Handmaiden of the Lord just to see and to talk to a wretch like him. Thrilled with the homage he would soon pay, trembling lest he should be weighed in the balances and found wanting, and in pressing need of a men's room but unable to express so dishonorable a frailty on so auspicious an occasion, he entered the chateau greatly preoccupied with himself, too preoccupied to marvel at its architectural splendors or to appreciate the exquisite decoration of its many rooms and corridors.

With one notable exception, the chateau had been left as it came from the munificent hands of Cyrus Dewayne Pritchard. That exception had to do with certain objects of art. Landscapes and still lifes remained where they had been hung, but works of pagan inspiration or of secular themes had been taken down and consigned to the flames, and all statues of unclad or of immodestly clad bodies had been removed and smashed to bits with sledge hammers. Crosses, chalices, carvings of the Last Supper, and such like replaced the offending statues when physically and aesthetically possible; and paintings and prints of biblical art, especially crucifixion scenes, were hung where naked gods and goddesses had once disported themselves shamelessly in praise of Bacchus. The fine taste and superb hand of Cricklet could be discerned in the disposition of the sacred art that enveloped all comers to the chateau like a great cloud of witnesses.

To his persistent shame and current dismay, crucifixion scenes, particularly the more lurid ones in which the nakedness and horrid contortions of Jesus and the dying thieves were emphasized, caused Manly to have erections. It had been so since childhood and was still a cross of incongruity that he bore. Trying intently to compose his mind for the imminent appearance of the Handmaiden and to disregard the increasingly insistent demands of his bladder, he felt himself stiffen against his right pant leg as he sat in the presence of two large grisly paintings of Christ's crucifixion (one by Mantegna, the other by Antonello Da Messina) placed on opposite walls of the audience chamber in which he awaited the Handmaiden. Immersed in misery, he did not sense that she had come until the fluttering of her attendants caught his attention.

But *there she was!* and Manly arose as best he could without revealing his

92

deplorable condition. She was, indeed, pink and white and plump all over just as Scott Truesdale and Emory Plunkett had said. She was wearing a plain yellow dress, much the same color as the stuccoed parts of the chateau, and a purple pillbox hat with a large yellow cockade on it. Several nondescript women, whom Manly took to be ladies-in-waiting, fluttered about her like ministering angels.

"Ah, Miss Alice," said Scott Truesdale, "may I present to you Manly Plumwell from Nickel Plate?"

"You remember, we told you we would try to bring him today," said Emory Plunkett, quickly getting his word in edgewise.

The Handmaiden fixed her amazing eyes upon Manly and, without so much as a hint of greeting, said sternly, "We don't believe in honky-tonk down here, young man."

Dead silence reigned. Manly's mouth, set to greet the Handmaiden, fell open but remained speechless. Then one of the nondescript ladies-in-waiting twittered a reiteration, and another took up the refrain, "Oh, no, no honky-tonk here."

"I'm sure Mr. Plumwell never thought for a moment that we countenanced honky-tonk," said Emory Plunkett.

"Nor hanky-panky either," added Scott Truesdale decisively.

"No, no," murmured Manly; nor hurdy-gurdies either, he thought to himself, his mind making a preposterous association.

Satisfied, apparently, that young Mr. Plumwell had not misjudged life at Big Bend, the Handmaiden raised her right hand as though in benediction and said a hurried prayer. Every head was bowed, and two of the ladies-in-waiting fell to their knees for good measure. "Heavenly Father," said the Handmaiden, "we beseech you to look with favor upon this young stranger in our midst; deliver him from communism, humanism, evolutionism, modernism, socialism, secularism, and all of the other godless 'isms' that afflict mankind, and lead him in the paths of righteousness; make him temperate and sober as regards strong drink, and give him the strength to subdue his flesh against its passions, in the precious name of Jesus, Amen."

With those issues tended to, she turned on her heel and bustled out of the audience chamber to the accompaniment of reverberating "Amens." For a few moments, Manly was left alone with his bursting bladder and the two crucifixion scenes that seemed to taunt him, saying, "Subdue your flesh; subdue your flesh!" When Scott Truesdale and Emory Plunkett returned after a short but cherished walk with the Handmaiden (who was, even then, departing for fields white for harvest), Manly was able to hint sufficiently at the uncouth needs of his body to be directed to a men's room.

Enormously relieved but dazed and disturbed, he tried to make sense out of the preceding moments. Why had she said to him, "We don't believe in honky-tonk down here"? Did she suppose that he approved of it? Could she possibly have heard of his doings at the Pilsudski County Free Fair? Was it meant as a reproach? Or was he too spiffily dressed to suit her? Did he look like a city-slicker or one of those rich hoods in gangster movies? Or, to his mortification, had she seen the impertinent bulge in his pants? Was that why she had specifically requested that he might have divine help in subduing the passions of his flesh? One thing was clear: Manly felt horrible and did not know where he stood as he emerged, pale and shaken, from the men's room.

"You need not fear," said the magnificent voice of one of the Five. In words delivered so convincingly that each utterance was its own attestation, the voice went on, "You would, most assuredly, not be here today, if you had not already been chosen to attend Big Bend Bible School, preparatory, if it is God's will, to your acceptance into the royal priesthood. All that remains at this juncture is your own acceptance of our acceptance. You may attend our school, free of charge, if you so desire. It is our belief that you will choose to do so, that our prayers for you will be answered. The Handmaiden's comment about honky-tonk that you mistakenly took to be directed against yourself was just her way of sharing with you what King Jesus had laid on her heart at that moment. Even we who stand closest to her sometimes require prolonged periods of prayer, meditation, and Bible study before we fathom the full meaning of her utterances.

"The case in point," said the one whose eyes nailed Manly to the spot, whose noble brow bespoke intelligence, whose strong, clean-cut jaw could emit no falsehood, "is very simple, yes, very simple indeed; the Handmaiden's reference to honky-tonk was, I am convinced, just her way of restating Jesus' meaning when he said, 'Enter ye in at the strait gate: for wide is the gate, and broad is the way, that leadeth to destruction, and many there be which go in thereat: Because strait is the gate, and narrow is the way, which leadeth unto life, and few there be that find it.' At Big Bend, we bear the Lord's cross in season and out. In truth, we never put it down. We have no time for frivolity, neither do we know levity nor secular insouciance. The Handmaiden simply wanted you to know that."

Still overawed, even if less intimidated, Manly simply could not doubt the one who had spoken thusly. Breathless and immobilized in the magnetic field of conviction generated by the presence in whose company he sat, it was compellingly clear to him how Iskander Moutsopoulos, formerly a stellar rug salesman, had become Big Bend's professor of preaching and other forms of Christian persuasion.

"But sir," he ventured to ask, still mystified as to how it had all happened, "how did the Chosen People in the Holy Nation hear about me? How did the Handmaiden know where to send such marvelous young men as Scott Truesdale and Emory Plunkett (angels to me, really) to seek me out? How did they know that I was lost in my sins? How did they know that I needed Jesus in my life?"

The belief-compelling voice said, "Since you will, perhaps, find others like yourself, one day soon, in the same inspired way, it will be better for you to experience it first-hand than to hear from me how the Holy Nation operates in this aspect of its evangelism."

"Yes, sir," Manly replied timidly but with a thrill of anticipation rippling up his spine.

"And now, Lord Jesus, may that day come soon for Manly Plumwell, if it is thy will," intoned Iskander Moutsopoulos, standing with his right arm aloft in benediction.

"Amen," added Manly Plumwell, knowing, even as he said it, that the die for his life had been cast.

Chapter Three

Two themes recurred in Herbert Plumwell's conversations with his grandson. One was designed to punish Manly when he was naughty; the other to reward him when good or, more precisely, to inspire him to be good. "You'll be sorry when I'm dead and gone," the old man used to say prophetically, whereupon Manly would creep off and cry in a secluded corner of the house that might as well have been his own private wailing wall, so frequently did he use it for that purpose. On other occasions, Herbert would say, "You know, Manly, all of this is going to be yours someday," whereupon he would swing an arm in an arc of 180 degrees or more, taking in the house, the barn, and the two large lots on which they stood.

Herbert had a strong sense of place and property and a powerful loyalty to Nickel Plate, which he believed to be the garden spot of the world. Hoping to instill the same fervent sentiments in Manly, the old fellow began to promise the property to the boy when he was little more than a toddler. Then, when Manly's parents died in Lake Superior, Herbert intensified his efforts, for it was no longer a matter of Manly's inheriting the property sometime in the distant future but rather in the not-too-distant future. The old fellow sincerely wanted the lad to have his patrimony, but he also wanted him to aspire to it, to be worthy of it, and to cherish the idea of passing it on in unbroken succession to Plumwells yet unborn.

Early in August, about six weeks after he returned from his momentous visit to Big Bend, the Probate Court ruled that Manly John Plumwell was indeed the rightful heir to the properties of Herbert and Marynell Plumwell. But, since Manly had already planned to leave for Big Bend by the middle of September, he decided to rent the house. That way he could subsidize himself, spare Big Bend any unnecessary expenses in training him to be a royal priest, and divert the savings to meet other needs amongst God's peculiar people.

Although Manly could not have known it at the time, he would neither produce offspring nor retain the ancestral property. If Herbert Plumwell could even have imagined such distressing eventualities, he would not only have said, "You'll be sorry when I'm dead and gone," he would have added,

"Just you wait until I come back from the dead; you'll be good and sorry then," or "Just you wait until we meet on the other shore, because, mister, I'm really going to give you a piece of my mind."

It has been said that the Protestant Church choir is the one great unsolved problem in the kingdom of God. This is not true. Sex is and will, no doubt, continue to be so until the saved of earth become as the angels of heaven already are, neither marrying, nor given in marriage, nor even thinking the thoughts that lead to either. Since Alice took this to be an eternal truth, she did everything she could think of, most especially in the household of God at Big Bend, to subdue carnality, to dry up lubricity, to reduce tumescence and all tendencies thereto. More than that, she tried to destroy or, failing that, to distract, derail, and divert the evil imagination lurking behind sexuality. Her reasons for doing so were many, even if not all equally cogent.

Psalm 51:5 made it clear to Alice that in God's view all humans were surely shaped in iniquity and conceived in sin. Her own experience certainly ratified this, for she still shuddered at the recollection of her parents' sensual abandon in their moonlit bedroom that night so many years earlier. On evangelistic journeys throughout the southern mountains, she was scandalized to learn that a virgin was jokingly referred to as any girl over six who could still outrun her brothers. That what happened to girls under six did not count for or against virginity set her teeth doubly on edge. Then, too, she knew that many of the so-called Christian orphanages peppering the Appalachian landscape were most certainly misnamed and that some were positively satanic. From firsthand confessions, she discovered to her horror that girls, in particular, in many orphanages had carnal knowledge thrust upon them early and repeatedly. Deplorable though the rape of minors was, especially in so-called Christian orphanages, Alice found it preferable to some of the seduction techniques that came to her once innocent ears, for in addition to threats, extortion, and naked force, these involved heresy or, worse yet, blasphemy. Three such episodes haunted her and contributed much to the draconian measures she took to crush the serpent of sex at Big Bend.

The first involved a foster father/orphanage director in Pike County, Kentucky. He managed to convince a ward of fourteen, as delicious to look at as she was dullish, that God had chosen her of all women to bear a Messiah-child for these last times and that he, her loving foster father, had been selected to deliver the divine seed to her sacred receptacle. Unlike the Holy Spirit, who needed to overshadow the Virgin Mary but once, the loving foster father obsessively overshadowed the girl throughout her pregnancy. When the sacred receptacle was delivered of a baby girl and began to weep bitterly over not having a son, and hence no Messiah-child, the sordid tale began to leak out. Soon the temporarily repentant bearer of the divine

97

seed confessed all. With her teeth on edge, Alice marveled that God could find it in his heart to forgive so shameless a wretch. That it could not be doubted was a sore test of her faith in divine justice.

The second episode that ravaged the Handmaiden's ear occurred in the mountainous northwest corner of South Carolina. It involved an orphanage director who was a part-time Pentecostal preacher, but more literate than most. By chance he found a volume of amatory poetry in a secondhand bookstore. One of the poems celebrated a seduction that was said to have occurred early in the rise of Christianity in one of the Greek cities, probably Corinth. It concerned a theologian and a beautiful girl of childlike faith with intellect to match. The first article of the theologian's catechism was that since the devil was the most awfully wicked of all beings, he shouldn't be allowed to enjoy roaming about on earth but should be forced to stay in hell. If he got out from time to time, well, then he should be driven back as soon as possible and as often as necessary. In fact, it was every Christian's duty to do so. The second article of faith maintained that each woman contained hell within her own body, tucked away out of sight between her legs. The third article was that each man bore Satan on his body as a kind of appendage. Whenever the appendage became proud and rampant, as it often did, lifting its haughty head, it should be thrust into hell. Discovering that acts of piety and pleasure need not be opposed to each other but can be welded into a harmonious whole when consecrated by faith, the Corinthian girl put Satan in his place many times with the enthusiastic help of her tutor. Since, as the Preacher said, there is nothing new under the sun, it should surprise no one that that which succeeded in Corinth should work in South Carolina.

In terms of deceit and lust, the third episode was equally disgusting to Alice but even worse theologically, for its logic was, in fact, too close to her own for comfort. This time the orphanage was in West Virginia, the participants distressingly familiar. The seducer arranged for the seducee (so to speak) to have extra sessions of Bible study. She was, after all, a bit slow; or was it that she was especially good? In any case, the seducer read rather more than sound doctrine required certain passages from Genesis (6:1-4) where it says in part, "And it came to pass, when men began to multiply on the face of the earth and daughters were born to them, that the sons of God saw the daughters of men that they were fair; and . . . the sons of God came in unto the daughters of men . . ." Between readings, the seducer rhapsodized on the intriguing unions in question and took pains to make clear to the girl, who was herself very fair to look upon, just what the Bible meant by "coming in unto the daughters of men." When these enlightening lessons had sunk in, he read a good deal from John's gospel, especially 1:12-13, which points out that born-again Christians are the sons of God. Since he had confessed his faith long years before and was at the time of seduction a Nazarene minister, it followed that he too was a son of God. Furthermore, since Genesis reveals no displeasure on God's part over his sons' going in unto women, what harm could possibly come of it, if then and there he were to go in unto her even as his brothers had gone in unto her sisters in olden times? For the life of her, she could think of no reason; so, it came to pass that she found out what it was like to have a son of God go in unto a woman. The Handmaiden, of course, treasured all of God's word, but, in truth, treasured some parts less than others. Judging from her failure to use Genesis 6:1-4 as a text for any of her sermons or even to recommend it for prayerful study, this passage in question can hardly have been a favorite.

As anxious to stamp out love-making as St. Paul had been, Alice grasped at the same straws, one of which was the conviction that the world was about to end, cataclysmically, at any moment, or at least the world as presently constituted. A geneticist named Frankson, made cunning by Satan, sought to entrap her. He professed to believe with all his heart that one should certainly not be making love these days, so near at hand was the end, but "How," he wondered aloud in mock confusion, "could it also have been near at hand 1,900 years ago when St. Paul exhorted (I Corinthians 7:29) even those duly married to avoid sexual dalliance with each other in view of the impending distress?" Alice was momentarily shaken. She knew there was an answer, but she knew that it had slipped her mind. Stalling, she urged Frankson (who was having a hard time keeping a straight face) to have faith and to pray until illumination came, as it surely would. Forsaking her own advice, she besought Dr. Van Hook. "Brother Emmet," Alice said, appearing to be almost academic in her interest, "how do you understand St. Paul's exhortation to husbands and wives to live as though they had none in view of the impending distress, i.e., the passing away of this world?"

"I don't know that I take your full meaning, Miss Alice," he said warily.

"Well, let us suppose that Satan gets at a weaker brother on the ground that since the world is still here nearly 2,000 years later there could hardly have been any reason for the Apostle to exhort husbands and wives not to come together because of the speedy end of the world. That could also cause a problem for unbelievers."

"Let me turn to God's word and pray about it, and I will give you my considered opinion as soon as possible," Emmet assured her and hastened to his study.

It took him less than a single night of prayer to find the answer. It lay, in fact, in one of the Holy Nation's favorite epistles (in II Peter 3:8) where the Scripture notes that with the Lord a day is as a thousand years, and a thousand years as a day.

Exchanging knowing glances with Emmet but betraying no hint of the relief she felt, Alice said, "Yes, of course, that is the answer."

"Indeed so," he agreed, deeply satisfied that God's word had shown yet again that it could answer all questions put to it, even those it raised itself.

Loathing the very idea that any royal priests might be found naked at the end of the world in each other's arms, lovingly, and operating on the axiom that sex never satisfies for long but lures its participants back for more, futilely, Alice decreed that there should be no sexual contact of any kind among students at Big Bend. Each female student was to be called "Sister" and treated accordingly; each male to be called "Brother" and treated as such. Conversation between the sexes was to be limited to communications essential to work, worship, or study. Small talk was frowned upon, and amorous murmurings were forbidden. No sparkle of sexual excitement could lighten the eye, quicken the step, or wreathe the face in smiles. Dating was not allowed, on campus or off; courting was unthinkable, marriage impossible.

Fearing propinquity like the plague, Alice segregated males and females as much as possible, at work, at study, in chapel, at prayer meetings, and in living arrangements. There was no need to segregate them at play, there being no play at Big Bend. After all, the New Testament knows nothing of play and authorizes neither humor nor light-heartedness. According to its pages, the awesome end of the world is always at hand for the individual, at least, if not for the entire family of man, and one must stand ready for it in fear and trembling, with none but pious thoughts on one's mind. Hence, the sheer good humor of being alive as a mortal man or woman on this earth on any day at any moment, together with levity and high spirits, were all out of the question. At no time were members of opposite sexes to stand, walk, or sit closer to each other than six inches. Cricklet, who had a good eye for distances, was especially charged with enforcing that rule. A former, but fallen, member of the Holy Nation, who had become coarse in his apostasy, observed with black humor that the six-inch rule wasn't so bad if a man had nine inches.

Married couples seeking admission to Big Bend had to live as though they were not married and abide by all the rules for single people. For the duration of their studies, their hands could not be used even for private clasping and caressing, their arms were to remain empty, their lips could not touch either in greeting or in parting—to say nothing of more tender communications—and their bodies had to remain separated, rigid, and unbending. Needless to say, the married couples who had previously found carnal knowledge worth having and who looked forward to periodic refresher courses in the future (end of the world or no end of the world) sped through their studies and left Big Bend hurriedly.

Alice's ban on sex did not extend to all the peculiar people but only to those at the Bible School. For the Lord's sake, those who would be royal priests of the pulpit smoldered and burned and suffered. But, on the brighter side, none of them has yet been overtaken by the awful end of the world, and, therefore, none of them has been caught at its advent doing what she feared most.

"'As a jewel of gold in a swine's snout, so is a fair woman which is without discretion,'" she said one day, quoting Proverbs 11:22 to the Five who sat attentively around a conference table in what had been the chateau's billiard room.

"Amen to that," chanted the biblical scholars, Dickinson and Van Hook.

100

"Yes, that is indubitably true," asserted Iskander convincingly.

Cricklet said nothing but nodded in agreement as he looked back on his own marital disasters, reproaching his wives under his breath. Though not in disagreement, Mordecai neither gestured nor spoke but reflected intensely on just how much such a jewel of gold would bring at current prices.

The occasion for Alice's quotation of Proverbs was a recent painful explusion from Big Bend. Cricklet judged that a girl named Olive Hornsby had flagrantly broken the six-inch rule with one Roscoe Waterman and, according to other information reaching Alice, had repeatedly offended by "batting her eyes" at several different boys. Clearly unable to subdue her passions and altogether lacking discretion, Olive was cast out of Big Bend, weeping, and denied all hope of ever becoming a minister in the Church of the Chosen. When last heard from, she was under the watchful eye of her pastor at home and in grave danger of losing her citizenship in the Holy Nation.

A hush fell over the Five when Alice, with an ineffable but characteristic look on her face, proceeded to announce that the unhappy episode had caused the Lord to vouchsafe another revelation to her. "Mine eyes were led by the Spirit to the words of Peter (I Peter 3:7), the rock upon which the Church of the Chosen is built, and his words, addressed to those who would be holy women, are that they should not adorn themselves with braided hair, with decorations of gold, or with finery. Then the Spirit led me to Brother Paul's words (I Timothy 2:9) where he says that he wills women to adorn themselves in modest apparel, with shamefacedness and sobriety; not with braided hair or gold or pearls or costly array. Henceforth, brethren, there must be neither braided hair nor jewelry of any kind at Big Bend. Moreover, the Lord tells me that neither perfumes nor cosmetics may exist among us."

The Five never thought of themselves as merely bright whereas Alice was a genius, but that is much the relationship in which they stood to her. When she announced something that was not in Scripture as though it were, they took it to be scriptural, and when she interpreted existing Scripture in novel ways, they gave up the traditional interpretations at once. When she spoke darkly, they blamed their own lack of sight, and when she uttered incomprehensible mysteries, they reproached themselves for lack of faith. Thus, it was not a matter of ratification when she banned all jewelry and fancy hairdos, all perfumes and scents (except those of soap) and cosmetics. It was simply a matter of promulgation. And so it was that Olive Hornsby indirectly made the women at Big Bend plainer and in some cases less desirable than they otherwise might have been. Satan, it seemed, had been foiled again, or had he?

A large measure of the beauty that launched a thousand black ships against Troy must surely have reappeared in Persephone Xenakis, the coed at the University of Florida who married Iskander Moutsopoulos while still a girl blooming into womanhood. Consumed with passion for each other during the early years of matrimony, their ardor cooled immensely after their conversion and was at a low ebb during Manly's days at Big Bend. By that time, Iskander had long since been rekindled by his first and most persistent love, namely, persuasion, not persuasion in general nor for the sheer art of it, but for King Jesus.

Unassuming and apparently contented, though largely ignored by her Christ-consumed husband, Persephone seemed so utterly oblivious to her beauty that men of all ages (even at Big Bend or, perhaps, most especially at Big Bend) yearned for private moments and for secret places in which to say (by seeming to ask) such things as "But don't you know how stunningly beautiful you are?" or "Has no one ever told you how exquisite you really are?" or "Is it possible, can it be, that you do not know how devastatingly desirable you are?" But, of course, those things could neither be asked nor affirmed. Nor could any man say to her, "How desperately I love you." Even less could any man say, "Dear God, how I envy him whose lover you are," for that would have compounded sin by adding envy to lust.

Although Persephone was married, was, in years, a mature woman and the mother of a little girl, she too remained a girl, eternally blooming into womanhood. She was, in fact, the Snow White of Big Bend, its resident Sleeping Beauty. Now, the devil, perceiving his opening, came and whispered into every man's ear, saying, "Wake her up; for pity's sake, wake her up; don't leave her that way. Put your lips to hers gently and part them; touch some vital spot which when touched lovingly will awaken her from the terrible coma of self-ignorance in which she languishes."

Able to carry on an indefinite number of conversations at once, the devil, while tantalizing the men with thoughts of Persephone, whispered to the women at Big Bend thusly: "My, how plain you look, dowdy almost. But, then, I don't suppose there's much you can do having to wear those long, white, shapeless dresses. What are they, some kind of uniform meant to look antiseptic? Of course, those lavender, purple, or yellow kerchiefs you're required to wear around your necks help a little, but when every other woman has to wear one and always in one or the other of those three colors, it gets monotonous, doesn't it? Oh, by the way, what is that scent you're trailing? Can it be Lava soap? Don't tell me its Fels Naptha! What a pity you can't do something a little bit alluring with your hair or perk yourself up with a bit of gleaming metal here or there, perhaps a bracelet, pin, or a necklace with something precious in it to add a flash of color."

In that manner the devil turned most of the women at Big Bend, whether on the staff or in the student body, into green-eyed monsters, especially in Persephone's presence, for what did it matter to her that cosmetics were banned? Her lustrous skin had no need of them, and there was always about her person the sweet fragrance of a baby fresh from the bath. What good would jewelry have done her, even if permitted? She would have adorned it; it could have added nothing to her. What difference did it make that the dresses at Big Bend were long and plain, revealing nothing but lumps?

Persephone could have been draped from head to foot in gunnysacks and still, merely by her presence, merely by gliding by, have achieved what many a beauty queen could not have accomplished even in costly and revealing attire.

Whenever and wherever she walked among the men at Big Bend, their hands fell idle at work momentarily, their eyebrows rose, their pupils dilated, their hearts skipped a beat. More, of course, could be said about their physical reactions to her, but modesty forbids. Cricklet, who effected to ignore women but had a sharp eye for beauty, hoped that she might aid him in designing some new plastic stained-glass windows. She was, after all, artistic. Montefiori needed her for what he took to be her natural business acumen, and Dickinson solicited her help with his contingency plans for the last days and Armageddon. A woman's point of view on such portentous goings-on should not be ignored. Van Hook, while reading the lesson in chapel one day, caught a glimpse of her unexpectedly and misread Psalm 11:4 as, "The Hord is in his lowly temple," not once but twice.

It is written (in I Pet. 5:8) that the devil prowls around like a roaring lion seeking whom he may devour. This is not always true. At Big Bend he flitted hither, thither, and yon, or sometimes just hovered in the air, looking much like Cupid except for the sly smile on his face and an occasional malevolent look in his eye. So successful was he at his Cupid act that he even made an ally of Alice in one particular. She and Satan were, of course, unequally yoked in all other ways much as a member of the Women's Christian Temperance Union is unequally yoked to a bootlegger when both team up to keep a town or a county dry by preventing all local sales of legal liquor. Still and all, the Handmaiden of the Lord and the Lord's archenemy were as one in the hope that Persephone would fall into sin. The devil wanted her to commit a mortal sin so that he could deprive God of her and cast her, writhing, into the everlasting lake of fire. Alice would have been contented with a venial sin, any venial sin, so long as it sufficed to expel Persephone from the Lord's household at Big Bend. The toxin of her beauty was too virulent to be tolerated. It poisoned the men with lust and the women with envy.

But Alice and the devil were both balked in their desires for her lapse into sin, because Persephone was as good as she was beautiful. In fact, she embodied the entire catalogue of virtues that St. Paul demanded of holy women. She gladly allowed Iskander to rule over her, kept her head covered in church, and never spoke out there but always asked for his explanations of Scripture at home; nor did she ever admit him to her body without first engaging in a lengthy season of prayer. In personal relationships, she was modest and unassuming, loving and helpful, and neither a slanderer nor a gossip. She was, in fact, extraordinarily abundant in the fruits of the Spirit. Most galling of all to the devil and Alice alike was the fact that she was eminently sound in doctrine. The Handmaiden had but to announce a new revelation or interpretation and Persephone subscribed to it at once, in childlike faith. So, for her part, Alice fumed over the spot of infection that was Persephone and agonized over the lamentable congruence between her own will and Satan's. For his part, the devil had to content himself with a harvest at Big Bend that did not include the beautiful one who ravished men innocently.

To her credit, Alice did not knowingly share any other purpose with Satan, nor did their fellow feeling in regard to Persephone lead her to give any quarter to the ancient enemy of mankind. Certainly, she did not permit him to construct a workshop at Big Bend out of idle hands, nor did she willingly give him a single moment in which to snare victims made unwary while taking their ease. She saw to it that there was neither ease nor leisure time for the people at Big Bend, staff and students alike. Life there was an unending round of work, work, work, worship, study, and memorization; work, work, work, worship, study, and memorization.

Big Bend was to a very large degree a self-supporting community. It produced much of its own food and a fair share of its fiber. That which was not consumed on the premises was sold on the open market, the proceeds being used to purchase other necessities. Although a few professionals and skilled laborers were employed the year around at the estate, the great bulk of the work was done by the students themselves. Nor were they aided by labor-saving devices. It wasn't that Alice had theological objections to modern machinery nor that she feared creeping modernism in things mechanical; it was just that she wanted each student to be bone tired at bedtime every night.

And, so, it was by hand that the male students slopped the hogs, sheared the sheep, milked and butchered the cows, pitched the hay, shouldered the grain, fed the animals, and shoveled the manure. They plowed the ground, harrowed the soil, and cultivated the fields on foot with horses and mules. They felled the corn with corn cutters and laid low the wheat with scythes. They strung fences, shoed horses, kept the buildings on the estate in repair, painted and roofed them as needed, built new buildings and renovated old ones, especially as the need for dormitories increased. They dug ditches, did plumbing, chopped wood, made bricks, and laid stone fences to nowhere in particular. Nor did they toil on and ever on with their bodies open to the air rejoicing. On the contrary, they often worked wringing wet with sweat, for even on the hottest days they were expected to wear coveralls when doing dirty work or to be attired in jackets, long-sleeved white shirts, and ties on all other occasions except in the privacy of their rooms.

Meanwhile, the female students drudged at woman's work, never really finishing anything, for there was always more of the same to do. They baked the bread, cooked the food, laid the tables, and washed the dishes. They did the laundry, did the ironing, and kept the fabrics and furnishings at Big Bend spotless and in good repair. They swept, mopped, polished, dusted, and scrubbed endlessly. And, as the seasons dictated, they tended the vegetable gardens, picked the fruits and berries, canned and preserved the produce of

Big Bend, plucked and gutted the chickens, ducks, and geese, rendered lard, and made mincemeat.

Whenever she was not otherwise occupied, Alice prowled around Big Bend ubiquitously, much as the devil was thought to do, not seeking whom she might devour but whom she might spur on to harder work, whom she might drive deeper into wholesome exhaustion. When she came upon a male student staggering, like a beast of burden, under too heavy a load or straining his guts hauling some huge thing or other, she would quote hearteningly from an old hymn, "Work, for the night is coming, when man's work is done . . . work while the night is darkening, when man's work is o'er." When she chanced upon a female drudge bending over her work with red chapped hands and with fingers whose skin being cracked hurt to the bone, Alice would say encouragingly, "Remember, young sister, Jesus is on his way even now. Our King is coming, oh, yes, he surely is. Yet a little longer, and this life will pass away, and we shall be with him in glory." When she came upon those who were reeling under the requirement to learn at least one new Bible verse per day without forgetting any old ones, or when she encountered students whose minds were benumbed by hours of daily reading in the King James Bible, she would recite II Timothy 2:15: "Study to show thyself approved unto God, a workman that needeth not to be ashamed, rightly dividing the word of truth." To all and sundry, in season and out, she announced with profound certainty that the Lord never laid on a person a burden too heavy for that person to bear. Thus, hard labor and strenuous study were to be sources of rejoicing and not of complaint.

It never occurred to the Handmaiden nor to those who remained steadfast in the household of God at Big Bend that any final night that might really fall would nullify their lives, make futile all their labors, and obliterate their every hope. With no such faithless notions to enervate them, they worked on and toiled ever harder the closer the final night was thought to be. And when, exhausted on their beds, they slipped into sleep realizing that it was only an ordinary night that had come and not the final night, they renewed their faith and looked forward not to the dawn of just another day but to the dawn of the everlasting day of the Lord when they would go to be with him in glory.

Except for the few female students who, over the years, had batted their eyes at men or walked provocatively and who had been speedily expelled from Big Bend for their insufferably coquettish ways, Alice felt fairly confident. If the young women there went to bed exhausted each night and either prayed themselves to sleep, as was recommended, or had headaches or other miseries which, though not recommended, were not thought to be altogether bad, she believed that they might be spared the evil imagination.

Less confident that she could defend the male students from the evil imagination than she could the females, Alice was, in fact, absurdly overconfident. Since a majority of the students at Big Bend had, at any one time, come there straight out of high school, and since over half of those were boys who, like Manly, were eighteen to twenty years old, Alice had her work cut out in trying to shelter many who were easy prey, indeed, for the devil. After all, sexual commotion is truly vehement in young males, and the delectation they take in the mere idea of the opposite sex is morose quite beyond the comprehension of any lifelong virgin who is happy with that estate.

Since Alice knew more of divine economy than of human economy and since she was much more familiar with the ways of God than with the ways of a man with a maid, it is not surprising that her various attempts at crushing the serpent of sex were not always successful. She never knew and could not learn that a healthy young male, even when bone tired, is not equally tired all over, that one whole system of such a creature is ready to rise to undertake love's work whenever beckoned. It never occurred to her that minds bored to oblivion with much Bible reading and benumbed with many memorizations would seek escape in the effortless imagings of love. Like many a saint before her, she was perpetually blind to the fact that where there is no play, there the sportive element of sex is enhanced, the delightsome games of love recreational and restorative in themselves. So, despite her best efforts, the ghost of Onan haunted Big Bend, much seed being scattered. Unnatural acts occurred, and natural acts took place in circumstances fraught with danger and drenched in guilt. Though expressly forbidden, furtive glances lisped of love and flickers of interest between men and women spoke in erotic codes secretly. Nor was Manly spared.

Big Bend's own Dr. Emmet Langhorne Van Hook asked with a pronounced Kentucky twang that belied his classical learning, "Just what kind of work do you think you might be cut out for, Brother Plumwell?"

"I . . . I really don't know, sir," replied Manly, awed by Dr. Van Hook.

"Well, then, did you come from monied people?" probed Emmet, thinking that perhaps Mordecai ought to have been brought in on the interview.

"No, sir, my folks were just ordinary people, but I never had to work much except for the time when I clerked in a hardware store, and of course took a few odd jobs for pocket money."

"Of course, we don't do a retail business here," Emmet mused aloud.

"My grandparents raised me, Brother Van Hook, and they were retired farm people, but I always lived in town, in Nickel Plate, that is, and not on a farm."

"So, you never even did any day labor on a farm during summers, is that right?" asked Emmet with something close to reproach in his voice.

"No, sir, I mean, yes, sir, that's right, I never did."

Making a steeple out of his fingers and pushing them up tight under his nose, Emmet asked, "How about construction work—such as building houses, for example—ever do anything like that?"

"No, nothing like that, but I did paint my grandmother's house once, after my grandfather died."

"The whole house?"

"Yes."

106

"Even the high places and cornices and the like?"

"Sure."

"Not afraid of heights then, is that it?"

"Oh, no, sir, I'm not afraid of heights; in fact, I sort of like to be up on top of things, always have. I like to climb trees too. In fact, my grandmother used to say I could climb just like a monkey."

Emmet, who was a strong antievolutionist, grimaced at the thought of likening a man to a monkey in any context. Recovering himself, he said, "That settles it then."

"It does?" Manly replied, more than a little perplexed.

"Yes, higher maintenance, including roof detail and painting, is your primary assignment, and depending on the work load and seasonal requirements, we may give you a secondary assignment. But most of the time you will stick with your primary assignment. I think it safe to say that we will find plenty for you to do. Not too many hereabouts seem able to take the high work. In fact, we have some who appear to get dizzy with one foot squarely on the ground and the other equally squarely on the bottom rung of a stepladder."

"Yes, sir," said Manly, taking his leave glumly. He had never relished hard physical labor and had thought that since he was able to pay for his keep at Big Bend he might be spared at least some of the more strenuous toil he had heard about shortly after arriving. But he was not to be spared. After all, Alice wanted him to drop into bed exhausted like everybody else.

During the first two weeks Manly's primary assignment was sheer hell. His feet hurt from standing on ladder rungs hour after hour, his thighs groaned with fatigue from climbing up and down, up and down. His neck ached from painting overhead, and his shoulders hurt from supporting first one arm then the other outstretched full length painting with a four-inch brush. Much of the time he had to work with thirty-two- and forty-foot extension ladders. Alice would have no truck with the light-weight metal ones that did not contribute sufficiently to exhaustion. Although nearly six feet tall, Manly was slightly built and had his hands full positioning, raising, lowering, and taking down the thirty-two-footers, and invariably had to have help with the forty-footers.

Up went the ladders, and up went Manly. Then down he came and over went the ladders grudgingly, sometimes to the left, sometimes to the right, and up he went again to continue his work. While standing halfway up on the ladders he made them sway so as to extend them or to retract them. Up he went with tools; down he came again. Up he went with paint and brushes; down he came again. Sometimes he had to take a blowtorch to layers of old paint, cracked and curled, and then scrape away the residue with a scraper until the naked wood appeared; only then could he apply fresh paint. Sometimes he puttied windows; sometimes he trimmed sash; sometimes he painted cornices, holding on to the top rung of his ladder with one hand and reaching behind him with the other far to the left or to the right, painting blindly.

Sometimes, in the glowing sun, he laid rolled roofing; other times, hand over hand by rope, he hauled seventy-five-pound cans of tar up to roofs on the very edge of which he stood looking straight down. Sometimes, he patched bad spots with roofing cement; other times he laid shingles. Nor did he merely go up and down. Sometimes he went laterally out onto steeply pitched roofs. Sometimes he leapfrogged along ridge rolls, and other times he teetered on swaying trestles slung between tall ladders.

But it wasn't all bad. Once his muscles were hardened, his aches and pains disappeared even though he was usually dead tired at night. Also, he liked to be up on top of things as he had told Bro. Van Hook. There was usually a breeze along the rooftops, and Big Bend was indeed beautiful when seen from on high. Best of all, the unusual perspectives he enjoyed let him hold and caress certain objects with his eyes that his eyes weren't supposed to be on at all. As the pressures of life at the Bible School mounted, Manly began to find even the plain Janes of Big Bend insufferably attractive. In ordinary circumstances, at ground level so to speak, he could no more than glance at them before averting his eyes. But that was not true of his primary assignment, which took him to strange places, left him frequently alone, and gave him a wide variety of vantage points from which he could see but not likely be seen.

Unless they happened to notice the ladder he was on, the girls and younger women at Big Bend seldom looked up, in a terrestrial sense, nor did they customarily sweep their eyes along the higher reaches of the buildings on the estate as they went about their work. Hence, they often walked in Manly's presence unself-consciously, not realizing that he was just above their heads, appraising them. His different altitudes, often changed, gave him new and promising angles from which to view unsuspecting specimens of womankind.

Then, too, there were the windows whose sashes needed trimming. While tending to such tedious work, Manly would often peer courageously into a room from the upper right-hand or the upper left-hand windowpane, hardly the kind of place from which women would ordinarily expect a man's eye to be fixed upon them. Furthermore, even when he was seen, he became an expert at feigning, at seeming to focus on his work while in fact looking elsewhere and seeing sights far more fascinating than any afforded by window sash.

Although he never saw anything really exciting, he was, nevertheless, titillated often and occasionally entranced by unexpected glimpses of girls who were blissfully unaware of his elevated presence. He was also devastated by Persephone almost daily. Thus, it came to pass that Manly's old Adam began to rise, phoenix-like, out of the ashes of remorse, repentance, and heartfelt protestations to God that, for Jesus' sake, he would never again abuse himself. But as often as he repented, he again put his hand to self-abuse; and as often as he sought divine forgiveness, just that often did he suffer the same old guilt anew, and for good reason. Worse than that, Satan sent a succubus to him.

He did not know her name. He had seen her in the flesh only once and briefly, but he recognized her face and was familiar with a great deal more of her as well. She was the dancing girl from the fair whom he had held in his arms, whom he had carried tenderly when she was hurt. Not only did he remember her in reality but also in the unreality of subsequent fantasies in which she had come to him gratefully, so eager to please, at the beck and call of his imagination. Now she came again, but whereas she had been loved with an unalloyed love in the past, in the present she was suffered over as well as yearned for, hated as well as loved.

He seemed to be hunting in woods where he had sometimes rambled as a child, back home near Plumstone Creek. He was surprised to be carrying a gun. If he had been able to speak to himself, he would have asked, "Is this a dream or am I really hunting?" but no words of self-interrogation came, leaving him to wonder mutely what he was supposed to be doing. Then, unaware of his presence, she appeared before him, walking at right angles to his path through the woods. When she saw him, she ran, not with fear, but with exuberance, enticing him to pursue her. As she ran, the articles of her clothing flew away one by one, leaving only her long hair for a covering, but it did not cover her, for so fast did she run that her hair undulated in her wake parallel to the earth.

Manly tried to sprint to her side but could not. Why could he not catch up? He was taller than she. His stride was longer. He was younger. But every step was a defeat. Was it that he sank into quagmire each time one of his feet fell to earth? Was there some awesome magnet that rooted him to the spot just below the humus of the woodland path? Were there no bones in his legs from the kneecaps down? He could not fathom why he could not move, nor did he know why she, running easily, did not outdistance him altogether and vanish from sight. But he could see the muscles in her back ripple as she swung first one arm ahead of her then the other. He could see a half-circular line come and go under each buttock as she put first one foot to the ground and then the other. On occasion he could see a bit of one breast or the other, rising and falling, as she twisted this way and that, following the sinuosities of the path.

As he reached for her as though to drag his reluctant legs after his arms by an act of desperate will, she looked back at him smiling, urging him with inviting eyes to catch her. For some mysterious reason, she was bound and determined to run and could only be his if he overtook her and captured her. Since no fear troubled her face and no alarm racked her beautiful body, he knew that she wanted his imprisoning arms around her, but it was not to be. In vain did he try to outrun her; in vain did he plead with her to stop; in vain did she try to slow down that they might be together for at least one loving moment.

When he awoke, he sat up abruptly and tried to drive all recollection of her from him. Trembling with determination to be pure, he lay down again intending to focus his mind on holy things and holy things alone until sleep returned. But sleep did not return; lust would not let him relax. Finally, will power melting under the fierce heat of desire, he indulged once again in the odious secret vice. How the Lord Jesus must despair of a moral weakling like him! How God must loathe such a debauchee!

Manly was sitting in chapel for the regular noon service. Bro. Dickinson led them lengthily in prayer. Everyone in the pews sat in an attitude of contrition, bent forward, hands clasped reverently. Every head was bowed; every eye was closed. Although he was by no means alone, Manly sat in isolation in that he was not close to any other worshipper. Yet, as he prayed he sensed a presence to his left, then felt human warmth against his face, and finally became aware of pressure along his left side from shoulder to foot. Tilting his head to the right and twisting his neck to the left, he peeped through half-opened lids and saw her sitting there smiling at him with her left index finger at her lips, shushing him. Although clothed, she was shivering and seemed frail, in pain perhaps. The next thing he knew, she had begun to wiggle and worm her way onto his lap, assuming his attitude, paralleling his body, and facing forward as he was. Choking back an urge to cry out, he looked about in horror fully expecting to be expelled from Big Bend swiftly and surely. But all about him eyes were closed, heads bowed, shoulders hunched. As he tried to push her off his lap before it was too late, she took his hands and guided them up under her blouse until they came to rest on her naked breasts, whereupon her whole body, quivering with long-sought delight, danced upon his lap. Then the fountains of his great deep burst, and he awoke with a squeal to find himself and his pajama bottoms wet and sticky with the pent-up liquid of love. Nor was God the only one who would know how craven he was in the presence of imperious desire, for his very sheets would testify against him when they went to the laundry, and his pajama bottoms would cry aloud in accusation. All Big Bend would learn of his sins of impurity.

He was sixty feet up in the air, straddling the ridge roll of the chateau's highest roof. In his left hand he carried a large mortarboard on which rested a heavy load of mortar with a trowel sticking out of it. Using his right hand for balance, he began to leapfrog slowly toward a massive chimney at the far end of the roof. Why was he going there? Was it to cement some loose bricks into place or to dump mortar down the chimney onto the swifts nesting therein? He did not know. In any case, as he neared it, she materialized out of nowhere, smiling and strutting her stuff, leaping and dancing before him as though he were her lord and master. Then, before he could come closer, she lay down on the ridge roll with her head pointed away from him, supported her hips at the small of her back with her hands, her elbows positioned on either side of the ridge roll, and began to pump her legs as though riding an imaginary bicycle, upside down in the sky. Manly did not know whether or not she wore panties, nor did it matter, the effect being the same. Upon awaking with a start, he abused himself vigorously and fell back into bed shaking. Suffused with warmth, he fell asleep quickly, but all during the following day he was cold with remorse and self-hate for letting himself lust after the one who came to him in dreams.

Standing on a ladder, Manly peeked into the upper left-hand pane of someone's bedroom window. Whose? Why was it so brightly lighted? It was brightly lighted because night had fallen, but why, then, was he still outdoors painting in the dark? That was not clear, nor did it matter, for suddenly there she was prancing around and around in a large circle in the middle of the bedroom floor. As she rounded toward him, she took off her top hat and threw it away, then her cape, then her skirt, and finally her panties. Bathed in mellow light and caressed only by air, she thrust out her breasts, then her pelvis, with its curly delta pointing to ineffable pleasure, and then her breasts again. At that point she saw him watching her. But did she cower with shame? No. Did she scream with indignation? No. Did she reproach him for lust or accuse him of violating her privacy? No. She held out her arms to him. She beckoned to him with her hands, her finger stretching out to touch him. She seemed to open her entire being to his coming. Could he come to her? Could he, with her arms pressing him close, enter into her? No, he could do nothing but watch her in futility. He couldn't even think of putting down his paint and brush. He couldn't move a muscle to open wide her window. He couldn't smash it in with his foot nor leap to her side. When he awoke from his dreamy paralysis, erupting with semen, he realized that she had been miming, just for him, the dance she and the other girls had done at the fair. For a fleeting moment he felt deeply grateful that she had come, even if only in a dream and even if sent by Satan to tempt him. When he returned to reality, theologically as well as physically, he got out of bed, cleaned himself as best he could, and tried to dry the bottom sheet of his bed. Then he fell to the floor on his knees in the wintry cold of his room, the inner man quaking with self-contempt as much as the outer man shivered in the cold and shook against the bed.

When she did not come to him in dreams by night, she came to him in dreams by day. When she did not come to him unbidden in dreams, she came to him bidden in fantasies. When she did not ravish him unexpectedly, he seduced himself with images of her intentionally. So preoccupied was he with her that he had difficulty reading the Scriptures long enough and intently enough to satisfy his teachers, to say nothing of God. He also found it difficult to memorize one new Bible verse per day, difficult to worship God in a way pleasing to the Most High, difficult to pray with purity and all but impossible to do so with total concentration on holy things. Satan was clearly winning, and for some inscrutable reason God was, at least, letting it happen. Defeated time and again, unable to bolster his will sufficiently to resist his temptress, and too ashamed to keep on promising God that he would never again have impure thoughts nor do impure deeds, Manly cast about desperately for help of any kind, secular as well as sacred. In that manner he found his way to the library.

The library at Big Bend was a ragtag affair at best. Cyrus Dewayne

Pritchard had cared more for the bindings of books than for their contents. He had hired an interior decorator to help him in stocking his library and in arranging its books, in singles and in sets, so as to be most appealing to the eye. When the Handmaiden arrived to take possession of the estate, she found an exquisite Gothic room in one corner of the chateau. It was paneled throughout in solid golden oak with great exposed beams overhead supporting a rococo ceiling in blue and gold. Under her feet was a floor of multi-colored Italian marble on which were scattered rich and sumptuous rugs, some Oriental, some European. Approximately 8,000 volumes lined the walls, two stories high.

Initially, Alice paid scant attention to the books except to take momentary delight in their beauty, but some had to be thrown out at once to make room for a jumble of Bibles, concordances, and sacred histories brought from Soddy-Daisy. Then, when a set of erotica was found among Pritchard's books, she was rocked with revulsion. Alice spoke much of depravity, but when she actually encountered it, it undid her. Those horrid books, whose very titles made her gag, occasioned agonized reflection over the legitimacy of his conversion. How, for example, could a born-again Christian (with due allowance for his having been very rich) have retained in his library for as much as an instant after conversion such titles as *Venus in the Cloister, or the Nun in Her Smock; Adultery on the Part of Married Women and Fornication on the Part of Old Maids and Widows, Defended by Mary Wilson, Spinster, with Plans for Promoting Same; The Diary of a Nymphomaniac; The Love Cabinet of Madame De Pompadour; The Battle of Venus: A Descriptive Dissertation of the Various Modes of Enjoyment of the Female Sex, with Some Curious Information on the Resources of Lust, Lechery, and Licentiousness, to Revive the Drooping Faculties and Strengthen the Voluptuous and Exhausted; A Night in a Moorish Harem; Ten Years of the Life of a Courtesan—Detailing Her Lessons in Lust, Her Seduction and Voluptuous Life, the Piquant Penchants of Her Various Lovers* (Illustrated), and many, many others?

Those books, some in numbered first editions and most in costly bindings, were consigned to purifying flames hurriedly, indignantly. The empty spaces were filled with hymnals, books on miraculous conversions and other divine deeds, ancient and modern, and volumes of approved sermons, mostly from the nineteenth century. Book burnings soon became an annual event at Big Bend, much like spring cleaning and at the same time of the year, not so much because the remaining books of Pritchard's collection were offensive but because many in the Holy Nation contributed books to the Bible School that were deemed more valuable from a spiritual point of view. Since Alice had little use for books, except for the One Holy Book, and did not intend to make any additional space for unnecessary volumes, it was simply a matter of disposing of existing books whenever better ones arrived. So, many a classic of world literature, beautifully bound, was consumed by the flames of successive springs.

Accordingly, the book collection at Big Bend was motley. Still and all, it contained a volume that promised Manly some help from his affliction, at the outset at least. Finding it, however, was not easy. He watched the library for several weeks trying to decide when it was least used. Settling on a Monday evening at 8:30 (sermon preparation being at its lowest ebb at that time), he crept in with hunched shoulders and a hangdog look. Casting furtive glances this way and that, he tried to find out whether or not any medical texts for popular consumption had survived the vernal holocausts.

In the depths of his misery, he had remembered coming upon something called *The Family Physician* in his grandmother's attic. As a little boy he had been intrigued by it for its colored pictures of internal organs. Moreover, it had contained some specially designed pages with flaps that could be turned in such a way as to let the beholder proceed straight through the human body from belly to backbone. There were also some line drawings of what he now knew had been erect penises. Yet, if memory served him correctly, they had all been bent the wrong way, due to diseases no doubt. When, one day, his grandmother had crept, cat-like, into the attic and caught him and a playmate looking at pictures of diseased penises, she had spoken no word, but, glaring at them, sent him and his friend packing. Needless to say, he never saw *The Family Physician* again, for it met a quick end. But, as he remembered it, the book had contained some prescriptions and home remedies for various diseases. Just possibly, Big Bend's library might contain such a book, one with help for him.

So, on a Monday night in early spring, Manly began his search for secular assistance in overcoming his most egregious moral weakness. His search ended in failure that night as it did on the following Monday night. Clearly, no such book reposed on the ground floor. On the third Monday night, he peered through the French doors leading to the library and saw only four people: one, the dour lady at the circulation desk, the other three, students, amorphous lumps bent over works of divinity. Manly climbed the ladder to the catwalk above with a professional aplomb that belied his anxious spirit. Finding himself alone with no would-be climber in sight, he calmed down and began a methodical search. Moments before the library was to close for the night, he found the prize he had been seeking. It was called *The Home Medical Advisor: A Thoroughly Reliable Guide,* by a Mr. James Gothicus MacGowan, M.D., late of Edinburg, and published in 1869. Although the antique tome contained no colored pictures of internal organs and no line drawings of diseased members, its index had an entry on "Masturbation (Onanism)," which was lumped under "General Diseases" and was sandwiched between "Gravel of Stone in the Bladder (Calculus)" and "Blood with the Urine (Hoematuria)" on the one hand and "Pox (Syphilis)" and "Clap (Gonorrhoea, Gleet)" on the other. Since time was very short at the moment, it took another furtive visit to the library for Manly to copy the entry, including certain prescriptions. Here is what he copied:

This is a very degrading and destructive habit, indulged in by young people of both sexes. There is probably no vice which is more injurious to both mind and body, and produces more fearful consequences than this. It is generally commenced early in life before the patient is aware of its evil influence, and it finally becomes so fastened upon him, that it is with great difficulty that he can break off the habit.

Symptoms: The symptoms produced by this vice are numerous. When the habit begins in early life, it retards growth, impairs the mental faculties and reduces the victim to a lamentable state. The person afflicted seeks solitude, and does not wish to enjoy the society of his friends: he is troubled with headaches, wakefulness and restlessness at night, pain in various parts of the body, indolence, melancholy, loss of memory, weakness in the back and generative organs, variable appetite, cowardice, inability to look a person in the eye, lack of confidence in his own abilities. When the evil has been pursued for several years, there will be an irritable condition of the system; sudden flushes of heat over the face; the countenance becomes pale and clammy; the eyes have a dull, sheepish look; the hair becomes dry and split at the ends; sometimes there is a pain over the region of the heart; shortness of breath; palpitation of the heart; symptoms of dyspepsia show themselves, the sleep is disturbed, there is constipation, cough, irritation of the throat; finally the whole man becomes a wreck, physically, morally, and mentally. Some of the consequences of masturbation are epilepsy, apoplexy, paralysis, premature old age, involuntary discharge of seminal fluid, which generally occurs during sleep, or after urinating, or when evacuating the bowels. Among females, besides these other consequences, we have hysteria, menstrual derangement, catalepsy, and strange nervous symptoms.

General Treatment: First of all, the habit must be abandoned; this is the first and most important thing to be secured, for unless this is done, every other treatment will be without avail. Everything should be done to strengthen the morality of the patient, and to raise his self-respect. He should cultivate the society of virtuous and intellectual females. Everything lascivious must be avoided. His mind should be directed to some employment or amusement, that will engage his attention without causing fatigue. He should avoid solitude and never be left alone more than is necessary, and above all he should never be permitted to sleep alone. The patient should sleep on a mattress, and be lightly covered with clothes. Frequent bathing and washing of the private parts should be employed, as well as sitting baths. The treatment of this disease should be undertaken only by a skillful physician.

Combining elation with ladder-climbing skill, Manly descended from the catwalk in a manner the like of which the dour lady at the desk had never before seen. One of the amorphous lumps also looked up in wonderment as he bounded off the ladder onto the floor and scurried through the French doors. Safely back in his room, he devoured again and again his handwritten copy of the symptoms, diagnosis, and various treatment plans for his condition. What a relief it was to know that a brilliant man like Dr. James Gothicus MacGowan had understood the morally vicious nature of the disease, and what a godsend that there were definite medically approved steps a person could take to cure it!

Among the three prescriptions he took down, one called "allopathic" recommended:

Diluted Nitric Acid............................. 4 drachms.
Diluted Muriatic Acid .... 4 drachms.
Syrup of Orange Peel............................ 1 drachm.
Water

Mix thoroughly; dose, a teaspoon in a wineglass of water, before each meal.

Although Manly did not know what a drachm was, he presumed any druggist would.

The second prescription, called "herbal," consisted of:

Red Peruvian Bark................................2 ounces.
Chamomile Flowers .... 1 ounce.
Compound Infusion of Roses ....6 ounces.
Port Wine .... 1 quart.

The ingredients were to be mixed and left standing for several days, followed by frequent shaking. The recommended dose was a wineglass full three or four times a day. At first that seemed better to Manly than the former prescription, because it contained no acid. But it contained alcohol, which was worse, for he could not risk bringing wine into Big Bend, even for medicinal purposes, nor could he safely hide the concoction while dosing himself with it. Moreover, it was recommended for those who had not yet been debilitated by the disease. That left him in a quandary, for he did not know how bad off he really was, and of course he could not compare notes with any other miscreant-sufferer. Certainly, he was debilitated morally, but perhaps not yet physically.

The third prescription, one called "eclectic," posed the same problem but in the opposite way. It contained:

Chloroform .... 1/2 ounce.
Tincture of Ginger .... 1/2 ounce.
Sulphate of Quinine .... 15 grams.
Aromatic Spirits of Ammonia..................... 2 drachms.

The dose was to consist of twenty-five drops in a wineglass of buttermilk, to be administered three times a day. It was specifically designed for the debilitated. Sorely abused though his poor body was and defeated though his spirit definitely was, Manly feared the full dose (and loathed buttermilk) lest it ravage his whole body in unexpected ways. Moreover, he did not know what percentage of dilution would meet his needs. Too little would do little good, no doubt, and too much might damage beyond repair the Temple of the Holy Ghost which was his body. Reluctantly, he chose the allopathic remedy.

While pondering the imponderables of remedy aɪd dosage, something that should be left to a skilled physician but couldn't be in his case, Manly's early elation was blighted by additional fears, his initial sense of relief dismantled, piece by piece, by insuperable difficulties. Although he had the old Nash with him, he had not yet been allowed to go out into the world to preach. Accordingly, he could not make a mad dash to a drugstore while on a routine preaching mission. To have produced what might have been taken as a plausible reason for leaving Big Bend briefly, he would have had to lie, no light matter for a born-again Christian, even to overcome an abomination to the Lord.

If, with downcast eyes, he had said to anyone in authority that he needed to have a prescription filled, eyebrows would, no doubt, have risen in suspicion of one who had hitherto taken no medicine and had been known to have had no medical consultations while at Big Bend. Terrified at the thought of lying to the Handmaiden or to any of the awesome Five, Manly consoled himself with the realization that cowardice was one of the symptoms of his disease. But that thought occasioned new anxieties. Had his sheepishness already given him away; had his depravity been discerned, its cause accurately and contemptuously diagnosed; did his hair really have split ends, or was that symptomatic only of female offenders against the Temple of the Holy Ghost? Regrettable though it was, Dr. James Gothicus MacGowan had not made that point clear.

At least as unnerving as the prospect of lying to the Handmaiden was the awful scene he imagined, repeatedly, at the drugstore in Kimballton. He knew nobody there, but in his mind's eye he kept seeing a baldheaded man with a predatory gaze, standing in white with tier upon tier of pill bottles crowding in on him from three sides. Manly also saw himself stepping up to the high counter behind which the raptorial pharmacist not only counted pills out of big bottles, putting them into small bottles, but also seemed to count the cost of each pill. Manly was, of course, well dressed and businesslike, at least to casual observation, his hair carefully combed, his clothes spic and span, his shoes black and shiny. He saw the pharmacist's guarded, quizzical look and heard him say with a hint of flinty suspicion, "What can I do for you, young man?"

"Do you know what a drachm is?" Manly blurted out. It probably sounded foolish, but when acid was at issue, one could not be too careful.

Looking insulted and superior, the man said between clenched teeth, "Of course I do. I'm a registered pharmacist."

"Well, then," Manly replied, his thumping heart belying the reassurance he should have felt, "I would like four drachms of diluted nitric acid."

"Oh, you would, would you," mused the man, narrowing his eyes.

"Yes, sir," said Manly as evenly as possible, "and four drachms of diluted muriatic acid too."

"Muriatic acid too?" questioned the man, his eyes now as widened as they had been narrowed a moment earlier.

"And," Manly quavered, his voice high and reedy with tension, "a drachm of syrup of orange peel."

"Syrup of orange peel!" bellowed the man, a great light dawning inside his head and shining out through his eyes at Manly. "Oh, you and your kind disgust me, parading in here as big as life and trying to get medicine without a proper doctor's prescription."

At that, Manly turned and fled from the drugstore, but not before he heard the man hiss the words, "You filthy self-abuser, you!"

Running pell-mell toward the car, he could see and hear the druggist telling his employees (except for the girl at the soda fountain) about the damned pervert who had just compounded his sins of impurity by trying to circumvent the medical profession and dose his loathsome disease all by himself.

"I like business as well as the next person, but there's a limit to what I'll do to get it," the druggist said self-righteously. Manly also saw the heads of employees nod vigorously in agreement.

So great was the tumult of his emotions, so extreme the pendulum swing between elation and abject fear, that he could only dither impotently and never act on his newly acquired, medically approved advice. But one kind of impotence led to another, and for nearly three weeks he thought he had, at last, been delivered from the scourge of his flesh, without the medicine he had so desperately wanted. But, alas, the phoenix of desire arose one day from the ashes of impotence with as grand a beating of wings as any with which it ever had on previous occasions mounted up from the ashes of self-contempt and repentance.

It should go without saying that Manly revered the Handmaiden almost to the point of adoration, that he was awestruck by the spiritual giants who surrounded her, and that he counted himself most fortunate to have been able to study God's word at Big Bend. Yet, everybody there in authority conspired against him (it seemed in his darkest moments) in that the one thing that might have helped him most in his dreadful relapse was systematically denied him. Dr. MacGowan had clearly said that one suffering his condition should cultivate the society of virtuous and intellectual females. Manly knew that he was surrounded by the most virtuous females, and he presumed them to be intellectual as well. Nevertheless, he was denied the very society that so abundantly surrounded him, that he, and perhaps others, needed so much. It may have been just as well, however, that the Handmaiden had made society between the sexes next to impossible, for whatever his virtues, Dr. James Gothicus MacGowan had not been altogether up on iatrogenic diseases.

At a more reflective point in his life, after unending years of sexual desire, defeat, and distress, Manly would seriously question why God had arranged for human reproduction as he had. Presumptuous or not, why, he wondered, could God have not made the insistent promptings of sex more like the gentler prickings of conscience? Why couldn't there have been a still, small voice within that said, quite simply, "It is your duty, whether you like it or not, to be fruitful and multiply"? Why, in general, did it please God to make sex so demanding, so unrestrained a craving, so imperious an appetite, refusing to be filled, and why, in particular, was he, Manly Plumwell, so lambent with lust all the while, so preoccupied by the evil imagination, so goaded by his own flesh to penetrate and to participate in female flesh when what he really wanted more than anything was to be pure and ethereal, like the angels above?

If you've never been submerged in a place like Big Bend nor exposed to it in some vital way or other, you'll have a hard time comprehending what it's like. It isn't like being in a public school or college or university. You might think that the courses there would resemble some of your own courses in literature and history, but not so, even though the written word is read much (also memorized) and even though something called sacred history is delved into minutely. But, with effort and imagination, you can get an inkling of what it's like. What it's like will surprise you.

Imagine that you're strolling alone on a warm lazy day. Your walk takes you into an empty open area, into a remote corner of a very large city park, perhaps, or, better yet, out onto rolling meadows on the outskirts of town. Wherever the place, there's a newness about it that fills you with a sense of discovery. You're in no hurry and not at all anxious. Happy to be alive and relieved to be at leisure, you wander down an inviting path. After looking all around and about for quite a while, you gaze inwardly, every footfall propelling you deeper and deeper into a delicious daydream. Lost in your sauntering reverie, you are unaware of bearing down on an enormous billboard, as big as a barn, nor do you perceive that a gigantic mural has been painted on it, a work so obviously inspired by Italian Renaissance painting that it might have been done by a resurrected master of the time. Oblivious to what looms before you, you amble on until you nearly ram your unsuspecting nose into it. In the nick of time, you stop and stare at the sight before you, not knowing what it is you are beholding. The mural is so vast and you are so close to it that it's almost as though you had stepped into it. From your perspective, the surface on which it is painted is as big as all outdoors. When you look up, the sky at the top of the mural and the sky overhead appear to be the same sky, the clouds of the one close kin to the clouds of the other. As you look to the extreme left and right, the hills of the mural are continuous with the hills leading away from the spot where you stand, the trees of the one marching in step with the trees of the other. The path on which you stand leads directly and almost irresistibly into the heartland of the mural, the sod at your feet the green of the grass at the bottom of the painting. Breathing deeply and shaking your head, thereby retrieving your wandering wits, you resist the bewitchery of the mural and decline to step into it. Rather, you back up a few paces to survey it whole.

It is clear that the landscape in the mural is not of a piece with the place where you stand, nor is every physical feature found on Planet Earth depicted therein. There are no polar ice caps; the Sahara is not there; the Himalayas do not appear; and no rocky windswept coast shows up. Still and all, much appears that is familiar, and nothing in itself, of an earthly sort, goes beyond easy belief. There are hills and dales, meadows and woods, gardens, grain fields, and wild places. The gentle hills in the foreground lead to plumper hills in the middle distance, and these advance toward distant mountains rising to craggy peaks, dusted with snow, where trees dare not climb and grass cannot cling. Here and there, rocks crop out, and springs well up making rills that trickle and tumble to a river lazing along, in the center foreground, toward its meeting with the sea. Grapes and cherries abound, and orchards cap the nearer hills with numberless points of color made by apples and apricots, peaches and plums peeking ripely through the leaves of their respective trees. On a fat hill in the middle distance, woolly sheep congregate to create a cumulus cloud adrift on an emerald sky. Into the wildwood above, hunters and their hounds go marauding. Stags bound into thickets, does stand stock-still, rabbits lie low, and wild fowl cower. In the valley below, fishermen bend over dark pools trying to lure fish from the secret places with promises of free food.

Everywhere on the flat lands and habitable slopes of the foreground, the works of humankind can be seen. Hedges planted by forgotten peasants quilt the land and constrain the paths that run to and fro through the countryside. In the middle distance, slightly to the right of center, sits a walled city, medieval in aspect and situated in the middle of a great web of roads and bridges leading to it. Protective walls of stone reach out from it, some extending to an arm of the sea that laps at one flank of the city, others leading to the river that glides before its gates. Watch towers and redoubts punctuate the walls, their verticality being answered by the spires and bell towers of churches and the steeples and domes of public buildings within the city. Dark ships nose toward its docks, the wind puffing their bright sails. Colorful caravans of animals plod toward its markets. Human beings from all ranks and walks of life stream into its vortex. Behind the city's walls in buildings shuttered against the light, men and women, duly married to each other if good Christians, merge their bodies to replenish the earth; midwives pluck the fruit of the womb; and babes are given the breast. In the city's

119

streets, on its commons, and throughout the hamlets that dot the hinterlands, children play or are busy at their parents' bidding. The butcher, the baker, the candlestick maker, the alchemist, the weaver, the blacksmith, and the herbalist ply their several trades. Nor are the learned at rest. Divines dispute doctrines, attorneys argue the law, barber-surgeons wield their knives, sometimes cutting hair, sometimes human flesh. Outside the walls, peasants and pluckers of all sorts, shepherds and swineherds, milkmaids and horsemen tend to the work of their hands. Horses are shoed, cows are milked, hogs are slaughtered. Inside the city and in the countryside alike, priests, morticians, and gravediggers do their bit to close the book of life on those whose tasks are finished. The whole of human life is not depicted in the painting, but there is more than enough to satisfy one's sense not only of earthly reality but of human completeness as well.

In the top center of the mural, high and lifted up, you see the King of all creation, enthroned in glory. In his left hand he holds a blue globe surmounted by a golden cross, the symbols of creation and redemption, the totality of his work. The Imperial Person appears as one of majestic masculinity, dominant and dominating. His regal presence bespeaks authority, and purple is his garb, ermine-trimmed. Wise beyond comprehension, he knows his own mind perfectly and in so knowing, knows all—the past, the present, the future, the far, and the near being equally pellucid to him. His all-seeing eyes are gravid with cosmic strategy; his lips need not move to command. Self-doubt does not furrow his brow, nor does his head rest uneasily beneath its golden crown, for there is none like him, and no one to challenge him. His right hand, uplifted, commands all creatures to keep silence before him except for those celestial choristers who praise his holy name and laud his deeds forever and a day. Though he needs nothing, being perfect, and can do all things, unnumbered cherubim and seraphim, angels and archangels hover about him in endless ministration. Cumulus clouds of pink and purple frame his throne; sun, moon, and stars pay blushing tribute to the luminosity that pulses from him effortlessly. Its rays, lighting the most distant reaches of creation, also illumine the way for the Holy Spirit to glide, like a gentle dove, to the waiting world below. Dazzled by these sights, your eyes blink and beg to turn away, but no sooner do you rest them than your ears take up the tale. Harp and harpsichord, trumpet and organ, strings and tympani tell you that the great Handel himself is in heaven, where in perpetual exuberance he composes coronation anthems, monarchial marches, and kingly choruses for the Majestic One. "Hosannas" and "hallelujahs" rumble melifluously in the heavens and reverberate throughout the whole creation.

On a skull-littered hillock in the left foreground, the work of redemption is completed, the First-Born of all creation dying in human form, lamb-like, the blood of atonement gushing from his riven side. The Father has sacrificed his only begotten Son and is exceedingly well pleased. The uncomprehending mourners who huddle, despairing, at the foot of the cross do not yet know that the ransom of redemption is paid. They who have been with him so long and still do not know must yet be persuaded by the ultimate miracle, his resurrection from the dead. Behind and to one side of the cross, unperceived by the wretched ones who mourn the Messiah's death, stand the spectral figures of prophet, priest, and king. As though newly aroused from eternal slumber, they smile wanly at the salvation whose seed they planted but upon whose fruit they could not feast. In them the past is present, and in their descendant, dead on the cross, the sacred history of Israel is finished, its *raison d'être* fully explained. Not only is the past present, the future is now, for behind the cross, on its other side, is a new tomb, ready to receive the body of King Jesus. But the tomb gapes open, not yet sealed, and in so doing foretells how it will be three days hence, for death can in no way keep this king, nor can a tomb, even though sealed with stone, delay his appointed ascension to the One above from whom he descended with saving love. Could the grief-stricken of Calvary's hill but perceive the immediate future, they would not weep but would, rather, rejoice exceedingly, for, unbeknownst, it has pleased God from the foundation of the world to give them the free gift of eternal life. Yet a little longer and they will know and, knowingly, will preach the good news to all nations.

Scattered here and there toward the bottom of the right foreground are what look like jagged portholes in the earth's crust. Through these you see flashes of red and orange made murky by vapor and smoke and set against abysmal black. You are looking into the infernal world, into the bottomless pit of torment and unmitigated grief. Your nose and ears cannot help uniting with your eyes in perceiving the ghastly realities of hell. The stench of hair singed eternally and of human flesh ever burning but never consumed, together with sulphurous fumes, assault your nostrils. Pandemonium pounds your ears as demons squeal and gibber in delight at new and more excruciating tortures. Meanwhile, their writhing victims, having no rest, cry and scream in unendurable pain, alternately swearing in vain rage at their torturers and pleading for deliverance in pitiful futility. In the center of it all, Satan slithers in dragonesque form, spewing threats and fire from his snout as he looks over his shoulder in reptilian rage at the premonitory tomb above. He knows what it means. He knows—and how he loathes the knowledge!—that the Christ cannot be kept in the underworld and that in rising from the grave will save many faithful ones from infernal fire, pestilential torture, and endless misery.

As if nearly bumping into a billboard standing in the middle of nowhere and containing a huge mural were not surprise enough for one day, an art critic appears as if by magic, introduces himself to you, and begins to ply his trade effervescently. Liberally festooned with historical knowledge and eager to enlighten you, he says, as though you had asked, "What we have here is a work reminiscent of . . . of . . . oh . . . a Carpaccio, I would say. There are stereotyped symbols of faith in it, to be sure, but note, if you will, that these symbols are treated as though they were ordinary solid objects. The wings on the angels, as you can see, are painted as realistically as the wings on the birds, just as though both kinds of wings were of the same stuff. In short, the whole work is representational, i.e., it portrays its subject matter, whether natural or supernatural, in the way in which people (in Western culture at least) ordinarily perceive the world. God's face, if you look closely, is that of a middle-aged human male, albeit a majestically grand one and well able to frighten the wits out of mere earthly kings and princelings. By the same token, the devil is recognizably reptilian, rather like a crocodile, and equally frightening. Heaven above and hell at the bottom together with the landscape painted in throughout the center of the picture—looking very like the Italian countryside, circa 1500—constitute one perspectival unity. The supernatural realm is not superimposed on our natural world as though it were an alien sphere nor does it intrude unnaturally into human history. On the contrary, the celestial is one with the terrestrial, the clouds framing God's throne much like ordinary cumulus clouds, though arranged a bit more reverentially—as befits their theological function in the picture—than one usually finds them in the run-of-the-mill atmosphere, so to speak. And, hell, ah yes, hell, just look at hell. It is much like looking through a peephole in the door of a furnace into whose hungry flames you have just thrown a half-dozen shovelsfull of very soft coal, except, of course, that that would be a most unlikely place for a crocodile. God's heaven, you will notice, hovers very close to earth, and the Holy Spirit, represented by that dove in the top center, descends through earth's atmosphere just as though it were the same as heaven's, his wings equally usable in either sphere. Satan, of course, could easily clamber through any one of those holes in the crust of the earth—and, my, my, how frightfully thin that crust is—and prowl around, as I believe Scripture says he in fact does, seeking those whom he might devour. The souls of the dead depart the church militant here below and ascend to the church triumphant above—not a very long trip you'll note; meanwhile, the wicked, no doubt, are those creatures falling headlong through the earth's crust, toward the bottom of the picture there, to feed the flames of hell. Angels wend their ways up and down between heaven and earth, carrying out God's decrees, and demons, doing their dirty work, scramble up and down between the world and the underworld. Yes, it's all of one piece and visually very well integrated. In summation, the entire painting is realistic in that every item, factual or fictional, is portrayed with what almost amounts to photographic verisimilitude."

Upon concluding these gratuitous and crisply delivered opinions, the effervescent art critic bids you adieu and departs, his destination as much a mystery as his point of departure and the reasons that brought him your way. It is most fortunate, however, that the art critic paused to give his impromptu lecture, because it contains a key for understanding the peculiar people at Big Bend and all others of their populous tribe. In a nutshell, the difference between such people and you is that instead of backing off to look at the mural coolly, critically, and contextually, and remaining outside it, they walk into the mural through faith (whether acquired slowly through nurture or suddenly through dramatic conversion) and proceed to live their lives in it as though nothing remotely like that had happened. The moment they cross the threshold, the mural ceases for them to be a two-dimensional illusion of three-dimensionality and becomes three-dimensional and veridical. From that moment on, they live and move and have their being within it. It becomes their world, and a tidy world it is, all wrapped up in itself, each of its parts verifying the reality of its other parts (for those whose vision it is). Within the great mural, every item (whether terrestrial or celestial, natural or supernatural, mythological or historical) is equally realistic and, to the eye of faith, equally real. As amazing as the idea of life in a mural (as it were) may seem to you, it is not miraculous, nor is it rare. Every true-believer inhabits some such mural.

There is another avenue you can and really should take toward imagining your way into Big Bend. Think of yourself in a darkened theater enjoying a live performance. The theater is intimate. Your seat is excellent. You can see and hear very well. Since the drama is engrossing, there is scarcely a sniffle here, a cough there, or a shuffling of feet anywhere. The lighting and backdrops for the various scenes are superb. The costumes are appropriate and neither cheap nor shoddy. The stage settings and props revealing careful researching are just right. The highly professional players are brilliantly cast. Moreover, they are giving a great performance. The direction bespeaks sensitive comprehension of the playwright's intentions. As a whole, the production is flawless, powerful, and convincing.

The play, adapted from a prize-winning novel, details the saga of a large, complicated, and sometimes confounding family, spanning four generations. Thus, there is birth, growing up, growing old, and dying on stage. The old refrain of rags to riches to rags again is played out, but at different tempos by various branches of the family and to the varied accompaniment of exploitation, ruthlessness, loss, ruination, and despair. Much of lust and love are acted out: open love, secret love, hopeless love, accepted love, forbidden love, love fulfilled, and love lost. There are legitimate births and illegitimate births, fidelity and betrayal, marital and nonmarital alike. Politics makes its appearance as do acts of justice and injustice, of fair dealing and unscrupulousness. There is a full measure of violence, much tenderness (sometimes ill-gotten, sometimes well-deserved), and instances of principled compassion together with unprincipled forgiveness. There is long-suffering, short-suffering, and intolerance. Some family members traverse their own private hells, coming out ravaged but emotionally whole; others, too delicately balanced, go haywire no matter what; and here and there lurks a touch of madness. Toil and travail and triumph take their turns on stage as do wealth, leisure, boredom, and folly. Indifference and deep concern, pessimism and optimism, cynicism and idealism, faith triumphant and the failure of faith, loss of self-regard and salvation, guilt and redemption play their parts. Replete with meaning and purpose and surcharged with a sense of destination, the play makes you feel as though human life in all its essentials is being encapsulated on the stage before your eyes. And brooding above the drama is what you take to be the presence of God, the unseen author and director of it all, despite other names on the program.

It is, you conclude, meant to be a profoundly religious play, clearly Christian in inspiration. More than just powerful and convincing, the play is captivating, compelling. You feel its insistent, pervasive tug, are really caught up in it, and empathize deeply with its various players; but you remain rooted to your seat. To your amazement, others are not so firmly rooted. Here and there, now and again, individuals in the audience leave their seats and move down the aisles toward the stage. Some spring up, stride forward purposely, and vault onto the stage. Others rise slowly, shuffle forward hesitantly, and clamber onto the stage as though moving in a dream. Still others are coaxed and led and need helping hands. You notice that those who go forward are young and old, male and female, well-dressed and not-so-well-dressed. You presume correctly that some are learned, some ignorant, some cultivated, some boorish, some strong in character, others weak; in short, a cross section of humanity.

Insofar as the players notice the newcomers, they register neither surprise nor annoyance, and no disruption occurs. The drama proceeds smoothly as though nothing untoward had happened. Many of the newcomers behave as though they were merely extras in a movie spectacular, making it clear to you that they also participate who only stand and wait. Others begin to assume bit parts, to speak and move about, and still others insert themselves effortlessly into the drama in integral ways. Astounded at such goings-on, it dawns on you that the people standing before you, professional players and newcomers alike, have forgotten that they are in a theater, that they are on a stage, that they are doing a play. For them the play has become human life itself; its story has become the whole of human history; the stage has become the universe. The players are equally oblivious of the audience and of themselves as players. Since nothing left out of the play is taken as significant by the players, the busy, banal, everyday world outside the theater has simply ceased to exist.

Manly and his cohorts at Big Bend knew that they were men and women of faith and made much of it, congratulating themselves and rejoicing greatly. The more intense their faith became, the more consuming, the more richly they thought themselves blessed. They also believed that miracles were wrought by faith but were oblivious to the precise nature of the miracles in question. They did not realize, for instance, that their faith had carried them, unsuspectingly, across an enchanted threshold into a mural (much like the one on the billboard) and that the mural had then obligingly ballooned around them into cosmic reality; nor did they know that faith had empowered them to step unself-consciously into a dramatic performance, thereby transforming the play and the stage on which it was being enacted into the whole wide world. In the beginning (for Manly and all his kind) there was credulity; then there was belief in (to them) plausible, agreeable ideas; finally, there was faith, transforming faith, a faith so puissant that it could turn fiction into fact effortlessly and fact into fiction with equal ease. That was the kind of miracle, so to speak, that had been wrought among the peculiar people of the Holy Nation, and nowhere more dramatically than at Big Bend.

"Do I believe in miracles?" asked the Handmaiden with rhetorical indignation, looking much pinker than usual. "Of course I do," she thundered in reply to her own question while preaching in chapel one day. Alice had gone to the University of Northern Iowa the preceding week to participate in a spiritual awareness week. During her visit she had expounded on miracles at length. In view of the bewildering variety of events she had included under that rubric, a philosophy professor, mild mannered to all appearances, had asked her to supply him with the essential properties of miraculous occurrences so that in the future he would know how to distinguish such happenings from perfectly natural events but of a rare, unexpected, or surprising sort. Wary of a snare laid by Satan, Alice had replied with a hint of rebuke in her voice, "I believe in miracles, because, Praise God! I am a miracle myself," and had moved on quickly, amidst scattered applause, to consider other questions, leaving the philosopher to fend for himself should he ever have to make such distinctions.

"Sensing that the professor was a profane person who was merely sporting with the Lord, I answered him saying, 'I believe in miracles, because, Praise God! I am a miracle myself,'" said Alice, hammering the pulpit for emphasis. "Amen to that," said the biblical scholars, Dickinson and Van Hook, in unison. "Oh, yes, Jesus," murmured Montefiori, the old Jew made new. "I, too," announced Iskander crisply, reflecting on the miracle whereby God had delivered him from the sponge diver's lot. Among the Five, only Cricklet remained silent. Meanwhile, taking cues from their spiritual betters, many students joined in, announcing that they too were miracles, and none more loudly than Manly.

Without knowing anything about the essential properties of such happenings or needing to know, the peculiar people at Big Bend discerned many miracles of diverse nature in the great mural of faith that encompassed them. Miracles were the mighty works of God; that's what they were; and the spiritual man could identify them. As for the faithless philosopher at Northern Iowa, "Well, he was only pretending to want to know how to tell a miracle when he saw one," said Alice, spawn of Satan that he is, she thought but did not say.

The Handmaiden and the Five were past masters at transmuting hard questions into hostile, but softer, ones. True to their kind, they practiced this alchemy, because hostile questions were easier to deal with. After all, those who asked hostile questions didn't really want to know the truth anyway, so there was no need to indulge them with carefully thought out answers, patiently delivered. In reality, they were just tempting the Lord and baiting his chosen people. As such, they were agents of the Evil One whether they knew it or not. People like the philosophy professor at Northern Iowa were mockers of the gospel, perverters of sound doctrine, and deceivers of the innocent rolled into one. For the sake of the innocent, the salvation of weaker brothers and sisters, the victory of the Lord Jesus, and the greater glory of God, those who asked what looked like hard but were in reality only hostile questions had to be shown in their own true light and subdued, else the devil might win, and in winning take all. So, when Manly and his fellow students (and those who had gone before at Big Bend and those yet to come) were not praying or reading the Bible or memorizing their verse for the day or practicing their preaching or other persuasive arts, they were trying to master the alchemical techniques that enable the faithful to inhabit their own murals as though each picture were the whole of reality.

If saving knowledge requires one to claim literal truth for his own particular picture of reality, then other pictures—rival pictures all—must be perverse delusions inspired by the Evil One. Accordingly, even though there were rumors of different pictures, i.e., of other religions, at Big Bend, no one bothered to learn about them; no good word was spoken of them, nor did they receive so much as an understanding nod. Certainly no one looked at them appreciatively, nor was credence placed in them. At best, they were but the ragings of the heathen frantically searching, but in vain, for the one true God and his salvation.

Similarly, if eternal felicity demands the confessional recitation of one and only one dramatic script, divinely inspired, then all contrary scripts and all contradictory lines are lies, not merely untruths nor innocent mistakes, but lies, inspired, of course, by the prince of lies and spouted by his pawns. There were also rumors of philosophy at Big Bend, but, again, nobody bothered to investigate such corrosive murmurings of the intellect. The peculiar people knew that philosophy had no consolations worthy of the name when compared with the priceless gift of eternal life. Philosophy, with its vaunted logic, was but the vanity of vanities, the futile onanism of unregenerate minds. Its multitudinous pages were useless except as mines to be plundered for homiletical gems or jeweled maxims with which to ornament sermons. As for science, well, it was tolerated only as long as it was noncontroversial, as long as its so-called laws could be tamed by the overarching will of God, leashed to his purposes, and brought to heel. Insofar as any scientist (such as those horrid evolutionists) cast doubt on a single line of inerrant Scripture or tried to paint a picture different from the biblical picture, they were not really scientists but merely so-called scientists, the dupes and tools of Satan sent to jeopardize the immortal souls of innocent school children and to deceive even the elect of God if possible. The Handmaiden and the Five and all who received their tutelage knew that there was, and could be, no real conflict between true religion and true science. That they could say this without knowing any science might seem brash, might even seem to disqualify them from making such a judgment, but not so, for they knew true religion, and that was more than enough.

At least four times out of ten, whenever Bro. Dickinson led a worship service at Big Bend, he called upon the assembled host to read responsively certain biblical passages assembled by his own hand. Slightly (but ever so reverently) edited, his responsive reading was devoured as though it were manna from heaven. Even when he was not leading the worship, others would often invite the people to participate in his rich feast. It went like this:

Leader: The fear of the LORD *is* the beginning of knowledge: *but* fools despise wisdom and instruction (Prov. 1:7).

People: The fear of the LORD *is* the instruction of wisdom; and before honor *is* humility (Prov. 15:33).

Leader: The fear of the LORD *is* the beginning of wisdom: a good understanding have all they that do *his commandments* (Ps. 111:10).

People: The fear of the LORD prolongeth days (Prov. 10:27): The fear of the LORD *is* a fountain of life (Prov. 14:27).

Leader: For it is written, I will destroy the wisdom of the [worldly] wise, and will bring to nothing the understanding of the prudent [intelligent] (I Cor. 1:19).

People: Where *is* the [worldly] wise [man]? where *is* the scribe? where *is* the disputer of this world? hath not God made foolish the wisdom of this world (I Cor. 1:20)?

Leader: For after that in the wisdom of God the world[ly] by [their own] wisdom knew not God, it pleased God by the foolishness of preaching to save them that believe (I Cor. 1:21).

People: For the preaching of the cross is to them that perish foolishness; but unto us which are saved it is the power of God (I Cor. 1:18).

Leader: For the Jews require a sign, and the Greeks seek after [worldly] wisdom (I Cor. 1:22).

People: But we preach Christ crucified, unto the Jews a stumblingblock and unto the Greeks foolishness (I Cor. 1:23).

Leader: But unto them which are called . . . Christ the power of God, and the wisdom of God (I Cor. 1:24).

People: Because the foolishness of God is wiser than [the worldly wisdom] of men; and the weakness of God is stronger than men (I Cor. 1:25).

Leader: For ye see your calling, brethren, how that not many wise men after the flesh [in a worldly way], not many mighty, not many noble, *are called* (I Cor 1:26).

People: But God hath chosen the foolish things of the world to confound the wise; and God hath chosen the weak things of the world to confound the things which are mighty (I Cor. 1:27).

Leader: And base things of the world, and things which are despised, hath God chosen, *yea*, and things which are not, to bring to nought things that are (I Cor. 1:28).

People: That no flesh should glory [boast] in his presence (I Cor. 1:29).

Leader   But of him are ye in Christ Jesus, who of God is made unto us
&   [real] wisdom, and righteousness, and sanctification, and redemp-
People: tion: That according as it is written, He that glorieth, let him
           glory in the Lord (I Cor. 1:30-31).

Nothing pleased Endicott more than to expound on his favorite responsive reading. His legal training had given him a certain feeling for what is known as systematic theology among more recondite believers in main line Christian denominations. Trying to make sense out of what the Old Testament says about fear and human wisdom and what Paul says in the New Testament about foolishness and divine wisdom and also about the useless wisdom of the worldly wise, he said (over and again in various ways), "No matter what the learned of this world know, no matter how much they know, they do not and can not possess saving knowledge. No matter how wise scholars may be in worldly ways, according to the flesh, they are lost, their wisdom availing them nought in that which matters most.

"Since God could not abide the boasting of the wise, could not tolerate the pretentions of philosophers and the certainties of scientists, he purposely chose to prevent such people from knowing anything at all about him through their own natural powers; and not knowing, they forfeit eternal life. Ever since Eve, deceived by the serpent, reached out her proud hand to seize the fruit of the tree of the knowledge of good and evil, God has been aggrieved by the self-glorification of mere mortals. So, to confound those who offended him with their intellectual arrogance, he chose something really moronic with which to show them a thing or two."

Accompanied by loud "Amens" from Bro. Van Hook and numerous nods of approval, Endicott always put it that way to heighten the effect. After all, as he never tired of pointing out, the word "foolishness" in "the foolishness of preaching" comes from the Greek word *moros*, the word from which we get our English word "moron." "Yes, indeed," he would say, a look of triumph flashing in his otherwise watery eyes, "God chose the folly of the cross, the moronic message that we preach, to save those who believe in this foolishness and at the same time to confound those who trust in their own unaided powers, in their own human understanding, in their own puny logic. Oh, they'll lay snares for you with that logic; they'll try to trick you with it so as to embarrass you, hoping to discredit the gospel. But be of good cheer, for God has already confounded them by putting spiritual truths beyond their comprehension.

"And don't worry about the facts or the so-called facts that they throw at you, like so much sand in your eyes. God has put the one fact that they need to know most of all, but can not know, completely off limits to them. But you know that fact; I know that fact; everybody in God's Holy Nation knows that fact: we all know it, not because of any strength of our own, but because, Praise the Lord! God has revealed it to us. It is the fact that Jesus died for our sins, paying our debt to God with his own precious blood, that we might live forevermore in glory. Brothers and sisters in the Lord, hold fast to that one fact, to that one bit of saving knowledge, and not even the gates of hell can prevail against you, let alone boastful unbelievers!'"

No compilation of Bible verses inspired the peculiar people more than Bro. Dickinson's responsive reading, and no interpretation of Scripture did more to underwrite their mission than his oft' repeated exposition of the mind of St. Paul (so to speak) on the saving foolishness of God and the futility of worldly wisdom. It transformed their initial fear that God might consign them to eternal flames into something infinitely precious. It turned that fear, whose reality no one of them could doubt, into saving knowledge. How marvelous that merely by fearing God they had become wiser than the wisest of natural men! Where are your Platos and Aristotles, your Einsteins and your Nobel Prize winners? Lost in sin, that's where! So, with fear as the strait gate and with faith in foolishness as the narrow way, the peculiar people stole a march on the rest of the world and hastened on, rejoicing, to their eternal home.

Did they need other kinds of knowledge as they made their pilgrim way? No. Did they need to know logic or use it fairly? No. Did they need to know philosophy or to examine their basic assumptions? No. Did they need to know secular history so as to put their beliefs in perspective? No. Did they need to know psychology that they might comprehend alternative explanations of their own religious experiences? No. Did they need to defer to the high and the mighty of intellect who did know such things? No, for God had scrambled the brains of such people, meanwhile endowing his chosen ones with self-certifying experiences that could be interpreted only in the one way in which they were in fact interpreted. What a boon to the ignorant that God had chosen them to shame the learned! What a stunning, ironic, but well-deserved trick he had played on the wise of this world by choosing the moronic to humiliate them! What a joy it was for the meek and the lowly, for the despised of this world, to know that God had confounded the high and the mighty, through the folly of the cross, and that he would one day deliver them over to eternal consternation!

Does the fact that the peculiar people had to preach a message incomprehensible to unaided human intelligence mean that they, themselves, were unreasonable, that they had to become irrational or, worse yet, crazy? Certainly not. They were at least as rational as the average man on the street and a lot clearer about their priorities than most. In light of their goals, no behavior was more rational than theirs. With the sanest kind of self-interest, they wanted to escape the flames of eternal hell and be united with God and their loved ones in heavenly bliss forever. The Holy Bible, the book that God had had written inerrantly, made it crystal clear that he would brook no disbelief in his being, no refusal to do his sovereign will, and no self-glorification in his presence. Accordingly, life for the peculiar people was simply a matter of believing in what God had clearly said about himself in his written word and in having faith, foolish though the world might think it, in the saving work of his living Word, his Son, the Lord Jesus Christ. To have questioned God, his being, his book, his Son, his salvation—to have doubted any of this was as unthinkable as it was terrifying.

To run the risk of eternal damnation was not in anybody's self-interest but was, rather, a crazy thing to do; that, at least, was the way they saw it at Big Bend. Let philosophers question the being of God; let sophisticates parade their scepticism; let scientists trumpet their agnosticism. Such people already had their reward, and a paltry reward it was. As for the future, well, the worldly wise were staring eternal hell straight in the face and didn't even know it. If they were so smart, why, then, were they behaving so irrationally? If the people at Big Bend were crazy, as some of their critics said, then, they assured themselves, they were crazy like foxes.

Sovereignty was written large in the script at Big Bend. Every day every voice there assured and reassured the despot above of how truly magisterial he was. He was Lord of lords and King of kings, a monarchial personage against whom the greatest of earth were but the basest of lackeys. Over and again they made joyful noises to the Lord with such enthronement hymns as "Come, Thou Almighty King" and "All Hail the Power of Jesus' Name." Every day every knee there (even the arthritic ones) bowed and scraped before him repeatedly. It was not that Alice had scattered prie-dieux about the premises nor that she had installed kneelers in the chapel. It was just that all were expected to pray on bended knees by their beds before sleep and that all were to be ready, upon the decree of inspiration, to drop to their knees in prayer whether in chapel, in class, at table, or even at work, circumstances permitting.

Once, at an evening service before Manly's time, Alice had been sorely vexed by a bat that had gotten into the chapel. As it dive-bombed her repeatedly in the madcap way of its kind, she bobbed up and down, and sometimes lurched sideways, behind the pulpit trying vainly to keep her composure while proving that Job had foretold the coming of Jesus the redeemer. Finally, unable to endure more of the bat's skitterings above her snowy white hair, she stopped preaching and said, "Dearly beloved, the devil has been after me this whole week; let us fall to our knees that we may pray this Satan-sent creature out into the darkness where it belongs." Thereupon 150 or more people fell to their knees in silent supplication. Since every head was bowed and every eye was closed, no one knew how the bat discovered how unwelcome it was nor how it found its way out; but out it went and quickly too, its departure being classified, ever after, as a minor miracle. In Manly's day, Big Bend was still alive with stories about how the Holy Ghost had chased the bat back to Satan from whence it had come. "And you ask us if we believe in miracles," they said to one another, mocking unbelievers. "Of course we do!"

Far more miraculous, however, was the fact that extreme deference to sovereignty at Big Bend somehow exalted those who debased themselves. The more the peculiar people groveled in the presence of God, casting themselves against the floor, the more firmly they felt the everlasting arms beneath them, buoying them up against the fall. The more they acknowledged how truly terrible it would be to fall into the hands of an angry God, the more they felt assured of his fatherly forgiveness. The more they emptied themselves of any personal worth, the more replete with divine purpose they felt, the more significant their lives became. The more they deprecated themselves, while at the same time boasting in the greatness of their wonderful savior, the more exuberant they felt, the more purged of vanity. The more ready they stood to sacrifice themselves, the more grandiose their mission became as soldiers of the cross. Undeserving of any good thing though they were, the Lord would surely remember each and every one of them when he came in his glory with all of his angels to inaugurate the heavenly kingdom and from that time forth and even forevermore.

A lump of fear formed in Manly's throat and nausea nestled in his stomach as he paced to and fro before the door to what had once been the billiard room. At that moment he was two-thirds through his second year at Big Bend and about to be sent out into the world on a trial basis. But how was he to go, under what circumstances would the Handmaiden and the Five let him make his way? That was the $64,000 question. Manly did not have long to wait for the beginning of the 1 P.M. appointment designed to provide the $64,000 answer. He had scarcely begun to pace in earnest when the door fairly flew open.

"Do come in, Brother Plumwell, and stand at the foot of the table, if you please," said Iskander, enunciating each word with the finality of graven stone. In the center of a long table, and directly opposite Manly, sat the Handmaiden of the Lord, her chair resting on a raised platform, judging from the height of her head. On her right sat Dr. Emmet Langhorne Van Hook, and on his right Bro. Endicott Peabody Dickinson. After closing the door behind them, Dr. Iskander Moutsopoulos returned to the empty chair on Bro. Dickinson's right. To the Handmaiden's left sat Dr. Mordecai Montefiori, and on his left Bro. Clifton Marsh Cricklet. Although it did not occur to Manly, Alice had arranged the Lords Temporal of the Holy Nation on her left and the Lords Spiritual on her right. Dickinson, who was both, sat on the Handmaiden's left when the meeting involved property acquisition and the like and on her right when the meeting involved spiritual matters. Shaking from head to toe, it could have hardly mattered less to Manly that day where Bro. Dickinson had come to roost.

"Brother Manly John Plumwell," said the Handmaiden, transfixing him with eyes made doubly piercing by their proximity to the nimbus of her snowy white hair, "you have grown in spiritual grace and in stature and in favor with God and man to a point at which the Five and I believe that you are ready to be sent forth into a perishing world as a royal priest. On a trial basis, I should add," added the Handmaiden for effect.

131

"I understand," squeaked Manly, fearing he had spoken out of turn.

"I have summoned you here for the Lord's sake that these who have instructed you in God's word and who have superintended your life and your work among us might speak to you plainly, that together we might determine how best you might serve God's Holy Nation in these last days."

As busy as only the possessed can be, the Handmaiden and the Five found time (no, they made the time!) to monitor the spiritual growth of each student, and never were they more meticulous than on those occasions when it came time to send forth a royal priest or priestess in the making.

Holding high her right hand as though to invoke the Lord's presence, Alice declared in measured tones, "Brethren, we are assembled here to judge, with fear and trembling before the Great Judge above, the fitness of this young brother to serve the New Israel. Speak of him as the Spirit moves you that we might, upon your testimony and with much prayer, look upon his heart."

"Dear God," wailed Manly involuntarily to himself as the ordeal began.

"Miss Alice," Emmet twanged, "Brother Plumwell came to us with hands uncallused and innocent, you might say, of a trade. The circumstances of his life had been such as to spare him the need to do manual labor. It may be presumed, accordingly, that he neither knew much of the dignity of labor nor of the real value of a dollar."

At that Manly shifted his weight from one foot to the other, dreading what one of Harvard's own might say next.

"But," Emmet continued, surveying them all, "since he has been at Big Bend, Brother Plumwell has certainly learned about the dignity of labor and about the importance of work well done." Then with a poker face, he launched into a description of Manly's work on higher building maintenance and concluded with, "I believe that he has come to do good work, but, in truth, there are so few of us who have dared go as high as he, so few who have dared hang so precariously as he from this, that, or the other handhold that we really don't know just how well he cemented the top brick on the highest chimney on the chateau back into place. The Lord knows, because he can see all, even from above, but we surely don't." At this, Emmet laughed raspingly; Alice smiled from ear to ear; and the remaining members of the Five chuckled, rejoicing that Christians could have a good time just as well as other people, that they too could laugh at good clean humor.

Manly beamed, but only briefly, for Emmet went on disconcertingly.

"In view of his fearlessness of high places and in light of what he has learned here about hard work and how to do it, there is no doubt in my mind that Brother Plumwell could find part-time or full-time employment, at good pay, in connection with weekend and evening preaching and pastoring."

A sinking feeling superseded the nausea in Manly's stomach. Most emphatically, he did not want to be sent out into the world under those conditions. He did not want to have to support himself as a house painter or

132

roofer while serving a church. He wanted a congregation that could support him as he labored full-time for the Lord. Moreover, although he did not admit it to anybody, he wanted a really big church, not for the money nor for the prestige, but because he relished the idea, the Lord willing, of thundering down at hundreds of people every time he mounted the pulpit.

"I believe that concludes my comments," said Emmet, sitting down.

Next the Spirit moved Mordecai to speak. He did so without leaving his chair, since he was so short of stature that his head was about as high and about as visible as it would have been had he stood up. "Brother Plumwell," he said with almost infinite regret over one so benighted, "knows next to nothing of economics, of the market, of money and banking, or of financial management. He cannot, of course, be blamed for this, since he was not apprenticed to me at any time while here."

The economic matters referred to were so far beyond Manly's ken that he didn't even feel apologetic about his ignorance. Those were matters he would simply take to the Lord in prayer if and when the need arose.

"But," continued Mordecai, "I would like to speak a word on his behalf. Unlike Ananias and Sapphira in the . . . oh . . . ah . . . Book . . . of . . ."

"Acts 5:1-10," interposed Emmet helpfully.

"Thank you, Brother Emmet, thank you. Brother Plumwell here made a clean breast of his financial affairs when he first arrived, told us that he could largely support himself out of rental income at little or no cost to the Holy Nation. That counts for a great deal in my book."

Hearty "Amens" resounded around the table, while Mordecai silently calculated the savings so achieved, and Manly beamed anew.

Cricklet, the consummate architect and master builder, had real trouble being charitable toward anybody who was not, and probably never could be, more than a mere maintenance man or decorator where buildings were concerned. Insofar as Manly was only a ladder climber, albeit a daring one, a roof patcher, and a paint dauber, Cricklet was not favorably impressed. "However," he said, looking at no one in particular, "Brother Plumwell here has been blessed by the Lord in having fair to good talent as a cartoonist and illustrator. He has taken my course in chalk art and can draw biblical scenes quite effectively, especially if he can pencil in the outlines ahead of time."

"Would you like to tell us why you think that that's so important?" Dickinson asked importantly, feeding Cricklet a well-rehearsed line.

"Well," replied Cricklet, making a bad face at the thought of sin, "with all the degradation and seductions of television keeping whole families glued to their sets night after night, it's increasingly hard to get people out to evening worship services. Now, if any of our royal priests can compete with that kind of demonic influence, it's those who have artistic ability of some kind, those who can use a little showmanship for Jesus' sake. With more experience and greater confidence, Manly here ought to be able to pack people in during prime time most any night of the week, also brighten up Sunday school classes, vacation Bible school in the summers, and the like.

In fact, as soon as he can solo freehand and stop having to use guidelines, people will almost think that a miracle is being performed before their very eyes."

"Oh, thank you, Jesus, thank you for Brother Plumwell's wonderful talent," said Alice fervently.

Dickinson and Van Hook chimed in with syncopated "Amens."

Iskander, capturing every eye present, opined that chalk art was a marvelously persuasive technique, and Mordecai, noting that people would pay good money to see such spectacles, adjured Manly to pass the collection plate each time he put on a chalk art performance.

"Oh, yes," intoned the Handmaiden.

Dickinson took the floor next, rising ponderously and reading from some notes scribbled on what looked like a piece of paper retrieved from a wastebasket: "Brother Plumwell has already read the Bible through twice since being here and is on his third reading now, having reached Habakkuk."

"Haggai, as of today," Manly blurted out proudly.

"Haggai? Well, even better than I had dared to hope," said Endicott, accompanied by titters of approval from the others.

"And he has memorized by his own count (and I have no reason to doubt him on the basis of evidence he has shown me over and again) 347 verses from the Old Testament, nicely distributed, and 273 verses from the New Testament. Moreover, in citing these passages, he is able to range over the whole of Scripture adeptly so as to juxtapose the verses in most apposite ways, yes, most apposite ways. He is truly fluent in citing the Lord's word and does so joyously."

"I concur with this appraisal," said Emmet gravely, "but, beholden to truth as I feel myself to be, it should be noted that his admittedly facile knowledge of the Scriptures is only a prima facie knowledge. Quite often deeper spiritual truths escape him; allegories elude him with ease, I am afraid; and as for metaphors, similies, and the hyperbolic in general, well, they are frequently quite beyond his grasp at this point in his spiritual growth."

"Ladder climbing, painting, roofing, hard physical labor, and part-time preaching, here I come," said Manly to himself in dismay, blushing for all to see at Emmet's indictment.

Finally, Iskander arose, nailed each person to the spot with a glance, and said flawlessly, thrillingly, "Reverend Handmaiden and Esteemed Brethren in the Lord, you see standing before you [here he gestured dramatically at Manly] one whom the Lord has favored. And how, you ask, has this one been favored? He has been favored with an alert mind, a retentive memory, and a fluent tongue. To these endowments for which, to be sure, he can take no credit, he adds a characteristic for which he can take considerable credit, a characteristic which also adds credit to us all in our labor for the Lord. There is none among us, no, not one, whether male or female, who is more particular than he in matters of personal grooming. He is always as well accoutered, even at manual labor, as circumstances permit. At a time when, and in a place where, impressions count for much, whether first impressions or subsequent impressions, Brother Plumwell is a paladin of appearance. With continued growth in the Lord, with requisite experience, and with the presence of God resting upon him and abiding with him, I predict that he will, one day soon, come to project a powerful presence, attracting and gladdening the hearts of those who are already saved and reaching out, magnetically, if you will, to those who are lost and perishing in their sins. In my view, he has all the essential constituents of a masterful persuader of men. And of what will he persuade them? Why, of the greatness and glory of God, of the grace and goodness of our Lord, Jesus Christ, and of the Great Commission being carried out, even now, by his chosen people, the New Israel. In summation, I believe that we will, God permitting, rejoice ere long, and even boast in the Lord, over the mighty way in which he will empower his most zealous servant, Manly John Plumwell, in proclaiming the good news of everlasting life."

Every eye in the room remained riveted on Iskander as he sat down, but no lips moved, nor was there any sound. After a long pause, Alice found her tongue and said, "Brother Plumwell, is there anything on your heart that you wish to add to what has been said?"

Manly's heart was torn asunder too completely to permit an answer. On the one hand he was fairly bursting with the need to confess his sins of uncleanness, to bring out into the open the truth about the thorn in his flesh that led him into almost continual pollution, that they might judge the whole man standing before them, the wickedness as well as the weaknesses and the strengths already mentioned. But to admit to his awful onanism was mortifying beyond endurance and, therefore, unthinkable. Furthermore, since prayerful contrition on his knees before the Lord had brought him no cleanness, what reason was there, he sincerely wondered, to think that con-fession to mere mortals would matter. He also wanted to cry out, "I don't want to work as a painter or a roofer full-time, part-time, or any time. I want to be a full-time preacher preaching often and to many, to *many* I tell you, persuading hundreds and hundreds to repent of their sins before it is too late and to accept Jesus as their lord and savior"; but to say any such thing was also unthinkable. It would be vain; it would be insubordinate to the Hand-maiden and the Five; worse, it would be sorely offensive to Almighty God. Thus, Manly merely moved his mouth up and down but said nothing, so great were the contradictions fighting within him.

"Then, if you have nothing on your heart to say, Brother Plumwell, would you kindly step out into the hall and await our prayerful decision?" asked Alice, looking much like a doting grandmother by that time.

No sooner had he managed to say "Yes" than Iskander had the door open for him, guiding him from the room. Manly's agonies continued in the hall, for the control that the Handmaiden and the Five exercised over those going out into the world was absolute, their decisions beyond appeal.

The Holy Nation grew populous, rich, and mighty on a steady diet of doomsday preaching. According to this preaching, our wicked world has long since hurtled beyond the point of no return on the road to calamity. Every next moment may witness the return of the Lord Jesus, with his winnowing fork in hand, to separate the wheat from the tares, the tares to burn in unquenchable fire forever. Should anyone think that the Day of the Lord has been delayed so long as to have been effectively cancelled, the idea is at best but an illusion of human perspective, at worst a delusion of the devil. No, the Day of the Lord is always at hand and ever to come. Nor will those who die before that Day escape its consequences.

Once this message has been preached, certain obvious questions must be asked: "Are you saved, brother? Are you saved, sister? Are you numbered with the good grain or with the tares? Where will you spend eternity? In the bliss of heaven by the waters of life or in the blistering heat of hell, in union with God or in league with Beelzebub, with your loved ones in joyous reunion or forever separated from them in ghastly isolation?"

Preaching this message and asking these questions is what the peculiar people did, and still do, best and most often, using every evangelistic technique common to American sectarian Christianity and some besides. Never content merely to proclaim the message and ask the questions in church and in revival meetings, over radio and TV, through books and pamphlets, indoors and out of doors, they also devised a particularly effective but laborious and time-consuming method of seeking those who would be most vulnerable to their message and most receptive to their questions. They read obituaries.

Yes, all members of the Holy Nation able to do so were called on to read the obituaries in every local paper available and then to take appropriate action. Appropriate action involved evangelistic visits to as many of the bereaved as possible, especially to those who appeared to have no faith, or to those who were weak in faith (i.e., those who were neither clearly born-again nor active church members), or, most especially, to those who remained crippled by their loss long after most people have recovered and resumed normal life. That was how Manly had been found. Unknown to him, someone in or around Nickel Plate was a member of the Holy Nation, and that someone had learned of the devastation wrought by his grandmother's death. For whatever reason, that unknown person had not contacted him directly but had called in professional assistance, so to speak, assistance that had come in the form of Scott Truesdale and Emory Plunkett, the angels he had entertained in disguise.

Although Manly never ceased thanking God for those angels who had come to him in his deepest despair and had led him, rejoicing, into the Holy Nation, he really did not want to join them in their kind of evangelism, not even for a short time and certainly not for the time of his initial testing. No, he wanted his own pulpit. Somehow or other he knew that he could do much better preaching to an established congregation (and, of course, serve God much better too) than by going out into the world to meet complete strangers, individuals who had been identified solely by their bereavement and subsequently selected by his superiors for personal evangelism. Furthermore, Manly liked to work alone, to move at his own speed, to do things his own way. It set his teeth on edge to think of being unequally yoked with some other young man arbitrarily (one he might not like very well) and sent out into the world, two by two, to rove hither, thither, and yon in pursuit of targeted individuals. But it was certainly better than hospital evangelism.

Royal priests and priestesses minister to their congregations much like the ministers and priests of such so-called Christian groups as the Southern Baptists, the Catholics, and the Mormons (who have all been deceived by Satan and misled by false prophets, popes, and revelators). Accordingly, they minister to the sick, the halt, the blind, the lame, and those possessed by demons or otherwise afflicted in hospitals. But the new Jews do far more than make routine hospital visits for the sake of their suffering brethren. Although they do not exactly chase ambulances, they do haunt hospitals, particularly the public waiting rooms close to intensive care units and on surgical floors. There are still not enough new Jews nor do they have enough time (nor are they all sufficiently dedicated) to hover outside of every intensive care unit in every hospital in the country all the time nor to loiter around every waiting room and every alcove of every surgical floor; and, of course, there were far fewer in Manly's Bible school days than now. Nevertheless, as many members of the Holy Nation as possible are set to this kind of work, particularly some of those being sent out from Big Bend for a time of testing.

Iskander, the best of the Five in psychology, laid down the pattern for hospital evangelism. The evangelist was always to be well and conservatively dressed and carrying a Bible. The evangelist was not to be pushy but retiring and serene and was to project a helpful, hopeful image. The evangelist was not to refer to himself or herself as a royal priest or priestess, as a new Jew, nor, above all, a peculiar person; nor was the Holy Nation to be mentioned at the point of first contact. "To do so," Iskander said, "might be too jarring to the ears of those already under heavy stress if not in shock." Nor was there to be any hint that the loved one undergoing the knife or feebly clinging to life in intensive care was in spiritual jeopardy. The evangelist was to wait until someone said something like, "Oh, Lord, I just pray to God that Mama [or Dad or Gramps or Sonny] is going to pull through." The evangelist was then to say something like, "Pardon me, I couldn't help overhearing what you said. I'm a minister of the gospel and would be very pleased to pray for your loved one." Then, kneeling and displaying the Bible for maximum effect, the evangelist was to emphasize the graciousness of God and to extol the power of his everlasting arms to keep from falling all those unto whom he extends his infinite and preserving love. Almost imperceptively, the prayer was then to change its focus from the one imperiled on the operating table (or wherever) to those who wept, sighed, hoped, and suffered in the waiting room. Where, wondered the evangelist aloud, would they spend eternity? Would they ever again on this earth look into the living eyes of their loved one? More importantly, would they ever again in the world to come look into the living eyes of their loved one? Would they all be reunited in endless joy with God in heaven above or not? What would the living, whose eyes still looked upon the light of earthly day, do that very day to insure life on the endless day to come?

Hospital evangelism was a glorious ministry and very fruitful of converts for the Holy Nation. Manly had no doubt of that or of its imperative need, but he wanted to stand tall in his very own pulpit. He wanted to be lifted up above the heads of those who, sitting at his feet, heard him preach again and again with great power and authority the messages that God would have him, Manly Plumwell, deliver to a sinful and perishing world. But, of course, he would do what he was told. He would accept the role of hospital evangelist without a whimper if that were the will of the Handmaiden. Even at its worst, it would be far better than having to undertake a mission of church extension, for that kind of ministry could be very rough indeed sometimes.

Shortly after the Lord had delivered Bro. Dickinson to the Holy Nation, thus completing the Five at her side, Alice received what she called an "illumination." Excitedly she assembled them, saying, "Brethren, as I have traveled the length and breadth of this great land, especially through the countryside and in small towns, I have seen many abandoned church houses and many others about to be abandoned, about to be abandoned because God has removed his Spirit from the congregation which once worshipped in those houses of his. Oh, Brethren, what a great pity it is to see those houses empty; what a great waste!"

Before she could finish her last sentence, three of the Five had also received illuminations almost simultaneously, each being tinged differently.

"Miss Alice," said Mordecai, with savings glittering before his eyes, "if we could only use those buildings, appropriate them, so to speak, without having to buy them, we could house new congregations without having to make substantial capital outlays and without saddling new congregations with the immediate need to launch expensive building campaigns."

The Handmaiden nodded at Mordecai reinforcingly as she thought back to the time when for little more than a song she had bought an abandoned church house and lot in Soddy-Daisy, Tennessee. But before she could speak again, Endicott had announced triumphantly, "And for all practical purposes we could acquire many of those buildings not only free of charge but with no questions asked, no legal questions, that is."

"Pray, do go on," Alice encouraged him.

"We would have to avoid buildings belonging to congregations which, though weak, were part of a tightly knit, centrally controlled denomination, and we would have to take a hands-off policy toward buildings totally or partially financed by denominational monies."

"Why so?" asked Emmet, thinking that he knew but wanting to be seen and heard taking part in the sharing of other people's illuminations.

"To avoid litigation over questions of ownership," said Endicott briskly.

"But we have *you* to tend to that sort of thing," Emmet rasped, not wanting to be put down and, thus, trying to interject a light and diversionary note to their deliberations.

"Quite so, and we are prepared to defend ourselves in court if need be, but we must avoid all unnecessary legal costs."

"Amen to that," declared Mordecai, squirming uncomfortably in his chair at the very thought of needless expenditures.

"But," continued Dickinson, seizing the floor impulsively, "if we can find church build . . . ah . . . er . . . 'houses', as Miss Alice calls them, whose dying or dead congregations underwrote the entire expense of putting them up and whose church governance was strictly local, then I believe we could gain use of and effective control over a great many church houses, church houses that are currently under-utilized or abandoned altogether."

"Yes," said Cricklet, abruptly standing up as much to his own amazement as to that of Alice and the brethren, "and what were once terrible eyesores can be turned into gems of simple beauty for the glory of the Lord and the inspiration of new Jews."

Murmurs of approval and "Amens" curled around the meeting table.

"I can do wonders, and inexpensively," he assured them, "with paint and minor alterations to the facades of frame structures—steeples, too, if any."

"Most of the abandoned church houses Miss Alice is talking about are frame structures with wooden siding of some kind or other," opined Emmet.

"Yes," agreed Cricklet, "and as for the sanctuaries, well, just give me some moldings, some valances, some velvet cloth for choir loft railings and the like, some decent colored glass for windows, some paint, and some attractive floor coverings, and you'll hardly be able to believe your eyes."

"That would be money very well spent," said Iskander, also trying to get in on the illumination act, and not even Mordecai demurred.

Alice was so moved by the miraculous way the Five had comprehended her illumination without actually being told what it was, that she had them all kneel at their places around the table while she thanked God for the gift of his guiding Spirit. "Amen," she said fervently at the end of her prayer and under her breath, "Mother of pearl!"

So, it became incumbent on all new Jews in all of their peregrinations to keep their eyes peeled for what looked like under-utilized or abandoned church houses. Once these were located, judicious questions were asked: What kind of church is that? Do they have regular meetings? Is there a full-time or a part-time preacher? Who built that church house? Is the congregation intact? Are any of the charter members or other old-timers still active in it?

Meanwhile, Emmet and Iskander, in particular, were consulting with the Handmaiden and praying much for guidance as to how to go about appropriating the church houses identified as good prospects by the scouts of the Holy Nation. The result was known as a mission of church extension (a ministry of church extension simply being a long series of missions). Basically two kinds of people were sent forth on missions or ministries of church extension. Those who favored the latter, even volunteering for it, became professionals at it by dint of doing it. Generally, they were people who, having few ties, had a yen to travel and who, for whatever reasons, liked hardship, stress, and even a dash of danger in their lives. For a variety of reasons, Manly did not fear being sent as a pastor to an established church, but he did dread being sent forth on one or more missions.

Rumor had it, but it was only rumor (and he wanted no part of rumors), that some students were sent on missions of church extension punitively, or, if not punitively, then for purposes of severe testing. Since the deliberations of the Handmaiden and the Five were secret and since they were responsible to none but God, nobody could be sure where the truth lay, but some students were convinced that those who were weak in faith or who had not grown sufficiently in the Spirit or who had shown tendencies toward carnality, for example, were sent out on "do or die" missions. Manly knew that he had grown in grace and believed himself to be strong in faith; but God knew, he knew, and perhaps, just perhaps, the Handmaiden and the Five knew about his lamentable carnality. Because of it, he might find himself in very hard circumstances.

The paradigm for every new Jew who undertook a mission or a ministry of church extension was a certain Herod Agrippa Smallwood (Herod's very fecund mother always favored biblical names for her numerous offspring but had difficulty distinguishing between the good guys and the bad guys). At various times in his life, Herod had been a wrestler, a bartender, a carnival barker, and a roustabout in the Oklahoma oil fields. Just before his second birth, which occurred during the Handmaiden's great Kankakee revival of 1946, Herod had been on the verge of a life in crime as an enforcer for a small-time mob.

On the first Sunday (weather permitting) after he had been given the go-ahead to expropriate a church house and as many of its congregation as wished to come over to the Lord's side, Herod would appear out front just as the worship service got under way. Positioning himself at the corner of the church property or sauntering to and fro on the street or road passing by, he would await the lull that invariably follows the opening hymn. Then he would begin strumming on his very loud banjo (is there any other kind?) and would lift his powerful baritone voice in song:

O Thou Fount of every blessing, Tune my heart to sing thy grace:
Streams of mercy, never ceasing, Call for songs of loudest praise.
Teach me ever to adore thee: May I still thy goodness prove,
While the hope of endless glory, Fills my heart with joy and love.

Inside the church, eyes closed in opening prayer would pop open two by two, and here and there a head bent in silent meditation would rise and swing from side to side inconspicuously, much as a venturesome turtle surveys new surroundings.

"Mommie, Mommie," a piping voice was sure to say, "what is that noise?"

"Shhh," would come the inevitable answer.

The minister of the dying congregation, more than likely an overeducated wishy-washy liberal or a retired parson trying to eke out a few extra shekels in peace or a callow, spiritless youth, would try to proceed as though nothing untoward were happening. "I have chosen," he would say, "as our lesson for this Lord's Day morning to read a portion of the First Epistle of St. John, begin—"

Here I'll raise my Ebenezer; Hither by thy help I've come;
And I hope, by thy good pleasure, Safely to arrive at home.
Jesus sought me when a stranger, Wandering from thy fold, O God;
He, to rescue me from danger, Interposed his precious blood.

Having fallen silent during the anthem following the reading of the Scripture, Herod would commence again during the relatively quiet period when the offering was being received.

O to grace how great a debtor, Daily, I'm constrained to be!
Let thy goodness, like a fetter, Bind me closer still to thee.
Never let me wander from thee, Never leave thee, whom I love;
By thy Word and Spirit guide me, Till I reach thy courts above.

Noticing the stricken look on the minister's face and realizing that things simply could not go on that way, one of the more aggressive members of the congregation, usually a deacon or other male in authority, would march outdoors, just as the offering was being laid at the foot of the pulpit, to confront whomsoever or whatever was spreading consternation throughout the congregation. Once outside, the man in authority would see all 265 muscular pounds of Herod Agrippa Smallwood, his head tethered on a short bull-like neck but rolling freely about his burly shoulders as he sang to the heavens above.

"And what," the man in authority would say more graciously than he had at first intended, "do you think you are doing out here?"

"I'm glorifying God and praising his Son, my redeemer, the Lord Jesus Christ," Herod would say, exuberantly but innocently. Before the startled official could say more, Herod would ask in the sweetest way imaginable, "Won't you join me in praise or is there some other hymn you'd like better? You name it, or hum a little, and I'll sure pick it out if I can."

"But, but, but," would sputter the official, "we're trying to have a worship service here."

"I know," Herod would respond and then continue with something like,

"Don't you see, the Spirit of the Lord has led me to this place. I don't know yet exactly what he wants me to do here, but until I find out, I'm just going to praise his holy name and sing out what's in my heart."

"But you can't do it here."

"Why not?"

"Because you're disturbing our service."

"Well, I don't know about that—and I surely don't mean to be disrespectful—but I do know what's in my heart."

"But there's a law against . . ."

"A law against what?"

"Disturbing the peace."

"Can you show me anything in the Constitution or in any man-made law that says that a born-again Christian can't glorify God on a public street or highway in a free country like ours?"

"Well, no, I can't actually cite . . ."

"Even if there is such a law, I just ask you this: Which is greater, God's law or man's?"

By that time the official's wife would be getting nervous over what was delaying him. The voices outside would invariably rise even though the words would remain indistinguishable. Unable to bear the uncertainty any longer, the wife would slip out of her pew to go see if anything was wrong. More than likely, one or two of the remaining deacons, thinking that reinforcements might be needed, would also slip out of their pews and edge toward the front door, and almost certainly some of the more exuberant children would scoot out of their pews and rocket toward the front door with their embarrassed mothers in pursuit.

However the scenario developed in detail on a particular day, the results would be much the same when viewed from the pulpit. First, there would be distraction and inattention, the twin banes of any preacher. Then there would be glancing about, followed by questions, some audible, some inaudible, some put to oneself, some to others. Then one of the more aggressive men in authority was sure to slip out, followed shortly by his wife, followed by others in authority, followed by their wives, who would be overtaken by several children pursued by their mothers. After a time, none would be left in the pews save the extremely obese or phlegmatic, the seriously crippled, and those who, for whatever reason, were loath to move until it was definitely time to go home.

Meanwhile, Herod could see out of the corner of his eye that quite a gaggle of curious, anxious people was forming just inside and just outside the front door. When the perplexed reinforcements would push their way through the crowd and move uncertainly toward him and the dithering man who had come to deal with him initially, Herod would launch into his second selection of the morning. Able to induce ecstasy at will whenever singing, he would proceed to throw himself into what some would call a fit. With rapture written on his craggy face and with fervor in his fingers as he strummed the banjo, he would sing as few around that church had ever sung before:

Guide me, O thou great Jehovah, Pilgrim through this barren land:
I am weak, but thou art mighty: Hold me with thy powerful hand;
Bread of heaven, Feed me till I want no more.

Although the reinforcements seldom felt like tangling with a 265-pounder who was throwing a fit while praising God in the middle of a public thoroughfare, violence sometimes threatened, depending on how bellicose the Christians of a given congregation became over having their worship upset. Should forcible eviction seem liable to happen, Herod would fall to his knees and beg God tearfully to forgive him for any commotion he had caused. "Where the Spirit is, there there's commotion," he would remind God, loudly enough for all to hear. Invariably, he would end his prayer with a plea for guidance as to how he could serve those whom he had so unwittingly disturbed. Once on his feet again, he would plead to clamber over the roof of their church house in search of fugitive holes, or to service their septic tank if need be, or to work on the plumbing, or to fix the furnace, or to do just about anything to show how remorseful and repentant he was. He would then give a short, impassioned testimonial as to how the Lord Jesus had found him in Kankakee and would end by inviting them all to join with him in singing. By that time, the minister would have given up and would be standing in the doorway in shock as his erstwhile congregation prepared to sing on the grounds:

My days are gliding swiftly by, and I, a pilgrim stranger,
Would not detain them as they fly, those hours of toil and danger.

In the hubbub sure to follow Herod's concluding hymn, somebody would inevitably ask, "Say, mister, just who are you, anyway, and where do you hail from?" "Why, I'm Herod Agrippa Smallwood, servant of the Lord Jesus Christ. I come from a life of sin, and I follow wherever God Almighty leads me and always do his bidding." Numerous other questions would then be asked, but no matter what they were nor where they led, he would invariably work hree points into his answers: First, he didn't have as much as one thin dime on him; second, he did not know where his next meal was coming from; and third, he had no place to lay his head—each of which was true.

Nine times out of ten, some family would invite him home to have a bite of dinner. Eight times out of ten someone would find a place for him to sleep that night, if not on succeeding nights. In matters of food, Herod had the discrimination of a Komodo dragon and would eat anything set before him with evident relish. On the relatively rare occasions when no food was forthcoming, he would miss meals gladly and call it "fasting for the Lord." As for a place to sleep, well, he had slept on the front porch of many a church house, or in barns, corn cribs, garages (even in jail houses by request), or out

143

of doors in culverts or other sheltered areas. And, of course, his conscience would simply not let him leave a community until he had made up for the terrible disruption he had caused the previous Sunday morning. So, with endless hymns falling from his lips, he would do odd jobs for his new friends with incredible gusto (the dirtier and more disagreeable the job the better) and would "fix up anything that was busted," as he put it, at the church house as he had offered to do.

By Wednesday of his first week in a given area, he would be seeking work that would pay enough to keep body and soul together and would be showing keen distress that there was no mid-week prayer meeting at the church whose Sunday service he had so unwittingly disrupted. By week's end he would be sure that the Lord meant him to tarry where he was. By Sunday morning he would be inside the church worshipping with the congregation, a model of decorum, despite the furtive, apprehensive glances cast at him by the minister. By the middle of the second week he would be drumming up interest in having a regular mid-week prayer service. "Why, yes, I could and would lead it, if that's what folks really want," he would say. By the second Sunday he would be back in church and beaming all over as the preacher announced, with alarm, that there would be a prayer meeting at the church on Thursday night. On that night, Herod would sing and play, and pray, and testify fervently but decorously. From that point on the congregation would never be the same. Within two or three weeks the minister would receive notice that the majority of the congregation no longer wished to retain his services. Herod would then mount the pulpit on Sundays as well as on Thursdays, and in the course of a few weeks would let it be known that he was not altogether a wayfaring stranger; he was, rather, a disciple of Miss Alice McAlister, the famous Handmaiden of the Lord. He was also, it turned out, a royal priest of the Holy Nation and a member of the Church of the Chosen. At least five times out of ten, a new sign or bulletin board, painted in light yellow and purple, would appear on the church lawn announcing the name of the congregation and proclaiming affiliation with the Holy Nation Association of Churches of the Chosen. The Lord would then lead Herod elsewhere, and Big Bend would supply the congregation with a new part-time or full-time minister.

Emmet and Iskander wrote the script. Alice gave it her imprimatur. Herod mastered, adapted, and improved it. Others, imitating him with more or less success, played every conceivable variation upon it, some with joy and achievement, others in misery and defeat. Manly had no illusions about what might loom before him. He knew that he might simply be dropped off in a strange place, like an abandoned puppy, isolated from all assistance. If so, he knew that he would have neither money nor any guarantee of food and shelter, of hot baths and clean clothes. He knew that he might very well bungle the job beyond redemption, might be spurned, laughed at, roughed up, or simply chased away. In addition to the humiliation he would feel in any of these circumstances, he knew that should he fail, it might be taken as proof positive that he was unfit to be a royal priest. So consumed was he in imaging himself being turned away from Big Bend, so deep was he in dread of total rejection by the Holy Nation, that he did not, at first, hear Iskander open the door behind him, softly calling his name.

"Do come in, Brother Plumwell, and stand at the foot of the table, if you please," said Iskander for the second time that day. Then he returned to his place but did not sit down, the others rising to their feet. How grand and imperious the Handmaiden looked to Manly! How awesome the Five! How small and undone he must appear to them, he thought.

"Brother Plumwell," said the Handmaiden, "between now and next Sunday you are to prepare two sermons suitable for delivery at a morning and an evening worship service at the church—"(Did he dare to believe? Yes, oh, yes, he did dare to believe that he was being sent out to an established congregation!) "at Calico Corners on the Shadrach Plains about sixty miles south of Kimballton." (Thank you, dear God, thank you, Manly said to himself.) "We will provide you with a map to the home of a Mr. and Mrs. Jedediah Bantry and daughter with whom you are to take supper and spend the preceding Saturday night at their request. They will lead you to the church on Sunday morning and will look after your needs throughout the day. After hearing you twice, the congregation will decide whether or not they would like to have you as a part-time weekend preacher. During the rest of the week you would continue your studies here. Do you have any questions?"

"Oh, no, Miss Alice, none, thank you."

The Handmaiden then bade Manly and the Five to bow their heads in prayer while she, raising both arms high over her head and looking at the ceiling, addressed God aloud. She ended her prayer with a fervent plea that the Holy Ghost might deliver and protect Bro. Plumwell from all contact with communism, socialism, secularism, humanism, and any and all other kinds of godless "isms." Hands were shaken all around, and many wishes of "God bless you" and "Godspeed" were showered on Manly. He left the billiard room that day more elated than he had been at any time since bounding out of the library with Dr. James Gothicus MacGowan's prescriptions for the treatment of onanism secreted on his person.

Although he was not to depart for Calico Corners until mid-afternoon on Saturday, Manly slept fitfully the night before (as he had the previous night), so elated was he over his prospects. The former interdenominational church at Calico Corners had, he had learned, been brought into the fold some years earlier by none other than Herod Agrippa Smallwood. In the meantime it had been served by a succession of royal priests none of whom had remained very long. An intense residue of bitterness lingered in the community, setting men against the members of their own households, over the way Herod had splintered the congregation and had then, like a Pied Piper, led the most strong-willed and voluble (if not the largest) splinter, together with the church property, into the Holy Nation Association. If the congregation accepted him, Manly's tasks were clear. He was not only to convict and convert sinners, to comfort and encourage saints, he was also to lay the remaining bitterness to rest once and for all, if possible, and to cement the congregation firmly and finally into the New Israel.

When the long-awaited moment of departure arrived, the old Nash refused to start and then would run only momentarily. Having become lethargic from disuse, it would not budge until pushed. Sputtering into life at long last, but with churlish reluctance, it belched unburned gas and backfired, bucking and lurching absurdly until it was well down the boulevard leading to Big Bend's main entrance and the road to Kimballton. Under any other circumstances, Manly would have been furious at such an undignified departure, but, as it was, no chauffeur-driven minister plenipotentiary ever left on a mission of state more freighted with significance nor more swollen with self-importance than did he on that day of entry into the world.

Fifteen minutes later, while driving west through downtown Kimballton in search of State Highway 15, leading to the Paddy McMurtry Memorial Bridge over the Kinross, Manly suffered for a moment from something akin to déjà vu. There on his right, announcing itself in letters of flaming red and yellow, was the Kimballton Pharmacy, the scene of his imagined attempt at buying a cure for the secret vice. Surely he would need no such nostrums in the future, for he was soon to have his own church, soon to be caught up totally in preaching the gospel. Surely God would then empower him to leave all impurity behind.

Once on Highway 15 and headed south, the old Nash began a swift and serpentine descent from the bluff (on whose top Kimballton sprawled) to the McMurtry Bridge spanning the gray-green waters of the Kinross at a place called the Riffles by local river folk. After a short, non-serpentine ascent of the river's south bank, he reached the beautiful Shadrach Plains. He had looked away to them, wistfully, more than once while making roof repairs on the pinnacle of the chateau; and there he was, by God's grace, driving through them and enjoying every moment of it, enjoying himself, perhaps, more than a Christian should ever enjoy this world. "Good ol' God," he heard himself say in boyish tones, "Good ol' God!" Startled by the exuberant and childish praise he had spoken aloud and fearing that the Most High might think him far too familiar, Manly closed his eyes fleetingly, asked for forgiveness, and tried to set his mind on spiritual things.

Then, when he crossed a churning stream identified as Go Forth Creek, he recited Isaiah 2:3 aloud:

And many people shall go and say, Come ye, and let us go up to the mountain of the Lord, to the house of the God of Jacob; and he will teach us of his ways, and we will walk in his paths: for out of Zion shall go forth the law, and the word of the Lord from Jerusalem.

A short time later, bearing down rapidly on a sign indicating that Highway 15 intersected Run Ragged Road, 500 feet ahead, he mused over the origin of the name. It was not the whimsy of it that captured his attention but concern for the unknown person who had named it. Manly hoped earnestly that he or she had not been so harrassed by the drudgery of the world as to have been tempted to sin as a means of escape. With his mind occupied in that manner and with thoughts of his Sunday sermons rolling around in his head, he nearly overshot his turn onto Butternut Pike. Since Butternut Pike neither lent itself to sermon preparation nor to some associated biblical verse or other, Manly's mind came down to earth and remained there as he went his westering way in search of Umberland Road. Once he turned to the right off Butternut Pike onto it, it was simply a matter of pulling into the lane just beyond the fifth mailbox, or so his instructions indicated, and he would be at the Bantry place.

Tighter than a drumhead though he was, and having to swerve this way and that to avoid potholes in the lane, Manly still managed to note something peculiar about the white frame house toward which he drove, but he couldn't decide what it was. No sooner had he begun to back out of the car, clutching his overnight case in one hand and his omnipresent Bible in the other, than a side door burst open emitting three Bantrys who bore down on him in single file. Jedediah Bantry led the procession and widened his lead over the other two with every purposeful step.

What Manly saw when he turned away from the car and looked up was a burly bullet of a man in bib overalls. What he was about to experience was the missile-like impact Jed made on most people. Before Manly could utter a shy squeak of greeting, Jedediah exploded into speech with his usual combustive mixture of suspicion, hostility, and rectitude.

"I [to be pronounced "ah," for Jed hailed originally from up above Chigger Hill on Sand Mountain in northeast Alabama] reckon you must be that young preacher fellah that they was supposed to send down here from Big Bend; well, I'm Jedediah Bantry; most folks just call me Jed, 'n' I reckon you can too if that's what you'd favor; I don't stand on ceremony much; never did feel altogether easy in m'mind bein' called 'Mr. Bantry this' nor 'Mr. Bantry that'; course I expect, or maybe you might better say *demand* a right smart of respect from young-uns 'n' blacks 'n' such as that, but you look pretty growed up, so just go ahead 'n' call me Jed." Meanwhile the speechless Manly was pleading in silent anguish that the callused horny python wrapped in ever tightening coils around his right hand would please let go.

"This here's m'woman, Sate; now that name don't come from Satan like some folks ud like to make out; it's kind of a substitute for Sarah, which she never did like, did you, Sate? Anyway, she's made me a right good wife; oh, she takes out after me a right smart for speakin' m'mind too plain sometimes, but it's made me a better man I reckon, leastways that's what some folks say."

Sate ignored Manly's wounded hand proffered in greeting, nodded her unsmiling head, and said, "Pleased to meet you, Reverend, I'm sure."

" 'N' that young lady there that's just had her fifteenth birthday two weeks ago yesterday, that's Beatrice; she come to us kinda late in life you might say, but she ain't never give us no trouble like some of these young scalawags that's always in the news these days, seems like."

Holding back too far for Manly to have shaken hands with her anyway, Beatrice mumbled something and looked at the ground, because she was shy around men his age. Manly also mumbled something, and he too looked at the ground, not just because he was shy but because he had just been shattered by the most adorable girl he had ever glimpsed. Honey blond, very pale honey blond, was her curly hair, creamy white her complexion, lustrously brown her eyes. Not quite fully filled out, her figure was, nevertheless, as nearly perfect as was any in Manly's imagination. And, added to it all, there was a spiritual quality about her. What was it? Was it that her eyes were the width of a pencil line too close together? Was it that her face was ever so slightly too narrow below the cheek bones? He did not know nor had he as yet seen her spiritual air belied by the Mona Lisa look that sometimes played in the corners of her mouth.

"I don't reckon there's any sense gabbin' out here in the yard when we could just as well be inside settin' in comfortable chairs; so just follow me, Reverend," said Jed, striding off toward the house with Manly's overnight case in hand.

"Why don't you set there, Preacher?" said Jed, directing Manly to a platform rocker in the parlor.

"Why don't you go and fetch the lemonade?" asked Sate of Beatrice.

Beatrice said nothing, but departed quickly. A short time later, she thrust a tray at Manly on which four glasses of lemonade quivered and slid.

"Why, thank you . . . ah . . . Sister Beatrice," said Manly, hoping that the elder Bantrys had no idea of the effect Sister Beatrice had had on him.

"Why don't you set down with us for a while too?" Sate asked the girl, " 'cause we don't have to start up the supper just yet."

No, thought Beatrice, because the preacher got here too soon for that.

Meanwhile Manly peeked over the rim of his glass as the stunning girl drew an ottoman close to her mother's chair, sat down primly, folded her hands in her lap, and crossed one foot over the other.

"Why don't you tell us something about your studies, Reverend?" asked Sate, hoping thereby to edify Beatrice.

"I'd be proud to do so," said Manly, taking a deep drink preparatory to extolling his spiritual preparation at Big Bend.

But it was not to be. Jed had been sizing up Manly between gulps of lemonade and had decided that the preacher they had sent down was deficient. He certainly didn't look much like a he-man, thought Jed, him 'n' his fancy suit 'n' shiny shoes 'n' slicked down hair 'n' prissy look.

"Don't seem to me that men folks're as rugged as they used to be; why, when I was a boy, many's the time we'd work clean around the clock, 'n'

148

never did seem to get tired; but you take these young gillygaloots we got today; seems like they're wore out before they git started; then they got to take a break, coffee break ya know or time off for a sody-pop; and eat, why, my lord, they're all the time eatin' that danged stuff that comes all wrapped up in this here cellophane—then a little later they gotta go if ya git my point."

"Jed, hush your mouth," said Sate, glaring at him.

More than a Mona Lisa look played in the corners of Beatrice's mouth as she glanced from father to mother and back to father and ever so fleetingly at the new preacher to see how he was taking it; and Manly caught her at it.

"Well, Judas Priest, it just don't seem to me that a body can git a decent day's work done that-a-way," Jed grumbled, unchastened and wagging his head from side to side at the enormity of it all. "When I was still a fairly young shaver, my folks didn't have none too much to set before us, me and my three younger brothers, that is, 'n' I recollect as plain as day goin' off summers to try to make some money; went way up to Montana one time to work at thrashin' wheat—worst thing about that was they didn't have no idee of what grits was—well we worked from sunup ('n' b'lieve me it comes up early in that country) until sundown, 'n' it's still light up there until way into the night; many's the time I done blacksmithin' after dark just so's we could start up agin next mornin', but I cain't rightly say I recollect ever bein' what you'd call wore out; course I admit I'm a lot stronger'n most men, always was, but that's just the point I'm gittin at.

"Well, after I left home for good 'n' come up north to these parts, farmin' was awful bad a right smart of the time and money was tight; anyhow, I remember havin' to go to work in one of them danged factories over at Newcombe. First they'd put me on one job 'n' I'd jist about git the hang of it, 'n' they'd transfer me to another. Pretty soon I'd had a belly full of that kinda treatment, 'n' I said to one of the bosses, 'Seems like ya might could leave me in one place long enough to git it down pat'; well, ya wanna know what he says to me? he says, 'Why, man, ya keep breakin' the machines wher'ever we put ya', 'n' he went on to make out like I was sort of a bull in a . . . in a . . . whaddy-ya-call-it? a china shop; to make a long story short, I admitted right off that I'd broke a deal of machinery, but I says, 'Look, mister, I'm just too stout, ther's no mistakin' that, in fact, I don't know m'own strength, but you've got to admit that this must be pretty shoddy-built machinery you've got here to keep breakin' so easy'."

"Won't you excuse us, please, Reverend?" asked Sate. "Because Beatrice and me need to start up the supper."

Manly mumbled his assent.

With the women folks out of earshot, Jed's conversation took an earthy turn, nor was his "yea" simply "yea" nor his "nay" simply "nay" as is supposed to be the case with Christians, according to Scripture. He found vivid analogies between different kinds of bad luck, usually visited upon his enemies, and the way pigs could lose their nuts. He talked at length, and graphically, about the rare style with which a favorite bull of yesteryear used to mount his cows and "service them repeatedly," as he put it. He mentioned various sorts of excrement often and discriminatingly, using a vocabulary as rich as that of an Eskimo when referring to different kinds of snow.

The day's excitement, the hour and a half's drive from Big Bend, and Sate's lemonade (she had insisted that he have two refills) eventually rescued Manly from Jed's unending discourse. "Mr. Bantry, I'm sorry to break in, but I wonder if you could show me where the bathroom is?" he asked.

" 'Fraid I cain't do that, Preacher," Jed said hypocritically, "but if ya'll follow me, I'll show you wher' the privy is at." So, out into the kitchen they trooped—right past Sate and Beatrice they went, everyone remaining silent but everyone knowing—and out to a screened-in back porch they proceeded. From there Jed gestured dismissively toward an outhouse standing free and alone, looking much like a sentry in open range land in plain view for all to see and with a half-moon for an ear.

Making a direct approach to the privy was out of the question, because between Manly and it lay a rectangular garden plot, freshly plowed. With no discreet alternative available, he had to take the path along the garden's south border and two-thirds of the way up its eastern edge. As he made his unhappy way, he was sure that Jed was scrutinizing his every step and positive that Beatrice was watching him from the kitchen window, even if only in furtive glances. Only Sate would avert her eyes. Once inside the privy, Manly was too distressed to notice that it was a three-holer, nor did he ponder on what that had meant at the time it was built. Greatly relieved in body but not at all in spirit, he emerged a minute or two later just in time to see a car, speeding toward the Bantrys', slow down as though to let its occupants get a better look-see at the stranger stepping out of Jed's outhouse. If they were members of the church at Calico Corners, what would they think of him? thought Manly.

Jed stepped down from the back porch to greet him, or so it seemed, just as Manly realized what it was that made the Bantry house look peculiar. Instead of being scattered around it in the usual irregular, informal way, all the bushes and shrubs were planted in straight lines, and each line ran toward the house as though it were a spoke and the house were the hub of a wheel. "Sate put up quite a squawk about them bushes," said Jed, "but I know'd this ol' boy in the Extension Service down at Auburn, 'n' he allowed as to how if ya wanted to keep mildew 'n' rot 'n' vermin 'n' such as that away from the foundation of your house, ya ought to plant your bushes like I done."

Then in a surprisingly considerate mood, Jed said, "Preacher, I'm goin' down to the barn to do some chores; you're more'n welcome to tag along if you're of a mind to, but that pretty suit of clothes you're wearin' might git slopped on, and maybe you're tired and would like to do some Bible readin', or meditatin', or whatever between now and supper." With that, Jed, who had divined most of what was on Manly's mind, marched off toward the barn with a bellicose tread, needing no answer.

White predominated in the meal Sate set before them. It consisted of creamed white corn, creamed carrots, boiled potatoes in a milk gravy, Swiss steak, heavily floured, a pear and cottage cheese salad, white bread, and more lemonade. Jed peppered his fare so heavily and indiscriminately that he appeared to be eating into a great gray mound of something uniform and undifferentiated. After a few bites had taken the edge off his appetite, he commenced to talk again.

"People ain't always ate this well, Preacher; leastways I know I never had such refined food 'till I met up with Sate 'n' married 'er; why many's the time I been served adult'rated food; I 'member workin' at a grist mill over by Chatsworth, Georgia; the fellah that ran the place, ol' man Messer it was, give us bed 'n' board 'n' $2.50 a week back in the depression; I've seen things in his corn bread I wouldn't even care to mention; but would you b'lieve it? More'n once we got worms in the beans he set before us."

"At least you got some protein in your diet," said Beatrice.

"*What?*" roared Jed, disbelieving that Beatrice could be cheeky and thinking that he must surely have misunderstood her.

"Nothing," said Mona Lisa, "just forget it."

"You talk about foul water; why, Preacher, many's the time I've drank cistern water; most of the time is was all right soon's a body could git used to that musty smell there is about it; well, then, there was one time I got me some of it over about Tupelo, Mississippi, that was too rank for any of us to take; seems that a 'possum had fell into the cistern and drown'ded, or got dropped in; course, nobody know'd it at the time—"

"Jed Bantry," said Sate, profoundly vexed by that time, "you shut up that kind of talk at the supper table." Manly, for whose benefit she had spoken up, concurred strongly but silently, his complexion having begun to resemble the food.

After Sate and Beatrice had removed the dishes and bowls of uneaten white stuff from the table and had gone to the kitchen to prepare the dessert, vanilla ice cream and angel food cake, Jed began anew. "I reckon one of the main reasons why I've succeeded wher' lots of men ain't is that I was always a great one to plan ahead; try to foresee, ya might say, what was most liable to happen. The best lesson of that kind I ever got, I reckon, was up in Idaho; I was workin' in a lumberjack camp, 'n' we had this man cook; well sir, ever blessed mornin' when he washed up 'n' such like, he'd take out his prick 'n' soap it up right good so's he wouldn't have to wash his hands no more the rest of the day after—"

"What?" shrilled Manly, his face pinched in disbelief that a Christian man would talk to a minister of the gospel about such a topic in such a manner!

Thinking that the new preacher they'd sent didn't even know what he was talking about, Jed said, with squinted eyes and evident disgust, "Oh, you know, his peter, his cock, the thing a man pees with."

151

The only thing that saved Manly from being routed completely was the reappearance at that moment of Sate and Beatrice, bearing dessert. More than age and beauty differentiated the Bantry women, he noticed, for the corners of Sate's mouth were drawn down sharply, whereas the corners of Beatrice's mouth were ever so slightly but very definitely turned up. What kind of a nest had he gotten into, Manly wondered. Whatever the kind, nothing he had learned at Big Bend had prepared him for it. But worse was yet to come, much worse.

When Manly and the three Bantrys came to roost in the parlor later that evening, Jed felt the need to testify. "It may come as a surprise to ya, Preacher, but I ain't always been a Christian; in fact, I reckon I's what ya'd call a hellion when I's young; I'm ashamed to say it, but I've drank moonshine whiskey 'n' played cards for money 'n' kept comp'ny with some real sorry folks; but, then, when I's in my twenties, I got me a slew of carbuncles, 'n' I wouldn't care to tell you wher' they was all at neither; anyhow, didn't seem like ther' was no way to get shed of 'em, 'n' none of the doctors in them parts give me any relief. I don't mind tellin' ya, them carbuncles, or whatever they was, just about drove me to distraction—hurt, you talk about hurt!— but I guess I's like ol' Job, 'cause I never did curse God, but I sure talked to 'im pretty straight one time; I says, 'Listen God, this here's Jed Bantry talkin' to ya, 'n' I'm a white man; I ain't no danged black; I know I ain't never talked to ya b'fore, 'n' I sure ain't always done right, but if you'll deliver me from these miserable carbuncles, I promise to straighten up 'n' serve ya to the best of m' ability.' Well, it wasn't more'n a few days after that 'n' I began to improve, 'n' I ain't never had a sign of one since; I'll tell ya one thing, I've kept my part of the bargain, 'n' I'm right proud to say God's done his part too; ya know, it's a reg'lar covenant I made with him just like the Jews done in the Bible, course they didn't keep theirs; but I'm always ready to serve the Lord by telling the tale to anybody that's weak in faith or needin' to hear a testimonial."

Manly was sure Jed could have gone on indefinitely if bedtime had not come early in the Calico Corner area. By 9:00 P.M., Jed was yawning. By 9:30, each of the four had trekked out back preparatory to sleep.

"Night, Reverend," said Beatrice, looking boldly at Manly for the first time since he had come. Without waiting for an answer, she glided sensuously into a nearby room but did not, he noticed, close the door completely. Then Sate wished him a good night's rest and said that Jed would be along shortly to show him where to sleep. Moments later, Jed stomped in from outside, retrieved Manly's overnight case, and guided him to a door that led to an enclosed stairway. "You're to sleep in the spare room upstairs," Jed said, "so just turn left on the landin' 'n' cain't miss it." With that Manly began to climb the steepest, narrowest stairway he had ever encountered. Halfway up, he and everybody else in the house heard Jed boom out, "Oh, Preacher, ya better come back down a minute; I forgot to give ya somethin'."

What Jed had forgotten to give him was a chamber pot. "I don't know if

152

you've ever used one of these or not," he said loudly, "but ther' ain't no special knack to it, so I reckon ya could figger it out if ya needed to." With cheeks the color of old rose, Manly mumbled his thanks and mounted the perilous stairs, the pot in one hand, his overnight case in the other.

In six short hours, life with the Bantrys had traumatized Manly. Not even his fervent request for strength, said on bended knees by the iron bedstead in their spare room (which was little more than an attic), prevented him from emotional regression. As he fidgeted on the bed's lumpy mattress, suspended on sagging springs, he needed very much to have a strong loving mother bend over him, lay a cooling hand on his forehead, and assure him that everything would be all right.

As sleep, with leaden feet, began to rescue him from the day's manifold miseries, the sky, which had been heavily overcast, began to clear, the moon peeping now and again between parting clouds. As its light appeared, then disappeared, then reappeared, the nocturnal creatures of field and forest came out to hop, freeze, slink, and stalk; to cry, to sing, and to call. Having been cued thusly by light and sound, Tick and Bozo, Jed's coon hounds, began to bark and bay, to whine, to snarl, and to howl. Sometimes they whooped it up in unison, sometimes antiphonally between themselves, sometimes with distant dogs. Occasionally they managed to whine a canine calypso. All in all, it was an unparalleled performance the like and length of which Manly had never experienced. Before that awful night was over, the once odious chamber pot had become a faithful friend. Denied sleep, dangerously close to yelling profanely out of the window at Tick and Bozo, definitely thinking unchristian thoughts about Bro. Bantry, and subjected to erotic visions of the beautiful Beatrice, Manly used the pot over and again, nearly filling it.

Toward morning, during a lull in the canine concert, new agonies assailed him. What was he to do with the pot? He could not carry it downstairs, for that would mortify everyone—well, everyone except Jed. But, then, he couldn't abide the idea that Sate or, worse yet, Beatrice would have to empty it. In the remote event that Jed did it, and surely he wouldn't, he would have a new outrage to tell. Manly could already hear it. At mealtime somewhere somehow, Jed would say to someone, sorely affronted in the process, "Now you talk about a full pot; why, we had this preacher fellah that they sent down from Big Bend; he come 'n' took supper with us, 'n' spent the night; didn't seem like he drunk all that much, but let me tell you, he peed our pot clean up to the brim."

Manly decided that he must empty the pot before the Bantrys awoke. But how? After surveying the situation he concluded that he should not try to creep downstairs and thence outside with it but should, rather, try to empty it out of his bedroom window in what he hoped would be several silent, or nearly silent, pourings, not too much at any one time in any one spot. The bedroom's only window was already cracked open. But when he tried to raise it, it resisted, being badly warped. There was nothing to do but to hoist on it strenuously and hope that Tick's and Bozo's barking would muffle any strange sounds coming from the Bantrys' attic. After several muscle-straining tugs, Manly managed to raise the window sufficiently. But to his dismay, he discovered that no part of the window screen would budge in any direction. There was nothing to do but to enlarge a tear (of ancient vintage) in the screen and hope that none of the Bantrys would notice, or, if so, that they would think that a large bird had careened into it, tearing it.

In the delicate process of lifting the heavy pot over the window sill, elevating it at an angle so as to clear the bottom of the screen's wooden frame, and extending it with one arm through the ragged tear, Manly lost his grip. Straight down went the pot, in an upright position, crashing onto the flagstones below. For a split second, Tick and Bozo froze. Then they began to leap madly into the air, yelping in the happy anticipation that something furry would soon fall from any of the nearby trees. Meanwhile, Jed sat bolt upright in bed, not knowing what had awakened him. He did, however, know the many moods of Tick and Bozo and the endearing ways they had of voicing their feelings. Clearly, they thought that a gun had just gone off.

Noticing that the clock was rounding on 5:00 A.M. and already wide awake, Jed bounded out of bed aggressively, dressed hurriedly, and bolted off the back porch to see "what in tarnation" was going on. He reconnoitered vainly for quite a while before coming on the unnumbered splinters of something white that appeared to have crashed onto his flagstone walk at one side of the house. As other senses came to the aid of his eyes in the dim light of early morning, the enormity of it all dawned on him. "That gol-danged preacher has gone and busted our chamber pot!" he snarled to himself.

Later that morning the tension around the breakfast table was truly terrific. It was as though four conspirators had taken a vow of eternal silence about the one common topic uppermost in the mind of each.

Jed was clearly outraged, but uniquely silent, as he ate his breakfast with short, fast, decisive, wire-cutting chomps. On the few occasions when he spoke, he hissed as though steam under critically high pressure were rushing through an overloaded safety valve. To his credit, however, he neither exploded nor did he blurt out the question he most wanted to ask. Inured though she was to being affronted (after thirty years with Jed), even Sate looked more aggrieved than usual as she went about the labor of being a good hostess. She could have accepted what had happened with equanimity if she could have believed that the visiting preacher was just trying to get back at Jed, but in breaking their chamber pot there was the nagging suspicion that he was also striking back at her, at her home, at her hospitality. Manly merely imploded that morning under the pressure of avenging shame. If Jed had only come right out and said, "Now, see here, Preacher, supposin' ya just level with us 'n' tell us what ya thought ya's doin' breakin' our pot 'n' all," he would have answered truthfully, though at the risk of his very being. Since none of the Bantrys adverted to the horrid occurrence, and since he could not bring it up, Manly simply suffered in silence; but how he suffered!

Meanwhile, Beatrice exacerbated the entire situation by irritating Jed, distressing her mother, and mortifying Manly. Nobody had told her anything, of course, but she had done a little surreptitious reconnoitering and believed herself in possession of the essential facts. Although she said next to nothing, certainly nothing offensive, she too seemed under heavy pressure, but when the supercharged steam escaped from her it burst forth in inopportune giggles. Trying hard to be demure and looking with downcast eyes at her food most of the time, she found merriment in absolutely everything, it seemed, her face pink with glee.

In retrospect, Manly believed that he survived the remainder of that day only through the power of God and the grace of his Son. A neutral, but informed, observer at the church at Calico Corners might have thought that it was his professionalism that saw him through, but Manly would have pointed out that he was not yet a professional. Others might have suggested that he was a natural-born actor, able to forget himself completely in his assumed role, that he had a singular flair for the dramatic. He would have denied that he was an actor, for he had had no experience at all in assuming various theatrical roles and was unaware of having any dramatic flair. But it cannot be denied that a striking transformation took place that morning.

The haggard, shaken young man who had arrived in the Bantrys' tow, hardly knowing where he was or why, seemed to rise up with wings as eagles with every successive act of worship. The initial quiver in his voice disappeared as soon as he heard himself invoking the presence of the Most High; all hints of fatigue fell away as he lifted his rather good tenor voice in songs of praise; all uncertainties, or semblances thereof, fled as he read from the Holy Book. By the time he mounted the pulpit to preach, it was as though he had been renewed throughout. Although he wore no vestments that made him look bigger than life, no gorgeous apparel that made him appear good, or more than mortal man, it was as though the mantel of the prophets had dropped from the heavens and come to rest upon his shoulders. Girded up in that manner, he spoke as one having authority, and the people were well pleased. Had there been a single learned person among them that day, it would have been clear to that one that Manly did not really know what he was talking about, but his was a virtuoso performance nevertheless. Even Jed Bantry was taken aback, the pussy cat he had known having become an imperious tiger.

What Manly ate at the midday meal, whom he saw that afternoon, where he went, how he found time to review his message for the evening, and where he took supper all swam together, coalescing in oblivion. But once in the pulpit again, he was as incandescent as he had been that morning.

With no hope that he would be called as the pastor of the church at Calico Corners, Manly forgot what he said in farewell, forgot whose hands he shook, and forgot all family names represented in the congregation except for the one name, Bantry. When, an hour and a half later, he arrived back at Big Bend, utterly exhausted but safe and sound, one thing alone was clear to him. God had not been his co-pilot on the return trip; God had been his pilot.

God had no sooner begun to deliver Manly to Big Bend than Whisman Roberts, the chairman of the church board, called its members together prayerfully, then said to the other six, "Well, gentlemen, you don't have to be told why we're here."

"Course not," Jed said belligerently.

"I vote we go ahead and hire Brother Plumwell," said George Meechum, "because there's no doubt he's a Jim Dandy of a preacher; don't rightly know when I've enjoyed any sermons more than his'n."

"Ain't no two ways about that," said Brachen Rose.

Steve Pottinger allowed as to how Bro. Plumwell sure did give those evolutionists both barrels.

Whisman, a retired high school history teacher, agreed, saying that when Manly referred to H. G. Wells as "Heathen" G. Wells, he surely gave the devil his due. The others didn't know who H. G. Wells was but were well pleased that Whis was pleased.

"Wasn't no flies on his evenin' sermon neither," Brachen Rose opined.

"I never heard a description of the second coming of Christ that was any plainer nor the end of the world either," said George Meechum, "so let's go ahead and hire him."

Morris Johnson, who represented a faction of the congregation some of whom were still seething over the way the church at Calico Corners had been handed over to the Holy Nation Association, cautioned them with a hint of reproof in his voice against acting too hastily. "Ain't we gonna get to hear somebody else, maybe from some other trainin' school?" he inquired. Answered by silence, he continued, saying, "Sure seems to me like we should."

"For what we're willing to pay, it don't seem to me we can do much better," rejoined Brachen Rose.

"I'm with Brachen," said George.

"Me too," said Steve.

Mortimer Bruce, who was a gifted obstructionist and parliamentary niggler, was apprehensive of any business meeting that went too smoothly. So, he raised an objection on principle. "As a matter of principle," he said in a deceptively sweet voice, "I have to agree with Morris, not because I'm sore about water over the dam, but because principle is principle."

"Oh, I'm as sure as I am of anything that the folks up at Big Bend sent us the very best person available," said Brachen Rose.

"But we must decide between two or more who is best for us; that's the principle of democracy," Mortimer replied.

"We should at least get to hear somebody from a different school," said Morris.

"Now, Morris," Whisman Roberts lectured, "you know that there's only one training school at present training royal priests for the Holy Nation."

"That's as may be, but there's other schools aplenty and other preachers to choose from," Morris snapped back.

"Yeah," said Brachen Rose, "but don't forget what we can afford to pay."

"On principle," said Mortimer, "I think we have to consider more than a man's preaching on the one hand and what we can afford to pay on the other. We have to consider what kind of a person he is, how well he can pastor, how well he can lead."

Wondering why Jed had been so patient, so unnervingly quiet for him, Whisman said, "Well, Jed, there's your chance. You've had the opportunity to get to know Brother Plumwell as a person better than we have."

"If ya ask me, he ain't got the right name," said Jed cryptically.

"Plumwell?" asked George Meechum. "What is it, Jewish or something?"

"No," said Jed, registering disgust, "it's not that; I mean, he ain't very manly, if ya ask me."

"Don't talk in riddles," said Steve Pottinger.

"Come on, Jed, morning comes early around here," remarked Brachen Rose.

"Just take your time and tell us what's on your mind," said Morris Johnson, taking heart in Jed's caveat.

It was not lost on Jed's peers that he was uncharacteristically slow to speak that night, but what they didn't know was that he felt the need to proceed slowly, because, first, he was trying to gauge Manly's support, and, second, he knew that there was some risk to himself in what he planned to say.

"That preacher wasn't like nobody we've ever had to spend the night before," Jed observed.

"Come on, Jed, out with it," they all said at once in one way or another.

"Well, he . . . he broke our . . . ah . . . chamber pot."

"Broke your chamber pot?" chorused six voices as one.

"But what would an accident like that have to do with the price of wheat?" somebody asked.

"It wasn't no accident, if ya ask me," said Jed, narrowing his eyes.

"You mean to say that a minister of the gospel came right out and broke your pot on purpose?" asked Whisman incredulously.

"Anybody who'd break Jed Bantry's thunder mug on purpose has just got to be pretty manly, seems like to me," observed Morris Johnson loudly to nobody in particular.

"He never did confess to it neither," said Jed indignantly, "nor did he tell us he was sorry or nothin'."

"Well, did you make inquiries about it?" asked Mortimer.

"No, of course not," Jed replied, warming under the collar at the question. "Whad'ya expect me to do, just come right out at the breakfast table in front of Sate 'n' Beatrice 'n' say, 'OK, Preacher, out with it; how come ya broke our piss pot?' "

"It does seem to me as though there's a principle involved here," said

157

Mortimer testily, "for, after all, we Christians have a responsibility to be quite straight about the facts of a case before we make an accusa—"

"I suppose we could just tell folks to hide their chamber pots when Brother Plumwell spends the night and advise 'em to give him a slop pail instead," said Brachen Rose, breaking in on Mortimer and chuckling openly.

"I call the question," said George Meechum, who was afraid that he would not be able to fall asleep that night if the meeting grew any more animated.

"All right, let's vote," said Whisman decisively.

Manly was called to the church at Calico Corners by four and a half votes to two and a half as nearly as anybody could make out. Jed and Morris Johnson clearly voted "no." All the others voted "yes" except for Mortimer Bruce, who was still arguing points of principle when Whisman Roberts adjourned the meeting. It may be presumed that he would have voted a resounding "maybe," since many points of principle remained unresolved.

So, Manly went to Calico Corners to preach on a regular basis, two sermons every Sunday. One family would have him to lunch and dinner on Saturdays; another would give him bed that night and breakfast the next morning; and yet another family would provide him with dinner and supper on Sundays. Only the Bantrys refused to cooperate in that way. But it was to be expected and just as well, for Manly and Jed could not look each other in the eye and avoided each other like the plague; he and Sate were mutually civil but very, very distant; and he and the beautiful Beatrice were object of mirth and mirth personified respectively.

While Manly went about preaching on Sundays and sandwiching in as much pastoring and evangelizing as possible on what was left of each weekend, Jed went about fomenting trouble enough to expel Manly from the church at Calico Corners. In the process, however, he suffered a pyrrhic victory and, for once in his life, knew it. Jed was neither loved nor admired around Calico Corners but, at best, respected, much as one would respect a water buffalo. He was a blow-hard who blew incessantly, buffeting many egos in the process and causing emotional wind damage that rankled long after his stronger gusts had died down. Moreover, his oft' repeated maxim, "Never do nothin' that ya'd be ashamed to do on the steps of the church," was not taken seriously nor was it thought that he abided by it. One time he offered forty acres on which the congregation might plant wheat, the proceeds to go to the church. He also volunteered to fertilize the wheat if the congregation would buy the fertilizer. When, in God's good time, the wheat ripened, all who saw it were struck by how sparse and spindly the church's wheat looked in comparison with Jed's luxuriant and robust grain planted on forty adjacent acres. No one said anything openly, but no one forgot either. The upshot was that the harder Jed tried to oust Manly from Calico Corners, the more Jed's enemies plagued him, but spontaneously and not in concert, even though they all used the same weapon.

QUESTIONS PUT TO JED PUBLICLY: Might you be interested in buying a new chamber pot? Might you be interested in buying a used chamber pot? About what does a new chamber pot cost nowadays? About what does a used chamber pot cost nowadays? Is there a black market in chamber pots? How does one go about replacing a splintered chamber pot? Can they be bought from catalogues? Is it true that one can buy chamber pots with instructions for emptying printed on them? Did you, Jed, put instructions for emptying on the rest of your chamber pots?

QUESTIONS AND ANSWERS UTTERED IN PUBLIC IN JED'S PRESENCE: *Question:* How do you empty a chamber pot? *Answer:* I dunno, but Jed Bantry can tell you how not to. *Question:* Do you know Jed Bantry? *First Answer:* I've known Jed for better or worse. *Second Answer:* I've known Jed for richer or poorer. *Third Answer:* I've known Jed when he was well-off, and I've known him when he didn't have a chamber pot to piss in. *Question:* What does a loaded chamber pot sound like when it goes off? *Answer:* I don't know, but Jed Bantry's coon hounds do.

CREATION OF A NEW TERM: To "thunder mug" and "left-handed looking glass," amusing synonyms for "chamber pot" that were well known and often used among the old boys around Calico Corners, the proud new term "Bantry pan" was added, though it referred more precisely to metal slop jars. The term caught on so well that in unguarded moments even Beatrice began talking about Bantry pans around home.

GRATUITOUS OBSERVATIONS GIVEN PUBLICLY FOR JED'S BENEFIT: Give me a Bantry pan any old time to one of those flimsy chamber pots. Give me a Bantry pan or give me death. Bantry pans may bend, but they don't break. Bantry pans hold more. If elected, I promise you a chicken in every pot and a Bantry pan under every bed. A really good coon hound can tell the difference between a Bantry pan and a chamber pot any old night of the year.

Ridiculed wherever he turned, unable to flee his laughing tormentors, and clearly losing ground daily, Jed finally "took the bull by the horns," as he put it, and wrote to the Handmaiden of the Lord, detailing his plight exhaustively.

"Mother of pearl," said Alice, swooning momentarily at her desk, Jed's horrendous letter quivering in her hands. Like all personnel directors, the Handmaiden was well acquainted with human error, weakness, and folly. But, unlike many such folk, she also knew much about the devil's depredations. Due to him, more than one royal priest over the years had succumbed to lust and more than one had absconded with the collection plate (causing serious problems for the Holy Nation); but breaking the Bantrys' chamber pot was in a class by itself. With uncommon worldliness, Alice perceived at once and fully what might happen if someone trafficking in witticisms and mirth for the media (print or broadcast or both) were to get a hold of the chamber pot episode, especially if it led to serious disruption in the church at Calico Corners. After all, the Holy Nation could no more tolerate being the butt of bawdy humor than could Mr. Jedediah Bantry, and much, much more was at stake than in his case.

Alice took her problem to the Lord forthwith, and, as he had promised, he answered her even before she asked. Four days earlier, using a massive myocardial infarction as his tool, the Lord took his servant, the Reverend Elmer Titus Pearl, B.D. (YDS), home to be with him in heaven, leaving the Nickel Plate Christian Church without a pastor. On the very day when Jed's unparalleled letter reached her, that mysterious person, still unknown to Manly, who had first identified him to Alice as a likely ministerial candidate wrote her again. In part, here is what he wrote:

The way Manly buried his grandmother made an awful good impression on folks around here. They still talk about that bell tolling for her. And we know that he is as smart as a whip. He gave an awful good talk when he graduated from high school. Also he was always a good boy when he was growing up and quite spiritual, it seemed like.

I really believe if you could send him to us or we could call him back, however it might work out, he and I and maybe a few others could lead this whole congregation into the Holy Nation Association. Our building is in real good shape. The Christian Church (Disciples of Christ) is very weak in this state, and we don't identify with it much anyway except for baptism by total immersion and weekly communion. As far as the State Secretary of the denomination is concerned, he is as slow as molasses in January and won't be able to do much about it, if it comes to a showdown. If Manly just does good that is all it will take.

Another thing is we can't afford to pay a whole lot, but he still has the family property here, and it won't cost him much to live. He could even rent half of the house and still have plenty of room, unless of course he marries and has a family. Folks around here will give him lots of produce in season.

My wife and I and several others have been praying for this kind of opportunity for a long time now. We just ask God to please let you help us in getting Manly back in this way.

It was signed: "Yours prayerfully in the work of the Holy Nation, Josh Tharp, Chairman of the Board, Nickel Plate Christian Church."

Chapter Four

Whoever said that a prophet is not without honor except in his own country must not have foreseen Manly Plumwell's triumphant return to Nickel Plate. What a day of rejoicing that was to be! Exhausted but euphoric, he pulled into town just past midnight on the first Sunday in June. Nearly two years of grueling work at Big Bend lay behind him, as did his Bantrian nemesis at Calico Corners. He was free to start anew, free at last to give his all to the Holy Nation of King Jesus. The tired eyes of his early-rising renters greeted him (very late at night for them) as he stepped stiffly from the old Nash. A week earlier, he had notified those unsuspecting people of his imminent return and had given them a month or more in which to find other lodgings. In the meantime, they would all share the house as best they could.

Shortly after sunrise, while Manly slept as though drugged, Ikey Strubble scrambled out of his feather bed, looked lovingly in the direction of the cot on which the late Liz had lain for years, called to her by name as though she were still there, pulled on his coveralls, and breakfasted on goat's milk, corn bread, and coffee. Then, having done his chores out back, he returned to the house, anticipation glittering in his blue eyes. Setting an ancient flatiron beside the coffee pot on the wood-burning kitchen range, Ikey went off in search of his remaining white shirt, the cleaner of his two ties (a red one), and his only blue jacket. Stepping out of his coveralls he dressed himself completely except for his moleskin pants and shoes. The former he took to the kitchen table where, wielding the ancient iron with a heavy hand, he tried to force some creases into their legs. That done (more or less) he finished dressing and set out for the Christian Church on foot, his wreath of white hair pointing in all directions except up.

Once inside the church, Ikey swiped at the pews with a dustcloth, pushed and pulled a dust mop back and forth between them, guided an asthmatic vacuum cleaner over the runners on either side of the auditorium/sanctuary and up its center aisle, straightened the cloth on the communion table, and disposed of some leaflets left behind some other Sunday.

With the Reverend Elmer Titus Pearl, B.D., YDS, gone to his reward, the members of the Nickel Plate Christian Church decided to revert to their previous practice of having morning, rather than afternoon, services, Sunday school to be at 10:00 A.M., church to be at 11:00, beginning with the Sunday of Manly's return. That explained why Ikey was up and doing at the church so early, and it also explained what he did at 9:30. At that very moment, he urged his old bones up an abnormally tall stepladder propped against the east wall of the vestibule inside and at the bottom of the bell tower. Clinging to the bell rope with both hands, he jumped off the ladder and landed as lightly as a feather to the accompaniment of a single peal. For several minutes thereafter, the bell rang jubilantly, reminding Nickel Platers that services would begin in just thirty minutes. To those who knew, it also seemed to announce that one of their own had returned to lead them, the only native son, up to that time, who had ever "made a preacher," as it was put in those parts.

The pealing of the bell caught Manly unawares and sent shivers racing up his spine. He had already, even if groggily, prayed, shaved, breakfasted, read the Bible, and polished his sermon preparatory to the services he knew were to commence later that morning, but from long association with afternoon services in Nickel Plate, he had not expected to hear the bell at 9:30 A.M. As the shivers subsided, he guessed rightly that it was old Ikey ringing the bell, ringing it for *him*, for Manly John Plumwell, returned home in power and purpose to preach the gospel of Jesus. Hearing the bell reminded him of another day, of a day when it was tolled in love, and loss, and sadness. Would she for whom it had been tolled be pleased with his return as a royal priest? Yes, he concluded, deep down she would have been, but she would not have shown it and would have found niggling reasons for which to criticize him or at least to warn him against becoming too big for his britches.

When Manly reached the church a short time later, he was overwhelmed by the throng awaiting him. The broad cement steps leading up to the porch in front of the vestibule were jammed with people, waving, greeting him aloud, trying to get his personal attention. As he made his way up the steps, his emotions were running too high to see very plainly. Then, too, some of the children had grown so much during his absence that he could scarcely recognize them. But here and there he picked out familiar faces, faces that gladdened him enormously. Straight ahead with hand outstretched was Josh Tharp, looking deeply pleased as was his wife. To Manly's left slouched Harrison Bane, who, for a change, appeared to find life almost tolerable, and close behind him fidgeted Bokie DeBoer, eyes glittering as avidly as though a funeral were about to commence. And there to Manly's right was the girl, now quite a young lady, who had been so impressed with his baptismal bravery years earlier. "Mrs. Dr." Benny Oesterly, as she was customarily referred to, was also there (had she ever come to church before? Manly didn't think so). Scattered about were several of his public school teachers, to say nothing of his high school principal, also a majority of the matrons who had taken over the arrangements at the house when his grandmother had died, and several women, looking vindicated, who had held him up to their troublesome, resentful sons as a model of morality and deportment. Even some Presbyterians had turned out, a couple of families from nearby Dewmaker, and several people who had not darkened the door of the Christian Church since the day of Manly's second birth. When he finally entered the vestibule, there, holding the bell rope, stood Ikey Strubble, grinning from ear to ear. Beyond Ikey, through the vestibule doors, other friends and neighbors could be seen selecting their pews, and, outside, still more were arriving. What a day it was for a hometown boy; and as for the sheer number of people in attendance, well, it was Christmas and Easter rolled into one!

When, nearly an hour and a half later, Manly arose to preach, standing tall in the pulpit, the people looked at him in his new role and sensed a great change, marveling at it. They remembered a tense, aloof boy, bookish and withdrawn, who often seemed to be bearing the burdens of the world alone, a good kid, no doubt, but good, perhaps, more by default than by positive action, good more as a result of headlong flight from temptation than of confronting and overcoming it. But there before them stood one who seemed almost garrulous, so abundant were his words, so freely did they flow. He who had once been shy and retiring now seemed to be reaching out openly to each and every person in the congregation that he might share with them something as imperative to him as it was precious. Utterly at ease, yet completely in control, Manly spoke as one empowered with divine authority.

Pride and humility wrestled each other to a draw in the occupant of the pulpit that morning, even as the imperious side of his nature grappled with certain subservient tendencies. Just how he who, earlier in life, had been remote and unfeeling toward most of the people who sat before him could suddenly become their spiritual commander and simultaneously their servant, he did not know. But, then, he was aware of reinforcing presences in the pulpit not discernible to the congregation. Directly behind him, as it were, stood Iskander Moutsopoulos, the great persuader, and behind him, Miss Alice McAlister, *The* Handmaiden of the Lord, and behind her, the Lord Jesus himself, and behind him, God the Father, maker of heaven and earth and of all things therein. Surely they who had called him, taught him, and empowered him would not suffer him to fail. In truth, Manly had good reason to feel confident in his new situation, but in view of what was to happen to him, it cannot be said that he came out of Big Bend wearing the whole armor of God. Still and all, the Handmaiden and the Five had outfitted him well, very well, indeed. Chinks in his armor were not to appear for quite a while.

The members of the Nickel Plate Christian Church left the services that morning full of self-congratulation and loud in praise of their new preacher.

"You are the long-awaited answer to our prayers," said Mr. and Mrs. Josh Tharp in an aside to Manly.

"My, but wasn't that a good sermon!" said one of the town's matrons to another, the same judgment being echoed by many others.

"I'll say one thing; he never once mentioned the word 'values'," said one of those who had not attended services since the day of Manly's baptism.

"Why, that sermon was of professional quality," Mrs. Dr. Benny Oesterly was heard to say, a hint of surprise coloring her voice.

"They'd better get somebody good at the Methodist Church in Dewmaker," said one of the visitors from Dewmaker, "otherwise we'll all be coming over here pretty soon."

"Well, old feller . . . er . . . ah . . . I mean Reverend Plumwell," stammered Ikey, "I . . . I was right proud to get to ring the bell for you this morning, right proud, I'll tell you that."

With wordless thanks, but beaming all over, Manly grasped Ikey's right hand with both of his and pumped and pumped the old man's arm.

With everyone gone, Manly left to rejoin the Tharps for Sunday dinner, and Ikey set out at a brisk pace pretending for a heartening moment that he could tell Liz about it when he got home; but he knew better, for Liz had died nine months earlier.

The following Sunday morning, Manly arose early, went about his preparations for the day alertly, and left for the church at 8:30 to practice his sermon before Ikey was due to arrive to tidy up and ring the 9:30 bell. By 9:20 Manly had perfected his sermon and had retired to a classroom at the back of the church that also served as an office. Immersed in his Sunday school lesson, he did not note the coming and going of 9:30, but by 9:35 he sensed that something was amiss. What was it? The silent bell, that's what was amiss! Manly went to the vestibule, opened the double doors leading onto the porch, went down the front steps and out to the side yard on the east to look in the direction from which Ikey would most likely come. But Ikey was nowhere in sight. So, Manly returned to the vestibule, climbed the ladder, jumped off it holding onto the rope, and rang the bell himself.

By 9:45, early-arriving parishioners began to trickle in, but no Ikey. By 9:50, people were beginning to mill about on the porch outside and to gather in small knots in the vestibule, but still no Ikey. Manly told Josh Tharp and several of the elders and deacons about Ikey's unexpected absence, but no one could explain it, for punctuality had been one of his hallmarks. Although any one of several men or boys would have rung the bell gladly, Reverend Plumwell, asking for no help, rang the bell himself at 10:00. More unconscious than calculated, that action augured well for Manly. It told the members of his flock that he had not been spoiled at Big Bend, had not become hifalutin just because of his advanced studies. He was their new spiritual leader, to be sure, but by gum! he was still an ordinary person like themselves, a person who, even in his Sunday best, could and would use his hands when the need arose.

When (after church services) the last "Amen" was intoned, the last hand shaken, and the last "good-bye" said, Manly hurried out north of town to Ikey's place to find out what was wrong with the old codger.

Ikey was dead. That's what was wrong, Manly soon discovered as he bent unsteadily over the old man's body. To all appearances, Ikey had let loose of life as easily as he had clung to it. He did not appear to have resisted death, to have suffered its arrival, nor to have struggled in its grip. He had simply stepped through his kitchen door, coming in from the outside, and had fallen dead on the spot, leaving his body in an attitude of sweet repose, his face composed almost beatifically. "The simple fact is he didn't make any more fuss and bother about dying than he did about living," said Bokie DeBoer to the eager lot who garnered such tidbits in and around Nickel Plate.

Except for his fabled love for Liz, Ikey Strubble had not been greatly admired and never once honored in life. Marynell Plumwell had thought of him simply as pesky, and many of the better people in town had treated him more or less as though he were underfoot, particularly in his role as janitor at the Christian Church. Yet, in the months that followed his death, an indefinable loss was felt by many. In a strange way it was as though Nickel Platers had been denied an endearing quality in the life of their community. Two intensely blue eyes, always merry, and a ready, infectious smile had disappeared forever. A certain simplicity, comic to be sure but genuine nevertheless, had been taken from them. When people thought about it, no one could remember Ikey uttering a single mean or spiteful word about anybody, nor had he been known to complain even once about his sorely limited lot in life, no scintilla of self-pity ever souring his disposition. Perhaps, Nickel Platers concluded, they had not done justice to Ikey.

To Manly, Ikey's death was both an act of God and a gift of God. It was a gift of God in that it would bring people back to church again quickly, giving him the sudden opportunity to insert himself and what he stood for into their collective consciousness. His congregation had grown lax, being used to meeting but once a week. Only those with long memories could recall when Sunday evening worship services had been customary, and only those with the longest memories could recollect when mid-week prayer meetings had been common. It would, no doubt, take some doing, Manly reflected, to get his flock to feel the need to worship God more often than once a week. Meanwhile, funerals were the most effective way of getting them back into church more often than that.

"Never sell death short," Alice had said repeatedly to the students at Big Bend. Manly remembered the delivery of one such admonition particularly well. It had been uttered during his first year, in February as he recalled, at a Sunday night chapel service. Bitterly cold, the night was pitch black except for the ghostly snow that lay upon the land blanketing everything, every bush, every tree, every roof. As the wind gusted, sighing and moaning outside and rattling window panes inside, the Handmaiden reached one of those numinous moments in her preaching when goose pimples arose on the arms of her hearers, their spines being set to tingling.

"Dearly beloved," she said, "when the cold, clammy hand of death slices into the human family and denies the joyous warmth of life to one of our fellow mortals, everyone feels the chill—everyone.

"It's a penetrating chill," she added, wrapping her arms around herself unconsciously, "a chill that freezes the cockles of our hearts and turns to frost the very marrow of our bones. There is no way to drive that implacable chill out except with the warmth of God's love; no human shelter will suffice against it, nor wraps, nor blazing hearth, nor hot tears shed in grief; no, nothing but the Savior's sacrifice can restore warmth to those whose souls shiver and shudder in the chills of death's dark night."

Then, as though coming out of a kind of wintery reverie, Alice gave them practical suggestions as to how to evangelize effectively among sinful mourners. "Put them in death's deepfreeze," she said, "yes, indeed, put them in death's deepfreeze and really turn the temperature down, down, down until they see that their sins have contributed directly to the loss of their loved ones; make them see the death of those loved ones as that punishing road whose cold and tortuous path they must travel alone and on foot until their own heartfelt repentance transforms that frigid route into a thoroughfare to the warm light of God's saving, sheltering love."

Seldom has an inconsequential person, as the world measures consequence, ever passed his final rite with more gravity and grace than did Ikey Strubble on the Tuesday afternoon after his Lord's day death. Harrison Bane, remaining relatively sober throughout his mortuary ministrations, selected the best looking cheap casket/coffin combination in stock. He also bought, at personal expense, a white shirt, a blue and yellow tie, and a dark blue pin stripe suit for Ikey's bodily departure. Moreover, no head of state ever surpassed Mr. Strubble in having a chief of protocol who could order events and put people in their right places; Bokie DeBoer saw to that. As Manly looked down from the pulpit into Ikey's open casket, bowered with home-grown flowers, there was a look akin to patrician satisfaction on the dead face, pleased, it would seem, over all the fuss that was being made.

Ikey's was not a tearful funeral. Most of those who came to mark his passing came out of minimal respect or duty or curiosity. But as Manly concluded his sermon with a eulogy, eyes that had been dry misted over, one or two people cried copiously (if briefly), and even Bokie flicked away a surreptitious tear. "Naked he came into the world," said Manly, "and almost naked he remained in that he scarcely ever acquired more than the barest necessities of life. Yet, in his poverty, he never craved abundance, never worshipped mammon, never called upon charity. Moreover, he shared his life and slight substance, gladly and unstintingly, with one far more impoverished than he. As we, the living, part from him now, we do not leave him as a foundling on the doorstep of an uncaring cosmos, but rather at the door of one who will open to him the life everlasting. For, you see, our humble brother, Ikey Strubble, was the child of a king, the King of the Universe."

A little later, with Bokie at the wheel and Manly occupying the front passenger's seat, he who had never as much as owned a rattletrap rolled staidly in Harrison Bane's new Cadillac hearse to his final lodging in the poorest part of the Nickel Plate Cemetery. As the coffin was lowered into the earth, Manly, spilling tears unashamedly, whispered, "Till we meet again, old friend."

In the pulpit Manly spoke often of death and dying, of the imminent end of this world, of God's awful judgment, and of the endless miseries of the damned. He lingered long over stories, usually apocryphal, about the earthly end of assorted atheists, agnostics, infidels, and unbelievers. Too proud to humble themselves before God, too vain to repent, too arrogant to trust in Jesus, such miscreants were commonly believed to suffer death agonies of unimaginable intensity, to say nothing of forthcoming torments. Yet, when such people actually died, Manly could not bear to plunge their disbelieving kin into the deepfreeze of death, nor could he turn down the temperature on those unbelievers who had lost believing loved ones. Theologically, he should have held out little, if any, hope for those who, like Ikey, had not been members of the Holy Nation and even less for those who had not had a born-again experience.

But when apprised of the passing of an actual human being, when besought tearfully by the survivors of death to conduct funeral services for their departed, or when standing in the hushed presence of a corpse in its casket, Manly's humanity triumphed. Always grim, and sometimes contorted, his countenance told others that he, too, suffered their loss. No matter how somber and melancholy his words, no matter how nay-saying his theology, those words were, with but few exceptions, uttered so as to be dulcet and comforting to those who heard them. In ways bordering on the ironic, he became a popular funeral preacher. In addition to the members of his own flock who called upon him naturally when death sliced into their number, some who belonged to other congregations and some who belonged to none asked specifically for "that nice Brother Plumwell who always says such comforting things" to bury their dead, to intone the final public words on their behalf.

Thus, it came to pass, during his five years at Nickel Plate, that many lay at his feet: a babe but a few hours old; a little boy dead of scarlet fever; twin girls of three dead from drowning; a boy of eight unable to field a line drive at his head; a girl savagely beaten during an attempted rape; three of his younger classmates from high school, killed in a head-on collision following a nocturnal lark; a young mother and her child asphyxiated by an open gas grate; two young men struck down in connection with military service; a Dewmaker man murdered by a prowler; five women and six men, in their prime, consumed by cancers; seven men and two women, also in their prime, felled by heart attacks; and numerous oldsters, perhaps two dozen or more, taken by strokes, pneumonia, the flu, and what have you. Over them all, and with sincerity, fell his words, dulcet and comforting. With each interment a piece of Manly's own being seemed to be wrenched off and buried, yet he was not diminished, and praised God for it.

Weddings, of course, were another occasion for assembling people in church more often than regular worship services required, but Alice had developed no recipe for evangelizing wicked wedding guests, had made up no such phrase as the "hot pot of wedlock" to parallel the "deepfreeze of death," and would have cringed at the thought of turning the heat up, up, up at weddings. The Handmaiden, like the Lord's Apostle to the Gentiles, believed it best for people neither to burn nor to marry, but if the former, then by all means the latter, lest there should be occasion for the many sins of impurity.

By and large, Manly found weddings a far heavier cross to bear than funerals. At the latter, he had, perforce, to set his jaws, choke back tears, and keep his voice from cracking, but at least the emotions involved were straightforward. Weddings, however, unleashed wildly contradictory feelings. Throughout his Nickel Plate ministry, Reverend Plumwell suffered from the "St. Paul Syndrome" and might as well have been a monk, so womanless was his life. During those five years, no girl or young woman shattered his shell of sexual isolation nor imploded the loveless vacuum in which he lived. Several tried (and tried hard), but he shared no non-preacherly part of himself with any of them. He refused to be closeted with a woman socially, engaged in no tête-à-tête with one, shared neither table nor food, bed nor pillow. Except for shaking hands dutifully after church services, he permitted no woman so much as to lay a hand on him (with one horrendous exception). Accordingly, no loving lips met his; no sweet scent of womanhood filled his nostrils; no strand of girlish hair brushed his face, teasingly or tenderly; no breasts cushioned his chest; no feminine form filled his arms; nor did womanly warmth irradiate his being. He allowed himself to see no coquettish glances, to hear no suggestive stories, to laugh no naughty laughs. Since he had uncovered no woman's nakedness, had despoiled no virgin, had seduced nobody's sister, his conscience remained clear. But how like death's deepfreeze were his depressions; how chilling his self-hate!

Many parishioners noticed that his face frequently looked more stricken as he awaited a bride marching down the aisle toward him to join her intended than when he helped embosom the dead in their graves. And more often than not, his voice cracked upon reaching the supreme moment of the wedding service. He was able to say quite grandly, "Now, by virtue of the power vested in me by the State as a minister of the gospel," but was unable to say, "I now pronounce that you are husband and wife," without choking up, all the while trying to smile.

As for the wedding nights, well, he was an unwilling-willing participant in those too. No matter how resolute he might be at bedtime, no matter how strenuous his spiritual exertions, the devil would send the bride to him, most especially if she was pretty and approximately his age. He would see himself back in the church (or wherever), would see the bride marching toward him, not toward the groom, would see again her twinkling, triumphant eyes, her exultant smile and white teeth, her lustrous hair and radiant skin, her swelling bosom encased in white lace. Then the groom, asserting his rights, would emerge from the purple shadows in the bedroom of the wedding night, not in the church, and for a time Manly would become an unseen onlooker. It was the groom who would unzip or unbutton the bride's dress and kick away her shoes. It was the groom who would unhook her bra and remove her stockings, lavishing kisses on her newly revealed skin. It was the groom who would tip her onto the waiting bed and, with willing compliance, slip off her panties. It was the groom who would fall upon her, fastening his mouth to her lips or nipples and parting her thighs with caressing hands and venturesome fingers. Sometimes, if Manly had known the bride fairly well, the groom would conveniently vanish, leaving him to know her fully. But whether the groom disappeared or remained to complete the act of love, the vision would invariably be so evocative that Manly would erupt, polluting himself again. Then, like Sisyphus of whom he had never heard and burdened with guilt as Sisyphus never was, Manly would commence again to push the boulder of purity back to the top of Everest.

"Hi there, Manly, you old son of a gun, you," bellowed Elaine Beuhler.

"Hello, Elaine," replied Manly evenly, trying not to show his vexation over the vulgar way in which his kindergarten, grade school, and high school classmate had just greeted him.

"This here's Harlow, Harlow Wren," said Elaine loudly between pops from her bubble gum.

Manly nodded at the strapping, beetle-browed youth who stood next to her and proffered his hand.

Taking it, Harlow mumbled something, a greeting perhaps.

"Me and him want to get hitched," said Elaine redundantly.

Of course they wanted to get married. That's why Manly had insisted that they meet him at his office in the church for a session of Christ-centered marriage counseling.

Elaine was one of those bulky, ebullient, brash people who, having little discretion and less taste, season the social lump. She salted and peppered her popcorn, had been known to give four-roll packs of toilet paper to her favorite (and broken packs to her not-so-favorite) teachers at Christmas, and often talked (always loudly) at social events about scouring toilet bowls by hand or reaming out clogged drain traps. Manly had teased Elaine off and on until she reached puberty, at which juncture she began to take his chaffing as a sign of romantic interest. Recognizing his error, he back-pedaled furiously and left her alone as best he could. But throughout high school she continued to blare her interest into his deaf ears, to block his path at doorways, taunting him to push her aside, and otherwise contrived to recapture his earlier attentions.

As he led Elaine and Harlow through the sanctuary (it was more impressive that way) toward the classroom/office in the back of the church adjacent to the rear door, he knew that Christ-centered marriage counseling with Elaine would be trying at best. Even if she had not always been like a

169

wet dog shaking on people, Manly had reason to be unhappy with that particular marriage. Elaine was nominally a Presbyterian but had never known Jesus (of that Manly was sure) and rarely attended services anywhere. As for Harlow Wren, well, he was rumored to come from a godless family and was known to Manly only by reputation as a mechanical wizard and dead-eyed horseshoe player. But it was far better for them to marry than to burn (and burn he was sure Elaine did, and probably not with slow burn either). Furthermore, for old time's sake, he could hardly refuse her, and if he did not perform the service, somebody else would. Then, too, he reminded himself, God must never be underestimated. Perhaps it would be the Lord's will that he should reach out to some sinners at the wedding, possibly even to the infidel Wrens. Whatever the case, Elaine's nuptials would enable him to extend his influence for Jesus' sake.

Manly was about as well prepared to counsel people on sex, marriage, and parenthood as an orthodox rabbi to discourse on the virtues of pork chops, bacon, and ham, but, emboldened by the Holy Book on his lap, he proceeded to give Elaine and Harlow the God's-eye view of matrimony. Prepared to enshroud any embarrassment he might feel in stately cadences, he said, "Holy matrimony, you must understand, is an honorable estate, instituted by God during the age of man's innocence, before the fall into sin. Jesus, our Lord, endorsed the honor of the estate by gracing the wedding feast at Cana with his presence, and St. Paul commended it to be honorable among all men, if not entered into lightly or unadvisedly, but reverently and in the fear of God."

Then he announced that he would turn to the Lord's words in Matthew 19: 4-5, and did so, reading: " 'Have ye not read, that he which made *them* at the beginning made them male and female, and said, For this cause shall a man leave father and mother, and shall cleave to his wife: and they twain shall be one flesh?' " Without prior design, Manly glanced up at the end of the word "cleave" to see if those being instructed were attentive; as he did so he caught Harlow peering in the direction of Elaine's abounding breasts. He had no sooner finished the verse than Elaine, sitting on the edge of her chair with jean-clad legs widely parted and clasped hands dangling down inside her thighs, asked eagerly, "When are we gonna get to the juicy parts, Manly?"

It's as though the wretched girl wants to be titillated, thought the un-smiling minister as he leafed quickly to I Corinthians 7:3 (to get the Paul's-eye view) and began to read: " 'Let the husband render unto the wife due benevolence: and likewise also the wife unto the husband. The wife hath not power of her own body, but the husband. Defraud ye not one the other except *it* be with consent for a time, that ye may give yourselves to fasting and prayer; and come together again, that Satan tempt you not for your incontinency.' "

Since words failed Harlow as much as he failed them, he sat, mute and uncomprehending, and suffered Manly to read on, but Elaine burst out with, "And just what's that supposed to mean?"

"Well, it means," said Manly, "that before . . . before you come together with a person of the opposite sex in a . . . in a . . . carnal way. . . ."

"Does that mean before you do it? You know, make love?" Elaine interrupted brightly, warming to the text.

"Yes, yes," Manly agreed, "before you have sexual . . . ah . . . inter- . . . or relations, you should fast and pray."

"Pray first?" Harlow blurted out as clearly as incredulously, the word "fast" having been lost on him altogether.

"You gotta catch up on some back prayin', ain't you, mister?" Elaine chided Harlow at the top of her voice, prodding him in the ribs with an elbow and laughing uproariously. "And do without some meals too," she squealed between guffaws.

Red in the face and staring at his shoes, Harlow mumbled something that sounded to Manly like, "You too."

Hoping to avoid a complete rout, Reverend Plumwell turned to Ephesians 5: 24 and read: "'Therefore as the church is subject unto Christ, so *let* the wives *be* subject to their own husbands in everything.'"

"Oh, you don't have to worry none about that," Elaine assured him, " 'cause if I get out of line and don't play second fiddle to Harlow, I expect him to slap me around and straighten me up just like my daddy always done."

With at least one of the eternal verities still intact, Manly concluded the Christ-centered marriage counseling session as expeditiously as possible and went home with his teeth on edge, knowing beyond all doubt that Elaine and Harlow were fornicators.

It is a matter of record that the Holy Ghost performed no wonders of conversion at the Wren wedding, the only memorable thing about it being Elaine's wedding gown, which (no joking) looked tattletale gray to Manly.

Several days before Elaine and Harlow became one flesh with the blessings of God and State, Manly had had the misfortune of running into Elaine at the post office.

"Hey, Rev.," she said with her usual boisterous abruptness, "whacha doin' at 4 P.M. next Friday?"

"Why, nothing special that I know of," he opined.

"Good, 'cause then there won't be no reason why you can't come to me and Harlow's wedding reception."

No reason at all, and, so, there he was, hobnobbing with the godless Wrens and having to exercise great caution not to get the spiked punch or the bourbon candies or other polluted foods.

For his part, Harlow seemed to have gotten into a spirit more potent than any present in the fluids and foodstuffs on the reception table. Whatever it was, it made him loquacious and loud. To Manly's disgust, he overheard Harlow joking with some of his rowdy friends about the counseling session. " 'N' then the preacher says 'cleave' er 'cleaved' er sumpthin' like that, 'n' I thought the bastard meant the line where Elaine's boobs bump together;

s'help me God, I did; 'n' I ain't horse shittin' you sons a bitches either; that's what I thought he meant."

But worse was yet to come for Manly, something quite horrendous. As he tried to excuse himself from the festivities, Elaine, who had always liked him (but had a few ancient scores to settle), grabbed him as a wrestler might (pinning his arms and knocking his Bible to the ground), puffed her punchy breath up his nose, and kissed him wetly, sucking his lips into her mouth and gnawing on them for just under an eternity.

As Manly stumbled away in consternation, one of the elder Wrens said, "Looked like you had some pretty hot competition there for a while, Harlow."

"A bride gets to do any damn thing she wants to on her wedding day," Elaine roared above the hymeneal hubbub, "and I've wanted to do that for a long, long time."

Since even the devil must be given his due, it is only fair to note that he did not send visions of Elaine to Manly on her wedding night or, for that matter, on any other night.

Even when nobody else was listening, Manly lowered his voice while talking about certain topics with Josh Tharp and his wife, Maude, with Moses and May Middleton, and with Stuart Acton. Like the Handmaiden, Manly also had five very special disciples in Nickel Plate, each of whom had long since been captivated by her message and had become a secret member of the Holy Nation. Together they were what might be called "holy conspirators" in that they had all resolved secretly to break the ties that bound the members of the Nickel Plate Christian Church to the Disciples of Christ, the parent denomination, and to lead the congregation, after suitable preparation, into the Holy Nation Association of Churches of the Chosen. Some people, of course, would be lost to Satan in the process, but many, many more would be gained for the Lord, and it was, after all, his will they were doing.

Congregational in church government and only loosely bound to denominational headquarters, churches like the Nickel Plate Christian Church were sitting ducks for the Holy Nation. Moreover, such practices of the Disciples of Christ as adult baptism by total immersion, weekly participation in the Lord's Supper, and the call to repentance and confession of faith issued at the end of each worship service were compatible with the Handmaiden's views. So, those who spoke to each other in hushed tones as they planned their tactics could leave much as it was.

At first, Manly would preach rather standard orthodox fare, touching only lightly on the distinguishing beliefs of the Holy Nation Association; later, he would bear down increasingly on those beliefs. Meanwhile, his "five," as fair-minded lay persons, would give their "it-is-in-the-Bible" endorsement to each of the novel ideas he would touch upon and, then, as the

172

time grew ripe, would supply increasingly loud hosannahs.

As Professor Robert Paul of Hartford Theological Seminary used to insist, a Christian sect is just a group of Christians who have discovered something in the New Testament that the rest of the church has forgotten, or played down, and have proceeded to make a crucial defining issue out of it. Accordingly, the Seventh Day Adventists discovered that the New Testament does not authorize Christians to change their day of worship from the Sabbath to the Lord's day; the Jehovah's Witnesses discovered that the meek shall inherit the earth, not go to heaven; the Mormons discovered baptism on behalf of the dead; and varying Holiness groups discovered speaking with tongues and serpent handling.

What was it, then, that the Handmaiden of the Lord discovered?

First, like St. Paul, Alice discovered that she was a thoroughly trustworthy expositor of the gospel. Those who disagreed were not merely wrong but were false prophets, blind guides, and ravening wolves, scattering Christ's flock and devouring his sheep. In like manner the Apostle had viewed his detractors. Of her trustworthiness she could not doubt, for had not God delivered her to her parents' bedchamber that she might become acquainted with sin? Had he not made her to know sin that she might come to know grace? Had he not "come to her in heat" three times? Had he not announced to her, "It is well with thee," not once nor twice but thrice? Had he not given her the power of tongues? Had he not allowed her to receive the Holy Ghost and share him with others? Had God not empowered her to heal either in person or at a distance over radio and TV? Had he not made her a mighty fisher of men, allowing her to net not only the Five but the million and a half members of the Holy Nation, growing daily? Had he not blessed her with an abundance of riches and resources (mounting by the moment) wherewith to carry on his work? Had she accomplished any of those things on her own, or in concert with mere mortals? Certainly not! Was all that not proof positive that God was with her? Had any other person in history done such things apart from the power of the one true God? No, a thousand times no! It followed, therefore, in Alice's mind, that when God vouchsafed a revelation to her, it was true, and that was that. Who could deny it or who could resist her, with God on her side?

Second, she discovered, to her shame, that she had been neglecting an essential portion of God's word, a portion as important as the gospels or any of Paul's letters. Had not God chosen her, and her alone, to reveal that neglect to the world? Had he not impregnated her, as it were, with the seed of that revelation and sent her to Hazel Green, Kentucky, as though she were to be in confinement? Had he not prompted her, while there, to dwell on the one who was to become the rock upon whom Jesus would build his church? Had he not then guided her preoccupation with Peter to the epistles that bear his name, especially to the first of those epistles (2:9) wherein Christians are identified as a chosen generation, a royal priesthood, a holy nation, and a peculiar people? Had he not led her in the Spirit through the sinful city of

Knoxville and shown her the many denominations of wicked men and heretics, thus facilitating her gestation of his revelation? Finally, had he not
conveyed her safely to Soddy-Daisy, Tennessee, where that revelation was
delivered as the Holy Nation Association of Churches of the Chosen? Had
not its astonishing growth verified the validity of her discovery? Of course!

Third, while reading and re-reading II Peter 3:5-13, she discovered a
doctrine of cosmic proportions, one that was to become paramount in distinguishing the peculiar people from all who call themselves Christian but are
not.

Shortly after the fifth of the Five, Endicott Peabody Dickinson, joined
Alice and the others at Big Bend, she asked him one morning, privately and
in hushed tones, to come to her apartment in the chateau that evening
immediately after chapel. Then she said, "I would be much obliged, Brother
Dickinson, if you wouldn't mention this to a soul, and, oh yes, be sure to
bring your Bible." Dickinson, who did not yet know the Handmaiden very
well, did not perceive how uncharacteristic her invitation was, but Emmet
Langhorne Van Hook, who knew her well, recognized the oddity of the same
invitation when put to him. "Anything to oblige you, Miss Alice," he twanged
congenially; nevertheless, his eyes narrowed quizzically.

Needless to say, each Bible scholar was unprepared to bump into the
other outside the Handmaiden's door at the appointed time, and each was a
bit ruffled, having hoped to have her all to himself for a few precious, spirit-
filled moments. When Alice opened to their knock, her brows were knitted,
her eyes were as big as saucers, and she was more fussy than usual; that
much, at least, was evident to Emmet.

Once her brethren were seated in substantial chairs, she said, standing
before them with uncharacteristic self-consciousness, "I have called you here
that you might test a spirit—a spirit that I have recently received."

"It is not we who should be testing your spirit; it is *you* who should be
testing *our* spirits," said Dickinson grandiloquently.

"Amen to that," Emmet agreed.

"No, no, you don't understand," she said, waving her right hand before
their noses as though to hush them.

"Could you kindly give us some hint of what is on your heart, Miss
Alice?" Emmet queried gently, sensing that the spirit in question had made
her great as though with child and that she was about to burst with it.

"I believe that God has made clear to mine eyes a passage of Scripture
that he has withheld from the understanding of all others, that he has hidden
from other eyes for 2,000 years," she said in low, measured tones, "and if I
am not mistaken, *and pray God that I am not,* it will resolve a deep, deep,
deep mystery and will put to rout thousands and thousands and even hundreds
of thousands of scoffers and sceptics."

"And you want us to search the Scriptures with you lest you should be
deceived by a lying spirit, is that it?" asked Emmet gravely.

"You are so right, as usual, Brother Emmet," she said, transfixing him with dilated pupils.

"Do, please, go on, Miss Alice," Dickinson urged.

"By all means," Emmet agreed, shivering with anticipation and, simultaneously, warming to the night's work.

After a very long pause during which she seemed to be bolstering her courage, Alice opened her arms, holding her hands palms down, stared at the floor, and announced, "This earth upon which we rest is the second of three earths; it is not the earth God created according to Genesis, chapters 1 and 2. It is a replacement for that first earth; nor is it the one that is to come, the third earth; no, it is the second of God's earths." Then, slowly lifting her head until it lay far back, she raised her outstretched arms, the palms of her hands held up, and declared, "The heavens above are the second of God's heavens; they are not the original firmament; nor are they the glorious heavens to come; no, no, they are the second of God's heavens."

With her deliverances completed, Alice subsided onto a nearby chair as though her bones were melting. Then, having regained her strength and stiffened her spine, she said, "Have your Bibles at the ready, if you please, while I tell you the story of how this was revealed to me.

"You will recall, brethren, that I am just come from a great tent revival in Chillicothe, Missouri, and that I returned by air. Well, as the plane took off from Kansas City and passed beside the great skyscrapers to the south of the airport, a downpour of rain began, and strong gusts of wind buffeted the plane. Dark clouds made it seem as though night had fallen upon the city. Then, as we gained altitude, we climbed up into dense fog just above the skyscrapers. Up, up, up we climbed until, many thousands of feet higher, we emerged into God's glorious sunshine, leaving a wild sea of storm clouds below us. I thanked God for our deliverance from the wind and the rain and the fog and took out my Bible and began to read the story of creation.

"I read Genesis 1:1-2: 'In the beginning God created the heaven and the earth. And the earth was without form and void; and darkness was upon the face of the deep.' Brethren, that inspired me to look out my window at those fearsome dark clouds below, and I thought of how deep they were, thousands of feet deep, no doubt. Then I read on: 'And the Spirit of God moved upon the face of the waters.' As I looked again at that great sea of thunderheads beneath us, it seemed to me that I was moving upon their face too. But, then, I was struck by the sudden realization that nowhere does Genesis say that God made the great watery deep, just the heaven and the earth."

"Oh, God makes water in Psalm 95:5," said Dickinson, quickly biting his tongue over the unfortunate way he had phrased the point.

"I just knew it had to come from God somehow," Alice replied, further complicating Dickinson's frame of mind.

"Then I read in verses 6 and 7: 'And God said, Let there be a firmament in the midst of the waters, and let it divide the waters from the waters. And God made the firmament and divided the waters which *were* under the firmament from the waters which *were* above the firmament; and it was so.'

Then over in verses 14 through 17, it says that God put the sun and the moon and the stars in the firmament. At that point I was pierced to the quick, oh, yes, I really was, by the terrible thought that God's word might actually be mistaken about something."

"Surely not!" cried the Bible scholars in near-perfect unison.

"But, don't you see," said Alice (playing the devil's advocate for a time), "that God placed the heavenly bodies *in* the firmament, *below* those waters which were *above* it?" Then, strengthening her point, she cited Genesis 7:11 wherein God opens the windows of heaven, thus commencing the forty days and nights of rain which were to flood the whole wide world. She also cited Genesis 8:2, revealing how God restrained the rain by stopping up those same windows.

"I fear I don't quite catch your drift," said Emmet cautiously.

"It's ever so simple, Brother Emmet," Alice assured him, "because before the flood, rain fell from above, *from above*, mind you, above the stations of the sun and even of the stars, to say nothing of the moon; but it doesn't happen that way any more." Rising from her chair, she said, "Why, beloved, as I was riding in that plane, I looked down and could see the origin of the rain we get nowadays. It was falling from those clouds far below; but above me, way over my head in fact, was the sun, shining in all its glory. Rain doesn't fall on the second earth that way, but it did fall that way on the first earth."

While the Bible scholars stared at her, the Handmaiden sat down again, asking, "And what of the great deep? Who can tell me about the waters *under* the firmament?"

"Well," said Emmet, clearing his throat, "for one thing, the Noachian flood wasn't caused by rain alone, for Genesis says, somewhere, that the fountains of the great deep were broken open."

"Broken up," corrected the Handmaiden, "in Genesis 7:11, and stopped up in 8:2, just like the windows of heaven."

"Genesis 7:11 and 8:2," murmured the Bible scholars, fixing those passages in mind for future reference.

"Now, little children, what else do you know about the fountains of the great deep?"

Taking no offense at the way they had been addressed, Dickinson, for one, began flipping back and forth through the pages of the Old Testament. Reaching Psalm 24:2, he read aloud about how the Lord had founded the earth upon the seas and established it upon floods.

"There's an equally pertinent passage somewhere else in Psalms," mused Emmet, also rustling pages back and forth.

"Now, here's something!" cried Dickinson. "Right here in Psalm 148:4 where it says, 'Praise him ye heavens of heavens, and ye waters that *be* above the heavens.'"

"That's not exactly about the great deep," said Emmet reprovingly, "but it does support the Handmaiden's position magnificently."

After a few more minutes of page turning and application to cross references, the Bible scholars reached Psalm 136:6 at approximately the same time, Emmet reading aloud about how the earth was stretched out above the waters.

"Exactly," said the Handmaiden, growing ever more confident in the trustworthiness of her spirit, "the first earth was placed above the waters just as other waters were placed above the first heaven."

"Is it that way any more?" she piped rhetorically, triumphantly.

"Oh, no," said Dickinson.

"Isn't our earth today supposed to be like a round ball?"

"So they say," said Emmet.

"Isn't it supposed to sail through space around the sun?"

"Yes, that's what the astronomers tell us," agreed Dickinson.

"Doesn't our rain fall from clouds far below the sun, rather than from above it?"

"Certainly," they chorused.

"Does anybody believe anymore that our earth sits on pillars founded in the great deep?"

"No," said Emmet, "I shouldn't think so unless it might be those crazies in the Flat Earth Society."

"So," piped the Handmaiden again, her face glowing pinkly, "what these science people tell us today doesn't contradict the creation we read about in Genesis at all, does it? No," she answered herself, "it's just that the science people are telling us about how it is with the second heaven and the second earth, whereas Genesis is telling us about the first heaven and the first earth."

As the Bible scholars sat stock-still in their chairs, trying to absorb the full significance of what they had just heard from their revered Handmaiden and seen in God's word, Alice, who by that time was perched on the very edge of her chair, all but shouted, "Oh, little children, here is wonderful news for us all! The rock upon whom the Lord built his church knew all these things from the beginning and wrote them down for us, but we did not see them in their full significance until now."

"Oh, my stars, yes!" replied Emmet, a light dawning on him as his mind raced to II Peter, second—or was it the third chapter? yes, third chapter, but verse what?

"Brother Emmet," Alice queried needlessly, "do you have your Greek Testament with you?"

As he fished it out of a jacket pocket, she said, "Kindly turn to II Peter, chapter 3, verses 5, 6, 7, 12, and 13, if you please."

"Verse 5," said Emmet. Then he read effortlessly from the koine Greek (while Alice, who did not know the language, and Dickinson, who was just beginning to learn it, followed in the King James version): "'For this, they wilfully ignore the fact that there were heavens from of old and an earth that had been formed, and by means of water formed by God's word.'

"Verse 6: 'By means of which, the world that then was, perished, through

177

being flooded by water.'

"Verse 7: 'While the heavens and the earth that now are, by the same word, have been stored up for fire, being kept unto the day of judgment and the destruction of godless men.'

"Verse 12: 'Looking for and hastening the coming day of God wherein the heavens shall blaze, being on fire, and the elements shall melt with intense heat.'

"Verse 13: 'But new heavens and a new earth we are expecting, according to his promise, wherein uprightness will abide.'"

"Isn't that part about the world being on fire and the elements melting and all that just what these nuclear science people say an atom bomb explosion is like?" asked the Handmaiden.

"Yes, yes, more or less," said Dickinson, stunned by the thought of an actual cosmic meltdown at the end of the present wicked age.

"So, you see," Alice almost crowed, "when it says that the first world perished, being flooded by water, it doesn't just mean that all human beings were destroyed, except for the righteous Noah and the seven others on the ark with him; it means that the whole earth was destroyed and a brand new one miraculously put in its place by God before the ark came to rest on the mountains of Ararat."

Before the little group disbanded that night, there was much more page turning, many more examinations of cross references, and an abundance of praying, but the spirit sent to Alice, holding fast, passed every test. As Endicott Peabody Dickinson and Emmet Langhorne Van Hook (Ph.D., Harvard) stole silently, if shakily, to their separate quarters, dawn was not far off, and the morning stars did indeed sing together, for the peculiar people had their defining doctrine.

Apart from having "God come to her in heat"; apart from hearing him say, "It is well with thee"; apart from healing the sick merely by her presence, even if only on the air waves; apart from discovering that God viewed his chosen ones variously as new Jews, as royal priests, or as peculiar people; and apart from founding the Holy Nation Association of Churches of the Chosen, Alice had had no spiritual experience so ineffably exalting as that of God's revelation to her of having already created two heavens and two earths with one of each to go, after destroying the present heaven and earth with fire in the near future. In tones of stentorian ecstasy, she had cried aloud (well above the roar of four mighty engines), "Praise the Lord, oh, yes, Praise his Holy Name!"—this to the surprise of all, and to the consternation of not a few, as the plane bearing her moved upon the face of the thunderheads, east from Kansas City.

Except for being saved, for knowing Jesus, and tasting the grace of God through the instrumentality of his Handmaiden, Bros. Dickinson and Van Hook had experienced no spiritual sublimity to equal that which they felt that night when Alice, in the guise of having a spirit tested, revealed to them the doctrine of the three heavens and the three earths. Much the same can be said of the others in the household of God at Big Bend when the revelation reached them. The quickest to accept, of course, was Persephone Moutsopoulos, but not by very much, and in the course of a few weeks—or months at most—all the peculiar people had followed suit, becoming "three-world creationists," as it was put by some, or "second-world salvationists," as it was put by others.

The doctrine of three-world creationism was a boon of unparalleled proportions to the peculiar people. Like the Christians of St. Paul's time, not many of them were (or are) wise by worldly standards, nor powerful due to riches, prestige, politics, and the like. They tended to be people from the upper-lower or the lower-middle classes, faceless people who were largely ignored and who seldom stood in the counsels of the mighty. That God had chosen them from out of all the peoples and nations of the world, that he had selected them from out of all the religions and communions of mankind to proclaim the ancient and long-forgotten but divine truth of three-world creationism was as energizing to them as it was amazing. It gave each and every one of them a uniqueness as rare as it was precious. Indeed, knowing the Handmaiden of the Lord, following her, and holding fast to each of her revelations and teachings was like shaking the hand of the man who shook the hand that wrote MENE, MENE, TEKEL, UPHARSIN on a Babylonian wall.

With the doctrine of three-world creationism those who would never have applied to the peculiar people for instruction or reproof could be taught a thing or two, including the error of their ways; and they had better listen and believe if they knew what was good for them. With the Handmaiden's newest revelation, those who occupied exalted places on the second earth's totem pole could be put in their places with respect to the forthcoming totem pole of the third earth. If they did not change their ways, it would not go well with them at the end of the second earth when its elements would melt at atomic temperatures and its totem pole would burn with fervent heat.

The first to be taught a thing or two and put in their places (and none too gently either) were liberal Christians, those so-called Christians who, having acquired what the world calls education, presume to believe whatsoever pleases them, picking and choosing doctrines pleasant to their ears and discarding, simply throwing away, the rest of God's word as myth and ancient ignorance. Everyone from Alice and the Five down to Manly and the brethren in the pews believed that it would go harder on such people than it had in biblical times on those who had gone whoring after false gods. Since the so-called liberal Christians were commonly believed to live in cities, not to work with their hands (or to get dirty), to be rich, to drink strong drink, and to carry on shamelessly, the folks in Nickel Plate savored Manly's description in no uncertain terms of just what would happen to such perverse people when the elements melted at the ending of the second heaven and earth.

But according to the peculiar people, it would go just as hard, if not harder, on most of their fellows in the great factious family of American fundamentalism. Everyone who professed to believe in the Bible as the inerrantly inspired word of God but who did not subscribe wholeheartedly to the Handmaiden's revelation of three-world creationism was in danger of eternal torments excruciating beyond any that so-called liberal Christians might suffer. Nobody ever made that point more pointedly than did Dr. Iskander Moutsopoulos in a sermon (Number 156) delivered on the "Holy Nation Hour," broadcast nationally over a major network and available free of charge in printed form in response to cards and letters of request. Here, in part, is what he said, the printed text of course being but a pale reflection of the matchless way in which he said it.

"How is it that unbelieving scientists—especially those who hold and teach the godless doctrine of evolution—are able to ridicule God's word so easily, to hold the Holy Bible in contempt as mere myth and superstition? In large part, they have been able to do these despicable deeds through the willing complicity of many, many who take themselves to be, and who represent themselves to others as, Bible-believing Christians, but who at heart are not. By holding stubbornly (demonically, some might think) to the belief that the heaven and earth described in the first two chapters of Genesis are the same as the heaven and earth which we inhabit today, they have made the mockery of God's word easy; and by refusing to accept the revelation of the three heavens and the three earths, vouchsafed by God to Miss Alice McAlister in these last days, they have made that mockery believable.

"Listen to them, to the unbelieving scientists of our day: 'How is it,' they ask, 'that there was light (Gen. 1:3) before God made the sun and the stars (Gen. 1:14-16); do we not receive our light from the sun and the stars?'

" 'How is it,' they ask further, 'that it is supposed to rain according to Genesis? Why, from holes in the roof of heaven (Gen. 7:11), through which water from far above the sun and the moon and the stars is supposed to fall. But,' they chide, 'there are no such holes. See for yourselves. Send a rocket aloft, ascend in a balloon, or fly a plane into the stratosphere while it is raining below and look about for holes in the heavens.'

" 'And what of the great deep (Gen. 7:11)?' they ask in mock seriousness. 'Are we supposed to believe that the earth floats upon an ocean of water? Fly around the world, proceed to its underbelly, as it were, and see if you are at the top of an ocean of supporting water as you cruise over China or Australia.'

" 'Are we to understand,' they ask, 'that the first living things were grasses, and herbs, and fruit-bearing trees (Gen. 1:11)? Not so,' they cry out, 'but primitive replicating entities composed of chemicals or ancient single-celled creatures, neither plant nor animal.'

" 'Are we to believe,' they ask sarcastically, 'that the moving creatures of the sea and the winged fowl of the air were brought forth on the same day of creation as Genesis says (1:20-21)? Certainly not, for fishes, amphibians, and reptiles,' they announce loudly, 'antedated the fowl of the air by long ages.'

"This pernicious ridicule of God's word will endure until those whose minds have been clouded by Satan's lying spirit come to their senses; until so-called Bible-believing Christians recognize that the Apostle Peter taught the truth of the matter, in his second epistle, 3:1-13, well before Christendom fell into the false doctrine of one-world creationism; and also until scientists come to the realization that the current heaven and earth, which they study and about which they develop their various sciences, are not the same as the first heaven and the first earth that existed before the flood.

"But how shall mere scientists know the truth if their spiritual leaders do not? Shall the current earth cry out, 'I am the second earth'? Shall the present heaven announce, 'I am the second heaven'? No, certainly not, for this knowledge does not come from nature but from God's revelation, from a divine revelation already in the New Testament and clearly stated, but one that lay unseen by apostate eyes until God in his infinite wisdom, grace, and mercy enabled the Handmaiden of the Lord to perceive the truth of three-world creationism in these last days and to teach it to the people of God's Holy Nation.

"Woe to those who have eyes with which to see, but do not see; woe to those who have ears with which to hear, but do not hear; woe to those whose necks are stiff and whose hearts are hard; woe to those who scoff in these last days and teach others to scoff; woe to those who follow false teachers, to those who call themselves Christians but who also call themselves Catholic, Protestant, Eastern Orthodox, or anything but what God would have his chosen ones call themselves. Verily, verily, it were better for such as these that millstones be hung around their necks and that they be cast into the depths of the sea! Such was the watery fate of the wicked of God's first world, in the days of Noah; but this world, our world, even now hurtling toward destruction, has been stored up for fire, for melting elements and vehement heat."

At the point of writing, it is still unclear as to whether or not the doctrine of three-world creationism has "put to rout thousands and thousands and even hundreds of thousands of scoffers and sceptics," as Alice had expected. Satan, after all, loosens his grip on unbelieving scientists only grudgingly and offers very stout resistance to the Holy Ghost's efforts among them.

By a stroke of genius, amounting almost to a direct revelation from God, it occurred to her that those members of the Holy Nation who were also scientists might be recruited to make a public declaration of some sort, testifying to the fact that a person could be a born-again Bible-believing Christian and a tough-minded scientist at the same time. The result was a pamphlet entitled *"Scientific* Three-World Creationism." It described in simple but glowing terms the basic concepts of three-world creationism, deplored the evils perpetrated by those so-called Christians, liberal or conservative, who did not accept that inspired doctrine, and concluded with an impassioned defense of the idea that science and revelation are but two sides of God's truth. "We the undersigned," the signatories wrote, "testify that science and religion do not conflict, can not conflict, when each is understood properly."

In order of scientific prominence, the pamphlet was signed by Perry W. D. Hornbuckle (Ph.D. in biochemistry, U. of Illinois) who worked for the Abner Mott Pharmaceutical Co. of Hoboken, New Jersey; by Garner Oarsman Weems (Ph.D., U. of California, Berkeley), Research Associate at Purdue in ovoviviparology; by Klaus Gebhaardt (Ph.D., Oklahoma State), an authority on parasitic infestations of ichorous fluids in swine, connected with the Cooperative Extension Service in Mississippi; by four physicians (three of whom were in general practice, the fourth in proctology); nine oil geologists; seventeen engineers, mostly civil; six opticians; two dozen medical technologists; innumerable pharmacists; and one prominent mortician from Detroit who held the M.S. degree in geology in connection with his earlier love of paleontology.

Shortly after Manly's return to Nickel Plate, a jumble of tracts appeared on a table positioned along the rear wall of the sanctuary. The church members had long been accustomed to having Disciples of Christ literature back there, pamphlets, extra copies of Sunday school materials, several current denominational magazines, and the like, but the new tracts did not come from the Bethany Press of the Christian Board of Publication, as had the old ones, but from the Royal Priests' Press. The tracts in question bore such titles as *"Scientific* Three-World Creationism," "Salvation from the Second Earth," "Where Will *You* Be When God's Great Meltdown Comes?," "The Third Heaven and the Third Earth," *"More* About the Third Heaven and the Third Earth," "What God Wants His Chosen Ones to Call Themselves," "Why Peculiar People?," "God's New Israel," "How To Be A Royal Priest," "Miss Alice McAlister: God's Handmaiden for the Final Days," "Dr. Mordecai Montefiori: An Old Jew Made New," "From Sponge Diver to Fisher of Men: The Inspiring Story of Iskander Moutsopoulos," "Saved from the Southern Baptists: A Short Life of Emmet Langhorne Van Hook (Ph.D., Harvard)," "God's Master Builder: Clifton Marsh Cricklet," and "Rescued From Liberalism: The Saga of Endicott Peabody Dickinson." Manly's sermons grew steadily more powerful as they were increasingly peppered with references to the topics, teachings, and people of the tracts.

"Sakes alive," said Polly Stamper as she affixed the last clothespin to some bedding she was hanging out to air, "I never planned on being a Jew of any shape, size, or form."

"But don't you see, it's a spiritual teaching," replied Maude Tharp from across the back fence where she was transplanting some tomato plants.

"I still don't see any reason why perfectly good American Christian people have got to think of themselves as new Jews," Polly complained.

"Now, Polly, you mustn't forget that even St. Paul himself refers to Christians as the Israel of God in . . . ah . . . in Galatians . . . ah . . . 6: something . . . 16, I believe it is," Maude said testily.

"I suppose if I've got to be a Jew of any kind, I'd rather be a new one. The old variety never did appeal to me very much," Polly retorted, wagging her head and ending the conversation.

Kevin Kilpatrick said that it just didn't seem to make a whole lot of sense to him as he picked up his change and pocketed the small sack of machine screws he had just bought at Tharp's Hardware.

"What don't make sense?" Josh asked.

"Well, as near as I can get the picture, everything was just water at the beginning, an' then God sorta stretches the water apart in one place an' a great big air bubble forms, an' solid ground pops up outa water at the bottom of the bubble, an' that's the whole shebang, plus, of course, the sun and the moon and the stars and such as that."

"See here, Kevin, as long as it makes sense to God, that's what really matters. It's his world, and I don't see any reason to think he couldn't have made it that way. Who are we to tell him how to go about his business? In any case, that world is over and done with, and we don't have to worry our heads over it at all. It was destroyed by water like the Bible says."

"That kinda bothers me too."

"What does?"

"Well, when the flood come, it was supposed to be because the top of the bubble sprung some leaks, an' also geysers sorta popped up outa the ground, an' water rose up until it was over the tops of all the mountains."

"That seems perfectly reasonable to me. If you'd read the pamphlet called 'Scientific Three-World Creationism,' it'd explain it all to you."

"Maybe, but the thing that beats me is this: here's all this water, an' old Noah and his kin and all them animals floatin' around in the ark up over the mountain tops breathin' what was left of that air bubble, an' sometime while he's up there, the bottom kinda falls out, or the whole earth under that water just washes away so that when the ark comes down, it lands on the top of a brand new mountain that's settin' on a brand new earth that God made while there was still water all over the place, if you see what I mean."

"Sure, I see, but so what?"

"Then this big wind comes along an' all the water evaporates, an' now we got this second earth, so to say, sailin' through empty space. Why, all that space was wall to wall water just a short time before."

"The answer's so simple, Kevin, so simple! It was a miracle, that's all, or better yet, a whole string of miracles, lined up and waiting to happen when God wanted them to."

"Josh, I just don't know that I can swallow all of that."

"Look here, Kevin, you believe God can do miracles, don't you?"

"Yes, I suppose it's reasonable he can do whatever he wants to. He's all-powerful."

"You believe Jesus was conceived of a virgin by the Holy Spirit, right?"

"Oh, sure, the Holy Spirit could've done that with no trouble."

"And you believe Jesus changed water into wine and walked on the sea?"

"Yeah, I believe that all right."

"And he healed people and raised Lazarus from the dead?"

"Yes, I don't have no trouble with that."

"And, greatest of all, you believe that God raised Jesus himself from the dead on the third day miraculously, don't you?"

"Everybody believes that."

"And you believe that God is three persons in one?"

"Well, sure, but I don't pretend to understand it very well."

"And that Jesus took all our sins on himself when he died on the cross?"

"No doubt about that."

"Well, then, I just don't see why you're having so much trouble believing in the first heaven and the first earth."

"Maybe it's just 'cause the idea's kinda new to me, but it still don't seem to make too much sense."

"It makes as much sense as any of the rest of it!" Josh concluded emphatically.

While waiting at the post office for the Monday morning mail to be distributed, Moses Middleton, Stuart Acton, and Lonnie Atkins, a recent convert from Presbyterianism, fell to talking—largely for the benefit of the unsaved who also loitered in the post office awaiting their mail.

"Boy, oh boy," exulted Lonnie, adverting to Manly's two sermons on unbelief and atheism, preached the day before, "I sure wouldn't want to be that Bertram Russell feller, if Manly . . . er . . . Reverend Plumwell was ever to come face to face with him. Would he tell that guy a thing or two!"

"Oh, he'd put him in his place in short order," agreed Mose, "that Russell guy wouldn't gota word in edgewise. When Manly gets wound up, or riled, one, he's just irresistible. You talk about know the Bible, my goodness, he has a verse on the tip of his tongue for just about everything under the sun."

"And he sure gave the old Harry to whichever one of the Marx Brothers it was that wrote all that danged communist stuff," Lonnie burbled in praise.

"No, Lonnie, you're wrong there, the Marx fellow Manly was goin' after wasn't one of them brothers," said Stuart.

"Are you sure, Stu?" Lonnie asked, feeling squelched in the development of his panegyric.

"Positive. You ask Mose here, Lonnie."

"I b'lieve Stu's right, Lonnie," said Mose reflectively, not knowing anything more than that about the Marx in question.

"Well, whoever it was," said Lonnie, recovering as best he could, "Manly sure took the hide off 'im good and proper."

"Yeah, and that Darwin too, and all that unholy crew of evolutionists," said Stu.

"Stu, maybe you could clear something up for me," Lonnie said, "or you, Mose. Just what in the dickens is a modernist? It can't be just everybody that's livin' nowadays in the modern world, can it?"

184

"No," both agreed, "it ain't that."

"You want to answer him, Stu?" Mose asked.

"No, you go ahead," said Stu, who was a little uncertain himself, "and I'll help out if need be."

"Well, the best I can figure it out," said Mose, realizing that Manly hadn't been any too clear about it either, "is that modernists are a bunch of people who call themselves Christian but are really intent on rippin' up the Bible, just makin' a mockery of it in the name of higher education or something like that. Most of 'em are professors at these hifalutin schools, and I guess they're all socialists, or communists, and atheists to boot, leastways that's as best I can figure it out."

"That's about as clear as I've ever heard it put," seconded Stu.

"I just don't see why God lets such people live," mused Lonnie.

"It *is* kind of hard to understand," agreed Mose, "but God knows what he's doin', of that you can be gol-darned good and sure, and such folks as these atheists and communists and evolutionists and modernists and whatever other kinds of unbelievers there are, are goin' to get their comeuppance one day—and soon, too, unless I'm greatly mistaken."

"Oh, it'll come soon," said Stu, " 'cause the Bible says that the end is near when you see scoffers and sceptics aboundin', and loose livin', and such like."

"Heaven knows we got all of that now and more to boot," agreed Mose. "And if you ask me it goes hand in glove with all this higher education you hear so much about nowadays."

"Well, it makes me glad I'm simple," said Lonnie.

"Me too," agreed Mose.

"Simple, maybe, but saved," said Stu, smiling with deep satisfaction at the other two as he moved toward his box to remove some mail.

With their roles more or less reversed (Polly Stamper was pruning some leggy shrubs, and Maude Tharp was hanging out her wash), Polly said, "Why, I'm fifty-six years old. My life is at least two-thirds over. I have been a member of the Christian Church since I was knee-high to a grasshopper. Now, at this late date, I learn that Christians, who I had thought of as the salt of the earth, are supposed to be peculiar, that I am supposed to be a new Jew and a royal priest and I don't know what all. If God had wanted me to know all that, why didn't he tell me sooner, if it was so all-fired important? You know, I could have died and gone to my grave and never known about it."

"Now, Polly," Maude said with assurance, didactically, "you know as well as I that we didn't have any real Bible-believing preachers at the Christian Church most of the time when we went there before. Now that we do, it seems kind of strange, I admit. You have to remember, though, that Reverend Plumwell is not making up any of this. He is simply telling us what is in the Scriptures, and God put it in there, don't you forget."

The precocious eleven-year-old Koch twins, Krister and Kristin, were related to so many people in and around Nickel Plate, especially to the Hinterleiter and Waldenheimer clans, that they were called "Cousin-Brother" and "Cousin-Sister" respectively. Under Manly's tutelage they had truly become Spirit-filled and set on fire for the Lord. Fire, in fact, was on their minds much of the time, or at least the threat of fire, and they adverted to it often when picking on someone younger and weaker than they, when being picked on by someone bigger and stronger than they, or when engaged in their zealous evangelistic efforts among the heathen, including the local Presbyterians and the family's Lutheran kin out in the country.

"We're saved," they would chorus to any unsuspecting child who did not attend their church, "but you're not."

"I am so saved," the child would respond, not knowing what it was all about but not wanting to admit to any lack or defect relative to the twins.

"We have entered the strait gate," Krister would announce proudly.

"And have taken the narrow way that leads to life," Kristin would add.

"But *you* have entered at the wide gate and have taken the broad path that leads down to destruction," Krister would conclude.

"Destruction by *fire* at the hands of *Satan*," Kristin would add by way of a footnote.

"I have not!" the child would say.

"Have so."

"Have not."

"Have so."

"Have not!" voices rising with each assertion and each denial.

Or, when a potential convert would resist their evangelistic efforts and decide not to come to their Sunday school and church, they would say, "We're ready for the Lord's return, but you're not."

"Just as much as you guys," the uncomprehending potential convert would assert.

"We will be spared the flames, because we're of the elect of God," they would retort, "but you're *not*."

"Will too be spared."

"Won't."

"Will too."

"Your house will burn up and all your toys," Cousin-Brother would affirm angrily.

"And your sidewalk, and your bike, and your wagon will melt and . . . and your . . . your sod will smoulder," Cousin-Sister would add for good measure.

"And you, and your dog, and your cat will be consumed with fervent heat!" Cousin-Brother would screech.

Or, when getting the worst of it, Krister would squeal at his tormenter, "We will be avenged!"

"Yes," Kristin would yell, pounding on Krister's attacker, "we will call upon the Lord to heap burning coals upon your head!"

"And your worm will never die," Krister would hiss between howls of pain.

After an evangelistic encounter with the Koch twins, many a younger, weaker child would return home in tears, nauseated and unable to sleep. Some would have nightmares about their pets' burning up but their worms not. Others, especially boys, would go home so enraged that they couldn't eat for short periods.

Anxious parents, wondering aloud at how religion, of all things, could make such behavioral changes in their children, fretted over what to do with the young Kochs and their evangelism. Pagan parents tended to shrug off the problem easier than did the local Presbyterians. The pagan mothers would normally say, "Now just you stay away from those awful twins." The pagan fathers would opine (when their wives could not hear) that what Krister needed was a punch in the nose and that Kristin needed her little ass kicked. For their part, the Presbyterians tended to smoulder much as the sod was supposed to do according to Kristin. Some thought that their minister should have a word with the Reverend Manly Plumwell—Manly, of all people, such a good boy before he had gotten in with that gang at Big Bend. The Lutheran relatives out in the country were also ignited with righteous indignation over the Koch twins, kith and kin or no kith and kin, for the Lutherans had Moses and the Prophets, and the Lord and the Apostles, and Luther on their side and did not need religious correction from any latter-day backwoods Handmaiden of the Lord.

Said one Nickel Plater to another, "We never had anything like this religious bickering around here before that Plumwell kid came back to preach."

"Lord, no, everybody in the two churches was good friends, and even the folks that didn't go to no church was as nice and neighborly as could be."

"And you know, there's some families that's been split right down the middle by all this religious fracas—torn completely apart!"

"I wish there was some way to restore peace and harmony to the town."

"What do you suggest?"

"Beats me. It's a free country, I guess."

Indeed, what can be done about a preacher who is merely preaching what he finds in the New Testament, and what can be done about the people in the pews who take what the preacher says to heart?

Of such as the Koch twins is the Kingdom of God.

"I had always thought that I was going to go to heaven when I died," said Polly, speaking to Maude through damp sheets that obstructed their views of each other, "but now I find out that I'm going to stay right here. Of course, it's going to be a new earth, not this one, but still . . . ."

"But still what?" questioned Maude, remembering all the times she had tried to get the point across to Polly that God could make the third earth just as nice as any heaven she might have thought she was going to inhabit over on the other side.

"I had always been taught that I would hear the last trumpet and would wake up, would come up out of my grave, and would float up into the air to meet Jesus, and that all of us Christians would just keep on going until we got to the mansions of heaven up yonder."

"Now, Polly, you know as well as I do that II Peter is not the only place that talks about a new heaven and a new earth. The Book of Revelations also talks about that in chapters 21 and 22."

"I always thought that was kind of poetical-like."

"Polly, I don't know what is going to become of you if you keep on in this rancorous way. The new heaven and the new earth is a revelation of God's; otherwise it wouldn't be in the Book of Revelations, would it? Kind of poetical-like, my foot! You sound like one of those liberal modernists Reverend Plumwell is always talking about. The next thing I know, you'll start up the way Elmer Titus Pearl used to with all that talk about values that nobody understood."

Picking up the empty clothes hamper, Polly marched off saying that she had never hoped to be of those liberal whadyamacallits and that she had never before given a hang for old Pearl but that it was all sounding better to her with each passing day.

"Not going to divine services this morning, Blanche?" Dr. Benny Oesterly asked his wife in bantering tones.

"No, and not for some time again, if ever," replied Blanche, sipping from her third cup of coffee and not yet dressed properly for the Lord's day.

"I had thought for a while that you were enamored of the Reverend Mr. Plumwell," piped Benny in his high-pitched voice as he meticulously remounted a stamp in his favorite album.

"I went at first out of sheer curiosity, as you very well know."

"Yes, but you were so impressed that you went back, and quite regularly for a time, if I am not mistaken."

"I did, and that surprised me. But I went more out of fascination with the preacher than anything else."

"And at your age, too," chuckled Benny piercingly.

"Don't be a cad, Benny. The Reverend Mr. Plumwell doesn't interest me in the slightest as a man, as a potential dinner guest, as a bridge partner, or in any social way. Pray God he doesn't feel the need to pay us any pastoral visits! No, socially he's stiff, if not awkward, brittle, and oh-so-serious. It's as though the coming of the Kingdom of God depended entirely on his never letting his hair down, on never having an ordinary relaxed good time."

"I don't see why you went to church as often as you did, then."

"You could answer that by hearing him a few times yourself, Benny. He is a dazzling pulpiteer, make no mistake about that."

"Ah, no thanks, my dear," said Benny, looking up from his stamps, "that's what I have you for. Doesn't the Good Book say somewhere that an unbelieving husband can be saved by his wife?"

"Listen, old man, don't depend on me to get you past the Pearly Gates," said the much younger Blanche.

"I don't expect to pass those pearly portals myself, pious wife or no pious wife," Benny replied. "But it doesn't surprise me that young Plumwell has the gift of gab. Old Herb didn't say too much around the house, I dare say, having to contend with Marynell and all, but out with his cronies he could talk a blue streak—swear one, too, if the need arose." Whereupon Benny laughed. "Then, too, Manly's father was a pretty slick talker and a good salesman. Runs in the family, no doubt. Genes will out, you know."

"In any case, I haven't heard his equal since I left Hiram College," Blanche said, referring to the denominational school in Hiram, Ohio, where she had received her very sound undergraduate education and in the process had heard many a sermon in chapel.

"Do you want to regale me with details as I mount these new stamps?" Benny said invitingly, seizing a little package containing new acquisitions.

"The strange thing is he loses all his awkwardness, all his stiffness, when he steps into the pulpit. It's as though it were his true home."

"I can understand that," mused Benny.

"And he's good-looking—not a matinee idol or anything like that, but good-looking without being distracting, if you know what I mean."

"Can't really say I do," said Benny, becoming more interested in mounting stamps than in trying to visualize Manly Plumwell in the pulpit.

"Then, too, he always looks as though he had just stepped out of a bandbox, always fresh and clean and clothes well coordinated. Must have a good eye for color. Anyway, it's hard to take your eyes off of him in the pulpit."

"Anything else?" asked Benny, his interest clearly flagging.

"He has an excellent voice, well-controlled, a pleasure to hear, and, surprising though it may be, he uses excellent diction without being prissy."

"Can any good thing come out of Nickel Plate, huh?" queried Benny.

"It's not that bright people can't come out of places like Nickel Plate," Blanche responded, "it's just that you don't expect to hear such superior diction here in the backwoods."

"Probably had a good speech teacher at that religion school," Benny observed realistically.

"But all this," Blanche announced, "is just the *conditio sine qua non.*"

"Please, Blanche," Benny cautioned her, "remember, I'm just a country doctor, so use terms I can understand."

Ignoring Benny's attempt at humor, she continued, "You have to presuppose qualities like these just to be a candidate for pulpiteer of the order I have in mind, the order this kid has already attained."

"Well, I'll never," said Benny uninterestedly, meaninglessly.

Speaking more to herself than to him, she went on, "It's as though he were a master salesman handling the top of the line. And when in doubt, he has a guidebook that just can't go wrong. You'd think that the Almighty wrote every word in the Bible just for Manly Plumwell. As for knowing God's mind, why, he knows it better than God does."

"Get your duds on and get to church, woman," Benny shrilled in mock command. "How dare you risk not hearing a golden-throated orator like this Plumwell?"

"Because he's a fool, Benny, talented to be sure, but a fool, a damned fool, and so are the people who listen to him week by week."

"Aren't you being a little hard on him, Blanche? He's still just a boy; surely he'll learn."

"Yes, he's just a boy, but, no, he'll never learn. He has no historical sense whatsoever, and he doesn't really respect the biblical text either. He doesn't really try to find out what was meant by those who first delivered those words to those who first received them. He just roams up and down the Bible ripping out any and all verses that seem to cohere with whatever tack he happens to be on, but without any understanding of the times, places, world-views, and circumstances in which the textual materials developed. Things that are meant allegorically, he takes literally, and things that are meant literally, he twists into metaphor. When it suits him he uses reason as best he can, but he's not very logical; when it doesn't, he discards it as mere human cunning. And misrepresent, my God! how he misrepresents positions that are not his own, including the Bible's. Then he attacks his own misrepresentations hip and thigh, boldly, bravely; and those boobies in the pews think that righteousness has triumphed again."

"Sounds like a regulation fraud to me," Benny observed without indignation, "but what could anybody have expected to the contrary?"

"It's not that simple, Benny. It's not that Plumwell knows he's a bunco-artist nor that the people in the pews are innocent victims of a swindle, or anything like that. The people in the pews *want* to buy the religion-product as much as the people in the pulpits want to sell it. It's reminiscent of Voltaire's observation that if God didn't exist, we humans would have to create him. If the Plumwells of this world didn't pop up spontaneously, the people in the pews would manufacture them."

"There's an element of that kind of thing in medicine, too," said Benny with rare candor, thinking of his all-purpose nostrum, "Dr. Benny Oesterly's Remedy," and observing to himself for the hundredth time that if he hadn't marketed it, somebody else would have. It had helped a lot of people, too, if their many glowing testimonials could be believed.

Except for unbelief and the free movies that were shown downtown on Saturday nights during the summer months, there was not enough sin in Nickel Plate to occupy Manly full time. In dealing with unbelief he was doing about as much as he could. He inveighed against it twice on Sundays, gave a sermonette regularly at the Thursday night prayer meetings, taught an adult Bible class throughout the year, and instructed children in vacation Bible school during the summers. Furthermore, he regularly distributed tracts from the Royal Priests' Press along the length and breadth of Nickel Plate's diminutive business district, and, most effective of all, no doubt, he set his

190

congregation afire with evangelistic zeal. The Koch twins made up but one of a dozen or more teams assisting him in spreading God's word in and around the community. There was still unbelief in Nickel Plate, to be sure, but not because the people there had not heard of God's word and will for their lives. Thus, pagan Nickel Platers had no excuse for their unbelief, nor could the Presbyterians continue to plead ignorance of the true gospel.

The free movies were a very different, even if only a seasonal, problem. The merchants of Nickel Plate, including Josh Tharp and several other members of the church, had for several years sponsored the free movies (projected onto the side of a brick building standing alone and painted white) so as to attract people to town in the hope of drumming up business on Saturday nights.

On the good side, the free movies really did stimulate business, thus enlarging the tithes and offerings of the church's merchant-members. They also attracted large aggregations of people, which facilitated the wide distribution of tracts, and it could be argued that the movies, questionable as they might be, kept many impressionable youths from being attracted to even less desirable places, events, or activities.

The movies were almost always western or crime-buster in type, old (having been produced in the 1930s), and straightforward. Right was portrayed as right, wrong as wrong, and right invariably triumphed. When mentioned at all, religion was mentioned with respect. It did, however, bother Manly to learn (he himself did not exactly attend the movies but could not help looking up now and again on those occasions when he passed out tracts) that Catholic priests always seemed to be portrayed more sympathetically than did Protestant ministers. Even a rabbi came off looking better than a preacher in one gang-buster picture.

Then, too, the murders and mayhem in the movies could, if viewed from the proper perspective, be used as object lessons. The deceit, drunkenness, and greed portrayed therein could, with divine help, be useful in illustrating how original was man's sin, how universal its influence. In the cases of those who had richly deserved it, execution, whether carried out legally or as the result of bushwhacking, might have a sobering effect, Manly hoped, on the viewers, especially on the young ones.

The greatest threats posed by the free movies, of course, involved the sins of impurity, of sensuality. Generally, such sins were only suggested, but sometimes they were recommended, it seemed, and on a few occasions were shamelessly depicted, or so Manly had heard. Would that he had seen just how brazen those few episodes had been! he thought, wondering what other people found attractive in such depictions of carnality.

With hard-core sin at low ebb in Nickel Plate, with the community about as evangelized, proselytized, and polarized as it could be, and with the need to extend his influence farther afield for JEsus' sake (Manly had commenced to lay heavy stress on the first syllable of the savior's name), he looked toward Dewmaker as the field whitest for harvest.

191

Dewmaker, a scant two miles to the south, was Nickel Plate's twin town. Physically, each was the mirror image of the other, being equally populous, give or take a few souls, and composed of similar kinds of people, socially and economically. But the moral and spiritual climate in Dewmaker was deplorable. Except for two families whom Manly had converted, there was not a single three-world creationist in the whole town. The largest church was Irish Catholic. How they were said to pack away the beer and ale, to say nothing of whiskey! The second largest church was Methodist, its congregation spiritless and heretical, even if teetotaling. The smallest church was a minuscule Episcopal congregation whose members were popish (it was rumored) and were given to tippling very hard spirits, as was known by all. Worse than that, Dewmaker had not one but two beer gardens, except for which the town would have been depopulated on Saturday nights during the summer months when Nickel Plate's free movies were in full cry. Then, during Manly's third summer back home, a new outrage was perpetrated in Dewmaker. The town hall was made available to young people for dancing— mixed dancing, round dancing!

With the blessing of the church board and the aid of several strapping lads in his youth group, Manly decided to serve JEsus by making a hit on the already infamous Dewmaker dance hall. On the Sunday morning before the hit, he preached a powerful sermon in which, using a sophisticated combination of science and Scripture, he fixed the exact location of hell. Of course, its position had already been demonstrated to him and to his fellow students at Big Bend by none other than Bro. Emmet Langhorne Van Hook (Ph.D., Harvard), but Manly did not mention that point, leaving it to his flock to suppose that it was he, Manly John Plumwell, who had first located the infernosphere precisely. Here, in part, is what he said:

"Hear the words of JEsus, how he said in Matthew 18:8-9, 'Wherefore if thy hand or thy foot offend thee, cut them off, and cast *them* from thee: it is better for thee to enter into life halt or maimed, rather than having two hands or two feet to be cast into everlasting fire. And if thine eye offend thee, pluck it out and cast *it* from thee: it is better for thee to enter into life with one eye, rather than having two eyes to be cast into hell fire.' There can be no doubt then, chosen friends, that hell is fiery, for JEsus himself says so. Also, in the Book of Revelation 20:1-3, John, who received his revelation from God, says, 'And I saw an angel come down from heaven, having the key of the bottomless pit and a great chain in his hand. And he laid hold on the dragon, that old serpent which is the Devil and Satan, and bound him a thousand years, and cast him into the bottomless pit . . . .' And so, we have two conditions for hell, well attested to in these and other passages of Scripture. Hell is fiery. Hell is bottomless.

"Now, you might think of 'bottomless' in the sense of a tub with no bottom, or a pail, or a tank of some kind. But that would be a mistake. You might also think of 'bottomless' in the sense of a shaft having an entrance but no end, a shaft infinitely long. But that too would be a mistake. Look about you, look anywhere, and you will find no infinite shaft in God's world.

"Chosen friends, how privileged we are to be living in this modern age of science, for science, properly understood, daily confirms the truths of God. What do astronomers tell us our earth, *the second earth*, is like? Why, the second earth is like a great ball afloat in the oceans of space. Other kinds of scientists, the ones we call 'geologists,' tell us that if a person goes down into the earth far enough, the temperature of the rock increases, and at a steady rate. If memory serves me correctly, at a mile down the temperature is 90°F, but at two miles down, 120°F, and so on, hotter and hotter the deeper one goes until one reaches the very center of the earth itself.

"Now just suppose, chosen friends, that you were at the very center of the earth, and suppose that you wished to go somewhere from there. Why, any way that you chose to go would take you up, up, up toward the surface of our round earth. Don't you see, chosen ones, that if you could only go up, *and could not go down*, no matter how hard you tried, you would be in a place with no bottom, a bottomless place and a fiery place, infernally hot, the very conditions that must be met, according to the Bible, for a place to be hell. Yes, hell is the very center of the earth."

Then, so as to bring hell much closer to home for his own purposes, Manly said in his most humble-but-know-it-all tone of voice, "The Scriptures do not expressly say so, but in my opinion, hell has its outposts, outposts that are not exactly in the center of the earth, but that are connected with it, of course. One of those outposts is very close to us, I fear. Where? you wonder. If you were to draw an imaginary triangle connecting the dance hall and the two beer gardens in downtown Dewmaker and were then to dig down into the earth anywhere inside that triangle, I am sure you would reach a fiery outpost of hell. In my view, chosen friends, that brings hell much, much too close to home for comfort. Would that we might drive it farther from us! Please join me in praying that, if it is God's will, this might be done."

The hit on hell's outpost in Dewmaker began inconspicuously. Just before 6:00 P.M. on the targeted Saturday, Manly drove south from Nickel Plate, ascended a tree-covered moraine, and coasted down into the natural partial amphitheater in which Dewmaker lay. Once on Main Street, he headed straight for the village hall, a yellow-brick building with a facade of russet sandstone, and parked directly in front of it. Then, leaving the car, he walked eight blocks to the Amos Burdick home where he was to take supper by prearrangement.

Although Manly did not bolt his food, Mrs. Burdick had scarcely cleaned the table of dessert plates and coffee cups before he began to excuse himself, saying "thank-you" to her and "good-bye" all around. Furthermore, he walked the eight blocks to the village hall much faster than necessary, for when he slipped behind the wheel of the old Nash to observe the goings-on for a time, the building was still locked. Presently, a man with "village employee" written all over him sauntered up and unlocked the front double doors on either side of the building, went inside, and switched on various lights. Then came two teen-age boys lugging a phonograph too large to be a portable, followed by a girl struggling with a topless cardboard box jammed with a motley batch of old 78-records. It was 8:15. The dance usually got under way by 8:30, according to Manly's information.

During the intervening fifteen minutes, kids from twelve to twenty or thereabouts began arriving from all directions. A few came alone. Most came in couples, boy with girl; but some came in pairs, boy with boy and girl with girl; and not a few came in loosely knit groups, odd as well as even in number. The kids were noisy but not rowdy, merry, to be sure, but not high, and were well behaved. Some of the girls wore dresses, but most were casually attired in blouses and jeans, matching the way the boys had dressed in shirts, open at the neck, and jeans or slacks. None of the kids were what Manly considered dressed up. The whole scene spoke of a relaxed good time and promised nothing more than some rugs well cut.

Into the hall went the young people, hailing friends, yelling smart sayings or harmless taunts at each other. Out again they came, looking for tardy friends or partners temporarily lost in the crowd. Across the street they went to a drugstore; back again they came with pop and popsicles, Eskimo Pies and popcorn. They formed into knots; the knots came undone and trailed off, were re-tied, and trailed off again. Some kisses were lightly planted on lips and cheeks. There were some hugs. A few ribs were poked or tickled. Here and there, boys threw playful punches at each other or entered into mock combat over girls laughing at the attention being showered on them.

Street lights came on, and the interior of the hall began to glow brightly against the deepening dusk. Through one set of double doors, Manly could see some young people swirling in each other's arms to music that he did not recognize. Was it boogie-woogie or the big band sound or "Turkey in the Straw"? He did not know and did not care, having studiedly avoided such machinations of the devil as dance music, of whatever kind. In any case, the dance was under way; the time for the hit, less than half an hour away.

He who has made himself a eunuch for the sake of the kingdom of heaven will, if he is still young and healthy, have serious difficulty remaining an unmoved onlooker as youthful dancers hold each other tightly, flirt, tease, and kiss. Manly knew that it would be a time of testing for him, that he would have to gird up his loins against the devil's assaults on that very part of his body. But, on guard though he was, being fortified with prayer and pure intentions, he was in no way prepared for the tigress who suddenly strode into view, seizing his attention and monopolizing it. Who was she? Where had she come from? What was her name? How could he reach out to her? She was a motherless young woman of nineteen who lived with her father and her two older brothers. She came from a farm twenty miles south of Dewmaker. Her name was Tampa Rhine. Neither then nor later could he reach out to her in the sense he had in mind initially.

With every step she seemed intent on reaching a preselected spot, yet

194

before arriving at that spot, she appeared to change her mind and select another. To and fro she went on the sidewalk in front of Manly, first to the west, then the east, then north across Main Street and back, then into the village hall and out again, then to and fro some more. As she moved in her decisive, yet random, manner, her hair, swept up and flowing back from her forehead, seemed to form tongues of black flame driven by a gale. Merely by being present, merely by living and moving, her body seemed to declare, "I am elemental woman; I am untamed; I am flesh and blood, but too feral to be ensouled."

Perhaps she was beautiful, perhaps not. With piercing brown eyes, deeply set, with her brows in a (perpetual?) frown, and the corners of her mouth drawn down, who could tell? Perhaps she was truly statuesque (she was, in fact, five feet, eleven inches in her stocking feet), but with her shoulders hunched forward a bit, her sinewy arms slightly akimbo, and her whole body tensed as though she were about to spring, it was hard to say. Manly thought that her figure might have been magnificent, given elegant clothing, but her purplish plaid blouse, faded jeans, and heavy shoes spoke to that point ambiguously at best.

Whatever the case, the stunning effect she had on him was heightened by the girl who accompanied her, a girl so nondescript that to have called her mousie would have been to overstate the case. Manly did not wonder about that girl's name (it was Eloise Creel), nor did he remember a thing about her except that she wore a dress and that everywhere *the* girl (Tampa Rhine) went, the lamb was sure to go, but always half a step behind.

So entranced was he by the dominating member of the pair that he did not notice Lonnie Atkins' station wagon (with the loudspeaker recently installed on its roof) pass by. On its second pass, he saw it inching toward him from the west but was not ready to act. By the time it had circled the block and returned, he was ready. Gauging the flow of traffic well, he backed out and drove off, leaving the station wagon to park in the space just vacated. He proceeded several blocks to the east, found a parking space, jumped out, and set off as briskly as his dignified role in life allowed. Five minutes later, he slid onto the front seat of the station wagon on the passenger side, thus joining three pious boys from his youth group, each of whom was big and strong.

Applause and the babble of voices coming from inside the hall indicated that a record had just been played through and that it would have to be flipped over or replaced. Within a few seconds the strains of Glenn Miller's "String of Pearls" wafted out of the hall, and the dancers went at it again, holding each other tightly.

Suddenly, the deep-throated sound of bells burst through the front door of the hall and seemed to settle from the ceiling. Dancers close to the phonograph or near the back of the hall were not so quick to recognize that something was amiss as were those who went swirling by the front doors. One boy, whose head was set to ringing by bells, cried out, "What in holy hell is that?" Another boy, his sense of rhythm utterly ruined, yelled, "What the fuck is up?" and embarrassed his very ladylike date. "Jesus God," murmured a girl, more aptly than she realized. Some of the more superstitious dancers thought for a moment that their sins had found them out and that their souls might be required of them that very night.

As the unnerved dancers stopped dancing and crowded toward the front of the hall to discover what was happening, they saw a station wagon, alien to Dewmaker, with a loudspeaker on its roof. From that loudspeaker, pointed straight at the village hall, came the hymn "Holy, Holy, Holy, Lord God Almighty" arranged for carillon performances. Inside the wagon sat a grimaced young man dressed in a dark suit, white shirt, and tie. Beside and behind him sat two big boys, recognized by some as Nickel Platers. Another big boy sat far back in the wagon overseeing a turntable and various electronic components.

The social chemistry might have been explosive that night but was not. Instead of pelting the station wagon with pop bottles or rocking it furiously or ripping out the wire to its loudspeaker, the dancers brought their phonograph out onto the sidewalk in front of the hall, plugged it into a socket in the foyer, turned the volume up as high as it would go, put on record after record, and entered into a spirited competition with Manly's hymns of praise and songs of salvation. Since the Lord's loudspeaker was much more powerful than the kids' phonograph, they resorted to clapping in rhythm to their music, and many began to sing along at the top of their lungs, thus augmenting the devil's tunes. But in terms of sheer volume, the forces of righteousness had the better of it.

Before long, some of the local clowns began to caper around and around in every available spot, pretending to dance to "My Blue Heaven" and "When the Roll is Called Up Yonder" simultaneously. Others quickly followed suit. By the time "What a Friend We Have in Jesus" began vying with Jelly Roll Morton's "Winnin' Boy Blue," a full half of Dewmaker's youth appeared to have St. Vitus's dance. The Lord's name was taken in vain more that night than during several months of normal dancing in Dewmaker. One girl, with a look of profound disdain on her face, turned her rear toward Manly and wiggled it audaciously. Numerous up-your-ass gestures were displayed for his benefit (and to his mortification), and the terms "fuck you" and "screw you" could occasionally be heard above the din. Even when they couldn't be heard, elementary lip reading sufficed.

By the time "All Hail the Power of Jesus' Name" was set against the "Maple Leaf Rag," every store in downtown Dewmaker was emptied of patrons and proprietors, except those that carried items of carnival fare. Even the beer gardens were emptied, except for the inveterate drinkers, as bartenders and casual drinkers alike stood outside in open-mouthed wonder at the goings-on.

How the news that hell was poppin' in downtown Dewmaker reached the free-moviegoers in Nickel Plate is anybody's guess, but it did, and that, coupled with the fact that the movie was the dullest of the season, emptied

Nickel Plate in short order, first to the amazement of its merchants, then to their chagrin. By two, by three, then by the dozen, and finally by the score, automobile engines could be heard starting. Then, out of Nickel Plate people roared, heading south in an unbroken line to find they knew not what.

Once in downtown Dewmaker, there was nothing for the lead car to do but to circle several blocks and try to follow the last car to arrive, thus making an endless procession of cars. Not everybody understood what was happening at the village hall, nor was everybody's ear good enough to disentangle "I'm Always Chasing Rainbows" and "Nearer My God To Thee," but whatever was going on was vaguely musical and very loud. Hoping to enter into the spirit of the brouhaha, some drivers began to honk their horns. Soon a majority of drivers joined in, especially when passing the village hall. Moreover, many passengers as well as drivers lifted their voices in whoops as if to cheer contestants on, and some emitted raspberries. With "Dipsy Doodle" set against "Onward Christian Soldiers (arranged for organ and trumpets)," with nearly a hundred automobile horns blaring anarchically, with coordinated clapping and uncoordinated yells, whistles, and raspberries rending the night, Dewmaker settled in for a seige of cacophony unparalleled in the annals of Pilsudski County.

So peaceful was the eastern part of that county where Nickel Plate and Dewmaker nestled, so crime-free was it, that the people in the two towns and in the countryside for miles around had but one deputy sheriff to police them. At the time of the exodus from the free movie, Mr. Clay Thurber, the deputy in question, was talking with Josh Tharp, the latter being totally innocent of any complicity in keeping him occupied. It just happened to be Clay's Saturday night to show the badge in Nickel Plate. He and Josh were swapping fish stories when the sound of many motors being started reached their ears.

"What in the Sam Hill?" said Clay.

"Beats me," replied Josh, observing that it was too early for the movie to be over.

Since there was nothing illegal about people leaving a free movie in droves, Clay adverted to a nice mess of bluegills he had caught recently. But the din of departure, followed by unearthly calm, broken only by the free movie playing to itself, nagged at his professional conscience. "I just have a sneaky feelin' I'd better go have a look-see," he said.

"Sure thing," Josh agreed, inviting him back whenever he wanted to "chew the fat" again.

With his ears guiding him, it didn't take Clay long to find his way to Dewmaker, but once there, what was he to do? An endless line of cars was circling the downtown area bumper to bumper as best as he could fathom the spectacle, and a "god-awful racket," as he put it later, was coming from the heart of town. Since nobody in the procession paid the slightest attention to his flashing blue light, and since his siren could not be heard above the din, he parked his official car and set off on foot, still mystified.

By the time he reached the center of the tumult, the bells of "Holy, Holy,

Holy, Lord God Almighty" were being pitted against the "Beer Barrel Polka," and everybody seemed to be having a rousing good time—everybody, that is, except for the wretched occupants of the station wagon parked in front of the village hall. The biggest complaint reaching Clay was that supplies of certain types were running dangerously low. Those who popped corn could not keep up with demand, and Dewmaker had been licked clean of Eskimo Pies and popsicles of every kind. Soft drinks were in very short supply, and ice for fountain drinks was running low. Merchants who had remembered to haul out noisemakers left over from the previous New Year's and Halloween celebrations were jubilant, however, having sold every item.

Even after Clay had gained reasonably accurate information as to the sequence of events, he was loath to act, so great was his respect for religion, so great was every citizen's belief in the right of a minister and his youth group to play sacred songs and melodies. But, despite the absence of complaints, the peace was being broken. So, Clay ambled up to Manly's side of the station wagon and said, "Evenin', Reverend."

A weak "hello" was the best Manly could manage.

"I don't expect there's much more good you can accomplish here tonight," Clay observed gently.

"No," said the voice of defeat.

"If you'd like to leave, maybe I could help squeeze you through all this traffic and see you on your way to Nickel Plate," Clay offered.

With real relief, Manly said, "Please do," to him, but with real agony he said to himself, "My God, my God, why hast thou forsaken me?"

No amount of praying on bended knees by his bedside could make Manly feel better that night, nor could he fall easily into the salvation of sleep, so fast and furiously did his mind race from one bitter thought to another.

After an epoch of tossing and turning, *she* sprang at him, not the visitor (long since worn out by fantasy) whom he had helped at the fair, not Persephone Moutsopoulos, not any of the brides whose wedding nights he had shared, but the astonishing one, the singular one, whom he had seen on the prowl earlier that night. He wished very much to pray for her. He would pray for her. She needed his prayers even if she did not know it. He knew (how he knew he did not know, but he knew) that she was in mortal danger of carnality. He feared that she would succumb to seduction and hoped desperately that it would not be so. Why had he converted the energy that pulsed from her every pore into the single force of sexuality? He did not know. Why had he associated the wild vitality of her being with sexual voracity alone? He did not know, but he did not feel guilty over having done it. To him, she was sexuality incarnate, and that imperiled her soul. That was why she needed his prayers, and she would have them.

Would that he knew her identity! Would that he dared ask someone, anyone about her! (But that, of course, he could not do.) Would that he could go to her! (But how, where?) Would that he could reach out to her, could touch her, could tell her that she had a soul, that it was her most priceless possession, that it could be saved unto eternal life.

He saw her down on her knees. Had she learned the awful fact of sin? Had its weight driven her down? Had contrition paralyzed her in that remorseful posture? To those questions he had no answers, nor did he need any, for he had come in time, had found her as JEsus had found the lost sheep. Lovingly (was it with Christian love alone?) he reached out to her, brushing a strand of hair from her forehead, just to have an excuse to touch her. As he did so, he told her of God's wondrous love (and enjoyed the sight of her), told her of how JEsus had died on the cross for her (how alluring she looked on her knees!), told her of how he, Manly Plumwell, was a minister of the gospel come to share the good news of salvation with her (how she would thank him!), and told her of how they could be together in God's Holy Nation then and there and how, after death, they could inhabit the new heaven and the new earth, world without end. Bidding her to rise from her knees and extending his hands to her, he helped her to her feet. Gone were the hunched shoulders, as she stood before him, gone the arms held akimbo, gone was the intensity of the hunt that had driven her to and fro in Dewmaker on dance night. Facing him, her eyes level with his and alive with hope, the lines of her face softened with relief (or, was it love?), she laid her strong hands on his arms, smiled a half-smile, and was gone. He could not bring her back then, nor did he wish to, for with her strong hands sleep had seized him.

Manly was not the only one who could not fall asleep easily that night. Exhausted though they were, Mr. and Mrs. Earl Spaulding also had trouble, and so, too, did Letitia Davenport, but in her case the difficulty came more from embarrassment than from the monstrous racket that rose out of downtown Dewmaker and settled over the whole hamlet, stabbing ears and assaulting sensibilities.

Letitia Davenport was a widow of sixty-seven years at the time when the outpost of heaven in Nickel Plate sent forth mighty men of valor to smite the outpost of hell in Dewmaker. Upon being widowed, five years earlier, she left Buffalo, where she and her husband had been in business, and returned to her ancestral home, a twelve-room house of carpenter Gothic set on an acre of land overlooking downtown Dewmaker.

Her dear friends, Earl and Beth Spaulding of Buffalo, had at last responded affirmatively to her frequent entreaties to visit her. She had tried to make the visit more alluring by remarking on how very noisy city life was with all the traffic and factories and jangling activities. In contrast to the hurlyburly of Buffalo, she had praised the pastoral calm of Dewmaker, "whose evening stillness is broken only by the falling of flower petals and the parachuting of dandelion seeds," as she put it in the most euphuistic of her letters.

A compulsive driver once he was on the road and no lover of motels or of unnecessary expense, Earl rolled Beth out of bed at 4:30 A.M., EDT, for the 500-mile drive to Dewmaker. Although they arrived in good time for Letitia's delicious dinner at 6:30 P.M., CDT, it was clear that they were spent, being as old as she and less robust. By 8:30 (which was 9:30 their time, she remembered), she began to urge her yawning guests to retire and soon led them, acquiescing easily, up an ornately carved open staircase to the spacious guest room at the front of the house, the room that adjoined the porch overlooking downtown Dewmaker.

Not yet sleepy herself, Letitia tended to a few things that needed tending to, laid out a fresh tablecloth for breakfast, and sat down to read the *Pilsudski Clarion-Crier*. Then came the sound of mighty bells ringing out "Holy, Holy, Holy, Lord God Almighty." Dropping her paper in disbelief that such a sound should be heard on a Saturday night, Letitia stepped out onto the front porch only to hear answering sounds mingling with the pealing hymn in a most disconcerting manner. In due time, of course, the blare of many car horns was added to the distressing serenade. As the original din became a monstrous racket and then transcended itself into quintessential pandemonium, Letitia nearly swooned with shame, her face red and her conscience stricken. What would the Spauldings think? What had she done to these good people, the friends of many years? How could she face them in the morning or, for that matter, ever again?

After a night of fitful sleep, she arose early and tried unsuccessfully to work off her anxiety with busy work. After doing every conceivable thing she could toward getting breakfast in the absence of those who were to eat it, she began pacing around the house, wringing her hands and rehearsing apologies. When, at last, she heard the Spauldings creaking their way down the staircase, she went to meet them as bravely as she could, but with dread in her heart and a dozen apologies on her lips. Having done some rehearsing themselves, the Spauldings descended the stairs arm in arm.

"And what was it we heard last night?" asked Earl.

"Was it the sound of flower petals falling?" asked Beth.

"Or was it the sound of dandelion seeds parachuting?" asked Earl.

"Or both?" both inquired.

Then three old friends shared an uproarious laugh.

"It was worth the whole trip just to hear whatever that was in your town of pastoral quiet," observed Earl, his eyes watering with mirth.

"I simply can't wait to get back to Buffalo to tell certain people," said Beth in gleeful anticipation as she named the names of mutual friends.

Relieved that her dread had been unfounded and not very worried about becoming the butt of jokes in Buffalo, Letitia made a sumptuous breakfast.

Over their second and third cups of coffee, she told the Spauldings what she had learned (over the phone the previous night) about the commotion.

Letitia Davenport was an Episcopalian, "neither high nor low, broad nor narrow, but right in the middle where all decent, rational, well-balanced people ought to be," as she put it. Wherever that placed her on the total Christian spectrum, it was clear to the Spauldings that her charity stopped short of "that awful Plumwell person." "It's just a shame," she said, making a bad face, "the Christian Church over in Nickel Plate was such a pretty old church, and now they've gone and painted it yellow and trimmed it in purple and had some famous architect in to spruce up the inside. The Disciples were such nice people, too, so neighborly, but now they've become just a bunch of fanatics like the Southern Baptists, or the Nazarenes, or the Jehovah's Witnesses, and others of that caliber. Why, they think they're the only ones that are going to make it to heaven. Everybody else is wrong and going to hell, according to them. If anything, they are more hateful toward other Christians than they are toward the unchurched."

"There's a lot of that kind of nonsense infesting the country nowadays," said Earl, who was a Mason (and therefore a theist) but not a churchman.

"Of course, in his way, I suppose that Plumwell's done great things," Letitia said grudgingly, "because he's more than doubled the membership and has the whole lot of them going to church every time the doors are opened, and that's often. According to a Presbyterian friend of mine—whose family has been split right down the middle by religion of all things—the members of Plumwell's congregation are giving their money to the church like it was going out of style. They've even bought a church bus so they can haul people in from the country, mostly children. And that's worrisome, too, because from what I hear, they believe in some pretty weird things and are just indoctrinating those innocent children with it."

"But that's what religion does," said Earl evenly. "It provides children with authorized answers to questions they hadn't even thought of asking yet and teaches them all about the supernatural before they are old enough to understand the natural order of things. Of course, if you don't get the kids before they can think for themselves, you don't get them at all, I guess, or at least not so many of them."

If Letitia thought that Earl's opinions applied to Anglicanism, she did not let on.

"Just what religious group are we talking about?" asked Beth, wondering what the Disciples in the Christian Church over in Nickel Plate had become.

"Oh, mercy me," said Letitia, rolling her eyes heavenward, "I don't know what they call themselves now; the Holy Association or something like that . . . "

"My God!" said Earl animatedly and breaking in, "you don't mean the Holy Nation Association of Churches of the Chosen, do you?"

"Why, yes, yes, I believe that is it," said Letitia reflectively.

"The ones that have this backwoods handmaiden?" asked Beth.

"Now that you mention it, I believe they are supposed to have some latter-day prophetess—Alice somebody, as I recall."

"I had always thought of the Disciples as a fairly moderate, reasonably well-educated group," mused Beth, wondering how a congregation of such people could be taken over by the Holy Nation.

"Well, except for three or four of the old, old families, including Polly Stamper's, I believe they've all swallowed it hook, line, and sinker," said Letitia, "and, of course, that Plumwell person himself was baptized into the

Disciples Church as a boy, and now he's no better than a Trojan Horse for that Holy Nation bunch."

"Listen, Letitia, let me tell you a little story," said Earl. "I have a friend at the office who went to a picnic some time back. It was hot and sticky, and the bugs were simply unbearable. Well, as he was standing there with a plate full of food, he heard somebody—a person he didn't know—say what sounded like, 'Those accursed Egyptians!' At first he thought he must have heard wrong, but no, a little while later this person says, 'Those wretched Egyptians!' My friend said he knew there were lots of kinds of prejudice in the world but that he had never heard anybody before get so fired up over Egyptians of all people. So he said, 'Pardon me,' and asked, 'Did I hear you mention the Egyptians?' Just then the guy swatted at some gnats or whatever and said, 'Yes, you heard right.' Well, to make a long story short, the enemy of the Egyptians was a member of this nutty Holy Nation sect. It seems that they believe that all insects, creeping and crawling things, were destroyed in the flood which ended the first heaven and the first earth in the days of Noah and that there weren't any bugs at all on what they call the *second* earth, the one we're supposed to be on, until Pharaoh refused to let the Jews leave the country. To make Pharaoh change his mind, God was supposed to have sent a batch of plagues, if you remember your Bible stories. In any case, that's where flies, gnats, and mosquitoes are supposed to have originated. If it hadn't been for Pharaoh and the Egyptians, we wouldn't have bugs at our picnics. My friend kept a straight face at the time, but now when he wants to have some fun with unsuspecting friends, he waits until the bugs are thicker than spatter and then sort of yells, 'Oh, those accursed Egyptians!' or 'A botch on all Egyptians!' He's gotten many a laugh out of it." Again, the three old friends laughed in unison, but not so long or so loudly as they had earlier at the foot of the stairs.

Collecting herself, Letitia, who knew the *Book of Common Prayer* far better than the Bible, said that she just did not see how people could believe such things.

Earl observed that not only could people believe such things, and all too easily, but that people had suffered and died for ideas no better than that second earth stuff and the origin of bugs in Egypt.

Beth said that folks used to believe that there was a fool born every minute but that with the birth rate what it had become, there must surely be one or more fools being born every second.

Whatever the rate of such births, one of the "fools" in question was seething at that very moment. Manly had not taken the events of the previous night in good grace, nor had he put them behind him. Anger consumed him, justifiable anger, to be sure, but anger nonetheless. He could no more doubt the rightness of his action at Dewmaker's dance hall than he could believe that God would look down from on high with favor at sensual dancing, casual kissing, not-so-inadvertent breast bumping, and loose talking, to say nothing of the profanities, in word and deed, that had been heaped on him, a minister of the gospel, and on his pious assistants.

JEsus had clearly said in John's gospel (14:13-14), "And whatsoever ye shall ask in my name, that will I do, that the Father may be glorified in the Son. If ye shall ask anything in my name, I will do *it*." The whole congregation of God's Chosen in Nickel Plate had prayed twice on the Sunday before the hit and once on the Thursday night preceding it that a nearby outpost of hell might be driven back from their midst, and they had asked that it might be done in JEsus' name and for his sake. They had not asked the impossible of the Almighty One. They had not asked him to do away with the beer gardens in Dewmaker. They had neither tempted nor tried him with anything of that magnitude. They had merely asked his help in throwing a lifeline to the devil-deceived youth at the Dewmaker dance hall lest evil claim them altogether. In beseeching God as they had, the peculiar people had sought neither personal gain nor privilege through their prayers. They had sought nothing petty, nothing ignoble. On the contrary, they had merely had the high-minded goal of cleaning up a certain moral cesspool in a neighboring town. Their prayers and actions were not aimed against the people in that town but were for them, that they too might put their minds on higher things.

If God had not yet answered their prayers concerning the dance hall in Dewmaker, Manly did not know what to do beyond waiting; but waiting how long? Certainly he had no stomach for making a second hit on the wretched place and would need to have a very straight directive from the Holy One of New Israel before he could face that prospect again. If God had already answered his (and his congregation's) prayers concerning the dance hall, then the answer was not so straightforward as the request had been, for the dancers had not fallen to their knees in tearful repentance, seeking forgiveness. Was there, then, some overriding factor, some lurking sin in his life or in the corporate life of his congregation, that had forced the Omnipotent One to refrain from answering in the straightforward way desired? If so, and if God had already answered their prayers, but obliquely, then what was his answer, how could it be found out, and what must they learn from it?

Those questions and more, too, Manly took up in his hastily revised sermon that morning. When, upon arising, he had tried to think through the debacle of the previous night and all the considerations it raised, he had felt frustration compound his anger and confusion burden his already heavy heart. It was plain for all to see that he had arrived at church with his spirit cast down. But once he was launched into his sermon, his own words heartened him (by God's grace, of course), and his confusion was parted even as the Red Sea had made way for the Children of Old Israel on their march to the promised land.

"Can God be doubted?" he asked, looking stern.

"No," he answered, striking the pulpit.

"Does he use his word to deceive his chosen ones?" he asked, making a peak of his eyebrows.

"Certainly not," he replied, smiling.

"Does not JEsus say that he will do whatsoever those who believe in him ask in his name?

"He does.

"And did we not ask in his name that he should help us drive sin from our neighboring town?

"We did.

"Why, then, was God silent last night? Why did he not act? Why did not a single young sinner come forth in repentance? Why does Dewmaker remain as much an outpost of hell as ever?

"The sceptic would say [Manly warned them, wagging a forefinger] that God does not hear prayer; or that hearing, cannot act; or that he does not care to uphold righteousness; or, worst of all, that there is no God."

A hush of horror fell over the congregation at the mere mention that there might be no God.

"Be not deceived, chosen friends," Manly said, pulling them back from the abyss of God's nonbeing, "God is. He cares, he hears, he answers, and he will not suffer Satan to triumph in the end.

" 'Why, then, did he not answer our sincere prayers for Dewmaker and show forth his mighty power in a straightforward way?' you ask.

"Well, sometimes he *delays* his answers to test the faith of those who call upon him, or, simply, to do his pleasure in his own good time. God will not permit himself to be put under a timetable in answering prayers. Who are we to force him to act at our pleasure rather than at his?

"Other times he *refuses* to answer, because what we have asked for is not really in the spirit of JEsus, even though asked in his name.

"And, on still other occasions, God *cannot* answer, because we have asked for something he knows to be sinful, even though we may not. It would be against his nature to answer sinful prayers. That would be something he could not do, even if he wanted to.

"Most often, perhaps, he refuses to answer so that he may punish and correct those who have called upon him, punish and correct them for their sins—sins of omission as well as sins of commission.

"After much prayer and soul-searching, I am convinced that that is why he did not act last night."

Following a dramatic pause, which caused his parishioners to feel increasingly uneasy, he said, "I take the blame for our failure in Dewmaker on myself, yes, all of it on myself."

Although none had been inclined to blame him, thinking him courageous to have done what he did in Dewmaker, they were relieved that he had taken the full responsibility. It exonerated them and heartened them too, for it showed what a big man they had leading them. It was hardly a secret that Manly had been deeply wounded by the Dewmaker debacle. But there he was, less than a full day later, taking all the blame on himself and triumphing over his pain.

Then and there he ended his sermon with an unrehearsed prayer: "O God, let thy servant be despitefully used that he may learn patience; let him be despitefully used that he may walk with a more tranquil step the tightrope which is strung between hatred of sin and love for the sinner; let him be despitefully used that through ministrations to him, when his spirit is cast down, thy matchless grace may shine forth to all thy chosen ones of the Holy Nation here in Nickel Plate. Thy servant asks these things in the name of JEsus and for his sake, that thou, Father, mightst be glorified in thy Son."

During his remaining days in Nickel Plate, Manly *was* despitefully used, and on numerous occasions. God answered that part of his prayer in a very straightforward way, but the rest of it was answered even more obliquely than were his many prayers concerning the sinkhole of sin in Dewmaker, where, if anything, dancing seemed to have increased in popularity.

Alice did not believe in Santa Claus, nor did the Five, nor anyone trained at Big Bend. Thus, holding fast to the word of God alone, the leadership of the Holy Nation was united in opposition to all mythology, including that which had grown up in the United States, around the so-called secular side of Christmas (as though there could be a secular side to the incarnation of the Second Person of the Trinity through the agency of the Holy Ghost and the vehicle of the compliant virgin!). Yet, no sooner was Halloween over than the blasphemous charade was cranked up annually. With well-nigh omnipotent commercial interests assuming the fertilizing role of the Holy Ghost and the great American public taking the part of the compliant but not-so-virgin mother, a secular bastard was born that threatened to replace the one whose birthday Christmas really was. No longer did the Star of Bethlehem outshine the luminaries of the night. It was being eclipsed by the blinking red nose of a juvenile reindeer named Rudolph. Bethlehem was losing out to the North Pole as the place of keenest geographical interest to children. The sands of Palestine had already given way to the snows of North America, palms to pines, camels to reindeer (of the older variety, having nonluminous noses); and the benign visage of the First Person, about to give his only begotten Son, was put into deep shade by the jolly white-whiskery face of Santa together with his innumerable helpers all dolled up in identical, highly stylized outfits. The heavenly host was clearly being upstaged by hordes of elves and Santa's helpers, and at the rate at which things were going, Frosty the Snowman might well become a yuletide personage with which to reckon. Even the carols were being threatened by such frights as "White Christmas" and "Waltzing in a Winter Wonderland." How the Handmaiden despised "Waltzing in a Winter Wonderland"!

Little wonder, then, that clergymen and concerned Christians from many denominations, including the Holy Nation, rose in protest crying, "Let's put Christ back in Christmas." None, as you might expect, uttered that cry more stridently than did Brother Plumwell, and he, too, loathed "Waltzing in a

205

Winter Wonderland."

Temporarily stymied at sermon preparation one day, Manly decided to walk, rather than drive, to the post office for his mail. Since he normally developed his sermons by talking them through point by point while pacing around the house or the church, he knew that the walk would not be a total waste of time (for he could think as he walked), and it would give him a needed breath of fresh, albeit frosty, air. It was the first Friday in December. The sermon he would preach two days hence was to be the second in a series of three on the theme, "Let's put Christ back in Christmas." As he neared the post office, walking very briskly, a novel but valid point flashed upon him. The Magi had not given gifts to each other but had brought them to the Christ child. Although the New Testament did not forbid mutual gift giving, it nowhere authorized the practice at Christmas. What it clearly established was the giving of gifts to JEsus, and that could be done in the modern world only by supporting his work on earth. As a first step in weaning his flock from secular Christmas observances, Manly decided that he would make the point he had just received and then urge them progressively to spend less and less on each other each year and more and more on the local church and the Holy Nation.

Thinking such valid, if novel, thoughts as these, he scarcely acknowledged the people who hailed him as he entered the post office. Since the single item he withdrew from his box contained a first-class stamp, he assumed it to be a personal letter. But, then, noting that the envelope bore no return address, he concluded that it would be junk mail of some sort. It was, however, far worse than that. The envelope contained a newspaper clipping, folded several times, of what to Manly was the most obscene photograph he had ever seen. The picture was of a man smiling inanely and standing by a large billboard that displayed the slogan, "KEEP THE M●A●S* IN YOUR CHRISTMAS PLANS." Below were the words, "Shop Downtown and Save," followed by "Free Parking Thru Dec. 27." At the bottom of the billboard in smaller, but disgustingly legible, letters were the words, "*Merchant's Association of Saranac." Below the picture, the clipping said, "Jamie Cuthbert, President of the Merchant's Association of Saranac, stands proudly by one of the five controversial signs his group recently put up."

"Do you need help, Reverend Plumwell?" asked one of Nickel Plate's deplorable Presbyterians, thinking that Manly had been stricken and might fall.

"No, no, no, no," he mumbled softly, barely aware of the question.

"Bad news or somethin', Reverend?" one of the local pagans asked solicitously.

"Yes, yes," he said, gathering his wits, "but not of a personal sort, no, no, nothing of that kind.

"Saranac, Saranac, Saranac," Manly hissed as he stamped up Main Street toward Rumsey Road and home. Everybody knew that that contemptible big-little city of 55,000 (in the recreationally developed part of the Kinross Valley) was the most notorious place east of Las Vegas. It catered to tourism and the convention trade, had more bars and strip joints than any other place of its size in the state and the lowest per-capita church membership of any city in the entire country, or so some said. And now the moral degenerates in the Merchant's Association had parodied a sacred slogan, and, worse than that, the sleazy, tasteless newspapers had gotten hold of it and turned what might have been merely local sacrilege into national blasphemy. Even those who denounced it most loudly most often would publicize it. Manly was not merely angry, he was enraged. Hate entered his heart and would not be dislodged.

About a week later, he suffered another nasty shock at the post office. After emptying his box, he walked to a tall table nearby to sort his mail, a couple of bills, a church paper, several pieces of fourth-class trash, and what looked like a Christmas card. Upon glancing at the card, he uttered an involuntary squawk and jammed the card back into its envelope so fast and violently that he tore it wide open. To the surprise of several people who had been vaguely aware of him, he dashed out of the post office and roared off in his car.

In hours of subsequent remorse, he knew he should have thrown the jolting thing away at once, but he had not; perhaps he could not. As he looked at it in the security of his bedroom, desire and revulsion fought titanic battles in him. It was a Christmas card all right, but unlike any he had ever seen. A beautiful girl knelt by the foot of her bed, her hands held high in supplication, her yearning face fixed on the ceiling and the heavens beyond. From her red, luscious lips poured the words, "Ah, Men! Ah, Men!" Through her bedroom window, the blue-black of night framing his ruddy face, was Santa staring at her lecherously. Since she wore a see-through nightie, Santa could be presumed to see, as well as the card's recipient, her saucy breasts with their impertinent nipples, her narrow waist, her sensuous hips. When the card was opened, the merriest of Santas imaginable was pulling off his red pants, and the girl lay on her bed, her head propped up on billowing pillows, her legs, bent at the knees, open in sensuous invitation, and her arms outstretched to receive him. Although the words, "Merry Christmas," in association with that erotic scene filled Manly with loathing, the scene itself extorted a libation to love from him, not once but several times. Nor did he throw the card away until it had lost its magic.

Suspicions began to haunt him, uncertainties to disconcert him. At first he had believed the newspaper clipping about keeping the MAS in Christmas to be informative, but perhaps not, perhaps it had been sent to vex him. The erotic card (postmarked in Dewmaker but bearing no return address) had certainly been meant to distress him. In late January, thinking his persecution over, he received an envelope (postmarked Pilsudski) that contained a booklet showing certain well-known cartoon characters engaged in obscene acts. It was very provocative and caused pollution in the sight of God. On Valentine's Day he received an anonymous letter (mailed in Nickel Plate) containing the following typed message: "According to the wisdom of God, delivered to the Fathers, it is a mature man's responsibility to marry and produce offspring, if possible. What masturbators do, when abusing themselves and expending semen for no purpose but shameful pleasure, is as bad as murder. This is what Isaiah meant when he said (in 1:15), your hands are full of blood." The letter was decorated with several pairs of hearts, drawn by hand, each pair being pierced with an arrow. Manly hurt as though he had been jabbed by a two-tined pitchfork.

Although a month's respite followed, he went to his mailbox each day as though it housed a venomous but beautiful serpent. Then came an anonymous letter (postmarked in Dewmaker). It contained a clipping which read, "Prof. Joachim Hertz Hillel, one of the most eminent of modern biblical scholars, has found linguistic evidence indicating that Jonah may have been incarcerated for three days in a house of ill repute rather than imprisoned in the belly of a great fish (usually described as a whale) as was formerly supposed. Prof. Hillel also believes that the well-known phrase from the Twenty-third Psalm, 'Thou preparest a table before me in the presence of mine enemies,' ought to read, 'Thou preparest a sword before me in the presence of mine enemies.' " Thoroughly disgusted, Manly took the clipping to be proof positive that what so-called modern biblical scholars did was satanic. Nevertheless, he could never think of Jonah in quite the same way again, and that was very, very vexatious to him.

Ten days later, another anonymous letter arrived (postmarked Dewmaker). Its message was spelled out with letters and words cut from various papers and magazines. The top line said, "Here is something you can clobber the Catholics with." The rest said, "Sexually, the Catholic husband may do with his wife as he pleases, according to Canon Law. He may have intercourse with her whenever it suits his pleasure. He may fondle or kiss any organ of her body at will. He may also have unnatural intercourse with her provided that he concludes his actions naturally, i.e., such that she is not prevented from conceiving." Manly would have loved to bludgeon the Catholics with their disgusting sex ethic, but he could not speak of such things from the pulpit or in Bible classes in such a place as Nickel Plate, and his tormenter knew that. But he could and did lust in his heart after several girls and young women unnaturally (as best he understood what that meant) even as he had already lusted after them naturally. His tormenter knew that too.

"What sort of tomfoolery is he up to now?" asked Polly Stamper, over the phone, to a friend who continued to attend what had been the Nickel Plate Christian Church. "Persecution? Persecution of who? Of true Christians! Well, I never. Why do you suppose he'd devote half a dozen sermons to persecution all of a sudden?"

Polly had lived among true Christians all her life and had been a true Christian herself since her early teens. She had never been persecuted; quite the contrary, she had been praised. She had never known any decent, God-fearing, hard-working, American Christians who had been persecuted. Every-

208

body agreed that such folks were the backbone of the country. Not knowing church history nor being acquainted with sectarianism, she had never heard of Christians' being persecuted, except in olden times. What Polly had in place of learning was common sense (plenty of it), and what common sense told her was that if there was going to be any religious persecution (and there wasn't going to be any), the Christians were going to do the persecuting, not be the persecuted, certainly not in a Christian country like the good old United States of America. The very idea that Christians (Christians, mind you!) would be persecuted in Pilsudski County made her laugh derisively.

"Maybe, at long last, his conscience has got to pricking him," she said to her telephone caller, triumph crackling in her voice.

"Mine would, I know, if I'd had the gall to come back to my home church and steal it right out from under people's noses. Well, that's exactly what he did. If you don't believe it, ask yourself what they call that place now. That's right, The Nickel Plate Church of the Chosen. Does it say Disciples of Christ at the bottom of the sign like it used to? No sirree, it says, The Holy Nation Association, and in purple—*purple!* I don't know about you, but I'm good and happy to have Brother Plumwell persecuted, or think he's persecuted; either way as long as it gets rid of him. Harsh or not, that's the way I feel, and I'm not the only one.

"Listen, I've got to go. No, something on the stove. Keep me posted, bye."

"I'm kinda worried about Brother Plumwell," said Stuart Acton.

"Me too," replied Josh Tharp, as the two sipped coffee in the back room at the hardware store.

"Lately, he just looks like somethin's bedevilin' him all the time."

"Yes, his spirit's cast down, and it's made him kind of waspish, whatever it is."

"I hate to say it," said Stu, "but you know, Josh, he kind of reminds me of my cousin, Morely, that works over at the hospital for the criminally insane."

"How's that?" Josh asked, slightly alarmed.

"Well, you know before he went to work over there, Morely stood just as straight as an arrow, but after he'd been there a while, it just seemed like you could see his shoulders get rounder and rounder. I didn't want to embarrass him or anything, but I mentioned it one time, and he just kind of laughed and said that anybody that had to go around in open wards with all them nuts just got to hunchin' their shoulders, sort of expectin' to get whacked between the shoulder blades most any minute, I guess."

"Manly needs a vacation, that's for sure," said Josh, "he works altogether too hard with no breaks at all."

"That's the truth," agreed Stu, "he's on call for the Lord twenty-four hours a day, every day of the year."

While strolling together to the village library to check out some novels or other light reading, Maude Tharp and May Middleton fell to talking in

209

whispers as befitted the sensitive nature of their topic.

"I just wish he wasn't so tense all the time," said May.

"And so hunted, you might almost say, especially lately," Maude went on.

"He's bound to be lonely, living all alone the way he does."

"The simple truth is, he needs a wife the worst way."

"Yes, if he had a good woman to keep him company and do for him, I believe he would take a better attitude toward the world and would stop making all those allusions in the pulpit, if you know what I mean, to . . . well, you know, about sexual topics."

"He kind of embarrasses me once in a while," said May, shuddering slightly, "even though he is circumspect about it, or tries to be."

"Me too," agreed Maude, "and more for him than for myself."

"I don't know what's to be done about it, though. There's several nice girls around here any one of which would make him a good wife, and would be willing too, unless I miss my guess."

"And twice that many women who'd love to have him for a son-in-law."

"You're so right, but he just won't let himself have anything to do with women except preach to them and teach them the gospel. Of course, that's far and away the most important thing and what he's here to do, but, still, he might at least *look* at a woman as a woman sometime."

"Needs to get married?" Polly Stamper hooted over the phone to the friend who kept her posted. "He may need to get married," she said in calmer tones, "but who needs to get married to *him?* Certainly no woman in her right mind. It would take a pretty strong-minded one, if you ask me, somebody who could lay down the law to him. Of course, there are women like that, his grandmother for one. She certainly kept old Herb in his traces . . .

"The Handmaiden? Well, I don't pretend to know anything about that Handmaiden person, though I have heard that she can make men jump through her hoop with no trouble.

"But, listen, seriously, if you know of any girl or young woman fool enough to think that she wants to get hooked up with Manly Plumwell, send her over here so I can talk to her first. Bye."

Nickel Plate's most persecuted true Christian (perhaps its only one) was so immersed in his persecution that he did not notice the change as the town sank closer to the very low level already reached by Dewmaker. Not until the noon hour of Easter Sunday did he notice it, and when he did, it nearly made him give up the good fight. He was conveying several aged people to their respective homes after the morning worship service. He had already helped Miss Amy Flanders into her house and was taking the Westons to their place when, passing through downtown Nickel Plate, he was stunned and infuriated to see old Bud Driscoll (a ne'er-do-well from north of town) playing pool with a teen-age boy whom he did not recognize, *playing pool on Easter Sunday* in a building that had stood vacant for many months.

"Aaaaiiiiiieeeeeeee!" squealed Mrs. Weston as Manly hit the brakes, the

210

better to observe the outrage.

"What in thunder's goin' on, Reverend?" asked Mr. Weston, reaching for his wife's trembling hand.

"Would you look at that!" Manly hissed through clenched teeth, pointing at the odious game in progress.

"Kind of tasteless, ain't it?" mused Mr. Weston.

"Tasteless is hardly the word!" Manly erupted. "Easter," he said loudly as though preaching to a whole church full of people, "is the time of the year when all decent people, not just Christians, but all decent people might be expected to give thanks for what the ever-living Son of God did for mankind, coming to earth to die for us, going to hell to preach to the spirits imprisoned there, and rising from the dead on Easter morning in triumph over Satan and death, and what do the Bud Driscolls of the world do? Do they humble themselves? Do they give thanks? Do they stand respectfully in church before God? No, they profane the holiest day of the year by playing pool in broad daylight for all to see."

"I sure disapprove of it," said Mr. Weston, "but I guess it must be legal and all, because whoever started up that pool hall in the old McLaren Building back there must have had to get a license to do it."

Manly had not heard so much as a whisper about starting a pool hall in Nickel Plate, did not know of anybody involved in it, knew nothing about licensing procedures, and was ignorant of any legal recourse that decent people, if not true Christians, might take against such a sacrilege as pool playing on the Lord's day, especially when it was also Easter. In time, of course, he would inveigh against it from the pulpit, hold it up to God's contempt in Bible classes, and excoriate it in private conversations; but at the moment, he was too heartsick even to contemplate the future.

Why anyone with Manly's theology should have been surprised that Satan was winning the day throughout the world and would continue to do so until the coming battle of Armageddon when God would triumph once and for all over the ancient enemy of mankind, is hard to understand, but for the time being he was physically enervated and spiritually undone. The only thing he felt energetic enough to do was to creep up behind old Bud Driscoll and pitch him head over heels into the bottomless fiery pit, something he could have done just then with a good will.

In the weeks following Easter, Nickel Plate's part of the world opened itself to the warming sun, and Manly opened himself, a crack at least, to the world's new warmth. The sacrilege done by the Merchant's Association of Saranac would not be repeated at least until after Halloween and thus could be forgotten for a time. Neither Nickel Plate nor Dewmaker was growing appreciably more sinful at the moment, nor would the Dewmaker dances begin again for several months. Best of all, Manly's persecution by anonymous letters had stopped, although he remained fearful that it might commence anew at any moment. For the time being, however, he stood a bit straighter, squinted at people less suspiciously, slept somewhat better, and was a little sweeter natured.

Early in May a letter arrived that lifted his spirits almost as much as his anonymous mail had cast them down. The letter said in part: "So, if you can talk your church board into releasing you, we would be right proud to have you preach us a week's revival series here at the Probasco Ridge Community Church. I think our people are ripe for conversion to the Holy Nation. Your reputation as a powerful preacher who is sound in doctrine has been spreading far and wide and is well-known to the Handmaiden and the Five at Big Bend. You could stay with my wife Ethelene and myself in our parsonage and would not have to worry about expenses. The church would cover your travel down and back, and would take up a nice generous love offering for you." It was signed, "Bro. Humbert V. Sohmer, RPP1."

The complimentary close reminded Manly that in his travail he had not paid sufficient attention to the "illumination" that had arrived earlier in the year from the Handmaiden concerning the letters "RPP1." and "RPPw." and the correct uses thereof. From the day so long ago and the place so far away when the Lord had first led the Handmaiden's eyes to I Peter 2:9, she had been perplexed about that which "RPP1." and "RPPw." had resolved. When the Lord's rock had written of Christians as a royal priesthood he had not distinguished them into ranks respecting special honors or functions. Hence, it seemed to follow that all true Christians were equal except insofar as the Holy Spirit showered different gifts on different people at different times in different measures. Some could speak with tongues some of the time; some could heal some of the time; some could handle dangerous serpents and drink poisonous potions some of the time, and so forth. Certainly Peter had made no distinctions between priests and people, clergy and laity, as did the Whore of Babylon, the Catholic Church, the church that had the gall to claim the rock as its first pope.

But it was also clear that the Holy Nation needed leaders identically indoctrinated to keep its dogmas pure and to teach them faithfully, leaders who would accept as gospel all of the Handmaiden's revelations, illuminations, and directives, who would appropriate church properties in the approved ways, and who could conduct such ceremonies as weddings in conformity with the laws of the land. Although all members of the Holy Nation were free to do whatever the Spirit bade and empowered them to do, still and all, a somewhat standardized clergy was needed and had in fact developed. The problem was how to make the necessary distinctions between royal priests and royal priests and yet retain the essential spiritual equality of all; and a vexing problem it was.

Singly and as a group, the Five had pressed Alice repeatedly to resolve the problem, but she resisted their every attempt, saying to them gently but emphatically, "Jesus will let me know in his own sweet time, but my own sweet time will be to let you know just as soon as he lets me know." At about the time when Manly was being despitefully used by the obscene cartoon booklet (which, inexplicably, he kept), Alice was "being chastened by the

Lord," as she put it in whispered asides to her intimates, by a bladder infection. While answering one of its nocturnal demands, she received the "illumination" that resolved the long-standing problem of how everybody in the Holy Nation could be a royal priest even though some were more priestly than others and some more royally royal than others. True to her word, Alice notified the Five at once, calling them by phone, one after the other, between 3:07 A.M. and 3:19 on January 23, a night none of them would forget.

Before a week had passed, the "illumination" was on its way by mail to all who had been indoctrinated at Big Bend for their information, implementation, and transmission to the remainder of the faithful. Henceforth, all who had been so indoctrinated were to use the letters "RPP1." in all communications involving the official business of the Holy Nation, and all other members were to use "RPPw." until further refinements could be made. The letters stood for "Royal Priest of the Pulpit" and "Royal Priest of the Pew" respectively.

Although some problems remained for Jesus to clarify (after all, Alice and the Five had not been trained at Big Bend, and Herod Agrippa Smallwood had gotten much of his training on the job so to speak and never did remain long with a given congregation), the "illumination" nevertheless proved to be of great benefit to the Holy Nation "just as the Lord intended it to be," as Alice put it, pleased as punch with her "illumination." It gave status even to the least of the peculiar people, for whenever such people were up and about the Lord's business, they could proudly append "RPPw." by word or pen to their names, and whenever the leader of a congregation came in contact with the high and mighty of so-called Christian groups, he or she could use the slightly more honored "RPP1." Thus it came to pass that on religious talk shows or panels of religious (or so-called religious) experts, in the papers or magazines, or in printed programs handed out on college campuses and the like, one could find the participants being identified or introduced as the following illustrates: Father Aloysius X. McIvor, S.J.; the Rt. Rev. Reginald K. Flamsteed, B.D., M. Div.; Dr. J. Clendennon Mercer (D.D., Piedmont-Delta Baptist Bible College); Bro. Humbert V. Sohmer, RPP1.

With the blessings of his board heartening him and the good wishes of his flock still ringing in his ears, Bro. Manly J. Plumwell, RPP1., fared forth to conduct a week of revival services at the church on Probasco Ridge, something he had never before been invited to do. When he left Nickel Plate, humming a hymn, it was early afternoon of June's second Saturday. Probasco Ridge was about twenty-two miles from Nickel Plate, twenty miles south of Dewmaker to be exact. Not even the village hall of that wretched place could dampen his spirits as he passed it, heading south for an adventure in the Lord's work. Within ten miles the landscape changed from gentle rolling farm lands, with an occasional moraine, to long finger-like ridges, heavily forested, that led up to the Andaman Plateau. With light traffic and only one intersection to watch for, he found himself at the Probasco Ridge

Community Church in little over half an hour. From there he had but a mile of sylvan road to travel to reach the parsonage and the Christian fellowship of Bro. Humbert V. Sohmer, RPPl., and his wife, Ethelene, RPPw., strangers to him in fact, but siblings in the service of Jesus.

Contact with the Sohmers was wonderfully restorative of Manly's self-esteem. Being in Humbert's presence did much to restore his confidence in his abilities, for, except in matters of personal grooming and fastidiousness of dress, Humbert was no rival, certainly not in gifts of the Spirit. More than once that week, Manly lifted his eyebrows in surprise that the Handmaiden and the Five had allowed Humbert to go straight to a pastorate from Big Bend without first having to undertake a mission of church extension. Furthermore, being in Ethelene's presence restored his ability to see the spiritual side of a young woman. In truth, she was not the sort of female whom the devil could easily use for inciting lust in men. Except for her bones, whose prominence and abundance were plain for all to see, Ethelene was a wraith, merely a wraith, and one exuding an acrid scent. Never still, except when engaged in some spiritual exercise or other, she worked prodigiously, taking over Manly's complete care in addition to her regular duties at church and home. She polished his shoes each morning, darned his socks, mended his clothes (preventively in most cases), washed and ironed them, cleaned his room daily (supplying fresh flowers), fed him splendid food on those occasions when a family in the church did not invite him to dine with them, and washed, waxed, and vacuumed the old Nash the day before his departure from Probasco Ridge. Except for the proprieties involved, she could and would have shampooed his hair, scrubbed his back, and clipped his nails, finger and toe; and all without so much as inciting a scintilla of lust.

So dazzling was Manly's preaching that week, so spectacular his chalk drawings of biblical scenes (he no longer needed to pencil-in guidelines beforehand), the people of Probasco Ridge thought themselves bathed in celestial light. Only Humbert was put in the shade; nor was he too dense not to notice, nor too humble not to care.

Thirty-one convicted sinners, ranging in age from eleven to seventy-four, confessed to faith in Jesus as their God and savior that week. Eleven other people transferred their membership to Probasco Ridge from a variety of so-called Christian congregations elsewhere, and an indeterminate number of sinners teetered on the brink of life's greatest decision, that of becoming Christian.

Something called the Holy Nation Association of Churches of the Chosen rose high in the estimation of nearly all who attended the revival. Keen interest and respectful attention were gained for a relatively unknown but singular person who modestly let herself be known as the Handmaiden of the Lord. Major gains were made for the old but only recently re-revealed doctrine of three-world creationism, and all the scoffers, sceptics, and evolutionists, together with the modernists, humanists, and communists, on Probasco Ridge were put on notice that the day of judgment was at hand.

Although the church was progressively well filled with each successive sermon, there was standing room only at the Friday and Saturday night services. Manly had chosen those times to exhibit his chalk art, the better to daunt the devil and attenuate his influence on the youth of the area who might otherwise have been tempted to dally with sin at the time of their lives when Satan was believed to be most active.

Collections of money ran high, and there was a 23 percent increase in commitments to tithing. Manly's love offering, taken up during the concluding service, came to $152.06, of which he publicly returned a tenth to the church at Probasco Ridge amid tears of delight and sighs of admiration.

Nothing, however, did more to unite Humbert and Manly in Christian fellowship than tracking Otto (Smut) Graeber to earth. Despite his blubbery bulk and slow gait, no greased pig was more elusive to the clergy than he. Smut's parents and grandparents, his brothers and sisters, his uncles and aunts and cousins, his wife and clamorous children had all tried time and again to get him to accept Christ and attend church with them regularly, but to no avail. Moreover, they had implored every minister at the Probasco Ridge Community Church, over the years, to see Smut, to persuade him to accept salvation. What a poor place heaven would be to the rest of the Graebers without Smut!

From time to time, advertently or inadvertently, various parsons, including Humbert, had seen Smut from side or rear views but always putting distance between himself and them. It was as though the wretch had his own early warning system designed especially for escape from clergymen.

It wasn't that Smut was exceptionally sinful. He was as decent, neighborly, and law-abiding as most other people on Probasco Ridge. He did not speak out against religion, nor did he lay straws before others in the free exercise thereof. Except for a few pet swear words, he was not uncommonly profane. Never having been in grace, he had not fallen from grace, and, so, was no apostate; neither was he a heretic, never having come close enough to Christianity to qualify. It was just that Smut never thought nor spoke of God, Christ, church, salvation, heaven, or any other spiritual topic. Not only did he find the story of Jesus uninteresting, he found theology incomprehensible or, when comprehensible, less than trivial. Since he did not divide beliefs into saving and non-saving varieties, it did not matter to him whether God was one in one, three in one, or ten in two. But none of this per se caused him to flee the clergy. It was just that he could not stand them. Something about them, something indefinable, set him on edge and put his nerves to jangling. So, he avoided them, and in so doing perfected his art.

As Humbert and Manly ranged far and wide, day by revival day, making evangelistic calls on potential converts, visiting shut-ins, and exhorting boys and girls along country lanes to come to the meetings (bringing parents and friends) to see Bro. Plumwell's pictures if nothing else, Humbert had no intention of wasting time on Smut Graeber. But proceeding north on the Pringletown Pike, they saw (a third of a mile ahead and on a hill to their right) what Humbert knew to be Smut's house. Suddenly, something dark moved around from behind the house, raising a lazy cloud of dust. It was a car leaving the farmyard and proceeding down the dirt driveway to the pike. From earlier futile attempts at cornering Smut, Humbert knew the driveway to be at least a thousand feet long and badly rutted.

Putting the picture together more by inspiration than by conscious thought, and whooping in delight, Humbert floorboarded his nearly new Dodge, aiming it at the mouth of Smut's driveway. At that point, the bank on the right side of the pike was high, Smut's driveway being cut into it deeply. The result was that for the first sixty-five feet (or the last, depending on whether one was coming or going) a car could not be seen from the pike, nor could its driver see traffic to the left or right. Anyone who valued his skin slowed to a snail's pace before turning onto the Pringletown Pike from that driveway.

Humbert, knowing all this, hit the brakes while his protesting tires were still on the blacktopped pike, then swerved expertly to his right in such a way as to plant all four wheels on the driveway's dusty gravelish mouth. Meanwhile, Smut proceeded blindly through the sixty-five-foot defile toward the pike, his early warning system not working. Out of nowhere came a black car sluing to a halt before his startled eyes, mere inches ahead of his front bumper. As a fog of yellow dust billowed and swirled around both cars, a barrage of gravel rattled off Smut's Ford.

Then out of the blockading vehicle bounded two dark-suited, Bible toting young men who could only be preachers. True to his heart, Smut jammed his car into reverse but gunned the engine so hard that his rear wheels could not effectively grab the dry, loose surface of the steep driveway. Thus, he went nowhere, but he did return the preachers' fire, pelting them with grit and gravel, especially from their kneecaps down, and assaulting them with a counterblast of dust.

"Sheeeiit!" he growled in self-contempt as the hounds of heaven closed in on him.

Smut's attempted escape wreaked an earthy vengeance on his pursuers, each fastidious by temperament, for as they stood by the side of his car they were, to all appearances, growing out of the ground, earth from earth, ashes from ashes, dust from dust.

"I'm Brother Humbert Sohmer, minister at the Probasco Ridge Community Church," said Humbert, trying to dislodge grit from his mouth.

"Oh," said Smut, holding his head humbly and avoiding Humbert's gaze.

"I'm just real glad, yes, real glad, to get the chance to meet you," Humbert prattled on, sticking his arm awkwardly into Smut's left front window.

"Uh huh," replied Smut, shaking hands limply.

"And this here's Brother Manly Plumwell, the pastor of the Church of the Chosen of the Holy Nation Association over at Nickel Plate, who's come to conduct a revival for us."

216

As Smut mumbled something that ended with "ta meet ya," Manly exuded delight over how the will of the Lord JEsus had brought them together.

To that Smut said nothing.

"Crops doing well?" Humbert asked by way of an introit to the serious business of winning a soul for Christ.

"Fair to middlin' I guess," murmured Smut, beginning to sweat profusely as the temperature in his Ford climbed, the sun beating on it, its engine still running.

"Been working hard?" Humbert went on cheerily.

"Sort of," Smut grunted, suddenly interested in his car's brake pedal.

"Brother Graeber," said Humbert, "there's something I just want to ask you, and it's this: What does it profit a man if he gains the whole world and loses his soul?"

Knowing nothing of the Bible and misunderstanding the intent of its rhetorical questions, Smut said slowly, "Well, the profit would be considerable, I reckon, but I couldn't put no dollar figure on it."

"What?" piped Humbert, hardly believing his ears.

"Well, with the price of land what it is, I ain't got no way of figurin' the profit a body'd gain from the whole shebang," said Smut thoughtfully.

With his face close to Humbert's, as both stood pressed together looking down on Smut, Manly tried a different tack, saying, "Mr. Graeber, there is no other name under heaven whereby a man must be saved than that of Jesus Christ . . ."

"One name like that ought to be plenty," said Smut, breaking in and daunting Manly as he had daunted Humbert earlier.

"Smut," Manly continued, overcoming his distaste for Otto's nickname, "I want you to know here and now that JEsus loves you, he really does."

At that Smut shuddered visibly, for any and all talk of love made him uneasy, at least as uneasy as being caught by a preacher.

As incredulous as though he had just been told that Buddha had always shown him compassion, Smut blurted out, "Why would he?" being under no illusions about being a lovable man himself.

"Because it is his nature to love," Manly chimed in.

"Well, if he can't help himself, I guess there's nothing to be done about it," Smut sighed, poking sweat out of the corners of his eyes with a fat forefinger.

"Don't you want Jesus to love you?" Humbert asked earnestly.

"I can't rightly say I want any man to love me, especially not a dead one," said Smut slowly, sounding serious.

"But he is not dead; he came back to life; he did that so that he could go to heaven to prepare a place for you in his Father's house," declared Manly, his voice rasping with tension.

"Now, that's what I'd call real spooky-like," said Smut, eyes downcast, drops of sweat dripping from his uncombed hair and making rivulets down his bulging cheeks.

"I guess I just have one more question," Humbert said, "and it's this: Have you ever thought where you're going to spend eternity?"

"Nowhere."

"*Nowhere!*" said the two royal priests as one.

"But a person's soul has got to be somewhere," said Humbert.

"Not if it ain't no more," Smut replied blandly.

"You don't think you'll either be in heaven or hell?' asked Manly, exhausting all the possibilities he cared to admit.

"I don't reckon I'll even be, let alone be anywhere," Smut observed, looking miserable at having to answer what were to him dumb questions but not concerned about not being eternal and, therefore, not being somewhere forevermore.

With the sun broiling them through their dark suits, with sweat running down their backs and into their shorts, and with frustration cornering them as surely as they had cornered him, the hounds of heaven said, "Good-bye, Smut," in barely civil tones, and trudged back to the waiting Dodge.

Smut Graeber was not a sensitive man, but he did feel slightly nauseated for a few minutes after his encounter with the clergy, mostly because of lingering self-contempt at having been caught, especially in broad daylight. Actually, he had found talking with such people to be less traumatic than he had always feared. Nevertheless, as he went about his daily routine, he solemnly rededicated himself to a clergyless life.

Humbert and Manly returned to the parsonage in silent dejection, having no need to speak, for they shared common thoughts. They had just encountered an alien being—not just an ordinary sinner who (though he had not yet done so) knew that he should repent of his sins, believe in the Lord Jesus, and accept the free gift of eternal life—an alien being who was deaf to the drums of the drummer after whom they marched, who found no allure in the drama of salvation, and who was blind to supernatural realities, seeing only the trees and streams, the hills and dales, the sod and rocks of Probasco Ridge, together with the works of men that clung to its contours.

Moreover, they, who truly believed that cleanliness was next to godliness, were filthy. Dust and grit and dried sweat made the hair on their respective heads feel like conglomerates. Free-flowing streams of sweat had plastered dust to their faces or deposited silt down their shirt collars. Every intersection of threads in their outer clothing contained a rubble of dust, and underneath it all, they stank. Upon reaching the parsonage, they soaked in a hot tub, first Manly, then Humbert. Meanwhile, Ethelene turned their jackets' and pants' pockets inside out, shook the grit out of their cuffs, and took the vacuum cleaner to everything that could not be laundered.

With the revival's concluding service only hours away, Manly asked Humbert to leave him at the church so that he could practice his final sermon in peace and quiet. It was 4:00 P.M. on Sunday when they arrived, Humbert saying, as Manly waved him off, that he would return in an hour. Before going inside to practice, Manly paused a moment to hug the place he had come to love.

The church, a simple frame building of white clapboard, was well proportioned and dignified, its bell tower especially pleasing just then against the afternoon sky. Sitting on a knoll in the middle of a large corner lot, the building, looking fresh and serene, nestled among oak, locust, and cedar trees. It faced east, Probasco Road running past its front side. On its south side was Humphrey Lane, a narrow dirt track leading west between rocky pastures, then plunging down into dark distant woods. Directly behind the church, extending for 150 feet or more and along its entire north side, was a well-tended cemetery, shaped like a fat L. Trying to fix the scene in mind for happy recollection, Manly entered the building to practice.

He had decided to call the last sermon of his series "My Last Sermon," and to preach it as though it were his final sermonic effort just before death. That approach boiled things down to fundamentals and underscored the imperative nature of the gospel. It was especially effective when a cemetery lay nearby. He would not only tell them what he thought was most crucial, most deserving, to be said by one about to depart life, but would also bid them to consider what those whose remains were but a few feet away would say, if only they could. Surely the dead on Probasco Ridge, the good and the bad alike, would agree with him that they, the living, should accept Christ without delay.

As Manly paced around the sanctuary, nearly finished with his sermon preparation, the ground beneath the church shuddered as though some heavy animals were running nearby. Then came several sharp cracking reports followed by the sounds of cows bawling. Above the thudding and the bawling, a husky voice yelled something indiscernible. Moments later, the voice, which had come much closer, said clearly, "You goddamned fuckin' cow, get the hell outa there."

Manly was chilled by such talk, especially in the shadow of the church and on a Sunday too, but he was reluctant to intervene in any way. Despite four years of public ministry, he was still shy, and, moreover, he did not want the mood of his sermon preparation to be shattered by a confrontation.

Then came a slightly varied sequence of sounds consisting of "Oh, piss, piss on you, you sod," whack, whack, whack, assorted bovine sounds uttered in fright or pain, and "Jesus H. Christ, you fuckin' cows would have to go and do this."

That did it! Manly ran through a room at the back of the church and unbolted the door leading out toward the cemetery where the profane racket originated. In the name of JEsus, he would reprove whomsoever it might be, kindly (even shyly) but firmly.

Squinting at first as a sunbeam stabbed his eyes through the branches of a cedar tree, he quickly focused on the scene. Eight or nine cows had broken down the fence dividing one edge of the cemetery from the pasture beyond. They had wandered into the cemetery, had torn up some flowers, pushed over some canisters and other decorations, and had left droppings here and there.

Far more startling than the sight of the cows, however, was the fact that *she* was there, trying single-handedly to drive them back through the broken fence into their pasture, clubbing them with what looked like a hoe handle minus the blade, and swearing a blue streak. There could be no mistake. It was *she;* it *was she*; the singular one, the riveting one, he had seen at the Dewmaker dance on that fateful night nearly a year earlier.

For the first time since childhood, Manly lost self-control. Knocked off balance by surging emotions, he ran pell-mell at her, jumping over low-lying grave markers and swerving like a dervish around taller headstones and other monuments.

Frustrated by the stupid cattle and unable to round them up easily because of the impeding gravestones, Tampa Rhine was unaware of Manly until he was almost upon her. Astounded at seeing a well-dressed young man bounding over headstones as he bore down upon her, she whirled to meet him, clenching her hoe handle.

When he reached her, he did something he had never done. He laid his hands on her, on a young woman, and did so voluntarily, or at least without invitation. He meant no harm. He meant only to reach out to her, to touch her. He meant to hold her right hand in genuine Christian love, not just for the purposes of a ritualized handshake. He meant to put his left hand on her upper right arm or shoulder to assure her that he had come, perhaps in the very nick of time, to help her, to help her out of a life of sin, not simply to lend a hand in driving some dumb cows back into their pasture.

But Tampa Rhine did not see any of it that way.

"Get your goddamned hands off me, you perverted sod, you," she yelled, baring her teeth and shaking free.

"I've wanted to see you for so long, so very long," he said, sighing with hope and yearning to touch her again.

"Oh, stuff it," she exploded. "I don't even know you."

"I've prayed for you over and over again; I've prayed that I could get a chance to talk to you," he yelled at her, hoping desperately that she would believe him.

"Can it," said Tampa. "I don't need no prayers from you or anybody else."

"Oh, but you do, you do," said Manly, admiring her angry beauty and forgetting the gospel for a fleeting moment.

"You don't even know me," she said in disgust, keeping the hoe handle between them, poised for attack.

Catching his breath and feeling more collected, he said, "I . . . I saw you one time last summer at a Saturday night dance in Dewmaker."

"I didn't see you," she replied, squinting at him, trying to figure out who in hell he was.

"I was sitting in a station wagon parked out in front . . ."

"Oh, Jesus H. Christ," she broke in (Sunday, a dark-suited young man, the Probasco Ridge Community Church in the background, placards advertising a revival plastered on every damned thing that could hold one, the summer dances in Dewmaker, a station wagon out in front, a loudspeaker, bells and gospel music, all falling into place), "are you the low-down turd that played that gospel crap so screwin' loud we couldn't even dance?"

"Yes," he admitted, but without pride.

"You ought to be ashamed of your fuckin' self, mister, doin' a shitty thing like that," she hissed, brandishing the hoe handle at him.

Crushed beyond belief and unable to absorb any more abuse without lashing back in unchristian anger, Manly pivoted and ran toward the church, tears stinging his eyes, grave markers grazing his ankles and skinning his shins. Upon reaching the back of the church, but with his head still down and his eyes still watering, he ran squarely into Humbert Sohmer.

Manly's sermon that night was strident and shrill. It was also ominous, being laced with references to persecution and to how this world could be expected to treat the true Christian despitefully.

The Great Pilot of Manly's life as surely saw him safely home to Nickel Plate that night as he had guided him safely home to Big Bend on the night after his dreadful stay with the Bantrys at Calico Corners.

While the old Nash rolled on through the night, automatically to all appearances and without incident, Manly was assaulted by three-pronged agony. The first prong was Humbert Sohmer. How long had Humbert stood at the back of the church? What had he seen? What had he heard? What conclusions had he drawn? What might he say, and to whom?

From many compliments on his preaching and from numerous indirect comparisons, Manly knew that he had outclassed Humbert by far. So, envy might well consume him and tempt him to cut Manly down to size by using the cemetery episode. Should even a breath of it reach Big Bend, the consequences could be very serious, partly because Manly was not sure of what he had done. Had he merely taken that wild young woman by the hand and patted or caressed her shoulder, or had he seized her, attempting to embrace her? Unless his memory improved, he could not in good conscience deny the latter, because he simply did not know the lengths to which he had gone, especially while she was fighting him off.

From the moment at which Manly had blundered tearfully into Humbert and thereafter, the latter had been very considerate and supportive, but, of course, that could change. As they stepped into Humbert's car to go to dinner, he said, "That was Tampa Rhine you just tangled with."

"I had no idea who it was," Manly said, bitterly rejecting the identity he had yearned so long to know.

"She's noted for her quick temper and a vulgar, profane tongue."

"Oh," Manly said, sounding uninterested.

"She keeps house for her father—he's a widower—and two older brothers; works like a horse and all the time too, from what I'm told."

"She doesn't even have a stepmother?" Manly asked, looking for anything neutral to say.

"No, the old man never remarried, too mean for that, from what I hear."

"I don't suppose they're believers?"

"According to most folks, they're outright atheists, the men at least."

"Have you tried to reach them with the gospel?" Manly inquired, not unwilling to find something to hold against Humbert.

"Oh, yes. Shortly after I came here I went to their place, and a great big tall dog—a wolfhound of some sort, I guess—came out and menaced me. He didn't offer to bite, but he kept bumping right into me, and snarling, and carrying on; and what was worse, at least one of the Rhines was in the house at the time. I called out, but not a soul paid the slightest attention, so I just started backing toward the car with that monster snarling and bumping into me every step of the way."

"That's very distressing," Manly observed sympathetically, forgetting his own distress momentarily.

"Yes, well, I didn't intend to subject you to that kind of treatment, so I didn't even suggest that we make an evangelistic call on those people. They know where the church is, if they want to come; it's right next door to their place, as they know perfectly well."

"Thanks," said Manly, but without thankfulness.

"Hardly anybody on Probasco Ridge has anything to do with the Rhines. They're just so coarse and profane, well, downright mean would be a better way to put it, I guess."

"I suppose a lot of men hang around that girl," Manly pretended to observe, interested but disinterested in the answer.

"Oh, no, she doesn't have any use for men from what I hear tell, and probably with good reason, having to put up with the three she does. She doesn't seem to have any close friends at all except for a girl called Eloise Creel from over around Pringletown. Besides, she works all the time, like I said."

Not all the time, Manly thought as his first sight of her skittered into consciousness and out again.

The second prong of his agony was Tampa Rhine. He had grown accustomed to being right, nor in his line of work could he afford not to be. The eternal fate of unnumbered souls depended on it. Quite often he had been likened to Billy Graham, who in spiritual matters had never been known to be wrong to those who made the comparison and complimented him thereby. After one of his sermons on Probasco Ridge, a dowdy gray lady with holy fire flashing in her eyes paid him the supreme compliment, whispering behind her hand, "I suppose I shouldn't say this, but . . . well . . . what I mean is . . . I . . . I think that St. Paul must have been a lot like you." *Not that he was a little like St. Paul but that St. Paul must have been a lot like him!* Lest he exceed the saint in boastfulness and thereby risk apostolic retribution, Manly disclaimed any such likeness hastily but couldn't suppress a smug smile.

It was, of course, quite true that no one with whom he came in daily contact knew the Scriptures as well as he. In fact, some had said, marveling, that talking with him was like having a conversation with the Bible, because, as likely as not, he would respond by reciting verses of Scripture without end, or so it seemed. Furthermore, no one whom he knew, except for his masters at Big Bend, could argue him down on doctrinal matters, nor could anyone, in his humbly held view, fault him on the soundness of his sermons. Although he never said so in so many words, aloud at least, he was convinced in private that few if any as young as he knew God's mind better. How, then, could one so versed in knowledge of the divine being be so wrong about a mere human being as he had been about Tampa Rhine?

From the moment when first he saw her, Manly knew that men, made wily with lust, were stalking her, that men of many ages were, even then, trying to hunt her down that they might invade her body. Once invaded, it would not matter to her by whom nor how often it happened again. That, at least, was his fear, and it was from such a dreadful fate that he had sought to save her through his prayers, and, if possible, his personal ministry. Yet, if the truth were admitted—not just known, but admitted (as it must be before all-knowing God)—it was he, Manly, who was in more danger of carnality than was Tampa. Humbert Sohmer had made that clear, even though he had not known what he was doing. Tampa had nothing to do with men, had seen too much of manhood in her odious father and coarse brothers, had only one close friend, Eloise Creel, and that friend was a mouse and no man and a female mouse to boot. How could he have been so desperately mistaken? But, even worse, what did that particular mistake say about him, about his purity, his spirituality in the eyes of the Holy One of New Israel?

Nor was that his only mistake. In his imagings and other spiritual raptures involving Tampa, he had envisioned her vital elemental energies being devoted to the Holy Nation because of his ministry. He had seen those blazing eyes softened to the ember-glow of love, and all because of the love of JEsus shown forth to her in him, Manly Plumwell. He had seen those powerful arms and strong hands put to the Lord's work, because he, as a royal priest, had cared enough to reach out to touch her in Christian love. But when he had reached out to touch her in reality, she had shaken him away as though he were a rapist, had brandished a hoe handle in his face, had vilified him, and had squelched him mercilessly for trying to do the Lord's work at a summer dance in Dewmaker.

No single name can be put on the amalgam of feelings Manly felt for, about, and against Tampa Rhine as he rode toward Nickel Plate through the indifferent darkness of that starless night. Nor did sleep seize him, once he was safely home and in bed, with comforting images of her strong hands.

Manly's encounter with Tampa in the cemetery reopened each and every wound despitefully inflicted on him subsequent to his prayer for the tutelage of such treatment. That was the third prong of his agony, and he suffered it

223

daily as long as he remained in Nickel Plate and bled from it profusely but did not learn from it, nor did it profit him in any secret way. Moreover, an element of deception relative to it entered his life. Often in public in the pulpit (and in private life too), he quoted Paul (from II Cor. 4:8-9): "*We are* troubled on every side, yet not distressed; *we are* perplexed, but not in despair; Persecuted, but not forsaken; cast down, but not destroyed. . . ." There was, however, far more yearning in his voice that it might be so than joyous declaration that it was so. In short, while still professing that he bore his cross lightly, he bore it very heavily indeed.

In the fall of his fifth year, he suffered a gash too deep to heal.

Elaine Beuhler Wren had walked out on her husband, Harlow, temporarily at least, and returned to Nickel Plate to live with her parents. Since Manly had not heard that unwelcome news, he took no precautions to avoid her. She had in fact been back in town for nearly a month before their paths crossed. Looking more unctuous than usual because he was wearing one of the black suits he normally reserved for funerals, Manly bent over to open his mailbox at the post office. As he withdrew the day's mail, a voice behind him snorted, "Fancy meetin' you here, you old son of a gun, you." Releasing the steel trap he had momentarily made of his jaws, he turned to Elaine with an indifferent, "Why, hello there," hoping vainly that she would not embarrass him further in the presence of the motley crowd of mail seekers milling around the post office.

"Just what have you been up to anyway, you devil?" she inquired loudly, batting her eyes salaciously.

"Why, the same sorts of things as usual: preaching the gospel, ministering to the needy, burying the dead," he said, cataloguing his work less for Elaine's benefit than that of the others who couldn't help overhearing their conversation.

"And baptizin' too?" Elaine asked eagerly, leading him on and smiling from ear to fat ear.

"Yes, yes, baptizing too; in fact I baptized three people just two Sundays ago."

"Is that when you tracked the water over to the door of the women's dressing room?" Elaine cackled, having a merry time in her typically thoughtless way.

At the vision of water on the floor, Manly turned as white as a sheet and fled the post office.

Up to that point in his Nickel Plate ministry, he had baptized 153 people, immersing each of them totally in the watery tomb. Sometimes the baptistry was readied for the immersion of one person alone (delaying it was thought to be dangerous to one's eternal weal), but generally several people were baptized, one after the other, at the end of a given worship service. Sometimes the converts would all be young (but seldom below the age of puberty), sometimes older, and often of widely varied ages. Sometimes the converts would all be of one sex, but most often both sexes would be represented. The baptismal service to which Elaine had referred had been unique in that it was the first time in Manly's ministry that the ritual had been conducted for women alone.

At that time, the convert who cheered him most was Rose (Rosy) Pegler, the girl with the long lion-colored hair who had been so impressed with his own baptismal bravery well over a decade earlier. Rosy, an ebullient creature normally bold and quite athletic, was afraid to stand up in front of a formal group of people and terrified at the prospect of having to say anything in public. More than once she had asked Manly, pleading with him almost, to hear her confession in private and to baptize her in secret. He had wanted to comply for more reasons than one, but fears, theological as well as personal, had stayed his hand. He promised Rosy, however, that he would write to the Handmaiden seeking a directive in the matter. Alice in turn had taken the matter straight to the Lord. There was every reason to believe that Jesus was still considering it, surely but slowly, when to everybody's surprise Rosy arose one Sunday morning and reeled forward to take Manly's hand outstretched in invitation to eternal life. At the same time, but with prior notification, Pauline Mason, a harried young mother of four, and Esther Wilbanks, a fetching widow of thirty-six, received the same hand. After hearing their confessions of sin, accepting their attestations of repentance, and leading them in affirmations of faith, Manly announced that the three would be baptized into newness of life at the end of the evening service one week hence.

The floor plan of Nickel Plate's Church of the Chosen was simplicity itself. One entered the vestibule, centered on the south side of the building (at the base of its bell tower), and proceeded north through double swinging doors into the rectangular (about 38 feet by 72 feet) auditorium/sanctuary, the center aisle of which led down and directly to the Lord's table from which (at every Sunday morning worship service) the elders of the congregation dispensed bread cubes and grape juice in memory of Christ's broken body and shed blood.

Centered directly behind the Lord's table and elevated about a foot above the main floor level was the podium in the front center of which stood an ornately carved (but portable) pulpit. Behind the pulpit was an antique settee on which the minister sat when not standing to sing, pray, preach, or otherwise lead his flock.

Centered directly behind the podium and elevated a foot above it was the platform (loosely called a "loft") on which the choir members sat, the lower part of their bodies being shielded from the congregation by a velvet cloth of winey red suspended on rings hanging on a brass rail that extended across the front of the loft and part way down its left and right sides. An upright piano reposed on the main floor to one side of the loft and an ancient organ on the other side.

Centered directly behind the choir loft in the north wall of the sanctuary was a broadly arched aperture whose bottom was a foot above the level of the loft. Two velvet curtains of the same winey red color hung behind the aperture. When closed, they served as a door or a screen; when opened, they revealed the baptistry.

The baptistry was, in effect, a rectangular tank twelve feet long east to west and four feet wide. Three steps led into it from the door in its west end and three from the door in its east end. When standing in it, minister and convert were in about three and a half feet of water. Once the podium was shorn of its pulpit, the choir loft vacated, and the baptistry curtains opened, those who sat in the pews could watch the proceedings rather well but could see only the heads and torsos of those awaiting watery entombment and symbolic resurrection.

As soon as the ritual was over, each male convert climbed the three steps to the west and then descended into a multipurpose room at the back of the church that served as a Sunday school classroom, men's dressing room at baptisms, and robing room for choir members about to process through its sanctuary door to the choir loft. Each female convert departed the baptistry to the east and descended into a room of similar shape and functions.

The area at the back of the church behind the baptistry and to either side of it looked like a large C done in block-letter fashion. Although the areas to the west and east of the baptistry were separated from the sanctuary by a permanent partition and by lockable doors, no permanent partition segmented the areas in question. To give privacy at such times as baptisms and to minimize noise during Sunday school sessions, wooden folding doors had been installed. At one end they were anchored into the back (north) wall of the baptistry and at the other end into the north exterior wall of the church.

At the very instant it dawned on Manly that the baptismal candidates were all female and eyeable, especially the smooth and supple Rosy, the devil slithered through a chink in his armor and invaded his heart. At the end of his morning sermon on the baptismal day, Manly did not give his normally impassioned invitation to shuck off the life of sin and put on Christ instead, but offered a tepid suggestion that there might be some there who might wish to consider repentance. At the evening service, his hope that no male would answer the Master's call was so perfervid it might as well have been a prayer.

With the hymn of invitation ended, no unwelcome males having presented themselves, he nodded affirmatively at the candidates and their towel-bearing assistants. As their entourage disappeared into the back room on the east, Rosy shaking like a leaf and nearly swooning with fright, Manly slipped happily into the back room on the west, whereupon Lonnie Atkins, who had succeeded Ikey as janitor, proceeded at a fast but ungainly clip to open the baptistry curtains. Then, with a helping hand from Josh Tharp, Lonnie wrestled the heavy pulpit off the podium. Meanwhile the choir members processed from their loft and took pews on the main floor, leaving an unobstructed view of the baptistry. Throughout it all, May Middleton played dirge-like variations (on the organ) of "Lead, Kindly Light, Amid th' Encircling Gloom."

Within a few minutes, Manly entered the baptistry from the west wearing the white shirt and black tie in which he had just preached, but having changed into white trousers and rubber-soled black shoes reserved for that purpose. How happy it would have made Ikey to know that Manly had not "fetched a rubber suit" along with him when he returned from Big Bend but that he would always make it a practice to descend into the cleansing stream of baptism dressed much as the candidates were—often at a heavy price, because whenever there were male converts, it meant that he had to undress, dry himself, and dress again in the presence of others, something he detested.

Once he was properly positioned and the candidates were ready, Manly normally baptized without further ado. Then, remaining behind when all others had departed the baptistry, he would offer a fervent prayer for the newly resurrected. But he proceeded differently that night. As though bidden by the Spirit, spontaneously, he turned away from Pauline Mason, who stood poised for descent, and faced the congregation. Then he prayed as follows, taking a leaf from St. Paul (Rom.6): "Merciful Father, Redeeming Son, Guiding Spirit, we call upon ye, as One and yet as Three, to over-shadow us all with thy protective presence as we participate in acts of death and dying, in the death and dying of three precious souls who have come to bury their carnality and to entomb their bondage to Satan, a bondage whose wage is eternal death. Quicken them that they may arise purified from their watery grave and that they may enter joyously into thy bondage, a bondage whose wage is eternal life. Let it be so, we pray, in the name of God the Father, the Son, and the Holy Ghost. Amen."

Then he turned to receive the waiting Pauline, who entered the water with tears dripping off her cheeks but arose with a shy "Hallelujah" on her lips. Esther Wilbanks descended with the confidence of one who is absolutely sure of what she is doing and arose serenely as though to say to the whole world, "Of course it was the right thing to do." But poor Rosy! She was like a metal superstructure too rigidly framed and vibrating in a storm. Nor did the suppleness return to her lovely body as Manly raised her into newness of life.

Rosy had scarcely stepped out of the baptistry when Manly offered a perfunctory prayer and was gone.

He was gone that he might peek through a crack, any crack, there might be in the wooden folding doors (warped over the years) that would stand for fleeting moments between him and his new converts. But a noise (imaginary, perhaps) drove him away from the doors and from any possibility of seeing sights of the kind that he had yearned for forever, it seemed. Frustrated, angry with himself over his fear, and obsessed with the need to behold a young woman naked, he reentered the sanctuary, his face white and drawn, to complete the rituals of the night.

The pine planking of the back room, stained, waxed, stripped, and waxed *ad infinitum* (and deeply worn), had preserved for a time the record of his quest for the unholy grail. Someone had seen the record, had interpreted its message, had spoken of it. Elaine had heard it; Polly Stamper, who despised him, had also heard it no doubt and could no more keep quiet than Elaine, though for different reasons; and Blanche Oesterly, who was rumored to have spoken contemptuously of him, might also have received the news. Indeed, unnumbered women might have heard and tattled on him far and wide. Pauline Mason, Esther Wilbanks, and Rosy Pegler would surely hear of it, and only Rosy would forgive him. If confronted, he would simply have to lie as to why he had sloshed his way to the folding doors and back that night, but lie he would. Short of blasphemy, God's mercy knew no limits.

Expecting the axe to fall here if not hereafter, Manly wondered why he had not already been called to give an account of himself before the elders and deacons of his congregation. Then, three days after Elaine's devastating revelation, he was sure the execution of his earthly sentence had come. As he paced around the house, working fretfully on his next sermon, he noticed an old black Packard hesitate at first and then park parallel to the house along Rumsey Road. No less a personage than Bro. Emmet Langhorne Van Hook, Ph.D., RPPr. (Royal Priest of the Professoriate) alighted from it and began to march darkly (in a black suit, shoes, and string tie) toward the house. Manly fell back in apprehension wishing to God that his grandmother were still alive to get the door and be his buffer long enough for him to get a grip on himself.

Since neither was given to small talk, Emmet got right to the point. "Brother Plumwell, the Handmaiden has sent me your way on a matter of considerable gravity."

"I know," said Manly, drawing his lips together in a thin line, awaiting chastisement.

Trying to make sense out of the answer, Emmet paused, then went on, "As you know, Miss Alice is most Christ-like in being considerate of youth."

Manly nodded in agreement, hoping he was still young enough to qualify for the Handmaiden's considerateness.

"And, naturally, she wants to daunt the devil's work among the youth of our nation as much as possible."

"Of course," Manly agreed, his dread mutating into curiosity.

"So, you see, that is why I have just visited Algonquin State University in the extreme northern part of the state."

"No, frankly, I don't see."

"And why I have stopped off here on the return trip to visit you," Emmet continued. "The point is, Brother Plumwell, many of the colleges and universities of this country are becoming prime breeding grounds of infidelity to the Lord. They are letting godless professors teach modernism, communism, humanism, and secularism."

Since Manly had long inveighed against those odious "isms," it was reassuring to hear from a learned man like Bro. Van Hook that they really existed, but in point of fact, he did not have a good grip on any of the evils in question, knowing only that God was dead set against each of them.

"Then, too, college life is fast becoming a quagmire of sensuality, to say nothing of dope, drink, and oriental mysticism," Emmet declared, shaking his head in reprobation as he ticked off each evil.

"To make a long story short," he said, tiring of the suspense he had created, "the Handmaiden wants as many royal priests as we can prepare to invade—and I use the word advisedly—to invade as many campuses as possible to take up the good fight against Satan on that rapidly developing front."

"I see," said Manly, still in the dark as to how it might affect him.

"An Algonquin merchant who was very sympathetic to our cause died recently and bequeathed the Holy Nation a small dry goods store he had owned and operated. It is down at the heels just now and in a neglected part of the town, but Brother Cricklet assures us that the building is sound and has good possibilities. What the Handmaiden wants is for someone we can trust to go there to establish a campus ministry and develop a congregation of the Holy Nation in conjunction with it. She thinks that someone might be you. Mind you, it would be a pioneering effort for us."

"But I never even went to college," Manly expostulated, nameless fears haunting him.

"We know that as well as you," said Emmet with some asperity, "but I believe that you could earn an undergraduate degree, which, together with your RPPl., would be enough, in the first two and a half years of your work there. I've just talked with some of the academic officials about that."

"You have?"

"Yes, and I let it be known where I took my doctorate," said Emmet, looking exceedingly smug. "The upshot is that I am now reasonably sure that some of your work at Big Bend would enable you to get advanced placement in certain departments, thereby accelerating your progress. Furthermore, I believe you could by-pass some requirements by demonstrating competency through examinations."

"I see," said Manly blindly, totally ignorant of such matters.

"It would not be a bed of roses," Emmet went on, making a steeple of his fingers. "No sirree, it would not. Whoever goes to Algonquin or any place like it nowadays will find some very hardened types indeed, inveterate unbelievers, if you take my meaning."

At the mere mention of inveterate unbelievers, Smut Graeber and Tampa Rhine hopscotched through Manly's mind, making him grimace.

"You would find Jews aplenty," Emmet continued, "and I do not mean to refer simply to those who live in their sins under the Law, not knowing grace; I mean antinomian Jews of the worst kind. They are simply infesting physics departments, not to mention psychology. And then there are *those* biologists! Almost without exception, they're evolutionists, being sure to spread their pernicious Darwinism whatever else they do. And so-called liberal Christians too! You talk about an epidemic, well, believe you me, Brother Plumwell, they are also pandemic on university campuses. English, history, and social sciences departments simply abound with them. I don't mind telling you, young man, the life of a royal priest expounding three-world creationism in such a place would be an uphill battle every step of the way."

The more Emmet expatiated on university-related evils, the more Manly realized that he had never before really encountered hardcore sin in its more rampant forms.

"But the Lord didn't command us to pack air mattresses, did he? but to bear our crosses!"

"Very well put, sir!" Manly enthused, making a mental note of that to use in a forthcoming sermon.

Then, as though he had just heard the Lord say, "Emmet, get yourself back to Big Bend," Bro. Van Hook arose, shook Manly's hand, and wheeled toward the front door.

"Couldn't I serve you a cup of coffee or . . . or . . . of . . . ah . . . tea?" Manly managed to ask.

"No," replied Emmet, "no, there's no time for refreshment. The Hand-maiden has had a strong presentiment that the time of Jesus' return has grown very, very short, and I must say, I agree with her."

"But surely, you could just sit and relax for a few moments," Manly urged him, noticing how very long and yellow of tooth he looked.

"I shall have all eternity in which to relax," Emmet said over his departing shoulder, "but now I must work, for the night is surely coming."

"Fare ye well, then, sir," said Manly, unconsciously imitating his grandmother.

With that, Emmet was gone, hastening south to tell the Handmaiden the result of his trip to Algonquin State University and of his subsequent conversation with Bro. Plumwell of Nickel Plate.

Manly walked through the house floating on air, each and every burden of the past year having tumbled from his shoulders to the ground. For several hours he marched or skipped or paced from room to room, now whistling, now singing, now humming the sprightliest hymns in his repertoire. It was foolish, he knew, to feel so elated, for he had not been chosen to go to Algonquin. No more than a mere possibility had been presented to him; yet for the moment that mere possibility promised escape from the millstones of despiteful use and suspicion that were grinding down his spirit daily in Nickel Plate.

But within a few days of Bro. Van Hook's visit, a new millstone began to take shape, so to speak. One by one the nameless fears he had felt (at the thought of going to college) received their names. He might fail his classes at Algonquin. He might seem to be a dunce to his fellow students, all of whom would be younger than he. He might suffer intolerable cuts at the hands of arrogant, sarcastic professors. Three-world creationism might be ridiculed, the Holy Nation might be made the butt of highbrow humor, its pioneering ministry might become a laughingstock—all because of him.

As each newly named fear took on identity, each of the old millstones repositioned itself on his shoulders, leaving him more weighted with misery than before. Added to it all was his dawning realization that he had done about as much as he could do in Nickel Plate. He had more than tripled membership and attendance, had more than quadrupled giving, had led the congregation in purchasing a church bus and in constructing an education building, but, despite all, the pool of potential converts was drying up. The bus had reached the limits of its effectiveness, and not even the assistance of the Koch twins and of other zealots could keep the congregation growing much beyond its present size. The whole enterprise had become a kind of holding action. Nor could Manly be sure of success at that, his reputation having become what it was in various circles and his sermons increasingly repetitious.

The harder he had to work for each new convert, the more important each potential convert became. The more important each potential convert became, the more devastating the loss Manly felt over each one who had "rejected JEsus," as he liked to put it, but had, in fact, merely eluded him. Although he did not recognize it, his evangelism became less the doing of the Lord's will and more the doing of his own will. He believed sincerely that he was representing JEsus and his cause alone but was, in reality, representing himself, feeding his own ego more and more. Feeling himself increasingly boxed in, not knowing where to turn, the persuasiveness of his sermons took on an air of desperation, and some of his attempts at evangelism became overbearing and high-handed.

Autumn came, but no word arrived from Big Bend respecting Algonquin. Early winter came; still no word. The dead of winter came; silence. Resigned to slogging on in Nickel Plate indefinitely, Manly ranged far and wide tracking down converts. One such person was Addie Hodger, who lived in a desolate, weather-beaten farmhouse eleven miles northwest of town. Her husband, Bert (whom Manly had known but not liked when they were schoolboys), worked in a grist mill in Pilsudski and was about as spiritual as Smut Graeber. Addie had come to church a few times the preceding year, bringing along her little boy, Artie, had exhibited wide-eyed wonder at the doctrine of three-world creationism, but had ceased to come. Manly visited her on several occasions thereafter, expressing the fervent hope that she would return to worship with them, only to be put off with what he took to be one lame excuse after another.

Desperate for converts, and with nothing to lose, he put chains on the car and made his perilous way (one January day) over icy roads and through mounting drifts to Addie's place.

Disposing of the pleasantries in jig time, he looked at her mesmerically and said, "We have missed you sorely at worship for some time now."

"Oh, I miss comin' too," she replied with fair candor, "but it just seems like Artie's been sick so much of the time."

As though on cue, Artie coughed croupily in an adjoining room where he was at play.

"Nothing would please us more than to have you become one of us,"

Manly said, his voice tense and imperative.

"Oh, I've thought about it plenty, tryin' to get back and all, but it seems like every time I do, Artie gets down with somethin' new."

A gust of wind roared by, the rickety old house shuddering in its wake. Addie said, "Brrr," and hugged herself tightly. Artie coughed again, at first hacking high in his throat, then rattling phlegm deeper down.

Manly went on compulsively, "JEsus needs you, Addie; he needs your belief, your devotion, your commitment, your assistance; and you need him, oh, yes, you need him, more than you can ever imagine."

"It's not that I'm unwillin', Reverend," she remonstrated in a whiny voice, "it's Artie. He has these awful bad respiratory things, infections, you know. In fact, he ain't supposed to be here today. He's supposed to be in school, but he's down with it again."

Hack, hack, hack, hack, Artie went on, making dry, sore sounds.

"But couldn't Bert look after Artie long enough each week for you to hear the Lord's word?" Manly inquired in such a way as to affirm that Bert most certainly could do that much for her on Sundays when he did not work.

"Oh, I couldn't trust Artie with him," Addie said, "no, I wouldn't even trust a dog with Bert, let alone anybody that's sick."

Artie went hack, hack, hack, hack, hack, hack, endlessly it seemed, and with each repetition, Manly's anger rose; why, he did not know, but it was so.

Above Artie's continued hacking, he said, succumbing to onrushing rage, "Perhaps we should ask the Heavenly Father to take Artie home."

"What?" cried Addie, astounded.

With Artie rattling phlegm in his throat disgustingly, Manly said, "I said, 'Perhaps we should ask the Heavenly Father to take Artie home.'"

"You can't mean that," Addie squealed, making an anguished face.

"Nothing should stand between you and doing what is right," Manly declared, suddenly rising, "no, nothing should be allowed to keep you from accepting JEsus and from becoming a member of his Holy Nation. Your immortal soul is at stake, woman, and you quibble about a kid's cough." With that, he grabbed his coat and stalked out into a gust of wind that nearly flattened him.

At about ten o'clock that night, a pickup, weighted in the rear with cement blocks and running on oversized snow tires, slipped and slid and strained its way through snowdrifts to Manly's place. A menacing figure in stocking cap, mackintosh, and arctics moved laboriously through fifteen inches of new snow up to the door of his front porch. The figure pounded the porch door as though to waken the dead. Startled, Manly dropped the concordance he had been leafing through and went to the door, heart pounding.

Bert Hodger stamped in and, refusing to take off hat or coat or arctics (or to sit down), thundered without preamble, "Did you enjoy the burleque show that night when the stripper fell in your lap?"

Stunned, silent, and as white as the snow outside, Manly recovered enough to recite a favorite passage (Gal. 2:20): " 'I am crucified with Christ; nevertheless I live; yet not I, but Christ liveth in me: and the life which I now live in the flesh I live by the faith of the Son of God, who loved me, and gave himself for me.' "

"Well, mister, I don't know nothin' about that, but if you ever darken the door of my place again, I'm gonna spread that story about you all over Pilsudski County, and if you ever even so much as hint that you'd like to have God kill my kid so my wife can come to that damned church of yours, I'll break you up so bad you won't even have a lap for no bare naked stripper to fall into."

Much later that night, trembling over what had happened and fearing presumption on his part, Manly wrote a terse letter to Dr. Emmet Langhorne Van Hook. It said: "I have prayed much about the Algonquin situation and now believe it to be the Lord's will that I should go there. If the Handmaiden concurs, I am at your disposal at your earliest convenience."

Chapter Five

With each passing day at Algonquin State University, Manly's fears of higher education abated. So well did he do in his courses that he cited Romans 8:28 in his first annual progress report to Dr. Van Hook, who wrote back, saying in part, "Yes, indeed, all things do work together for good to them that love God, to them who are the called according to his purpose." From preliminary talks with various academic officials Emmet knew better than Manly that ASU supplied the ideal setting for the Holy Nation's pioneering campus ministry.

Under the dynamic leadership of President Sythian MacGilvary (who knew what was good for ASU "student-wise" and "appropriations-wise") and the imperious influence of Dean Dirk Smalley of the School of Education, Algonquin was nothing if not innovative. In addition to a respectable number of ordinary undergraduate curricula, ASU had one very attractive curriculum called "The Career Curriculum," or "CC" for short. CC, administered by the School of Education, was designed to provide university credentials to people who were already well into their careers but who possessed no degree.

"It's not experience these people need; it's not formal education these people need; it's not a lot of academic or professional requirements these people need; it's letters after their names they need; it's degrees they need," Dean Dirk Smalley declared irresistibly at a meeting of the Board of Trustees. Thus CC was born, and thus people who were into everything from hooking rugs to honey dipping, from selling cable TV to white water rafting could tailor-make their own curricula (with certain limitations, of course) and acquire the desired letters after their names.

Needless to say, CC was the fastest growing curriculum on campus and a source of great strength to the School of Education, the dominant School at ASU, the others in rapidly descending order being Arts and Sciences, Music and Theater, and Home Economics and Nursing. In short, CC brought hundreds of people to ASU who would never have entered a university otherwise (including Bro. Manly John Plumwell, RPP1.).

Perceiving at once the advantages of CC, Emmet tailor-made Manly's curriculum. He was to major in adult education and minor in speech communication and art. Proceeding toward his degree in that manner, he would not be imperiled by a so-called liberal education. Indeed, with that kind of curriculum, getting a liberal education would be impossible.

Emmet's choice of a major field was a master stroke for at least four reasons. First, nobody who attended classes regularly and who could answer such questions as "How do you *feel* about this?" or "What is *your reaction* to that?" had been known to fail. Since there could be no wrong answers to such questions, failure was impossible. Second, adult education professors were most considerate of the clergy, viewing them as fellow educators and custodians of the highest moral values. Third, since the adult education professors could be depended on to know little of the Bible and less of dogmatics, nothing prejudicial to the Holy Nation was liable to be taught. Fourth, since Manly was to function in an academic community (largely with people of college age or above), it was only natural that he should major in something that had "adult" in its title.

Emmet's choice of speech communication as a minor field was also masterly. Since the name of Iskander Moutsopoulos was still highly esteemed, Manly was able to by-pass "Public Speaking I and II" and get full credit. As might have been expected, he excelled in the more advanced speech courses he took and learned to read the Scriptures aloud more dogmatically than before as a result of his course in oral interpretation. Although Emmet knew speech professors to be less pious on the whole than adult education people, and more articulate, he thought it unlikely that a student minoring in speech communication would encounter much that would be prejudicial to new Jews; and he was right.

Since Manly was moderately talented at drawing, being able to do chalk art pictures without using guidelines; since it would be good for him to continue using that medium in his evangelistic efforts at Algonquin; and since there would be nothing detrimental to three-world creationism in drawing classes, again, the choice was brilliant.

Actually, Manly's CC resembled a liberal arts curriculum more than most, for with Emmet's direction or approval, he took courses in English, history, political science, mathematics, science, and philosophy (yes, philosophy, but via the foundations of education, of which, more later).

Since his grammar and diction were good, his vocabulary above average, he was allowed to by-pass freshman English, yet receive credit for it. He also demonstrated knowledge equivalent to that expected of students in a course in the English Bible as literature. A directed reading course in the Puritan divines of early America rounded out his literary studies. Since he knew the Bible better than the directing professor and could distinguish parable from putative history as well as he, and since neither knew anything about the history of Christian thought or philosophical theology, he did very well.

Lamentably ignorant of history in the view of Algonquin's historians, Manly took the year-long freshman sequence in the history of civilization.

Emmet thought it a safe subject, believing that Manly could be exposed to it and remain just as he was. It was not that he learned no new facts; it was just that he learned nothing from them, all of his presuppositions remaining precisely what they had been, no new supposition entering his mind nor disturbing any of the old ones. Such was the beauty of the subject.

The history department was filled with learned folk who knew a great deal about what had happened but none of them knew for sure (at any deep level of explanation) why what had happened had happened. Those who believed that history was made by great men could not deny that God had made the great good men what they were nor that Satan had made the great bad men what they were. The historians who subscribed to the notion that ideas, exalted thoughts, and visions had uplifted mankind from barbarism could not deny that God had planted the good ideas and visions in the minds of those who had had them, nor could anyone deny that it was Satan who had sent lying spirits (or was it God, in view of I Kings 22:23 or II Thess. 2:11?) to those whose ideas and visions had been bad, ignoble, and barbaric. Not even the sole economic determinist (but not a Marxist) in the department (an irresolute person who feared for his position and wanted to curry friendships) could deny that economic man was just another name for man in the service of mammon rather than God. As far as any of the historians knew, original sin was as good an explanatory category as any other and a lot better than most. There was, of course, no confessed Marxist on the staff, it being agreed that ASU had not yet reached that level of maturity.

As a group, Algonquin historians were convinced that there was no science of human behavior, but, knowing nothing of genetics, neurophysiology, behaviorism, or anthropology (either physical or cultural), they could not be sure. Being tolerant and urbane, they were content to live with a great deal of uncertainty about causality in human affairs and to entertain the widest variety of interpretive concepts, including the will of God. Manly was as ideally suited for his studies in the history of civilization as it was for him, being taught the way it was. As one of Algonquin's philosophers was overheard saying, "Any halfway coherent mythology that a student really believes in will do all the good and more for that student than the freshman sequence in the history of civilization, the latter merely confusing the student with facts."

"Submit yourselves to every ordinance of man for the Lord's sake; whether it be to the king as supreme; Or unto governors, as unto them that are sent by him for the punishment of evildoers, and for the praise of them that do well." So said the Lord's rock (I Pet. 2:13-14), and, not surprisingly, the Lord's apostle to the Gentiles agreed, saying (in Rom. 13:1-4), "Let every soul be subject unto the higher powers. For there is no power but of God: the powers that be are ordained of God. Whosoever therefore resisteth the power, resisteth the ordinance of God: and they that resist shall receive to themselves damnation. For rulers are not a terror to good works, but to the evil. Wilt thou then not be afraid of the power? do that which is good, and

236

thou shalt have praise of the same: For he is the minister of God to thee for good. But if thou do that which is evil, be afraid; for he beareth not the sword in vain; for he is the minister of God, a revenger to *execute* wrath upon him that doeth evil." Although they were members of a Holy Nation and were new Jews, royal priests of the pulpit and pew alike were super-patriotic Americans and law-abiding to an astonishing degree. Little wonder then that Emmet had Manly take courses in local, state, and federal government that he might know something of the ordinances of God for these latter days. But, in light of what Bro. Dickinson was up to, there was an ulterior purpose.

At about the time when Manly was being despitefully used by anonymous mail, Alice and the Five articulated some conclusions as curious as they were momentous. First, the federal and state governments had secretly adopted a godless religion and were promoting it to the detriment of the true faith. Second, the godless religion in question was humanism, its promotion being undertaken in the public schools. Third, its most insidious manifestations occurred in biology courses, textbooks, and classrooms, but elsewhere as well. Fourth, the insidious manifestations in question had to do with the godless theory of evolution developed by the demon-inspired Darwin.

"It is Satan's master stroke," said Alice vehemently, "his finest hour by far."

"But what can we do?" clamored four of the Five, close to despair.

"I think I know," said Bro. Endicott Peabody Dickinson.

Even as Manly was studying political science, Dickinson was looking for just the right situation, the right community, the right public school system, and the right court in which to engage Satan in litigation. Dickinson would argue that the public school system was coercive; that, as coercive, it was in a position to violate the students' right to the free exercise of religion; that it did so by teaching them only one point of view in courses touching on the origin of life and mankind. Under the guise of science, the public schools were forcing children to learn the godless religion of Darwin. Since Dr. Perry W. D. Hornbuckle (the well-known Ph.D. in biochemistry from the University of Illinois) had already proved that scientific three-world creationism was scientific, what possible justification could there be for not giving it equal time and emphasis in all relevant courses in the public schools? Yes, thought Emmet, aware of the forthcoming litigation, we royal priests ought to know more about the government and how it works, especially its courts. Without recognizing it, Manly was a pioneer in more ways than one.

He rounded out his curriculum with courses in three other fields. He took something called "Business Mathematics Education, I, II," work that Emmet thought might be useful in church management and budgeting. He also took a course called "General Practical Science for Non-Scientists," which was taught by a dietician in the School of Home Economics and Nursing. Emmet thought that that might make him a bit handier around the building that was to serve as the Algonquin Church of the Chosen.

Finally, he took "The Foundations of Education I, II, III." Since it was a commonplace among students that all one had to do to master the material was to hear it once, and since the same content was delivered in each of the three courses, Manly, hearing it three times, had the material well fixed in his mind. It was there, for all practical purposes, that he took his work in philosophy, the names of several philosophers being mentioned together with such words as "realism," "idealism," "rationalism," "empiricism," and "existentialism." It was commonly believed by the professors (but less commonly believed by most of the students) that there were some relationships between some of the philosophers mentioned and the philosophical works on the one hand and certain educational practices on the other. What the relationships were and whether or not they were consequential was never made clear to the students. Manly did, however, learn how to quote famous philosophers and other weighty thinkers out of context, a device that made his sermons more powerful—around Algonquin at least.

"Under no circumstances take anything in the philosophy department," Emmet warned him, "because they put reason above faith and are all sceptics and humanists deep down."

"I won't," vowed Manly.

"And nothing in the religion department, because religion professors around universities are all modernists and the worst hypocrites in the world."

"I won't."

"Avoid biologists like the plague; they're all evolutionists. Don't ever let one get in a position of authority over you."

"Yes, sir . . . er . . . ah . . . no, sir."

"Steer clear of psychologists; some of them may *seem* nice, but they're a queer lot and have really nasty minds, together with profane tongues."

"No need to worry about that, sir."

"And, finally, keep your distance from sociologists and anthropologists. The former are all socialists or worse, and the latter are as abhorrent as biologists and the psychologists rolled into one."

"I will."

Manly embarked upon his higher education the summer after he realized it was God's will that he leave Nickel Plate and go to Algonquin. Once there it took him only two summers plus two full academic years to be graduated. Thus, Bro. Manly John Plumwell, RPP1., acquired the letters "B.S. Ed." after his name, and with high honor. So exemplary had his CC been that advisors in Dean Dirk Smalley's office used it as a model of what could be wrought by a strongly motivated student well into his life's work. For Manly to have accomplished so much in so short a time and yet to have remained so much what he was before matriculating might seem noteworthy. But not so; ASU students did (and do) it all the time. In fairness it should be pointed out, however, that his work there, especially in the foundations of education, made him considerably craftier in handling abstract ideas than he had been.

Like Bro. Van Hook, Bros. Dickinson, Montefiori, and Cricklet preceded Manly to Algonquin: Dickinson to conclude legal matters relative to Embery Howland's bequest of his dry goods store, Montefiori to examine the economic situation and determine the size of Manly's subsidy while in school and in the initial phases of establishing a congregation and campus ministry, Cricklet to renovate the building that had housed Howland's store.

The building was a simple, two-story, rectangular structure of yellow brick sandwiched between a meat market and an auto parts store. Cricklet converted the second story into an apartment for the minister (at the front of the building where there were windows) and into a large, multipurpose room with many folding doors and moveable partitions, the two areas being connected by a spacious kitchen that could be used for social occasions as well as by a minister on a daily basis. Access to the second floor could be gained by an internal stairwell leading up from the church office/pastor's study on the first floor at the rear of the building. Access to either floor could be gained by an external stairway that led to an alley and parking lot in the rear.

When facing what had been Howland's Dry Goods Store, the customer entered by a door at the extreme right. Cricklet built a wall from floor to fourteen-foot ceiling along the entire length of what had been the sales area of the store. Three quarters of the way toward the back of the building, the resulting corridor connected with what had been a private work area, the area that Cricklet made into the church office/pastor's study. At the front of the building the long corridor, which communicated at that point with the sanctuary/auditorium, served as a vestibule. At the rear it served as a robing area for the choir or a staging area for processions. Folding doors, strategically located along the length of the corridor, gave it flexibility and privacy as needed.

Except for the front door at the extreme right, the entire front wall of the first story of the building was composed of two large plate glass windows. Immediately behind (or inside) those windows, Cricklet built frames for four panels of his plastic stained glass. Each panel ended in a Gothic arch at the top.

The panels told the story of three-world creationism. When viewed from inside, the first panel (on the left) told the story of God's creation and destruction of the first heaven and the first earth. Blues, grays, and greens predominated as the waters of the great deep deluged the first earth. Close inspection of the saga (which was to be read, so to speak, from top to bottom) revealed the twinkling lights of the sun, moon, and stars of the first firmament, the tempting serpent, the succumbing woman, the fall of man, and the saving ark of Noah. The second panel began at the top with the ark safely resting on Ararat, the pinnacle of the second earth, and ended at the bottom with the emergence of Christ from the tomb, as much of sacred history as possible being sandwiched between the two scenes. For that panel Cricklet used a full palette of color. The third panel could be read from bottom to top or from side to side as well as from top to bottom. It represented the end of the second earth and the second heaven. Blazing reds, angry browns, sulphureous yellows, and stabbing orange opened the eyes of the beholder to fervent heat as the elements melted, popping and cracking. The fourth panel, the one to the extreme right, depicted the third heaven and the third earth. Since it was surrealistic, it did not commit the beholder to any particular physical geography. Translucent blues, inviting lavenders, and sumptuous purples gave intimations of the opulence to come, the ever-greens of the leaves of the trees of eternal life bespeaking endless refreshment for the souls of the saved.

The four panels that Cricklet designed could not be compared in jewel-like effect with any of the great rose windows of any of the major European cathedrals, nor was he an artist to compare with Matisse or Chagall, but what he did was very beautiful, very moving, a veritable invitation to step into an enchanted world not only rich in beauty but laden with meaning.

Overhead, he carried out the Gothic motif with exposed beams arched upward with beauty, though not with true function. From the ceiling he hung beautiful eight-sided chandeliers with plastic panels of his own design. Recessed colored floodlights, to compensate for the absence of windows in the sanctuary, answered the panels of the windows and the chandeliers. At eye level, richly stained veneers and velvet cloths here and there completed his work. To the uncritical eye, the interior of Algonquin's Church of the Chosen was better than any of the college Gothic on campus and on a par with many a legitimate work of Gothic art. So seductive was the church physically as a place of reverence, taste, and beauty that many also took it to be a place of intelligence and truth.

A computer search at Big Bend revealed the names of sixteen people in and around Algonquin who were on the Holy Nation's mailing list. Since several of those were heads of households, it could be assumed that Manly would find a viable nucleus around which to develop a new congregation. Among those identified, the most important were Dr. Atherton Landis, Assistant Professor of Family and Child Development in the School of Home Economics and Nursing (and his wife, Mabel), Mr. Garvis James, Assistant Director of Buildings and Grounds at the university (and his wife, Mona), and a bachelor librarian at ASU named Rollo Skeeds.

With the nucleus of his new congregation, Manly was able to proceed much as he had at Nickel Plate, preaching the same sermons, conducting the same rites of passage, making pastoral calls, distributing tracts, and teaching the same doctrines in the same way in Bible classes. It was as a campus minister that he was embarking on the unknown. He felt as he imagined a person who had just been blinded would feel. There he was in darkness at noon, keeping his balance awkwardly at best, feeling his way, groping, stumbling, fearing a wire across his path, putting each foot down tentatively, tapping clumsily with a white cane, straying off the path, off the sidewalk, off the road, straying into one desolate place after another.

At a time when there was unprecedented cooperation between mainline

Protestant groups, between those groups and Catholics, between Catholics and liberal Jews, and between liberal Jews and progressive Protestants, Manly appeared as an alien from a distant age, indeed, as a throwback in the eyes of many. At a place where the ecumenical movement was succeeding daily (as picayunish differences in doctrine were discarded) in ministering to students from broken homes and checkered pasts, in ministering to those who were threatened by a burgeoning war or left distraught by it, to those who were increasingly alienated from society and sunk in anomie, to those who were damaging themselves to a shocking degree with dope and drugs, Manly came as a competitor or, as seen by some, a predator, so hard did he strive to convert students from other religious denominations rather than from unbelief, sin, or self-destruction.

He couldn't go to the Episcopal College Center or to the Wesley Foundation and say to their directors, "I'm new in town and new to this racket and not very well prepared for what I'm here to do. Could you give me some pointers and a little help along the way?" He couldn't go to the Newman Club and say to those in charge, "I know there's a lot that divides us, but we have enough in common to cooperate in ministering to some desperately needy young people," nor could he say to the counselors of the small B'nai B'rith Hillel group, "We share to a very great degree the same tradition, so let's be friends and do what we can to preserve that tradition against an uncaring world." No, he could go to none of those religious centers, could speak to none of their professional leaders; for those leaders were his enemies. No one of them accepted the Handmaiden's tutelage; no one of them was a new Jew; no one of them believed in three-world creationism. They were, therefore, all heretics, apostates, and perverters of the gospel, even the local antievolutionists of one-world creationism. Nor could he turn to the noncampus clergy of Algonquin for help, solace, or encouragement. He was alone and, temporarily at least, blind in a strange land.

But not all the denizens of that strange new land were strange. At the beginning of each new term, ASU's admissions office sent a computer printout to every campus minister, giving the church membership or preference of all new students. Thus was Manly led to his own, and they in turn led him to others of their kind. Members of his congregation, from both town and gown, gave him additional leads, and, then too, he found birds of his own feather in nearly every class he took. Had he been more sophisticated, he might well have been amazed, if not appalled, at the number of kindred spirits there were at ASU.

As a whole, Algonquin students were more ready to believe than to think, far more open to articles of faith than to items of knowledge, more given to things of the spirit than to things of the mind, and withal incompetent to tell which was which. Manly found plenty of them who were receptive to the story of JEsus as he told it and who accepted three-world creationism with open-mouthed enthusiasm. "That's a really neat doctor . . . or . . . I mean doctrine," said one boy, a freshman in accounting. "Oh, wow,

241

what a groovy belief, really realsville," burbled a girl spaced out on marijuana. "It kind of blows my mind, you know, but it does explain a lot of questions I had about the Bible and stuff like that," said a senior in lab technology. "It's really cool, man; it's right in the Bible in Peter-something," said several students trying to convince an unbeliever on the steps of the student union.

The problem was that many who really "dug" the Handmaiden, who hung on her every miracle, and who rejoiced in three-world creationism also had ears easily tickled by other beliefs, by beliefs that were abhorrent to Manly and to all new Jews. The believing-ones of ASU awaited the emergence of Atlantis from the sea, expected the Great White Ones of Venus to alight at any moment, believed with the Brotherhood of the Rosy Cross in the sixth (spiritual) sense of man (or of ancient man at least), pored over books of astrology more than they read the Bible, and were ready to drop out of school at a moment's notice to search as questing pilgrims for the sacred city of Shamballa. Indeed, they believed all things, hoped all things, and trusted all things enticing.

And were they ignorant of the Scriptures? God, they were ignorant! When a mature student asked Manly in all seriousness to expound on what the Book of Revelations had to say about the four Norsemen of the Acropolis, he knew just how ignorant they were.

And were they dismissive of authority? God, they were dismissive! With the authority of the family in shambles, with the authority of organized religion in question (including the Catholic Church and its pope), with academic authorities acting like ninety-pound weaklings, and with the authority of the secular authorities a paper tiger more often than not, how could the Bible hold out against the erosion? How could God? Closer to home, how could Manly? Indeed how could he keep his footing when everything that he stood for was in danger of being swept away, not so much by a torrent of unbelief as by a miles-wide flow of imbecility that rolled on and ever on?

And were they carnally minded? God, they were carnally minded! Of all the sins at ASU, the sexual ones distressed him the most, not so much because of their frequency or even their variety, but because of the insouciance with which they were committed. Nothing drove that home more forcefully than a mimeographed glossary that Atherton Landis thrust into his hands one afternoon during his second term at the university. Having just attended his science class in Wheelwright Hall (which housed the School of Home Economics and Nursing), Manly stopped in to see Atherton for a much-needed moment of Christian camaraderie.

Since in speech as many roads lead to the subject of sex as in religion lead to Rome, sex came up. Dithering, Atherton pulled a sheet of paper from a folder on his desk and toyed with it. As conservative as Manly in sex ethics, but married and not so naive, he said, "Perhaps I . . . I shouldn't let you . . . ah . . . see this bit of filth, but I suppose you have to know as well as . . . ah . . . I what we Christians are up against in these latter days."

242

Assuring Atherton that his ears had heard many a confession and that he was no stranger to sin himself, Manly took the proffered sheet.

Leaning back in his chair, Atherton said, "Here's the story that goes with it: It seems that a certain vulgar student named Caudrell or Caudell or something like that, a female no less, in that blessed psychology department of ours, began referring to any girl who was known to have had sexual relations as a 'laid maid' or a 'made maid.' In no time, a virgin came to be known as an 'unmade maid,' and from there on it simply took off. What you have in your hand is a glossary of spin-offs from that humble beginning here at good old Algonquin. Read and weep."

Manly read:

allayed maid: one who has just been talked out of, or has otherwise lost, the last of her fears about going all the way (see *swayed maid*).

ambi-aid maid: a newly coined term not widely accepted that refers to one who is equally enthusiastic about pursuing the orgasm with persons of either sex (not to be confused with a *ladies-aid maid*).

belayed maid: one who has become the exclusive sexual partner of another person, usually but not necessarily of the opposite sex; a steady.

betrayed maid: one who has done it with someone who kisses *and* tells; one who mistakenly thought she was a *belayed maid* or had belayed her partner.

cool-aid maid: any sexually experienced female who teaches a sexually innocent male how to do it with her.

delayed maid: any female who has become a senior or (ugh!) a graduate student while retaining the tokens of virginity, but not necessarily on principle (see *staid maid*).

fade maid: one who is known to have been sexually active but who has desisted for a time due to various concerns or inhibiting factors (see *jade maid*).

flayed maid: one who allows herself to be screwed masochistically or otherwise to experience sex-associated pain.

glade-maid: one who does not mind having intercourse, occasionally at least, while lying or otherwise positioned on grass, sand (as on a beach), or other natural surfaces out of doors.

grade maid: one who tries to get high grades in areas other than carnal knowledge and may sacrifice the latter for the former.

inlaid maid: one who is too fastidious to be a *glade maid* but who will do it on such man-made surfaces as satin sheets, naugahide, shag rugs, etc., especially indoors.

jade maid: an oriental cookie; in the sense of jaded (see *fade maid*).

ladies-aid maid: a Lesbian (see but do not confuse with an *ambi-aid maid*).

laid maid: one who is known to have participated in her first act of sexual intercourse, especially recently (see *made maid*).

made maid: see *laid maid.*

man-made maid: redundant; thought to be in bad taste by some, being prejudicial to mere boys.

marmalade maid: a young girl above puberty but not yet of normal college age who has been taken to bed by an upperclassman, a graduate student, or other older male.

mislaid maid: one who has gotten pregnant unintentionally.

paid maid: anyone who does it for money, a call girl, hooker, or prostitute (see *trade maid*).

played maid: one who will engage in heavy sexual play including oral sex but will not permit intercourse.

raid maid: a policewoman, perhaps a decoy, attached to a vice squad or otherwise engaged in enforcing sex laws especially as they relate to the unmarried; a Dean of Women or other female campus functionary charged with impeding, suppressing, or preventing the exercise of academic freedom to have carnal knowledge.

re-laid maid: too obvious to need definition, you ninny, you!

relayed maid: one who has had sexual relations with several partners seriatim such as fraternity brothers; one who will engage in group sex.

remade maid: one who taken to be a female originally but wishing to be male has undergone a sex change operation; one who taken to be male but wishing to be female has undergone a sex change operation (not known to apply to anyone at Algonquin at the time of compilation).

repaid maid: one who has been screwed vengefully or has had condign justice meted out to her sexually.

replayed maid: a *played maid* who does and doesn't what she does and doesn't with more than one partner.

sashayed maid: one who is in the process of being seduced (whether she knows it or not) by being taken to many dances (especially discos), parties, drinking bouts, etc.

spade maid: one of African descent.

splayed maid: see *flayed maid,* and use your imagination!

staid maid: one who retains her virginity on principle as for example a nun, vestal virgin, or perhaps a Dean of Women, etc.

swayed maid: one who has been persuaded to make love forthwith (see *allayed maid*).

trade maid: see *paid maid.*

unmade maid: a virgin, especially one who is not a *played* or a *replayed maid.*

waylaid maid: one who has been raped or is the victim of an attempted rape.

Manly did not weep, but he did shudder with colliding emotions, being as repelled as he was enticed, as enticed as repelled.

"Except for the exception made for the remade maid," Atherton observed somberly, "those cute terms are not just idle vulgarities, not just innovative pornography put together by foul-minded students with nothing better to do. They actually name kinds of people, kinds of people who are to be seen all over this campus. Why, when you have 7,500 students at a state university nowadays, you have just about everything there is sexually—all the lust, all the depravity, all the perversion you can imagine."

Being no stranger to sin by his own bold admission and having heard many a confession, Manly could hardly admit how torn asunder he was over what he had just seen, but he wished that Atherton would shut up. Atherton, however, went on glibly (but censoriously) giving Manly fascinating new evils to imagine with every breath. Finally, adverting to the Lord's work which would brook no delay, Manly arose to go.

"I could get one of these for you if you'd like it," Atherton offered, making a bad face as though the glossary stank.

"No, no, there's no need for that," Manly almost shouted, making a bad face in return. Nor was there, for with one avid reading the delicious-detestable thing had become a perdurable part of his consciousness, effortlessly. Nor did he, could he, look upon girls and young women as innocently as before, for the enticing-repelling, delicious-detestable thing was ever ready for pigeon-holing pigeons. Upon seeing any early blooming teenybopper (the town of Algonquin was full of them) he could not block *marmalade maid* from his mind. When driven at various times from campus sidewalks by coveys of girls chattering noisily, he could not keep the glossary's labels from vaulting into consciousness, begging to be used. "Hey, Brother Plumwell," yelled *delayed maid*, "use me on that homely, shy, awkward, lumpy one bringing up the rear." "Use me, use me, oh, please, use me on that prim, proper, reserved, fastidious one," insisted *unmade maid*, "before she gets *allayed* and *swayed* and *made*." "Look at that one with the thick glasses, and the high forehead, and the flat chest, and the enormous bundle of books," piped *grade maid*, "if I don't fit her, I can't imagine what does." Whenever Manly chanced upon an amply endowed girl casually dressed and lollygagging around a boy out of doors on the grass or in the arboretum, he couldn't resist using *glade maid*, and every time he espied a boy getting a quick kiss from a girl in a campus building, *inlaid maid* clamored for application. Despite his best efforts to the contrary, he found himself appraising all the unmarried women of his flock, wondering which among them were *unmade* (if really *unmade*) merely because *delayed* or due to being *staid*. Once when a distraught member of his mid-week Bible class remained behind to confess to having gotten pregnant after a wild party, he blurted out, "So, you were *sashayed* and got *mislaid!*" Would he even recognize a *paid maid* if he saw one? he wondered. Might a *cool-aid maid* ever accost him with his own free instruction on her mind? How could he minister to a *flayed maid* or a *ladies-aid maid*, should either one come to him for spiritual guidance? About to enter the church one day, an especially noisy semi-truck and trailer rig caught his attention. The name on the truck was Peterbuilt. Aren't we all? he thought in an unguarded moment, whereupon the whole horrid glossary paraded through his mind, each label skipping and gamboling as it went. Was there to be no end to it? No, not so long as he remained at ASU. Even then, in what for him was an idle moment, a philosophy professor was

245

dashing off an addendum that was to include *accolade maid, afraid maid, degrade maid, evade maid, blockade maid, re-maid maid, retrograde maid,* and *scaid maid* (an *afraid spade maid*). Manly resolved to pray for all the fallen maids at Algonquin, each becoming in that way a *prayed maid*.

Were ASU students carnally minded? God, they were carnal! Was their carnality a heavy cross for the Holy Nation's pioneering campus minister to bear? God, what a crushing weight it was! But, as Bro. Van Hook had put it so splendidly, Jesus hadn't called on his disciples to "pack air mattresses" (would that be *glade maid* or *inlaid maid*?), but to "bear their crosses." So, Manly slogged on, stumbling but not falling, toward his own Calvary.

Ironically, the fields at ASU whitest for harvest involved some of the departments against which Emmet had warned Manly most vehemently, for example, the religion department. As a whole it was opera buffa. Each of its four professors embodied a curious but different blend of the academic and the religious. Each was naive in believing what he believed; each was guileful and dextrous in resorting to so-called higher theological truths whenever it became important to flee lower nontheological truths; and each was paternalistic in steering students away from readily available but disagreeable information prejudicial to the favored religion. The department labored under two delusions: first, that the academic study of religion would deepen and broaden the students' religiosity and, second, that they would benefit from learning what they did not want to know, namely, the precise meaning of their sacred texts and the actual historical development of their favorite religion(s). But the students didn't give a hang about any of that. What they wanted were spiritual highs; they wanted their minds blown. Failing that, they wanted to feel warm, good, clean, protected, buoyed up, and exonerated. At a bare minimum they wanted their favorite texts to keep saying what they had understood them to say since childhood. They wanted those texts to speak to their particular problems, peccadillos, and preoccupations in the decade of grace 1960 or thereabouts. They could not have cared less what a bunch of illiterate shepherds had understood upon hearing the same information in 1960 B.C., give or take a thousand years. Since the religion professors could not deliver the goods the students wanted, there was grumbling, disaffection, and uncertainty. Such indignant complaints reached the dean's office as, "I guess I know what I believe, but that's not what they teach in the religion department," and "Unless you are really strong in faith, you better not take any religion courses." What a wonderful opportunity ASU's religion department was for a certain pioneering campus minister!

Then there was that haven for sick souls known as the psychology department. Since majoring in psychology at ASU was cheaper than psychoanalysis or other expensive therapies, many "sickies" entered the department bent on acquiring sure-fire do-it-to-yourself therapeutic techniques. Some students, lusting after power over other people, entered the field because a knowledge of psychology was supposed to confer upper-handsmanship on those who possessed it. Still others (those with a keyhole mentality) studied psychology because they enjoyed probing in dark places, especially when those places were lubricious. But what did these various seekers find in their studies? They found numbers and the need to quantify everything in sight; they found statistics, testing, and more statistics. Such frights as neurophysiology and biochemistry also confronted some of them. Among the human terrors that confronted all of them were the behaviorists, would-be despots wielding laws of human behavior, according to rumor. Furthermore, they were embroiled in spirited quarreling, on principle, between the behaviorists and the non-behaviorists and collided with numerous prima donnas on the psychology faculty who were quarrelsome but not on principle. To cap it off, the department had of late gotten a strain of intractable rats that were turning the labs in animal learning into shambles. The result was a large number of aggrieved, painfully self-preoccupied, guilt-ridden young quantifiers. Manly intuited opportunities to minister to the "sickies" and the "screwups" in the department but also sensed that he must tread warily around the professors, people who were notorious for blowing their stacks and delivering themselves of venomous profanities under the guise of catharsis. Yes, he would walk warily, but he would walk.

The philosophy department was part of the price President Sythian MacGilvary paid for getting Algonquin upgraded from a teachers' college to a state university. It was commonly believed by his peers that nothing did more to make an aspiring institution of higher learning appear to be serious about academic respectability than the presence of philosophers. So, for public relations purposes, Sythian went on record as one who had always believed philosophy to be a beautiful subject and posed as one administrator who was doing all he could to hasten the glad day when Algonquin could boast of its own genuine, albeit small, department. Privately, of course, he knew that philosophers, especially at their most innocent, could be dangerous, their activities boat-rocking to administrators, their subject matter troublesome to students and parents alike. At its worst, he wanted a department that would simply be irrelevant (except for public relations); at its best, one that would be an adjunct to the religion department.

With the appointment of Sterling Armistead (Ph.D., Princeton) as the first department head/faculty member of philosophy, Sythian realized as many of his fondest hopes for the department as he could reasonably have expected. An ethereal Anglophile, Sterling was far more desirous of levitating to empyrean realms where he could behold Truth, Beauty, and Goodness in their pure, primal, and permanent forms than of ministering to earthbound individuals always gravitating downward into carnality. Thus, he turned from the Episcopal ministry to theology and thence to philosophy. For reasons the profane mind cannot grasp, his rational mysticism and recondite pursuits attracted many of the same intractably naive and invincibly ignorant students as did the religion department. The result was that the philosophy department grew in numbers and in favor with Sythian MacGilvary.

Committed to writing a definitive work proving logically that such categories as "temporality," "transience," and "ephemerality" could not have Platonic Forms as their referents (whereas "eternality," "permanence," and "perdurability" could and did), Sterling mislaid many a university form, failed to appear on time, if at all, at meetings called by his administrative betters, took a detached attitude toward budgetary matters (even though the philosophy budget was "permanently" small), and often overlooked those particular transient loci of carnality known as students.

With the census in philosophy rising at the same time Sterling was ascending above and beyond sublunary concerns, the administration appointed a new department head, one Kiefer Maddox, an ebullient pragmatist from Johns Hopkins. Kiefer seemed perfectly safe to Dean (of Arts and Sciences) Hamilton S. F. Braniff, to Vice President (of Academic Affairs) Jay Graves Roberts, and to President MacGilvary. Prior to his appointment, Kiefer had cheerfully declared that students at a place like ASU ought to have every opportunity to study the nonrational, the uncerebral, and the noncognitive as well as the rational. Furthermore, though not orthodox, he was most respectful of religion, knowing it to be an enormous force in human life, helping people by the droves to realize their goals. Since it worked in achieving many of the things people wanted, it was good, and being good, was true too. Best of all, Kiefer was a hail-fellow well met, a joiner of clubs, an enthusiastic participant in committee work, and a booster of the Algonquin Braves every time any team bearing that proud name took to the playing field or court. In short, he was as American as apple pie. To say that the department grew under his leadership would be to put it mildly. So, another faculty member was added.

Algonquin's third philosopher was Rhadamanthus Reid. Named for the just and great judge of the underworld in Greek legend (by his classicist-mother and jurist-father), he was nurtured in a staunchly Presbyterian home in the town of Jackson in "Bloody Breathitt" County, Kentucky. Despite his name and nurture, the lanky lad left home in the fullness of time to play basketball at the University of Kentucky, incidentally studying chemistry while there. Distressed that he had shown no bent for the classics and none for the law, the elder Reids were pleasantly mollified when he entered the University of Michigan to earn the doctorate in philosophy. True, they could have chosen happier specialties than symbolic logic, the philosophy of science, and epistemology (the theory of knowledge), but he could have done worse, as his earlier inclinations had shown. By the time he reached Algonquin, he was a genial giant of a man with a moustache to match. So committed to teaching philosophy did he become, so splendid a colleague, and so much a father confessor to his adoring students that the administration lost its initial unease over his appointment.

Such, then, was its philosophy department when Manly was a student at ASU. Neither totally irrelevant nor perfectly a handmaiden to theology, still

248

and all, it served its purpose and did not rock Algonquin's boat. Though he took no courses in the department, being dutiful to Emmet, Manly was increasingly attracted to it, especially as he neared graduation. Like the religion department, it clearly had its quota of lost souls; like psychology, its screwed-up souls. Indeed, some psychology students, traumatized by behaviorism, had fled to philosophy seeking the consolations of existentialism and phenomenology. With his degree in hand, Manly decided it was high time to establish contact with ASU's philosophers and to begin making evangelistic forays among their students. What he did not know was that a momentous change was about to occur in the department.

"Yes, sir, Kiefer, what can I do for you?" asked Dean Hamilton S. F. Braniff, rising from his desk to greet his philosophy head.

"I want to be like you, Dean," said Kiefer even before he had sat down.

"You what?" the dean shrilled, not always ready for Kiefer's humorous sallies.

"I'd like to try my hand at administration at your level or at the academic vice president's," replied Kiefer, bursting with enthusiasm.

"Fine, fine," approved the dean, reflecting momentarily on his own satisfying lot in life, "but how do I fit into your plans?"

"By supporting my candidacy for a Harrington Full-Stipend Grant to study administration in higher education."

"For how long?"

"One year or possibly two."

"And what happens to the department while you're off and gone?" asked the dean, putting on a grave air so as not to be thought a pushover.

"Sterling can surely manage for a year or two," said Kiefer mischievously.

"Perish the thought!" Braniff erupted, ready for Kiefer's humor for a change and even emitting a deanly chuckle.

"Seriously, there's no reason why Rad couldn't serve as acting head, and we could seek a temporary replacement for me at the instructor's or assistant's level—the woods're full of good young people—and could even save the university some money out of my salary."

"So, you're asking for three things," the dean recapitulated, "(a) you want our support for your candidacy for one of the Harrington Grants, (b) you want a leave of absence for at least a year, subject to possible renewal, and (c) you want us to help you get so damned good, you'll leave Algonquin for a nice plum somewhere else."

"Except for part (c) that's it exactly," replied Kiefer diplomatically.

"Let me talk with Jay about it," the dean said, rising to signal the end of the conversation, "and I'll get back with you soon. You know, of course, that I'll support you to the hilt, but I wouldn't want you to leave us permanently."

"Thanks a lot, Dean," Kiefer said, smiling broadly, "see you around."

The announcement Manly read in the *Algonquin Daily Messenger* to the effect that Prof. Kiefer Maddox had won a coveted Harrington Grant to study university administration at Cornell for a year left him unmoved and undeterred in his plans for evangelizing the philosophy department. However, the late-August sequel to that early-June announcement opened his eyes with interest. "DeWulf Appointed to the Philosophy Department," said the caption above a picture of the appointee. Below the picture, Manly read: "Dean Hamilton S. F. Braniff of Arts and Sciences announces the appointment of Dr. Adrian DeWulf as Assistant Professor of Philosophy. Dr. DeWulf comes to ASU directly from Columbia University where he was recently awarded his doctoral degree. DeWulf also holds the B.A. degree from Chadron State College in his native state of Nebraska and the B.D. degree from Texas Christian University in Fort Worth, Texas."

"Very, very interesting," Manly mused aloud to himself in his office, knowing that "B.D." stood for "Bachelor of Divinity" and that Texas Christian was affiliated with the Disciples of Christ, his boyhood denomination. There might just be some common ground, some useful common ground, between this DeWulf person and me, he thought. Then, he looked at the picture and said "dark," referring to DeWulf's hair and deep-set eyes, and "sharp," referring to his angular but well defined features. "Looks more like a hawk than a wolf, though," he added aloud, looking at the dark eyes made beady by thick convex lenses.

Manly was not the only one put on the wrong track by Adrian's B.D. degree. Relevant Algonquin administrators were also misled. So trusting were they that they understood what B.D. meant and what it implied that no one of them was given pause by the word "Gothic," which Adrian had printed on the line following "Church Preference" on his application form.

Laying the *Messenger* aside, Manly returned to his desk where, pausing often to pray, he worked on evangelistic strategies for the coming academic year.

Meanwhile, the dark, sharp one with the raptor's gaze (who was soon to play a decisive role in Bro. Plumwell's life) was taking a sentimental trip around the Columbia campus and saying "good-bye" to as many of his philosophy professors as he could find. For their contributions to what had been, incomparably, the greatest educational experiences of his life, Adrian expressed his gratitude to Ernest Nagel, John Herman Randall, Jr., and Arthur Danto; also to Horace Friess and Joseph Blau of the religion department for letting him sit in on some of their lectures and seminars and for other kindnesses too. Each bade him farewell quickly, each shuddered slightly or otherwise grimaced (it seemed) to think that a Columbia man should be going to a place like Algonquin State University (wherever it was), and each returned at once to his research, absorbed. Thus dismissed but far too respectful to impose further on the time of such men, Adrian descended the stairs of Philosophy Hall and left by its southwest door. Passing Kent Hall, to his left, he turned south and went across the great yard to Butler Library. Once inside, he went straight to the philosophy reading room, made the sign of the cross together with a wry smile before the portrait of John Dewey hanging therein, and whispered "good-byes" to three acquaintances, one of whom was the student librarian on the reserve desk. Outside again, he paused before turning left onto College Walk to look for the last time at the Alma Mater sitting regally with arms outstretched on the steps to Low Memorial Library. Then, glancing up at the lions' heads dotting the cornices of the older buildings, he turned west and departed the "Colossus on the Hudson" at Broadway and 116th Street, a lump of farewell forming in his throat.

Early next morning, Adrian headed west across the George Washington Bridge, driving his blue '53 Chevy station wagon, laden to the gills and pulling a small U-Haul trailer groaning under the weight of his books. If he had felt free to go home again, he would have driven as straight as possible on as much four-lane highway as was available to the town of Valentine, nestling in the dunes of north-central Nebraska. Only then, only with the sands of home in his shoes again, would he have doubled back to Algonquin. But he was not welcome at home. So, he chose a meandering route, to be driven lazily, lovingly. If it took three or even four days to make the normal two-day trip from New York City to Algonquin, no harm would be done. A certain Rhadamanthus (what a name!) Reid had written, as acting head of philosophy, to say that he knew of a place to stay which he thought Prof. DeWulf would find acceptable and that it could be held for a few days into September.

West of Paterson, New Jersey, Adrian took State Highway 23 and went northwest through lake and hill country until he reached the point where New Jersey, New York, and Pennsylvania touch. There he crossed the Delaware, picking up U.S. 209, first driving along the river's west bank then turning west-southwest into the heart of Pennsylvania. At Millersburg he crossed the Susquehanna by ferry and took State Highway 17 to U.S. 322, angling west-northwest toward Ohio. When he felt like it, he would stop and take hikes into the woods or to waterfalls, or he would pause to picnic at roadside parks or on splendid overlooks. Sometimes, he would climb down under bridges to wade in the cascades of mountain creeks or to skip flat rocks off the glassy tops of water holes. Sometimes, he would stop the car abruptly and bound out of it, binoculars in hand, to look at a bird. At dusk, on the first evening, a feathered rainbow catapulted out of a creek-side bush, before his very nose, and disappeared. "Holy Clones!" he yelled, concluding moments later that he must have seen his first painted bunting. "No, it can't be; it's too far north," he announced to the great out of doors. "But what else could it have been?" he questioned the darkening sky. Trusting his identification, he condoled the little bird, muttering, "Poor boy, you'll die an untimely death; too far north, too far."

Although they were not the hills of home and could not delight him in the same way, the beauties of rural Pennsylvania, natural and man-made alike, were enormously refreshing to Adrian's spirit, a spirit that had been caged on Manhattan Island for four years of almost unremitting toil. Past fieldstone houses and antique barns, some brightly painted, he went; through quaint villages, reminiscent of Europe, he crept; down into and through numberless valleys and up and over unnumbered ridges he weaved his way, noticing here and there woodlots and pastures making checkerboards of green and elsewhere grain fields, timbered hills, and rocky eruptions creating corrugated quilts of many colors. More than once, the Alleghenies caused "How beautiful, how very beautiful!" and "Wow, what a view!" to cascade from his lips willingly, enthusiastically, but without prior intention.

Adrian DeWulf never intended to become anathema to his parents, but once that happened (for reasons over which he had no control), he embraced the secular world gladly, not needing their blessing. During his third and final year of ministerial training at TCU, he experienced two paranormal episodes that were linked with his conversion to irreligion. Each experience occurred during a service at the Prairie Road Christian Church of Mineral Wells, Texas, the church he served as a part-time minister on weekends. On the first Sunday in December he launched a series of sermons on the incarnation of God in Christ. With the choir sitting in their loft on his left as usual, with the church about as well attended as usual, with most people sitting in their favorite pews as usual, with everything as normal as it could be, he adverted, while preaching, to the biblical text he had read earlier, picked up his Bible, lying open on the pulpit, and read from Colossians 1:15-20: " 'He is the image of the invisible God, the first-born of all creation; for in him all things were created, in heaven and on earth, visible and invisible, whether thrones or dominions or principalities or authorities—all things were created through him and for him. He is before all things, and in him all things hold together. He is the head of the body, the church; he is the beginning, the first-born from the dead, that in everything he might be preeminent. For in him all the fullness of God was pleased to dwell, and through him to reconcile to himself all things, whether on earth or in heaven, making peace by the blood of his cross.' "

While attempting to explain the full significance of what he had just read, it seemed to him that he had stepped out of himself, backing up. Somehow, inexplicably, the real Adrian stood behind and to the right of his own bodily manifestation. He saw the back of his own head, saw his body arching slightly over the pulpit toward the people, saw his arms outstretched toward them, his hands poised as if holding them. Equally without explanation, he heard himself preaching, seemed to be listening to himself as if to a recording of his own voice. Then, as effortlessly as he had become his own observer, his own auditor, he stepped back into himself, a fully integrated entity again, congruent in all his aspects and parts.

"That was a good one, as usual," said one man, shaking Adrian's hand at the end of the worship service.

"Howdy, Preacher, how yew?" said a second man.

"You doin' all right this mornin', Brother DeWulf?" someone asked routinely.

"Say, I really did enjoy that sermon," said a woman sincerely, laying a hand on his forearm.

"That was a beautiful message, so timely too," said a second woman, equally sincerely.

"It was a good exposition, but there are some points I'd like to take up with you sometime," said a physician who doubled as the congregation's thinker.

As far as Adrian could tell from listening carefully to their comments— comments that were as typical, predictable, and banal as ever—nobody had noticed anything out of the ordinary in his sermon or sensed anything amiss. So occupied was he during the balance of the day with small talk, eating, pastoral calls, and last-minute sermon preparation that he could not reflect further on the curiosity he had undergone that morning.

Courteously declining invitations to stay the night in Mineral Wells to escape the expected blizzard, Adrian drove off in pitch darkness toward Fort Worth as quickly as he could, following his evening sermon. Between gusts of slanting wind slamming into his station wagon, making him fight the wheel, he reflected, catch as catch can, on his ecstatic experience of that morning. With imagination leaping to the aid of memory, he saw himself standing outside himself, saw himself hearing himself. He had not criticized himself as he had been trained to do, had not faulted his thought nor disparaged his delivery. He had merely listened, attentively to be sure, but in a detached way, across an abyss. While standing outside himself he had not thought to ask, "Is what you say true or false, good or bad, right or wrong, wise or foolish, realistic or unrealistic?" He had simply listened, understanding what he was saying but unmoved by it, disinterested in it.

While running it all through his mind again, to the accompaniment of the wailing, hissing, thundering wind and the weaving of the car, a certainty so paralyzing that he could not doubt it overtook him, overwhelmingly. He had not known *what* he was talking about that morning. He *had never known* what he was talking about when he spoke theologically or discoursed on Christian metaphysics. *He never would know, never could know!* Oh, he knew the text, knew the commentaries on the text, knew theology well enough, and knew what his teachers had taught him; but that was it, *that was all!* At no time had he been speaking the truth about God, knowing it to be the truth. He had been preaching rumors and rumors of rumors, had been discoursing at enormous length and repeatedly on hearsay, and mouthing theological fabrications made up out of the most circumstantial of circumstantial evidence, if evidence at all.

Suddenly, the winds had a companion: the snow, not merely falling snow but snow driven slantwise against the car, the ground, the road signs, arrows of white streaking through the beams of his headlights. Nor did their companion quiet the winds. Unabated, they roared on, surging against the station wagon, buffeting it, almost forcing it into flight. In times of retrospection, Adrian often wondered why he had not raged within himself that night as the weather had raged without. Instead there was a stillness about him like the stillness of the land under an eiderdown of snow. He did not storm against himself over having been a fool nor did he blame himself for having misled his parishioners. At the moment, he simply knew with certitude, calmly, quietly, serenely, that when speaking of God *he had never known what* he was talking about.

In the days following immediately upon his deliverance from the blizzard, he was suffused with the realization that, theologically speaking, his sermons could be epitomized as follows:

"Dear friends, brothers and sisters in the Lord Jesus, I speak of holy things this day, of God himself. Being perfect, as Scripture says (Matthew 5:48) and as theology has shown, it follows that God has perfect taste, aesthetically. Being without peer or precedent, he is nonetheless a demanding deity (jealousy being his name, Exodus 34:14) and seeks all glory, laud, and honor for himself. Having an inexhaustible appetite for praise, he takes enormous satisfaction in having his children extol him continually. Likewise, any structure consecrated to his worship is pleasing to him whether it be a hut of daub and wattle or a Norwegian stave church. But, my friends, being beautiful himself, having perfectly exquisite taste, and relishing exaltation exceedingly, he has architectural preferences; yes, by virtue of his very nature, he has architectural preferences. Thus, it follows, I sincerely believe, that he favors the Gothic in ecclesiastical structures, for the Gothic is clearly the most exalted and exalting style in architecture. And he wants us to favor it even as he does. Far be it from our God (who is also compassionate and understanding) to belittle any building devoted to his worship; nevertheless, he does not find beam-and-column construction sufficiently exalting and, thus, not especially suitable for his worship. Respecting the columns used in such architecture, neither Corinthian nor composite capitals find favor with the Most High, being far too preoccupied, as they are, with the creation (symbolized through plant leaves) and not enough with the creator. If his houses are to have domes, he prefers them to be founded four-square on squinches rather than placed on pendentives, or so it was said in olden times and attested to by saints. Such, anyway, is my belief. Moreover, since our God is the God of light (Psalms 104:2), it follows that he is not too partial to the Romanesque; no, it is too dark, too massive, too earthbound, too thick; nor are passageways created by the barrel vault as pleasing to him as might be, for the barrel vault leads the eye back to the earth. It is, in short, subterranean in feeling and chthonic. God, on the contrary, dwells in the heavens and does not burrow in the earth, as it were. Moreover, it can hardly be doubted that he frowns on the bulbous domes of Russian ecclesiastical architecture, erected, as they most often are, on tubular towers. Such structures are earthy in a different sense and far too suggestive of the flesh to suit him who is spirit and truth. No, no, my friends, it is the Gothic God loves, the Gothic with its pointed arches transcending themselves; the Gothic with its ribbed vaulting, its flèches, spires, and pinnacles, each and every one pointing all eyes heavenward where God sits enthroned; the Gothic with its lightness and luminosity of rose and clerestory windows bathing the faithful in celestial light; the Gothic with its vertical spaces eliciting effortless praises from the Lord's worshippers far below. You ask, dear friends, how I know these truths; why, from revelation as recorded in the sacred Scriptures, from theology, the fruit of our own God-given rationality, from holy tradition, from the eye of the beholder, and from the believer's heart, yes, from the heart. Amen."

Fantastic though the epitome of his own preaching seemed to Adrian, it was less fantastic by far than Colossians 1:15-20 and many another of St. Paul's presumptions. The realization that he, Adrian DeWulf, had been trying to persuade people to believe such effusions, to convince them, to convert them, left him speechless and paralyzed. So, for the moment, he left his life to habit and continued to be what he had been.

It was the night before Christmas when Adrian underwent the second curious episode. He had gone to the Prairie Road Church to participate in a special service including the presentation of a pageant, gift giving, and carol singing. The last carol to be sung was "O Come, All Ye Faithful," his favorite. Often when singing it (and sometimes merely when hearing it), he had been enraptured with a sense of participation. He would see himself as one of a numberless multitude of the faithful drawn from all times and places and peoples. Joyously, their joy bounded only by reverence, the faithful would commence the triumphant procession to Bethlehem to "behold Him, born the King of angels!" Nor did the pilgrims in that procession grow weary and drop by the wayside as they streamed from the four corners of the world to Bethlehem's manger; because, overhead, invigorating "choirs of angels" and all the "citizens of heaven" sang in exultation, giving "Glory to God, all glory in the highest!" Not only did none grow tired in the endless procession of adoration, the faithful all arrived simultaneously before the first-born of all creation reborn as man in infant form, hailing him individually, and yet as one, "Yea, Lord, we greet Thee, born this happy morning. . . ."

But as the good people of the Prairie Road Christian Church of Mineral Wells, Texas, sang "Adeste Fideles," their spiritual leader, whose lips had fallen silent as though he were in a stupor, did not lead them, nor was he with them at all except in body. He was standing on the sideline watching as they, together with countless other Christians, passed him by on the road to Bethlehem. He did not criticize their going, did not belittle their faith, did not carp at them for bending their knees, but he was *not* with them, was *not* making the trip, was *not* about to bend his knees, would *not* salute any Lord, born on that day or on any other. When the members of the congregation ceased their singing that night, the new Adrian DeWulf, who knew he had been reborn before their unsuspecting eyes, dismissed them, as in a dream, with a memorized benediction.

While driving west from Mineral Wells to the country home of Karl and Dora Potter, where he was to spend the night and take Christmas dinner, Adrian suddenly felt free as never before. Unable to abide the cramping confines of his station wagon, he brought it to a halt on the roadside, turned off its lights and motor, flung open the door, and stepped out buoyantly into the icy night. There, with only starlight to guide him, he strode, bareheaded, upon the all but limitless prairie beneath the infinitudes of space, and, then and there, celebrated his new-found freedom and tried as best he could to fathom it.

It was not the freedom of the libertine that he felt, not the freedom to exchange his staid habits for the life of uninhibited pleasure, nor was it the freedom of the criminal helping himself remorselessly to what was not his, nor the freedom of the psychopath doing as he pleased with no respect for his victims and deaf to their cries for mercy. No, it was a very different kind of freedom. Without knowing the metaphors of mural and theater, Adrian had, nonetheless, backed out of the great mural of faith onto a landscape devoid of spirits and their teeming world. He had absented himself from the Christian drama of salvation, had departed the theater, hardly knowing what he was doing, and had stepped into the great out-of-doors. No longer was he a fulcrum for faith; no longer did he have to prop up God with his belief so that God could then explain the universe. He was free from all that and, being free, saw the world through eyes no longer bewitched by belief. Throwing back his head, smiling broadly, he looked at the stars for what they were, seeing them for the first time as atomic furnaces, crucibles of new worlds. God had not put them there so that he, Adrian DeWulf, could have light by night as he strode the open prairie, nor were they the heralds of Hebrew holidays and sacred seasons as Genesis would have it. No, the stars were not artifacts, nor was he. Both he and they were natural, each to be taken on its own terms. Neither existed for the sake of the other, nor did common purpose bind them together. Gone was the need to explain the cosmos by a biblical deity too ignorant to have made it, too incompetent to have run it, too quixotic in his love to have cared for it. "You shall know the truth, and the truth shall make you free," Adrian murmured to himself freely, shivering in the night air, but from elation, not from the chill of winter. As he slipped back into the station wagon to conclude his journey to the Potters' place, he knew that he was alone, very much alone, but he was not lonely. He also knew that he was but a transient speck of conscious substance in an enduring universe immense beyond conception, but he was not intimidated. He was free, and that was more than enough, for his freedom also made him brave.

But such freedom is dear when purchased by a clergyman. What was he to do with himself? He had spent four years in college pointing toward divinity school. He had spent two and a half years in divinity school pointing toward a professional degree in religion and had but a scant six months to go. Since he was already ordained, he had gone beyond the point of no return emotionally. Having solemnly committed himself to life in the Lord's service, he had had elders' hands laid upon his head, setting him aside as a very special kind of person, reserving for him a very special kind of work. Ceasing to be the special kind of person he was supposed to be and ceasing to do the special kind of work reserved for him was not like a mere change in occupations. It was not as though he were a chemist deciding in mid-career to be a physicist, a physician becoming a college president, a hairdresser turning into a performer. It was far more like treachery, was, in fact, worse than treachery in the eyes of many, since apostasy was also involved. Rejection in various forms would follow. Bridges would be blown up, even though he had not set the charges. Darkness would descend, obscuring his face and the faces of many whom he loved. Could he, a non-believer, continue to preach on weekends? That was no idle question, because he did not preach simply for practice nor to fulfill requirements. He preached to support himself while in school, being trained for nothing else. If he continued to preach, what would he do when next he was served the Lord's Supper—spurn it? Unthinkable! Worse than that, what would he do should someone at Mineral Wells repent, confess to faith in Christ, and seek membership in the Prairie Road Church? Could he honestly hear such a confession? Could he baptize the confessing person conscientiously, validly? No, not honestly, not conscientiously. In the silent anguish that followed his expulsion from faith to freedom, he talked to nobody about the emotional explosions that had overwhelmed him but muttered often to himself, "You shall know the truth, and the truth shall make you free, but the price of freedom is excruciatingly high."

In deciding what to do Adrian chose in each case what he believed to be the least of evils. Although he no longer relished theology, he would continue working toward his divinity degree and would keep on preaching until he had it. He had not ceased taking the Bible seriously and still cared that it was given accurate exposition. So, he would simply tell the believers at the Prairie Road Church what was really in the book they took to be holy but about which they were so abysmally ignorant. Moreover, whether Jesus was (*a*) pure God, (*b*) God-man, (*c*) pure man, or (*d*) none of the above, he had preached a moral message that Adrian could still endorse in good conscience. As for communion, well, he would play the game and drink the grape juice as usual. If anybody sought baptism, he would conduct the rite. After all, in theology, it is God who saves, not the hands that do the immersing. As for his future, he would apply to several different graduate schools for admission as a doctoral candidate in philosophy.

The professors at TCU who wrote letters of recommendation for him concluded to a man that he merely wished to carry out his ministry in some way that required more formal education than did the pastorate, nor did he disabuse them of their spurious inferences. The people at the Prairie Road Church entertained similar notions when he resigned as of the forthcoming first Sunday in June. Not being told otherwise, his friends also reached similar conclusions. No member of either group realized that there was an apostate in their midst. Although he did not lie to his parents in the infrequent letters he sent them, he left them to believe, more through vagueness than anything else, that he was remaining in Texas, for the time being at least, to continue serving his church.

257

With his degree from TCU in hand, with his final sermon (not only at Mineral Wells but of all time) preached, and all restraining ties to Fort Worth neatly cut, Adrian disappeared into nearby Dallas. There he lived in a hole in the wall in a cheap rooming house in a shoddy part of town and took on as many jobs as he could, eating on the run and leaving himself just enough time to get sufficient sleep. Early the following September, he would go to New York City, to study philosophy at Columbia. Even with the promised scholarship, it would take every cent he could earn and more.

Will and Clara DeWulf could have been bowled over with a feather when he turned into their driveway unexpectedly on the Wednesday night following Labor Day. Clara had just stepped into the living room to call Will to supper when she saw the blue Chevy station wagon roll to a stop. Hurrying to the kitchen to set an extra place, she left him to greet the youngest of their three children and the only son. The oldest child had died long since of cancer. The second child, fifteen years older than Adrian, lived in California and did not keep in close touch with her parents.

"Well, well, well, stranger, what brings you to these parts?" yelled Will, descending the front steps arthritically.

Even before he had slipped out of the car completely, Adrian yelled in return, "Oh, I was just passing through this neck of the woods and thought I would look you and Mom up."

"You come to the right place, I'll say that much," Will said, bantering happily.

As the two shook hands, Will asked, "How have you been, son?"

"Fine as frog's hair," Adrian answered using the comical phrase his grandfather had taught him when he was little more than a toddler.

"And you, Dad?"

"Oh, I'm just about right, I guess," said Will stoically, knowing that his arthritis had left him anything but just about right.

As Clara materialized in the front door to greet her son, Will noticed that the station wagon was packed up to the roof and on the roof, too, with what looked like every blessed thing Adrian owned. "Wonder what that means?" Will murmured to himself, resolving to ask outright if Adrian didn't clear up the matter voluntarily.

Throughout supper (which turned out to be one of Clara's minor miracles of multiplying fishes and loaves), Adrian kept the conversation away from himself and his potentially disturbing future by asking about the weather, the gardens, beef prices, how things were going in Valentine in general, and all about his old friends, where they were and what they were up to.

After washing up the dishes, Adrian and his mother joined Will in the living room where he was taking it easy in his stocking feet after another tiring day at his combination saddle shop and blacksmith shop where he continued to shoe horses despite the arthritis.

Pointing in the direction of the driveway with the stem of his corncob pipe, Will said leadingly, "Looks like you've got your car pretty well loaded."

"Yeah, it's so full it rode on the rear axle all the way from Texas," Adrian replied, smiling boyishly, "mostly because of all the books lying around in it."

"You leavin' Texas?" Will asked.

"Yes."

"I mean movin', are you movin' for good?"

With a flicker of hope enlivening her face, Clara broke in before Adrian could answer. "Are you going to settle closer to home, son?"

"No, not any time soon anyway."

"Well then, where are you goin'?" Will inquired, his voice rising.

"To New York City."

"*To New York City!*" Will and Clara chimed together.

"Yes."

"Well, my stars, aren't there any Christian Churches closer to home that you could serve?" Clara asked wistfully.

"I'm going there to go to school, to Columbia University, not to serve a church."

"You gonna spend your whole life in school?" snorted Will, himself an eighth grade drop-out.

"No, but for what I want to be, it takes a lot more school."

"But we always thought you wanted to be a minister," said Clara, dropping her handwork.

"Why, yes," interjected Will, "we supposed that's why you went down to Texas, to learn how to be a preacher."

"I did, but I don't want to be a preacher anymore."

"You're not going to become a missionary or anything like that and go traipsing all over the world, are you?" Clara asked apprehensively, foreseeing a childless old age with her only daughter in California and her only son in Timbuktu.

"No, no, not a missionary," Adrian nearly yelled, shuddering at the thought, "no, I want to be a philosopher."

"*A what?*" said Will, his voice rising more in challenge than in query.

"I want to be a philosopher."

"What would you *do,* being one of those, I mean?" Clara asked, baffled and wondering how she could explain the evening's revelations to her neighbors and to the folks at church, people who had always followed Adrian's career so admiringly, so hopefully.

"I would teach philosophy at some college or university and write," Adrian answered uninformatively.

A reflective period followed (the calm before the storm) during which Adrian wondered if he would have to tell the whole story of his defection. He wanted to dish it out in installments, to tell them on that occasion only that he had left the pastoral ministry and to defer if possible as long as possible the news that he had left the church, that he was no longer a Christian, that he did not even believe in God. Meanwhile, each of his parents reviewed the past wordlessly but in tandem. He had been an "awful smart boy," everybody had said so. He was curious, questioning, persistent, and sometimes belligerent in a know-it-all way. But it always seemed that the church had the answers that satisfied him. Will and Clara, ignorant of higher education and fearing its reputed deceits, had been anxious about him throughout the four years he had spent at Chadron State. He had, however, come through those years unseduced and unperverted to all appearances. At Texas Christian, he had become more liberal religiously than they liked, of that they were sure. Little things he had written in his letters and remarks he had dropped during his one visit home (two years earlier) convinced them of it and made them very anxious. But nothing had prepared them for the bombshell that he was leaving the ministry, leaving it for something called philosophy, something that sounded suspicious to them.

Not fully believing what he had heard, Will broke the silence, saying, "Well, are you gonna serve a church on weekends in New York City like you done down in Texas, or what?"

"There aren't very many Disciples in that part of the country, Dad," Adrian said with perfect candor, hoping that his father would drop the subject.

"There must be lots of nondenominational churches in a big place like New York that would be willing to have a Disciple minister," Clara observed, "because our denomination has always been noted for being cooperative with other sincere Christians."

"No, I wouldn't look for any nondenominational church to serve," Adrian replied abruptly, decisively.

"Well, why in Sam Hill not?" asked his father, increasingly aggrieved by what he was hearing.

"Yes, why not?" Clara chimed in before Adrian could have answered, had he wanted to.

A long pause ensued before he could bring himself to say, "Because I . . . I have left the church; not just the ministry, but the church itself." Looking at their faces, he knew that he might as well have said, "I have taken down our flag, I have taken down Old Glory, have trampled it into the dust, and renounced my country."

"Well, now," said Clara scoldingly, "just what kind of a Christian do you think you can be if you don't belong to a church?"

Aware that he could not dole out the truth of his defection in installments as he had hoped but that he would probably be forced to tell the whole story then and there, Adrian said as levelly as he could, "I have left the church, because I am not a Christian any longer." At that, Will's jaw went slack, Clara's face turned ashen, and each appeared to be diminished, shriveled up somehow. The impact of his words, "I am not a Christian any longer," was as great as if he had said, "I have committed incest with my sister repeatedly."

When Will found his tongue, it was with fury. "I suppose the next thing you're gonna tell us is that you're one of those goddamned atheists."

"Oh, not an atheist too!" Clara squealed, too horror-stricken to scold Will for his profanity.

"Look," said Adrian, sitting on the edge of his chair, his hands out, palms down, as though to still the raging sea, "I have never made an affirmative declaration of the nonexistence of God, if that's what you mean by 'atheist', because that would be a faith position like making an affirmative declaration of the existence of God, only the contradictory, but I must say that I do not know what the word 'God' names, properly speaking, and, therefore, do not—"

"Well, do ya or don't ya believe in God?" Will thundered. "Just answer me that, and don't give us none of that hifalutin educated palaver."

"I don't believe in . . . in the God you two believe in, the God of the Bible, that is; I don't believe in that God at all." Adrian could not have devastated his parents more had he said at table earlier that evening, "Look, I don't eat your kind of food any more, because I'm a cannibal now and eat only human flesh."

Clara rose up from her armchair, then fell back into it as though faint, then rose up again with the heels of her hands jammed into the sockets of her eyes, and stumbled to her bedroom sobbing. Meanwhile, Will had to exercise herculean restraint to keep from whipping his belt out of its loops and slashing it across Adrian again and again.

"Look what you done to your mother!" he shouted, his eyes glistening with tears, his face red with surging blood. "Now you get out of this house and don't you come back until you've come to your senses. Everybody but you educated fools knows that there's a God; there couldn't be no world otherwise, and we wouldn't even be here."

As Adrian stalked out of his boyhood home, as stricken by that time as his parents, he heard his father saying, "You're more'n welcome to come back whenever you come to your senses, but not before," accompanied by his mother's distant muffled wailing. Out into the night he went alone, driving first to the southeast, then east, on U.S. 20 toward Chicago and New York City far beyond.

During his four years at Columbia, the prodigal son from Valentine, Nebraska, failed to "come to his senses" as his father understood the phrase. Measured by that meaning, he took ever greater leave of his senses, his "palaver" becoming increasingly "hifalutin" and "educated," his contact with the common man ever more tenuous. He who had merely left the faith became its enemy.

At Columbia he was reconciled to science as the dominant mode of modern knowledge. Since science spoke no word of God, could speak no word, it was clear to him that Christianity was scientifically unsupportable. Then, too, the more he studied philosophy in general, the more he realized that Christian theology was suspect, and the more he read such philosophers as Hume, Russell, Dewey, and Ayer, the more he realized that it was disreputable. Moreover, the deeper he delved into the great ethical thinkers of the West, the more obvious it became that Jesus' ethics of love was ill-defined and poorly worked out, that it was in fact very thin stuff. But it was his light reading, his reading during the summers while grubbing for money, that wrought the greatest emotional change, making him disgusted with himself and feeling a fool. Quite by accident, he came upon S. G. F. Brandon's book, *The Fall of Jerusalem and the Christian Church.* That led him to *The Messiah Jesus and John the Baptist* by Robert Eisler. From there he turned to works by Loisy and Guignebert and eventually to the popular book, *Why Jesus Died,* by Pierre van Paassen. Intrigued by what he read, sometimes stunned, and, in the end, more liberated than ever, he was led to believe (no, compelled to believe!) that the flesh and blood Jesus had been a wonder-worker made king for a day, that whatever his religious views may have been, he had been arrested for sedition and executed by the Romans as King of the Jews. It was inescapable: The Jesus of history had been a messianic pretender, a very great one, no doubt, but in the last analysis a pretender and a failure.

For reasons hidden to history, if not altogether mysterious, he who had failed as King of the Jews had been elevated, in faith, to King of Humankind; he who had died was proclaimed as alive, eternally alive; he whose righteousness had been at the most only conventional was said to have been divine love incarnate; he whose teachings were fragmentary and ambiguous at best was preached as the Word and Wisdom of God. Surely there had been other sides to the story of Jesus. Surely there had been opposing voices. Why had they been quiet? As Adrian read the Imperial Edict of 333 he knew, for therein the Emperor Constantine gave Christians, bishops and laity alike, the right to obliterate all writings contradictory to the teachings of the established church. No wonder there was so little historical evidence of the life of Jesus external to the gospels! It had either been consigned to the flames or expurgated by Christian censors. To Adrian's initial surprise, the Columbia library itself had such mutilated texts among its many treasures. Jesus' enemies had silenced him, but Jesus' church had silenced them.

Just as a pirate on a grand enough scale becomes a conquering head of state, so fraud on a grand enough scale becomes social fact, and superstition, suppressing its rivals, crowns itself as true religion. That was how Adrian had become a Christian. His parents, pious, innocent, and ignorant, had brought him to it as though it were the veriest common sense, more natural than second nature. But how could he, even as a child, have sucked it in so greedily? How could he have been so gullible? How, when reading the Scriptures or hearing sermons, could he have lifted up every valley so blithely? How, when studying theology, could he have made low every mountain and hill of contradiction so easily, leaving a boulevard upon the resulting plains for his credulity to tread? Although Columbia abounded with students far more brilliant than he, he was no fool; yet, he had been a fool, and a recent one too. He could forgive his parents. They had merely been what had been expected of them in their time and place and had done what they had thought was right. But he could not forgive himself, nor could he forgive his professors at Chadron State. Had none of them known better than to practice the faith so uncritically or to give lip service to it so glibly, confirming their students in it so thoughtlessly? Least of all could he forgive his professors at Texas Christian. They of all people with whom he had come in contact up to that time should have known better, should have realized how tenuous their faith in Christ ought to have been in light of the historical Jesus. No wonder they had talked about the scandal of the gospel and had discoursed on the paradox of the eternal, universal God incarnate in the temporal, particular man from Nazareth. Yet, faith had seemed to rest upon them so easily, it was hard for Adrian to believe that they were really scandalized by the gospel, as they should have been, or confounded by the paradoxes of theology.

Some people, realizing that they have been defrauded, can shrug it off, making light of themselves. Others can take it as a good lesson but then forget the better part of it. Still others may cry aloud bitterly but lift no effective finger against it. But it was not in Adrian's nature to respond in those ways. He would confront the defrauders, pious though they might be, and unmask their fraud. If they used illogic, he would use logic. If they persisted in fictions, he would marshal facts. If they would be serious gravely, he would be serious comically. If they exalted faith above reason, he would raise its price scandalously. If they would cite Scripture, he would poison the well, citing it to their disadvantage. As for the defrauded, well, he would extend a helping hand to them, lifting them from their knees to their feet, if they would stand; would share his courage with the timid; and would breathe Columbia's free air into those whose lungs could receive it. All that and more, too, he would do, in season and out, insistently.

While sipping on his second Singapore Sling at a party one night, Adrian began to tell jokes. "It seems that there was this Pentecostal preacher," he said, "who always preached by inspiration. He would open the Bible and put his finger down at random on some verse or other, would then read it aloud, and commence to preach under the Spirit's guidance. One Sunday he turned to the book of Joshua and read, 'And Joshua threw his saddle on his ass and rode away.' At that point, the preacher turned white, began to tremble, and couldn't speak for quite a while. Finally he said, 'Brethren, I've been a Bible-believing Christian for forty years, but there has just got to be a mistake here; it must have meant to say, 'And Joshua threw his ass on his saddle and rode away.' "

As the mixture of laughter and derisive hooting died down, Betty Pruitt, who was a nursing instructor at St. Luke's Hospital, said, "Tell your Christian Science joke, Adrian."

After a thoughtful pause, Adrian said, "Betty, you're probably the only woman here old enough . . . er . . . ah . . . mature enough to get the point. Tanya and Natalie over there and any other Barnard beauties we have in our midst [here he craned his neck, looking about] will be too young and innocent; no, I take that back, not too innocent, just too young to get the point." Ignoring the disdainful looks and scurrilous jibes aimed at him by the beauties in question, Adrian went on to suggest that probably none of the males at the party, with the possible exception of his fellow philosophy students who had taken all knowledge as their province, would understand it either, but he would tell it anyway.

"Oh, thank-you, thank-you, all-wise one," Tanya chanted, Natalie joining in.

Bowing in their direction, Adrian said, "Well, there was this newly widowed, little old lady with more money than sense. She wanted to get in touch with her country and see America at the grass-roots level. So, she just hopped on the bus whenever she felt like it and went wherever she wanted to. One night, in Montpelier, Idaho, or some such place, she went for a walk after supper and chanced upon a number of well-dressed people going into a building identified as the Christian Science Meeting House. She didn't know what that meant, but, feeling lonely, she followed them in and sat down in the back. The occasion turned out to be one of the testimonial services Christian Scientists have periodically. Each person would stand up in turn and tell what his or her life had been like before Mary Baker Eddy had come into it. One woman said that she had had St. Vitus's dance and rheumatism at the same time and was very uncomfortable until Mrs. Eddy showed her that her pain wasn't really real but was due to her own bad thoughts. A man said that he had had lockjaw and a tapeworm simultaneously, and so on. Well, this little old lady had never experienced such a gathering before, but she was caught up in it and really wanted to participate, even though she was ignorant of Christian Science and had never heard of Mrs. Eddy. So, she stood up and introduced herself and said, 'I know nothing of Christian Science or of Mrs. Eddy, but I just want to say that Lydia E. Pinkham has certainly done wonders for me.' "

True to Adrian's expectations, the laughter did not come all at once but in staggered outbursts, as different people at different times got the point.

"While you're at it, tell the one about Jesus and the woman taken in adultery," said Dee Martin, a graduate student in religion at Columbia.

"All these stories parch a person's throat," Adrian observed, dramatically taking a big drink of Singapore Sling.

"Only if you feel up to it, of course," Dee said, qualifying her request and pretending to be put upon.

"As those who are familiar with John's gospel will know," said Adrian, effecting a look of vast erudition, "Jesus comes upon this mob about to stone a woman caught in *the act,* and says to them, 'Let him who is without sin cast the first stone.' Moments later a big rock sails through the air and goes splat right by the poor wench's feet. Jesus turns around to see who has thrown the stone and says with asperity, 'Oh, Mother, why did you have to go and do that?' "

To that one there was much laughter.

Basking in his success as a raconteur and feeling elevated by virtue of his second Singapore Sling, to more of which he was helping himself for the sake of his poor parched throat, Adrian said, "And, then, there was the rich Jew who stopped in a small town in Russia to—"

"Are religious jokes the only ones you know?" broke in a first-year girl from Union Theological Seminary, a newcomer to the group.

"Holy Clones, no, I take all kinds of jokes as my province," he replied.

"He knows a lot of horny ones too," said Natalie, smirking.

"Also horny religious ones," Betty added.

"Why doesn't he just tell those?" an unidentified male voice muttered.

"Have you got it in for religion or something?" asked the Union girl testily.

"Perish the thought!" Adrian said, his voice dripping with irony to the accompaniment of numerous chuckles from those who knew him best.

"I think you're really kind of irreligious," said the Union girl perceptively.

"I, irreligious?" said Adrian, standing up, "I who bear the mark of religion in my flesh?"

"In your flesh?" the girl exclaimed, taken by surprise.

"What have you got, the stigmata or something?" asked Tanya banteringly.

"No, my foreskin was taken from me and given to the Holy One of Israel."

"*What? Oh!*" said the girl, answering her own question as she blurted out the words.

"Oh, hell, he just means he's been circumcised," said a male graduate student, also from Union Seminary.

"That's just for good health," announced a second nursing instructor from St. Luke's.

"The hell you say," said Adrian, still on his feet and warming to verbal combat, "it was the way a bunch of goddamned, primitive, ignorant, superstitious, benighted Jews ratified their make-believe covenant with Yahweh, their equally make-believe god."

"Just a minute, goy," said a Jewish senior from Barnard, "what do you mean 'ignorant'? Don't you know that Jews have won more Nobel Prizes per capita than any other people?"

"Not the ones I'm talking about, sweetie," said Adrian. "The ones I'm talking about may have gotten the annual Jehovah Prize for unnecessary and mutilative surgery, but no Nobel Prizes."

"It's a well-known fact that circumcision cuts down on penile cancer," declared the second nursing instructor, hoping that medical practice might be vindicated.

"That's pure humbug," Adrian announced loudly, "that's what the quacks want the parents of baby boys to believe. Look, if instead of circumcising boys, the Jehovah Prize winners of olden times had removed one ball from each baby boy, our modern and very scientific obstetricians and G.P.'s would justify the operation on the ground that it cuts testicular cancer in half. Such surgery as that would be a very high price indeed to pay for the alleged benefits, don't you think?"

"Speaking of price," said one of Adrian's fellow graduate students, who was professionally interested in medical ethics, "it's a pretty penny the scientific quacks you refer to make off circumcisions. Just imagine dressing up a purely ritual operation in scientific garb, making it routine because it's traditional, and then having the gall to charge for it as though a great health benefit were being conferred. You know, medical people are as ignorant of human evolution as priests are. Neither seems to have noted that Mother Nature provided males with foreskins and intended that they should get to keep them. It's unnatural to whack 'em off. In fact, it's a crime against nature and, therefore, immoral."

Relishing that bit of sophistry, Adrian sat down, saying, "I'm a born-again pagan myself, and I want a peter to match. I want to be whole again as Mother Nature intended me to be."

"It really is too bad about you," said Dee Martin, not taking him seriously. Meanwhile, Natalie was playing imaginary sad music on an equally imaginary violin.

Undaunted, Adrian declared, "I think I may get over the psychological scars of Christianity if I live to be eighty or ninety, but I'm never going to get over the physical scars. Every time I'm in my birthday suit and see my poor mutilated member, it cries out in reproach, 'Ah, thou who thinkest thou art free from superstition, thou bearest the mark of superstition in thy very flesh.'"

"Could we please talk about something else for a change?" complained the Union Seminary girl.

"I tell you what," said the graduate student interested in medical ethics, "if there were only enough money in it, our medical benefactors would cut off our foreskins while we're babes as usual and put them on ice, so to speak. Then, upon demand later on, they would thaw them out, find some way to stretch them to fit, and would sew them back on again—peterplastic surgeons, you might say."

"You know what?" Adrian asked loudly of nobody in particular, "I'm gonna found an organization called 'CUTS, Circumcised Unbelievers Traumatized by Surgery'; no, wait, I'm gonna call it 'CUTOFFS, Circumcised Unbelievers Triumphant Over Foul Foolish Surgery', and raise hell with those sanctimonious witch doctors who perform unnatural acts for profit on helpless little boys, that's what I'm gonna do." Winking at his friend in medical ethics, he called out, "Any joiners? What about you, Betty? Women can join too, you know. And you, sir, and you there, Miss Christian from Union Seminary, what about you?"

Such, in brief, was the dark, sharp one with the raptor's gaze who was

266

wending his way across the Alleghenies toward Algonquin State University to teach philosophy and to set people free from superstition and religious fraud.

When Adrian saw the maroon billboard that pictured the seal of Algonquin State University in white and also welcomed people to the home of the Algonquin Braves, he fished a sheet of paper out of his shirt pocket. On it Rad Reid had written, "Proceed north 2.7 miles beyond the sign welcoming people to the home of the Braves. Turn left onto County Road 37, turn right onto Tamewood Road, then right again onto Borealis Drive, and follow it to 1138, which will be on your left."

A few minutes later, Adrian found himself looking up at what was surely one of the tallest and highest moustaches in the western hemisphere, if not the world.

"Professor Reid?" he inquired.

"The very one," came a booming voice from somewhere behind the moustache.

"I'm Adrian DeWulf."

"So, you're here, huh?" said Rad, pumping Adrian's hand. "Well, come in, come in."

"Thank you, sir."

"Could I get you something to drink?" asked the giant. "Bourbon or Scotch?"

"No, no thank you."

"Moonshine or bathtub gin?"

"No, thanks, nothing for me just now."

"Something softer, perchance?"

"Oh, no."

"Mayhap an uncarbonated beverage such as coffee, Sanka, tea, or Postum."

"No, I'm fine, really, I'm fine."

"Milk, maybe, or water?"

"No, I'm not at all thirsty."

"Broth, consommé?"

"No, no," Adrian said, beginning to smile.

"Hot chocolate or Ovaltine."

"No, not even one of those," Adrian replied, laughing openly.

"One or more fruit juices?"

Still laughing, Adrian said, "I guess what I really need are directions to the place you wrote about earlier where you thought I might hang my hat for a while."

Beckoning him to follow, Rad proceeded through the house and out into the back yard.

Borealis Road followed the crest of a ridge running east and west. Below them in a broad but shallow bowl lay the town of Algonquin. The northern rim of the bowl was formed by the Algonac Hills, some of which stood over

750 feet above the bowl below.

"Beautiful," said Adrian, "really beautiful!"

"See that building with the Norman tower to the left center there? That's the Administration Building. If you sight to the northeast about 500 feet, you can see just a corner of the main gate to the university. Go straight north of that gate for three blocks, then turn two blocks to the east. That will put you on Litany Lane. You'll be looking for number 5, apartment 2A."

"Litany Lane?" asked Adrian, laughing more than he had meant to.

"What you have to realize," said Rad, grinning, "is that this place almost got the God-awful name of Christianopolis foisted on it."

"Holy Clones," Adrian said, turning the corners of his mouth down.

"As a gesture of good will, the city fathers who had fought to retain the name the place had when it was just a trading post let some of the streets be renamed to suit the horde of religious immigrants who came here in the 1870s. So, we have Anthem Boulevard, Trinity Place, Glory Road, Litany Lane, and one or two others that slip my mind."

"Wonderful, just wonderful!" Adrian said humorously, almost giggling.

"Anyway, when you leave here, just go to the next intersection and turn left. At the bottom of the hill, you'll come out onto Dormitory Drive. Take the first left you come to, and you'll wind up going right past the main gates down there, then three blocks north, and two to the east, as I said earlier. Well, now that you've seen where to go, come on back into the house and have a seat."

"Thanks, but I really need to get settled as soon as possible or I'll have to pay extra for the U-Haul I'm pulling," Adrian pointed out.

"Well, okay, just go on down to Litany Lane, and meanwhile I'll call the landlady, a Miss Grace Moore Mistledine, and tip her off that you're on your way. Miriam—that's my wife—and I had wanted you for dinner tonight, but it seems that we're in demand at a social event, and . . ."

"Oh, please, think nothing of it," Adrian broke in.

Shaking hands, the two, who had warmed to each other instantly, parted.

Litany Lane was a narrow street, only two blocks long, on either side of which stood antique row houses, built of brick, two and three stories high and standing a scant ten feet back from the sidewalks. Between the sidewalks and the street, ancient oaks crowded together, their roots buckling the concrete, their branches forming a canopy over front yards little bigger than postage stamps.

Number 5 was a narrow, but very deep, three-storied structure whose bricks had long since been painted white, its shutters, newly green. The flagstones leading to the house did not bisect the front yard but rather led to a front door at the extreme right-hand side of the building as one faced it. Once inside, a long hall extended straight back about half the depth of the house. While proceeding down the hall, Adrian passed a door on his left, identified as 1A, which led to the front downstairs apartment. At the back of the hall, he had to turn 180° so as to climb the long stairway to the second floor, As he reached the second floor landing, he came face to face with a small bathroom whose door stood ajar. Upon turning 90° to the right he saw a door marked 2A. If he had turned another 90° to the right he could have proceeded down a hall much like the one below, but not so long. At the back of that hall a second staircase, paralleling the one below it, led to the third floor where Miss Mistledine lived. Several creaks on the stairs above and to one side of him indicated that someone was descending, the landlady herself, no doubt.

Grace Moore Mistledine was surpassingly ugly, having no redeeming feature at all. Adrian averted his eyes from her as they shook hands lest his contracting pupils notify her anew of how hard she was to look at. Once inside apartment 2A, she spoke of its qualities abstractedly and answered most of his questions about it by remarking on how many fine proposals of marriage she had received while young. Of course, there had always been some serious flaw in each of the young gentlemen who had sought her hand. It was clear to Adrian that serious and prolonged distress during young maidenhood had soured into desperate preoccupation with middle maidenhood. He could only hope, and did so fervently, that old maidenhood would free her from her torment.

After many irrelevant answers, composed of marital musings, to certain pointed questions that he had posed concerning the apartment, Adrian decided on two courses of action: First, he would take the so-called apartment, would move in that very afternoon, as a matter of fact; and, second, he would avoid Grace Moore Mistledine as much as possible. Although he would never win the "Mr. Handsome Contest" of any year, Adrian did not want his own reasonably good looks to serve as yet another reproach upon his landlady-to-be.

"Litany Lane," he mused with a wry smile after moving in. "What a laugh the characters in the old gang at Columbia will get when they see my return address, if I decide to favor any of them with my cards and letters."

Adrian had two good reasons for referring to his new home as a so-called apartment. First, the bathroom into which he had looked when climbing to the second floor turned out to be his, but it was separated from the rest of the apartment, having no communicating door. So, every time he answered a call of nature or went to bathe, he had to parade out into the hall in plain view of anyone ascending the stairs or of Miss Mistledine making one of her rare descents from above. As for the rest of the apartment, well, it was just a big old room that had once been the front bedroom on the second floor when the whole house had been occupied by the Mistledine family. Second, Adrian's kitchen turned out to be one half of a large walk-in closet that had stretched originally across the entire west end of the room. It contained a diminutive sink, two small metal cabinets (one for food, the other for pots, pans, and dishes), and an ancient hot plate with two burners, which rested on a built-in shelf. A card table and three folding chairs completed the kitchen-dining area of the room. The remaining half of the walk-in closet remained just that. The east end of the room contained two widely separated windows looking out into the great oaks in front and down onto the sidewalk below. Litany Lane itself was almost hidden by branches and leaves. A high double bed stood between the windows and extended toward the center of the room. A large, gray, overstuffed chair reposed several feet from the foot of the bed, more or less under a nondescript chandelier. On the south wall was a chest of drawers, on the north wall a desk beside which Adrian positioned his typewriter, its stand and accompanying chair. It was hardly an elegant apartment; it was certainly not the most convenient apartment; but it was cheap, quiet, and close to campus. What more did a young philosophy professor who was single, poor, and in debt need? Nothing really, especially if the Muse could find him there and would make him productive.

In the days following immediately upon his arrival in Algonquin, Adrian spent a lot of time on foot orienting himself to the campus and the town. He liked to know north, south, east, and west; liked to know exactly where he would end up if he were to go left or right from any given spot; liked to have the maps he carried in his head accurate in the smallest detail; and liked to know the names of all the buildings on campus and what they were used for. When he began to get acquainted with Algonquin, the campus was as quiet as a ghost town except for the workmen repainting lane markers and the like on the streets and except for the thuds, whacks, shouts, and whistle blasts coming from the football practice field. Meanwhile, the town itself seemed depopulated, the few people who were there, torpid.

But then, as if by a secret signal, the tempo quickened. Fraternity brothers and sorority sisters suddenly materialized, making ready for a wave of aspiring immigrants eager for membership in their respective societies. And to the sounds of football practice were added the sounds of the marching band practicing. Faculty members appeared abruptly, having just returned from vacations or emerged from their studies at home. Second only to "Hellos" and "Hi theres" was the question, "Are you ready for the onslaught?" followed by, "No, are you?" or "No, no way!" Dormitories that had been empty and quiet suddenly crawled with students moving in; cars, station wagons, and vans parked three-deep around them, each vehicle disgorging wardrobes of fall and winter clothing. New faculty were convened for hours of orientation to the university, departmental meetings were called, registration instructions were given and duties assigned. The two-day hubbub of registration itself came and went. All was in readiness for the fall term to begin. Adrian was incredibly excited as he strode from his office to meet his first class as a full-fledged assistant professor of philosophy. It was the early morning of his true calling and the beginning of a year unparalleled in the history of Algonquin State.

Chapter Six

In really important matters, i.e., in spiritual matters, President Sythian Mac-Gilvary was certainly a man of his word. The first two weeks of the fall term had scarcely passed before six men of God (three Protestants, two Catholics, and a Jew) descended on campus (from as many directions) to conduct a period of religious emphasis. At the barbeque supper (an annual affair) that Sythian had hosted for freshmen, their parents, and new faculty members on the eve of registration, he had promised as much. Before supper, he had convened his guests in the amphitheater adjacent to the picnic grounds in the arboretum. Standing on a natural limestone slab, which served as a podium, he announced the obvious, declaring, "Algonquin State University is, of course, a secular, state owned and operated institution of higher learning in a society that believes in the fundamental separation of church and state."

Or says it does, Adrian thought.

"In keeping with that cardinal principle," Sythian went on, "we here at Algonquin are scrupulous in maintaining the separation of the sacred and the secular. No narrow parochialism, I can assure you, is ever tolerated here nor allowed to deflect us from our educational mission; but, at the same time, the ASU family yields to none in its concern for the total student, and that, of course, includes the spiritual dimension, or the religious side you might say, of life."

After pausing to see how his oft' repeated words were being taken by the various constituencies semicircled before him, he said mellifluously, "We do three things here to minister to our students' religious and moral needs. First, we have a religion department composed of committed Christian scholars. Each has the highest earned degree, attesting to his scholarly attainments, but each is also an ordained clergyman, which shows that we don't believe in divorcing the free study of religion from religion in life, religion in action."

"And, so, they lived happily ever after," Adrian said sotto voce to the uncomprehending freshman faculty member (in political science) to his left.

"Second, this institution works closely with the various campus ministries in the different denominational centers adjacent to the campus and with the pastors of local congregations. At the beginning of each term, we send each minister, free of charge, a computer print-out of the incoming students' religious preferences. Moreover, we give all the clergy in Algonquin easy access to the campus and keep them in mind in building our library collection in religion. Also, and this should go without saying, we encourage the Algonquin student to take full advantage of the religious programs offered by the various denominational centers and the local churches."

Pleased as punch with the parental support his words seemed to be eliciting, Sythian went on, enthusiastically, to point out, "Third, we bring outstanding spiritual leaders to our campus to participate in what we think of as periods of religious emphasis. Now, whereas many schools do this once a year, we here at Algonquin do it twice, once early in the fall term, and once toward the end of spring. We think this begins and ends our academic work on just the right note." So saying, he smiled broadly and was rewarded by a sea of smiling faces and not a few rapturous looks. True, he did not see the saturnine expression on the face of his new appointee in philosophy, but even if he had, he would have remained undaunted.

President MacGilvary could have been a superbly effective public speaker had he only known when to shut up, but he did not. So, while some in the audience that night began to stand first on one foot, then the other, restlessly; while certain others squirmed on the rocky seats of the amphitheater; and still others fidgeted to get on with the barbeque, whose ravishing scent was almost making them drool; he droned on and on.

"There are many who fear the college experience these days, and rightly so," he said, looking threatened, "for many are the temptations, morally and academically, to transform freedom into license. But we at Algonquin believe, and we believe that the history of the institution will show, that we have struck just the right balance between our commitment to academic freedom and the integrity of scholarship on the one side and complete responsibility to the total student on the other." Then, softening his voice as though speaking intimately to each and every person there, he said, "You know, it is often said that free inquiry is corrosive of traditional values and truth, but that is not so. All truth comes from God. In the last analysis, there's no conflict at all between scientific truth or historical truth and religious truth. Young people, you have nothing to fear. You can study as freely as you like here at Algonquin and not have to worry about its undermining your faith, or the faith of your parents, or the 'Faith of our fathers, holy faith, the Faith of our fathers, living still'!"

With that, Sythian himself was still for a moment. Then he said, "In conclusion, I would like to end with the Lord's prayer . . ."

"I wonder which Lord's prayer," Adrian muttered to nobody in particular, "Buddha's, Krishna's, Mahavira's?"

". . . and I invite you to join with me. We can also let it serve as grace for the meal to follow."

As most of the other people in the amphitheater bowed their heads,

Adrian, unbowed and looking straight ahead, wondered if he would be able to keep his daily bread down. Having to go through the receiving line and shake President MacGilvary's hand before he could get his daily bread didn't help his dyspepsia any either, but a free meal was a free meal, and, as it turned out, he was able to eat heartily. In fact, the food was exceptionally good and abundant. Doubtless, the citizens of the state would be well pleased to know that their tax money was being so well spent in supporting Christianity at a secular institution of higher learning where the separation of church and state was also being scrupulously maintained, Adrian thought to himself sarcastically.

At first, he resolved to forego the pleasures of sniping at the various men of God imported by ASU to emphasize religion for an autumnal week. College teaching had proved to be more demanding of freshman professors than he had bargained on. Working up brand new lectures in three different subjects (introduction to philosophy, social ethics, and elementary logic) and trying to pace the material properly took more out of him than he had expected. Then, too, with the term already in its third week, he had to begin thinking about getting his first examinations made up. But his initial resolve evaporated after a knock on his office door early on the Tuesday afternoon of religious emphasis week.

"Come in," he said loudly, pushing his chair back from his desk and swiveling 90° to his left to greet the one who knocked.

Peeking around his half-opened door, the caller said, "I'm sorry to interrupt you, Dr. DeWulf."

"You haven't," he assured the girl who stood there, still half-hidden.

"I'm . . . ah . . . my name is . . . um . . . Claire Sumner, and I'm in one of your classes."

Looking alive to the situation but feeling quite deadheaded, Adrian began to ransack the file drawers of his memory in the hope of associating the girl with the unnamed course she was taking or the physical position she occupied in whichever classroom was involved.

"You probably don't remember me," she said, trying to be helpful, "but I'm in your class in social ethics."

"Oh, yes," he replied as though suddenly remembering the location of a prized object long lost. Although he had already met each of his classes over a half-dozen times, he had not yet sorted out his ninety-three students by course nor by classroom, nor had he distinguished them, one from the other, as individuals. He had been looking inward too much for that, had been too concerned with monitoring how he was doing as a lecturer, and had been showing off a bit too much, if the truth were known, to have noticed his students as persons.

"I sit about two-thirds of the way back in the row next to the wall on the . . . ah . . . on your left," she said, gesturing animatedly.

"Sure," he said, nodding affirmatively, "I remember you now." Then, pointing to a chair, he said, "Say, why don't you come all the way in and take a pew?"

"A pew?" she questioned, smiling broadly.

Smiling in return, Adrian could not help noticing the remarkable grace with which she moved and the beauty of her posture as she composed herself before him.

"Well, what can I do for you?" he inquired, getting his mind back on business.

"Ah . . . I'm a Coyote," she said, "and . . ."

"You don't say," he broke in, his Nebraskan's familiarity with coyotes causing a smile to play at the corners of his mouth.

". . . that is, I'm a member of the Kai Iota Epsilon sorority. Have you ever heard of it?"

"Afraid not."

"Anyway," she went on, "it seems that one of the religious leaders visiting campus this week—one of the priests, that is—is supposed to come to the Coyote House to lead a discussion tomorrow night," (when referring to the house, Algonquin students did not sound the e, but when referring to the girls who lived there, they did sound it, the plural being "Coyoties.") "and I wondered if you would be willing to come, sort of as my guest. Would you?"

"Well," he said, eyes rolling heavenward, "yes, yes, I guess I could come, but why me?"

"Why you? Oh, that's pretty simple really. When you were talking the other day in class about how . . . um . . . religious ethics boils down to . . . ah . . . unquestioned obedience to a monarchial figure taken by the believer to be absolutely dominant, some things seemed to click in my mind. You just made sense of certain things, that's all."

"Thanks very much," he said, looking at her appreciatively.

"And," she went on, "preachers just haven't been making much sense to me lately, and I doubt that the priest will tomorrow night either, but I'm not always sure how to respond to what they say."

"So you want somebody in the crowd who'll keep the opposition honest, is that it?"

"Sort of," she admitted, smiling conspiratorially and rising to leave.

"Oh, what time?" he called after her.

Peeking back in the door, she said, "If you could come a little before eight o'clock, I would plan to meet you on the front porch. Oh, yes, the Coyote House is straight across the yard from the tower of the Ad. Building."

"Fine. I'll see you then and in class tomorrow morning, too, I guess."

"Yes," she said decisively over her departing shoulder, "it would take wild horses to keep me away from your ethics class."

"Wonderful!" he announced to his empty room with its closed door.

When Adrian reached the Coyote House, quite a few girls were milling around its flood-lit front porch awaiting their boyfriends. Other girls, more enterprising or desperate, as the case may have been, had apparently gone across the campus to track down their dates and lead them back to the house. Adrian, eavesdropping on various conversations, was amused by Algonquin's boy-girl chatter, none of which touched on religion.

As she had promised, Claire Sumner was waiting for him, though he did not see her until she moved effortlessly through the crowd to his side. "Hi," she said with a slight wave, "here I am."

"So you are," he replied lightheartedly.

"Would you like to go inside now and get a good seat?" she asked.

"Lead on," he said. And she did lead on, and as she did so, he marveled again at the grace of her movements. Had someone taught her how to walk in that queenly fashion? he wondered.

Nobody in the rapidly filling social room took special notice of the casually dressed man with Claire as they took seats together on the back row against one wall of the room. Adrian noticed, however, that Claire took pains to save a seat on the side opposite from him. "For my date," she said, aware of his curiosity.

Their small talk, to which Adrian could easily have warmed, was short-lived, for in a matter of moments an enormous boy, almost beetle-browed and bursting out of his shirt-collar, entered with a black-garbed man in tow. After introducing the man to a tall, angular girl, the boy made a beeline for the chair Claire was saving. Meanwhile, the angular one rapped for attention and said nasally, "In case any of you don't know me, I'm Adele Blass, and I'm the student program coordinator for the Coyoties this year." Pausing for the chatter to die away completely, she continued, "We're certainly fortunate tonight . . . ah . . . and honored, too, to have as our religious emphasis week guest, Father Darius Nooper. Father Nooper, as some of you may know already, is the professor of . . . um . . . ah . . . moral theology at the College of . . ." (Here she looked at a three-by-five-inch file card secreted in the palm of her left hand.) "St. Joseph of Arimantha—"("Arimathea," Father Nooper corrected her hastily, a wan smile on his face.) "Oh, yeah, Arimathea, the College of St. Joseph of Arimathea, in Diablo Springs, Wyoming. He did his undergraduate work at Marquette University in Milwaukee and majored in . . . in . . . what is this?" she asked, looking from her card to Father Nooper, seated to her right. "Soteriology," the priest said softly, pleased to be of help. "Oh, yeah, sote-ri-ol-ogy." At that, several people, boys mostly, clapped. "And," Adele went on, ignoring the applause, "he did his divinity work at the Catholic University of America in Washington, D.C. Oh, yes, and he also did graduate work there, majoring in—" (Here she looked at her trusty card again.) "the . . . ah . . . philosophy of God."

Adrian, who had merely smiled at the thought of Father Nooper's work in soteriology, chuckled openly at his studies in the philosophy of God.

Except for his robust voice, Father Nooper was anything but prepossessing physically, being a slight man with translucent skin of alabaster, light hazel eyes, and sandy hair going gray. Expressing the keen pleasure he felt at being invited to the Coyote House and the honor he felt at being brought all the way from Wyoming to Algonquin State University, he reminded everybody that he had given the theme talk for that day at the morning convocation and said that what he really wanted to do was to answer questions rather than give another formal talk then and there to the Coyoties.

As murmurs of approval reinforced his wishes, he asked, "Any questions?"

Some seconds of nervous silence ensued during which Father Nooper looked from left to right and back again expectantly, openly.

Finally, a young man whom Adrian recognized as one of his own students raised a tentative hand and said, "Father, I'm not a Catholic, but I am a Christian, and I'd just like to observe that it seems like students, around here anyway, sort of get weaned away from religion while they're in college, if you know what I mean."

Making a steeple of his fingers, Father Nooper said, "I think there is much truth in what you say, but it need not be the case. If we only had more Newman Club workers on more campuses, many, many more, I believe we could stanch the flow, so to speak. I have made this point to my superiors many times, as I am sure others have too. If the church would only alter its priorities so as to increase the number of Newman Club centers on college and university campuses and would train more personnel to man them, I believe the tide could be turned."

"But don't you think there's a lot more to the problem than just that?" asked a second young man, quite mature in appearance. "Don't you think it's harder for us in this generation to believe than it was in your generation?" He hastened to add, "I . . . I don't mean to make light of your generation, Father, it's just that it seems to me there's an awful lot against belief now that wasn't around earlier."

Looking very understanding as he surveyed the fifty-odd people assembled to hear him, Father Nooper said, "It is certainly true that there are factors and pressures that have changed the religious situation on campuses, but I believe that the changes at issue are at base only superficial. Look at it this way. Human nature hasn't really changed, has it? Human sin remains the same as ever. Human need, the need for Christ and his church and redemption, is just what it always was. The message of the church is the same as it has been for almost 2,000 years and is as firmly based as ever. There may be more unbelievers nowadays than before, but there is no greater justification for it. After all, the Catholic faith is based on knowledge. We know that God exists, because we can demonstrate it by natural reason."

"Please demonstrate it," said a cool clear voice rising from the rear of the room.

Father Nooper's head jerked in Adrian's direction (as did many other heads including Claire's) as he sought out the precise source of the challenge. "You mean you don't believe in God!" he said reproachfully, hoping to put the challenger on the defensive.

"Whether or not I believe in God is hardly at issue; the issue is your

276

ability to demonstrate God's existence, as you say you can," Adrian said, as though setting a confused child straight.

Father Nooper, looking very sure of himself, said, "Well, we know that every single thing that happens has a cause, and we know that each cause, each mediate cause, that is, is itself the effect of an antecedent cause, which in turn is the effect of a still more remote cause, and so on. We also know that there cannot be an infinite chain of causes, that there has to be a first cause, and that, of course, is God. So there is no question about—"

"How do we know that there has to be a first cause?" Adrian cut in.

"You mean you don't believe in a first cause?" Father Nooper asked, horror tinging his voice.

"Whether or not I believe in a first cause is beside the point," Adrian replied patiently, looking very sober but relishing the exchange. "The point is that you have said that we can know that there is a first cause. As you are very well aware," he went on, needling the priest, "there have been thinkers all the way from Parmenides to numerous modern scientists and philosophers who have maintained the eternality of the universe, who have held the idea that the universe never came into existence in the first place and therefore had no first cause, and that it will never cease to be."

Hoping to score a direct hit on his tormenter, even if it meant aiming over the students' heads, Father Nooper said, "Yes, of course, and Aquinas himself was prepared to accept the notion that the catena, or catenae, of mediate causes was infinite, that there need not have been a *terminus a quo* temporally conceived, but, of course, that doesn't alter the fact that every contingent happening and every dependent being has to be supported and sustained by a first cause hierarchically conceived."

Although most of the students were lost at that point, they were sure more was to come; so, heads swiveled as one in Adrian's direction excitedly.

"Father Nooper," he said, "how do you respond to Bertrand Russell's terse observation that if everything has to have a cause, then God has to have a cause, whereas if there is anything that does not have to have a cause, it could just as well be the material universe as God? In your enthusiasm to account for the world, you mustn't neglect to account for the account of it."

Darius Nooper was about to say that God was a necessary, not a dependent, being when someone (whether by design or coincidence) let him off the hook by asking for his views on the role of women in the Catholic Church. Relieved from having to demonstrate God's existence, the harried priest said that he was certainly for women and that for some of their qualities he admired them much more than he admired men but that women must never aspire to the priesthood, because they were made of the wrong substance to handle such sacred objects as the body and blood of Christ in the eucharistic celebration and unfit by nature to preside over such sacred rituals as holy matrimony.

"But what I want to know is who did make God?" asked a girl who strongly resembled Raggedy Ann.

277

Dismayed, the priest mumbled something about not wanting to get involved in an infinite regress; or was it that he didn't want God to get involved?

"That doesn't seem like a fair answer to me," observed a second girl, a girl who looked like a proverbial china doll.

Together, but without being in league, Raggedy Ann and China Doll had prevented the Coyoties from scoring the highest grade average of any female group at ASU during the previous spring term. Together again, but still not in league, they held the priest's feet to the fire, so inspired were they by the novel ideas introduced by the stranger (to them) sitting in the back row. No sooner had Father Nooper answered one girl to his satisfaction than the other one was at him, and no matter how eagerly he sought to address himself to other types of questions, one or the other would yank him back to the question of God's antecedents. With no attempt at humor, Raggedy Ann brought the house down when she said, reasoning very well for her, that if the Virgin Mary was the mother of God, then her parents must have been God's grandparents. In the tumult that followed, Adrian stamped the floor in glee and laughed unabashedly for a great while. Claire was also vastly amused, he noticed happily, but her date was not, nor was he pleased with her rollicking laughter.

Despairing of all hope that he might remain on congenial topics, Father Nooper lectured the terrible twosome using dense medieval terms designed to squelch them.

"Father," said Adrian, breaking in and appearing to be helpful, "don't you think your terminology is unnecessarily scholastic? After all, these students haven't had the benefit of your rigorous training in antediluvian systems of thought nor in the antique vocabularies to match." Several "uh huh's" endorsed Adrian's point and rubbed salt into Father Nooper's wounds.

With most eyes fastened on him and only a few resting in sympathy on the seething priest, Adrian simply took the floor. Standing by his chair, perhaps a bit arrogantly, he transformed Father Nooper into a son and everyone else into a student, saying, "Don't you see that trying to explain all being, or reality as a whole, or the universe (call it what you will) with reference to God is the same as explaining a dark mystery with a much darker one? Call God a necessary being, if you like; call him an adorable mystery, if it pleases you; but do not presume to explain anything thereby, for in so doing you are simply transferring the hard questions about physical reality to the alleged nonphysical cause of it all. As long as you remain ignorant of what God is, of why he is what he is, of why he wills what he is alleged to will, and of how he executes his mandates, you will remain as ignorant of ultimate reality as before. In the presence of ineffable mystery, the pious thing to do is to remain silent, it seems to me."

With that gratuitous piece of advice ringing in his ears, Darius Nooper, his face aglow with indignation, said in a dry, rasping voice, "I came here to talk to students; I didn't come here to talk to a philosopher." Then, to the accompaniment of several "oh's" and "ah's" from surprised students, he excused himself, shook hands with Adele Blass and with someone Adrian took to be the housemother, and took his unexpected leave. Several Coyoties sped after his departing back, hoping to undo any damage that might have been done to the sorority's reputation for hospitality.

"Not since Pope Umbrage the Umpteenth touched the Host with the wrong finger has there been anything in Christendom as scandalous as this," Adrian said to Claire in mock horror.

"What?" she squeaked, utterly at sea but trying hard to fathom his meaning.

"Just imagine," he continued loudly, "a holy man leaving early! What is our world coming to? Usually, they stay, and stay, and stay, especially when there's a captive audience of students they can bamboozle. But this one is really skedaddling."

Not intending to change the subject but only trying to be polite, Claire gestured toward the mountainous youth on her other side and said, "Oh, Professor DeWulf, this is my date, Bucky Oaks. I would have introduced you two earlier, but there wasn't time."

"How are you, Bucky?" Adrian asked, not caring much nor needing to be told that Claire's date was really steamed up.

"Hi," Bucky grunted unpleasantly, spurning the professor's hand. (It was not until later that Adrian learned that he had been introduced to Mr. Anthony Starbuck Oaks, one of the biggest men on campus in more ways than one. Among other things, Bucky was Algonquin's stellar linebacker, a pious Catholic, and a student pillar in the local Newman Club.) By the time the introduction had been completed, a ring of students five deep, including Raggedy Ann, had formed around the three of them, and Adrian found himself answering questions animatedly put to him.

For quite a while, he explained to the students what Father Nooper had meant by such recondite terms as 'hierarchical causation', 'contingent being', and God as 'pure actuality'. Then, Bucky got into the act. Trying to play the part of the departed priest, he said, "There just has got to be a God, because there's either design in the world or it's just an accident." To that, several students said, "Yeah," and "That's right," but Adrian held his ground calmly, pointing out that the universe might be neither the product of design nor an accident. The mood at the moment, however, was too volatile for him to succeed in showing that being the result of an accident was not the same as having no cause, so he let the matter drop.

"Oh, pooh, there just *has* to be a supreme being," said Raggedy Ann.

Loath to go through the whole thing again, Adrian said, "Look, everybody, if we hang the whole universe on a sky hook, so to speak, but don't explain what the sky hook itself is hooked to, somebody is going to say, 'Hey, how does the sky hook hold the whole thing up?' "

"But where does that leave us?" Claire asked, the floor under her feet feeling a little like quicksand.

"Right where we always have been, You see, whenever we humans penetrate into reality as far as our kinds of minds will let us reach, we have to be content with stopping at that point, even if it is psychologically difficult."

"I'm not too sure I get it," she replied with a blank look on her face.

"Well, it just means that there are questions about reality that no human being can answer."

"Like what?" boomed Bucky, clenching and unclenching his fists.

"Like what philosophers call 'The Given'," Adrian said, "and it wouldn't matter whether 'The Given' was the matter/energy of this universe, or God, or some Super-Being above God. Whenever you reach 'The Given', you reach that which humans cannot fully comprehend, if at all."

With many eyes staring at him opaquely, incredulously, he went on: "It's like this, when we reach the most fundamental level that we are capable of dealing with, then we have reached the level at which we no longer have any terms in terms of which to think our way into anything deeper. Right?"

"Yeah, I guess, but it still blows my mind," someone mumbled with resignation.

"That's just dumb," observed Raggedy Ann, leaving the group.

"But what about the purpose of the universe?" asked a girl looking a little frightened.

"It almost certainly has none," Adrian said flatly, "and even if it did, we couldn't know what it was."

"But then our lives would lose all their meaning," another student said, in a complaining, whiny voice.

"Yes and no. Human life would not have any objective, cosmic meaning attendant on the so-called 'purpose of the universe', but within the universe and in the context of human society and individual purposes, it could certainly take on meaning and retain it. In fact, both of those things happen regularly."

"I think I'd kill myself if I didn't believe in God," said a boy dramatically, but perfectly seriously, several "me too's" following his dire assertion.

"Well, I know what I believe. I believe in what the Catholic Church teaches, and that's plenty good enough for me," said Bucky, still glowering.

"Oh, damn, here comes Miss Haskins!" Claire exclaimed regretfully. At that, the circle of students opened to admit a woman whose face looked to Adrian astonishingly like a goat's.

"Dr. DeWulf, I'd like you to meet Miss Nympha Mae Haskins, the Coyote housemother," Claire said, gesturing at the one with the capriform face who had just bustled purposefully into their midst.

"How do you do?" said the newcomer curtly as Adrian simultaneously expressed his pleasure at meeting her.

"It is to be expected," Miss Haskins announced, "that we would want in all things to conform to the rules, and that time has come, so exceptions would not be thought to apply."

While Adrian blinked several times trying to figure out what he had just heard, Nympha Mae Haskins, who was pious to a fault, looked daggers in his direction. "Oh," said Claire, coming to the rescue, "Miss Haskins just means that it's time for men to leave the sorority house now—university rules, you know—so, I'm sorry, but you'll have to go."

"Why, certainly," he agreed, wondering why one who looked so much like a goat could not be as forthright as the goats he had known. Aware that Claire wanted whatever seconds were left to be with the still-scowling Bucky, Adrian said that he could find his way out easily. Then, telling the students who were still clustered about him that he would be seeing them around and reassuring Nympha Mae of his keen pleasure in getting to meet her, he left in very high spirits, having forgotten how much fun religion could be and looking forward to the rest of religious emphasis week.

The following afternoon, he attended a panel discussion on "Christian Sex, Marriage, and Parenthood," conducted by Father Nooper and two of the Protestant ministers on campus for religious emphasis week. Arriving late, Adrian slipped into the meeting room unobtrusively and took a seat in the rear just in time to hear Father Nooper say in answer to a student's question, ". . . certainly not for pleasure alone and certainly not outside of holy wedlock."

"I just don't see how the church can teach such a narrow-minded thing," blustered the questioning student, who had all but admitted to having participated in sex for pleasure alone and outside of holy wedlock to boot.

"It is very clear and simple really," said Father Nooper, sternly but patiently. "Natural law itself teaches us that the propagation of the species is the purpose of sexuality. God made us sexual beings so that we could be fruitful, and multiply, and replenish the earth in accordance with his commandment. Sexual intercourse may be pleasant and may even contribute to a variety of marital values, but they are not its fundamental purpose. No, nature plainly shows us that the primary purpose of sex is procreation."

"I should like to comment on that," Adrian said loudly and clearly, rising to his feet swiftly and not waiting to be recognized by the moderator. "I presume, Father, that you, like the rest of us, eat food periodically to sustain your body."

"Of course I do," Father Nooper replied, distressed upon recognizing the questioner.

"And you would agree that the purpose of eating food is nutrition?"

"Certainly."

"Did you ever eat anything that you did not need to sustain you, that you did not need nutritionally?"

"I don't think," Father Nooper said warily, "that I care to engage in this kind of question and answer . . ."

"Oh, please do," Adrian cajoled him, "for the sake of the students here, for their edification, if not for our own."

At that a murmur of approbation wafted up from the students.

"Oh, very well; what was the question again?" asked Father Nooper guardedly.

"Did you ever eat anything simply because you liked the taste of it, some delicacy or other that you did not really need nutritionally, something that you did not require to sustain you?"

Thinking of the cakes of bishop's bread and the red raspberry pies that his mother and sisters sent him from time to time or were sure to set before him on his infrequent visits home, Father Nooper agreed reluctantly that he probably had eaten some delicacies simply because he liked them.

"And what of drink, that is to say, of the natural purpose of drink," Adrian asked, "is it not to enable us to maintain appropriate levels of bodily fluids, to prevent dehydration, for example?"

"I suppose so," said Father Nooper, seeing all too plainly where Adrian's dialectic was leading, even if the expectant students, whose heads were swiveling first one way and then the other, did not.

"I am wondering, Father, if you have ever drunk any liquids for reasons other than that of avoiding dehydration, possibly taken a shot of bourbon or of Scotch or, perchance, of brandy when a drink of plain tap water would have maintained your bodily fluids just as well?"

Darius Nooper knew that, to many Protestants, Catholics had the unsavory reputation of being tipplers and that this, if nothing else, gave the Roman Church a bad name in the minds of many. If he answered the question about drink by saying, "No," he would lie, for, in truth, he was inordinately fond of Irish whiskey and drank it whenever he could do so with impunity. If, on the other hand, he answered, "Yes," truthfully, he might do a disservice to the church and might even be set upon by a fellow panel member, the Reverend Rex Manchester from the First Methodist Church of Texarkana, Arkansas, an obnoxious chap who had already made known his rabid opposition to strong drink of all kinds and quantities. Drawing himself up to his full five feet, six inches and looking very grave, Father Nooper said, "I have, on occasion, drunk spirituous beverages, but I hasten to point out that our Lord drank wine and even turned water into wine at the marriage feast in Cana."

"Oh, Father, please let me assure you that I am no puritan moralist," said Adrian, gesturing deprecatingly and making a bad face at the mere thought of being classed with such benighted folk. "No, no, my point is simply that if nature teaches us her law to the effect that sexual intercourse is for reproduction and is never to be engaged in for pleasure alone, then nature also teaches that eating food is for nourishment and never for pleasure alone and drinking drink is for maintaining essential bodily fluids and never for pleasure alone."

"That analogy does not hold," Father Nooper declared piercingly to the accompaniment of several whoops, sighs of approval (or perhaps of relief), and hand clappings from assorted students.

"Father Nooper," Adrian said, his voice arching over the commotion, "you have sinned against the laws of nature and of nature's God, I fear."

"That is preposterous," Father Nooper shrilled, his face so flushed that his graying sandy hair looked white, "because in sexual relations there are two persons involved in a way in which they are . . ."

"And I can only hope that you will confess to your sins against nature," Adrian said, his voice overriding the priest's vehement tones. Thereupon, he sat down with many heads turned in his direction. Father Nooper also sat down resignedly, knowing that the students had already drawn the conclusion they wished to draw and that nothing he might say about the invalidity of the professor's analogical reasoning would make any difference.

Just then, Bro. Manly Plumwell arose and attracted the moderator's eye. Remembering the anonymous letter he had received back in Nickel Plate which the sender had said could be used for clobbering Catholics, he said, "Sir, I would like to address a question to the priest." At that, Father Nooper arose uncertainly, not knowing what to expect next. "Reverend Nooper—I call you that rather than Father Nooper, because the Scripture, in Matthew 23:9, says to call no man father on earth—Reverend Nooper, I have read that Catholic Church rules permit liberties to the husband of . . . ah . . . a sexual sort that are denied to the wife; to be more specific, that a husband is permitted to perform unnatural sex acts on his wife."

"The Catholic Church never condones unnatural sex acts of any kind," said Father Nooper, his voice quavering with outrage.

"Not even in marriage?" Manly asked querulously, fearing that his anonymous persecutor of yesteryear had misled as well as titillated him.

Leaping to his feet and speaking again without the moderator's blessing, Adrian said, "That gentleman over there has a point that you have either ignored or sidestepped, I fear, Father Nooper."

Hoping for vindication, Manly subsided onto his chair, keenly interested in what might transpire. Turning away from Manly, Father Nooper looked angrily at Adrian and braced himself for the worst.

"Father Nooper," Adrian said with a supportive, almost consoling, note in his voice, "I don't pretend to be an expert in Roman Catholic Canon Law as I am sure you are. In fact, I have never seen all the canons, my only acquaintance being with the condensed and adapted version of Jone-Adelman entitled *Moral Theology,* a version you may have in your personal library." Getting no response from the temporarily frozen figure that was Father Nooper, Adrian went on, saying, "Anyway, there's a canon, numbered 750, or 770, or somewhere along in there that says a husband may begin the marriage act—and I quote—'sodomitically', provided that he intends to consummate it in such a way that conception may result." Delighted in Father Nooper's stricken look, Adrian went on, "It goes without saying, of course, that the wife cannot cooperate willingly, must offer internal, but not external, resistance, and must take no pleasure in the sodomitical aspect of the proceedings, and, of course, the husband must engineer things in such a way as to avoid the grave sins of onanism and pollution."

"That's just the kind of disgusting thing I had in mind," said Manly, bobbing up cheerfully, still in the hope of clobbering Catholics.

"That's gross," shouted one girl. "It's horribly unfair to women, that's what it is," said another, a girl who was an active feminist. "It's just sick," said several others, more or less in unison. "It's ridiculous," said still others, all to the accompaniment of many sharp intakes of breath on the part of young women. For their part, the male students kept their peace but exhibited a variety of inscrutable, if thoughtful, looks.

"Would you . . . um . . . want to respond to any of these people?" the distraught moderator asked of Father Nooper.

"No," said the priest through clenched teeth, "I've already monopolized the floor, so perhaps you might turn it over to my fellow panelists here."

"I just want to say," boomed the Reverend Rex Manchester into the microphone before him, "that in the Methodist Church we believe that men and women are equal in God's sight, and that goes for marriage, too—it's a partnership all the way with equal pleasures and responsibilities for both parties."

As Rex boomed on and on, Adrian asked of the person on his left, "Who is that well-dressed man who brought up the subject of unnatural acts?"

"I think he's one of the campus ministers or maybe a pastor here in town, but I don't know his name," the person replied.

Moments earlier, Bro. Plumwell had asked of a student companion named Oscar Jiminie, "Who is that person talking about natural law?"

"Oh, that's Professor DeWulf," Oscar had answered, "you know, the new guy in the philosophy department."

"That's what I thought," Manly had replied, redoubling his interest in what the new professor was doing to Reverend Nooper.

With Rex Manchester steering the discussion onto safer, more boring, terrain, Adrian arose and left the session, grinning broadly.

Before the unsmiling Darius Nooper left Algonquin, the next day, for the safety of the College of St. Joseph of Arimathea in faraway Wyoming, he lodged a sharp protest with the Coordinator of Religious Affairs concerning the treatment he, a priest of the Roman Catholic Church, had received at the hands of a certain philosophy professor. As a result, a detrimental memorandum found its way silently into Adrian's file in ASU's Personnel Office.

Shortly after the end of religious emphasis week, Adrian had two visits in a single day relative to it. He hoped the first visit would not be repeated. As for the second, well, it could be repeated as often as the visitor cared to return.

"I'm Brother Manly Plumwell, RPPl.," said the immaculately dressed man standing in Adrian's doorway and reaching out stiffly to clasp his hand.

"I'm afraid I didn't catch all that," Adrian replied, feeling doltish over not having comprehended everything the newcomer had announced, especially

284

the part involving letters, strangely arranged to his ears.

"I said, 'I'm Manly Plumwell, RPP1.,' Royal Priest of the Pulpit, that is. I'm the campus minister for the Holy Nation Association and pastor of Algonquin's Church of the Chosen."

"My name is DeWulf," Adrian said, reluctant to reveal more than necessary about himself lest the one standing before him should find occasion to stay long or come again.

"I want to tell you how much I appreciated what you did to that priest at the session on sex, marriage, and parenthood last week."

"Aw, think nothing of it."

"I do think something of it, because I don't ever recall seeing one of the papists put on the run like that before, and it did my heart good. In fact, I've written my superiors about it."

You should have seen him the night before, Adrian thought to himself. Then aware that Bro. Plumming, or Plumbber, or whatever, was still standing, he invited Manly to sit down, but without much enthusiasm, and said, "Well, you set him up for me very nicely. I was content to show what a lot of bunk that natural law malarkey of theirs is, but then when you brought up the unnatural acts topic, it was great good fun to bring canon law into play. I'm only sorry that I didn't think to cite the encyclical, 'Bombasticus Gullibilitatus.' " At that, Adrian chuckled at his own private whimsy, whimsy on a par with the nonexistent pope, Umbrage the Umpteenth, whom he referred to from time to time.

"Perhaps," said Manly, not picking up on "Bombasticus Gullibilitatus" and seeking his opening warily, "perhaps, we were able to team up because we have something in common."

"We do?" Adrian responded, wondering what in hell it might be and hoping that it wasn't much.

"Yes, indeed," Manly went on, "because I noticed in the paper some weeks ago that you have a divinity degree from Texas Christian."

"Yes, do you have one too?"

"Oh, no, I just have my B.S. in adult education from Algonquin here and, of course, my RPP1. from Big Bend Bible School."

Unimpressed with his visitor's degree and chuckling inwardly at the RPP1. from some Godforsaken place called Big Bend Bible School, Adrian said, "Well, then, just what do we have in common?"

"I was thinking, perhaps, that you might belong to the Disciples of Christ, my old denomination."

"Oh, that. Well, I was a Disciple for a long time, but not any more."

"Neither am I any more; I saw the light years ago," Manly said triumphantly, thinking of the sunset hour, a decade earlier, when Scott Truesdale and Emory Plunkett had found him in misery on his screened-in front porch.

"So did I, see the light, that is," Adrian asserted, thinking of the wintry night when he strode free and alone upon the open prairie outside of Mineral

Wells, Texas. "I think we must have seen different lights, though," he observed warningly.

"I can only hope that everyone might see the same light JEsus shed on me," Manly said decisively, his eyes boring into Adrian with fierce sincerity.

"I don't suppose that's in the cards," the professor replied, bored and hoping to terminate the conversation.

"You have heard of the Holy Nation Association of Churches of the Chosen, haven't you, Dr. DeWulf?"

"Vaguely."

"And of Miss Alice McAlister, the Handmaiden of the Lord?"

"Yes, I've heard the name, but then I've also heard of Mother Ann Lee, Mary Baker Eddy, Madame Blavatsky, Aimee Semple McPherson, and Miss Lela G. McConnell," Adrian said dismissively, hoping that his visitor would get the point and leave well enough alone.

Of the six mentioned, Manly had heard only of Mrs. Eddy and knew as little of her as of the rest (except that they were all mistaken), but that did not prevent him from asserting knowingly, "Miss Alice McAlister is *truly* the Lord's handmaiden for these latter days. God vouchsafed to her a revelation that was overlooked for almost 2,000 years, a revelation in the Bible all along, but one that was completely ignored by so-called Christians until our time. I would surely like to tell you about it sometime." But, receiving no encouragement from Adrian, who had assumed a poker face so as to neither laugh aloud ror smile derisively, Manly said, sensing that the time was not yet ripe, "Perhaps we can go into that some other time. What I really wanted to do today was to meet you and thank you for routing that papist last week."

For the second time that day, Adrian said, "Think nothing of it."

"Well, good-bye, then, till we meet again," Manly said, rising to go.

"Farewell," Adrian replied lukewarmly, wondering what steps he might take to prevent their reunion. He had almost said that as far as religion was concerned he was very democratic and would as happily put to rout a royal priest of the pulpit as any papist, but he held his peace.

He had scarcely settled down to finish reading U. T. Place's "Is Consciousness a Brain Process?" when the second visitor arrived. Rapping on his office door even as she opened it, Claire Sumner stuck her head in pertly and said, "Can I interrupt you for a minute?"

"You already have," he responded in deadpan tones.

Flustered, she said, "Oh, I'm sorry, I . . . I didn't mean to . . ."

Smiling broadly, Adrian said, "You mustn't take everything I say so seriously. I am sometimes known to bandy words." Then, as he gestured at a chair, he played the pedagogue, saying, "You see, the locution 'Can I?' probes the issue of what the individual is able to do, whereas 'May I?' asks for permission to do something or other. Now, since you had already interrupted me, it was pleonastic to ask, 'Can I interrupt you?' See how simple the distinction is?"

Pretending to be sorely put upon, Claire asked with exaggerated precision, "Professor DeWulf, *may* I interrupt you?"

"Certainly, Miss Sumner, interrupt away."

"You know," she said, looking at him intently, "you really were fantastic at the Coyote House the other night."

For that he gave her a playful grin, both deprecating and smug.

"And, from what I hear, equally fantastic the next day at the sex thing in the afternoon."

"Oh, any halfway decent philosopher would have done as much. I didn't say anything that hasn't been thought and said for generations or even centuries," he replied candidly.

"Yes, but you put it into words so well—things that we wouldn't have been able to say back to that priest." It was really Adrian's self-confidence, his boldness in saying what he had said that had struck her most forcefully, but she was not bold enough to tell him that.

"Philosophers are supposed to be good with words," he said, understating the case and wondering if she had come just to compliment him on so trivial an achievement as that of disconcerting a priest.

"Of course, not everybody liked what you said," she went on with a wry smile on her face, "or did to . . . ah . . . to that poor man of the cloth."

"More's the pity," he declared earnestly, "because I think the Noopers of this world ought to have to put up or shut up; they've taken advantage of people far too long."

"My date that night—he's a Catholic—was spitting mad at what you said; and we even had a fight about it the next day," she volunteered.

"Are you Catholic too?" he asked, hoping it was not so.

"No, no, I'm not Catholic," she said slowly, thoughtfully, "but that doesn't mean that I know exactly what I am either."

"I don't think I follow," he said, trying to fathom the perturbation on her face.

"Well," she said, dropping both hands to her sides as though opening herself to fuller scrutiny, "I used to belong to the Church of Christ; do you know of it?"

"Ah, do I know of it!" he said, nodding vigorously. "The Southern Baptists or worse, if one can imagine it, of the Campbellite movement!"

"I don't know about that," she replied, mystified by his comment, "but, anyway, my home church in Heather, a little town down in the southern part of the state, was always fairly weak and struggling, and then one fine Sunday morning a really weird thing happened. A person named Smallwood, Herod Agrippa Smallwood to be exact, came by singing at the top of his lungs, and in no time the congregation had a knock-down drag-out fight, and presto, it became the Heather Church of the Chosen of the Holy Nation Association. It kind of amazed me, but my dad and mother were among the first converts, so to speak, not that they had to be rebaptized or anything like that, but they did change their allegiance and took me right along—I was thirteen—into the new denomination, or the true church as they call it."

Pausing in her discourse as though spent, chin resting in the palm of her left hand, her elbow planted on the arm of her chair, Claire asked, "Have you ever heard of the Holy Nation Association?"

"Indeed I have," Adrian replied, "and recently, too, and of someone named Miss Alice McAlister, the Lord's very own Handmaiden, if I am not mistaken."

"You're not mistaken, and I have some news for you," she said. "The Handmaiden and her new Jews—I mean the members of the Holy Nation— have at least one really far-out doctrine called three-world creationism. Have you heard of it?"

"No, I've been spared that so far," Adrian responded, chuckling and wondering if that was what Bro. Plumluck, or whatever, had been looking for an opportunity to reveal to him.

A long pause followed during which Claire seemed to be searching for the words with which to go on or, perhaps, for the courage without which she could not go on. Finally, she said, "At the end of my sophomore year, last spring, that is, I decided to major in psychology. Well, let me tell you, I'm in real distress. Some of the things I'm learning about human behavior are blowing me right out of the water in . . . um . . . relation to what my folks taught me and the stuff that was drilled into me in church and Sunday school. I'm not even sure I know who I am at the moment—maybe I'm going crazy."

"Believe me, I do understand," he said comfortingly, recognizing for the first time that behind that queenly carriage of hers, strong emotions were in painful torsion, that beneath her usually blithe exterior, there were gnawing doubts.

"And then, I get into your class in ethics—don't get me wrong, I love it—but sometimes you do bad things to me."

"I do bad things to you?" he asked, appearing to be startled.

"Well, maybe not bad things, but you do set students up and then pull the rug out from under them. Sometimes, when I have spoken out in class, I've been so sure of myself, only to have you wipe me completely out."

"But," he said, trying hard to remember specific instances when she had spoken out, "the points you've made have usually been based either on sheer feelings, amounting to knee-jerk responses, or have been simply reflexive and traditional, like loving mom and apple pie. If you don't fall through the floors of feeling and habit once in a while, how will I make you respect the imperative need for supporting your positions with fact and logic whenever possible?"

"Oh, I suppose you can't," she said, "but after a few of the pratfalls I've taken in your class, I need somebody to tell me what to think."

"No, you don't need any such thing!"

After staring at him for a long moment, amazed at his vehemence, she said, "Okay, maybe not tell me outright, but screw my head on straight for me."

"Help you screw your own head on straight would be more like it."

"All right, *help* me screw it on. Any suggestions?"

"First of all, keep on living."

"I'm not exactly suicidal," she answered, arching toward him, hands outstretched.

"I don't presume for a moment that you are. What I mean is that there is really no emergency, no objective emergency, over getting your head on right concerning the conflicts you are feeling just now between the traditional beliefs you've acquired and what you are being confronted with here. Just think what a strange world it would be if twenty-year-olds, like yourself, were perfectly clear in their minds about profound issues in religion, psychology, and philosophical anthropology. Twenty-year-olds are too young for that."

"Maybe so, but this twenty-year-old is really hurting a lot of the time."

"So, in addition to keeping on living, and learning, and maturing, and developing your critical abilities, and deepening your appreciation for facts, how about taking my course in the philosophy of religion next term?"

At that, her face lit up, and she said, "Hey, I'd love to do that. I didn't know you were going to teach it." Then, pausing, rolling her eyes heavenward, she said, "If only I can work it into my schedule."

"I really hope you can and will," he said animatedly, for he already knew her to be a good student. Besides, she was fun to watch and to talk to in class and very responsive to his teaching. With a little luck, perhaps, he could help deliver her from the superstitions that still hounded her, that still tried to drag her to earth before she reached full self-possession.

After she had gone, Adrian returned with some difficulty to U. T. Place's article. As he read, "What I do want to assert, however, is that the statement 'Consciousness is a process in the brain,' although not necessarily true, is not necessarily false. 'Consciousness is a process in the brain,' on my view is neither self-contradictory nor self-evident; it is a reasonable scientific hypothesis," he found himself whistling a very happy circus tune he had learned as a child. "What are you doing?" he asked himself, "going nuts?"

Adrian was gifted (or, perhaps, cursed) with the ability to tell outlandish tales as though they were sober fact agreed to by all who were informed. Not only could he keep a perfectly straight face while perpetrating his fictions, he was also able to look suitably grave, or soulful, or hortatory, or even pious while doing so. If questioned pointedly by incredulous hearers, he could look crestfallen; if challenged, aggrieved; if laughed at, hurt. Indeed, he often posed as though he, and he alone, were clothed in right and truth; all others being benighted or perverse. His first best opportunity at Algonquin to exercise his gift (or curse) came at a party given by the Reids on an evening in early October.

Directed by Rad's long arm, he made his way from the front door through the nether gloom of tobacco smoke and dim lighting to the dining room where a table sagged under a mountain of food. An enormous country ham from the hickory woods near Elkatawa (pronounced "Elkeetoy," but don't ask why) in Breathitt County, Kentucky, sat enthroned in the middle of the groaning board. Surrounding the throne were platters of southern fried chicken, tangy meatballs simmering in a chaffing dish, and a cast-iron pot of steaming burgoo. Piping hot rolls, biscuits (to go with the redeye gravy), and corn sticks, which Miriam baked while her guests ate, appeared continuously, as if by magic. Homemade cottage cheese and dill pickles from a nearby farm graced the table; also antipasto, piccalilli, coleslaw (in a horseradish dressing), and kidney bean salad. There were assorted crackers in profusion and flat, broad, fried noodles together with plum preserves, pepper jelly, cream cheese, and a smoked oyster dip, to say nothing of the green Spanish olives wrapped in a cheesy peppery pastry and baked to a golden crisp. On a nearby serving table reposed several pies (made from cushaws, Adrian learned later), Swedish pastries, and a Black Forest cake. Above the din of a dozen and a half conversations, Adrian could hear the clink of glasses and the plopping of ice cubes indicating that cold beverages could be acquired in the kitchen, a brightly lighted slice of which he could see through the pass-through counter. Although the Reids were not opposed to alien or exotic liquors, it was clear that they favored the bourbon whiskies of their native state, and strong coffee over weak coffee or tea, although the latter was available in straight and spiced varieties. "Holy Clones," Adrian exclaimed over and again to all and sundry as he dived first into one delicacy, then another.

He was positively raving over the homemade dill pickles and telling a bemused young woman that he believed the garlic in many commercial dills to be part of the international Zionist conspiracy when Rad came weaving his way through the crowd with a distinguished-looking man in tow. "Say, Adrian," he said, "I'd like you to meet Lucien Montmorency. Lu is a big dog in the physics department, an honest-to-God theoretician amongst a rabble of experimentalists."

"A real natural philosopher, then," Adrian said, catching Rad's infectious laughter and shaking Montmorency's hand warmly. "In what theater of operations do you conduct your *theoria*?" he asked, genuinely interested in the alert-looking man he had just met.

Trying to gauge his reply so that he wouldn't have to go into technicalities impossible for the layman, Lucien said, "Well, in addition to teaching, I make my daily bread working with the 'strong interaction' in atomic nuclei, but I'm . . . I'm really after bigger theoretical game, much, much bigger game." Pausing for effect, he went on, saying, "To make a long story short, I'm trying to fathom what holds it all together, including gravitational and electromagnetic forces as well."

"You might call Lu the mucilage man of Algonquin," Rad interjected, laughing above their heads.

"I know what holds it all together," said Adrian, deadpanning it and playing down his astonishing assertion.

"*You do?*" said Rad and Lu simultaneously, the former anticipating a low joke, the latter daring to hope, as only a physicist can, against insurmountable odds.

"Sure, do you want to know?"

"Do of tell course us," came their words in a rush and a jumble.

"Jesus," said Adrian, looking very serious yet pleased to share the secret of the ages.

"*Jesus!*" exclaimed Rad.

"Jesus?" asked Lu as though something had just gone wrong with his ears.

"Well, not in his capacity as a newborn in a Bethlehem barn nor subsequently as a carpenter in Nazareth, but in his capacity as the first-born of all creation."

"I cannot imagine what you're getting at, DeWulf," declared Lu, who was, nevertheless, far too pious to dismiss Adrian's view out of hand as the raving of an incorrigible crank.

"I trust that you two gentlemen are sufficiently conversant with the Scriptures to recall Colossians 1:17," said Adrian, looking at them sagely.

"It beats me," said Rad, stretching his moustache from ear to ear as he grinned broadly somewhere behind it.

"I should know that verse—I'm sure I do—but I . . . I fear that it escapes me at the moment," Lu admitted blankly, a strange sense of unease creeping over him.

"The context is simply this," announced Adrian didactically: "Earlier in the chapter, the Apostle Paul says that all things in heaven and on earth, whether visible or invisible—you have your atomic nuclei right there—were created in, and through, and for the first-born of creation. Then, verse 17 says that he (the first-born, that is) was before all things and that *all things hold together in him*. I've checked the Greek, and you can trust that translation. So, you see, it's pretty simple: it's Jesus who keeps those strong forces working strongly, and the weak ones weakly, and magnets attracting metal filings magnetically, and—" With that, Prof. Montmorency turned on his heel mutely and sought out other, more congenial, conversationalists, and Rad, laughing more than Adrian thought appropriate, sidled off to talk to other guests.

Adrian did not know strong drink until he was in his mid-twenties and at Columbia, but enough of his puritan past lingered to make him the soul of moderation, even while still a graduate student. By his own admission, however, strong drink had been known to elevate his spirits occasionally, even if never to addle them. With those spirits already elevated at the Reids' party and with yet another tall glass of bourbon and ginger ale in hand, he joined a covey of faculty wives plus a really cute new instructor in English, all of whom were being harangued by the mesmeric Melius Atarbaxes, the head of the foreign languages department. Melius had a Mediterranean cast of countenance, was easily offended, and choleric to say the least. He was also a compulsive promoter of himself, of foreign languages, and of European culture in that order. As Adrian wandered up to the group, quaffing his frosty drink, Melius was saying, ". . . and so I told him nicely, but decisively, that the foreign languages were most important because of the culture they taught to the students, if for no other reason." Staring exophthalmically at the really cute new English instructor, he went on to say, "Why, there are pictures in the textbooks that show the architecture and the painting, the cities and the hamlets, and the clothing of the different peoples, not to mention the stories, the sagas, the legends, the songs, and the spirit, yes, the spirit itself, of other folk." Gesturing frenetically, he concluded, "Yes, yes, yes, to be sure, the study of the foreign languages brings the people together, promotes the unity of mankind, and makes the peace and the concord which enables the humans of diverse origins and tongues to work together, to cooperate—"

"And to endanger God thereby," Adrian said loudly, his gaze clear and steady despite flushed cheeks.

"And to endanger God thereby," Melius repeated witlessly as though he were a parrot. Then as the meaning sank in and he began to scent the intimation, at least, of a slight, he said, "How you this thing can say?" his English syntax crumbling with rising emotion.

"If you remember Genesis, chapter 11," Adrian said earnestly, "you will know that mankind began with but one language of few words." Then, pausing to look at the electrified faculty wives plus the one really cute new English instructor, he asked rhetorically, "And what did they do? Why, it was so easy to cooperate, having just the one language of few words, that they started to build a tower right up to heaven."

"Thees ess reedeecoolus," Melius said, his pronunciation going the way of his syntax.

"Anyway," Adrian continued sincerely, "it scared the socks off God, so to speak, because he reasoned that if those primitive buggers could build a ziggurat right up to heaven with nothing but burned bricks and bitumen, then there would be no telling what more technically advanced humans like ourselves could do.

"Just imagine, if you will, what could be done nowadays with steel or reinforced concrete and all our sophisticated technology," he suggested, making a peak of his eyebrows worriedly. Then, as though she had responded affirmatively instead of merely looking at him dumbly, he said to the new cutie in English, "We could build a tower today that would go clean up to one of the lower decks of heaven and in no time people could pop right up into the place through one of the manholes in the golden streets."

"Eet ees madness these awful tings you are sayingguh," Melius erupted, shaking both index fingers at Adrian ferociously.

"Oh, it was a kind of madness all right," Adrian went on knowingly, "because God decided right then and there to confuse human tongues and make people from different countries sound as though they were just babbling— that's why they called it the Tower of Babel—with the result that they couldn't cooperate easily any more and threaten him with their pernicious competence.

"Of course, the thing that really disturbs me most deeply," continued Adrian, knitting his brows and speaking somberly, "is that people like you, Professor Atarbaxes, are trying professionally to undo the divine will in this matter."

Envisioning foreign languages classrooms at Algonquin even more depopulated than at present, should the theological ravings of the devil who stood before him become known to the students, Melius lapsed into what sounded like pure gibberish in English but was in Greek a rich and fluent profanity.

"My advice to you, sir," Adrian said, permitting himself the slightest smile lest he burst into uncontrollable laughter and spoil everything, "is that you have a care for your soul and look to its salvation." With that, he stalked off in a reasonable facsimile of righteous indignation.

"Harvey O. Ijjam," said Harvey O. Ijjam, reaching out his hand to take Adrian's in the smokey gloom of the family room, whence the latter had wandered.

"Adrian DeWulf," replied Adrian DeWulf, surprised by the abruptness of the dark encounter.

"Pleased to meet you," said Harvey.

"Same here," Adrian lied whitely. He had known Harvey for some time by name, sight, and field but had avoided him, Harvey being one of Algonquin's four religion professors.

After several moments of desultory chatter, Harvey said, "Say, I've heard of 'holy smoke', 'holy cow', and 'holy mackerel', but what is this 'holy-something-or-other' I keep hearing you say?"

"Oh, you must mean 'Holy Clones'."

"Yes, that's it," Harvey replied, smiling inquisitively.

"Well, you surely know what a clone is," Adrian said, making a question out of his observation.

"No, I can't say I do," Harvey murmured, looking thoughtful.

"Any organisms, or population thereof, sharing identical genetic information are clones," Adrian said as though it were a topic foremost in everyone else's mind.

"Hmmmmm," Harvey murmured, then said, "Such as?"

"Well, in nature, any individuals springing from a single zygote, such as identical twins, would be clones or any of the offspring—together with the parent—of critters that replicate or reproduce asexually, assuming no mutations. Of course, nowadays, in addition to cloning plants, scientists can clone some kinds of lower animals. If you take the DNA from any cell of a donor, insert it into an enucleated egg, and then reimplant it in a host or otherwise bring the ovum to maturity, you get a genetic replica of the donor, which is what a clone is."

"Fantastic!" Harvey exclaimed, taking a swig of Scotch on the rocks. "Still and all, I fail to see anything holy about it."

"Oh, mercy, no, there's nothing holy about it. What made you think there was?"

"Well, what are holy clones then?" Harvey asked, feeling as though he had been led on a wild goose chase.

"Gee, it's so obvious! I'm really amazed that you, a religion professor, haven't caught on," Adrian replied, effecting great surprise.

"You'll have to excuse me, but I haven't caught on," Harvey said, looking at Adrian a little petulantly and taking a deep drink.

"Holy Clones are God the Father, God the Son, and God the Holy Ghost," Adrian declared, lifting his eyes and his hands to the heavens.

At that, Harvey choked on his Scotch and spluttered, "You . . . you can't be—" (Here he coughed twice.) "serious!"

"Then why am I writing a book to be entitled *The Mystery of the Trinity Unmasked?*" Adrian asked with tongue deeply implanted in cheek.

"What in God's name do you propose to say in it?" Harvey asked, genuine concern etched on his face.

"As you know, from the very beginning, the holy fathers and doctors of the church realized that they had no words with which to describe adequately the mysteries of the adorable Trinity. Right?"

"Yes, yes, one has difficulty speaking of ineffable things," Harvey agreed, admitting without protest that it was pretty hard to describe the indescribable.

"But ask yourself why, specifically, they had so much trouble speaking of God the Father, God the Son, and God the Holy Ghost as having one identical nature or substance *(homoousias)*, yet being three distinct Persons *(hypostases)*, but in perfect unity."

"Well, why?" Harvey asked, a little put out at being instructed Socratically in his own field.

"Because the holy fathers and the doctors of the church didn't understand genetics, that's why; they didn't understand the double helix of the DNA molecule and, therefore, didn't have the terminology to match; but now we do."

"Oh, come off it!" Harvey exploded, "you don't really mean to tell me that the three Persons of the Trinity all have the same genes."

"Sure they do, spiritually speaking, that is," Adrian added with a fanatic glint in his eye.

"Just what in hell are spiritual genes? if I may ask."

"Just what in hell are Persons in the Trinity? Surely, they are not like human persons. No competent theologian ever supposed they were. Look, when speaking of the Second Person as the Only-Begotten Son, no sane theologian thinks that the Father begat the Son in a human way. No, no, it was all spiritual! And when speaking of the Holy Ghost as proceeding from the Father and the Son, nobody means that he does it in time, temporally, or that he proceeds from some one place where they are to some other places. No, once again, it's spiritual. So, when I say the Persons of the Trinity are

294

Holy Clones, I don't mean it literally; I mean it symbolically, like everything else that's said of the Triune Godhead. That ought to pretty well clarify what I mean by spiritual genes."

Harvey wanted very much to relieve himself by saying resoundingly, "Bullshit," but held his peace, for several persons passing, overhearing the conversation, had paused, fascinated by it much as a bird is said to be fascinated by a snake.

Moving closer as though to enlist him in a secret cause, Adrian said, "Harvey, I would really appreciate your critical insights on a certain problem that I haven't quite resolved, to my satisfaction anyway."

"On what?" Harvey asked, looking down his nose suspiciously as certain other people, upon overhearing the conversation, sped by.

"The double procession of the Holy Ghost, that's what."

"Well, what about it?" Harvey inquired, fearing a new outrage.

"As everybody knows, the Three Persons are not just eternally consubstantial without confusion; they're also distinctly three in operation as variously functioning Persons. The First Person does not proceed and is not begotten, but begets. The Second Person does not proceed and does not beget, but is begotten. The Third Person does not beget and is not begotten, but proceeds. So far, so good. The trouble is that the Third Person proceeds doubly from the First Person and the Second, and that breaks the symmetry. Now there's just no question in my mind but that I've solved the relationship of the First and Second Persons. They're clones, spiritually speaking, like identical twins. Don't be fooled by the fact that one is known as Father and the other as Son, because they are co-eternal, the begetter not having begotten the begotten in time. So the First Person didn't precede the Second temporally. But here's where I have real trouble. It looks to me as though the Holy Ghost is a clone of a different type; oh, he has the same nature, the same spiritual genes, I hasten to add; but he's a different type of clone, because he proceeds from both the Father and the Son, which means that he is a clone of each, the same substance twice replicated, if you see what I mean. So, the Holy Ghost is not a 'clone identical' in the sense of identical twins but is a 'clone replicate', if you see my point. The only way I can handle the problem of the double procession of the Holy Ghost is to reconstrue the Doctrine of the Trinity as 'Three Persons in One in Double Clonehood'."

"Did you say you were going to call your book *The Mystery of the Trinity UNMASKED?*" Harvey asked sarcastically.

"Gee, that's what I had hoped to do," Adrian fibbed.

"Damn it, man, you've made the whole thing more incomprehensible than it was before," Harvey protested.

"You think I should call it *The Mystery of the Trinity MASKED?*" Adrian asked, seeming to be disconcerted.

"Frankly, I don't care what you call it or *if* you call it," Harvey replied sourly.

"I just know I've made a big, big theological breakthrough approaching the Divine Persons as clones," Adrian declared, exuding self-confidence, "but I must admit that I'm still not perfectly satisfied with the idea of double clonehood. Let's see; what do you say to calling the book *The . . . The Mystery of the Trinity: Clarified and Profundified?*"

Wanting no part of the re-entitling process, Harvey said rather nobly, "I disagree with what you say but will fight for your right to say it." Then, responding to his wife's crooked finger, he terminated the conversation. On their way home, his wife, Ida, said to him crossly, "Why do you keep muttering 'bullshit'? Never mind, just stop it. It's not at all becoming to you."

Adrian enjoyed himself so hugely at the Reids' party that he was among the last to leave. Bidding him farewell at the front door, Rad said, "Say, that was a pretty big mouthful you made poor Montmorency swallow."

"Surely, he didn't believe what I said," Adrian responded in astonishment.

"Don't be so sure. Lu is of Huguenot stock. Of course there's no Huguenot church here, so he goes to the more conservative of the two Presbyterian churches in town, but he's there every time they open the doors. Anyway, Lu's so incredibly imaginative and so damned receptive to new ideas, especially theological ones, that he's going to worry his way through every nuance of that crazy stuff of yours about Jesus' holding it all together."

"Rad, did you ever hear John Herman Randall's quip about physicists?"

"No, can't say I have."

"He was always quick to point out that there is no greater threat to sound theology than a pious physicist."

To that, Rad laughed heartily, and Adrian said, "Maybe I'd better rush a book into print called *Electromagnetism, Gravitation, Nuclear Forces, and the First-Born of All Creation* and explain it all before Montmorency botches the whole thing up. But I'm not going to start before sunup."

"Better get an early start, though, because Lu's not going to sleep tonight. He could steal the march on you, if you're not careful."

While drying his hands Adrian looked at himself in the mirror above the lavatory, traced the line of his jaw, tried to peer through his eyes at what was behind them, studied his slightly bulging forehead, and asked himself, "Are there any brains in there? What are you going to make of yourself? Are you ever going to amount to anything? If so, when are you going to get at it?" Receiving no answer, but inspired by the questions, he snapped off the light, opened the bathroom door, and came face to face with Bro. Manly Plumwell, just then reaching the top step to the second floor of No. 5, Litany Lane.

"Well, well, hello there, Professor DeWulf," Manly said, brimming with Christian friendliness.

"Hi, what brings you to these parts?" Adrian asked, not really caring.

"I was making a pastoral call nearby and thought I would stop to see you, if you're free, that is."

"Step right in," Adrian said without enthusiasm, gesturing at the door to his so-called apartment.

As Manly sank down in the big gray chair at the foot of Adrian's bed and Adrian straddled his typing chair, his arms resting on its back as he faced Manly, each had incredibly different thoughts, not less different, perhaps, than those that representatives of alien species might entertain.

If Manly had paid Prof. DeWulf a visit that evening, or on any other occasion, concerning any merely personal affair of his own, he would have been ill at ease, for in such matters he remained shy and diffident, even after a first meeting. But doing the Lord's work was different. When he was up and doing it, he was an ambassador of the Most High, a plenipotentiary bearing God's nonnegotiable imperatives, a soldier in the army of King Jesus, a priest of the Holy Nation. In those roles he knew no timidity. He had been at Algonquin long enough to recognize dimly how little he knew of the world, but he knew God, knew that God knew everything, and that gave him an inexpressible confidence, a sense of perfect security. Thus, no complexities overwhelmed him, no superior knowledge daunted him. No, quite the contrary, ignorance of the kinds of knowledge known and taught, studied and learned at ASU was no drawback, for none of it was *saving* knowledge, none of it could redeem a man. If DeWulf were to resist him, were to harden his heart against God's Holy Nation and its message of three-world creationism, it would be because he had already succumbed to the god of this world and was perishing even then, as II Corinthians 4:3-4 put it, or it would be because he was being misled by philosophy and empty deceit as Colossians 2:8 said. If DeWulf were not only to turn a deaf ear to the message Manly bore but were to criticize him for bearing it, it would be a futile effort, for the unspiritual man can never judge the spiritual man. I Corinthians 2:15 makes that crystal clear. Since Manly knew the fear of the Lord to be the beginning of wisdom, he would, in all things, speak to please God as I Thessalonians 2:4 directed, not to please men, least of all educated men, boastful as they often were. Should he be ridiculed or despitefully used for speaking to please God, well, that would simply fulfil the prophecy of Matthew 10:22 concerning Christians. Thus fortified spiritually, Manly prepared to speak.

Although Adrian did not yet know the doctrinal idiosyncrasies of royal priests, he knew enough Southern Baptists, Church of Christers, Mormons, Adventists, and Pentecostals to predict what kind of mentality Manly would have. He would have an insatiable appetite to live forever and would believe with supreme egotism that the whole great universe was so contrived as to make that inevitable. Convinced of personal redemption unto everlasting bliss, he would, nevertheless, be haunted more or less continuously by the flames of endless hell. Distrustful of his own unaided intellect, scornful of his own human-heartedness, and unable to face life on his own two feet, standing with none but other human beings, he would have accepted Jesus as his savior-shepherd-master-judge on bended knees, neck bent, humbling himself

297

and crying piteously for mercy. He would go up and down and around and around in the circle that leads from God to God's Holy Book, from God's Holy Book back again to God. He would not know that no book can authenticate the God in its pages, that no God in its pages can authenticate a book. If the book speaks disagreeably of God, or of God's doings, the Plumwells of the world can be depended on to allegorize it, or otherwise trifle with it, until it speaks agreeably. If their favorite doctrines are not really in the book, they will plant them there, only to find them as they had claimed all along. Moving mountains is, after all, the least that faith can do. The only logic they will accept is the logic whose only axiom is the fear of the Lord; the only facts, those that cannot subvert faith. Such was the unwelcome person who sat before him, Adrian knew. The question was, How to handle him?

Insistently, as though there were not a minute to lose, Manly said, "I know that you know the story of JEsus—"

"Oh, I know the story all right; it's the facts I care most about."

"So I'll get right to the point. Did you know, Professor DeWulf, that we are not on the original planet Earth, that that one was utterly destroyed by water, that the one we're on now, the one that's reserved for fire, is the second planet Earth?"

Great Scott! Adrian thought, Plumwell is not just the garden variety of confused Christian; he's a crazy Christian. "No, I did not know that;" he said calmly but warily, "is it?"

"Yes, and I can prove it to you by the Scriptures."

Fat chance, Adrian thought, but said, "Prove away."

"Do you have a copy of the Holy Bible here?" Manly asked, surveying the room without spotting any book that looked like one.

"Yeah, I have an RSV somewhere."

"If you wouldn't mind getting it and following me through II Peter 3:5-13, it would really help."

Going to a pile of books dumped in one corner of his closet, Adrian returned, flipping pages. "II Peter what?" he asked.

"Start at 3:5," Manly replied, beginning to read and explaining three-world creationism fervently as he went.

Keeping an amazed eye on his guest, Adrian was overwhelmed with three thoughts. First, he had read II Peter numerous times but had not really seen the fantastic stuff Plumwell was revealing to him. My God! he thought, how could I have missed it? "You blind ass, you," he said to himself. Second, although it was as preposterous as any cosmology in the Bible, it was, by the same token, just as sound as any other. Great denominations had been founded on sands no more sinking than those. So, the Holy Nation had found something doctrinally significant after all! Third, he thought of the immense fun he could have with it. Forthwith he would add three-world creationism to his quiver of biblical absurdities. He would make jokes about it, would enliven parties with it, would discomfit the pious with it, and would show his students, especially in the philosophy of religion, how to the faithful no absurdity is too great to swallow.

But, at the moment, the problem was how to get rid of Plumwell. "I'll tell you what," Adrian said gravely, "I'm going to reserve judgment on this until I can get to the office to take a look at the Greek original."

"Do that by all means," Manly said, looking very smug, and well he might look smug, for he knew that the great New Testament scholar, Dr. Emmet Langhorne Van Hook, Ph.D. (Harvard), RPPr., had already taken a most careful look at the Greek original and found it to be incontrovertible.

"*Damn* it to *Hell*," said President Sythian MacGilvary with uncommon vehemence as he slammed down the *Signal Flare*, ASU's student newspaper. Then, stamping into the office of his private secretary, he said without preamble, "Miss Ellison, get Felix over here as soon as possible, certainly before I leave for Washington this afternoon."

Well within the hour, Felix Molineaux, the Assistant Dean of Student Affairs and Coordinator of Algonquin's Great Expectations Lecture Series, appeared, looking a bit rumpled and out of breath.

"Felix, how in the devil did this person, Chester Clydesdale, get an invitation to speak in the Great Expectations Series?"

"Why . . . I . . . well . . . let's see," said Felix. Then sitting down unbidden and gathering his wits, he said, "The same way as usual. We had several requests from various student organizations, one or two department heads, and just quite a few ordinary faculty folk who wanted to hear him. So, the Committee met and decided to offer the invitation. He's pretty hot property right now, you know, at least since he was written up in *Time* or *Newsweek*, whichever."

"Yes, I know he's hot; he's hotter'n the hinges of hell," Sythian announced loudly and then went on to say, "Speaking of hell, he doesn't even believe in it, and I find that pretty repugnant."

"But, President MacGilvary, I'm sure as I can be that you knew about the invitation and approved it," Felix said, hoping that not all the blame for inviting the radical theologian to campus would fall on him.

"I did?"

"I'm positive you did; otherwise I can't imagine that we would have gone ahead and issued the invitation—it's costing a cool $1,500, you know."

"Well, if I did, it must be because I confused him with Clydesdown at Southern Cal. Now, *he'd* be just fine, but I would certainly never knowingly have invited a man like Clydesdale to this campus. I'll get nothing but flak out of it for weeks to come, months maybe, or even years."

As Felix shook his head commiseratingly with Sythian, the latter said in some desperation, "I suppose it's too late to cancel the invitation—without causing a big stink, that is."

"Oh, I'm afraid so! Here it is almost Thursday noon already, and he's due in next Monday morning to speak to some religion classes throughout the day and then to deliver the public lecture at 8:00 P.M. Monday night, and by now it's pretty well advertised."

"I'd certainly like to salvage something out of this," said Sythian, still seething, "so, have you got any suggestions?"

After a long, thoughtful pause, Felix asked, "Would you . . . ah . . . yourself consider introducing Clydesdale on Monday night?"

"No! I don't even want to be on the same campus with him, let alone on the same platform."

"But, sir, if you could see your way clear to do it, I think you could picture Algonquin as being very brave by having Clydesdale here, very open-minded, progressive, etc., and at the same time could take the role of an educational statesman, if you see what I mean."

To that, Sythian made a buzzing sound in his throat.

"You, sir, could make it clearer than any of the rest of us, just by your presence, that Algonquin doesn't endorse what Clydesdale has to say for a minute but that we're absolutely committed to the free exchange of ideas, feel our responsibility to students to have such people here, and . . ."

"Oh, all right, all right. Thanks for your counsel, Felix."

The cause of the consternation at Algonquin was a prig and a popinjay who had, only recently, been appointed to the Cudworth Chair of Speculative Theology at Boston University. A brilliant expositor of ideas, Clydesdale had published five books in a little over nine years. First came *Divinity, Relativity, and Temporality,* a work written primarily with scholars in mind. Then came *Immortality: Divine or Personal?* a book with wider appeal. With *The Impotence of Transcendence,* Clydesdale caught the national eye and with *The Mutating Deity* reached number nine on the best-seller list of non-fiction books, holding that slot for three weeks. Only a few days before President MacGilvary took counsel with Felix Molineaux, Clydesdale's fifth book, *Love for the Loveless God,* had hit the market with great promise both to make him rich and his name a household word.

Adrian went to Schoolcraft Hall that Monday night to hear Clydesdale, not because he was interested in what the man might say nor because he was in need of instruction, but solely to hear the one reputed to have an absolutely incandescent delivery. Arriving at the auditorium early, he took a seat in the center of row "H" and began to jot down some ideas he was developing for an article. Vaguely aware that the hall was filling fast, he was surprised, nonetheless, when a familiar voice from almost directly overhead said, "Would it be okay if I sat here?"

Looking up at Claire Sumner, absolutely adorable in boots, blue jeans, and a knit sweater of many colors, he said, "Well, I . . . I don't know; I do have my reputation to think about, you must remember."

Startled by his response and therefore not completing the act of sitting down, but suspended in mid-air as it were, she asked, "And just what's that supposed to mean?"

"Oh, sit down, for heaven's sake," he said, reaching out and pulling her left forearm toward him sharply.

Once composed in the seat on his right she said, sounding miffed, "You know, you almost blew it."

"Blew what?" he asked, feigning incomprehension.

"There are plenty of people around here who really like it when I sit next to them."

"Hmmmmm, well; is that so?" he hemmed and hawed, smiling at her broadly, warmed by her presence, really pleased to see her.

In row "K," several seats to their left, Bro. Manly Plumwell watched, though unable to overhear them, and felt a pang of concern.

Then, very suddenly, the noise level dropped. Not only had the guest speaker just come onto the platform; there, too, was President Sythian MacGilvary.

"Why, look!" said some who observed the proprieties, "there's President MacGilvary." Others, much less formally, said, "Hey, ol' Sythy's here," and a few who thought the president to be a ruthless administrator said something to the effect, "I see Syth the Scythe is here; wonder who's going to get mowed down tonight?"

Then, striding to the lectern (catching every eye and silencing every tongue by his imposing, silvery presence), President MacGilvary said: "Good evening, ladies and gentlemen, faculty and staff, students and townspeople, and friends of Algonquin State University. It gives me great pleasure to initiate The Great Expectations Lecture Series for academic 1960-61. Our first speaker, Dr. Chester Clydesdale, Professor of Speculative Theology at Boston University, has amply demonstrated the popularity of unpopular ideas, his books having caused a national stir and attracted a vast market. It is not to advance the stir that we have invited him to Algonquin nor to endorse the ideas that he has espoused that we have asked him here tonight; no, it is to rise to our high obligations as a center of higher learning that we have invited him here; it is to carry out our public mission to present students with a diversity of opinions that we have asked him to visit our classes and to speak to this audience; it is to keep faith with our social mandate to be a conduit for the free flow of ideas, even ideas that we may personally find repugnant, that we have asked him to share his thoughts with us. Would you, therefore, give our speaker for this evening a rousing Algonquin welcome."

As the large audience did as bidden, President MacGilvary stepped aside with hand outstretched to welcome Chester Clydesdale to the lectern, but Chester, spurning the presidential hand, marched straight to it, red meerschaum pipe clenched between very square, very white teeth. For a long moment, he removed his pipe, looked at it solicitously, seemed to tamp it, and then lay it down on the lectern together with a large tobacco pouch and a lighter. Finally, he said icily, "With an introduction like that, I am charmed, I am sure, to be at a place like Algonquin. I trust that I shall not be alone in helping it carry out its high calling."

Then by virtue of unsurpassed rhetorical gifts, he proceeded to make his

301

unpopular ideas popular or at least palatable for at least as long as he expressed them. He argued for belief in a limited deity, pointing out that a God who was both perfectly good and absolutely all-powerful was inconceivable in light of the natural and moral evils abounding in the world. Moreover, he noted that the New Testament did not teach a God unlimited in power but rather a God unlimited in goodness. He came close to persuading the audience that the only immortality worth caring about was God's own immortality and capped the point by asserting that the New Testament, understood rightly, did not teach the immortality of the individual human being anyway. It would be enough, he pointed out, for each human being to have a place in God's eternal memory. Finally, he urged the audience to love God but not to expect him to love them, because for God to do so would require that he should have characteristics that no thoughtful, caring person would want him to have. Then, as icily as he had begun, he concluded his talk, leaving people suspended in mid-air, and strode back to his chair refusing to entertain questions as he had been expected to do.

As the huge crowd began to file out of Schoolcraft Hall, Adrian noticed that Claire was still in a daze. He had glanced at her often throughout Clydesdale's fantastic performance only to see her transfixed, mouth slightly open, appearing to be mesmerized. Clearly, she was still under the spell as she told Adrian "good-bye" and set off toward the Coyote House with several other girls whom she had joined at the auditorium's front doors. For his part, Adrian was hopping mad over the president's gratuitous and insulting introduction and planned to write a letter about it.

Manly, long since having forgotten the pang he had felt at the beginning of the lecture, was furious over what he had heard. It was really monstrous letting a so-called speculative theologian like Clydesdale loose on people, letting him inject his demonic venom into them. Clydesdale had obviously cut himself off from belief in the Scriptures, yet there he had been daring to show himself in public and pretending to tell people what was in the Bible, making it seem as though the New Testament did not teach the omnipotence of God, blatantly proclaiming that it did not teach eternal life for the saved of earth, and having the unmitigated gall to assert that God did not love individual human beings. Bro. Van Hook had certainly been right; intellectuals, especially in the field of religion, could be quite despicable.

Neither Adrian's nor Manly's anger abated quickly that night. The former stalked straight to his apartment where, bent over his desk, he wrote and rewrote and wrote again a scalding letter to the *Signal Flare*. Meanwhile, the latter prayed, on bended knees by his bed, as follows: "Dear God, Majestic and Holy One, if it be thy will, please let thy servant wax strong that he may blast thine enemies, that by the word of thy servant's mouth he may put to shame those who, in their insufferable boastfulness, pervert thy word, ridicule thy teachings, and make a mockery of the gospel of JEsus Christ. Let thy servant rise up with wings as eagles, run and not grow faint, and fight without flagging in the cause of righteousness. Inspire his speech to

302

confound the enemies of thy Holy Nation, refresh his spirit that he may not falter in contending with the worldly wise nor fall into the traps of their petty logic. Finally, please let thy servant blaze like a great light that those who live in darkness in Algonquin may see his light, and seeing it may see the Christ, the Light of the whole World, and thus come to thee. These things thy servant asks humbly in the precious name of thy Son, even JEsus. Amen."

The letter from a Professor DeWulf in the philosophy department reached the editorial offices of the *Signal Flare* too late for inclusion in the paper that appeared on the Thursday following Clydesdale's Monday night lecture. But the letter did appear a week later. Adrian did not see it until he went to the Braves' Cafeteria in the Algonquin Union to eat lunch that day. Merely noting the letter's inclusion, he put the paper aside until he had finished eating. Then, with nothing but scraps and half a cup of coffee left, he opened the paper to its editorial section and read his letter, well satisfied that it had been printed in full and without blemish. Here is what he wrote:

"I take it to be axiomatic that the editorial section of a student paper should be the province of students primarily, yet, on occasion, a professor or other outsider may be justified in intruding therein. Such an occasion seems to me to have presented itself recently. I refer to the public lecture of Prof. Chester Clydesdale delivered under the aegis of The Great Expectations Series. No less a person than the chief executive officer of our university felt constrained to introduce the speaker and to do so with a caveat, a caveat that was certainly perceived by the speaker, if not by everyone in attendance, to have been inappropriate and gratuitous.

"Given the advanced condition of both civilization and higher education in the United States, is there really anybody so ill informed that he or she must be told that a university does not necessarily endorse, nor need to endorse, each and every idea aired on its campus, anybody so misinformed as to presume that colleges and universities are idea-endorsing agencies, anybody so benighted as to believe that disclaimers ought to be announced before lectures are delivered or heard?

"Assuming for a moment that those who teach or lecture at institutions of higher education are to traffic only in endorsed ideas, eschewing all others, how will they discern between the two? Shall the president's office of each institution make it clear, its Board of Trustees, the House Un-American Activities Committee, the Holy Office of the Inquisition, some as yet un-specified but self-appointed fundamentalist vigilante, or some other worthy agency or individual not envisioned by this writer?

"The equanimity of theologians has not hitherto been a major concern of the letter writer, believing as he does that they should receive a great many more lumps than they normally get, but his heart goes out to Chester Clydesdale for the affront he suffered at Algonquin from what may have been self-serving and were certainly boorish hands."

Adrian had just finished rereading his letter and was scanning others when Claire slipped unannounced into the empty chair beside him and asked,

"Are you free—"

"No, but I'm cheap," he said without looking up.

"Oh, hell, you do that kind of thing to me every time," she said, sounding exasperated but really enjoying the peculiar kind of attention he lavished on her, even though it was momentarily vexatious. Then, forming her thoughts very precisely, she said, "I meant to ask whether or not you would be able to talk to me for a few minutes or would have to dash off to a one o'clock class, or go to a meeting, or an appointment, or anything of that sort."

"Yes," he said, smiling enigmatically.

"Yes what?"

"Yes, I would be able to talk to you for a few minutes without having to dash off to a one o'clock class, or go to a meeting, or an appointment, or anything of that sort."

"And do you not fear for your reputation, sitting here in plain view at a table in the cafeteria?" she asked with feigned sarcasm.

"No, for the moment, I do not fear that," he replied, realizing, nevertheless, that she had never before been so close to him, perhaps to be heard above the cafeteria's din. In any case, in the light of high noon that was streaming through tall windows nearby, he noticed that her eyes were gray with crystalline gems of green embedded in them, that her silky hair, glinting in the light, was the color of bittersweet chocolate, that she was rather dark complexioned as though she had a perennial tan, and that her teeth were straight, well-proportioned, and very white. Admiring her face more than he ever had before, he almost asked, "Do you also have money to go with your brains and your beauty?" Instead, he said, "So, what is it that you want to talk to me about?"

Leaning over the table, with her elbows on it, but twisting her neck to look at him squarely, she asked with some heat, "Just what did that character mean last week when he said that we should love God but that we should not expect him to love us?"

"Miss Sumner, if you'll simply sign up for my course in the philosophy of religion next term, it will all be made clear to you," he said invitingly.

"Look, I can't wait that long," she responded, opening her eyes very wide. "It has been bugging the very devil out of me for ten days now. I had meant to come by your office—even tried once—but there never seemed to be a good time, and there was no opportunity, really, in the ethics class."

"Well, Clydesdale thinks that we should love God if we love life. To a thinker like him, God selected only the best ingredients for a world—our world—out of a great number of alternatives. So, if life has been anything from fairly agreeable to a real ball, then the individual might appropriately and piously love the principle of choice that made it all possible." So saying, Adrian fell silent.

Claire almost said, "Look, smartie, that's not the part that's bugging me, and you know it," but she was not about to take such liberties with a professor, even jokingly. "Okay, but it's the part about not expecting God to love us that's giving me fits," she said. "Why, all my life it's been drummed into me that God loves mankind, that he loved us so much he gave his only Son."

"Yes, but you're thinking of an essentially Hebraic God."

"What other God is there?"

"Lots of others."

"Such as?"

"The God of the Greek philosophers."

"Thanks, but I don't get it."

"In a nutshell, let's put it this way: A God of love is a God in need, and a God in need is not a God indeed—that is, if you want him to be perfect."

"Riddles, riddles! My parents pay through the nose to send me here, and I come like a good little girl and work my tail off, and what do I get? Riddles! Right?"

Adrian threw back his head and laughed at the ceiling. Then, without preamble, but caressing her face with his eyes, he said, "In his greatest dramatic work, *The Symposium*, Plato shows that love is not a god, nor an object, nor a thing of any sort, but a relationship, a relationship uniquely compounded of poverty and plenty, or, perhaps more precisely, of want and wit, the wit to get what is wanted. Now, the beloved can be anything: a person, an object, or any kind of thing. It can be as transient as applause, as exalted as justice or righteousness, as lasting as a solid place in history. But the crucial point is that the lover needs the beloved, needs something outside himself or herself to complete life, to make it whole, to satisfy desire, something with which unity is indispensable to personal happiness or bliss. Without the beloved, life is just burning lust, empty yearning, unrequited love."

"I can see that," she said, her face more composed than at any time during their conversation.

"Now, is God said to be perfect or not?" Adrian asked her abruptly.

"Sure," she fired back.

"What needs would, or could, a perfect being have? What person, or object, or type of thing outside himself does God have want of, desire for, or lust after? With what does he need to unite himself to complete his being? Nothing, because only imperfect beings have such needs. As Aristotle put it, and I think I'm just about quoting, 'God is happy and blessed in and of and by himself by nature, not by virtue of any external cause or reason.'"

"My God!" she said, staring at her knees for a long moment, "so that's it."

"Yep, that's it. The Clydesdales of this world are just trying to have a philosophically respectable God, but one who still bears a faint resemblance to the celestial despot in the Bible, who, by the way, can be quite fatherly on occasion."

Adrian was about to tell her why ploys like Clydesdale's failed when she looked at her watch and said, "Oh, Lord! I've got to run. Mr. Oaks will be furious if I keep him waiting." Then, rising, she thanked him for his time, said, "Bye-bye," and was gone, hurrying from the cafeteria, but as a queen might hurry to hold court.

"I wonder what she sees in an oaf like Bucky Oaks?" he asked himself.

At about the time Claire left the cafeteria, Miss Ellison laid a copy of the *Signal Flare,* with items of greatest interest to him duly marked, on President MacGilvary's desk. Shortly thereafter, he said, *"Damn* it to *Hell!"* the second time in connection with Chester Clydesdale's unfortunate visit to Algonquin and added, "Who is this pipsqueak in the philosophy department who has the gall to write a letter like this?"

Oscar Jiminie jerked open the front door to Algonquin's Church of the Chosen and sped unevenly through the vestibule and down the long corridor to the church office/pastor's study, yelling jubilantly, "Oh, Brother Plumwell, I've got great news! Just guess what. Brother Plumwell, are you here?" Electrified, Manly looked up from his desk as Oscar careened into the room.

Recently converted to the Holy Nation, Oscar was a slightly roly-poly young man who moved with a hitch in his gait and had a moustache that resembled a whisk broom. Unable to decide on what he wanted to do in life, he changed from one curriculum to another so often that he was forever having to take prerequisites for whatever he had most recently elected to pursue. By the time Adrian arrived on the scene, Oscar had already been there nearly five years but was still only a junior. He didn't mind the delay in graduation, however, for he adored Algonquin, its people, its places, its traditions. When he was not loitering near some vending machine or otherwise eating or drinking (which was much of the time), he was busy passing stories about ASU from one admirer of the institution to another. He did not, it should be pointed out, delight in telling salacious tittle-tattle, though he told it sometimes, nor was there a malicious bone in his body. It was just that he loved to hear of, to get to the bottom of, to know thoroughly, and to speak often and eloquently of the best university in the country, of the most beautiful campus, of the most fabulous faculty, and of the grandest, most spirited student body.

"Oscar, Oscar, calm down, boy," Manly counseled him, fearing that too much exuberance immediately adjacent to the sanctuary might be impious and therefore offensive to God.

"Man, have I got news for you!" Oscar burbled.

"Well, then, out with it," Manly said, already infected with the lad's enthusiasm and smiling expectantly.

"You'll never guess what."

"What, what? Please don't make me guess; just tell me."

"Well, get ready. Just a few minutes ago, I was going from one wing of the Ad. Building to the other, and guess who had who in a corner on the third floor."

"Who, for pity's sake, *who?"*

306

"Professor DeWulf, that's who. He had ol' Rathbone backed right up into a corner, and I mean a corner in more ways than one."

"Ol' Rathbone" was Cecil (pronounced "Cessil," the "e" being short) Dement Rathbone, Algonquin's medievalist, a professor who taught half-time in the history department and half-time in English. Nothing fired his imagination more than visions of life lived in the thirteenth century with Albertus Magnus or St. Thomas Aquinas, whether in Paris, Cologne, or wherever. Cecil despised much in the twentieth century and deplored most of the remainder, being happy in the present, it would seem, only when he was marching in full regalia in some academic procession or other. When dressed in the cap and gown of St. Andrew's University and wearing his hood of violet-purple silk lined with white satin (symbolizing the Doctor of Divinity degree), he would appear, even though untimely born, to be somewhat reconciled to his century, and could even smile. This, then, was the Rathbone whom Adrian had cornered in more ways than one.

"But why are you so excited about that?" Manly asked, mystified.

"Because DeWulf was teaching him *three-world creationism,* and—no offense intended—doing as good a job of it as you can," Oscar said, tears of admiration spilling from his eyes.

Hardly able to believe his ears, Manly sank back into his chair, trying to absorb the significance of what he had just heard and saying, "Praise the Lord!"

Oscar also sat down, but on the very edge of the chair he chose, so keyed-up did he remain. "When I heard what was going on," he continued, "I just pretended to be looking at a bulletin board far enough away so they wouldn't think I was eavesdropping, but I got most of it anyway. DeWulf was just wonderful. He says to ol' Rathbone, 'How is it that one who is reputed to be as sound in doctrine as you doesn't believe in three-world creationism?' Then he cites from II Peter 3, verse 7 or 8, and says some words I couldn't understand, Greek I guess, and Rathbone just doesn't know what to say to that. He just stands there and takes it—oh, it was beautiful! Then DeWulf says in kind of a huffy way, he says, 'Well, if you are going to take the Scriptures seriously, as I do, then it seems to me that you have to take them all seriously and not just pick and choose to suit your taste. Mustn't you take 'em on all fours?' or something like that. Then ol' Rathbone says something in kind of a whiny voice about how the church had never taught that doctrine, and DeWulf answers and says, 'Well, if it's a choice between what the church has taught and what the Scriptures say, what then?' Believe me, Rathbone looks kind of squelched and doesn't have a word to say. He just shakes his head and says he has to be excused because he has an appointment somewhere, and then DeWulf says, and this is the most beautiful of all, he says, 'I'll just walk to the door with you, because I still don't feel that you recognize the gravity of three-world creationism,' so he sort of tags after Rathbone out of the hall and down the stairway in the tower."

Spent by his exertions, Oscar fell silent for a while, then said, "Gosh, won't it be wonderful to have DeWulf in our church?"

"Oh, yes, yes," Manly answered, almost daring to believe that it would be so but made cautious by the fact that Adrian had not contacted him concerning his conversion or his desire to enter the Holy Nation formally. "If he doesn't get in touch with me very soon, I'll go by to see him," he assured Oscar.

They meant to look a trifle intimidating, the three strapping youths who stood in Adrian's office. He recognized one as the surly student who sat on the back row, right-hand corner, of his logic class. Another he took to be a student who had dropped ethics early in the term. The remaining one was unknown to him but, to all appearances, was also a student. The ethics dropout said, "Professor DeWulf, we're members of the Campus Crusade for Christ, and we've come to complain about what we believe to be the unfair way you treat Christianity in class."

"How very coincidental!" he exclaimed, brightening to their complaint. "Why, just last week I received a letter from the Cartel of Confucian Carpenters carping about my treatment of Confucianism. Then, over the weekend a boy from the Brotherhood of Buddhist Bricklayers bitched at me over my handling of Buddhism. Now, I'm not sure, you understand, but I have it pretty straight that I should get set for a delegation from the Syndicate of Sikh Salmon Seiners. Of course, what I'm really worried about is that the Junta [here he pronounced the word as though it began with an "h"] of Hindu Hammersmiths will hound me about my handling of Hinduism."

At that juncture, the unknown student began to snicker uncontrollably, the other two looking at him reproachfully.

"I'm just hoping that the Menage of Moslem Morticians will stay off my back," he said, rolling his eyes and shaking his head dramatically.

Then, as though each had said silently but in unison, "Oh, hell! What's the use?" the burly youths turned on their collective heel and departed.

"Wait!" Adrian cried, "don't go yet. Don't you want to hear about the jam I'm in with the Junta [this time pronounced with a "j" sound] of Jewish Janitors, to say nothing of the Jain Gymnasts?"

Ever since he had learned that the Campus Crusade for Christ was active at ASU, he had been lying in wait for just such an opportunity. How very considerate of them not to have kept him waiting long, he thought, as he wiped tears of mirth from his eyes.

"How are you bearing up under the headship?" asked Dean Braniff as Rad draped himself over a chair in the dean's office.

"Fine, fine; I'm eating well, sleeping well, and not drinking any more than usual," Rad replied, chuckling.

"Good, good, and what of Sterling?"

"Sterling comes to class, and that's all we see of him. He's so wrapped up in that book he's been writing forever that he has no time for anybody or anything else. Of course, he never did know the season of the year or the day of the week, to say nothing of the time of day."

"How true," the dean replied, allowing himself a slight smile. Then he said, "Rad, the reason I asked you down today is that I've been getting some complaints—so has the Academic Vice-President, I might add . . ."

"About me?" Rad broke in, grinning.

"No, not about you; about the temporary person in your department."

"DeWulf?"

"Yes."

"Such as?"

"A delegation from a certain religious organization on campus came to see me the other day, one of whom is in Professor DeWulf's logic class."

"So?"

"Take a look at these examples he showed me from a logic examination," the dean said, handing over a sheet of paper.

The sheet contained the following: "Determine the validity of 'Mary and Joseph would have called their child Emmanuel only if the child had been extraordinary from birth. But they called him Jesus. So, he was not extraordinary from birth.' Determine the validity of 'Judas Iscariot cannot both have killed himself by hanging himself (Mt. 27:5) and died from disembowelment due to falling off a cliff (Acts 1:18). He did not die from disembowelment due to falling off a cliff, because it is well authenticated by ancient authorities that he hanged himself.' Supply the conclusion implied by the following premises: 'Our ideas reach no farther than our experiences. We have no experiences of divine attributes and operations.' "

Handing the sheet back to the dean, Rad said evenly, "Those are perfectly legitimate problems for beginning students in logic."

"Perhaps so," the dean murmured noncommittally, "but also take a look at another sheet I have here. The items on this sheet were compiled by the members of the delegation that came to see me. They say that everything on here is attributable to DeWulf and that every bit of it can be attested to."

Taking the sheet, Rad read the following: "1. The fish is a most appropriate symbol for Christianity, because there is a lot that's fishy about it. 2. Crucifixation is a psychological malady of Christians. 3. The Christ-creators don't really want to know about the historical Jesus. 4. In addition to being omnipotent, omniscient, and omnipresent, God is also, and most importantly, omni-compliant, being whatever his believers want him to be and taking on whatever values they want him to take on. Any other deity would be the devil. 5. The Messiah is always coming, never leaving anyplace, never arriving anywhere, but always coming."

Before Rad could respond, the dean thrust a third sheet into his hand, saying, "And, here's more of the same. The vice-president received this complaint: 'Prof. DeWulf said, "Blessed are the gullible, for they shall believe

309

whatever they want to; blessed are the ignorant, for they shall know no restraints on their credulity," and he said, "Faith is the assurance of wish-fulfillment, salvation through faith alone being the ultimate example of every-thing for nothing." Finally, he said that a fool for God is still a fool.' "

"So, what are you asking of me, Dean, or, perhaps, telling me to do?" Rad asked, feeling a cold lump in the pit of his stomach.

"In simplest terms, you'd better tell him to lay off and be quick about it."

"Dean Braniff," Rad said slowly and coldly, "is ASU an arm of the church?"

"No, of course not, and you know it's not, but ASU has to live in the world, and the world it lives in is overwhelmingly Christian."

"Let me ask you a different kind of question then," Rad went on. "Have you heard any good things about DeWulf or only bad things, assuming that what you have shown me is bad."

"Yes, I've heard some very good things and from some very reliable sources including a faculty wife in his ethics class—all the more reason why you should talk some sense into this young man. It would be quite un-fortunate if a promising career were blighted at the outset because the person in question rides an antireligious hobby-horse too much of the time."

Rad left the meeting with the dean deep in thought, troubled, and of two minds sharply divided.

Adrian was not acquainted with the all-knowing Oscar Jiminie, nor could he have guessed that Rathbone had scarcely retreated from the Ad. Building before Manly Plumwell learned of his (Adrian's) spirited exposition of three-world creationism. So, though he fully expected to see the royal priest again, he was by no means prepared for the encounter when Manly, smiling broadly, burst into his office with only the briefest tap on the door.

"I thought you might have called me by this time," Manly said, sitting down without invitation.

"Called you! Whatever for?" Adrian asked, momentarily mystified.

"Why, about three-world creationism, of course."

"Oh, that," Adrian said, smiling, but not thinking of the Rathbone in-cident.

"Did your Greek New Testament bear me out?" Manly asked, feeling supremely confident and looking it.

"Absolutely!"

"So, what do you think of it now?" Manly asked triumphantly.

"Fantastic! Just as fantastic as anything in the Bible and just as sound doctrinally as any of it," Adrian responded with merriment, but convincingly.

Mistaking the merriment for enthusiasm, Manly said, "Praise the Lord!" Then, his face aglow with expectation, he asked, "When would you like to confess your faith and unite with us?"

"Confess my faith and unite with you!" Adrian fairly shouted, with

310

something akin to horror in his voice.

"Why, yes."

"Brother Plumwell, I fear that you are on the wildest of wild goose chases."

"Fighting off disappointment that bordered on dismay, Manly stammered, "But, it . . . it was my belief that you had accepted three-world creationism."

"How could you have gotten any such preposterous idea as that?" Adrian asked, really puzzled.

"You were overheard explaining the belief very convincingly to a certain professor."

"Oh, that!" Adrian exclaimed, a light dawning on him as he remembered old Rathbone backed up into a corner and trying to get away. "Look," he went on, "Rathbone makes a damned nuisance of himself parading his pious medieval mentality around here, deprecating everything that's happened since anno Domini 1300. I simply asked myself why he should have a medieval mind. Why shouldn't he have an antique mind or an archaic mind? So, I decided to confront him with something really antediluvian, and at the time I couldn't think of anything better than that fantastic stuff you showed me in II Peter."

In a hoarse whisper, little more than a croak, Manly asked, "You mean it was all a . . . joke?"

"Yes, it was a joke, but not just a joke," Adrian said. "In my view, people of intelligence and education, like Rathbone, ought to know better than to believe Christian dogmas of whatever vintage. But if they persist, then I want them to take it straight and believe all of it."

Not taking Adrian's bait, not asking why he should care that Christians take the full gospel straight, Manly asked in the gravest tones he could muster, "Professor DeWulf, aren't you a Christian?"

"No, I'm not a Christian, not in any sense of the word and by no stretch of the imagination."

Manly had never assumed that Adrian was a true Christian but had taken it for granted that he believed himself to be somewhere within the pale of Christendom. So, he had been prepared to deal with heresy alone, not with apostasy. "Well, why aren't you a Bible-believing Christian, if you don't mind my asking?" Manly asked, a measure of his self-possession having returned.

"Because Christianity is scientifically unsupportable, philosophically disreputable, and historically fraudulent," Adrian said decisively, hoping thereby to put an end to Plumwell's pestiferous visits.

Looking very pale, Manly left Adrian's office abruptly and in misery, his emotions having been brutally wrenched around 180° in a matter of moments. As he stalked off toward the Church of the Chosen in the dusk of a wintry evening in November, he heard no salutations, though two were delivered, and saw nobody wave at him, though several people did. Upon arriving at the church, he threw off his overcoat, dismissed all thoughts of pre-

311

paring his evening meal, and went straight into the sanctuary. There, with no light except that which seeped in from the street through Bro. Cricklet's four panels depicting three-world creationism, he paced around and around and around agonizing over DeWulf, what to do about him, and whom to rescue from him.

As Manly circled the dim sanctuary, strode in righteous indignation up its center aisle between ghostly pews, stepped up onto the podium, pausing behind the pulpit, or dropped to his knees to pray in its deep shadow, many thoughts flooded his mind. Among them was the realization that his evangelism had not been conspicuously successful among the faculty and better trained support personnel at ASU. Mostly he had met with polite disinterest in the Holy Nation or cheerful indifference to its message. But not since the horrible encounter with Smut Graeber on Probasco Ridge had he met anybody so unspiritual as Adrian DeWulf, and never had he met anyone anywhere who openly rejected Christianity, rattling off reasons, even bad reasons. DeWulf's awful words, "scientifically unsupportable," "philosophically disreputable," and "historically fraudulent," kept playing in Manly's head as though they were on a broken record, a record that could not be taken off the turntable, could not be unplugged, could not be stopped, but went on and on and on. What had he meant by "scientifically unsupportable"? Did DeWulf not know that this was God's world and that science was just the study of this world in its various physical aspects? Since it was the study of one of the things that God had done, how could that study not give evidence of God's existence and God's creative power? Everybody at Big Bend knew that there was no conflict between science and religion—true science and true religion, that is. Moreover, the people who had written the pamphlet "*Scientific* Three-World Creationism" had proved that the doctrine was scientifically true, and nobody could disprove it. Just because it took a miracle on God's part to create a new world while Noah was afloat on the waters destructive of the first world did not make the belief false nor unscientific. Bro. Van Hook had made that point over and over again.

What nonsense must DeWulf have had in mind when he said that Christianity was philosophically disreputable! At its very best, philosophy was nothing but natural theology, nothing but the recognition that the Maker's mark could be found on what the Maker had made. Any reasonable person— and Manly knew himself to have enough God-given brains to be reasonable—recognized that the world was like a great mechanism. One had only to watch the stars and the constellations wheel across the night sky to know that. It was clear to common sense that the world was not a natural occurrence, something happening spontaneously, unaided. Quite the contrary, it was an artificial thing. It had required creation by another, and all but the most perverse fools knew that that other was God, God the Father of the Lord JEsus Christ. At its worst, philosophy was merely the speculation of weak, limited, corruptible, fallen human beings. What easy prey such creatures were for the devil and his deceits! How prone they were to boast of their worldly

312

wisdom and to aggrieve God most sorely with their boundless vanity. As for the logic philosophers were always flaunting, well, anything and everything persuasive of true faith was logical and nothing, nothing at all, dissuasive of true faith was logical. Logic, of course, had its limited uses. Manly knew that. It could be used to make false religions put up or shut up. It could be used to devastate alien faiths and heresies, but it could never be turned against the true God, for his ways were past finding out, nor against the true faith, for it was above and beyond reason and appeared as foolishness to those who were wise as the world judges wisdom but were perishing nonetheless. Let those whose speculations did not begin with their fear of the Lord call Christianity disreputable if they liked. That would be the greatest mark of commendation they could bestow upon it.

The worst, but most outlandish, thing DeWulf had said was "historically fraudulent." What on earth could he have meant by that? Manly wondered in rage and revulsion. As unable to fathom it as he was disinclined to do so, he knelt by the pulpit to ask God that his ears might never again be assaulted by such blasphemy. But the prayer did not suffice to stop the horrid din in his head. Historically fraudulent, historically fraudulent, historically fraudulent! At Big Bend Manly had heard dark allusions to so-called New Testament scholars and their higher criticism, such names as Bauer, Strauss, and Wellhausen having been uttered infrequently but always in contempt, the name of Albert Schweitzer also added from time to time in the same vein. It was well known that such people were the spawn of Satan and that their so-called historical work in no way brought sinners to Christ, in no way conduced to the work of redemption, but perverted the minds of men and destroyed faith. What did so-called historical knowledge matter anyway? God had handed down his autographs to the inspired writers of Scripture, and out had come the books of the Bible, the gospels and the epistles. The gospels spoke of JEsus and delivered to their readers and hearers all the information that was necessary to redemption and the life everlasting. Where could fraud have found entrance? How could it have weaseled its way in? Where could it have lodged? Nowhere! No way! God would not have permitted a single deceptive jot or tittle to invade his revelation, to worm its way into his saving message for mankind. So, what did DeWulf mean by "historically fraudulent"? Why did such a heathen as he rage as the heathen always seemed to rage? Why could they not simply accept Scripture as revealed? Why could they not receive its message of salvation in humble gratitude on their knees?

As Manly paced around and around and around and prayed, reflected on Adrian's apostasy first in one grim way then in another, and agonized over it, a definite kind of evolution occurred in his thought-feelings. Upon arriving in the sanctuary, he had wanted, quite simply, to deliver Adrian over to Satan for the destruction of his flesh, even as St. Paul had dealt with certain men as recorded in I Corinthians 5:5 and in I Timothy 1:20. But, unable to sustain that pitch of righteous anger for more than an hour, he fell back to the softer, more charitable, tactic of making a public example of him, of causing him to disgrace himself because of his blasphemy, of humiliating him for his faithlessness. Manly pleaded with God and prayed exhaustingly to be the instrument for doing just that. Finally, after two and a half hours had passed, his anger transmuted itself into a passionate desire to convert the raging heathen. Perhaps God, in his infinite wisdom, had sent DeWulf to Algonquin to try his (Manly's) faith. If so, how wonderful if, with God's help, he could overcome any hidden weaknesses in himself and then go on from strength to strength to find the power to bring DeWulf to his knees at the base of the very pulpit where he himself had pleaded and prayed only moments earlier. But, before that could happen, Manly was sure that Adrian would have to be humbled, and he, Manly John Plumwell, would have to find a way to make a public spectacle of him to convict him once and for all of his intellectual arrogance. Yes, it was clear that he would have to hound DeWulf, would have to become a kind of hound of heaven, ever tracking him down, ever snapping at his heels, ever heading him off, ever driving him toward the foot of the cross. What a triumph of divine huntsmanship it would be, the raging heathen tamed and made a Christian!

Although it was still early in November, there was already a skiff of snow on the ground, and it was very cold, as cold as the "tip of a witch's broom handle," as Adrian liked to put it when in polite company. He had gone to feed french fries to Theophrastus. Theophrastus had descended on him early in the term, perhaps as early as the first week of October, he thought. Adrian had gone to Jim-Jam's Hamburger Palace for one of their delectable hamburgers garnished with fresh mushrooms. He had also purchased a sack of their unique french fries (made only from potatoes that had begun to shrivel and cooked with their skins still on) and a large Coke. Since it was a ravishingly beautiful day in one of Algonquin's golden-scarlet autumns, he had taken his fare back to the campus, where he planned to eat on a bench under a tree. Relishing each morsel, watching pretty girls go by, and delighting in the breeze that rippled the leaves on the golden and scarlet trees, he was momentarily alerted to he knew not what, something or other that seemed to be falling in his hair. Smoothing it down, he noticed some tiny specks in the palm of his hand, but paid no further attention to them. He had scarcely taken another bite, however, before there was a second diminutive cascade of bark and fragments of lichen. Looking up and behind him he saw a fine fat fox squirrel hanging upside down and begging as surely as if it had been holding both paws palms upward. Remembering numerous happy encounters with squirrels in Riverside Park, just to the west of the Columbia campus, Adrian fished out a french fry and presented it to the moocher from on high. That initial encounter blossomed into an enduring friendship between him and the one he came to call Theophrastus. Why that name had popped into his head so fast and so decisively, he did not know, but it had. Several times a week thereafter, he would take french fries to the same locality and wait for Theophrastus, who was by that time a well established pan-handler, to come twitching down a tree.

On the frigid day in question, Adrian had already lunched in the warm cafeteria but had, nevertheless, braved the cold to go to Jim-Jam's just to get the salty ration that Theophrastus loved so much. Unaware that anyone was near, Adrian gave french fry after french fry to the squirrel, which hung blithely by the claws on its hind feet while holding each piece of potato with its front paws and munching in the frenetic way typical of squirrels. As he gave an especially succulent-looking piece to the little animal, he spoke to it: "It's more blessed to give than to receive; that's your view respecting me, isn't it, Theo?"

"Making like St. Francis, eh?" said a voice close to his ear.

Startled, Adrian turned abruptly, while Theophrastus scooted up the tree to the protection of an enormous branch fifteen feet overhead.

It was Harvey O. Ijjam. Harvey had come striding along, his color up and a big smile wreathing his face at the sight of the reputed *bête noire* of the philosophy department feeding a squirrel on that icy day.

Once over his momentary fright, Adrian said, "No, I'm not exactly making like St. Francis. I've never even mentioned the gospel to Theophrastus up there nor have I preached to a bird all day."

"No, I suppose not," said Harvey banteringly, "but did I hear you say 'Theophrastus,' 'proclaimer of God'?"

"Yes, you did," Adrian had to agree, wondering again why that name had popped into his head with such force and why it had seemed so right.

"Sounds all very Christian to me," Harvey observed, turning to go.

"Well, of course, I *am* the only true Christian in Algonquin," Adrian announced.

"*What?*" Harvey asked, turning back to look squarely at the young philosopher, wondering whether or not his ears had deceived him.

"I said, 'I *am* the only true Christian in Algonquin.' "

"How can you say such a thing as that?" Harvey asked, genuinely intrigued by the assertion.

"Because I'm the only one around here who accepts Jesus for what he really was."

"Well, what was he?" Harvey asked rhetorically, silently ticking off every theological interpretation he could think of.

"A leading member of the Palestine Liberation Organization of the time," Adrian announced. "Of course, it wasn't called that in those days, and the enemy was different, not Israel, but Rome and its occupation force."

"You can't be serious!" Harvey said, barely above a whisper, suddenly as chilled in spirit as his body was chilled by sharp gusts of wind that were cutting across campus and swirling around buildings, intensified.

"I am absolutely serious," Adrian replied, as chilled as Harvey physically but warming to battle.

Convinced that Adrian wasn't joking as he might have been with that

315

preposterous trinitarian clonehood business at Rad's party, Harvey asked, "But, really now, how can you say such an outrageous thing?"

"For one thing, the cleansing of the Temple—driving out the money changers and all that—was not the pious act that Christians like to make out of it; it was clearly a seditious act and was taken as such by the Romans. Furthermore, if you recall the episode in which Pilate is pictured as giving the people their choice between Jesus and some prisoner or other—and the people chose Barabbas—Mark makes reference to an insurrection in which Barabbas had committed murder. 'What insurrection?' you might ask. It's also interesting to note that according to Luke 22:35-36, shortly before Jesus was taken captive by the authorities, he exhorted his disciples to sell articles of their clothing so that they could buy swords." Sensing that Harvey was about to break away on some pretext or other, Adrian hastened on, "And don't forget Matthew 10:34 where Jesus says that he did not come to bring peace on earth, but a sword. The following verses make it clear that he was involved in something so divisive that it was going to tear families apart, exactly what one would expect of an insurrection—some people urging moderation, or even pacificism, and others, like the Zealots, urging violence." Catching Harvey by the forearm, restraining him from leaving, Adrian said, "Don't forget that there was a member of the PLO among Jesus' disciples. Luke calls him 'Simon the Zealot'—not just a zealous person, spiritually speaking, but a member of the PLO of the time. Matthew softens it to 'Simon the Cananaean,' but it's a historical fact that Cana, like the rest of Galilee, was a hotbed of sedition. Now, as for 'Messiah', it meant, as you perfectly well—"

Making good his escape, Harvey strode off with distressing images of the young Yasir Arafat flashing before his mind's eye, images in lurid color, images in three-dimensionality. "Oh, shit! *Leader of the PLO, indeed!*" Harvey hissed between clenched teeth as he stormed toward his office, oblivious of the wind. "Shit, shit, *shit!*"

Harvey's flight left Adrian all alone, for Theophrastus would not come down, having had enough french fries for one day or, perhaps, too much religion.

The Handmaiden received an illumination to the effect that much of the moral rot afflicting modern man was due to existentialism and confusion in dress. Of existentialism in general she knew next to nothing and of its Christian forms absolutely nothing, so she took it to be totally godless (whatever it was) and lumped it with other evils such as humanism, secularism, socialism, and communism. From early in the history of the Holy Nation, Alice had resolved that among royal priests the sexes would dress themselves as God had intended: the men in shirts and pants or suits, the women in blouses and skirts or dresses. Deuteronomy 22:5 made it abundantly clear that any deviation from these approved modes of attire was abominable in the sight of the Lord. But it was no longer enough for royal priests alone to dress as God had decreed. According to Alice's illumination, it was imperative that the Holy Nation do everything possible to prevent godless dress among the members of the various denominations (so-called Christians) and non-Christians alike. The Handmaiden was convinced that the twin evils of existentialism and confusion in dress had led directly to an insurgent feminism that was in many ways directly contrary to God's will for womankind and to a marked, if not an explosive, increase in the number of women who were shamelessly expressing masculine interests in carnality; "brazen hussies," Alice called them.

The directive to royal priests (of pew, pulpit, and professoriate alike) to do battle with existentialism and confusion in dress reached Manly at about the time Algonquin's unofficial glossary listing the different kinds of maids was updated to include such entries as: *accolade maid, brigade maid, cockade maid, good-grade maid, promenade maid, retrograde maid,* and *weighed maid.*

In order to carry out the Handmaiden's mandate, Manly reasoned that he ought to learn something about the evils in question and also find strategic ways and means of placing himself such that he could speak out on God's behalf effectively. Thus, braving what he feared would be an auditorium full of brazen hussies, Manly, Bible in hand, attended a public forum on "The Liberation of Women" sponsored by ASU's Coordinating Committee for Women's Activities.

The forum was moderated by Sasandra ("Sassy") Muldoon, an officer of the Student Government Association. Sassy was a broadly based young woman with abounding breasts and a cherubic face surrounded by ringlets of golden hair. In short, her appearance was such as to inspire male comments of the very types she reprehended most. The members of the panel were Dr. Pamela Mountcastle, a young instructor in political science; Rachel Hacker, a senior in sociology; and Josephine Lovejoy, a curvacious, left-leaning, graduate teaching assistant in the English department. To get the ball rolling, Sassy called on each of the panelists to tell horror stories of discrimination and injustice, of sexual harassment and affronts to womankind, of exploitation and repression.

Dr. Mountcastle, a spare and angular woman, spoke with scarcely concealed indignation of a well-known women's university that had an all-male administration except for the Dean of Home Economics and pointed out similarities in the power structure at ASU. From there she launched into a general indictment of male-dominated college and university administrations, ending with the observation that it was women who really supplied the brains behind the various administrations but from poorly paid secretarial positions.

Rachel Hacker, who had done a survey on such matters, spoke of applications from women for faculty positions that were simply pitched into wastebaskets after being laughed over and of various male-inspired myths that ruled faculty hiring, among which were (*a*) the belief that the intelligence of a woman was inversely proportional to the size of her breasts; (*b*) that good-looking, and therefore socially desirable, female colleagues made second-rate scholars; and (*c*) that only ugly, masculine-oriented women had a chance of becoming first-rate academically. Rachel, her tangled hair obscuring her eyes, also spoke of the shabby treatment accorded to faculty wives in teaching positions, treatment that consisted not only of low pay but of temporary appointments that never gave job security nor opportunities for sabbatical leaves and the like.

Josephine Lovejoy spoke animatedly of the male patters, pinchers, fondlers, and kissers whom female faculty, especially graduate teaching assistants, had to put up with; of sexual innuendoes; and of prurient preoccupations on the part of major professors and department heads, always males, it seemed.

With the formal presentations ended, Sassy, her breasts cantilevered astonishingly toward the audience, invited questions and comments. In the course of the next few minutes, speech became heated at times, words increasingly coarse. At one point, Sassy referred to American society as this "prickocracy" in which we must live, Dr. Mountcastle softening it to "phallocracy." Much was said of "so-called male superiority" and of "male chauvinism," and many more horror stories were told, including some about the subservience of American wives to their husbands.

Muttering "prickocracy" over and over to herself while trying to maintain a semblance of order, Sassy Muldoon noticed something black and vertical to her extreme right. It was Manly. Sorely vexed by the tenor and direction of the discussion and sensing that the time had come for God to be heard, he had stood up to catch Sassy's attention. Acknowledged by her, he introduced himself, saying, "Manly Plumwell, RPPI., pastor of Algonquin's Church of the Chosen and campus minister for the Holy Nation Association." After letting that sink in, he continued, "I'd like to make three points that I believe are worthy of our consideration. First, the problems we've heard about tonight would never have taken place if mankind hadn't rebelled against God's will for the sexes, the family, and society. Second, in what matters most, men and women are perfectly equal in God's sight."

"God!" said somebody profanely.

"And just what is that?" Sassy asked, her eyes very wide, her pupils dilated, making some of the boys close enough to see her well think of bedroom eyes.

"Salvation unto eternal life," Manly announced.

"Jesus Christ!" exclaimed an unidentified female voice.

Scowling briefly at the profanity, Manly said, " 'For as many of you as have been baptized into Christ have put on Christ. There is neither Jew nor Greek, there is neither bond nor free, there is neither male nor female: for ye are all one in Christ Jesus.' Galatians 3:27-28."

Speaking icily into the microphone before her, Dr. Mountcastle said,

"Right now, we women are not all that concerned about divine justice in the hereafter. We're concerned about human injustice in the here and now; we're concerned as American citizens with certain constitutionally guaranteed rights that are being denied us; we're concerned about equal treatment at work, in the school, at play, or at home as wives."

"Ah, yes," said Manly, brightening, "but that brings me to the third point that I would like to make. Our Heavenly Father has not decreed that males and females, men and women, should be equal in all respects."

The target of many surly, if not hostile, looks, Manly hastened to add, "You must realize that this is not what I, Manly Plumwell, a mere man even though a minister of the gospel, am saying on my own authority; it's what God is saying." Then, opening his Bible, he said, "Right here in I Corinthians, the eleventh chapter, it says that just as Christ is the head of every man, so the head of a woman is her husband, and in verse 8, it points out that man was not made for woman but woman for man."

"Yeah, and it wasn't Adam that was deceived by the devil either, but the woman that was," said Oscar Jiminie, popping up at Manly's side, trying to be helpful.

"Aw, Christ," Rachel Hacker boomed into her microphone, "that's just the way a bunch of old-fashioned, male chauvinist Jews thought God wanted things to be. He doesn't really want there to be any differences between men and women. He created us to be free and equal."

"You're goddamned right he did," shouted a strident female voice from somewhere far to Manly's right.

"Christ, yes!" said several other young women.

Hitherto silent and unnoticed, but enjoying himself immensely, Adrian stood up abruptly and shouted above the hubbub, *"Women will never be truly free so long as they keep on swearing with male deities!* You call God 'he' and think of the deity as a male—a king or a father—and you're all the time saying 'Jesus Christ' or just plain 'Christ,' and he was a man." Then, hamming it up, he said imploringly, "How long, O Mother Goddess, how long will this sex keep on doing this thing? When, Dear Mother in Heaven, will they start saying such things as 'Holy Mother Demeter!' or 'By the black heart of Kali!' or 'Oh, Isis!' or 'Yin-damn you yangs!' and such like?"

Adrian had meant only to have some fun at the expense of religion (thus interjecting a bit of humor into an increasingly tense situation) and to disconcert Manly. He did disconcert Manly, but he also disconcerted a majority of the females there that night. Josephine Lovejoy felt as though she were running, naked and ashamed, a gauntlet of major professors and department heads, all of whom were laughing derisively, surrounding her with ridicule. Rachel Hacker realized as never before how manacled, hand and foot, she was by her culture. Dr. Mountcastle, looking very pale, temporarily forgot about human power structures and put her mind on the divine power structure. Sassy Muldoon's hitherto surging breasts seemed to sag, probably because what she had just heard caused her to bend limply over the lectern, and numerous girls in the auditorium looked stricken.

Disquieted by the eerie silence that settled over the crowd, Adrian said, "Look, I'm for the liberation of women. I'm wholeheartedly for feminism and for every relevant equality. The devil made me say what I said, and he's a *male,* don't forget."

Without being told that it was all over, people sensed that the meeting had been shot down, mortally wounded, and, so, began to leave, jamming the aisles of the auditorium and the corridors leading from it. Adrian was able to move at will, however, for he was so completely shunned that empty space surrounded him wherever he stepped. Moving with good speed, unimpeded, he overtook Manly, who seemed to be staring at the beautifully undulating buttocks of some girls in jeans just ahead of him. "The heavens declare the glory of God; and the fundament sheweth his handywork," Adrian said aloud as he passed by.

When Manly reached his office at the church and looked up "fundament," he gave himself over to righteous anger.

Catching up with him in the hall after the ethics class, Claire, her eyes wide in mock horror, asked Adrian, "Just what did you say at that feminist meeting the other night?"

"I can't remember a thing about it," he fibbed, looking at her twinkling eyes blankly.

"I suppose senility would affect the memory of a man as old as you," she said, catching her breath, fearing that she had spoken too sarcastically. But when he agreed cheerfully that that must surely account for his lamentable lapse, she said, "Anyway, it must have been a heavy message."

"Why do you say so?" he asked, mildly curious.

"Because you've got half the girls on this campus trying out new kinds of profanity, to say nothing of new experiments with obscenity."

"Such as?" he asked, grinning from ear to ear.

"Well, 'Yin-damn you yang' or 'yangs,' and 'Yin-damn your yang' have both caught on like wildfire," she said. "And one of the Coyoties in Greek and Roman mythology has come up with the term 'Cybele cunted,' but nobody seems to understand exactly what it's supposed to mean; and a girl in comparative religion has begun swearing by the 'Holy Ass of Astarte,' I believe it is. Also, it may interest you to know [here she looked all around to see if they were being overheard, then put her lips close to his right ear] that 'frig' is now being capitalized and spelled with two 'g's."

At that, Adrian exploded with laughter, finally managing to say, "Damn! Why didn't I think of that?" and "What a wonderful use for the holy name of the old Norse goddess!"

"And that's not all; there are other examples, but really too gross for me to mention," she said, leaving him laughing at his office door as she disappeared around a corner on the way to her next class.

When Candace ("Candy") McIntyre was elected queen at the time of the 1960 homecoming football game, Professor O. K. Grampian could no longer contain himself. It wasn't that he was angry at Candy personally, no, not at all, but at something she represented, represented most thoughtlessly, represented most impiously as he saw it.

Candy was by all accounts ravishingly beautiful, far more beautiful than any of the other contestants that year and more beautiful perhaps than any homecoming queen for a decade or more. She had long flaxen hair, tawny skin, and sky blue eyes. At five feet, ten inches, she was statuesque. Moreover, she was poised, superbly proportioned, and magnetic, so magnetic that only the most inhibited of males could keep from finding some pretext or other to shake her hand, take her by the arm, pat her back, encircle her waist, or kiss her avuncularly. She also had excellent taste plus the means to dress very smartly, had a good fund of dietary knowledge, had real expertise in personal grooming, and was assiduous in following a physical fitness program, including yoga exercises. In short, she always kept her stunning self in the pink of condition. As a result, she was no long shot in beauty contests, her election as the homecoming queen for 1960 being but one more stepping stone to greater future triumphs.

It was none of that, however, that disturbed O. K. Grampian; it was what Candy said about her election that set his long teeth on edge unbearably. Every time she was interviewed by the papers, every time she was confronted with a microphone, whether for broadcast or merely for amplification, she made comments that seemed blasphemous to him, and made them in the fluted tones of a ten-year-old, breathlessly; all of which made him grind his teeth the more. On the night when her homecoming triumph was announced she spoke to an enormous crowd in the field house, saying, "When I entered the homecoming contest—"(here she took a shallow but noisy breath) "I just knew (breath) that I didn't have a chance (breath), not a chance to win (breath), not a chance with all the really beautiful girls (breath) who had planned to enter (breath). But I believed in my heart (breath) that for reasons I didn't understand (breath) it was God's will for me (breath) to enter the homecoming queen contest (breath). Now that he has let me win (breath)—and I thank you, God, I do (breath, head back, eyes rolled upward)—I just want you to know (breath) how much I appreciate (breath) everything that you students have done (breath) to help me to fulfill his will (breath) with your many votes (breath). I could not have made it (breath) without your many prayers either (breath). They gave me so much strength (breath). In closing, just let me (breath) acknowledge the help that mattered (breath) most, the help of Almighty God (breath). I prayed and prayed to him (breath) to be Algonquin's homecoming queen (breath), if it was his will (breath), and he granted me my wish (breath), so, I want you all to know (breath) that I plan (breath) to dedicate my life to him (breath) and to Christian service (breath). Thanks so much (breath), and God bless you all (breath), and may the love of Jesus (breath) be in all of your hearts (breath)."

After multiple exposures to Candy's views of her triumph and of God's part in it, O. K., unable to restrain himself further, wrote to the editor of the *Signal Flare* as follows:

"It is with a heavy heart that I write, yet I feel compelled to do so. To remain silent would, for me, be an act of moral cowardice. Moreover, not to speak out might well stifle a witness greatly needed, as I see it, in this day of the progressive vulgarization of profound religious concepts.

"I have taught at ASU for twenty-six years and have during that time formed many deep attachments to the institution, including attachments to, and interest in, its various athletic programs. I have even found value in such tangential activities as beauty pageants and the like.

"In that which follows, I do not intend to attack any person, activity, or institution as such, and I am quite prepared to admit that that which I do propose to attack is innocent in motivation, even well-intentioned, but is nonetheless deplorable and, yes, well-nigh blasphemous.

"Let us consider the hundred thousand million billion stars of the known universe. Let us contemplate the myriads of mighty galaxies wheeling in space and hurtling outward from one another toward far horizons.

"Let us also ponder the atom, that diminutive solar system, building block, and dynamo of the universe. Let us also think of molecules and crystals, of acids and bases, of substances and attributes, and of all that constitutes the extensionality and solidity of the world of everyday experiences.

"Let us additionally think of Mother Earth, four and a half billion years in process, developing into a fit habitat in which after millions of years of evolution there stands erect a creature, a singular creature, MAN, the being in whom the universe is conscious of itself.

"Having reflected on all of these marvelous yet commonplace facts of modern knowledge, what are we to say of God? Is he not an immensity greater than the immensities of space, an essential foundation for all being, enormously more profound than any individual being, a principle of choice regnant over every discrete process, over every particular type of thing, over every determinate reality? Is he not to be taken as the ground for the order and structure of causality, of all life, purpose, personality, and value in the cosmos? Of course!

"Yet we learn that, for mysterious reasons, he prompts a particular young woman to enter a beauty contest so that she may be Algonquin's homecoming queen, and at what? At an annual football game, hardly an event of cosmic proportions! And, spurning the petitions of all others, he answers the prayers of that one, the winner. What do we presume him to do to bring these marvels of design to pass—stuff ballot boxes, send delusions, change people's minds, deprive voters of their free will in the matter, compelling them to vote as he chooses, or what?

"How pathetic is the deity who concerns himself with such trifling affairs as beauty contests and contrives to defeat particular athletic teams that others may win. How sad, how appalling that someone, anyone, were to devote his or her life to such a piddling god!"

Pushing away his lunch tray and opening the *Signal Flare,* Adrian, sitting by himself in the cafeteria, laughed aloud upon reading O. K. Grampian's letter. He wanted to go home that very instant to compose his answer, but it made more sense to return to his office first and then go to his two o'clock class. As soon as the class was over, however, he went straight to Litany Lane rather than back to his office lest students or colleagues or the phone distract him. Grampian's letter was simply too good to ignore. Furthermore, he wanted his rejoinder in the next issue of the paper while the topic was still hot. Nestled in his big gray chair, clipboard on his lap, he wrote, and rewrote, and polished his rejoinder. Then he typed it as follows:

"It is no light matter to take issue with so learned and seasoned a colleague as Prof. O. K. Grampian of ASU's religion department. Nevertheless, I am constrained to comment on his views respecting what God does and does not do.

"In the days of yore, when the universe was looked upon as though it were like a watch, or other machine, or a structure of some sort, i.e., an artifact, it was to be expected that people would think of God as a watchmaker, an inventor, an architect, or a designer of some sort. But, in these latter days, we have had increasingly persuasive reasons for doubting that the universe is like a watch, or piece of machinery, or a building, or like ANY THING AT ALL in our experience, least of all a product of artifice. As the universe has become curiouser and curiouser, that which is supposed to have caused it, and even now is supposed to be sustaining it, has become increasingly attenuated. Gone is the consummate horologist, the preternaturally gifted inventor, the quintessential architect, the master designer. In their place, nowadays, reside such honorable, perhaps, but vacuous concepts as 'Being-Itself' and the 'Ground of Being,' compliments of a certain Prof. Paul Tillich.

"Since Being-Itself is no thing (certainly no thing of religious interest to 99.9999% of the people) but is most likely just nothingness (which is of interest to no one except the excessively morbid), and since the Ground of Being is the very opposite of *terra firma,* being utterly unsubstantial, it is no wonder that many are finding God curiouser and curiouser, too curious to pray to, to expect anything of, or to entertain hopes about. Although the Incarnation of Being-Itself in the man Jesus of Nazareth may not cast doubt on his mother's perpetual virginity, it does cast a queer light on the issue of her womb. What it would mean to call Mary the Mother of Being-Itself beggars imagination.

"It is understandable that so recondite a man as Prof. Grampian would want a deity as philosophically respectable as possible, but such is not to be had in our day. It is understandable that he would want a God as compatible as possible with the world that science is describing, but that deity has absconded. It is understandable that he would want a deity who, in William

323

James's wonderful words, 'does a wholesale, not a retail, business,' but that kind of deity is tantamount to no deity at all for the 99.9999% of the people alluded to above.

"On the contrary, those who have an appetite for the supernatural require a God who is in the retail business exclusively, a God who numbers the hairs on our respective heads (how very nice to get to number the hairs on Candy McIntyre's beautiful head!) and whose eye is on every sparrow that falls. That such a God should not have his eye upon the lovely contestants who fell in competition with Candy is unthinkable. Of course, he let her win and made the others lose. Moreover, if he who watches over Israel neither slumbers nor sleeps, then surely he has time to tend to point spreads, to fix football games, horse races, cockfights, and the like, to say nothing of answering prayers by putting hexes on the enemy and spells on the beloved. In short, he is a God of battles, a God of all kinds of competition in life, letting whomsoever he chooses win and defeating all others for his own mysterious reasons.

"Much has been made of God's omnipotence, omniscience, and omnipresence, but not nearly enough of his omni-compliance, yet here is where his perfection reaches the nth degree. He is the quintessential handyman, ever ready to do what his devotees want and need him to do."

To O. K. Grampian's dismay, his testy letter won the sympathy vote for Candy in her subsequent bid to become Miss Algonquin, a contest she won far more decisively than she had won the homecoming competition.

The part Adrian's letter played (if any) in his own eventual silencing is difficult to assess, because irony in religion is hard for people to understand. Some thought he had come to Candy's aid, thus putting old Grampian in his place. (Whatever the case, O. K. stopped speaking to him.) Others thought he had made a mockery of God and were outraged. Still others, having feared that he was an atheist, took heart in his letter about God, for no atheist could have written such a letter, as they saw it. Let it suffice to say that after the letter, no fewer wanted him to shut up than before.

For her part, Candy continued to worship and serve the God whom she believed had made her so very beautiful, and paraded her lovely self before the multitudes, unruffled by the theological turmoil she had caused.

After prolonged prayer and stressful consideration of his options, Manly decided on guerrilla tactics of a sort. He would seldom, if ever again, go to DeWulf's office. No, he would not beard the lion in his den. Moreover, he would not engage DeWulf in spiritual combat in open meetings. No, he would not suffer Father Nooper's fate if he could help it, nor would he let himself and his faith be confronted and ridiculed as had happened at the recent feminist meeting. Swearing by female deities indeed! May the Heavenly Father have mercy on their souls, he thought. What he would do, Manly decided, was to jab at DeWulf when he least expected it. He would try to embarrass, or at least surprise, him, would try to catch him off guard, would present him with problems and questions that only a Christian could answer, and he would do it in public but not at formal meetings. He would do it outdoors and indoors, on the walks and lawns of ASU and in the halls or common rooms of campus buildings or around town, at the post office, the laundromat, or anywhere their paths might cross. DeWulf simply had to be put down for JEsus' sake that he might subsequently be raised to newness of life as a Christian and a royal priest.

Adrian, however, had already seen too much of Manly. The latter was not a foeman worthy of his steel and was, therefore, not much fun. Yet, everywhere the professor went, the preacher was sure to go, or so it seemed. It hadn't dawned on Adrian that Manly had ceased coming to his office, nor had he recognized anything resembling different tactics in the latter's new ubiquitousness. Nevertheless, it was as though Adrian had suddenly acquired a tail.

In the hall after the ethics class one day (shortly after Manly had instituted his new tactics), Claire and another Coyote and the Coyote's boyfriend were pursuing an ethical question left unresolved in their minds at the end of the hour. After hearing them out, Adrian said, "Look, whether the topic is sex ethics or not, the question is: Are moral principles objective and external to the human species or are they psychologically endogenous to us and to our social experience? In other words, do we find moral principles, as a prospector might find precious metals? Do we find them in some holy black book or other, on tables of graven stone, in the inspired teachings of a messiah? Or do we have to manufacture them ourselves, so to speak, out of our own experiences, thoughts, choices, and decisions, and then have to modernize the product from time to time as changing values and conditions dictate?" Unnoticed, Manly had silently joined the group, Oscar Jiminie in his wake.

Staring intently, looking anxious, Claire said very slowly, "But, if I understand what you're saying, then . . . then that means that we have . . . ah . . . to take responsibility for deciding what is right and wrong, good and bad, rather than discovering it or receiving the information in some supernatural way or other."

"Exactly!" Adrian exulted, admiring her, even loving her a little, and savoring to the full the joy of the successful teacher.

"I'm going to pray for your soul, Professor DeWulf, I really am, teaching that kind of thing!" Manly blurted out, horrified himself and startling everybody else.

"It wouldn't do you any good," Adrian fired back, annoyed.

"How do you know that?" Manly asked sharply, never having met anybody who would spurn well-intentioned prayers in so cavalier a way. Even Smut Graeber would have said, "Go ahead and pray for me if you want to."

"Because I've committed the unforgivable sin," Adrian announced decisively.

"You *what?*"

"I've blasphemed against the Holy Spirit."

"And just how did you do that?"

Smiling, Adrian said, "You should surely know how to do it; you're an expert on sin. Anyway, since I'm quite perfectly Godforsaken, you shouldn't waste your breath on me."

Distressed by the exchange, Claire and her fellow students found excuses for going elsewhere quickly, and Adrian marched off to his office, daring to believe that he had finally gotten Plumwell out of his hair.

"Do you think he really has?" Oscar asked, his mouth agape.

"Has what?" Manly asked as though he had just been jerked out of a captivating daydream.

"Blasphemed."

"No, no, I can't believe that; he doesn't even know what he's saying, and furthermore, he doesn't even know how," Manly assured the youth.

"Wouldn't it be awful if he had!" Oscar exclaimed, thinking of the endless inferno of hell.

"It would be awful for DeWulf all right," Manly agreed, clamping his jaws together righteously. And, although he didn't say so, he knew that it would also be bad for him, because more than anything else, he wanted to play a prominent role in the humbling and saving of Adrian DeWulf. That was one triumph he really wanted to revel in. But it could never be, if DeWulf had really committed the unforgivable sin. He doesn't even know what he's saying, Manly assured and reassured himself, resolving to stick to his new tactics, to keep on plugging away, no matter what, to redouble his efforts, if need be.

"Are you ready to go?" Rad asked, poking his head in at the top of Adrian's door.

"Sure, just let me grab my coat."

So saying, the two set off across campus for Tamewood Hall. Rad needed to see Frank Callisto, the head of the chemistry department, about some requests soon to be sent to the curriculum committee for action. He could have conducted his business with Frank over the phone but thought that Adrian might like to meet some of the "prickly characters in chemistry," as he put it. Furthermore, Rad thought the walk might provide a pleasant opportunity for giving Adrian some fatherly, friendly advice. On several occasions he had tried to tell him to button up his lip on the general topic of religion but had been unable to find either the stomach or the tongue with which to do it.

As they left the Ad. Building and angled northeast toward Tamewood, Rad said, "Well, now that you've been here the better part of a term, how do you like it—Algonquin, college teaching, and all that jazz?"

"Algonquin is not exactly Columbia, is it?" Adrian asked, smiling a little

326

ruefully.

"No, nor Michigan either," Rad answered, his moustache twitching at the mismatches mentioned. Then, after a pause, he asked, "Otherwise, how are things?"

"I really like teaching," Adrian replied, "and a few of my students are quite good, and I like my classes, and I like working with you very much, and Sterling—whoever and wherever he is—causes no trouble, but, God Almighty! this place is pious on the whole, isn't it?"

"Well, you have to remember that it's sort of the northern annex to the Bible Belt," Rad agreed.

"Do you know a certain microcephalic named Manly Plumwell?" Adrian asked, "a local divine who dresses most unctuously and pesters the living hell out of me?"

"Sure," said Rad (who knew everybody), "but not well."

"If you're given to prayer, you might pray that you never get to know him well. He's the blue ribbon winner in the invincible ignorance category."

"Cognitive knowledge isn't everything," Rad observed, chuckling.

"That's lucky for Plumwell, because if it were, he simply wouldn't make it."

"You say he pesters you?"

"Does he pester me! He's all the time coming up behind me unexpectedly in public places and saying inane things, not to mention earlier unwanted visits to home and office."

"Maybe he likes you," Rad said, his eyes twinkling merrily.

"I'm trying to discourage that."

"How?"

"By devoting myself to giving him a really hard time. I see to it that he never wins. For example, I was in one of the bakeries downtown recently, whence I had gone in pursuit of goodies. The place was crowded, and I was standing in line minding my own business. Well, from out of nowhere, Brother Plumwell materializes and says in those tense, fanatic tones of his, 'Professor, if you were walking along a deserted beach and you came upon something shiny half buried in the sand and you reached out and picked it up and discovered that it was a watch (here he jerked his watch off and shook it under my nose—sort of an audio-visual performance, you might say), wouldn't it be logical to assume that it manifested design and purpose and wouldn't you conclude that it was made by a watchmaker?' I agreed gladly and said, 'Brother Plumwell, the next time you're walking along a deserted beach and see something shiny in the sand and pick it up and it turns out to be the universe, then you could go ahead and make the point you're driving at with impunity.' I'm not sure he got the message, but it did shut him up."

As Rad's laughter at the absurdity of finding the universe on one of its own beaches died away, Adrian continued, "At intermission the other night—the night the St. Louis Symphony played—I was enjoying certain female attentions in the lobby when who should break into my idyll with Pascal's wager but good ol' Brother Plumwell. In tones that would have been funereal if they had not been much too loud, he said, 'Doctor, doesn't it make good sense to wager on the existence of God, because if you believe in him and he doesn't exist, then you haven't lost anything; but if you gamble on his existence, having faith in him, and he does exist, then you've gained everything, eternal life, that is?' 'Oh, yes indeed,' I said, pitching my voice so as to sound as funereal as his, 'unless it happens that God absolutely despises gamblers of all kinds and automatically sends them to the lowermost pits of hell.' I gained the impression that he did not stay for the second half of the concert after that."

Satisfied that Rad was enjoying his stories about the pestiferous one, Adrian offered another. "The other day, a very good student of mine, a certain Miss Claire Sumner by name, and I were feeding Theophrastus— Theophrastus is a campus squirrel with a lust for french fries—and who should chance upon us, scaring the hell out of Theophrastus, but Manly Plumwell, RPP1. For contextual reasons that eluded me then and still do, he said out of a clear blue sky, 'You agree, don't you, that the absence of evidence is not evidence of absence?' 'Oh, indubitably,' I said, 'but the absence of evidence is not evidence of presence either, so why not just be an agnostic about whatever it is you have in mind?' Then he said, 'It's because we know so little that we must believe so much,' and I countered with, 'But there is a great deal that you could know that you don't know, so you're believing much more than necessary.' The girl with me took a sharp breath as though she were embarrassed, and Plumwell looked positively stricken, and Theophrastus didn't come down again, and that was that."

"I think you're being a little too hard on Plumwell," Rad suggested, hoping thereby to introduce the distasteful topic he had been deferring.

But Adrian broke in, saying, "Oh, no, he likes to be despitefully used. That proves to him that he's a true Christian, because that's what happens to true Christians."

Laughing darkly at the illogicality Adrian had just exhibited, the two almost bumped into Dr. Bobby Duke Donough, just then departing Tamewood Hall by a basement door together with a gaggle of students.

"Why, Bobby Duke!" Rad exclaimed, "long time no see."

"Hey there, philosopher," Bobby Duke replied cheerfully.

Looking from Bobby Duke, a lumpy, rumpled man with a baby-face, back to Adrian, Rad said, "This is Adrian DeWulf; he's taking Kiefer's place this year." Then he said to Adrian, "This is Dr. Bobby Duke Donough, professor of biology and parasitologist *extraordinaire*."

"Wonderful!" Adrian said effervescently as though he had been hoping to meet a parasitologist his whole life long. "I'll bet you could clear up a problem I've been having in theology," he continued, feigning hopefulness.

"I'd be right proud to if I could," Bobby Duke said sincerely in a thick southwestern drawl.

Dear God! DeWulf's off and running again, Rad thought.

"It seems I was reading this big book called *Systematic Orthodox Theological Doctrines* by Dr. Didymus Lightfoot," Adrian said (making up the names as he went), "and it raised the question of the origin of parasites and their place in the divine economy, but it left me in quite a quandary as to whether God created these avengers before Eve ate the forbidden fruit or afterward. In other words, do parasites antedate the Fall, or are they part of the general curse God put on the ground in Genesis 3:17, or were they divinely appointed at the time of the plagues on Egypt, or what?"

As Rad fought off a snicker and Adrian maintained his customary poker face, anticipating a good laugh later, Bobby Duke, empathizing with Adrian's alleged confusion, said slowly and thoughtfully, "Different Bible authorities have different opinions on that. There's a Dr. Bart Siemas at a Nazarene school out in California that thinks there were some types that were created on the fourth day when swarming things were brought forth in the waters and certain other types that were created on the fifth day when the creeping things were created. On the other hand, there's Brother Elwyn Davies, a Welshman down at Abilene Christian in Texas, that thinks that no parasites got started before God cursed the earth after the original sin took place and entropy got started. As for myself," [here Bobby Duke looked painfully perplexed] "I have to admit I haven't made up my mind yet, because I don't think the Bible speaks clear enough on that point. In the last analysis, it may be something we're not supposed to know, just not supposed to know."

Even Adrian, who thought he had already encountered every kind of religious absurdity, was stunned—but not too stunned to have further sport. "What does a person like yourself have to look forward to?" he asked.

With confusion piled on perplexity, Bobby Duke stammered, "I . . . I . . . I don't think I get your point."

"Well, there surely won't be any parasites in heaven, will there?"

"Lord have mercy! whoever thought there would be?" Bobby Duke said, showing some alarm at the drift in the conversation.

"But how could you be happy in such a place?"

"How could I be happy in *heaven*?" Bobby Duke asked, hardly daring to believe his ears.

"Sure. You spend your whole life studying something that interests or even fascinates you, and then you wind up in a place where there won't be any of that sort of thing. After all, a mathematician can keep on doing mathematics in heaven, and a musician can keep on playing—religious music on harps at least—but what are you going to do with all your free time?"

Meanwhile, several students, chancing by but arrested by the conversation, paused, circling around the trio, waiting expectantly for Bobby Duke's reply, but he remained mute, dithering, it would seem. Sensing that the time had come to push on, Adrian said to the still speechless Bobby Duke, "If you get any revelation or make any big scientific breakthrough on the etiology of parasites, I'd be greatly obliged to you if you'd share the information with me." With that, he disappeared into the bowels of Tamewood, hoping that Rad was right behind him.

Outside, as the curious students began to flake off in different directions, Bobby Duke stood his ground as though rooted. His friendship with Kiefer Maddox and Rad Reid had mollified most of his animosities toward philosophy, but the encounter he had just suffered had brought them all back again, intensified.

Inside Tamewood, Adrian, grinning from ear to ear, punched Rad playfully and said, "Why didn't you tip me off as to what kind of a curiosity you were introducing me to?"

"Honest to God, I didn't know," Rad answered, stretching his moustache with a broad smile. "I knew he was a pious guy, but I didn't know any biologists any more believed in Genesis literally."

"You know, you're kind of naive in some ways," Adrian said, assuming the fatherly role and explaining what he meant as they sought out Frank Callisto.

And Adrian was right, for Dr. Bobby Duke Donough was and is by no means exceptional. Born forty-seven years earlier in Ben Hur, Arkansas, the youngest of eleven, he had been raised in a family as rich in religion as it was poor in the goods of this world. So accepting was he of that religion, so uncritical of it, that he was in high school before it dawned on him that the church he belonged to was the Holiness Church, not the Holy Nest Church as he had often announced. At Harding College, where he did his undergraduate work, he was confirmed in the divine creation of all animal species (and of man) by fiat in days of twenty-four hours each, and at the University of Arkansas, where he received his doctorate, no serious challenge to his "Holy Nest" religious mentality was ever mounted. Furthermore, even as he stood rooted to the spot trying to figure out whether or not he had just been made fun of, he was teetering on the brink of conversion to the Holy Nation at the hands of Bro. Manly Plumwell, three-world creationist *extraordinaire*.

"What you've got to recognize is that scientists are some of the most child-like, most naive, most dogmatic people in the country outside their little specialties," Adrian said, wagging an index finger far below Rad's nose.

"Well, of course, most of them haven't had the benefit of any philosophy in their education," Rad mused.

"*Exactly!*" Adrian replied loudly, knowing that the woods were full of Bobby Duke Donoughs but perplexed as to how it could still be so in higher education in modern scientific America.

The last issue of the *Signal Flare* to appear before the Christmas break between terms contained Adrian's third letter. For several years he had become increasingly angry over the absurdly favorable treatment the media accorded Christianity, publicizing its faith as though it were fact. Accordingly, he wrote:

"Now that the silly season is upon us, there will be such an excess of good will that otherwise tough-minded editors will carry highly suspicious pieces on the Star of Bethlehem. It will be suggested that it might have been an unpredicted comet, a conveniently exploding star, or the conjunction of Jupiter and Saturn, or the conjunction of those planets plus a comet or supernova. But notice, whatever the source of the alleged light may have been, it behaved in a most aberrant way, most unlike a comet, a supernova, or planets in or out of conjunction. It led a bunch of Magi (magician-astrologers) from their interview with King Herod to Bethlehem and then hovered over the very building where the babe was born (Mt. 2:7-11). The reader is urged to try to follow a star sometime. Follow Sirius, for example, or even the moon, and see where either will lead. Upon more serious reflection, perhaps there is no reason to go to such frustrating lengths. Simply note, dear reader, that the story of the aberrant star is part and parcel of a tale that includes the genealogy of the man who was NOT the babe's father (Mt. 1:16; Lk. 3:23) and also contains instructions to call the child Emmanuel (Mt. 1:23) rather than the common name Jeshua (Jesus in Greek), which he was in fact called. How strange it is that the tough-minded people in the various media can't recognize a pious cock-and-bull story when they're confronted with it but palm it off each year as though it were new, or at least history."

As far as the calendar was concerned, Adrian's letter was well timed, but as far as circumstances at ASU were concerned, the timing couldn't have been worse. Since it appeared just as the students were plunged into the final examination period, it was ignored. But the campus ministers, who had easy access to the *Signal Flare*, and the local clergy, who received complimentary copies of it, did not ignore the letter. On the contrary, many of them, including Manly, were incensed, taking public issue with the (godless?) professor from their pulpits and in the pages of the *Algonquin Daily Messenger*. Manly's letter to the editor said in part that to achieve the so-called "aberrant behavior" of the Star of Bethlehem was a mere nothing to him who had already made *two* heavens and *two* earths and was about to make a third of each. In Manly's view, the Star of Bethlehem was not an ordinary star, nor a comet, nor a supernova (whatever that was), nor planets in conjunction, but rather more like a cordless floodlight moving along sedately just ahead of the camel-mounted Magi and then pausing directly above the manger for their convenience.

Adrian rejoiced in Manly's response and lay in wait for him to point out that the biblical text says "star" and means star, not cordless floodlight.

Claire rapped on the door and stuck her head in, saying, "I know I'm bothering you . . ."

"I don't mind being bothered," he interjected, looking up from a great pile of final exams and thinking, as long as it's you.

331

"... but before I leave for home in a few minutes, I'd like to know how I did on the ethics final."

"You passed it," he said, pretending to be reassuring.

"Oh, thank you very much," she replied, cocking her head and making a face.

"And you passed the course too," he continued, reaching for his roll book.

"Would it be asking too much to inquire as to the margin by which I passed?" she asked, effecting a mildly sarcastic tone.

Rustling the pages of his roll book and pretending to have a hard time finding her name, he finally said, "Hmmmm, according to this, you made a 98.5% on the final, giving you a 96.5% average for the term. Too bad about that first test that wasn't so hot."

But Claire wasn't worried about the not-so-hot first test. On the contrary, she let out a little whoop of delight and held up both hands giving the "V" for victory sign. "Straight 'A's'," she exulted, "which means that . . . that I can go home again."

"What on earth do you mean by that?" he asked, puzzled.

"Well, you see, my parents take great delight in my academic success, as measured by 'A's', but they worry about me extravagantly, and they always want to know what I have learned, and who taught me what, and what was said, and whether or not I'm still true blue in my beliefs, especially in my religious beliefs, and, well, you know very well what you've done to me this quarter, don't you?" So saying, she smiled a little ruefully.

"I have a vague idea," he said, genuinely concerned over the music she might have to face because of him and showing that concern plainly.

"Depending on how the third degree goes, I'll just have to remain silent at points or fib, I guess," she said, "or there'll be holy hell to pay."

"Somewhere, John Dewey says, 'Let us admit the case of the conservative: if we once start thinking, no one can guarantee where we shall come out, except that many objects, ends and institutions are doomed. Every thinker puts some portion of an apparently stable world in peril and no one can wholly predict what will emerge in its place.' Is it possible that you could make that kind of point to your parents?"

"No," she said decisively, "they'd never understand a word of that, and the worst of it is, I'll have to fib most about the ethics class—delicious irony, eh what?"

"They understand training but not education, is that it?" he mused.

"By the way," she continued, turning to leave and not looking squarely at him, "I won't be able to take the philosophy of religion with you next quarter." At that, she saw him stiffen his whole body and clamp his jaws as though to deal stoically with enduring and unavoidable pain.

"If you can't, you can't," he said evenly, making no attempt to urge her to change her mind or rearrange her schedule or whatever.

"Have a nice vacation," she said, smiling.

"You too," he replied, but with no smile, a light in his life having just gone out.

As she opened the door, Adrian saw the hulking figure of Bucky Oaks standing in the hall waiting for Claire and scowling in the direction of the office.

"That bastard is putting pressure on her to stay away from my classes," he said subvocally to the empty room, "and away from me, too, I dare say."

On the long road home to Heather, Claire had surprisingly little time for Bucky and the other kids in the car, bound for their several homes in the southern part of the state. She was thinking over and again of Prof. Adrian DeWulf, of the way he had looked when she had lied to him about not being able to take his course in the philosophy of religion. There is no doubt that he likes me, she exulted to herself, really likes me. And it was no small thing to her that one whom she had come to respect enormously should care for her, not only as a student, but as a person, as one torn between duty to parents and the need to be herself, to become autonomous. That he did care for her in all those ways she could not doubt. What a good feeling that was!

The school year at ASU was divided into four equal terms. Students could enter at the beginning of any term and could be graduated at the end of any term. Thus, with the final exams for the fall term over, there was nothing to do but to let those who had made the grade be graduated. Since Sterling Armistead was, as usual, nearing the completion of his book and did not wish to participate in the graduation ceremonies, and since Rad needed to be out of town on family business on commencement day, it fell to Adrian, wearing hastily borrowed regalia, to represent the philosophy department. Three things pleased him about the ritual: the trumpet fanfare by Josquin des Prez that served as the processional, the beautiful recessional by Gabrieli, and the sight of Cecil Rathbone with a smile on his face, wearing the colors of St. Andrew's. Three things disturbed him: the religious aura that surrounded the entire affair, the fact that President Sythian MacGilvary did not know how to conclude his remarks but went from anticlimax to anticlimax, and the extreme parochialism of his comments. No sooner had Adrian shed his regalia than he sped straight home, settled himself into his gray chair, clipboard on his lap, and began to write a letter, compulsively. Since the *Signal Flare* would not be published for another three weeks, and since his complaint would be untimely by then, he wrote to the local daily.

"It is understandable and justifiable that private educational institutions with close ties to a parent religious denomination would wish to suffuse their academic ceremonies with the sacred, but is it justifiable that a secular, state-supported institution with no religious ties should do so? Surely not!"

Before he could commence the second paragraph of his letter, Claire came to him unbidden and dwelt in his consciousness for a time. It was not so much that he was able to focus on her face clearly as that he could sense her presence, serious yet humorous, bold yet needy, fresh yet seasoned. What secrets of her being does she hide behind those gray-green eyes, big and clear and luminous? he wondered. Then, losing his grip on her presence, he resumed work on his letter.

"Those of us who were treated to the recent commencement services at ASU heard the presence of a particular deity invoked at the outset and received his benediction willy-nilly at the conclusion. During the proceedings, the President of the institution spoke often and much of that deity and of a certain Jesus of Nazareth, a presumed relative. There was no mention of alternative deities nor of other prominent founders of religions such as Muhammad, Buddha, or Lao-tzu, yet students of Arab, Indian, Chinese, and southeastern Asian countries were being graduated. Furthermore, it was made to seem that ASU exists to produce trained builders for the kingdom of a particular god, as though he couldn't take care of such matters himself, and that loyal service to that kingdom is as important for ASU graduates as good citizenship in the various countries they represent or as contributing membership in ASU's alumni association."

Then Claire cracked open the door to his consciousness again and slipped in. How much does she really care about Bucky Oaks? he wondered. If she likes him a lot, does that make her a *played maid* or even a *laid maid,* in the argot of Algonquin, or is she a *delayed maid* or even a *staid maid?* Whatever the answer might be, it was a well-kept secret as far as he knew. Still and all, it was an interesting topic, and he was curious about it.

"In view of the great prominence given to Jesus of Nazareth, called the Christ, at the recent commencement, I cannot but think of other messianic pretenders, noteworthy for their absence. Was a single good word spoken of Judas the Galilean? no; of Bar Kokheba? no; of Sabbathai Zvi? no, not a word! How much more parochial can a commencement exercise be? Perhaps there are others in Algonquin who would like to join with me in forming a group to Celebrate All Messianic Pretenders (CAMP), or Honor All Messianic Pretenders (HAMP), or Remember All Messianic Pretenders (RAMP) the precise name of the organization to be chosen later."

Instead of signing his letter, "A. DeWulf, Apt. 2A, 5 Litany Lane," Adrian identified himself as an assistant professor of philosophy at ASU. Thus, those who surveyed many of the state's dailies for public relations purposes were almost certain to see it and to bring it to Sythian MacGilvary's attention. When he saw the letter in the press digest given him, shortly after its appearance in print, he said more than "*Damn* it to *Hell*!" He acted at once.

334

Chapter Seven

The new year and the new term began happily for Adrian, but also ominously. First came the happiness, happiness heightened by surprise. Then
came the ominous news.

On the opening day of classwork, he met his students in the philosophy
of religion enthusiastically, to be sure, but not so enthusiastically as he would
have had Claire been there, but she was not there and would not be; thanks,
no doubt, to Bucky Oaks, the bastard! Adrian introduced himself and his
grading policies to the students (some of whom looked uncommonly apprehensive), stated his office hours, and gave his phone numbers. Then he
called the roll, taking time to master the pronunciation of each name and
trying to associate each with its owner's face. Next, he began to introduce the
subject matter so that those who had enrolled believing the course to be a
glorified version of Sunday school might think better of what they had done
and drop it early without penalty. Finally, he gave a preview of the assignments and the approximate dates of exams. Midway through the list of
assignments, the door opened and in came Claire, turning every head and
handing him a class card picked up late. Each smiled at the other fleetingly
but knowingly, triumphantly, two people who rejoiced in each other's company again.

He had known that their paths would cross on campus, if only infrequently, and that she would find reasons to come to his office even though
she could not take his course in the philosophy of religion, but now he would
see her five days a week, regularly, in addition to other encounters. She was
so good to look at, such fun to teach, and so worthy of rescuing from the
religious make-believe of her girlhood that he would be inspired. She would
not know it, for he would not tell her, nor would the other students in the
philosophy of religion know it, but he would exceed himself because of her.
Both knew, without saying so, that she would do her best work for him.

Later that morning, Rad stepped into Adrian's office from his own office
using the communicating door. "Did you have a good vacation?" he asked,
making an attempt at his usual joviality, despite the ominous news he bore.

"Yes," Adrian replied, smiling, "really nice. I went to Chicago—as I told you I might—to spend the holidays with an old friend from Columbia. And you, did you and yours have a good break?"

"So-so."

"Rad, I hate to say this, but you look like something the cat dragged in. What's wrong?"

"I feel like something the cat dragged in, that's what's wrong." Then, pausing, trying to find the stomach to go on, Rad said, "I'm the bearer of bad news, and I'm at least partly, perhaps substantially, to blame for it."

"Well, out with it, man," Adrian encouraged him, studying his face and wondering what on earth it could be.

"There is no chance that you'll be able to remain with us next year even if Kiefer elects to stay away that long," Rad said bluntly.

"I hadn't planned on that anyway," Adrian said evenly, hiding his disappointment.

"I know, and that's good, but what's worse is that you may not be allowed to remain to the end of the current academic year."

"*What?*" Adrian cried, sitting bolt upright, his whole body stiffening.

"You're only here now because of the disruption your summary release would have caused at the last moment," Rad said, "and you won't be here this coming spring term, unless you change your ways."

"Change my ways?"

"Well, some of them."

"Am I derelict in my duties?"

"No, quite the contrary."

"Am I thought to be incompetent in my field?"

"Far from it."

"Is my teaching not up to Algonquin standards?"

"Your teaching exceeds Algonquin standards from what I've been able to learn."

"Am I believed to be guilty of moral turpitude or of unprofessional conduct?"

"Certainly not the former, but maybe the latter in a very special way."

"Tell me all about it," Adrian said challengingly.

"Adrian, I really can't think you don't know, but if you don't, then I bear great responsibility, because Dean Braniff told me midway through the fall term to set you straight, for your own good, but I couldn't find the heart to do so."

"Okay, Rad, discharge your duty and set me straight."

"Well, to put it mildly, the shit really hit the fan when you wrote that letter attacking MacGilvary's handling of the most recent commencement, which, by the way, was like all the others he presides over. Moreover, earlier you jabbed a long hot knife between the administration's ribs with your letter about the Christmas star. Nearly every preacher all over hell's half-acre complained about that, to say nothing of the ASU trustees who also receive

336

the *Signal Flare*. In brief, they all want to know if the state intends to support atheism, if ASU is harboring an atheist, and if so, why. Then, too, you provoked a storm of student complaints on the general topic of religion."

"Rad, I have three questions," Adrian said angrily. "First, am I or am I not an American citizen with the right of free speech? Second, is there or is there not academic freedom at ASU? Third, did MacGilvary mean or did he not mean what he said about free inquiry and the free exchange of ideas at the barbeque he hosted last fall?"

Looking Adrian squarely in the eye, Rad said, "To the first, yes, but institutions have rights too. To the second, yes, but by default, i.e., we are free as long as nothing happens that causes political or public relations problems for the administration. To the third, MacGilvary meant what he said as he understands it, but he's none too bright and not courageous at all in matters of academic principle."

After a long pause, Adrian said, "Rad, tell Dean Braniff, and tell him to tell his overlords, that I am a member of the American Association of University Professors, and a member of the American Civil Liberties Union, and that I have a liberal lawyer friend who yearns for opportunities to engage in litigation involving the denial of civil liberties. Finally, tell him to tell them that I am prepared to play the role of Samson and to pretend that Algonquin is the temple of the Philistines, which is not too far from the truth. In short, if I am brought down for anything but justifiable reasons, I will do as much damage as possible in my fall."

Rad lost no time in telling Dean Braniff what Adrian had said—later that very day, in fact. Shaking his head sadly over one so promising but so innocent of the world as Adrian, the dean told Vice-President Graves, who in turn told President MacGilvary, who in turn exclaimed, "Why, that impertinent whelp!" as he dialed the number connecting him with ASU's attorney.

The new year began joyously for Manly but turned sour very quickly. On the first Sunday of January, Dr. Bobby Duke Donough, his wife, June B., and their eldest child, Donny Lum, came forward at the invitation, extended at the end of the morning worship service, to join the Holy Nation. Manly was so moved upon extending the right hand of Christian fellowship to Bobby Duke that he had to be very careful to keep his voice from cracking. It was far and away the most significant conversion he had ever had a hand in, for it spoke volumes about how true science and true religion did not and could not conflict but how they could be united in a single individual. Bobby Duke's conversion also conferred legitimacy on the doctrine of three-world creationism in Algonquin and opened new avenues for proselytizing on campus. As Manly concluded the service, thanking Almighty God profusely for his part in leading the Donoughs into the true church, the thought of Adrian DeWulf crossed his mind. How long, oh Lord, how long? he wondered, sighing inwardly as he called the Lord's benediction down on

Algonquin's new Jews.

With the winter term at ASU under way, Manly resumed his guerrilla tactics aimed at neutralizing Adrian's pernicious influence and eventually converting him. It did seem to Adrian that Manly was absolutely everywhere on campus all the time, but it did not occur to him that he was the object of the minister's pursuit, nor did he know that there was another person on campus on whom Manly was especially concerned to keep his eye and by whom he wished to be seen. Thus, it was not unusual that Manly would saunter up and join some students (including Claire) who were asking Adrian questions in the hall one morning after their philosophy of religion class. He had assigned several essays on the general nature of religion, which had raised questions concerning various non-Christian religions. Fascinated, some of the students had wanted to know more than there was time to divulge during the regular class session. Pleased over their interest, Adrian had made certain comparisons between the figure of the Christ on the one hand and the figure of the Buddha in Mahayana Buddhism on the other and had begun to speak of Lao-tzu when Manly could take no more.

"Professor DeWulf," he asked challengingly, "just how do you explain the fact that the bones of Buddha, the bones of Muhammad, and those of the person you were just now mentioning lie in their tombs to this day, whereas the tomb of JEsus Christ is empty and has been since the first Easter Sunday?"

"Well, to start with," Adrian said, "he may not have been dead when placed in it, and—"

"*Wasn't dead?*" Manly screeched as students' mouths fell open.

"Brother Plumwell, if you remember the order of events in John's gospel, Jesus is given a drink of something, loosely called vinegar, whereupon he promptly gives up his spirit. Then, when the soldiers break the legs of the two thieves crucified with him to hasten death, it is discovered that Jesus is already dead, surprisingly soon for death from crucifixion. But, then, when a soldier pierces his side with a spear, blood and water are said to have come out, indicating that he was still alive, though comatose. In short, he may have arranged his 'death,' so to speak, through a drug in the vinegar to insure his so-called resurrection, upon being revived later, and also to insure an empty tomb and all that that would mean in the minds of certain people."

Manly had never heard anything so awful, the very hearing of which was like a blow to the pit of his stomach, a blow that left him nauseated, unable to speak, and scarcely able to stand. Mercifully, DeWulf kept the students' attention riveted on himself, making it possible for Manly to back away unnoticed and wobble out of sight before fleeing to his church for refuge. There, on bended knees by the pulpit, he prayed as though giving himself a pep talk. It was true; the other gospels didn't say exactly what John's gospel said. Doubtless, John intended a spiritual teaching that could be harmonized with the other gospels—with sufficient ingenuity and prayer. JEsus was certainly dead when he was laid in the tomb; otherwise his soul couldn't have

338

gone to the underworld to preach to the spirits in prison there, nor could he have broken the bonds of death by coming back to life. That's what the Bible said, and that very fact proved the Bible true. Moreover, the resurrection of the Lord JEsus from the dead was the one fundamental fact of Christianity, a fact absolutely crucial to faith. There could be no doubt that the everliving Christ lived, and was alive at that very moment, for he lived in Manly's heart. Manly's own redemption, which he could never doubt, proved that over and over. The resurrection of JEsus Christ from the dead was the only way—well, perhaps not the only way, but certainly the best way—for God to endorse and certify the message of his Son and to prove that the Son was King JEsus.

Although Adrian may not have realized just how preoccupied he was with it nor known just how much time he spent doing it, he knew that he was quick to pounce on religion, especially Christianity. But, as he saw it, he attacked it only where and when it deserved to be attacked and only when right and truth were on his side. He never made a straw man of it that he might make a great show of pushing it over, nor did he ever portray it as being more fraudulent than he believed it to be. Furthermore, except for an occasional letter to the local paper, he confined his attacks to academic situations and to people who, ideally at least, were in a position to know better than to keep on believing in the inanities of religion. What was most important, perhaps, was that he was always prepared to put up or shut up, to give hard reasons of a logical or factual kind for his antireligious opinions. Then, too, his assaults did not emanate from mere spite alone but were driven by a kind of benevolence. Although not a Marxist, he did see himself as a liberator or would-be liberator of human beings through the "philanthropy of atheism," to use Marx's words.

And now his philanthropy was in jeopardy, at Algonquin at least (to say nothing of his job), for every single one of the intellectual pygmies in the higher administration was against him. Had they heard him out? No. Had they given him a chance to defend himself, a chance to put up or shut up? No. Would they have understood his views if they had heard him out? No, not without considerable effort at grasping the arcane issues in question and much more will to expend in that effort than any of them had hitherto exhibited. As a result of his disagreeable situation, Adrian was infuriated, except when teaching, and went around with a chip on his shoulder. It should come as no surprise, then, that he chose that time to pick on Bro. Manly Plumwell. Nor was that difficult to do, for Manly seemed to be omnipresent, popping up here, showing up there, lurking around everywhere.

Striding toward Antrim Library one day in early January, mulling things over angrily, Adrian approached the Westering Biological Laboratories just as Manly stepped out into the wintry air. Manly had gone to Westering not so much to give succor as to receive it, to draw strength from his most illustrious convert, Dr. Bobby Duke Donough. "Hey, Brother Plumwell, I've got a spiritual problem that you could probably help me with," Adrian almost yelled.

Still determined to bring the apostate to Christ, and still hopeful even if edgy, Manly said as evenly as he could, "I'd be glad to help if I can."

"I was reading the Scriptures recently, as I am given to doing," Adrian said, his words lilting, his tone bantering, "and I discovered in Matthew that Mary Magdalene and another Mary who went to Jesus' tomb on Easter Sunday morning saw an angel in white sitting on the rock that had previously sealed the sepulchre."

"Yes, that's right," Manly asserted as though he himself had been an eyewitness. "So?"

"Whereas in Mark, the two Marys mentioned don't see an angel outside the tomb but, rather, see a young man in white inside the tomb," Adrian went on.

"Well, you have to pay close attention to the context," Manly said, trying hard to remember precisely how they might differ.

"Oh, I do, I do, I assure you, and that's the problem," Adrian continued. "Now in Luke, the two Marys, accompanied by one or more other women, saw two men in dazzling apparel somewhere on the premises but no angel; and in John, Mary Magdalene, apparently unaccompanied by any other woman, saw two angels but no man. Well, you can imagine my consternation. I want to know what I'm supposed to believe in, one Mary or two, seeing one man or two, or one angel or two? What do you or your Handmaiden of the Lord have to say about that?"

"She's never said anything about that that I know of," Manly answered tensely, "because . . . because there's really no problem at all."

"*No problem*? How can you say there's no problem?" Adrian shrilled. "God's inerrant Scripture has anywhere from one to three or more women seeing anywhere from one to two men to one to two angels, and you say there's no problem!"

"I do know one thing for certain," Manly announced, his voice high and dry with tension, "and that is that no matter what *you* think, there are no mistakes in God's Word."

His mission accomplished, Adrian strode off toward Antrim Library, leaving Manly alone with the mocking snicker of a passing student ringing in his ears. As usual, when under spiritual duress, Manly dropped everything and made a beeline toward his church. There, in his office-study, he pored over the relevant texts looking in vain for the miracle that would make them one. Not finding it, even after an hour's search, he could only speculate that God was using the variations in the Easter story to test the faith of true believers like himself, even as Jesus had tested doubting Thomas and the men on the road to Emmaus; or, perhaps, God had allowed what looked like inconsistencies, to human beings, but were not so to him, to appear in the Scriptures that he might ensnare sceptics like DeWulf.

As though God had not tried his believers and tripped up his unbelievers enough with variety in empty tomb tales, Manly also discovered to his grief that in Matthew, Mark, and Luke no disciple is said to have been present with Jesus on the cross and the women who followed him, including his mother, watched the grisly proceedings from afar; whereas in John's gospel, Mary was present at the foot of the cross as was the one known as the beloved disciple. And, as though that were not more than enough, the risen Jesus is reported in Matthew 28:10 to have told his disciples to go to Galilee but in Acts 1:4 to have charged them not to depart from Jerusalem. But, thought Manly sighing, God's ways are past finding out, faith in those ways an old rugged cross the believer has to bear. For him, however, the tribulations of faith were intensified, because that devil, DeWulf, knew all the hard passages and just how to weight the believer's cross.

Two days later, at the end of the day, Adrian walked downtown to his favorite bakery. As he left a few minutes later carrying a box containing six cinnamon crisps, three Bismarks, and three Long Johns, he saw the car parallel-parked directly in front of the bakery drive off. No sooner had it left than a black Plymouth bore down on the empty space. A plate on its front bumper said, "God is My Co-Pilot." "Why, bless my soul! if it isn't the royal priest himself," Adrian said half aloud, squinting into the darkened car as Manly crept by, stopped, and began angling backward. Standing stock still in the middle of the sidewalk, Adrian noticed that the back bumper bore a medallion in the shape of a cross and also a sticker saying, "Clergyman on Duty." Stepping to the front of the car just as Manly, head down, emerged from it, Adrian said in tones designed to carry, "Brother Plumwell, I'm going to report *you* to the heresy investigation division of the local ministerial society."

Startled, chagrined, and hoping to God that none of his parishioners passed to or fro, Manly said testily, "Ahhhh, DeWulf, what do you mean by that?"

"God is either all in all or he's nothing at all," Adrian announced righteously. "He doesn't take a back seat to anybody, nor does he play second fiddle to any man. He is the *pilot* of your car, not its co-pilot." Giving Manly no chance to get a word in edgewise, Adrian said, "It all reminds me of a Mother's Day card I saw once. It had the audacity to say, 'Since God couldn't be everywhere at once, he created mothers.' Why, that's one of the most blasphemous things I have ever heard. Everybody who knows anything about God knows that he is everywhere at all times; otherwise he wouldn't be omnipresent. By the same token, your bumper plate is blasphemous. I must say I fail to see why you don't sit on the passenger side of the front seat and leave all the driving to God."

Tight-lipped, looking neither to the left nor the right, Manly stalked straight ahead into the bakery, leaving Adrian, smiling broadly, behind.

Several days later, feeling drained at the end of his afternoon class, Adrian went to the basement lounge in the Ad. Building to get some refreshments. As he stepped out of the stairwell he saw Manly gesturing animatedly as he harangued a gaggle of students. Stepping up on the new Jew's blind side, Adrian, looking benign, listened for a while in peace, but when Manly said, "Look, students, there is simply no way we human beings can comprehend just how great the God of the Bible really is, no way at all even to imagine his greatness," Adrian could restrain himself no longer and broke in, saying, "But it's easy enough to see just how *little* he is."

Whirling around, fighting to keep his composure, Manly hissed, "And just what's that supposed to mean, pray tell?"

"Why, he's like a two-bit dictator in a banana republic having to have praise, and honors, and medals heaped on him all the time, and he's so damned jealous for fear he won't get all the goodies that he condemns innocent unborn babies for the sins, or the alleged sins, of their great-great-grandfathers. He also sends lying spirits to people and hardens their hearts and then holds *them* responsible, and . . . and he prescribes capital punishment for homosexual contacts and banishment for any husband and wife who make love during any part of the wife's period."

Then, leaving the entire company breathless and aghast, Adrian marched off to get some coffee and doughnuts even though he was no longer feeling listless.

Unable to regain the students' attention or to restore the desired mood, the best Manly could do was to snarl, "Come Judgment Day, I certainly wouldn't want to be in DeWulf's shoes."

"Me neither," echoed Oscar Jiminie, his moustache fairly bristling with indignation over the way his revered spiritual leader had been put down.

Opening the *Signal Flare,* Adrian smiled devilishly as he noticed the piece announcing that the Spiritual Explorations Brown Bag Faculty Luncheon Club was to meet the following Monday at noon in the Powwow Room of the Union. Bro. Manly John Plumwell, RPPl., was to speak (his to be the fourth presentation of the season) on the topic, "This is My Faith."

Adrian, who had never before attended a SEBBFLC (pronounced "seb-fluk") meeting, was the first to arrive on the appointed Monday. In fact, he reached the Powwow Room so early he had to stand and wait until a janitor unlocked its doors. Once inside, he went straight to the chair in front of the lectern as though laying claim to it. He had dressed for the occasion in his most funereal suit of charcoal gray and wore a tie of tiny geometric designs in black and blue. Not content with a shirt that was merely white, he had chosen one with French cuffs that he might wear his matching cuff links and tie bar of sardonyx. Needless to say, his socks were black as were his newly polished shoes. In short, he looked as unctuous as anyone could who held his lunch on his lap and who had advertising in purple and orange from Jim-Jam's Hamburger Palace on every piece of paper about his person.

Manly had coveted the opportunity to address the SEBBFLC people ever since he had learned of their existence. He knew that the Lord had blessed him beyond most men with the power of the spoken word and that, given half a chance, he could speak eloquently of the Handmaiden and persuasively of the Holy Nation. Moreover, he was convinced that to hear three-world creationism expounded correctly was to accept it—if one were a Bible believer, that is—and surely there might be one or more such persons in SEBBFLC even though the organization was largely composed of liberals and modernists and other so-called Christians.

Working through the friend of a friend, diplomatically, Atherton Landis managed to persuade Lyman Tinker (botanist, liberal Methodist layman, and program chairman of SEBBFLC) to invite Manly to speak and respond to questions. Although Manly knew his faith backward and forward, he practiced his talk intensely throughout the morning of the appointed Monday and was so keyed up that he had no stomach for lunch. Dressed as unctuously as Adrian, and looking much like his nemesis, he arrived at the Powwow Room exactly at noon, leading a phalanx of supporters, chief among whom were Atherton Landis, Bobby Duke Donough, Rollo Skeeds (the librarian), Garvis James (the Assistant Director of Buildings and Grounds who had never attended a faculty function of any kind), and Oscar Jiminie, dressed to kill and looking more like a young instructor than the old student he really was.

Upon entering the Powwow Room, Manly's first feeling was one of elation over the large audience. But his second feeling was one of sudden dismay, for there, squarely in front of the lectern, sat Adrian DeWulf, the devil's champion. Since Manly had never dreamed that the apostate would appear at such a function, he had not prepared himself for that eventuality and, thus, felt utterly undone. There was no doubt in his mind that in the end the Lord JEsus would win the war against all unbelief and apostasy, but in the meantime, right then and there to be exact, he (Manly Plumwell) might go down in battle ignominiously, not only in the presence of the so-called Christians assembled to hear him but also in the presence of a number of sheep from his own flock, sheep who depended on the strength of their shepherd against the wolves of disbelief.

Invited to sit down while Lyman Tinker brought the chattering, paper rattling group to order, welcomed visitors, made announcements, and introduced the speaker, Manly prayed in fear and trembling that he might be a Gibraltar against the apostate's expected ridicule, a tower of strength against the winds of outrage with which DeWulf would surely assault him. The sword and the fire to which the saints and martyrs of yesteryear had been put seemed almost benign to Manly compared with his thoughts of Adrian's impaling humor.

As Lyman Tinker completed his rather self-serving introduction, Manly arose stiffly, arms at his sides, and walked to the lectern, not standing upright but hunched forward. Never before had he so dreaded speaking to a group, and never before had his sheep heard such a quaver of uncertainty in their shepherd's voice as Manly exhibited during the opening sentences of his presentation. But, as he proceeded, refusing to make eye contact with

Adrian, he felt the Lord's anointing power suffuse his whole being, and the words began to flow freely, as usual, intensely and persuasively.

What a rug salesman Plumwell would make! Adrian thought, not knowing that Manly was the product, in part at least, of one who had been a rug salesman of stellar quality.

When Manly concluded the formal part of his presentation, having reached a very high pinnacle of emotion indeed, the applause was heartening and genuine. Even those SEBBFLC members who had initially questioned his invitation and who remained dubious of his doctrines agreed that he had acquitted himself well. Adrian also clapped but only decorously and not long either, for he had his hand up in no time that he might ask a question.

He had no hope of educating Manly, but he did think that he might help to set straight some of the benighted faculty members who had come to hear Algonquin's royal priest of the pulpit. As soon as he was recognized by Lyman Tinker, he stood up and said, "Brother Plumwell, before I ask my question, I would like to applaud you for the definitive way in which you brought three-world creationism to the attention of the Christians assembled here. Thus expounded, it is as sound a doctrine, biblically, as anything else Christians believe."

As Adrian uttered those ironic words, the royal priests of the pew, who had come to hear and to cheer their leader, smiled smugly, not catching the irony, but Manly did not smile, for he knew that some sort of outrage was in the making. Refusing to say, "Thank you," or even to nod, he waited stonily for Adrian to go on.

"My question centers around your description of how God came to the young Alice McAlister 'in heat three times,' as you say she put it, and said to her, 'It is well with thee.' "

"So?" Manly asked, staring intently at his tormenter, trying to envision the trap he was about to spring.

"Did you ever read *The Doors of Perception* by Aldous Huxley, published a few years ago?"

"No."

"In that book, Huxley recounts how—under the influence of mescaline and other hallucinogenic drugs—he had paranormal experiences astonishingly like some of those reported by the great mystics."

"So?" said Manly for the second time.

"So, the issue is this: Did the Handmaiden actually feel the presence of God hotly and really hear his voice auditorily, or was her brain merely in a paranormal condition on those occasions? Is it not possible that what she took to be God was no more than the results in consciousness of a peculiarity in her blood chemistry, for example, at that moment?"

"Look," said Manly, "God can work any way he wants to. If he wants to, he can speak directly to a person, or, if he wants to, he can alter a person's nervous system and speak that way. It all depends on how God wants to communicate."

Smiling either at Manly's craft or at his ignorance (Adrian knew not which), he said, "But sir, you miss my point rather badly."

"Sounds like *just* the right point to me," Bobby Duke Donough said, breaking in, his gloating tone accompanied by approving noises from the other royal priests of the pew.

Shifting his ground quickly, Adrian said, "But in your theology, Brother Plumwell, the devil can do the same things, can't he?"

"The same as what?" Manly asked, buying time.

"Speak directly to the individual, if he wants to, or alter the person's nervous system so as to cause delusions and false beliefs."

"Yes," Manly replied, having to agree but feeling himself on increasingly firm ground nevertheless.

"And God can do the same things, right?"

"Look, God is good and doesn't cause delusions and false beliefs the way the devil does," Manly said, disdain coloring his voice.

"Oh, the Bible disagrees with you there," Adrian said mischievously, "because in II Thessalonians 2:11, it is written that God sent a strong delusion upon certain people to get them to believe a lie, and in I Kings 22:23 he is said to have sent a lying spirit to certain prophets, and in II Corinthians—chapter and verse escape me just now—Christ refuses to remove the veil from over Jews' minds, leaving them to misread the Law of Moses."

"Jeez!" grumbled one of the three liberal Jews who had attended the SEBBFLC meeting out of an excess of broad-mindedness, a Jew from Brooklyn.

"But," Manly retorted harshly, "those people to whom he sent a strong delusion were wicked people."

"I thought all human beings were wicked and . . . and fallen in God's sight," Adrian replied, doing his best to look and sound Calvinistic.

"That's just awful," interjected a liberal Christian somewhere in the back who believed in angels and archangels but not in devils and demons, also in heaven but not in hell.

"And don't forget," Adrian continued, wagging an index finger at Manly, "that the devil can disguise himself as an angel of light, so you see—"

"Can't anybody else get a question in edgewise?" a questioning woman muttered in the general direction of Lyman Tinker, who seemed undone by what had become the most animated SEBBFLC meeting he had ever attended.

"See what?" Oscar Jiminie asked loudly enough for Adrian to overhear.

Turning from Manly to face Oscar, Adrian said, "The point is simply this: How can we be sure it wasn't the devil in disguise, and not God at all, who came to Miss Alice in heat and deluded her with that business about all being well with her? We mustn't forget that the devil is magisterially deceitful and could easily impersonate divine personages."

At that, a howl of anguish arose from the royal priests of the pew, augmented by sympathetic cluckings from many others, but above their protestations, the royal priest of the pulpit thundered, "I'll tell you one thing, DeWulf. When the Lord JEsus returns in power and glory to judge the quick and the dead, you'll know who it is all right enough."

"How will I know it's not the devil in disguise?" Adrian bellowed over the hubbub. "After all, he wants me in hell too, I suppose."

"Oh, you'll know!" Manly exclaimed, "you'll know!" Then, perceiving the meeting in shambles, he turned toward Lyman Tinker hoping that the latter might do something about it.

As might have been expected, Manly won the sympathy vote that day, but Adrian's spirit was not cast down as he left the Powwow Room. In fact, it was elevated, especially when the really cute young English instructor whom he had seen at Rad's party the previous fall sidled up to him and said, "Professor DeWulf, I was quite interested in what you had to say about Huxley until all that crap about the devil in disguise sidetracked everything."

"The point I was trying to make," he said, rejoicing in the proximity of a face as friendly as it was cute, "is that you cannot justifiably assert that God has appeared to you or spoken to you until you have ruled out all other explanations of the experience in question. It seems pretty clear that biochemical changes in the brain or changes in brain-wave patterns self-induced by meditative techniques, and the like, can cause paranormal experiences. So, though I have no doubt of the Handmaiden's experiences, I have the greatest doubt about her interpretation of them."

"Yes, I see that and probably even agree with it," she said thoughtfully, heartening him. "But," she continued, "I believe all that talk about God's deceits and the devil's disguises was beside the point, and detrimental."

"Beside the principal point, yes," he averred, "but a very serious point indeed, methodologically speaking, for Christians, including hopeless meatheads like Plumwell. After all, if you're going to believe in God and Satan, in various supernatural agencies that can get inside of your skin and make you hear voices, and in so-called saving truths and in beliefs that may condemn you, then you had damn well better be sure who it is or what it is that is communicating with you. The eternal felicity of your very soul depends on it."

Trying to insert herself into the magical ambience of orthodox Christianity, she finally said, "I guess I see what you mean."

"So, the DID Principle," he said in a moment of sudden inspiration, "by which I mean the Devil In Disguise Principle, is crucially important epistemologically."

"Do you think I could come by to talk about these things at greater length sometime?" she asked, laying a graceful hand on his arm.

"Of course. Just name the time," he said enthusiastically as their paths parted.

It was the following Saturday afternoon when Adrian's and Manly's paths crossed again. On that occasion Manly not only received no sympathy vote, he was left utterly disconsolate. Adrian had walked downtown from

No. 5, Litany Lane, to leave a pair of pants with his favorite dry cleaner. Returning home a different way, he passed Algonquin's Church of the Chosen and noticed, on a bulletin board, that Manly was to speak the next day on the topic, "What Makes God Vomit," Revelation 3:14-16 being given as the text for that day. Halfway between the church and the main gates to the campus, just before he was to turn right toward Litany Lane, he came upon Manly talking intently to three students, one of whom was Claire. Another girl (a Coyote) and a boy unknown to Adrian were also parties to the conversation. Walking silently on crepe-soled shoes and slowing down as he neared Manly's back, Adrian heard him say petulantly, "You mean to say that you've actually gone to the Catholic Church with this Bucky Oaks person?"

"Yes," Claire admitted a little defiantly, her color rising, "but only because Bucky wanted me to, not because I believe in it."

"I wonder what your parents would think if they knew?" Manly asked, making no attempt to hide the threat implied by his tone of voice.

"They'd be furious," she said candidly, noticing Adrian's approach but giving Bro. Plumwell no hint of it.

"I'm sure you know," he declared, holding a forefinger close to her nose, "that the Catholic Church is not a full-gospel church, and—"

"Neither is yours," said a voice that Manly was trying hard not to hate.

"It most certainly is," Manly retorted, turning and thinking of how the Handmaiden had restored the long overlooked doctrine of three-world creationism to gospel preaching.

"Do you heal the sick in your church?" Adrian asked.

"I do not," Manly replied, "but Miss Alice has, and others too."

"Do you raise the dead?"

"No."

"Neither you, nor Miss Alice, nor any other new Jews raise the dead?"

"Not that I know of."

"In the tenth chapter of Matthew, Jesus tells his disciples to heal the sick, cast out demons, and raise the dead. Was that directive ever revoked that you know of?"

"No," said Manly reluctantly, "I suppose not."

"Why don't you do those things then?"

"Because the Lord has given various gifts to different Christians, that's why."

"Do you take up poisonous serpents and drink deadly things in your denomination?"

"No," said Manly, angered by the word "denomination."

"Why not?"

"It is written that you shall not tempt the Lord God, that's why," Manly said righteously.

"That's a cop-out. The Scriptures don't say that you would be tempting God or toying with him in doing those things. Somewhere in Luke—chapter

10, I think—it says that Christians have been given authority to tread on serpents and scorpions and that nothing shall hurt them."

"That's your interpretation," Manly said lamely.

"Interpretation, hell! Moreover, the ninety-first psalm says that believers can trample lions underfoot and dragons too—Komodo dragons, I suppose."

At that Manly merely looked contemptuous and refused to speak.

"It's really too bad you Christians don't do more of those sorts of things," Adrian said, rubbing it in, "because then I think your numbers would be greatly reduced and the noxious influence you wield over people might be weakened."

Deeply bruised though he was from Adrian's rough handling, Manly was less distressed for himself than he was for Claire. Most emphatically, he did not want her to hear the awful things DeWulf was saying; no! no more than he wanted her to stay away from his church, as she had been doing, nor to fall prey to Catholicism; but he could think of no way to stop her ears from hearing, no way to shelter her from the spiritual filth that apostate was spewing from his mouth.

Not really wanting to maul Manly any more but intent on rescuing Claire from any influence the royal priest might have over her and to deliver her altogether from the shackles of Christianity, Adrian said to Manly, wagging a forefinger under his nose, "No, despite the doctrinal hobby-horse you ride, you're not about to follow the full gospel any more than other Christians. You're not about to give away your jacket as well as your overcoat. In weather like this, you'd freeze, and you know it. And you do take thought of the morrow; you do plan what you're going to say rather than waiting upon the Spirit to do your speaking for you. And you're certainly not persecuted for your faith as Jesus predicted his followers would be; no, you're praised for it, and paid for it, and treated as a leader in society, at least by some."

Shifting gears, Adrian went on, "You know what I'm going to do? I'm going to help you follow the Lord's command and send every student I run across who needs money to see you for it, because, according to full-gospel teaching, Christians are supposed to give freely to those who ask of them, not expecting to receive in return. In fact, I think I may even apply for some funds right now." With that, he held out his right hand, palm upward, mockingly.

Then, noticing that the other Coyote and the unknown boy had slipped away in the heat of battle and recognizing that Manly was livid, that he had been pushed dangerously far, Adrian said softly, "Claire, I'll walk you wherever you were going." It was the first time he had ever called her by her given name, and that fact was not lost on her. How easily, how naturally he had said it. Nor was it lost on Manly that the two proceeded toward campus as close to one another as though they had been walking arm in arm. Never before had he been accused of hypocrisy, and seldom, if ever, had he felt so horrid.

The Dodge Praeville sex scandal rocked Algonquin State as nothing had ever rocked it before. Dodge was a junior from Milwaukee majoring in economics, and an amateur photographer of rare artistry. Perceiving a market at Algonquin and on other campuses for what were commonly called "dirty pictures" but what he called "photographic erotica," he proceeded to turn his hobby into a thriving business. Two of his accomplices were proctors in Callowell Hall, the men's dormitory where he lived. The proctors managed to supply him with a double room featuring a nonexistent roommate, the latter providing space for Dodge's equipment. The proctors' sentry duties plus a Do Not Disturb sign, which one of them had swiped from a motel, provided him with the requisite peace and quiet at crucial times. They also helped to get his so-called business associates into and out of the dorm without attracting attention. This was not extraordinarily difficult, since Dodge's favorite times for shooting were between 4:00 A.M. and 8:00 A.M. on Saturday mornings, when the campus was still sleeping off Friday night, and between 6:00 A.M. and 10:00 A.M. on Sunday mornings, when the campus was either asleep or in church or both. His third accomplice was a maintenance man who kept a former storeroom in the basement of Callowell, which had been turned into a darkroom, under surveillance at crucial times and under lock and key at all other times, the lock being impossible to open with any key issued to campus personnel. Occasionally, the maintenance man, who was young and of craggy appearance, also posed in varying degrees of nudity and in varying stages of tumescence. Dodge's business associates (two-thirds of whom were female) were generally ASU students, although one of his most engaging models was a certain *marmalade maid* who was only a junior in high school.

Possessed of excellent entrepreneurial skills, Dodge devised a system whereby the more salacious the photograph, the higher the price per print and the greater the cut for the models. His system was a classic example of how the free enterprise system can utilize incentive while at the same time stimulating it. Indeed, his models, most of whom were very shy and awkward at first, soon strove to outdo themselves. Moreover, in recruiting, he also spoke of the "piece system," by which he meant "the better the piece, the more money in the system." In that manner, he was able to attract stunning young women and handsome young men to his enterprise. Dodge was, undeniably, a multifaceted genius. With his mild manner, soothing voice, democratic ways, and persistent sensuality, he was able to banish his models' inhibitions and inflame their prurience with ease, sometimes in one fell swoop. "Just posing for Dodge is like having an orgasm without the messy part," said one girl who insisted on anonymity. "When he looks at you or turns his camera on you, it's like being fondled all over deliciously all at once," said another girl, equally interested in anonymity.

Dodge had read somewhere that the next great breakthrough in erotica would come only when ways could be found that would turn on females as readily as males could be turned on with words or pictures. So, already knowing of male sensuality, Dodge focused on female sensuality in more ways than one. Being the kind of young man who, when he was well known by them, could loosen young women's tongues, he spent many rewarding moments with his would-be models educing their sexual fantasies and exploring, with a kind of free association, the nuances of their sensuality. As each one poured out the secrets of her carnality, Dodge looked at her caressingly and, in looking, saw visions, visions that he might subsequently capture on film. Despite the ungodly hours when he snapped his pictures, testosterone levels rose, love juices flowed, bidden and unbidden, and sighs of desire were emitted by Dodge and his associates. Given the erotic delerium he could conjure in his models and the mastery of his photography, it is no wonder that his business was brisk. All went well from the point of its inception in mid-October of the previous year until the middle of January, 1961, when one or more sleepless inmates of Callowell, or early risers therein, became unduly curious over certain unexpected arrivals in the wee hours of weekend mornings.

Sythian MacGilvary had long known the ecstasy of Algonquin's presidency. With the arrest of Dodge Praeville and several of his associates on a breath-taking variety of morals charges, Sythian came to know the agony. Caught flat-footed with no contingency plans for dealing with such an eventuality as that of hosting a studio for photographic erotica, Sythian acted with impulsive rectitude. Not content with suspending Dodge, pending a full investigation and appropriate legal action, Sythian summarily expelled him from ASU. That ill-advised act was to cause enormous grief. In the first place, the expulsion did not suffice to avert the public relations disaster that Sythian had instantly and accurately foreseen, and in the second place it opened a can of legal worms that prolonged the period of adverse publicity.

As though the "bare facts" (as one Chicago daily put it) of the Algonquin sex scandal were not enough, a New York tabloid caught wind of the term *marmalade maid* and ferreted out ASU's unofficial glossary of maids, which it proceeded to publish in its recently updated form. The news of Dodge's arrest had, of course, no sooner hit the campus than *portrayed maid* was added, designating any female who posed in the buff, posturing pruriently or acting salaciously for an artist or photographer. Then, as the names (or rumors of names) and life stories (or rumors of life stories) or photographs of certain portrayed maids began to surface, new terms were added. When it was discovered that one of Dodge's models was both frigid and rich and had posed mainly for the excitement of it all, *escapade maid* entered the glossary. Any likely female who was coy about whether she had or hadn't posed, or did or didn't practice what she posed, was known as an *evade maid*. In due course, the term came to designate any female who refused to disclose what kind of a maid she was. *Parade maid* entered the glossary, designating one who was willing to strut her stuff but not to share it with anyone interested in more than the eye's delights, and *charade maid* was included to refer to one who pretends or entices but does not deliver, i.e., a cock tease. Thus, through the aforementioned tabloid, ASU's glossary of maids became the common property of American college students, being vulgarized in the process, naturally, and coming to include such questionable entries as *administrative-aid maid, cascade maid, degrade maid, grenade maid, jock-aid maid, par-layed maid*, and *touchéd maid*, most of whose definitions are too tasteless to be printed. Sythian, of course, was truly mortified by that kind of publicity but not more so than when he learned that *Seraglio*, the notorious magazine for ostensible gentlemen, had contracted with Dodge and certain of his associates to feature some of their more dazzling efforts. Inevitably, ASU came to be known as ASS U, and the school was soundly attacked for fostering immorality by several of the more venal state legislators who hoped thereby to rehabilitate their own moral credibility with the voters. More seriously, personal sources of gifts and monies dried up, chief among whom was Mr. Estes Bantermann, a long-time benefactor, who suddenly broke his promise to give his estate, Sylvan Dells, to ASU as an off-campus center for continuing education, giving it instead to nearby Laurentian College. Most seriously, the *Signal Flare* seized upon Dodge's expulsion as the basis for a spirited attack on ASU's administration.

A reporter for the *Signal Flare* discovered that, in kicking Dodge out, old "Syth the Scythe" had by-passed the Discipline Committee and had acted on a provision, hitherto unused, in the "Braves Behavior Code (BBC)" enabling the president to take definitive action whenever an emergency threatened the well-being of the university.

Armed with that information, the editor of the paper accused President MacGilvary of "high-handed, despotic, and un-American tactics" in expelling Dodge. "Elsewhere in the United States," the editor wrote, "a person is presumed to be innocent until proven guilty, but at ASU, one is punished first, conviction, if at all, coming later." Ending with the observation that the president's drastic action had subjugated Dodge to double jeopardy, the *Signal Flare* offered the accused every form of succor and assistance at its disposal.

Heartened by the editorial, Dodge not only conferred with his attorney concerning his defense in city court but also explored the possibility of legal action against Sythian MacGilvary and ASU, charging that his civil liberties had been violated. Nor was Dodge at all reluctant to disclose such legal explorations to the media, the result being a number of news stories variously captioned, "School May Be Sued for Rights Violation," "Algonquin State in Denial of Rights Case," and "Student to Sue College Prexy."

Felix Molineaux, Assistant Dean of Student Affairs and a principal mouthpiece for the administration in time of trouble, wrote to the *Signal Flare*, pointing out that attendance at ASU was not a right but a privilege and that the institution had the right, in law, to discipline those privileged to attend in ways it would never dream of disciplining those not privileged to attend.

The *Signal Flare* responded editorially by pointing out that the constitutional rights of the privileged are guaranteed as surely as those of the underprivileged (those not allowed to attend ASU), that not even so exalted a code as the BBC could nullify the rights of American citizens in attendance. Furthermore, the paper challenged the administration to show how "Dodge's caper" had created an "emergency for the university."

Felix had wanted to write back saying that anything that embarrassed the administration (especially the president), that alienated state legislators and the general public, and that made fund raising more difficult than normal was an emergency, but Sythian would have none of it, because it seemed to him to be self-serving as stated. "I have been guided by the highest ideals in this matter," he told Felix heatedly, "and have acted only on principle, not on expediency!"

The sociology and political science clubs co-sponsored a student symposium on the topic, "What Constitutes Lewd, Indecent, Obscene, and Sexually Disorderly Conduct?" Other campus groups debated such topics as "Freedom of Expression," "Artistic License," "The Human Body as Natural Beauty," and "Sex as a Mode of Communication." The conclusion most often reached by the various symposia, forums, etc. was that the ASU administration was repressive of students.

Meanwhile, the clergy, local and regional, were stimulated into what can only be called homiletical frenzy, no less by the topics being discussed on campus than by that which had provoked those topics in the first place.

A letter to the *Signal Flare*, co-signed by more than a dozen students, said that since "obscene" means "offensive," "disgusting," or "repulsive," and since President MacGilvary's expulsion of Dodge Praeville was offensive, disgusting, and repulsive, it followed that the president had acted obscenely. The letter ended by asking why the Board of Trustees had not expelled him from the presidency as he had expelled Dodge from the student body.

With pressure building and no end in sight, Sythian, tearing his silvery hair in private, called the Board into extraordinary session, hoping for a vote of confidence. That proved absurdly easy for him to get, one of the Trustees, a Mr. Redford (Red) Hepple, volunteering on the spot to defend President MacGilvary at a rap session with the students in general or their representatives.

Two days later, Red, who was the owner of the Braves Buick and GMC Truck Company in downtown Algonquin, returned to the campus to meet with the officers of the Student Government Association and the editorial staff of the *Signal Flare*. As the fiery session proceeded, the plight of Dodge Praeville was largely forgotten in favor of subsequent disputes between students, student groups, and the school paper on the one hand and Red and ASU's administration on the other. The students laid claim to rights that the Constitution did not guarantee and that the Supreme Court had not imputed to them. Red laid claim to institutional rights that the framers of the Constitution had never dreamed of and that the Justices of the Supreme Court had only dreamed of, and then only in their most fitful sleep. Finally, with his patience wearing very thin, Red moved the dispute to different footings.

352

"Listen," he said, "if you Yahoos want to attack the administration, you should attack it for the way it has always bent over backwards to coddle you people." At that, a great clamor arose, pommeling Red's reddened ears. "If I'd had my way," he roared, "I'd have closed the school paper down the very minute it attacked President MacGilvary's handling of this awful, disgusting Praeville affair." Cries of "Censorship," "It's a free country," and "What about freedom of the press?" rent the air of the Powwow Room. When, at last, he could be heard above the din, Red, in a moment of high inspiration, yelled, "Listen, if any of you can show me any place in the New Testament where it says the students on a school paper have the right to attack the administration of that school, like you have, then I'll believe it." Stunned by the challenge and clearly unequal to it, the students could only mutter impotently among themselves, and thus the meeting ended.

After reading the issue of the *Signal Flare* that contained the transcript of the students' meeting with Trustee Hepple, Adrian, still smouldering over the threat of his own early dismissal, wrote the most injudicious, the most intemperate letter of his life. It ended with the incendiary words:

"If Mr. Redford (Red) Hepple can show us anywhere in the New Testament where higher education is mentioned, hinted at, or even conceived of, or if he can show us anything in its pages even remotely resembling a university, or if he can point out any person in it occupying a position even faintly like that of a trustee of a university board, then perhaps we can take seriously his otherwise utterly inane ethical challenge to the students. But, of course, he cannot. The incredible incongruity of his challenge has simply escaped him.

"It is hard to be sanguine about an institution of higher education any of whose directors can give vent to anything so fatuous, and it is to be feared that he is not alone. Indeed, as we consider the composition of Algonquin's Board of Trustees, one of whom is a former state forester, another of whom is the pharmacist-owner of a drugstore chain, another the manager of a logging operation, another the administrator of an osteopathic hospital, another a hydraulics engineer, another an oil geologist, another a purveyor of mortuary paraphernalia, in addition to Mr. Hepple, the owner of a Buick-GMC dealership, they resemble nothing, in educational background, so much as the members of the Central Committee of the Presidium of the USSR."

If Sythian had not been consumed with the Praeville public relations disaster and momentarily loath to face additional troubles, Adrian would have been fired on the spot. Even Rad was aghast at the letter.

True to form, Manly hurried to his church, lurching with emotion, after Adrian had all but proved him a hypocrite and had then walked off arm in arm, to all appearances, with the one person Manly wanted most of all to return to the fold. Back in the sanctuary, where his spirit had so often been rejuvenated, he paced and prayed, prayed and paced, and stared for long moments at Bro. Cricklet's wonderful windows. Finally, he slumped onto the podium near the pulpit, eyes closed, face in his hands, elbows on his knees. As cold within his skin as the January night was cold outside the church, images of his life's worst moments skittered into consciousness, and out, and back again pell-mell. He saw his grandmother on her deathbed, glistening with yellow sweat, and felt himself being driven deeper and deeper into the permafrost of depression by the pile-driving force of her death. He was in the cemetery on Probasco Ridge daring to reach out to Tampa Rhine with something additional to Christian love, only to be seared by the blowtorch of her profanity and blown away by her rage. There stood Jed Bantry, bullet-shaped and abusive, thrusting a chamber pot at his guest and bellowing his sarcastic conviction that even that guest, poor excuse of a man that he was, would know how to use the thing in time of need. The pot was evaporated by Elaine Beuhler Wren, leering at him in the post office and laughing explosively about a telling trail of water from the baptistry to the folding doors of the women's dressing room at the church in Nickel Plate. Elaine's obscene prattle gave way to Bert Hodger, snarling with rage, ". . . if you ever darken the door to my place again, I'm gonna spread that story about you [and the burleque dancer] all over Pilsudski County, and if you ever even so much as hint that you'd like to have God kill my kid so my wife can come to that damned church of yours, I'll break you up so bad you won't even have a lap for no bare naked stripper to fall into." He was on a forty-foot ladder at Big Bend nearing one of the chateau's many roofs. His hands, not yet callused, were protesting the wire handle of the paint pail that he transferred from one sore hand to the other; his thighs, not yet toughened by climbing, rebelled at every new rung, up or down. He was exhausted, dazed by all the memorization required of him in his studies, and despairing of ever becoming a royal priest, but then *she* had come to him, the Handmaiden of the Lord, and she had said to him, "Be of good cheer, young Brother Plumwell, the Lord never, ever burdens one of his own with more than that precious one can bear. Oh, he ladens us to the breaking point, but he does it not to break us but that we might grow stronger to do his wonderful work. Praise His Holy Name!"

Heartened by those recollections of Miss Alice in his early days at Big Bend, Manly opened his eyes in the darkened sanctuary, lifted his head, and rose up refreshed. The Handmaiden's words were, after all, perfectly true. The Lord had not burdened him to the breaking point. He had borne all the burdens of his past and triumphed over them, or at least survived them, to do pioneering work for JEsus and his Holy Nation at ASU. Most likely, God had greater challenges ahead for him, Manly thought, with which he could not contend successfully without first having overcome the apostate. Surely he could handle anyone if he could handle DeWulf. If he could only handle DeWulf!

No longer pacing in distress, Manly began to stroll more self-confidently up one dark aisle and down another. No longer praying that he might triumph over the apostate, he pondered anew as to how he was to do it. Turning up the center aisle for the umpteenth time, the words of Emmet Langhorne Van Hook suddenly rang out in his head: "You must remember, young brothers and sisters in the Lord, it is sin that unites us, not just those of us who have been redeemed by the Blood of the Lamb, but unites all humankind everywhere and at all times. Yes, we are all one in our common sinful humanity. That is the bridge between every one of us and every other person. It is not that we Christians are sinless, just that we are forgiven." With those words resounding in his head, Manly discovered a new way to approach DeWulf, a way which he would act upon at once, a way that, with God's grace, might also help him get his mind off that fascinating, repulsive Dodge Praeville person and the awful sex scandal that had engulfed Algonquin, causing Manly and many others to pollute themselves in God's sight.

So, he gave up the guerrilla tactics he had adopted (tactics that had failed miserably) and resorted to the way he had previously renounced, i.e., he began to visit DeWulf in the latter's office again, but with a difference.

Aw, God, it's Plumwell, Adrian thought as the royal priest followed his own rapid knock into the office.

"I hope I'm not interrupting anything," Manly said, all smiles.

"Nothing that can't wait," Adrian answered, putting a marker in the book he had been reading and setting it aside reluctantly.

"Professor DeWulf, I think I owe you an apology," Manly said, embellishing his words with sincerity.

"Whatever for?" Adrian asked, apprehensive of the bathos of which Christians were sometimes capable.

"I have often spoken to you in anger," Manly confessed, "and . . ."

"Oh, think nothing of it," Adrian said hurriedly, dismissively, trying to forestall any breast-beating Manly might do.

"But I do think of it, because I've let my own self-love come between us in many of the . . . encounters we've had."

"Look, you and I both maintain our views vehemently, and they just happen to be in vital opposition, that's all," Adrian said reassuringly. "There's no need to take intellectual combat personally, I assure you."

"Be that as it may, I don't feel that I've manifested the love of my Lord JEsus to you the way I should have personally, and I bear a heavy burden because of that. In fact, my contacts with you, especially recently, have made me realize just how prideful, just how sinful, I really am sometimes."

Intellectually sinful because of the things you could know and should know but don't, Adrian thought but left unsaid.

"And," Manly continued, making a peak of his eyebrows, "I hope that you can find it in your heart to forgive me for the disrespectful ways in which I have . . ."

"There's nothing for me to forgive you for," Adrian said earnestly, protestingly, holding his hands out, palms down toward Manly.

"Still and all, I'm sure I've given you occasion to think ill of me and to

355

reject my Lord and my God because of my failures," Manly went on, "but knowing that there are no hard feelings between us does lighten my burdens."

At that, Adrian merely looked at Manly, unwilling to continue what to him was a pointless conversation, and the latter, sensing that the time to leave had come, arose and left with a friendly, "Thanks ever so much for your time, and God be with you till we meet again."

Leaving Adrian behind in his office (feeling slightly unclean from the unwanted apologies that had been heaped on him), Manly made two left turns, bounded down the tower stairs of the Ad. Building, went out onto the snowy campus, and strode toward Wheelwright Hall where Atherton Landis had his office. As a professor of Family and Child Development, Atherton had to traffic continuously in psychological concepts, jargon, and literature, some of which he could bend to his own fundamentalist Christian purposes. He had often tried to entice Manly to make use of carefully selected psychological musings in his sermons and pastoral counseling sessions, but Manly, ever wary of psychology and psychologists, had always resisted. "After all," he pointed out to Atherton, "God's Word has everything in it I need to know about human nature." But having put his relationship with the apostate on a more promising foundation, Manly decided that psychology might be another girder in the bridge he was building.

Atherton was both pleased to see his pastor and free at the moment "to discuss some things in general," as Manly put the purpose of his visit. And discuss some things in general they did, profitably for Manly, or so it seemed at the time. The only thing that bothered him was that Atherton seemed more intensely preoccupied with the Dodge Praeville affair (alluding to it distressingly often) than professional considerations warranted. The result of that was speedy self-abuse on Manly's part, but, still and all, the visit to Atherton had been worth it to get a better grip on what some of the great psychologists had had to say about religion.

"Look, I'm not a psychologist; I don't know about all that stuff," Adrian protested, feigning ignorance in the hope of forestalling a pointless conversation with Manly.

"I'm sure you know a lot more about it than I do . . ."

Sure I know a lot more about it than you do, Adrian thought as Manly burbled on.

"And I would really like to get your opinion on some psychological teachings, from a philosophical point of view, that is."

"I suppose there's no time like the present," Adrian replied dubiously, putting his overcoat back on the hook from which he had just taken it preparatory to walking home at the end of a blustery day. He was not surprised at seeing Manly per se (though the hour was a bit unusual), but he was surprised at seeing him again so soon (a scant two days following their previous encounter). The greatest source of surprise, however, ought to have been the change in Manly's mood. Gone was the confessional air, the apologetic tenor, of their last meeting, and gone was the abrasiveness of their

356

earlier encounters. Acting as though all had been forgiven and forgotten (though Adrian had neither asked for forgiveness nor given any nor forgotten anything), Manly exhibited nothing short of ebullience as he sat down to talk about psychology, from a philosophical perspective, that is.

Unaware that he was the target of a one-man crusade and oblivious to the fact that Manly had subjected him to a variety of tactics designed to humble him first, then to convert him, and was, even then, trying out a new ploy, Adrian asked, a hint of resignation coloring his voice, "Now what is it exactly that's on your mind, Brother Plumwell?"

"I'd just like to hear what you think of what the great psychologist Jung had to say about religion."

"Which was what?" Adrian asked, knowing that Jung had had a mouthful and then some to say about religion but that he had never said any of it the same way twice, not prizing clarity and coherence.

"That among all his patients the problem was fundamentally one of finding a religious outlook on life."

"I never know from one minute to the next what that guy means," said Adrian. Then, with a smile playing at the corners of his mouth, he asked, "By the way, have you read much Jung?"

"No, not much," Manly admitted reluctantly, "but what I just quoted makes good sense to anyone, like myself, who deals with spiritual problems."

"Except that you didn't quote it correctly, and in the correct form it doesn't apply to me at all," Adrian answered, refusing to take Manly seriously and deflecting the conversation from its original course.

Straining to keep his composure, Manly said, "How can you say that?"

"Because what Jung said was that of all his patients in the second half of life, beyond thirty-five or so, he had found the problem to be the lack of a religious outlook. Since I'm still in the first half of my life, it doesn't concern me. Come back in six or seven years, then we'll see."

"I should think," Manly said very deliberately, "that if spiritual problems underlie mental illness in people over thirty-five, then the roots of those problems would start earlier in . . . in the sins of youth."

"Could be," Adrian admitted breezily, "but Brother Plumwell, you can't take much comfort in what Jung said, because he didn't mean the same thing by 'religious outlook' that you do, not by a long, long, long shot."

That left Manly, who had never read a word of Jung, tongue-tied.

"Of course, you know that he progressively gave up orthodox religious beliefs after his famous dream," Adrian mused, looking over Manly's head at the ceiling.

"What famous dream?"

"Why, the one he had when he was about twelve or so, the one in which he saw God drop an immense . . . ah . . . turd on a beautiful cathedral, simply smashing the whole thing, just smothering it in, if you'll excuse the expression, 'shit.'" As Manly grimaced at that odious image, Adrian went on merrily, observing that that's exactly what Jung would have felt like doing if he had ever heard of three-world creationism—just crapping on it.

"Do you know Atherton Landis?" Manly asked, changing his subject abruptly but clinging to his goal stubbornly.

"No, but I've heard the name mentioned; why?"

"He was at a meeting of psychologists not long ago with the great psychiatrist Karl Menninger and heard Menninger say that what we need to do in dealing with people is to get 'sin' back into our vocabulary again."

"'Sin' is a theological concept having to do primarily with anything that's offensive to God; what would a psychiatrist know about such things?"

"Why wouldn't he?" Manly asked lamely.

"Psychiatrists are trained to deal with human beings in various psychosocial contexts, not with what offends God a little bit, pisses him off quite a lot, or gets him madder'n hell. Psychiatrists don't know anything about such things, any more than you or I do."

Trying hard not to be affronted but grasping for straws, Manly said, "A lot of famous psychologists, including some of the really great ones, say that we are religious because it's our nature to be that way."

Then, before Manly had a chance to add that it was God who had made man with a religious nature, Adrian cut in: "You mean it's our biological nature to be religious due to the way primates like us evolved, or what?"

"*No!* No, we're not animals; we didn't evolve; God created us exactly the way we are," Manly all but shouted, showing sparks of temper as the old bugaboo of evolution came up.

"So you say."

"So the *Bible* says!"

"So the Bible says; so what?"

"Well, it is God's Word, you know."

"So you say."

"No, *it* says so; God doesn't lie."

"Brother Plumwell," Adrian said, hoping to end their futile conversation, "have you ever discussed these subjects with Abe Bronznowski in the psychology department?"

"No."

"Well, he's the very one you should see. He also has a fabulous cure that he thinks is a lot better than Jung's. I simply cannot urge you enough to see him at your earliest convenience. Would you do that? You could mention my name if you like."

"All right, I will," Manly promised, feeling a strong need at that moment to do something definite, something decisive, rather than thrashing around with DeWulf any longer, getting nowhere. When Manly finally pulled himself out of the quagmire of their conversation and left the office, Adrian waited for him to get out of earshot, then laughed at the ceiling with explosive barks, his eyes watering with glee. What great good fun it was just to anticipate the riot of Manly's first meeting with Abe Bronznowski! Indeed, every few minutes, as Adrian slogged his way home through three inches of new snow, he laughed uproariously (insanely, a chance observer might have thought) and was still chuckling as he climbed the stairs at No. 5, Litany Lane.

Abraham Bronznowski, a primatologist by training, a profane evolutionist by conviction, and the foremost exponent of dendrotherapy at ASU (or maybe anywhere else on God's green earth), descended—quite literally descended—into Adrian's life. He had done so on a clear crisp Saturday morning early in the preceding November. Adrian had awakened on the morning in question with an overpowering yen for some freshly baked cinnamon rolls. So, he had dressed quickly, not bothering to shave, and had set off at a good clip toward the nearest bakery. Straight ahead of him at the end of Litany Lane a silvery ladder angled up into the reddish brown leaves of a gigantic oak. Just as he reached the base of the ladder, a wiry little man of uncertain age, almost as brown as the oak's leaves, plummeted down the ladder carrying a cat.

"What fun!" Adrian exclaimed for want of something better to say.

"Yes, yes, how very true!" exulted the man, who then deposited the cat gently on the sidewalk and said, "Now don't you worry, Eartha, I'll be glad to get you down whenever you get chased up a tree again." Straightening up and turning toward Adrian, he said intensely, "See, I pluck all the neighbor's cats out of trees when they get up and can't get down again."

"How very enviable and . . . and how very admirable!" Adrian replied, bemused and bantering.

Taking those words to be heartfelt, and thus a recommendation of Adrian's worthiness, the man (who turned out to be Abraham Bronznowski, dendrotherapist) began to pour forth a torrent of words, his eyes snapping with excitement and his hands carrying on a supportive conversation of their own.

"When I was just a little kid, of maybe three or four, back home in Hickory, North Carolina, I had my first proto-orgasmic experience up a tree. I was hanging from this branch, see, and trying to hook my legs over it. Well, I just couldn't get up the steam to do it, so I started to kick my legs like I was riding a bicycle, see, thinking that I could get up some momentum that way and swing up and over. I couldn't, but the kicking was as good as if I'd shot my wad. (Of course that didn't happen until almost ten years later after a boy played with my pecker for a half hour or more.) Anyhow, I sure climbed a lot of trees trying to recapture that first proto-orgasmic episode. God, it was good! I guess people thought I was crazy all the time up in trees riding a bicycle to all appearances. But what did those bastards know about it? Then, later on, I read Hooten's book, *Why Men Behave Like Apes and Vice-Versa,* and it really turned me on. In fact, I even read it up in trees. Anyway, when I got to Wisconsin, see, to study with Harlow, it occurred to me that for a fuckin' latter-day monkey like man, climbing trees ought to be like going home again—not geographically, see, but temporally, over millions of years.

I mean in evolutionary terms. Anyway, I'm getting ahead of my story. I studied the importance of clinging to various kinds of monkeys, see, and created some real loonies by depriving juvenile monkeys of handholds and the like. God, they just flip their lids when you put 'em in environments where they can't grab ahold of anything or climb up into anything. Later on, I turned my attention to autistic children and got some interesting results. Shit, I thought when I was hired here I was going to get to work with a variety of retardates, using my theories, but at this goddamned place all the retardates are in the administration and not the labs where I need them. See, I've theorized that what I call 'dendrotherapy'—climbing trees, clinging to branches and the like, or swinging on branches and bars—is therapeutic under certain circumstances for certain dysfunctions. Hell, if I can ever get out of this fuckin' place and get a decent position at a university that's got some visibility, because it's respectable, and not just a crap-heap like ASU, I might get some professional recognition. Of course, in a goddamned Christian culture like ours, people think you're bananas whenever you go up a tree unless it's to get a fuckin' cat down. How in the hell can you help people when the very thing they need to be doing—especially to relieve stress situations and certain kinds of anxiety-producing environments—is looked on like it was crazy? By God! if the neighbors around here got their own cats down out of the trees, they'd all be a hell of a lot better off for it. Of course, then I wouldn't get all the fun and all the benefits I do, but still, you'd think these fuckin' assholes would have enough sense to realize that trees hold security for animals like us. Goddam it, if I didn't get to climb a fuckin' tree every now and then, I'd feel so insecure I'd blow my stack and start screaming at the wife and kids. Why, shit, I even chase cats up trees, when nobody's looking, so that I can save the little sons of bitches. Otherwise I wouldn't be able to climb trees at all without being laughed at, or ridiculed, or looked on like one more schizy psych-prof."

Adrian, as you might imagine, was absolutely delighted with Abe Bronznowski and doubly delighted that Manly was going to meet him.

The next time he saw Manly (after Manly had promised to talk with the dendrotherapist), Adrian didn't know whether to laugh or head for the hills. He was walking toward Antrim Library—it was mid-morning—and Manly, apparently very excited, was angling across campus as fast as his ministerial dignity would permit. "Hey, Dr. DeWulf," he yelled, "wait up." His next words convinced Adrian that there was no need yet to head for the hills. "I've got some great good news." Then, still a dozen yards away, he added, "You might really be interested in this." Finally, coming to a stop, Manly said breathlessly, "I just got a letter from Holy Nation headquarters, and guess what."

"What?" Adrian asked, as cold as the snow that carpeted the ground.

"The Handmaiden of the Lord, Miss Alice McAlister, has accepted an invitation to speak *here* during the religious emphasis week this coming spring."

"So?" Adrian said, turning down the corners of his mouth.

"Aren't you even the slightest bit interested?" Manly asked, fighting off plunging disappointment.

"Brother Plumwell, why in the hell should I take delight in learning that the high school drop-out who cooked up three-world creationism is coming to an institution of higher learning, so-called, to spout off her superstitions to the dumb-dumbs—faculty and students alike—who don't know any better than to go hear her?"

"Oh, you're so dogmatic," Manly hissed, "so judgmental, so quick to reject anything that has to do with true Christianity. Why, you won't even give other people a chance to make their point."

"Have it your way," Adrian said, about to push past the royal priest on the way to the library.

Catching his arm, restraining him, Manly said fervently, "Dr. DeWulf, Miss Alice is the most powerful, the most Holy Ghost-inspired person, and the greatest religious leader in the world. If you'd only listen to her, you'd know that nobody can do the things she does without God. You know, your very soul is at stake, your salvation is hanging in the balance, and yet you won't even listen to the message of the Lord JEsus. You just turn your back on God. I know that if you'd simply go to hear his Handmaiden one time, your questions would be answered and your doubts put to rest once and for all. Please say that you will."

"Brother Plumwell," Adrian retorted icily, "if I should go to hear this Handmaiden of yours—and I almost certainly won't—then I would do so just for the curiosity of it all, sort of like going to a carnival to see the freaks. From what I've heard from you about your Miss Alice, she must be one of the prize simpletons of our time. Now, if you'll excuse me, I want to get to the library—to improve my mind."

Claire came. Sticking her head into Adrian's office after the briefest of knocks, she said, "Could I bother you for a while?"

"No, I don't think you could," he answered.

"Aw, damn!" she said, visibly disappointed. "Maybe some other time, then?"

"No," he said.

"No what?" she asked, confusion compounding her disappointment.

"No, I do not think that you could bother me just now, nor do I think it likely that you could bother me at any other time. I just do not think it's part of your nature, Miss Sumner, to bother me. So, why don't you just get yourself in here and stop making a scene?"

"You know, I don't take this kind of treatment from anybody else but you," she announced, standing over him and making a fist, but hardly able to keep from laughing. She had sworn to herself that she would not let him catch her that way again, but he had done it, and with the greatest of ease.

"So, what's on your mind?" he asked, looking at her appreciatively, delighting in how superbly her mind was housed.

"I just want to talk to you for a while," she said. "I know I'm wasting your time, but I just want to talk for a while."

"Okay, so take a pew and talk," he said, closing the book on his desk, not at all begrudging her the time he would have spent finishing it.

That afternoon, they spoke of many things collected loosely around themes of religion, self, psychology, and sex—not love, but sex. Draped over an office chair, more graceful than a cat, she initiated their talk with religion. After all, that legitimized her visit, made the waste of his time (if waste it were) professionally acceptable. Of course, to Adrian, her being there needed no legitimizing, but that was his secret (one she could not have known for sure), and she was not presumptuous about her intuitions respecting him. Laughingly adverting to the fact that the kids in his philosophy of religion class were at sixes and sevens as to whether or not he was an honest-to-God atheist, Claire, screwing up her courage, asked him pointedly, "Are you?"

"Emotionally, yes; logically, no," came the speedy answer. Then, breaking into the quizzical silence that enfolded her, he added, "In terms of feeling and action, I live as though there were no supreme being, but, logically, the question of divine existence depends on what, if anything, the word 'God' names, names properly and uniquely." Hearing the words clearly, reaching for their meaning, but not fully grasping that meaning, Claire settled on noting that some of the kids thought that he was actually an agnostic and not really an atheist. "Look," he said, leaning toward her intently, his hands outstretched, palms up, "everybody is an atheist, an agnostic, and a believer all rolled up in one, but not about the same thing. Everybody denies existence to gods he thinks are nonexistent, just make-believe; everybody keeps an open mind about possible deities, as we humans comprehend possibility; and everybody affirms whatever deity or deities he believes in." Seeing uncertainty settle on her face, he said, "It's like this: you're an atheist yourself respecting Zeus and all the gods on Olympus, right? Right, and yet if you fully comprehend Plato's idea of a finite, craftsman deity, I think you'd be intrigued by it all and would probably say that it might be possible, but that you did not know, probably could not know. So, you'd be agnostic about that. But, with respect to Spinoza's deity, I think you'd have to agree that that God exists, if, that is, Spinoza was using the term 'God' properly."

"Which was what?" she blurted out, eyes wide with curiosity or, perhaps, hope.

"Which was that God is the causal order and structure of the universe, the nomological framework in which all happenings happen. Although I do not use the word 'God' in that way, I would be a believer in God's existence if I were convinced that that was the uniquely proper referent for the term."

No longer able to breathe the rarified air of his philosophic altitude, Claire descended quickly, pointing out how enormously different, how incredibly free, his thoughts were from the cut and dried stuff she had been

362

taught as a child. From that springboard she dived into reminiscences about herself (her increasingly sweet self to him), about her girlhood in the little town of Heather, about her parents' property out in the country, about her cats and dogs and the pet rabbit to which she had been so very good, about being brought up in the Church of Christ, and about her conversion, more or less, to the Holy Nation. How natural she was, he thought, how vivacious in recollection, how adorably unself-conscious as she relived her salad days. Then, when she began to slow down, he picked up a similar tale and told her of Valentine, of the sand hills of his home, of his college days at Chadron State, of TCU, of the Christmas Eve of his deliverance when he bestrode the Texas prairie free and alone, and finally of his expulsion from home. As each spoke of self to the other, encouraged and encouraging, the yawning gulf that usually separates professor from undergraduate shrank, becoming a mere strait over which each could leap with a little effort.

"Dr. DeWulf," Claire said, breaking in on his last reminiscences (always painful to him), "why are people religious?"

"Beats me," he said, making a wry smile.

"Come on, tell me," she went on, thinking he was teasing her.

"That's in your field."

"Psychology?"

"Sure, and anthropology, and probably, in the long run, biology."

After a long pause, she tapped his knee with a forefinger and said, "Yeah, but philosophers take all knowledge as their province—you said so yourself in class the other day—so, out with it."

Laughing at her cajolery, and loving her for it, he said, "Dear God—so to speak—I wish I knew! If I did, I'd rush into print and become famous, then I'd spend as much of the rest of my life as necessary trying to find an antidote for it."

"You really detest religion, don't you?"

"For its brainlessness, yes. It's so powerful and so blind. It scrambles brains and gets otherwise sensible people to go goose-stepping off after this father-figure and that messiah, this guru and that charismatic leader, this holy book and that sacred object."

"But it does meet needs."

"Of course, but intensifies those needs and increases gullibility in people, gullibility of the worst kind."

"But in a religion where God is love, that's not so bad, is it?" she asked a little wistfully, hoping to spare idealized Christianity.

"Is 'God is love' the same as 'Love is God'?" he asked sharply, startling her.

"Oh, I . . . I guess so, sure," she replied slowly.

"What kind of love, just any old kind?"

"Meaning what?"

"Well, take sexual love, for example. Do lovers create deity when they make love? Is that what it means to say God is love?"

"I think I'll be an *evade maid* and pass on that one," she said, a smile wreathing her face.

"I see that you're familiar with Algonquin's famous, or is it infamous, glossary of maids?" Adrian observed, laughing with her.

"Listen, I know every entry in it by heart," she said triumphantly, "and a flesh-and-blood example to go with just about every entry."

"Who would have thought it?" he mused aloud, wondering again just what kind of a maid she was and simultaneously feeling distaste at the thought of Bucky Oaks' nuzzling around her, probably knowing what kind of a maid she was. "I've decided, Miss Sumner, that you are a *cade maid,* in a certain special sense of the term," he said, plunging deeply into his vocabulary.

"A *what?*" she asked, her eyes widening as she ticked off the entries in the glossary, unable to believe she had missed one.

"A cade maid," he answered, pretending that it was the commonest term in the English language.

"Is that really a word?" she asked, sitting bolt upright, eyes twinkling.

"My dear young woman," he protested, "surely, you don't think I would make up a word, do you?"

"To vex me, you would," she fired back, trusting that intuition.

"Oh, perish the thought!"

"How do you spell it?"

"P-e-r-i-s-h."

"No, damn it, I mean whatever kind of maid you mentioned."

"C-a-d-e m-a-i . . ."

"I can spell 'maid'," she roared, looking put upon.

"Very good."

"What does it mean?"

"We have dictionaries," he said, then observed that there might not be one big enough for the job in his office at the moment.

"So, why don't you just tell me?"

"Students are encouraged to do some things on their own," he said loftily.

"Oh, come on, tell me."

"If I were a maid," he continued, "you could call me a *caid maid,* of words, that is."

"We're the same kind of maid! according to you?" she asked incredulously.

"No, this is different; this is 'c-a-i-d,' not 'c-a-d-e'."

"I suppose there's no point in asking you what a caid maid is."

"No, I wouldn't think so," he said, trying to sound mysterious.

"I'll get you for this," she erupted, resolving then and there to look up some big new words to spring on him.

Thus went the afternoon, ranging from banter to serious talk about her course in human sexuality, and from it to religion, and then to psychology, and back again. "Oh, my God!" Claire said suddenly as she glanced at the window above and behind him, "it's pitch black outside."

Looking over his shoulder, then at his watch, Adrian said, "No wonder; it's almost six o'clock on a winter's night."

"I know," she agreed, "and I've got to get myself [she almost said, 'my ass'] to the Coyote House, and on the double."

"So, get moving, girl," he admonished her, rising and helping her into her coat.

"Do you happen to know when I got here?" she asked in disbelief.

"No, but early," he replied, laying a hand on her shoulder.

"Just a little after two," she said, amazed at how they had abolished time.

"And there's still more to talk about," he mused.

"So, why don't you walk to the Coyote House with me, or part way, at least, and keep talking?" she asked, cocking her head to one side invitingly.

"Indeed, why don't I do that very thing!" he said, as though making a great discovery among unnumbered possibilities.

Unknown to them, it had misted late in the afternoon. Then the temperature had plunged. So, as they left the sidewalk and angled across the lawn toward the Coyote House, their feet crunched through an icing of ice into the cake of snow below. As they neared the House, talking continuously, except for punctuating laughter, a burly figure came toward them, looming darkly. "Oh God, it's Bucky Oaks," Claire said, sounding anxious to Adrian. Then, putting on a cheerful air, she greeted the hulking boy with a perky, "Hi, there." Bucky merely grunted at her and said nothing to the professor.

Turning from them, Adrian said to Claire, "See you in class tomorrow," and set off toward Litany Lane.

Bucky's next words were, "Where in hell have you been the whole afternoon?" Adrian could not hear her response above the crunch of his feet, but he was sure he heard Bucky respond, saying, "You bitch, you," or something like it, equally ugly.

What a damn shame she can't seem to get that jerky jock out of her life, Adrian thought, making a bad face.

The next day, February 7, 1961, was to be a day whose magic moments he knew he would never forget. The day dawned with leaden skies and bluster, threatening snow. At the office, he met Rad early and asked, "What do you think my chances are of being able to stay and teach through the spring quarter?"

"I haven't heard word one about that," Rad answered, "but in view of your diatribe in the paper, the one against our prominent trustee, Red Hepple, to say nothing of earlier attacks on ol' Syth, not very good, I should guess. So, prepare for the worst, and hope for the best."

The remainder of the work day went as usual, except that Claire did not attend class. That disturbed Adrian, because it was not like her to miss class, not his class anyway. Doubting that there was any objective cause for alarm, still and all, he couldn't get her out of his mind. That lout, Bucky Oaks, had been very angry when he had left her with him the previous evening.

About ten o'clock that night, Adrian, curled up in his big gray chair, tossed away one book and grabbed another. He was planning to write an article but first had a lot of background reading to do. No sooner had he started on the book he had just taken up than he heard a shy tapping on his door. Having had very few callers while at Algonquin and expecting none at that moment, he was more than puzzled. In fact, his eyes were narrow with suspicion as he opened the door and peered into the dimly lit hall. Claire stood there, not with the queenly stance she usually effected so effortlessly but with shoulders hunched and with uncertainty, if not consternation, etched on her face.

"I really need to talk to you," she said huskily.

"Why, certainly," he answered gravely, all thoughts of teasing her, as he usually did when she popped in on him unexpectedly, banished.

She could see the hesitancy in his eyes as he asked her in, and she knew how scrupulous he had been in treating all students professionally and equally, in giving no hint of his true feelings toward individuals. This might be the first time, she thought, that he had ever admitted an Algonquin student to his apartment. Moreover, she was a girl, they were alone, and she was required by curfew to be elsewhere very soon. In fact, she was not supposed to be where she was at all but was, rather, presumed to be in the Coyote House at that very moment, not having checked out properly. Similar thoughts raced through Adrian's mind, but, then, Claire had made no claim on him to treat her differently from other students, and he had given her no explicit reason to think that she had gotten closer to him than the arm's length distance at which he kept most people, colleagues and students alike.

Before he could offer her his one comfortable chair, she had pulled his typing chair away from its place by the typewriter stand and had sat down on it, but without taking off her coat. So, he sank into the gray chair, mystified and a little apprehensive. He was, of course, secretly delighted to see her, but resolved that she should not know that secret. No sooner was he seated than Claire, without preamble and as though talking to an intimate friend of long standing, began to pour out a tale of woe. "Since last evening, Bucky Oaks and I have been fighting just about every minute we've been together—that's why I missed class today." (Bucky had, in fact, physically prevented her from attending.)

Adrian said nothing to that disagreeable news but merely looked at her intently, waiting for her to go on.

Wiping her eyes, she continued shakily, "He demands that I drop your course."

Chilled by that prospect, Adrian pointed out to her, unnecessarily, that it was too late to pick up a replacement course and that if she dropped it, she'd lose the credit hours.

"Oh, I'm not worried about that," she said dismissively. "It's that he doesn't want me to study with you, or hear what you have to say, or even be with you in your office, or talk to you at all. He'd probably kill us both if he knew I was here right now."

Not really needing to ask why, Adrian, nevertheless, asked why.

"Because he hates you—I'm sorry to say it, but he hates you—and has ever since the night when you put that priest on the defensive at the Coyote House during religious emphasis week last fall. Bucky's a very, very big Catholic, and he thought I was going to join his church just for him. But ever since that night—ever since I got to know you—he knows that's out."

"I've never done anything to take you away from Bucky Oaks," Adrian protested self-righteously, as he thought how much he'd love to do so, and for more reasons than one.

"I know that, and I've told him so," she said, dissolving into tears (also for more reasons than one). After that, the conversation did not devolve on Bucky alone. On the contrary, Claire began talking about everything that concerned her.

As the night sped on past the curfew hour for Coyotes, the typewriter chair, bearing a gesticulating Claire, inched ever closer to Adrian until the two were knee to knee, her jean-clad thighs parted with unconcern. As she talked on and on with accelerating abandon and as Adrian responded, at first with measured concern, then with fair wisdom, and finally with burgeoning affection, each fell into the yawning vortex created by the other. The gulf between them caused by differences in age, in education, and in pedagogical roles narrowed to nothingness. At some point in their conversation, Claire, still gesturing, held one of Adrian's hands in her own, and his response was so fast as to be no response at all. Knees no longer touched knees in chance encounter but were being patted, calves and thighs soon being caressed.

No doubt it took an act of intention on somebody's part, perhaps an invitation was spoken, or perhaps their bodies spoke in voiceless communication. Whatever the case, Claire, her coat long since fallen to the floor, found herself enfolded on Adrian's lap in his big gray chair. Her eyes, which had earlier welled with tears of anger, were now brimming with tears of love. Chaste kisses gave way to less chaste kisses and were soon interspersed with the confident laughter of love.

In the magic moments that followed (hours in reality) the magnetic field of their new-found love seemed to need no human agency to work its miracles. It locked the door and turned off the light. It removed clothing, dropping various pieces in carefree piles between Adrian's gray chair and his bed. It threw off the bedspread and turned down the covers. It banished inhibition and melted all reserve. It created a sensuality so wise that no learning was needed for them to know each other, no art required to be one. And, forbidding all remorse, it let them spend and be spent in love. When fully spent, it blessed them with deep and childlike sleep in each other's arms, sheltered and sheltering. And thus, the night passed.

As the new day dawned, Claire and Adrian ratified the night with love's lubricity and whispered, each into the other's ear, that they would never again be separated. Then their love (so spontaneously given) began to exact the price of its suddenness, a price initially paid in the coin of confusion. Claire had planned only to talk with Adrian about the hell she was going through with Bucky, to warn him of possible trouble, and then to slip back into the Coyote House as furtively as she had slipped out. The question was whether or not she had been missed. Almost certainly she had, but maybe, just maybe, she had not. At Algonquin it was very serious when a sorority girl was absent overnight without permission, especially when she had checked in properly (leading the housemother to believe that all was well) only to slip out again. Claire could only guess at the additional penalty for having made unexpected love with a faculty member who also happened to be her teacher—something on the order of forty lashes at high noon on the campus green, no doubt. No, in some ways worse than that, for there were precedents at ASU in which girls had been expelled from school and embroiled in almost endless hassles with their parents. Adrian's uncertainty, simple in comparison with Claire's confusion, stemmed from any adverse effect their love, if known, might have on his future employability at Algonquin. Then more than ever (almost infinitely more) he did not want to be separated from the joy, delight, and love of his life, even for a short time. It had been made amply clear to new faculty that ASU frowned on student-faculty fraternization (to say nothing of sex relations), and understandably so. As the lovers dressed and breakfasted hurriedly, dithering all the while, one thing was clear. An ordinary day lay ahead of them which they had to get through—somehow.

Claire did not want to see any of her sister Coyoties that day. She did not want to have to fend off their sly looks, to explain herself, or to hear the bad news that the housemother knew of her absence, nor did she want to be seen by anyone who might notice that she was wearing yesterday's clothes, somewhat the worse for a night on the floor.

"Hey Claire," yelled the Coyote who looked like Raggedy Ann, "where were you?" then added, "you devil, you."

"No comment," Claire said in dismay.

"Well," Raggedy Ann went on, "you'd better get your ass over to the House first thing, because Nympha Mae's madder'n a wet hen at you, and Bucky, well, he's really pissed off."

"Bucky knows too?" Claire gasped in disbelief, instantly nauseated.

"Oh, sure, everybody knows you were out all night, but not where, who with, or doin' what."

Not a single word in her first class registered on Claire that day. She had far too much to mull over. By the end of the hour, however, she had sorted things out tentatively. She would go straight to Nympha Mae Haskins and admit her guilt but would not reveal where she had been and would thus leave unanswered the inevitable question as to whether or not she had been with anybody. In taking that tack, she wasn't so much trying to protect

Adrian from ASU's administration as from Bucky Oaks. She didn't know much about his troubles with the former, but she could easily envision potential trouble with the latter. As for herself, she felt a paramount need to buy as much time as possible, time in which to comprehend what had happened, to think, and to plan. Beyond that, she wanted to keep her parents in ignorance as long as possible. Their first reaction to the news that she had broken the particular rule she had broken would be horror mixed with hurt. Then, if and when they discovered that she had fallen in love with an atheist, had actually made love to him, and, worst of all, wanted to marry him, they would be incensed, following which all hell would break loose. They hadn't even learned of her year-long involvement with Bucky (she hadn't dared to tell them), because they held Catholics in contempt, as did all new Jews of the Holy Nation. No words, of course, could express the loathing they felt toward atheists (though they knew none). To learn that their own flesh and blood had been one flesh with an atheist would, she supposed, be tantamount to perpetual banishment from her family. Even though that gut-wrenching result of her love could probably not be avoided, it might be delayed for a little while at least.

As Claire hurried across campus between morning classes to be confronted by Nympha Mae Haskins, she could not imagine how Bucky Oaks had discovered her absence, but in due time it became clear. During the previous day, he had kept her virtually a prisoner in his car as they had cruised hither, thither, and yon, fighting away the hours. That's why she had not attended Adrian's class. Ricocheting between anger, tears, and occasional feelings near to panic, while he raged at her over the way she had been treating him, she finally threw open the door, as he slowed for a red light, and bolted toward the Coyote House, arriving just in time for dinner. Eating little (and that hurriedly), she then went straight to her room, refusing to socialize with any of her sisters that night. Fortunately, her roommate had gone to the library to work on a term paper. Overpowered by the urge to be with Adrian, to pour out her tale of woe to his understanding ears, and to warn him against Bucky, who had sounded murderous, she slipped through her bedroom window onto a roof, went across it and another, lower roof, bent double like a fugitive, and then down a vertical fire escape fixed to the northwest side of the Coyote House. As she dropped to the ground, she had an hour in which to get to Litany Lane and back again before the 11:00 P.M. week-night curfew.

Within fifteen minutes of her stealthy departure, Bucky Oaks, cooled off by then and feeling a little repentant, came to make up with her. Miss Haskins herself was in the entrance cubicle when he asked the girl on the desk to ring Claire's room. When after several rings there was still no answer, Nympha Mae dispatched the girl to look for Claire in person. But Claire was not to be found. This vexed Nympha Mae sorely and angered Bucky anew. Driving him and several other boys from the premises at 10:55 P.M., Nympha Mae grudgingly altered her plans for getting to bed early that

369

night and resolved to hover about the entrance hall until the miscreant appeared. At midnight, she notified campus security, the city police, and the sheriff's office of a missing person.

Bucky was also on the alert for the same missing person. At first he merely stalked around campus looking for Claire in some of the likelier spots. Toward midnight he jumped into his car and began cruising along the fringes of the campus, flicking on his high beams as he turned down dark residential streets. Only after a half an hour did it occur to him to look for DeWulf's place. Bucky was not angry at Adrian because he knew him to be a rival for Claire's love; he was angry because he knew the professor to be a disastrous influence on her religiously. He was angry with her, not simply because she spent too much time with DeWulf in particular, but because in spending time with anybody else, she denied that time to him, to Anthony Starbuck Oaks, the biggest "Big Man On Campus." By the time Bucky had thought to check a campus directory (the city phone book had not yet included Adrian), No. 5, Litany Lane, was asleep to all appearances. So, Bucky passed by, not realizing how great a loss he was suffering—at that very moment.

Nympha Mae Haskins was on a very high horse indeed when Claire marched into the Coyote House and abruptly said, "I slipped out last night without permission. I didn't mean to be gone past the curfew. I know that what I did is a serious infraction of the rules. I am not at liberty at the moment to . . . to tell you where I was. What will the punishment be?"

Such frank admissions and such a straightforward question startled the housemother out of the convoluted harangue she had prepared and into what was, for her, a most direct answer. "The immediate ensuing of house arrest is to be expected upon such an infraction and loss of social privileges. Since mandated, your appearance before the University Discipline Committee is not to be avoided, next meeting on Monday, February 13, leading to possible notification of parents, if uncooperative, and possible suspension or expulsion."

So, for the time being, Claire was under house arrest, meaning that she had to be in the Coyote House every evening from dinner time until the first class period of the next day. Dating was prohibited as was attendance at games, concerts, etc. Weekend activities were severely limited, and only official or parental callers were allowed by phone or at the House in person.

However, since love is the child of wit and want, as clever at reaching the beloved as desirous of the beloved, Claire was able to circumvent her house arrest both before and briefly after her hearing before the discipline committee. If the secrecy of night is denied to desire, the hubbub of daylight will do; if leisure for languorous love cannot be had, there are compensations in fleeting moments of high-intensity affection. Claire went to classes a bit earlier than usual, stayed afterward a bit longer than normal, spent an uncommon amount of time in the library, and could not seem to finish her labs on time, or so she said. Occasionally, she was seen going into the Union cafeteria for lunch, but, strangely, nobody could recall seeing her leave. Meanwhile, Adrian occupied his office much less than previously and did a great deal more of his writing and research at home than before so as to finish a paper prior to a hastily invented deadline. Since No. 5, Litany Lane, was but a short walk from the center of campus and since a variety of people came there and went away unnoticed, it was no great problem for the beloved ones there to rob the academic day of precious minutes. Moreover, they found that the pace of their lives had so accelerated that much of love could be spoken and much be shared in moments of brief encounter. It was only when separated that they dallied with dreams of all the things they would do when they could be together openly as often and as long as they liked. And, so, their days were lived in love and in thoughts of future love, the difficulties to come seeming surmountable.

Claire's appearance before the discipline committee went much as she and Adrian had expected. In her favor were the facts that she had hitherto been a model of decorum and propriety, that she was a top student, and that she had not been linked with any crime during the period of her absence. Against her were the facts that she had broken a very serious rule in full awareness of what she was doing, that she had not divulged all relevant information, and that she had been unable to suggest any extenuating circumstances. Her grudging admission to the committee that she had indeed been with someone during her absence and that she felt the need to protect that person counted little one way or the other. As anticipated, her house arrest and loss of social privileges were continued indefinitely and her parents were to be notified and invited to attend the committee's next weekly meeting. These actions were intended to be both punitive and extractive of further information. Her parents' pressures, if any, and her response to those pressures together with how forthcoming she chose to be at the next session would determine whether she was to be put on social probation, to be suspended for a stated period of time, or to be expelled from Algonquin.

The day following Claire's hearing was St. Valentine's Day. It was also the anniversary of those magic moments, one week earlier, when their mutual love had burst upon them in carnal epiphany. That love was by no means to be denied on February 14, 1961, even though one of them lived in dread of a family row to end all rows plus possible expulsion from ASU and the other was sick with certainty that he would lose his position, thus blighting his career at its birth. Despite all, they slipped out of town briefly (a dangerous thing for Claire to do), seeing nobody they knew (but being seen), and drove down Green Pond Road. Angling northeast from town, with the Algonac Hills on their left looming whitely against stormy skies, they saw seven deer within a few moments, more than either had ever seen in a single day.

"It's a sign," Claire exulted.

"Of what?" Adrian asked.

"That everything, absolutely everything, is going to work out all right for us, even if it takes a slew of miracles."

371

"Very well," he announced, "we—and I use the papal 'we'—decree that seeing seven deer in a single day is a mysterious and mystical sign, woven into the very fabric of reality, that one Claire Sumner and a certain Adrian DeWulf shall be infinitely happy together, world without end. Amen."

"World without end. Amen," she echoed, daring to believe those words.

Turning the car around, heading back to town, Adrian said, "Only one sign would have pleased me more."

"What?" she asked, all agog.

"Seeing a unicorn," he declared.

"Why a unicorn?"

"Beats me," he drawled, bewitched by her, his logic having gone lame. "I suppose you realize," he added, as they reached Algonquin's outskirts, "that you can no longer tame unicorns."

"What, why not?" she piped, feeling empowered by love to do anything.

"Because only virgins can tame unicorns, no *laid maid* ever having been known to do so."

As they entered his apartment some moments later, Claire said coquettishly, "Know something? I neither wish to tame any unicorns nor do I miss the power to do so."

As Adrian lay full length upon her, deeply embedded in her naked body but not yet moving, he said, "This is a time when I have a wish."

"What more could you wish for right now than you already have?" she asked, bemused.

"I wish I could be like one of those Hindu gods with six arms and hands, because then I could pet you practically all over all at once and make you feel super-good."

"Tell me about it," she said, smiling up at him. "What would you do?"

"With one hand I would hold your head or stroke your hair. With another I would caress your face and trace its beautiful lines. I would slip an arm under your neck and hold one bare shoulder with my hand. With the, let's see, the fourth hand, I would knead your breasts one after the other and play on your nipples with my fingers lightly. With my fifth hand I would reach under your bottom and cup your buttocks in my hand, as best I could, and with my sixth hand I would stroke the inside of your thighs and reach for your feet to play with your toes. Come to think of it, six arms and hands are not enough. I should have at least eight or maybe ten to do the job right."

Chuckling at his impossible dream, he began to move upon her rhythmically and then said, between quick kisses bestowed upon her half-opened mouth, "You just have to know that every movement and every good feeling is meant to tell you, to make you absolutely certain, of how surpassingly I love you."

When, fleeting moments later, the mounting tension in Claire's body broke in ecstatic release, she laughed with wild abandon and wept at the same time; and Adrian sighed deeply over and again as though to say, "It is finished; my life is fulfilled; all is complete."

372

In the afterglow of their love-making, he said, "Claire, please, please know that no matter how, nor how much, we might be separated, I love you as I have loved no other, and please be certain beyond any doubt that I will always want to be a loving presence in your life, no matter what may befall us." She had no need to speak or even to nod in assent to reassure him. The ineffable look on her face told him eloquently that she felt supremely confident of his love, that he would indeed always be a loving presence in her life, no matter what.

When she left—too soon, too soon—he felt like thanking God for her and for what had happened to them, but he could not do that, and she would take no thanks. So, he was bottled to bursting with emotions, the like of which he had never known.

Throughout the next day, their love languished. Except for a few minutes together in his office and the communal hour in class, they were separated. For a long time that evening he considered calling her, pretending that his was an official call, but in the end, he thought better of it. So, he tried to work on his article but failed, all the while fuming at the mess they were in. Meanwhile, Claire was stung repeatedly, as often as she read and reread the venomous letter she had received from home that day. Her parents were outraged. Her deeds would ruin them. She would be the death of them. They would arrive in Algonquin, at great inconvenience, on Saturday. They would stay through Monday (her father missing a day of work), at God alone knew what expense, to attend the discipline committee meeting. They were prepared to take drastic action. Only one thing in the entire letter could wrench a smile from her. That was their threat to have a serious talk with her pastor on Sunday.

The following day, Thursday, February 16, was the same old story except for a humorous exchange that lifted their load briefly. Slipping into his office after class, Claire said, "Professor DeWulf, could I possibly have a short extension on the written work I was supposed to turn in today?"

"Well, I really don't know, Miss Sumner, unless, of course, there might be extenuating circumstances sufficient to prompt me to leniency," he hemmed and hawed, hugging her tightly all the while and tickling her ear with breathy words.

"Oh, there are, there most certainly are," she giggled and squirmed as he began nuzzling her neck.

Pushing her away to arm's length, but still holding her shoulders, he asked in mock horror, "What, pray tell?"

"Well, I have been very hard pressed for ti—"

"Hard pressed!" he broke in with what he hoped was a lascivious-looking grin on his face, "hard pressed by what?"

"Hard pressed by you-know-very-damn-well what," she said, pretending to grab for his crotch, but merely patting his yielding flesh when her hand finally found its mark.

As they hugged and kissed their good-byes, he said, "Permission granted,

Miss Sumner, for . . . for anything you might want."

That night was a lionesque night, March having arrived two weeks early, or better yet, perhaps, a night straight out of Nordic mythology with all manner of malevolent spirits up and doing in the air. The wind was howling, the timbers overhead were creaking, and unattached objects were bounding helter-skelter across roads, over back yards, and through open spaces, anywhere the wind could go. Unable and unwilling to get Claire out of his mind, Adrian sat hunched over his typewriter trying unsuccessfully to make progress on his article, his fingers blundering over the keys. While pausing to ponder the proper construal of a particular point, the phone rang. Hoping against hope that it might be Claire, he said, "Hello!" exultantly into it before it could ring a second time. Then he said, "No, you're not upsetting anything terribly important," his voice laden with disappointment. "You need that tonight?" he asked, a little incredulously. "No, no," he replied to the caller, his voice dropping on the second "no." "I'm not doing anything that can't be interrupted. Furthermore, it might be seen as an act of charity on my part. Besides, the walk might be good for me. I seem to be stalled at the moment. Tell you what, I'll meet you at the office in about fifteen minutes."

Feeling slightly imposed upon but mildly amused over the opportunity to do a charity, as he had called it, Adrian went to the window beside his bed and looked out into the night. Cans, leaves, branches, and a shingle or two went speeding past the house, now fast, now faster, as the wind gusted above its average gale force speed for that evening. Then he drew the backs of his fingers across the windowpane to get some idea of just how cold it was turning. It would not take long to get to his office and back, but with the wind like that, he might get chilled in a hurry. Deciding that a wool sweater and a windbreaker with a hood would be enough, he left his room and descended the stairs at top speed.

Once outside, he had difficulty keeping his footing, but leaning low into the wind, he plunged ahead as best he could. Overhead, low clouds went rocketing along as though the jet stream had come down to earth to power them on their way. At times they caught the lights of Algonquin and reflected them downward, making vision easy; at other times the town's lights were lost in the twinkling dark, and it was hard to see. Now Adrian was about to be hammered by a bounding can, now clobbered by a big box of Kleenex perhaps, or was it Kotex? and at all times there was the pandemonium of the wind. It was just such a night as Halloween ought to be, a night when it was hard not to get spooked up. As he progressed, he began to warm toward his caller. It really was no imposition to be called out on that particular night. It was, in fact, a needed distraction.

Half-winded from his rapid pace and from having his breath sucked away now and again by swirling gusts of wind, Adrian reached the tower doors of the Ad. Building in just under ten minutes. Once inside, he took the stairs to the third floor two at a time, reached his office on the double, unlocked the door, went in, turned on the lights, went to a particular bookshelf, took down two books, sat at his desk, and waited for the caller to come. Since the matter in hand would not take long to resolve, and since he did not wish to encourage the caller in conversation, he left his sweater and windbreaker on, merely pushing the hood off his head.

Meanwhile, back at the Coyote House, the imprisoned Claire found a way to think of Adrian, to love him *in absentia,* and to please him, all wrapped in one: she finished the paper that had needed extra time. It was no part of her make-up to abuse anybody's permissiveness, certainly not his, and above all not the carte-blanche permission he had given her earlier that day.

After the night's rampage, the weather next morning was clear, still, and cold. Looking like an Eskimo, Claire left the House early enough to pop into Adrian's office before her eight o'clock class. She would give him a "Hi," a hug, a kiss, and her paper. Later that day, just before or just after their class together, they would have to talk about how much of the truth she was to reveal to her parents and to the discipline committee. All of it, she supposed, no matter what.

When she reached the third floor of the Ad. Building by means of the tower stairs, she went straight to Adrian's office door and knocked perkily. Her face was pink from the cold and the climb, and her heart raced almost as much from exertion as from love. Getting no response, which dampened her spirits at once, she went down the hall to the next office, Rad's, and knocked, hoping to find Adrian there or at least to learn of his whereabouts. Slurping a cup of steaming coffee, Rad greeted her jovially, though he did not know her. No, he had not seen Professor DeWulf that morning. Apparently he had not yet come in. "Perhaps the fellow's malingering," he observed, a smile crinkling the corners of his eyes and stretching his moustache.

After a moment's hesitation, Claire said, "Could you see that he gets this paper, please?" Even if there could be no "Hi," no hug, and no kiss, at least she could prove that she had thought of him, that she had been there, and that she had done her work, hard pressed or not, and in jig time too.

"Why not just go through that door that communicates between our offices?" Rad suggested, pointing, "and leave the paper on his desk yourself."

"Are you sure that's no trouble?" she asked.

"Nah, it happens all the time and among the best of people," Rad said, prattling and slurping more hot coffee.

Claire had scarcely stepped through the communicating door when staccato screams, unceasing, cut through the walls, the floors, the ceilings of the building, piercing the ears of everybody nearby. Students passing in the hall outside froze in their tracks at the chilling sounds. Students assembling in the classrooms across the hall quit their chattering, some in mid-word. Professors and secretaries in the offices directly below were jolted out of their day's beginnings. Students in the hall below gaped at the ceiling in disbelief, and those who approached the Ad. Building from the front door looked up, some in alarm, some in dread, trying to grasp what was happening. By the time Rad bolted through the communicating door, followed at once by Patti Ray (the departmental secretary), Claire was bending over—no, more nearly kneeling above—the prostrate form of Adrian DeWulf. Screaming without ceasing as though in so doing she could deny his death, Claire resisted all initial efforts at getting her on her feet, at leading her away from the gruesome sight (Adrian's skull had been caved in). Finally, Patti Ray, who knew her slightly, together with two sorority sisters who happened to be passing in the hall when frozen to the spot, managed to get her, stumbling blindly and choking on her tears, into Patti's car in the Ad. Building parking lot and from there to the Coyote House.

During the first hours of devastation after her discovery of Adrian's body, Claire lay in her darkened room on her bed in a fetal position and would not move. Nor would she, could she, accept expressions of love from her sorority sisters and other best girl friends who came to be by her side. Many a sympathizing tear fell on her behalf, but they brought no comfort, nor could she respond to them in gratitude. For her, at that terrible time, love could be no more. Nothing could replace what she had lost, and never again, she vowed endlessly, would she permit herself to be vulnerable to such pulverizing loss. It was infinitely better, she assured and reassured herself between sobs, never to have loved and, thus, never to have lost, than to have loved and lost as she had lost.

The grief that emanated from her fetal form, irradiating with deep sorrow all whom it touched, left little doubt as to where she had been the night of her absence from the sorority house and even less doubt as to her relationship to the one, now dead, with whom she had spent it. After all, a young coed does not grieve inconsolably over the loss of a mere professor, even should she stumble upon her teacher's dead body.

Nympha Mae Haskins perceived the truth at once, and, to her credit, felt no elation that a mystery had been solved. On the contrary, she, too, was deeply irradiated with grief and extended a kindness to Claire in thought, a kindness which she would present in person to the discipline committee, a kindness which would probably lighten any further punishment.

For Rad, the day of Claire's dreadful discovery was also a day of sheer hell and of pandemonium. Locking the communicating door between his office and Adrian's with trembling fingers and ushering out those who still jammed his office, he made three quick phone calls. First, he rang up campus security, trusting that they would carry on from there. Second, he called Dean Braniff, who took the news very badly it seemed. When Rad had a chance to collect his thoughts later that day, he wondered why. Adrian and the dean had not been close. In fact, they barely knew each other by sight. Third, he went to his files, took out Adrian's dossier, looked up the phone number of his next of kin, and put through a long-distance call to Valentine, Nebraska. Satisfied that he had reached Adrian's father, he stammered, "Sir, I . . . I hardly know how to tell you what . . . what I have to say, but . . .

but I do urge you to prepare yourself for a nasty shock. Your son, Adrian, employed here at Algonquin State University, is dead—worse than that, murdered!" Rad will never forget the eerie answer he received. "We knew he'd come to no good end," the voice said flatly. Throughout the rest of the conversation respecting the care and shipment of Adrian's body back to Nebraska for burial, after the police had finished with it, Rad kept hearing the words, "We knew he'd come to no good end," words uttered with distant regret perhaps but without present surprise, words unslurred by tears. Increasingly perplexed in the moments following the call, but unwilling to ring up again for clarification, Rad was brooding on those singular words and the precise sentiment they conveyed when Homer Podlacs arrived.

The High Sheriff of Algonquin County burst into Rad's office characteristically, i.e., while turning its knob he collided with the office door and sent it smashing against the nearest wall. Above his hips, Homer leaned forward precariously, as though defying gravity, and when walking lurched to and fro. Except for not being graceful, he reminded one of a sailboat tacking against strong winds. He also rammed people rather often and knocked not a few to the ground where the unluckier ones were trampled amidst profuse apologies. While young, he had inherited his family's seed and feed business. Prospering, he added a gristmill—more out of antiquarian interest than anything else—then a small elevator for grain storage. But, in mid-life, he grew as disenchanted with business as he became stage-struck with the many roles he could play as the High Sheriff of Algonquin County. Since he was a local boy who had always been genial and accommodating, was God-apprehensive (if not downright fearful), was usually forgiven the accidents his lurching body caused, and was widely known, he was elected with votes to burn.

When Rad called campus security, he supposed they would contact the city police at once, but not so, for, just then, jurisdictional disputes were simmering between the city police department and the sheriff's office. This led to brisk competition, especially in the investigation of high-visibility crimes. At the time of Adrian's death, Homer had the competitive edge for two reasons. First, he was a poker-playing crony of the new chief of campus security, and, second, his wife, Evelyn, was the executive secretary of J. Graves Roberts, the academic vice-president of ASU. This gave her privileged access to much official business. Moreover, she was the nerve center of a vast secretarial grapevine and a master of campus-wide tittle-tattle, all of which gave her husband the inside track in campus investigations. From his point of view, there was yet another reason for his suitability in investigating the high-visibility crime in the philosophy department. Once the introductions were over, he said, "You know, perfesser, you and me've got quite a bit in common. I've learned a lot, just an awful lot, of philosophy from meetin' the public over the years both as a businessman and now as the High Sheriff. I think we'll be able to cooperate real good in this case." Rad could muster neither the heart nor the energy to comment on Homer's point but mutely unlocked the door to what had been Adrian's office and led the sheriff in.

Adrian's body lay in a crumpled heap, his face on its right side, on the floor about two feet from and at right angles to his desk, which was pushed against the north wall of the office and parallel to it. The desk chair stood a foot and a half to the right of his body at about the level of his knees. The communicating door through which Rad and Homer Podlacs had just come was at the extreme east end of the wall in question. To the layman's eye, there was an area about the size of an average grapefruit above and behind Adrian's left ear which had simply been smashed in, blood and brains having gushed or oozed out, congealing in time with hair into a gory mass. There did not appear to have been a struggle, nor was the office ransacked, everything normal to it appearing to be in place. Since the offices in the Ad. Building were heated night and day in winter, and since Adrian had not removed his windbreaker, it looked as though he had planned to be in his office only briefly at the time of death. Also, since janitors emptied wastebaskets in every office after the regular teaching day, and since the building was locked to all but high administrators after 11:00 P.M., it seemed reasonable to assume that he had been killed sometime the previous evening. It was most unlikely that he had been murdered that morning between about 6:30 A.M. when the building was opened for the day and 8:00 when his body had been discovered by a student whose name, Rad had just learned, was Claire Sumner, a name which Homer was quick to jot down.

In the middle of the desk, in a tiny area apparently cleared for writing, lay two books which occasioned more than passing interest, particularly on Rad's part, although they provided no clue at the moment. One was Adrian's abridged version of Liddel and Scott, a basic Greek-English dictionary. The other was *A Greek-English Lexicon of the New Testament and Other Early Christian Literature* by Arndt and Ginrich. Only the front cover of the Lidell and Scott lay open, but the Arndt and Ginrich was open at pages four and five. Rad took sufficient notice of the page numbers to remember them.

"Doc, what kind of language is that?" Homer asked, pointing at the open lexicon.

"Greek."

Thinking somehow that philosophers ought to stick to philosophy, Homer asked, "Did he do stuff with Greek too?"

"He read Greek or at least knew his way around the dictionary. He was a minister at one time, you know, in an earlier life as he liked to put it."

"I guess that figures, him bein' a philosopher and all."

To that, Rad said nothing.

"Just gimme your impression, Perfesser Reid: Do these here books have any bearing on what happened to him, do you think?"

"I can't answer that. I don't know. DeWulf was rather compulsive about words. If he ever encountered one he didn't know, he couldn't wait to look it up, and then he would spring it on people just as if everybody knew it."

"Would somethin' like that have brought him out at night, especially on a night like last night?"

"Maybe. Certainly a little wind wouldn't have stopped him from coming back to the office to look something up. He didn't live very far away. On the other hand, I don't know why he would have cared that much about a term in Greek. Surely it could have waited until morning. As far as I know, he wasn't doing any research involving Greek usage, either philosophical or theological."

"You suppose he was trying to help someone with their studies?"

"Possibly, but at the moment I can't think of anybody needing help with Greek."

"Maybe somebody was out to git him and just happened to be around when he got here."

"That makes as much sense as anything I can think of," Rad said, suddenly aware of an immense sorrow creeping over him.

"Did he have any enemies you know of?"

"Only intellectual enemies."

"*What?*" asked Homer incredulously, standing almost straight for once.

"People who disagreed with him, you know, colleagues with different points of view."

Ignoring this, Homer said, "Did he seem worried about anything?"

"Yes, he was worried about losing his job."

"Why, wasn't he doin' good?"

"His work was excellent, but he held some very unorthodox views and was pretty vehement about them. These irritated a few people."

Knowing that Evelyn could fill him in on that kind of stuff best of all, Homer forged ahead, asking, "Any love angle?"

"Not that I know of, but maybe. I don't pry into the private lives of my faculty."

Thinking that Evelyn could check up on that too, Homer was about to excuse Rad for the time being when there was a hubbub in the hall as several people from the sheriff's office (including a photographer) arrived, together with an uninvited detective from the city force and an invited technician from the branch office of the state forensics laboratory in nearby Laurentian.

"I'll let you get back to your work and all, Perfesser Reid," Homer said authoritatively, "but be sure to stick around town, 'cause I'll probably need to talk to you more." Then, softening his voice, he said as though to confer a rare and special status on Rad, "If you think of anything that I should know, git back in touch with me right away. Just tell 'em who you are down at the office and tell 'em that I said to put you through right straight to me, that way we can sorta handle things at the top level, if you see what I mean."

"Sure," Rad said, looking one last time at the ghastly heap on the floor and shuddering. Once back in his office, he found massed therein a solemn delegation of students and a gaggle of people from the various media. It took all his force of character, much patience, and an inordinate amount of time to convince the people from the media that he knew next to nothing and that he would not reveal even that much at the moment. "See the sheriff," he said over and over again, "or talk with the people in university relations. I'm sure they'll be happy to share information with you as soon as they know anything." Ignoring their persistent clamor and refusing even to speculate, to say nothing of making interpretive comments, he finally shooed them out into the hall, towering over them, trying half-heartedly to intimidate them. "Now," he said tiredly, turning toward the students, "what can I do for you?"

To the accompaniment of earnest nods and grave looks, their spokesman said, "We know that Professor DeWulf wasn't religious, at least not in any ordinary way, but we'd like a memorial service for him this coming Sunday, and we'd like you to lead it." Without the vaguest idea of what he would say or how he would say it, Rad agreed in principle, if they would take charge of securing an auditorium and getting the word around. Before they left, the students suggested Woodbridge Hall as the best place and picked 3:00 P.M. as the best time.

Alone with his thoughts for a few minutes and unable to lift a hand to do anything, so tired did he feel, Rad kept thinking of music. With that one thought recurring, dominating his consciousness, he arose, after what seemed a great while, and stumped across campus on leaden feet. His destination was the office of S. Epristible Kirklin, Professor of Music, but so preoccupied was he with shock, sorrow, and bewilderment that he forgot to call to see if Kirklin were in. He was.

S. Epristible Kirklin was English, patrician, prickly, and no more than a half-step removed from virtuosity on the pipe organ. Only a minor miracle or a major disaster could have deposited him in Algonquin, and he would never say which. He regarded most of Algonquin's professors as peasants at heart and felt amused contempt toward nearly all of his colleagues on the music faculty. But when he sat before the great Holtcamp organ in Woodbridge Hall and proceeded to make it do his bidding, much was forgiven on all sides. Rad was one of the few Algonquinites whom Kirklin respected and one of an even smaller number allowed to call him "Priss" with impunity. It was a badly shaken Rad who appeared at the door of Kirklin's studio. "I hope I'm not disturbing you at a bad time, Priss," he said in a voice drained of emotion.

"Never, esteemed savant," came Priss' answer.

"I suppose you've heard about the dreadful business in my department, I mean the death of Adrian DeWulf, our new assistant professor?"

"I've heard people babbling about an unexpected death, or was it, as some claim, actual murder?"

"Murder, without a doubt."

"This is outrageous! Do the campus security officers give us no protection?"

"No, not really, nor can they, but you'll be relieved to know that Sheriff Homer Podlacs has taken the case in hand."

"That cretin!"

"He doesn't inspire too much confidence, does he?"

"At most, he inspires the pity one accords an imbecile."

"Priss, what I came for is to ask if you would be good enough to assist me in a memorial service for Adrian. A fair number of students, I should think, and probably a handful of colleagues believe it appropriate that we mark his passing."

"Quite."

"I came to you not just because you're the best damned musician around but because organ music would be appropriate, also because we would need to make the selections very carefully."

"Singular people though they are, do philosophers require singular music? Will the ordinary run of old masters not do?"

"Oh, it isn't that. It's that the deceased was not religious at all. Well, that's putting it mildly. He was vehemently antireligious. I wouldn't want us to bash in his memory with music offensive to his spirit the way his head was bashed in."

"His head was really 'bashed in,' as you put it?"

"Yes, literally, all the way from above the left ear around to the back center."

"Good God!"

"Good God, indeed, in a manner of speaking. Anyway, back to the music. I believe from something DeWulf said that he was fondest of baroque music, but he would not have wanted any kind of pious church music at his funeral, or, I should say, memorial service. No, that would be very inappropriate."

"That seems most curious, loving the baroque, I mean, and yet not liking church music. What was he, an atheist or something?"

"Mostly 'something,' but he was an atheist emotionally—or maybe it would be nicer to say that he was a humanist—in that the supernatural, whatever it is, played no part in his life. Logically, he claimed that God's existence was not the fundamental question. The fundamental question, as he saw it, was whether or not the term 'God', when properly and uniquely used, names a referent. Depending on what that referent is, if anything, God either exists or does not. In any case, whether it names an idea in people's minds or names nature or whatever, he didn't worship it, pray to it, or take moral orders from it."

"Well, whatever else you philosophers are, Rad, you are not peasants. Peasants do not think as did our departed colleague. I will not press you just now as to your views on deity."

"Thanks, Priss, and I do not joke."

"Musicians are believers, you know." With those words, S. Epristible Kirklin put his mind to the problem of suitable music for a pagan sophisticate done to death brutally. "Rad," he said after a minute or two, "I think I may have two selections in mind, either one or both of which would do. They are set to biblical themes, but they are not church music as such. Both are by Handel—he was all baroque and half-pagan—so we might have something here that would not be offensive to the shade or the non-shade, as the case may be, of the departed profes—"

Breaking in, Rad said, "Adrian did say something—was it to me or to a student?—anyway, something about his never expecting to get any closer to heaven than when he was listening to some of the great Handel choruses. Yes, I think your suggestion would be very appropriate."

"But, of course, I am not thinking of choruses, great or otherwise. We could not prepare choruses in short order even with a royal proclamation."

"Of course not, nor did I expect you to."

"No, but there are two magnificent funeral marches that come to mind. One comes from the oratorio *Saul* and is played in memory of the fallen King and his son, Jonathan, freshly slain in battle with the Philistines. From rumors I seem to have heard about your dead colleague, his iconoclasm was such that he may also have been slain by a Philistine—in a manner of speaking, of course."

"You have no idea of how truly you may have spoken."

"Now, the other dead march comes from *Samson* and is played for him as his body is returned from the havoc he wrought when he brought the temple down on his own head as well as on the Philistines'. Both pieces are short—four minutes perhaps—each is grave and moving and sublimely beautiful, but the latter is a little more triumphant and a bit sweeter in a good sense than the former. Is triumph an issue, I mean did DeWulf make any lasting impression? Did he die for anything, do you suppose?"

"Well, perhaps not, but he did have a fierce, if premature, kind of intellectual integrity, and that may have influenced some students positively. To keep this from dragging on any longer, Priss, I think your suggestions are splendid, and I leave it to you to play whichever one you like first or last."

"The *Saul* dead march first, I think, and then *Samson's*. Oh, Rad, where and when, if you please?"

"Does 3:00 P.M. this coming Sunday here in the Woodbridge auditorium sound all right?"

"By all means, let's conduct the service here."

"Many thanks, Priss. I'll see you then, if not sooner, and will get back with you at once should there be any change. And thanks again."

Rad returned to his office only to find the phone ringing off the wall. Incredulous friends, colleagues, and acquaintances simply had to know then and there what was fact and what was fiction concerning the dead man in the philosophy department. Between calls he merely stared at the wall in front of him, unable to compose himself, unable to work. Then, feeling like a zombie, he shuffled off to his one o'clock class and probably gave a lecture. He does not remember what, if anything, he said. At two o'clock he formally notified the students in the last of Adrian's classes for that day that Dr. DeWulf would no longer meet their class nor any other for that matter. When the students, most of whom had already heard the bad news, clamored to know what would happen to their class, he could only say vaguely, "We'll work something out and let you know." Then, realizing that he was hungry, he went to the basement lounge in the Ad. Building to get a bite to eat. Taking his snack back to the office, he nibbled on it abstractedly, stared at the wall some more, and answered additional phone calls. As their number decreased with the waning of the afternoon, he pulled himself together sufficiently to look at the day's mail. The first piece was an advertisement from Beacon Press. The second was a promotional reminder of a forthcoming lecture of special interest to faculty in the humanities. The third was a confidential memorandum from Dean Braniff, dated February 16, 1961. It delivered the second nasty shock of the day.

The memo said, "This is to instruct you to inform Dr. Adrian DeWulf, Assistant Professor of Philosophy, that his services to Algonquin State University will be terminated as of the last working day of March, 1961. His services will not be required during the spring quarter." The memo also said, "Kindly complete the termination form (enclosed herewith) and send it to the personnel office." In a handwritten note at the bottom of his memo, Dean Braniff put, "Put 'Inability to work with others' as the cause of termination and put 'No' in the blank asking whether or not you would rehire the person in question."

In addition to the termination form included with his memo, Dean Braniff sent a list of student complaints submitted to him and to his superiors, including President MacGilvary, concerning incendiary comments on religion which Adrian made during the winter term. Among these were:

"People who claim to have supernatural experiences deceive themselves and others, because they cannot tell the difference between a 'supernatural experience', so-called, and a natural experience whose cause is unknown and whose nature is unexplained at the moment.

"The Rock of Gibraltar is but shifting sand compared to the Rock of Gullibility on which the Christian Church is built.

"It is not so much the mystery of the gospel that ought to concern us as the fraud of the gospel.

"The Bible is no longer under lock and key, but those who read it reverentially are. They are still chained to its presuppositions and locked into its judgments. It is truly a bewitching book.

"The decisions that we take to be God's are but the decisions made by human beings like ourselves (usually in earlier times) who were under the impression that their own gut feelings were identical with their god's.

"The gullibility industry is one of the biggest of all growth industries.

"St. Paul was right when he said he was the foremost of sinners, if he meant by that the suicide of his own mind.

"Making up God's mind for him then changing it as the times require (without his noticing the difference) is one of the principal tasks of theology.

"No slavery is more complete than that of a mind enthralled by faith.

"If you ever visit a great cathedral, you will see a great playhouse come down to earth from the clouds, and inside a splendid land of make-believe.

"In some ways God is like an imaginary playmate from childhood carried over into maturity.

"Imagine a very learned zoologist who specializes in bears and who also takes literally the adventures of Goldilocks and the three bears. Such is the pious scientist.

"Religious beliefs are imagined solutions to problems real or phony.

"Just as a democratic person can do without a king, so an educated person in the twentieth century ought to be able to do without a lord, even the Lord Jesus.

"A 'spiritual truth' is any idea, no matter how false, outlandish, or absurd, about which a person is religious.

"Faith is another word for gullibility, just as superstition is another word for religion.

"All things are possible to the faithful, especially the power to utter untruths, if not outright lies, for the sake of the faith while keeping a clear conscience."

Pushing away the odious directives from Dean Braniff, Rad said in loud grief, "Good God, if Adrian hadn't been murdered, I'd have had to fire him today!" Rad was also aggrieved over being told what to put on Adrian's termination form. " 'Inability to work with others,' my foot," he growled. As for the 'No' he was supposed to put behind the question "Would you rehire this person?" why, hell, he would have written, "Yes, yes, yes!" if left to himself. In all the shock and confusion of that day, two things were starkly obvious. First, Adrian had angered certain powerful people at ASU over the unpopular things he had been saying about religion and had, without doubt, made himself a nuisance to public relations. Second, had he lived, he would have been denied his academic freedom by ASU's administration and forced to pay a high price indeed for speaking his mind. Rad could not deny that Adrian's views on religion were sizzling hot, but if a professor who is trained at the highest level in the philosophy of religion cannot express himself openly at a place like ASU without fear of reprisal, then higher education at such a place is a fraud. But, despite the narrowness Rad was witnessing at that moment, he could not really believe that anybody at ASU had caved in Adrian's skull merely for what he had been saying, nor could he believe that any citizen in as cultivated, as civilized, as progressive a town as Algonquin could have done it either. So then, who had done it and why?

Shortly before three o'clock on the Sunday afternoon after Adrian's death, darkly clad people began to converge on Woodbridge Hall, the building that housed most of the music department and also provided the best auditorium on campus. Rad and his wife, Miriam (who barely knew Adrian), were among the first to arrive. Once in the auditorium, she took a seat in the rear while he went down to the front row to await the time when he would make a few remarks and read what he believed to be a most appropriate selection. A good percentage of the students from each of Adrian's classes came, both from the classes he had taught during the fall term and from those he had been teaching at the time of his death. Abraham Bronznowski and several colleagues from various departments attended as did Dean Braniff of the School of Arts and Sciences. No member of the administration higher than he, however, deigned to come. Among the few local people who attended were the heavily veiled Grace Moore Mistledine, Adrian's landlady; one of the young couples also inhabiting her house; and a clerk, a girl, from his favorite bakery. As might have been expected, the clergy, the members of the religion department, and other religious workers in Algonquin stayed away in droves. Only the Reverend Manly John Plumwell, RPPI., came, the one among the clergy who had known the deceased best and had worked hardest to deliver him from apostasy.

In his sermon that morning, Manly had adverted to Adrian's death and had pointed out that for many the sad letters "R.I.P." could mean no more than "Rest In Peace" (even though Manly believed that sinners could expect no rest), whereas for the true Christians of the Holy Nation, the letters "R.I.P." meant "Risen In Power." Nor was Manly alone among Algonquin's clergy that morning in bidding his flock to consider the everlasting fate of such a one as Adrian DeWulf. As Manly sat in Woodbridge Hall awaiting the start of Adrian's memorial service, he fully expected some kind of assault on his Christian sensibilities. What could Reid, or any mere philosopher, or any person who was not a true Christian (which was about the same as not belonging to the Holy Nation) say on behalf of an apostate sinner like DeWulf? Certainly there could be no words of genuine consolation and none of triumph. "Risen in Power" DeWulf most certainly was not, nor would he rest in peace! That recognition was a bitter pill for Manly to swallow, for he had worked and prayed very hard (and suffered much abuse) to rescue the apostate before it was too late. "Too late" had come so very soon for DeWulf, sooner than any who had known him could have imagined!

Coeds do not normally include mourning attire in their wardrobes, death being too far from their expectations. Certainly that was true of Claire. Nor did she have the presence of mind, nor the energy, to try to borrow anything black. So, she appeared in the darkest winter outfit she had, a navy blue suit, and came with her head uncovered. Her eyes were dry, but she was so near to collapsing that two of her closest sorority sisters had to support her every step down the aisle to a middle point in the auditorium where they found seats. She was followed dumbly by her parents, who were very confused by it all and feeling badly out of place. Her sorority sisters, together with Nympha Mae Haskins, turned out en masse as did all her best friends (except for Anthony Starbuck Oaks), and all sat as close to her as possible, surrounding her with love and seeming to hover over her so as to extend any kindness possible or to meet her slightest need.

At three o'clock sharp, the prepossessing S. Epristible Kirklin strode from an anteroom in Woodbridge Hall and approached the Holtcamp organ, an instrument of surpassing power and beauty, really too good for Algonquin, given to it by a grateful alumnus. Then for nearly four minutes, the somber, measured, mellifluous strains of the dead march from *Saul* made all who sat there seem to arise and march to the very brink of Adrian's gaping grave. As soon as Kirklin had finished and taken his seat, scarcely breaking the spell, Rhadamanthus Reid, deeply moved by the music, drew himself up to his full six feet, seven inches and commenced to speak.

But Claire did not hear what he began to say, for *Saul's* dead march led to a cloudburst of feelings following which the flow of her consciousness became what it had been almost continuously during the two previous days, a river of grief in flood stage. Surging forward out of its banks, swirling amorphously, treacherously, it swept words, ideas, and images into her mind and out again just as houses and cars, trees and clumps of vegetation, animals and human beings are swept by on the flood tides of an actual river, swollen and on the rampage. Words came: "Sunset and evening star," "the silver cord," "the golden bowl be broken," "rest in peace," "sleep well." Oh (such a painful "oh"), that was impossible, according to Adrian. Adrian. Adrian appeared. She could see him so clearly! Jaunty, crisp, articulate, bursting with life, he perched on a corner of his classroom desk, one foot on the floor, the other dangling in midair, and said, "Notice how people speak of the dead as though they were still alive. See how the grammar of death feigns the grammar of life." A vision came. She saw her little niece, Eurydice, drowned at Sapphire Lake, lying in her casket, an arm around her Pooh Bear, followed by the words of Walter de la Mare, read at the graveside, words so poignant she looked them up and memorized them after the funeral:

> Here lies, but seven years old
>   our little maid
> Once of the darkness, oh, so sore
>   afraid.
> Light of the World—remember
>   that small fear,
> And when nor moon nor stars do
>   shine—draw near.

"Yes, people visualize themselves dead as though still alive. They lie in their graves as in a bed, they sleep, they await the resurrection, they see themselves ready to arise." She heard music, the music of the lovely, lovely Christmas carol, "Lo, How a Rose E'er Blooming," then to the music came the words of the last verse, words she had once learned as her part in a Christmas cantata:

386

Lord Jesus, till Thou call us
To leave our earthly plight
We pray Thee lead us onward
Towards those mansions bright
In God the Father's home,
And we shall sing thy praise,
When full spent is the night.

When full spent is the night—Eurydice, opening her eyes, pushing away Pooh Bear, calling for her mother. "But only the living lie down on a bed to rest, not the dead in their caskets," Adrian said, looking so very magisterial. Only the living await this or that event after their rest and make plans to act. The picture of her cousin came, a cousin killed in Korea. "Home is the sailor, home from the sea, and the hunter home from the hill." Then Adrian burst into view again, wagging a negative finger at a drawing of Robert Louis Stevenson. Stalking about the classroom, intense, taut, he declared (looking straight at her), "Trying to answer the question as to where one will spend eternity seems to involve a kind of post-mortem geography—an exercise in unreal estate." At that he grinned boyishly and faded from view. "But, 'when full spent is the night,'" she insisted, "'when full spent is the night' . . ." "Claire, sweetie, there is no good reason to believe that there is going to be a morning after, after the sunset, that is, but there's no reason to believe that there will be night either. As the final darkness falls on each of us, it extinguishes all our desires to see more light. That kind of darkness also abolishes the night and all its fears." Laughing, joking with his students, he said, "You might as well ask, 'What will I be in infinity?' as to ask, 'Where will I be in eternity?' "

The little toy dog is covered
with dust
But sturdy and stanch he
stands;
And the little toy soldier is red
with rust,
And his musket moulds in his
hands;
Time was when the little toy dog
was new,
And the soldier was passing fair;
And that was the time when our
Little Boy Blue
Kissed them and put them there.

She saw him lying on the floor of his office, his face ugly in death, his left eye dull and dry, staring vacantly, his crushed head indescribably repulsive to her but still he spoke, for he would not be silenced, no, not he, "Students, all you who have had your wits scared out of you by the horrid Christian hell, listen to Epicurus, who said, in a nutshell, that when life is, death is not, and when death is, life is not, and never the twain shall meet. It's dying that hurts, not death." A vision came, a vision of Flanders Field followed by the words, "THE GOOD DIE YOUNG," in block letters as white as the crosses of the Field, then the sound of *Taps* and the sight of red poppies swaying in the sunset, next the purple dusk, the valley of the shadow of death. "How about taking my course in the philosophy of religion next term?" "Hey, I'd love to do that." Then the lie to please Bucky, "I won't be able to take the philosophy of religion with you next term." "If you can't, you can't (trying to sound unconcerned, but really disappointed; she could still see it in his eyes)." "So, why don't you walk to the Coyote House with me, or part way at least, and keep on talking?" "Claire, I'll walk you wherever you are going (said earlier, the day he had rescued her from Bro. Plumwell's scolding)." "I really need to talk to you." "Why, certainly." "The seven deer are a sign that everything, absolutely everything, is going to work out all right for us." "I have loved you as I have loved no other." Then the cloudburst brought on by the sounds of *Saul's* dead march ceased, and the river of grief sank temporarily into secret subconscious places. With her eyes drained of tears for the moment, she lifted her drooping head and saw Professor Reid, heard him speaking, and tried to remember what he had been saying, but in vain.

"Thus," he said, opening a book, "in light of all the circumstances we know at the moment, it seems most fitting to read a few lines from Plato's *Apology,* from very near the end. Socrates has already been found guilty of atheism, of introducing new gods into Athens, and of perverting the youth of the city who had studied with him. Not only has he been convicted; he has also been condemned to death. Here is what he said to the members of the jury:

"'Let us reflect in another way, and we shall see that there is great reason to hope that death is a good; for one of two things—either death is a state of nothingness and utter unconsciousness, or, as men say, there is a change and migration of the soul from this world to another. Now if you suppose that there is no consciousness, but a sleep like the sleep of him who is undisturbed even by dreams, death will be an unspeakable gain. For if a person were to select the night in which his sleep was undisturbed even by dreams, and were to compare with this the other days and nights of his life, and then were to tell us how many days and nights he had passed in the course of his life better and more pleasantly than this one, I think that any man, I will not say a private man, but even the great King will not find many such days or nights, when compared with the others. Now if death be of such a nature, I say that to die is gain; for eternity is then only a single night. But if death is the journey to another place, and there, as men say, all the dead abide, what good, O my friends and judges, can be greater than this? If indeed when the pilgrim arrives in the world below, he is delivered from the professors of

388

justice in this world, and finds the true judges who are said to give judgment there, Minos and Rhadamanthus and Aeacus and Triptolemus, and other sons of God who were righteous in their own life, that pilgrimage will be worth making. What would not a man give if he might converse with Orpheus and Musaeus and Hesiod and Homer? Nay, if this be true, let me die again and again. I myself, too, shall have a wonderful interest in there meeting and conversing with Palamedes, and Ajax the son of Telamon, and any other ancient hero who has suffered death through an unjust judgment; and there will be no small pleasure, as I think in comparing my own sufferings with theirs. Above all, I shall then be able to continue my search into true and false knowledge; as in this world, so also in the next; and I shall find out who is wise, and who pretends to be wise, and is not. What would not a man give, O judges, to be able to examine the leader of the great Trojan expedition; to Odysseus or Sisyphus, or numberless others, men and women too! What infinite delight would there be in conversing with them and asking them questions! In another world they do not put a man to death for asking questions: assuredly not. For besides being happier than we are, they will be immortal, if what is said is true.

" 'Therefore, O judges, be of good cheer about death, and know of a certainty, that no evil can happen to a good man, either in life or after death.' "

Closing the book, fighting to keep his composure, Rad concluded by saying, "And so, to Adrian DeWulf, philosopher, teacher, forthright colleague, and friend, we say, 'Hail and Farewell!' " With that, he sat down, trembling, as Kirklin, the magnificent, if misplaced, musician, returned to the organ and, uniting himself with it in perfect concord, played the somber, measured strains of the dead march from *Samson*. Again the mourners seemed to arise and march toward the grave itself, but this time there was a touch of sweetness in the music that lifted the pall somewhat and gave a subtle hint of triumph. Somehow it seemed to say that life would be better because of the life that had been lost.

As soon as Sheriff Homer Podlacs had completed his investigation at the scene of the crime, had engineered the removal of Adrian's body to the regional forensics lab, and had settled some matters at his office (including an altercation at the county jail), he sped officiously to the Coyote House, in front of which he double-parked. Lumbering into the building, scattering Coyotes as he went, he came face to face with the housemother, looking more like a goat than ever.

"Howdy, mum," he said, "I'm Homer Podlacs, the High Sheriff of Algonquin County, and—"

"And I, sir, am Miss Nympha Mae Haskins, the housemother of the Kai Iota Epsilon Sorority here at ASU," she said with rare directness.

"Yes, mum, well, I'm here to investigate a murder that I believe one of your girls here, name of . . . [here Homer consulted his note pad] Summer, might know somethin' about."

"Sumner," said Miss Haskins, pursing her lips.

"What?" Homer asked, loath to believe that he had jotted down a wrong name so early in his investigation.

"The name in question is Sumner of the one you wish to question, there being no question of questioning a Summer here."

"Oh, I see," Homer said, not too sure that he did. "Anyway," he went on, "I'd be obliged to you if I could have a few words with the person in . . . in question."

"At the moment that is out of the question, it is to be feared, since a soporific has been administered, to you the subject in question would not be able, allowed even, to converse, Dr. Granger of the infirmary himself having counseled complete rest and prescribed it."

"Mum, I don't want to be ornery," said Homer, more confused than ornery, "but what you have to understand is that murder's been done, and me and the others involved in the case think time may be of the essence, so, you see, I need to learn all I can as quick as I can, and this here Sumners girl may have vital information, see." Homer already leaned toward the crime-of-passion theory and wanted to check into the "love angle," as he called it. Since the dead professor had been discovered by a young woman, that seemed to him a likely place to commence all further investigations.

Deeply mired in what struck her as a serious dilemma of authority, a doctor's on the one hand and a lawman's on the other, Nympha Mae finally gave in to Homer and led him to Claire's darkened room, crying in a loud voice as she did so, "Man on the stairs," then, "Man on the floor, man on the floor." For her part, Claire barely noticed Sheriff Podlacs and revealed little between nods into brief sleep. Yes, she had found Dr. DeWulf's body. Yes, she was one of his students. Yes, she was more than a student to him. No, she did not know who would have done such a thing. Her "no" sounded less certain to Homer than her "yeses," but he did not press her further at the time.

Daunted by the thought of taking notes on anything additional the housemother might care to say, Homer excused himself and left, kicking a small chip off the wooden frame of the front door as he did so. Once in the yard, he stopped the first girl he came to, the Coyote who looked like a china doll. China Doll was voluble, and Homer took voluminous notes, but became ever more distressed as he scribbled.

"She's just about the very last person I ever thought would do a thing like that," China Doll said of Claire emphatically.

"Do what?" Homer asked, pad in hand, pencil poised.

"Oh, you know, sort of go A.W.O.L. from the House and spend the night with a professor."

"I guess it's not too uncommon, though, in this day and time is it, Miss?" Homer mused as he wrote.

"It is a little if you've been going steady with somebody else for a year."

"Now just what is the connection, do you think, if any, between the perfesser the girl spent the night with and the one that got murdered?"

"Everybody says they're one and the same."

"Do you know that for a fact?"

"Well, no, not absolutely, but everybody's convinced they're the same, just like two and two makes four."

"When did this happen? The night the Sumners girl stayed out all night, I mean."

"Oh, let's see, about ten days ago, ah, Tuesday or Wednesday night of last week, I guess, yeah, Tuesday."

Counting back on his fingers, Homer finally said, "February seventh, huh?"

"Yeah, like I said."

"Now, Miss, you said earlier that this Claire-girl had been dating somebody else for a year or so?"

"Right, and we thought they were going to get married."

"Do you know who?"

"Sure, everybody does."

"Not me, Miss," Homer observed, arranging to sound officious and left out.

"It was Bucky Oaks."

Startled, looking up from his note pad, Homer exclaimed, "*Not Bucky Oaks, the football star!*"

"Sure, who else?" asked China Doll, sounding a little put out that anybody could be so dense.

Aw, shit, Homer thought, as well he might. Sheriff Podlacs yielded to nobody in his love of Algonquin's football Braves, among whom none shone more luminously than Anthony Starbuck Oaks, ASU's stellar linebacker. Why, scouts from the pros had begun coming to home games just to see Bucky, and Bucky alone, play. Moreover, Bucky was a pious Catholic, a co-communicant, in fact, at Homer's own church. Linking his celebrated name to a possible crime-of-passion was the very last thing the sheriff wanted to do.

"Yeah, Claire and Bucky were sure having lots of fights just before she up and went A.W.O.L. that night," China Doll went on, sighing a little and breaking into Homer's distraction.

"Goddam, I hate that like the devil," he said aloud to himself later as he sped off to undertake various investigations at Adrian's apartment house.

Grace Moore Mistledine was as unnerved by Sheriff Podlacs's unexpected presence in her establishment as she was by the news that one of her roomers had been murdered. As she unlocked the door, trembling, to what had been Adrian's apartment so that the sheriff could have a "look-see around," as he put it, she was having a hard time thinking of ways in which to work in anything about the excellent proposals of marriage which she had received when young.

"Well, it don't look like there's anything very revealing here, does it?" Homer said after a leisurely "look-see around."

"No, I shouldn't think so," Grace agreed, grasping all the while for an association between Adrian's unrevealing room and the heartbreaks she had caused in her many suitors.

"Oh, by the way, when was the last time you seen the deceased?" Homer asked.

"Ah, mercy me!" replied Miss Mistledine, "I seldom saw Professor De-Wulf. He wasn't very sociable, not much of a conversationalist at all."

"Speakin' of sociable, did you know he may have had a young woman in here overnight at least once, one of his students, that is, about ten days ago?"

"*No!*" she said in particular horror, no proper association being possible between that horrid possibility and the relationships in which she had stood to her various suitors.

"Now, as to last night, did you see him or know that he was in, or did you hear him go out or anything like that?" Homer asked.

"My stars! Well, I never!" said Miss Mistledine, reeling from multiple shocks.

"Yes, mum," Homer went on patiently, "now about last night?"

"I think I may have heard his typewriter going, sort of in bursts, you know, but with what the wind was doing to the timbers up overhead last night, all that creaking and moaning, it's hard to be sure."

"About what time was that, mum?"

"The typing, you mean? Oh, I don't know, maybe from eight to nine or nine-thirty."

"Nothin' after that?"

"No, I don't think so. Oh, I take that back. It seems to me I did hear his phone ring once, or somebody's down below."

" 'Bout when was that?"

"Maybe nine-thirty or a little later."

Subsequent inquiries made of others in Miss Mistledine's apartment house indicated that Adrian had probably been in his apartment on the night of Thursday, February 16, but that nobody had positively seen him come in or go out. And, yes, someone had typed in short bursts for quite a while. Of that the people in apartment 1A, directly below his room, were quite sure. Also, there had probably been at least one ring of his phone around nine-thirty or a little later. Nobody had heard a thing but the storm after that. A phone call to campus security informed Homer that a night watchman had checked every door on the third floor of the Ad. Building between 11:15 and 11:25 that night as was his custom. Adrian's door was locked as usual, and the black at the back of his transom window indicated that the office was empty.

With supper over that Friday night, February 17, Homer got his wife, Evelyn, into the investigation by suggesting that she might nose around a little concerning the love angle between the girl who had found the body and Bucky Oaks. "You mean that football player?" Evelyn asked. "Yeah," Homer replied, feeling terribly apprehensive. During much of the rest of the evening and well into Saturday morning, Sheriff Podlacs's home phone was tied up. On the basis of what Evelyn learned thereby, China Doll's information was confirmed and there seemed to be no way of keeping Bucky Oaks out of the investigation.

Believing the feed and seed business and his public services experiences to have taught him much of psychology, as well as philosophy, Homer liked to spring verbal surprises on people under investigation, or use other psychological ploys. So, on Sunday morning, he donned his sheriff's uniform and drove to the parish church of Saints Joseph and Jude well ahead of early Mass. Carefully selecting a parking place where his official car would be highly visible and from which he could observe all who entered the church, he waited and watched for Bucky Oaks. He did not, of course, know which of the morning's three Masses Bucky would attend, but he wanted Bucky to see him and his sheriff's car as he entered the church. Homer would be on the alert for any sign of apprehension, any change in Bucky's gait, any furtive looks, voice tremors, or whatever. At long last Bucky arrived for the eleven o'clock Mass, the third of the morning, sauntering along with several of his football buddies and seeming cheerful. Waiting until he was sure Bucky had seen his official car, Homer eased out of it and joined the throng of communicants streaming into the church in such a way as to draw near to Bucky. The two had seen each other at worship often enough, but never before had Bucky seen the sheriff in his full dress uniform at that time and place. If this surprised him, he did not show it.

"Mornin' there, Bucky," said Sheriff Podlacs, looking at the athlete intently, but trying to keep suspicion out of his eyes.

"Oh, hi, Sheriff," Bucky said, looking anything but apprehensive.

"Everything goin' all right with you?" Homer went on.

"Not too bad, I guess. How about you?" Bucky replied casually. He was not about to bring up the disaster in his love life at that point.

With that their exchange ended as others stepped between them on the way into the sanctuary. Crossing himself, Homer was relieved to see Bucky so cool, if not altogether convivial. But that in itself did not allay his worries and suspicions, because Bucky was renowned for being cool under pressure. J. R. "Drub" Arnholder, the head football coach, had made that point repeatedly as had Rip Ballou, the radio voice of the Algonquin Braves. Bucky could look as cool as an iceberg and then simply explode into fiery action, or he could seem as relaxed as a dozing tiger only seconds before lunging across the field to smother-crush an opposing back. During the slower moments of the Mass, Homer pondered the problem of where he would nail Bucky for a few questions, also which question he would use as an opener. After the ancient ritual of appeasement, of bowing and scraping, of hand-clasping and crossing oneself was over, Homer hastened out to await

Bucky. He wouldn't nail the athlete on the church steps in front of the whole congregation (too embarrassing for the boy) but would get him a half a block away where and when the people would have thinned out some.

"Oh, Bucky, hold up a minute," Homer said authoritatively at what he took to be the appropriate time and place.

Stopping dead in his tracks, Bucky turned to confront Sheriff Podlacs, expecting a word of praise or of appreciation as much as anything else, even though the football season had long since passed.

"How much did you dislike that murdered perfesser, Adrian DeWulf?" Homer asked, springing what he thought would be a surprise.

"Not nearly enough," Bucky snapped, scowling instantly.

Then it was Homer's turn to be surprised. Finally, he stammered, "I . . . I wonder if you'd care to . . . elaborate on that comment."

"Well," said Bucky, glowering in the sheriff's direction, "that bas . . . ah . . . that man [it was, after all, Sunday] not only ruined my girl's mind, he also seduced her, it looks like, and took her away from me." After their all-day fight on Tuesday, February 7, Claire had refused to see Bucky or to respond to his phone calls at the Coyote House and had assiduously avoided him elsewhere. Keeping him completely in the dark, she had merely said that she wanted to remain his friend but did not intend to date him anymore or see him in private. It was not until after he had heard the news of her appearance before the discipline committee on Monday, February 13, that it had dawned on him that there was probably a lot more going on between DeWulf and her than a meeting of minds.

"Bucky, where was you at 9:30 P.M. last Thursday night, the sixteenth of February?" Homer asked sharply, his chagrin at what could have been construed as an incriminating comment having lessened.

"I don't know right off hand," Bucky said, then added reflectively, "probably at Chief's pool hall."

"Anybody there with you?"

"Sure, lots of people."

"Did you get back to the athletic dorm in time for the regular check-in—eleven, isn't it?"

"Sure thing."

"Can you prove it?"

"Easy."

"What was you doin' between the time you left the pool hall and checkin' in?"

"Cruising around." Bucky had in all truth done a lot of cruising around since he and Claire had begun to fight. But had he been cruising around just then?

"Alone?"

"Yeah."

"Anybody see you?"

"I don't know. Why?"

"I'll let you figger that one out for yourself," Homer said. "How long did you cruise around, Bucky?"

"Quite a while."

" 'Bout when did you leave the pool hall?"

"I don't know. Chief, or maybe Eddie, down at the hall, could probably tell that as good as I could."

"You make any phone calls earlier that evening?"

"Don't think so. No, I'm sure I didn't; why?"

Ignoring the question, Homer said very gravely, "Bucky, until I say it's okay I don't want you to leave Algonquin without lettin' me know about it and tellin' me where you're goin' to."

"Sheriff Podlacs, you don't really think I rubbed out that DeWulf guy, do you?"

"Don't matter what I think, Bucky."

"Well, I can tell you now, I didn't. I'm a Christian like you, and Christians don't go around killing people, even people who use them as bad as he used me."

"Oh, I know that, Bucky, but it's also well known that you had somethin' against him, and I have to look into all angles."

"Yeah, but no more than lots of others," Bucky said. Then, exaggerating a little, he added, "This place is full of people who hated that professor's guts."

"It is?" Homer asked in disbelief.

"Sure, everybody around ASU knows it too," Bucky went on almost abstractedly.

Thinking of putting Evelyn onto the gut-hating angle right away, Homer said, wagging a finger at him, "Just don't forget what I said, Bucky, about leavin' town, will you? Because I really mean what I say about that."

"No," said Bucky, placid and unconcerned to all appearances.

"Win, lose, or draw, he's a cool one," Homer murmured to himself as he slipped into his car and drove home to lunch.

Sheriff Podlacs's home phone remained busy during much of that Sunday afternoon and well into the evening. The same was true of several successive evenings. Moreover, during the coffee breaks and lunch hours of all the days of that week, the caller persevered in her inquiries, even taking a peek at certain appointment books.

Homer had long since received an oral report from the forensics lab that determined the cause of death and fixed its approximate time. Neither bit of information was surprising. The skull of the deceased had been pounded repeatedly by a heavy, flat object, the first of whose blows had probably only stunned him or, perhaps, rendered him unconscious. It was one of the subsequent pulverizing blows (of which there had been at least six) that caused death. Contusions and abrasions on the victim's right forehead and cheekbone (the latter also being fractured) indicated that the skull had been pounded while the body lay on the floor. In addition to bones and hair, which had been driven deeply into the victim's brain, there were tiny specks of dirt, but it could not be determined whether they had already been in his hair or had been introduced by the murder weapon. Death could have occurred any time between about 9:30 and 11:30 P.M. In addition to Adrian's, there were only two fingerprints that could be lifted well from anywhere in the office. One of these belonged to Sly Wilson, the janitor who usually tidied up on the third floor. The other turned out to be Claire's. Not only had the murder weapon not been found, it could not be identified as to type beyond being described as heavy (perhaps five or six pounds), smooth, and flat, i.e., the part or parts used in delivering the blows had no sharp edges or points. With this information in hand plus what he already knew, Homer jotted down the following summation:

1. (a) Victim could have met somebody at office because of prior agreement to be there.
   (b) Could have gone to office because called at home on phone and asked to meet at office—people at apartment house think victim's phone rang, but nobody saw him or saw him leave after reported typing.
   (c) Murderer(s) might have met victim on way to Ad. Build. office and gone there with him.
   (d) Murderer might have come to office and come into office after victim went there for reasons unknown as of now.
2. (a) Don't seem that there was a struggle between victim and assailant(s).
   (b) Victim might have opened door to an acquaintance voluntarily by previous agreement or maybe not, maybe on spur of moment.
   (c) Nobody found so far that admits to having planned to meet victim that night or who just happened by before crime.
3. (a) Greek books on desk might mean something. Victim could have been at desk using them when clobbered.
   (b) No blood on desk or books, books could have been put there later.
   (b) If later, could be an attempt to cast suspicion on unknown person(s). *Who?*
4. Victim's clothes show he had not been in office very long and maybe didn't plan to stay very long. Might be indication of prearranged meeting for short time.

Summary

Looks like maybe DeWulf was setting at desk, maybe looking up something for somebody when that person (?) was standing just behind him and to his left (pretending to look at books (Greek?) over his shoulder) and smashed him in head. Victim falls and assailant bangs away some more. Might not have been looking at books but at a document (letter?) or something.

To do

1. See Sumpter girl again to get more on love-jealousy angle, also finger-prints.
2. Go back to Doc Reid and talk more about enemies of the kind he mentioned, also check him out and maybe get prints.
3. Wait on Evie to snoop around some more on the enemies stuff.

One week to the day after the discovery of Adrian's body, Rad said, "Come in," to the unseen person who pummeled his office door with thunderous blows. Thus arrived Sheriff Homer Podlacs. After greeting the half-rising professor, Homer sat down, missing the center of the chair, rearranged himself, then asked abruptly, "Doc, how much did you hate DeWulf?"

Rad was too much a logician either to be rattled by or to answer, off the cuff, a complex question like that one. His breath was, however, taken away by Homer's ploy, and he hesitated before saying, "I was very fond of Adrian, really I was. In fact, in view of the sorrow I can't seem to shake off, I guess I must have loved him, a little bit at least."

"Well, relax, 'cause that confirms my information," Homer said reassuringly, "but I wanted to hear it from your own mouth anyway." Then he filled Rad in on most of what was known, including some of his information on Bucky Oaks.

After seeing Claire on the day of her grisly discovery, Homer had revisited her once, getting her fingerprints and jotting down additional information. Though more forthcoming than she had been previously, she still had little to offer, and Homer dreaded the distinct impression she conveyed to him that she was protecting Bucky. "No, no, no," she kept insisting, "I do not know who could have killed Professor DeWulf." Not even when Homer prompted her with Bucky's name did she appear to place any credence in that possibility. "I keep telling you over and over, I do not know who could have done such an awful thing," she wailed, then wept at length. Homer left the Coyote House of two minds after his Monday afternoon visit with Claire. On the one hand, Bucky had been so cool, so utterly unperturbed after church the day before, that he just had to be innocent; on the other hand, there was something unnerving—and suspicious—about the fact that the girl most deeply involved in the whole sad affair would not make a connection, even in theory, between Bucky, her jilted boyfriend, and DeWulf, her dead lover. Was she protecting Bucky, because she still loved him, in spite of her love affair with the perfesser? Homer wondered over and again, fearing that that was the sort of information that not even Evie could worm out of her many contacts.

Tilting forward in his chair with a hand to his mouth, as though to foil an eavesdropper, he said, "Doc, I'm going to let you in on a little secret."

"Shoot," said Rad.

"You remember what you told me about DeWulf having what you called intellectual enemies?"

"Yes."

"Well, I'm here to tell you that that young man had people all over this campus, and in town, too, that detested him."

"For what, for God's sake?"

"For what he done to people's religion—ridiculin 'em and everything for what they believed in."

"Isn't it a bit strong to say that people detested him?"

"Not from where I'm settin' it ain't, not when I've probably got to find the motive to find the murderer."

Tugging at his moustache reflectively, Rad said slowly, "Sheriff, I guess you know (or do you?) that DeWulf was fired, as of the end of this term, the very day he was killed."

"Yep, I do know that." (Evie was nothing if not thorough.)

"Well, that's one of the ways of getting rid of detested people around a place like this, but not murder. No, no, people around universities don't murder their opponents, ideological or otherwise."

"Sure as shootin', somebody did," Homer said emphatically, scoring a point, "and I've got to try to find out who."

"Of course you do, but it's just inconceivable to me that your suspects, such as they are, could include any of DeWulf's colleagues or any of the officials at ASU."

"Doc," Homer said, "I've got a list of people on this campus that despised DeWulf, judging from what they said at one time or another, that's as long as my arm from the elbow down." With that he arose, caught his foot on the chair he had been sitting in (making a big noise), and surged this way and that getting out of Rad's office.

Although Homer had indeed exaggerated the length of his list, he had not exaggerated the depth of feeling that had developed in some circles against Adrian DeWulf. In very truth, Adrian was detested, despised, and loathed by a considerable number of Algonquinites, in both town and gown. Chief among the enemies on Homer's list were Mr. Redford Hepple and President Sythian MacGilvary. Red was absolutely furious and swore a blue streak when he saw himself and his fellow board members compared in print, in the *Signal Flare,* with the members of the Presidium of the Central Committee of the Communist Party of the USSR. His anger was intensified, moreover, by his failure to understand what "that son of a bitch of a professor" was getting at. With respect to the disgusting Dodge Praeville sex scandal, it still seemed perfectly sensible to him to say to the students who had attacked MacGilvary's handling of the affair, ". . . if any of you can show me any place in the New Testament where it says that students on a school paper have the right to attack the administration of that school . . . then I'll believe it." Evelyn Podlacs had found a person who could and did give a verbatim report of the blue streak of profanity which Red swore at the time.

ASU's hometown trustee lost no time in spouting off to President Mac-Gilvary. Elbowing his way one day into Sythian's very tight schedule, Red said, "Syth, I want you to get rid of that DeWulf bastard, and on the double. Nobody talks about me and . . . the other board members like he did and gets away with it." Red spoke so loudly that Miss Ellison, Sythian's private secretary, heard every angry word as though there were no wall and no closed door between them. She did not hear everything the president said in response, but she already knew his mind on that score. Way back during the previous fall term, Sythian had been angered—had even said, "*Damn it to Hell!*"—when DeWulf had attacked him in print over his handling of that wild and woolly theologian, Chester Clydesdale, who had spoken on campus. At that time, Sythian had dictated a negative assessment of DeWulf for insertion into his file folder in the personnel office. Then, after the commencement service at the end of the fall term, DeWulf had struck again, and it was not stretching things at all to say that President MacGilvary had been fit to be tied over it. In fact, he had told Miss Ellison then and there to remind him midway through the winter term to have DeWulf terminated. He would have done it on the spot, but he had not wanted to disrupt the philosophy department, all of whose plans for the winter term had been laid. Also, he wanted the university attorney to look into the situation. It would not be prudent, Syth knew, to remove even so lowly a person as a temporary faculty member on religious grounds. Moreover, according to Professor Reid, DeWulf had threatened the administration with legal action should he be removed for anything that might be construed as a violation of his civil liberties, one of which was complete religious freedom. As Red Hepple left, Miss Ellison heard Sythian say, ". . . so, don't worry, Red, DeWulf will be gone by the beginning of the spring term and will not, I repeat, will not ever have a chance of returning."

Evelyn Podlacs also discovered through Dean Braniff's secretary that he too had been irked, to say the least, by DeWulf's "lipping off all the time on religion" and using antireligious arguments in his logic exams and the like. Furthermore, Braniff had had it up to his ears with the many complaints about that new philosophy professor that flooded his office each week, members of the Campus Crusade for Christ being particularly vociferous in their displeasure. But, since he had not himself been attacked in print as had Red Hepple and President MacGilvary, he had no reason to be quite so aggrieved as they. Still and all, he was no friend of DeWulf and breathed a huge sigh of relief when the order to terminate him came down.

While pumping Braniff's secretary at lunch one day, Evelyn acquired unexpected information from the religion secretary who, passing by, paused at their table for a few minutes to talk. "Well," said the religion secretary, getting into the spirit of things, "Ida Ijjam, Harvey's wife, says DeWulf just made her husband very mad at a party one night, just got him to using very vulgar language, something he hardly ever stoops to. Ida even had to shush him up. Anyway, it seems that DeWulf made mockery of the Trinity, I think it was, or something like that, something about clones, whatever they are, you know, really crazy stuff."

"Anything more?" Evelyn asked, fascinated by the way her investigation was ramifying.

"Oh, there was another episode, but I guess I'd better not go into it."

"Why not?" Evelyn asked, seeming to relish the tittle-tattle for its own sake.

"Well, Harvey, I mean Dr. Ijjam, came into the office just after the noon hour one day a few weeks ago, and was he furious! I don't know that I've ever seen him so wrought up."

"Why, for heaven's sake?" Evelyn asked, adroitly leading the religion secretary on.

"Actually, he didn't tell me personally, but O. K. Grampian came into the office just then to get his mail and noticed that Harvey was pretty well steamed up and asked him if he was all right, and Harvey said, 'I don't mind telling you that I was just knocked off my pins a few minutes ago by that s.o.b. DeWulf, in the philosophy department. He announced to me, as cheeky as you please, that Jesus was really a leader of the Palestine Liberation Organization of the time, that he was involved in an insurrection—he even cited scriptural passages—and was crucified by the Romans for that reason.' Well, believe me, that really got to O. K., and he began to get about as upset as Harvey, not just because he was angry about that PLO stuff but because DeWulf had attacked O. K. in print for something he had written about that Candy McIntyre who was Miss Algonquin, you know. Anyway, O. K. said, 'Oh, that deplorable man is an absolute menace to this institution,' and Harvey agreed, and they ended their conversation by agreeing that we ought to get rid of DeWulf as soon as possible."

As the religion secretary prattled on, Evelyn began to feel as though she were sinking in a sea of information, information that would surely swamp her unless she could find the time to jot it all down fairly quickly, then organize it, and try to make sense of it all for Homer. When, after a few days, it became clear to certain key secretaries on campus that Evelyn was not merely curious about DeWulf's murder, as everybody else was, but was actually helping her husband, informants began to get in touch with her. In that way she found out about the nasty trick DeWulf had played on Cecil Rathbone, pious old coot that he was. One informant, who remained anonymous, said, "DeWulf, pretending to be a member of the new Holy Nation sect, did his damnedest to persuade Professor Rathbone to believe in something silly called three-world creationism as though it was his Christian duty to do so. Why, he even chased the poor old guy down the stairwell in the Ad. Building trying to get him to believe that stuff, but then Rathbone found out it was all a joke and got very angry. You know, he takes his religion pretty seriously."

Evelyn's ears really pricked up when another anonymous informant also mentioned the Holy Nation aggregation. That informant said, "It seems that

DeWulf turned a SEBBFLC meeting—you know, that brown bag faculty religion luncheon thing—into an absolute shambles the day when Reverend Plumwell of the Church of the Chosen spoke. Some folks think that Plumwell got in some good licks, but most say that DeWulf chopped the preacher's legs off at the knees and he didn't even know what was happening. DeWulf also sort of attacked the founder of that religion and said some pretty awful things about how God and the devil are alike."

"Was anyone else involved, you know, angry?" Evelyn asked, casting her net ever more widely.

"Yeah," said the second informant, "the people that were the maddest at DeWulf were faculty members from Plumwell's church, such people as Bobby Duke Donough, the parasite man; and Atherton Landis in family and child development; and Rollo Skeeds at the library; and some kid who's been hanging around here long enough to have a couple of advanced degrees named Oscar Jiminie."

"Oh, I know him, everybody does," Evelyn said, nodding her head.

"Well, he almost worships the ground Plumwell walks on, from what I hear," the second informant said, "and really got mad at DeWulf for what he did to the minister."

Other names, such as Lucien Montmorency and Melius Atarbaxes, eventually wafted Evelyn's way from other sources of information, but their owners, though put out with Adrian, did not seem to be aggrieved due to any kind of personal attack. Evelyn also learned of the feminist meeting that Adrian had thrown into consternation with his "ridiculous suggestion" that women would never be free as long as they kept on swearing by male deities, but no confirmed DeWulf-haters seemed to have emerged from that (to some people) tawdry episode.

Homer had developed a fair amount of poise and not a little gall over the years, but some of the identities that Evelyn revealed to him robbed him of both and filled him with dread. "How in the holy hell," he asked himself, "am I gonna confront Mr. Redford Hepple on this matter?" Hepple was one of the richest, most commanding, and best known people in Algonquin. Moreover, he was reputed to have a long memory for slights, and some said he could be rough as a cob when riled. Even to hold him under sufficient suspicion to question him about his whereabouts on the night of the murder might lead to a blowup, something Homer did not want to happen, not under his nose at least. "Anyway," the sheriff mumbled to himself, trying to paraphrase Rad Reid's point, "there's lots of ways of gettin' rid of people at a university without resortin' to murder." Red Hepple had known that and had acted on it. So, what motive would he have had to *kill* DeWulf? With that reasoning, Homer managed to avoid questioning the great man.

Sheriff Podlacs went through much the same agony with President MacGilvary. Sythian was a smoothie, everybody agreed on that, but he could be damned intimidating when he wanted to be. And the Lord knew he was a prominent man! Thus, as embarrassed at the thought of questioning ASU's chief executive as he was at the thought of confronting Hepple, Homer decided to try to find out surreptitiously where each man was at the time of the crime. So, Evie wrangled a peek, as best she could, at the business and social calendars of each, then Homer followed up by checking into whether or not the individual in question had actually turned up where he was supposed to be. Feeling similar anxieties over questioning professors, especially religion professors, concerning their whereabouts on the fatal night, Homer pursued much the same kind of surreptitious course in their cases as in the cases of Red and Sythian. Not only were these procedures indirect, they were time consuming, productive of unwanted gossip, and in some cases disquieting. Knowing what he did, Homer decided to lie low for a while, keeping an eye on all suspects, and waiting for something new, something unexpected or serendipitous even, to help break the case wide open.

Late on the Friday afternoon following Adrian's memorial service, Rad heard a diffident knock on his office door. Claire Sumner, her face drained of color and emotion, opened it a crack and asked if she could bother him for a moment.

"Please, have a chair," Rad said, half rising behind his desk.

Moving as though she might break asunder at any joint at any moment, she sat down slowly and said woodenly, "I'm Claire Sumner."

"Yes, I know. How may I help you?"

Speaking very slowly, as if the articulation of each word were a major accomplishment, she said, "I haven't really been in the world for a while, if you know what I mean."

"I think I do; better than that, I know I do," Rad replied in deep sympathy.

"It may seem strange to you," she went on, "but I haven't listened to anything people have tried to tell me or to ask me about Adrian, I mean, about Dr. DeWulf."

"I'm afraid there's precious little to tell."

"But, I mean I'm not even sure I know the basic facts about anything. Up to this point, I haven't wanted to know. I just wanted people to leave me alone. But, now, I seem to have to get it all straight. That's one of the reasons I'm here. I thought you'd know."

"I'm happy to share whatever I know, but it isn't much, as I told you."

"Why did he have to come here that . . . that awful night?"

"We don't know whether he was lured into coming or whether his being here was a coincidence. I'm inclined to think the former, but I certainly have no concrete evidence, nor do the authorities as far as I know, and there is no solid suspect yet, I guess from what I'm told." Rad considered mentioning Bucky Oaks, but thought better of it.

"Do you think he knew it was going to happen, at the time, I mean, just before it happened?" Claire asked, beginning to show emotion.

"Possibly, but there is no indication that he was alarmed. Of course, that would be impossible to prove, but there was no sign of a struggle. He seems to have been sitting at his desk looking up something, perhaps at the request of the person or persons who did it. It seems probable, although I don't know how probable, that he did not know the blow was coming, that he never knew what hit him. It's likely that he was looking away from it, not suspecting anything like it. Everything I know about head injuries, which isn't all that much, indicates that he died without pain, maybe instantly. The lab report also tends to confirm that as I understand it."

After a pause, during which Rad thought there was a flicker of relief on her face, Claire said, "I don't know if you knew it or not, but we, Adrian and I, had fallen in love with each other, well, really more than that, we were already lovers. That may be hard for you to understand, but . . ."

"Why should it be hard to understand? It's the most understandable thing in the world," Rad said, looking at her appreciatively. How beautiful she must be when not grieving, he thought as another flicker of relief seemed to relax her drawn face.

"We were planning to get married as soon as possible, as soon as I could figure out how to break the news to my parents. They couldn't possibly have accepted him right away because of the kind of person he was, religiously I mean, but I loved him so very, very much—I was happier than ever before in my whole life—I know that they would have come around in time, if we'd just had more time." No longer drained of emotion, her movements no longer wooden, she buried her head in her hands at the thought of their brief time together and cried uncontrollably.

Casting professional caution to the winds, Rad moved quickly to her side, lifted her from her chair, and held her very close, somehow protecting her, it seemed. "I know it's living hell for you," he said, "but think about Adrian for a moment. Unless one has died triumphantly for a great cause, what cleaner way is there to go, what more benign way to end it all than to leave life instantly, knowing no fear and having been filled with love and joyous expectations right up until the moment of departure."

Trying to remember as vividly as possible what it had been like to be young, to be a lover with his beloved, Rad said, "Having told me what you did this afternoon about Adrian and yourself, I know, and you know, that you were on his mind every moment he was here that night, even though he may have been looking up something for someone else, or thought that's what he was doing. With all of his mind most of the time and with more than half of his mind at every waking moment, he was thinking about you; you were an abiding presence to him all the while. He died young, but he died in love, and that's nothing to make light of. Many people, I'm afraid, lose love and die without it, having found a long life to be little more than long years of futility and disappointment and regret. It may be small comfort, but at least he was spared that." Adrian may also have died so much in love and so soon that there had been no reason and no time for a lovers' quarrel, Rad mused, envious of that blessing.

Sensing that her sobbing had become more gentle, more accepting, he released her from his arms and for some inexplicable reason used both hands to push back her hair on both sides of her forehead, then held her face gently. Not believing in life after death any more than Adrian had, but remaining hopeful toward even the slightest possibility of it (whereas Adrian had entertained no hope), Rad said to Claire, "As for you here and now, don't feel that you have to go it alone. Talk to Adrian just as you did when you two were temporarily separated. Call his name. Listen to him. Sense him close at hand. Let him be a living, loving presence in your life. Above all, remember him, and keep remembering him until you can smile again at his remembrance, or, better yet, until you can laugh at what I know must have been moments of great good humor the two of you shared."

After what seemed an eternity, she squeezed his right hand with hers, nodding affirmatively, thanked him with her eyes, bit her bottom lip upon turning from him, and left the office wordlessly but not woodenly. Rad's words reminded her poignantly of how Adrian had said over and again, marveling each time, that her love had made him feel "incalculably valuable." Indeed, hers was the loss, for Adrian had in fact (and she knew it) died feeling as he had said she made him feel, "incalculably valuable." Professor Reid was right; there could be no better frame of mind in which to die than that, if, that is, one had to die. But why did Adrian have to do the dying, why her beloved, and not another?

Shortly before noon the following Monday, Claire was back in Rad's office. "Dr. Reid," she said a little apologetically, "when I was here last Friday, I completely forgot the second reason why I came."

"Which was what?" he asked, smiling, pleased to see her appearing to be more vivacious than before.

"To thank you for the very, very kind and sweet thing you did for Adrian's memory; you know, the memorial service you conducted for him. I'm afraid I wasn't helpful at all."

"I'm pleased to hear your words of thanks, but I cannot really take any," he said gravely, "for I very much wanted to mark his passing, to make whatever gesture I could to his memory."

In the weeks that followed, the bond between the bereaved at Algonquin deepened. At one time or another, Claire told Rad everything about herself and Adrian and about the results of their love. She had been put on social probation for the rest of the term by the discipline committee, but that was no more than the house arrest under which she had been living, and it meant nothing to her. She was so far behind in her class work that she would probably have to take some "incompletes," but she assured him that she would stick it out and finish her junior year. Her parents had forgiven her, more or less, not knowing the depths of Adrian's paganism. Her relationship with Bucky Oaks was finished, period! yet she refused even to cast the slightest suspicion in his direction. The more Rad saw of her, the more he understood how easy it would be to fall in love with her. Ah, Adrian, how very lucky! How dreadfully unlucky!

Meanwhile, Bucky seemed to be doing very nicely without Claire. After his initial rage and his impotent cruising around, he began to date again, squiring several girls around campus, including Candy McIntyre, Miss Algonquin. Later, he settled on Theresa McClain, raven-haired, petite, gentle, and Irish Catholic. Homer Podlacs watched it all from afar, but intently. At no time had Bucky shown the slightest anxiety over his lack of an alibi, nor did he attempt to find or to fabricate one. He certainly was a cool one, Homer mused again and again admiringly.

Immediately after Adrian's murder, Algonquin, both in town and gown, reacted with righteous shock and outrage. It was unthinkable that bloody murder should defame ASU's fair name, that fatal violence should invade her sanctity, the sanctity of thought and learning. But, with the passing of a scant week, or ten days at most, editorials in both the campus paper and the local daily began to point out that the victim had failed to restrain himself properly, had failed to exercise just responsibility in the exercise of his academic freedom. Though no commentator or letter writer said so in so many words, the implication in the papers was loud and clear: DeWulf had brought it on himself. The fool hath said in his heart; there is no God, and hard is the way of the transgressor! Scarcely a month after Adrian's death, he was all but forgotten. Indeed, among some who missed him, the "miss" was perceived as good. Algonquin, it seemed, could do very nicely (thank you) with one less atheist or without any atheists at all. Thus, the zeal to find the murderer or murderers, so very intense initially, petered out day by day and at the end of six weeks ceased to exist in all but a very few.

Apart from Claire Sumner and Rhadamanthus Reid, the one person most affected by Adrian's death was Manly Plumwell. This was not due primarily to the loss of his principal target of evangelism. It was due to his rapidly intensifying interest in some of the gibes Adrian had hurled at him and at the Holy Nation. In short, what had once been the barbs of bitterest ridicule became the topics of keenest theological preoccupation.

Adrian and Manly had bumped into each other unexpectedly in a laundromat one night shortly after their unhappy exchange in front of Antrim Library the day when Manly announced exuberantly that the Handmaiden of the Lord was coming to Algonquin. After that disagreeable news, Adrian had stormed into the library cursing under his breath and reviling the society in which simpletons, nincompoops even, could be welcomed on a university campus provided only that the simpletons or nincompoops in question were religious. Meanwhile Manly had stumped off campus with something like hatred in his heart for the insufferable dogmatism of a certain so-called sophisticate who wouldn't even give the gospel a fair hearing. Fed up with Manly but unable to get the ignoramus out of his hair, Adrian said loudly in the steamy air of the laundromat, "I don't think it's right to give medical care to those who have profaned the Lord's table, do you, Brother Plumwell? By the way, where does the Holy Nation stand on that?"

"What in the world are you talking about?" Manly all but bellowed, forgetting for the moment that he had adopted a strategy of manifesting the love of the Lord JEsus to the apostate.

"Oh, you know," Adrian said as though Manly had merely been teasing.

"Well, I'm afraid I don't," the new Jew snapped, setting down his basket of dirty clothes.

"Why, surely," Adrian went on didactically, "you recall what the Apostle Paul, of sainted memory, said in I Corinthians, chapter 11, verse 27 and following, to wit: 'Whoever, therefore, eats the bread or drinks the cup of the Lord in an unworthy manner will be guilty of profaning the body and blood of the Lord. Let a man examine himself, and so eat of the bread and drink of the cup. For any one who eats and drinks without discerning the body eats and drinks judgment upon himself. That is why many of you are weak and ill, and some have died.' So, you see, Brother Plumwell, my position is that those who have fallen ill of profanation are merely experiencing condign justice and shouldn't receive medical attention. Of course, that would require physicians to know which diseases are the result of profanation and which are not. I was rather expecting—hoping even—that your Handmaiden would have made it all clear to you. In addition, I must say that I think those who die of profanation should be denied Christian burial. What do you say to that?"

"You're always busy tempting God, aren't you, DeWulf?" Manly answered lamely but loudly, never having thought about any of the things Adrian had just brought up.

Undaunted by Manly's retort, Adrian burbled on to another outrage. "Brother Plumwell, in your arduous studies of Holy Writ, have you come across any place where it says that the resurrected dead went ahead and sired more children?"

As most heads in the laundromat twirled in his direction, Manly said, "I have no idea what you're talking about, DeWulf, but I fear it's blasphemous as usual."

"Oh, you do too know what I'm talking about," Adrian asserted mischievously.

"Well, I don't!" Manly all but shouted.

"In Matthew 27, about the middle of the chapter," Adrian went on merrily, "it says that just after Jesus died on the cross, the curtain of the temple was rent in two, the earth shook, rocks were split, tombs were opened, and many bodies of dead saints were raised. And it goes on to say that these resurrected people went into the holy city and appeared to many, maybe even in the bedroom. I'm presuming, of course, that some of those resurrected people at least went back to their families and started life up again where they had left off. And, well, you know how propinquity breeds."

With every eye upon him by then, Manly said through clenched teeth, "The New Testament says nothing about the resurrected dead having any more children."

"Maybe church history does," Adrian persisted speculatively, "maybe there are a lot of Jews alive today who are the lineal descendants of the resurrected dead. Have you read much church history, Brother Plumwell?"

"No," Manly said explosively.

"Does your church baptize on behalf of the dead?" Adrian asked, changing the subject without warning.

"No, it most certainly does not," Manly replied, feeling himself to be on firm ground for the moment.

"I hate to see the Mormons get ahead of you new Jews on that score," Adrian declared, seeming to commiserate with Manly.

"There's no authorization at all for any such thing in the New Testament," Manly said authoritatively, seeming to get the upper hand.

"True enough," Adrian replied, sprinkling nodules of soap into a washing machine, "but when Paul mentions it in I Corinthians 15, he has nothing bad to say about the practice, and goodness knows he'd have jumped all over it if he'd thought it bad, because he was never shy about taking others to task; so, he must have thought it an acceptable practice at least."

To that Manly could find no answer.

Within days after Adrian's death, the barbs that had left the royal priest all but speechless in the laundromat became an obsession. Manly warned his parishioners again and again against taking the Lord's Supper in an unworthy manner, spoke darkly and often about the afflictions, sometimes fatal, of profanation, and tried in private to guess which diseases they might be (the most loathsome ones, he presumed). He also preached a sermon on I Corinthians 15:29, expounding on the ancient and honorable practice of baptism on behalf of the dead. But of all these ruminations, the most startling to his flock was the observation that converted Jews, like the great Mordecai Montefiori, who sat on the left hand of the Handmaiden, were the direct descendants of the resurrected dead mentioned in Matthew 27:52-3.

"*Mother of Pearl!*" exclaimed the Handmaiden as she read the letter from her pioneering campus minister expressing his deepest and most prayerful concern over certain points of doctrine. Obsessed by those points and still smarting under Adrian's earlier accusation (made the day he had rescued Claire from Manly's scolding) that the Holy Nation was by no means a full-gospel church, Algonquin's royal priest of the pulpit had taken his problems to the Handmaiden by mail. "If we are to be truly a full-gospel church," Manly wrote, "then it seems to me that we must have direct revelations, or illuminations at least, on the points I am raising herein." Then he proceeded to ask the Handmaiden a number of questions that left her quite breathless. Did she or did she not think that the converted Jews of history were the direct descendants of the dead resurrected at the time of the Savior's death? Should the Holy Nation, or should it not, let the Mormons stay ahead of them on the ancient and honorable (at least St. Paul had found no fault with it) practice of baptism on behalf of the dead? Weren't Christians commanded (still in modern times) to heal the sick and raise the dead? But did this apply to those who had fallen ill or died of profanation? Which diseases might be God's favorites in punishing profanation? Should a new Jew physician withhold treatment, and even palliation, from sick profaners, and what of Christian burial for profanation? Should a royal priest refuse to participate in a profaner's funeral? Manly ended his letter by expressing his keenest pleasure at the thought of the Handmaiden's coming to Algonquin in mid-May to participate in the spring term's religious emphasis week. He also expressed the fervent hope that she would have speedy revelations or illuminations on all the issues he had raised and that the two of them would be able to talk about it all at length and conclusively at that time. "It goes without saying," he wrote in a postscript, "that Algonquin's new Jews hope and pray that you will bless us with your revered presence at a worship service in our church if at all possible."

On the last Thursday in April, ten weeks after Adrian's death, Rad trudged home at the end of the day, still very much preoccupied with the unsolved murder, and found his wife upset. "What's wrong?" he asked after one quick look, not needing to be told that something was wrong.

"Read this," she said testily, tossing a piece of paper at him. The paper said, "Dearest Children, unless there is some compelling reason to the contrary, which you could convey to me by phone, Romulus, Remus, and I will visit you for several days next week. We plan to leave Jackson [Kentucky] on Sunday in the Buick and will expect to arrive in Algonquin, after a leisurely trip, on Tuesday, late in the afternoon we would expect. Love, Romulus, Remus, and Mother."

"Now, Rad," Miriam went on very intensely, "don't get me wrong, I'm very fond of your mother—she has many good qualities—but she doesn't mean *days,* she means a week or two."

"Could be," Rad said noncommittally.

"It isn't just the time I object to, you know," Miriam continued crossly, "it's those dogs. Well, not so much the dogs as such—I like dogs well enough—but the way she treats them, sometimes serving them like a slave and other times carrying on with them as though they were dunces in her classics class, and all the time making everybody and everything revolve around them."

Shortly after Rad's father died in 1955, two tiny black mongrel pups, as alike as two peas in a pod, appeared out of the blue on the front porch of Hypatia Kendall Reid. Bereaved, lonely, and lacking all purpose at the moment, she almost literally clasped them to her bosom, nourishing them, nurturing them, watching over them, exhorting them. Thus came Romulus and Remus to the Reid family.

"What can I do about the problem, if problem it is?" Rad asked, protest tinging his voice. After all, he could hardly tell his own mother to stay away, could he?

"Couldn't you ... ah ... isn't there any way you could get the point across that your mother is very welcome but not the whole menagerie—I mean, couldn't she leave those mutts in a kennel or ... or someplace?" Miriam asked, knowing that the answer would be "no" but protesting that answer in advance nonetheless.

"Ah, Miriam, you know that her whole life, since my dad died, is tied up with those dogs. Why, hell, she likes 'em better than she likes me any old day of the week," he expostulated.

"So, we're to have *mineral oil* on every single unguarded piece of fabric in the whole damn house, is that it?" Miriam went on, simmering with resentment. Her complaint about mineral oil was not, however, the raving of a demented housewife clutching at any straw to get her way. However and wherever Romulus and Remus sojourned, they got mineral oil on the overstuffed furniture, on coats hanging on hall trees, on jackets or sweaters inadvertently left over the backs of chairs, even on pant legs with the living legs still in them. In the mid-thirties, Hypatia underwent an appendectomy. Thereafter, upon her doctor's order, she drank a tablespoon of mineral oil, usually with a glass of juice or sometimes of tea, just before retiring at night. Twenty years later, when Romulus and Remus entered her family, she was still at it religiously. In fact she swore by mineral oil, attributing much of her well-being to it. As the dogs grew and became more humanized, they decided they should have what she was having, and she thought they should have what she was having too. So, even though they had not undergone appendectomies, they also began receiving their mineral oil, usually in milk but sometimes in canned broth or consomme, and on special occasions, such as the anniversary of their arrival on her porch, in clam chowder or homemade soup.

After getting their nightly nostrum, Romulus and Remus invariably undertook the lengthy chore of removing the mineral oil from their whiskers. Lap, lap, lap went their long pink tongues, first out of one side of their mouths, then out of the other, and finally out of the front, their tongues curling up and over their noses. Sometimes each one lapped the other's muzzle in fraternal cooperation, tails wagging, rumps swaying, while Hypatia exhorted them to continued altruism. But not even their best efforts, either singly or in cooperation, could remove all the cloying oils, especially when they had taken their medicine in a soup rich in animal fat. History does not record how Romulus and Remus first came to conclude their nightly ritual by rubbing their noses and wiping their muzzles on assorted fabrics. Perhaps Hypatia taught them, getting down on all fours and showing them how to approach and use a sofa or a hall tree laden with long coats. Perhaps Romulus alone first discovered the benefits to be obtained thereby and taught them to Remus by example, or perhaps it was Remus who made the great breakthrough in oil removal, teaching it to Romulus, or perhaps the twins fell upon it as one, guided by a common instinct. In any case, they became compulsive about it and would rub their noses vigorously on any person who tried to keep them away from the overstuffed furniture or various hanging garments.

"God, Miriam!" Rad all but exploded. "I don't want the residues of mineral oil, dog spit, and clam chowder seeping through my pant legs either, but, hell! I can't bring myself to tell my own mother that she can't come unless she leaves her family behind, or otherwise dictate terms to her."

So, the problem was settled, as each knew it would be, and in the course of time Romulus, Remus, and Hypatia Kendall Reid arrived, joining Rad and Miriam and their twins, Anita and Roxane, a season of pandemonium ensuing.

Even when visiting her only child and his family, Hypatia directed most of her speech toward Romulus and Remus, and when speaking to the non-canine members of her family spoke mostly of her dogs. In each case, she typically used couplets. If, for example, Romulus and Remus were up to something that bordered on bad taste, or was positively immoral, she would say sternly, "Cease, Romulus, and desist, Remus." Then she would repeat the words for purposes of fairness and equity as follows: "Cease, Remus, and desist, Romulus." If they persisted in questionable behavior, she would announce their need to recant and repent in no uncertain terms. If, on the other hand, they were obedient, she would croon of reward and recompense. Always up at the crack of dawn, she would greet the dogs, saying, "Let us rise, Romulus, and shine, Remus; let us rise, Remus, and shine, Romulus." Reluctance on their part to bound out of their warm beds was met with the words, "For we must be up and doing," expressed as an admonition. If other animals intruded where Hypatia thought they ought not to intrude, she would set the dogs on the animals in question, exhorting them to flush and pursue the offenders. After exerting themselves in that manner, Romulus and Remus would usually return panting and dangling their dripping tongues, to which Hypatia would say, "Do you huff, Romulus, do you puff, Remus?" and in perfect equity, "Do you huff, Remus, do you puff, Romulus?" Thereafter, she would suggest rest and relaxation to each in turn. On the rare occasions when the dogs had to be separated, she would bid them to say "Hail and Farewell" to each other (actually doing it for them). Ever and anon she warned them against snares and delusions, exhorting them to smite hip and thigh any particularly odious intruder on their domain (such as a rat), and reminded them that what was sauce for the goose was sauce for the gander, especially when feeding them, treating them to an unexpected morsel, or dosing them with mineral oil.

Always a pious Presbyterian and a regular churchgoer, Hypatia, however, became perfervid in one particular of faith, upon acquiring Romulus and Remus. Just as a believing wife can sanctify an unbelieving husband (according to I Cor. 7:14), so, she reasoned, can a believing owner sanctify an unbelieving pet, especially if that pet is a dog. Since eternal life in the spirit world was quite unthinkable to her without the spirits of Romulus and Remus ever present, and since they showed no signs at all of comprehending the gospel (much though she tried to get the point across to them), she

410

doubled and redoubled her efforts to live so as to sanctify them through herself. She also called their innocence and many virtues to God's attention in her multitudinous prayers, most of which focused on the subject of canine immortality. She remained a little sceptical of cats, parakeets, goldfish, and the like as candidates for eternal life, but never did she doubt that dogs, her dogs, at least, could qualify. Believing regular and frequent churchgoing to enhance her own sanctity, upon which so much depended, it is not surprising that early in her visit to Algonquin, she broached the subject of attending church on the forthcoming Lord's Day.

Rad, who had long since given up churchgoing, remarked that the girls could just as well take their grandmother to Sunday services. This caused Anita and Roxane to make very bad faces indeed and to protest rather stridently that that was an unfair proposal, one of the most unfair they had ever heard. Ignoring her granddaughters' protests, Hypatia delivered an impromptu lecture to Rad on the importance of filial piety and on the duties to which sons, especially only sons, are beholden. Unseen by her mother-in-law, Miriam grinned broadly, naturally, and spontaneously for the first time during the visit of Romulus, Remus, and Hypatia Kendall Reid.

Thus, it came to pass that Rad took his mother to church on the first Sunday morning of her visit, selecting for her edification the more conservative of Algonquin's two Presbyterian churches. The sermon, entitled "Oh To Grace, How Great A Debtor!" was delivered by the senior pastor, the Reverend Dr. T. Beadle Dunn, Princeton-educated all the way. His intent was to extol and magnify the love of God by emphasizing that grace, the grace God extends to sinners, is utterly unmerited. Reverend Dunn thought he could best make the point by showing what it was that grace had replaced, namely, the Law of Moses. So, he adverted to various capital offenses in the Old Testament and then dwelt at length on the punishments meted out, such as stoning, burning, decapitation, and mutilation. At an indeterminate point in Reverend Dunn's treatment of stoning, Rad said involuntarily, "Oh my God!"—surprising himself as well as others in nearby pews. "Cease and desist this instant," Hypatia whispered imperiously, as though upbraiding Romulus and Remus over some ruckus they had made. But Rad did not hear her, nor did he hear anything else in Reverend Dunn's sermon, so furiously, so intently did his mind start putting two and two together.

After bolting his dinner, scarcely noticing anyone in the family or saying a word, he excused himself and strode as fast as he could to the Ad. Building. There, in Adrian's old office, he looked again at the pages of the Greek-English Lexicon that had been open on the desk when Claire had found the body. Then Rad hotfooted it over to Antrim Library to look up the topic "Crime and Punishment" in various encyclopedias of the Bible and assorted reference works. After that, he loped across the yard in front of the Ad. Building to the Coyote House where he flabbergasted Miss Haskins with his authoritative insistence on seeing Claire Sumner at once. Claire was clearly puzzled but not unhappy to see him. Once they had positioned themselves in a far corner of one of the social rooms, he said secretively, "Okay, Claire, now tell me the rest of the story."

Registering disbelief at what she had just heard, she said, "What? Whatever do you mean?"

"I mean the rest of the story of your life."

"Of my life? Of my *whole life?*"

"Claire," he said insistently, unaware of his familiarity with her, "I'm now sure that I know the kind of person who killed Adrian. The question is: Which one of that numerous kind? I think the answer may lie with you. So, hit the high points of your life, especially after you got to Algonquin, then go on to the middle points, and, if need be, give me the lowdown on the low points too." At that he smiled, and so, too, did she.

An hour and a half later, Rad left the Coyote House and, after a thoughtful but brisk walk, arrived at home, amidst surprised looks, just in time for a light supper. Nothing he had heard from Claire had disappointed him. Everything he had heard conformed to the insight he had received in church that morning, and as always, when in her presence, he knew again how very easy it would be to fall in love with Claire Sumner, how easy to want to do good deeds for her, to want to protect her against . . . against any and . . . and all dangers. Immediately after supper, he called Homer Podlacs in the hope of arranging the earliest possible meeting. "Just name the time and place, and I'll be there," he said urgently. That same night, Rad went to see the sheriff.

Pushing on the door, which was ajar, Manly entered Rad's office punctually at 3:30 the following afternoon, saying, "Well, sir, here I am as I said I would be."

"Oh, hello there," Rad said, rising to take the Reverend Plumwell's hand and guide him to a chair.

Manly was very pleased over the invitation to visit Rad. He had made certain inquiries long since and knew the professor to be a lapsed Presbyterian. Reid, unlike the apostate DeWulf, was a philosopher who had a reputation for being gentle on religion, at least around students, and a reputation of living and letting live where faith was concerned. So, there was at least a chance, perhaps even a good chance, Manly reasoned, of winning him back to the Lord JEsus and of leading him into the bosom of the Holy Nation.

"How have you been getting along, Reverend Plumwell?" Rad asked as he settled himself into his desk chair.

"Oh, very well, very well indeed," Manly replied, lying whitely. "And how have you been, Professor Reid?"

"Not very well, to tell the truth," Rad said.

"I'm certainly sorry to hear that," Manly went on in his best pastoral fashion.

"You know, of course," Rad said, "about the terrible business involving Adrian DeWulf and all the disruption that has followed his death, to say nothing of the fact that the killer seems to have gotten off scot-free."

After a long pause, Manly said, "Well, for my part, I know that I did everything I could do to help him avoid his awful end."

"*What?*" Rad asked in surprise, not having expected the conversation to take that turn.

"I mean," Manly continued evenly, "that I did everything I could think of to offer redemption in the Blood of Christ to that man before it was too late, but would he listen to me? No, he resisted my very best efforts and my every prayer for his salvation. More than that, he ridiculed my church, the Holy Nation Association of Churches of the Chosen."

"Oh, well, I guess I didn't know about all of that," Rad mumbled, trying to size up Manly.

"I don't suppose there was any reason why you should have known all of it," Manly observed, "but I probably spent more sheer man-hours trying to bring him to JEsus than I have ever spent in witnessing to or in working for the Lord's sake with any other three people combined, or maybe even more."

"Yes, I guess he would have been a pretty tough nut to crack," Rad mused aloud as he tried to fathom the full significance of what he was just then hearing for the first time.

"Right, and look what it got him," Manly said intensely, "dead at an early age, unsaved, lost forever!"

Choosing his words very carefully, Rad said, "Since you worked with him so very hard—something I hadn't known about before—right up to the . . . to his untimely end, I wonder if you'd be interested in the particulars of the case?"

"Why, yes, yes, I . . . I would, but I didn't think any particulars were known, beyond the obvious ones that have been reported in the papers," Manly said.

"Oh, that was a police ploy to put the killer's mind at ease," Rad fibbed, leaning back in his chair and locking both hands behind his head. "No," he went on, "quite a lot is known about the crime."

"So, what is known?" Manly asked, sitting very straight in his chair and seeming to Rad to stiffen all over—though perhaps that was just Rad's imagination playing tricks on him.

Taking his hands down from behind his head and leaning forward as though to share highly privileged information with Manly, Rad said, barely above a whisper, "The simple fact is that the murderer tricked DeWulf into coming to his office. He called at about 9:30 on the night of February the sixteenth—that wild stormy night you may remember—and asked about some term in Greek, probably about the term 'agape' (love), judging from the pages in the Greek-English Lexicon left open on Adrian's desk. While he was sitting at his desk looking up the desired information, the murderer, standing behind him, leaned over and took a five-pound rock, or so, out of his

413

briefcase, or satchel of some kind, and struck him on the head. Then, when DeWulf fell to the floor, stunned or unconscious, the murderer kept pounding on his head against the floor, breaking his skull wide open." Without pausing for Manly to respond, Rad went on, saying, "Yes, he was stoned to death for blasphemy in general and for the special danger he posed to a certain young woman named Sumner."

As Manly sat in his chair staring, saying nothing, Rad said very grimly, shaking his head slightly as though in loathing, "You know, Brother Plumwell, the thing about it that was so bad, so very bad, was that it was done all wrong, the stoning, I mean."

"*Done all wrong?*" Manly all but shouted. "What do you mean, done all wrong?"

"Why, contrary to God's will, of course. As you well know, Reverend, the divinely authorized way, the biblical way, to execute an offender by stoning requires at least two witnesses to the crime. Also, the offender has to be led *out* of the city. Nobody is ever stoned on the spot. And, finally, the whole people do the stoning, never any one person and never by pounding on the offender with a rock or anything like that. No, the stones have to be *thrown* at the offender, first by the principal witness, then by everybody."

As Rad spoke those words, Manly's mouth fell open and his eyes stared wildly, as though (from Rad's perspective) the terrible realization had just dawned on him that he had forgotten something absolutely essential to carrying out God's will.

"As you well know, Brother Plumwell," Rad went on, reaching for a Bible, conveniently at hand, "Leviticus 24:25 says, 'Lift not thine own hand to strike a blasphemer, nor touch an offender, but call upon the whole people to cast the stones of judgment.'"

At that, Manly opened his own omnipresent Bible but was trembling so badly that he could not find the passage Rad had read. "What was that passage again?" he cried in great agitation.

"Why, Leviticus 24:25," Rad said, citing an existing chapter but a non-existent verse to go with the instructions about stoning he had cited.

Blundering through the pages again, Manly dropped his Bible, whereupon he leaped toward Rad, trying to grab the latter's Bible. But Rad saw him coming and rose to his full six feet, seven inches, holding his Bible aloft, far above Manly's frantic reach.

Panting and wild-eyed, Manly shrieked, "But it doesn't make any difference anyway, because we Christians live under grace, not law."

"Ah," said Rad, fending Manly off, "but the New Testament never authorizes any Christian to stone anybody, so the Old Testament still contains God's revealed will on stoning. No, Brother Plumwell, the murderer caused a terrible pollution by stoning DeWulf the way he did—the wrong way—and we're all going to pay a high price for it."

"I did not pollute this place, I *did not!* Do you hear me, Reid? I *did not*," Manly yelled, tears streaming down his face.

414

"I'm afraid you did," Rad said sadly as the tragedy rolled inexorably toward its conclusion. Unknown to Manly, Rad had positioned him in a chair so placed that he could not see Homer Podlacs come through the communicating door to Adrian's office in case anything happened remotely like what in fact did happen.

Beside himself, his arms hanging limply at his sides, Manly was completely vulnerable to the final horror that boomed in his ears as the High Sheriff of Algonquin County said, "Reverend Plumwell, I'm afraid you'll have to come down to my office for further questioning in the murder of Adrian DeWulf."

"I'll tell you one thing," Manly wailed as he whirled around to confront Homer, "and that is that I did *not* pollute this satanic place, because I obey God in all things, *do you hear?*" Then, whimpering, sobbing, wilting, and hiding his face in his hands and arms, he allowed himself to be led away meekly, as a lamb is led to the slaughter.

When Manly first laid eyes on Claire, he was far too preoccupied with himself to notice how lovely she was. Moreover, she was only one among several very attractive young women to show up at Algonquin's Church of the Chosen in the fall of 1958. At that time, he was also a college student (and of recent vintage), still unsure of himself academically, beset with school work, and laboring strenuously to establish his new congregation. In addition to his heavy workload, he was clearly stressed in trying to relate himself to students, many of whom were rather more advanced academically than he, and to people such as Atherton Landis who were intellectually far ahead of him. In short, trying to match himself to his own evolving ideas of the roles he was supposed to play was exceedingly difficult for him, especially since he spurned the very professionals who could and would have helped him.

Not only did he not notice Claire in particular during the first Sundays of her attendance that fall, but also he could not have noticed her much of the time, for she began to play hooky from church for the first time in her life, not yet having been included in Manly's college-age Bible class, just then developing. In most ways, Claire (the baby of her family) was a dutiful daughter to her elderly parents and took delight in pleasing them, especially in her school work. But religion was becoming a different matter. While still a little girl, she took the supernatural to be as real as the natural. God, his cherubim and seraphim, his angels and archangels, and the whole heavenly host were as real to her as her parents, her grown brother and sister, her aunts and uncles, and assorted cousins. Jesus was her sweet savior, always hovering above her bed while she slept, ready to take her soul to heaven should she die before she woke. And her church, the Heather Church of Christ, was a New Testament church. She did not know exactly what that meant, but there could be no doubt that it was a very good thing, because she knew the New Testament to be God's Holy Book.

Then came Herod Agrippa Smallwood, rolling his head and belting out hymns on the grass out in front of her church. That was followed shortly by terrible acrimony in the congregation. Families were sundered, their members shunning each other. People who had been lifelong friends and neighbors ceased to talk to one another and to speak well of one another. As she perceived it, her parents became fanatics on behalf of the new religion that had emerged from the spiritual melee in her church. The most disturbing, the most confusing part of the whole sorry episode involved the new certainties they espoused and superimposed on her, certainties that destroyed some of their earlier certainties, the old certainties in which she had been steeped. Loving her mother and father though she did, she couldn't help wondering if they had gone crazy. Outwardly, dutifully to all appearances, she followed them into the new faith, into the Holy Nation of new Jews and royal priests. But, unlike their wholehearted conversion, hers was half-hearted at best. Somehow or other, she never could get very inspired about the supposed goodness and near-infallibility of the Handmaiden of the Lord and never could swallow three-world creationism without choking on the "dumb stuff." Nevertheless, she went to church without protest and kept up appearances for the sake of her own peace and quiet.

When the fateful day came for her parents to deliver her by car to far off Algonquin State University, they spent much of the trip taking turns reminding her that she was not to change her (admittedly) good ways, her manners or her morals, just because she was going away to college. Most importantly, she was to go to church regularly. She was not to forget that the principal reason she was sent to Algonquin (rather than some place closer to home) was that the Holy Nation had just established a pioneering campus ministry there. No, she would not forget. Yes, of course, she would go to church regularly. But, with college life affording her more fun that she had ever had before and with Saturday night parties robbing her of sleep, she became a bit wayward in church attendance until Bro. Manly Plumwell, armed with her name and campus address, came looking specifically for her.

For him, it was the beloved curse of love at first (close) sight. However, being Manly and being a pioneering royal priest, he could not tell her what had happened to him. Moreover, he could not treat her differently from the other young people in his college-age Bible class, and, finally, could not, simply could not, let her intrude disruptively in his thoughts nor into his arduous preparations on behalf of God's Holy Nation. Of the various things he could not do, the last was the hardest not to do. As time went on, as he cemented her ever more firmly into different college-age projects, he could not keep from stealing more and more glances at her, more than he stole at any other girl. No, he simply could not help calling on her to respond to more Bible questions than he put to any other student, girl or boy, nor could he resist asking more help of her, relative to various church activities, than he asked of other girls.

It was in stealing glances at her that she most devastated him, quite oblivious to what she was doing to him just by being herself. Not only was she lovely to look upon, not only was she exceedingly graceful when she walked or moved in any way, but she also had a disconcerting habit (to Manly) of curling up on the floor or on the ground as the occasion presented itself. The first time she did so in his presence was at a midweek evening Bible class. With the chairs all occupied when she arrived late, she simply eased herself onto the floor between the chair whereon Manly sat and the other (students') chairs arranged in a semicircular pattern before him. Propping her left cheek against her left hand (made into a fist), her left elbow on the floor, she lay at his feet looking at him unself-consciously as he expounded the Scriptures. Her right forearm dangled languidly from her right side to the floor, her right hand very nearly cupped under her right breast. She wore a fuzzy plum-colored sweater that night, which emphasized the curves of her pert breasts, and she wore blue jeans, faded, soft, inviting to the eye, inviting to the hand. With her legs drawn up a bit, it looked to Manly as though she had been poured into her pants, the curves of her legs so round, her flesh so firm, her clothes so fully packed with the tabooed treasures of love. Manly could hardly go on and could not safely steal a glance at her in mid-thought or sentence. Only when he had completed a thought, only when he had put a mental period safely behind each completed sentence did he dare look down in her direction. She was also given to doing the same kind of thing at cookouts and picnics. On a Saturday evening in the spring, toward the end of her first year, she nearly drove him to distraction as she lay first in one position then another in the light of a leaping bonfire, the patterns of light and dark, of orange and purple, of yellow and bluish-blackish gray, making her look sensuous beyond anything he had ever seen. Of that he was sure!

Claire also had the habit of propping her feet and legs up whenever she was dressed for it and could. So, quite often, she would pull an empty chair up to her, its back toward her front, and then curl her legs around its back so that her feet could nestle together on the seat of the chair in front of her. So positioned, the juncture of her curving legs made an entrancing "Y," separating her sex from Manly's famished, imaging eyes only by the thickness of her jeans and the miniscule thickness of her panties. She was, indeed, a cross to bear, forcing him to position himself in the course of his expositions so that he could see as much of the forbidden junction as possible, thus exciting and re-exciting in his heart the sin of lust. How like the tawdry days of his boyhood when he had looked at girls' crotches in cartoon strips with a magnifying glass in the hope of seeing something the naked eye had missed! In addition to the exquisite articulation of her arms and legs, hands and feet, Claire's face was as beautiful to him as Beatrice Bantry's had been (back at Calico Corners) and a lot more mature, and she was as fascinating as Tampa Rhine had been that night at the Dewmaker dance hall, but infinitely more decent, more ladylike. What a marvel she was, and a Christian, too!

Then came the summer, and she was gone. How he missed her! How he hoped against all hope that she would write to him, would contact him in some way! But, of course, she did neither. What reason had she to be in contact with him, having no idea of how he felt about her? How mortally wounded he would have been if he had known her true feelings for him at that moment. Dutiful to her parents though she generally was concerning churchgoing, and respectful toward Bro. Plumwell though she was (as she would have been to any man of God), she already thought him to be as goofy as she believed three-world creationism to be, and in time she would come to think him profoundly ignorant as well.

Manly was mutely overjoyed at seeing her again at the beginning of her sophomore year and lost no time in working to reintegrate her as fully as possible into the Holy Nation's work in Algonquin. But she was more stand-offish than she had been before, he noted sadly, and by the middle of the year had largely deserted him due to a truly dreadful happening. Anthony Starbuck Oaks made his appearance in her life, and he, in addition to being a rival, was a Catholic, all of which distressed Manly beyond words, except in prayer. She was not, however, completely lost to him, because the very fact that Bucky was intensely pious in the Catholic way while Claire was neither (being an increasingly sceptical member of a Protestant pentecostal sect) tempered their romance, limiting it to rather tentative and cautious dating during the rest of her sophomore year.

Then came the second summer of her total absence from Manly's life. Again he was plunged into excruciating desire for her, for a call, a letter, a card, any word or scrap of information indicating that she remembered him, that she thought of him, that she cared even the tiniest bit for him as a man of God, if not as a person in his own right. But, as before, he received nothing from her.

At the beginning of her junior year, he had already resolved to do something decisive, even drastic, to separate her from Bucky Oaks and the spiritual threat he posed. By that time, of course, Manly had gained an unsuspecting ally in the form of Oscar Jiminie, who saw all, heard all, knew all, and could easily be persuaded to tell all to his minister. Oscar could and would be a second pair of eyes, a second pair of ears, could and would, in fact, duplicate all kinds of senses for Manly. Claire was vaguely aware that her pastor was omnipresent on campus and that Oscar Jiminie was a permanent and comic fixture wherever she went, but she had no idea of how intently they watched her comings and goings, of how solicitously, of how exhaustingly they watched over her for reasons known in full only to Manly.

Then came Adrian DeWulf, a new and, as it turned out, an even more virulent danger to Claire Sumner than Bucky Oaks had ever been. At least that was the way Bro. Manly Plumwell saw it. First was the stab of apprehension Manly felt when he saw Claire approach Adrian tentatively, yet hopefully, at the lecture given by Chester Clydesdale, the radical theologian. Although he could not overhear their conversation, he could sense that they were bandying words and relishing every moment of it. Then the stab wound was reopened when he saw them sitting together in the cafeteria several days after Clydesdale's odious talk. From his distant seat, partly hidden by a pillar, it was impossible to know that their topic was Clydesdale's ideas, but whatever the topic, Claire's face was alternately eager, perplexed, and enlightened. Meanwhile, DeWulf's face was happy, enthusiastic, and intent, his gestures animated in an explanatory way.

Then for the first time in Manly's life, jealousy—pure unadulterated jealousy—seized him with cloying hands and clutching fingers. That happened several days after DeWulf had turned the feminist meeting (which Manly had tried to inform with God's views on womankind) into a travesty. "The heavens declare the glory of God; and the *fundament* sheweth his handywork, indeed!" Manly had hissed to himself over and again as soon as he had looked up the word. Biding his time in a certain hall in the Ad. Building where he hoped Claire would soon pass after class and where he hoped above all that she would see him and would pause to speak, he was simply ravaged by what she actually did, passing him by without so much as a nod and not only catching up with DeWulf but also whispering something in his ear, then giggling and scooting off quickly.

Following that, two more disagreeable episodes involving Manly with Claire and Adrian occurred before the end of the fall term. The first of these took place when Manly and Oscar Jiminie came upon Adrian talking to Claire and a couple of other students after class. The subject was ethics, and what DeWulf was saying infuriated Manly. Unable to suffer any more of Adrian's godless moral relativism, Manly blurted out, to the surprise of all, that he was going to pray for the professor, whereupon Adrian had fired back that prayer would be futile, because he had committed the unforgivable sin, that he had already blasphemed the Holy Ghost. In the embarrassing exchange that followed, DeWulf clearly gained the upper hand quickly and firmly. Claire and her friends, distressed by the conflict, had simply melted away. Although Manly knew that he had come out of the encounter looking good in the dog-like eyes of Oscar Jiminie, he also knew, or at least suspected most strongly, that he had been diminished in the lovely eyes of Claire Sumner.

Then came an even more embarrassing encounter. Spotting Claire with DeWulf in the distance on a wintry day doing something together (it turned out that they were feeding french fries to a squirrel), Manly had hurried up, accosting the professor spiritually, in the hope thereby of getting Claire's favorable attention. The result was that DeWulf made the accosting pastor look a fool, pointing out as he did that Manly wouldn't have to take so much on faith if only he would learn a thing or two.

Near the end of the fall term, Oscar Jiminie reported to his pastor that he had just seen Claire go into DeWulf's office (she had gone there to learn her ethics grade for the term, but Oscar didn't know that). While loitering in the hall, timing her visit for Bro. Plumwell's information, Oscar saw Bucky saunter up, glowering. Then when Claire came out, she and the hulking Bucky went off together. No news could have disturbed Manly more, the one person he loved above all others consorting with a papist and an atheist. What, oh what, could he do to set her free from their seducing, perverting influences? Well, he could pray and did, lengthily, fervently, imploringly, on bended knees.

With respect to Claire Sumner, 1961 began as badly for Manly as 1960 had ended. No sooner had the new term gotten under way than Manly had come upon DeWulf talking after class to some students (including Claire) in the Ad. Building hall about various religions and religious leaders. Trying to witness to the eternal truth of the gospel, Manly had challenged the professor by asking how come the bones of other religious leaders like Buddha and Muhammad were still in their graves whereas the bones of JEsus were not. Then DeWulf had said that that was because Jesus might not have been dead when laid in the tomb, that since he might have planned his own resurrection appearances, he had had to remain alive throughout the time involved. At that, Manly had all but fled the scene, his stomach churning, his teeth grinding.

Even worse for him was to come, however. Manly had met Claire and two of her friends while walking close to campus on a Saturday late in January. Emboldened by desperation, he had come right out and asked her testily why she had done such a thing as going to Mass with Bucky Oaks. He knew that she had done so, because the all-seeing Oscar had seen them do it on two different occasions. Unsatisfied with her answer that she had not believed any of it but had merely gone to please Bucky, he proceeded to berate her, telling her that the Catholic Church was not a full-gospel church, when who should come sneaking up behind him, nearly scaring him out of his wits, but DeWulf announcing loudly that the Holy Nation wasn't a full-gospel church either. The grilling that ensued had left Manly completely mortified. Then, as if to rub salt in his wounds, DeWulf had walked off with Claire just as though she were his girl.

Next came the devastating news, delivered by Oscar, that Claire had been put under house arrest for having been gone overnight without permission from the Coyote House. Not even the information that she had apparently broken up with Bucky could make Manly feel better or could lessen any of his suspicions about the dreadful possibility that she had spent the night with DeWulf.

Finally, Valentine's Day came, one of the most awful days in Manly's entire life. While driving through town on a pastoral call, he had chanced to see Adrian and Claire drive past. He had then followed them for several blocks through a congested part of Algonquin and did not end his pursuit until Adrian's blue Chevy wagon turned east onto Green Pond Road leading out of town. At that moment, Manly knew what he must do, and quickly.

During the weeks and months immediately preceding the Valentine's Day of 1961, Manly's love for Claire had grown progressively desperate, shattering all hope of composure. She became his waking thought each morning, his fading thought each night. Whenever his consciousness flickered

420

alive in the midnight hours, she was there, not in his bed, not filling his empty arms, not overlain by his surging body, but standing there by his bedside, not looking exactly like an angel, not standing in long white robes, not wearing a golden crown, but there, nonetheless, blessing him by her presence and promising him that one day he would, through her, know the bliss that passeth all understanding. When in fitful sleep he dreamed, it was sometimes of her, but never often enough. Once he found himself ascending a spiral staircase. She was descending it. As they passed on a landing, she extended her left hand to him, and he boldly reached out with his left hand too and clasped hers for one dreamy moment too brief to measure. But, in wakeful memory, that moment marked an epoch.

Another time, he saw her fully clothed and in no apparent pain, yet lying spread-eagled on the floor. A heavy black object, perhaps a filing cabinet, lay upon her in such a way as to cover the right side of her body, beginning at the base of her neck and extending he knew not how far. Ever so gently so as not to add to the weight pressing her against the floor, he lowered himself upon her for an instant. No word was spoken, yet somehow he knew that all was well with her, and so he departed, reassured and strangely fulfilled.

On yet another occasion, he dreamed he was standing before his easel doing a landscape in pastels. To his right was a bean-bag chair in which Claire had curled up, half sitting and half lying. Manly kept backing up to look at his picture, trying to analyze what was wrong with its composition, trying to see how to improve on it for her. Then, taking pieces of black and umber chalk, he drew a tiny, curving, bare branch high on a tree in the foreground, and, lo, the picture was perfected. Stepping back, he lay down his chalks on a table behind him, then crumpled a piece of paper in his right hand and proceeded to drop it in the wastebasket at her right. As he leaned over her to throw the paper away, Claire took his left hand and guided it first to her mountain of love and then into the valley below. Simultaneously, she pressed her warm, sculptured lips to his. At that instant Manly awoke, but not to the bankruptcy into which reality usually plunges illusion. On the contrary, the dream had been so intense and so beautiful that he believed it better than any earthly love that reality had to offer him. For a long time Manly lay perfectly still, bathed in the dream's golden light, rocked in a cradle of luminous love.

In his waking life she became omnipresent. Morning after morning after breakfast, as he commenced his daily labors of the Lord, nausea born of yearning would well up from deep within and overwhelm him. It was as though he had a kind of morning sickness, a sickness associated with a desire that resisted delivery, that would never really be born, a hopeless love that could only be in prospect and never in reality. Even after the nausea subsided, he could not speak to God in prayer without her intercepting the message. He could not commune with Christ without her supervenience. He could not prepare his sermons without her delightful distractions, could not read the Scriptures single-mindedly, so great did she dominate his thoughts, could not keep his intentions riveted on what he was doing unless what he was doing was focused on her, imaging her, trying to foresee where she would be so that he too could be there to watch over her, and increasingly to protect her from one person above all.

For reasons he did not begin to understand but which he perceived to be a secret part of God's plan for his life, Manly could express no love in word or gesture or deed to any woman even remotely his own age. With such people he was futility incarnate, and in their presence utterly vulnerable. He could gain nothing, because he could venture nothing, and could receive nothing either, even when freely offered. The slightest rejection from any eligible woman, however revocable it might have been, however transient, would have shattered his brittle self and wounded him mortally. Yet, he needed to love so much and yearned for it so desperately! If he could have been honest with himself, blasphemous though that would have been, he would have had to admit that God's love did not and could not suffice, else why was he so miserable? Bursting with desire, yet compressed with paralyzing fear, Manly was as surely imprisoned as any wretch in solitary confinement anywhere. Unable to make his bondage tolerable, he tried to make it noble by convincing himself that he had freely chosen chaste impotence so that nothing he might ever say or do could offend any woman or diminish his person in feminine sight. By some mysterious mechanism he could thereby serve the Lord JEsus, he presumed, and give Almighty God the glory due Him.

A week after the Sunday morning in January of 1961 when Bobby Duke Donough, his wife, and his son joined the Holy Nation, Claire put in her most embarrassing appearance. Manly had just left the pulpit and descended to the main floor at the front of the sanctuary. From there he gave the call of Christ to a perishing world. "If there is anyone here this morning," he said in tones gravid with emotion, "anyone who does not know the saving grace of our matchless Lord, JEsus Christ, I invite that person to come forward now to repent publicly and to confess faith in JEsus as the Son of God come down below to save our souls." Not unexpectedly, a high school girl named Josephine Wilbrand moved out into the center aisle and came weaving forward to meet Manly's outstretched hand, her eyes brimming with tears. After surveying the congregation for another expectant moment and becoming convinced that no one else would answer the call that morning, Manly turned to Josephine, gave her the right hand of Christian fellowship, looked her squarely in the eye, and said, "Do you, Claire, repent of all your sins and confess your faith in the Lord JEsus Christ for the remission of your sins?"

Josephine was dumbfounded and deeply hurt. Reverend Plumwell not only knew her name but also knew her well and knew that she would confess her faith as soon as the day came when she could find the courage to step before all those people in church. Even though her eyes were brimming with contrition, she was not about to answer for another nor to confess to sins not hers; so she stood and stared dumbly ahead, waiting for him to make it right. For his part, Manly was mortified and seemed to be falling hotly into an abyss. There before him stood a lost and fearful soul about to make the supreme confession of her immortal life, and he had misnamed her "Claire," and embarrassed her, and upset her parents, and served his Master badly. Yet, despite his consternation, he could lodge no complaint against the omnipresent Claire.

As Adrian's station wagon turned down Green Pond Road, Manly was overcome with fear, fear for himself and fear for Claire in different ways and measures. He feared that he would lose her, but he had never had her. How could one lose that which one had never had? Yet, that is how he felt. What he did have was his image of her, and though he could hardly lose that, in any ordinary way, still and all, it could be shattered and lost in a different way. How he feared that! He feared for her as though she were his child. She was not his child and was in no extraordinary danger, to all appearances at least; nevertheless, that is how he felt about her. In sad moments, he wept for her, because she was not his. In happy moments, he shouted at the trees and in the open air, "I love you so much, Claire!" "Oh, Father," he said in numerous prayers, "you have no idea how much I love her." But he did not ask God for her nor for aid in bending her to him. He sought no control over her and, beyond trying to be where she might be, made no overtures to her. He carried on imaginary conversations with her, conversations of meeting, conversations of greeting, but never conversations of parting and never, ever of farewell. But there was a parting. She had left him and in her manner of departing had shattered his image of her, leaving him utterly desolate. She was in worse than mortal danger. She was in immortal danger, and he could not truthfully say "Farewell" to her, for she could not fare well in what she had done with the apostate. Thus, he resolved to destroy Adrian DeWulf into whose arms she had gone, spiritually at least and maybe carnally as well. For once in Manly's life, however, considerations of carnality were of little consequence. It was the spiritual poison of the apostate that imperiled her.

As he turned away from the blue station wagon bearing Claire down Green Pond Road and closer and closer to everlasting hell, Manly knew that he must give himself as a ransom, not for many, but for one; that he must lay down his life, if necessary, not for his friends, but for one person and one person alone—his beloved Claire. "Greater love hath no man," he mumbled over and again as he drove back to the church, tears cascading from his eyes.

All Algonquin was astounded to learn that the Reverend Manly John Plumwell, RPPl., pastor of the local Church of the Chosen, had been arrested for the murder of Professor Adrian DeWulf. Algonquin's royal priests, new Jews, peculiar people were not only astounded, they were also appalled. Only one of them, Atherton Landis, had sufficient presence of mind to act intelligently during the first hours after the awful news broke over the community. He put through a long-distance phone call to Big Bend. When the Handmaiden herself was put on the phone, she seemed neither to hear nor to comprehend what was being said, but asked Atherton to repeat himself over and over.

When the news finally got through to her, Alice called the Five into extraordinary session. As white as a sheet and clearly rattled, she led them in prayer, more to gain time, it seemed, than to lay her burdens on Jesus. Then she told them what had happened. From that point on it took only moments to reach an initial decision. Endicott Peabody Dickinson was to fly to Algonquin at once, using the Holy Nation's executive aircraft, dubbed "The Dove" and painted purple and gold. He was to assess the entire situation, especially the legal situation, and report as soon as possible.

Thirty-six hours later, give or take a few minutes, he was back, his face ashen, his eyes running. Thereupon, there was another extraordinary session. After laying many additional facts before Alice and the brethren, Endicott said, "Brother Plumwell maintains that he will plead innocent to the charge of murdering a certain Professor Adrian DeWulf, but he admits to all and sundry—gladly, I might add—that he did execute the man in question, righteously in his view. He believes with his whole heart, firmly and without qualification, that God commanded him to destroy this professor on grounds of blasphemy. Now I hasten to add that there is no doubt that the professor was a blasphemer, and a singularly notorious one at that. Moreover, a young woman was involved."

At that, Alice gasped and the brethren looked very grim.

"But," Endicott went on, "I am happy, as I know you will be, too, and relieved beyond measure to report that Brother Plumwell's relationship to this young woman was pure, blameless, and exemplary throughout, no charge of impropriety whatsoever being possible."

This was received with audible sighs of relief all around.

With his eyes running like a poodle's, Endicott continued, saying, "Plumwell maintains that he is prepared to give himself as a ransom for this one young woman and to lay down his life for his female friend just as our Lord Jesus laid down his life for the salvation of mankind, of those that believe, that is."

Alice greeted this with a look of alarm and bade the Five at once to bow their heads in prayer. During the prayer—a lengthy one because rambling— she received a revelation to the effect that the Holy Nation was to cut all ties with the accused, to treat him henceforth as though he were no more. After her prayer she announced, "Satan has surely entered into Manly John Plumwell; therefore he is not one of us." Then, paraphrasing I Corinthians 5:5, she said, "We shall deliver him over to the state for the destruction of his flesh." And that was that. No longer a royal priest of the Holy Nation, Manly was left to fend for himself alone and to defend himself, as best he could, out of his own resources.

More surprising, perhaps, than her decisive action in denying all solace and succor to Manly was the fact that Alice cancelled her forthcoming appearance at ASU as one of the distinguished participants in the spiritual emphasis week planned for the middle of May. She cited an indisposition as her reason for cancelling but refused to elaborate on it. That act was noteworthy, because it was the only time in her long and tireless ministry that she ever failed to show up at the appointed hour at the appropriate revival tent, church house, broadcasting studio, or platform anywhere to promote God's Holy Nation.

Thus, Algonquin was denied the presence of the Lord's Handmaiden, and Manly was left to go it alone, to face his uncertain future all by himself. Algonquin survived her absence well enough, but Manly was convicted of first-degree murder and sentenced to life imprisonment, to be served, the judge decreed, in the maximum security prison at Bartauk. The jury, composed of three Catholics, three Southern Baptists, two Lutherans, two Methodists, an Episcopalian, and a member of the Church of Christ, was especially hard on him, not because of any love lost on Adrian DeWulf, but because the majority of them had it in for the Holy Nation Association of Churches of the Chosen. So, Manly, no longer a royal priest, took the rap, in part at least, for his prior association with what the jury found to be a most arrogant and disagreeable sect. Manly did not remain at Bartauk long, however, being there less than three and a half years.

Epilogue

Twenty years have passed since Sheriff Homer Podlacs lurched—quietly for him—through the communicating door between what had been Adrian's office and Rad's and took Manly down to his office for questioning. That episode, together with all that followed it, still haunts the Handmaiden. Every time she thinks of it, she also remembers the horrid incident at Calico Corners when Manly broke Jed Bantry's chamber pot. "What a caution that young man was!" she sometimes muses aloud, echoing Manly's grandmother and shaking her very white head in distaste. She also says, ever and anon, "Praise be to God that nothing really detrimental to the Holy Nation came of either incident!"

In the decade before Manly's recruitment, the Holy Nation was the fastest growing religious body in the United States. During the sixties, the rate of growth began to fall. By the end of the seventies, it had dropped a little below the growth rate of the Mormon Church, also that of the Southern Baptists. But, with a total membership of 2,137,258 at last count—and still growing substantially—the Holy Nation Association of Churches of the Chosen remains a potent force in American religion and nothing to be trifled with. "Yes, indeed, Praise the Lord Jesus that that Manly Plumwell wasn't allowed to do any substantial damage!" Alice reiterates. All in all, then, Manly seems to have had little effect one way or the other on the fortunes of God's peculiar people.

As for the Handmaiden herself, there is still much of the eternal twelve-year-old in her make-up. But the grandmotherly air that could also be discerned when she was young now predominates. In short, Alice is getting old, and, as she says, "The Lord Jesus will be taking me yonder to be with him in glory most any day now." Of more concern to the hundreds of thousands who pray for her daily than her mere mortality is the fact that while still alive she is clearly losing control of the Holy Nation.

Emmet Langhorne Van Hook and Iskander Moutsopoulos are already locked in a preliminary but titanic battle for that control. It is a classic case of brilliant scholarship and doctrinal soundness on the one side battling with

426

great showmanship and public relations expertise on the other, fervor being equally apportioned on both sides. When the Handmaiden's hand falls from the tiller, one or the other will almost certainly emerge as the spiritual leader of the Holy Nation.

Mordecai Montefiori remains a beacon of new Jewry to old Jewry, beckoning Jews to renounce the old Israel in favor of the new. In so doing, he inspires Christians enormously and heartens royal priests everywhere. Moreover, he continues to manage all the financial affairs of the Holy Nation, receiving a deluge of gifts annually, maintaining an ocean of assets, and presiding over an Amazon of disbursements. But, despite his enormous abilities, indefatigability, and good intentions, the job is too much even for him and has been so ever since the mid-seventies when he lost track of just how incredibly wealthy the Holy Nation really is. It nettles Alice that she cannot seem to pry that information out of him any longer, but she remains patient and persistent in trying to keep up with the full extent of the assets and monies in the various pipes of her great organization. Since she and Mordecai are both failing in various ways, perhaps she will never know just how great in economic terms her work for the Lord Jesus has been.

Endicott Peabody Dickinson remains a loyal trooper in the Handmaiden's army, tending most competently to the complicated legal affairs of the Holy Nation, but he is increasingly becoming a nonentity in personality and is daily overshadowed by the others who make up the Five.

Clifton Marsh Cricklet retains the architect's eye for beauty. Since this includes feminine beauty, and since he is often beset by a spirit of fornication, he is equally often in danger of falling from grace. The Handmaiden and the other four of the Five do not know how very close he came to scandalizing them all by running off with a former Playboy Bunny young enough to be his granddaughter. Since they are not tempted as he is tempted, it could be argued that he is spiritually the strongest of the lot, but they would not see it that way.

Since Rad has always tended to be a permanent fixture wherever he has gone, it is not surprising that he is still at ASU and not many years from early retirement, if he chooses that option. More than likely, he will teach on until time decrees his departure. He has always been and remains now an outdoors man, roaming around in the woods whenever possible and doing a lot of what he likes to call "creek-stomping." At odd hours and on weekends he often hops in his old pickup and heads toward his all-time favorite spot on the north shoulder of Mintonac Mountain, the highest of the Algonacs north of Algonquin. A county road inches part way up the mountain's flank. From its terminus, one must use logging roads that are little more than tracks or trails. Since an easy congeniality exists between the nature-loving hometown boy who owns most of this timbered mountain and the nature-loving people of Algonquin, town and gown, the tracks and trails remain open, weather permitting, and free to all.

Rad usually parks the pickup on a little-used spur a scant 200 vertical feet from Mintonac's top. From there, he moves off in sylvan solitude on a circuitous and rock-strewn path that leads to the mountain's north shoulder. His goal is a glen at one end of which a large spring gushes out of living rock. At first the water forms a crystalline pool, then, as though testing its strength, it dashes over ledges and roils around rocks. Next, it rushes headlong down a U-shaped concourse of naked granite extending for 300 feet or more. Finally, with pioneering abandon, it disappears from sight down a series of secret falls and inaccessible cascades until it reaches Little Honeycomb Creek, 300 feet below.

Opposite the crystalline pool there is a natural ledge of granite, which at one point is exactly chair height for a man of Rad's size. Here he sits and sets his mind free, a thinker at one with water and rock, sky and life. The place never fails to work its magic. Ideas that are hard to deliver elsewhere beg to be born here, productive reflection is bewitched into being, and ideas, like water from the rock, burble effortlessly from their own secret springs.

Though he brought Adrian to this spot only once, it is here, far more than at the office or anywhere else, that Rad communes with Adrian's shade, a shade still vital after twenty years. He now recognizes that the young philosopher marked a turning point in his thought, that he became a source of enlightenment even though Rad did not want to see what Adrian persisted in illuminating.

When Rad was a little boy back in Breathitt County, Kentucky, his mother, Hypatia Kendall Reid, used to drum it into his head that the Heavenly Father sent his Son, Jesus, only in the fullness of time. "You see, Rhadamanthus," she would say gravely, "God very carefully prepared the world for the coming of our Lord and Savior. God raised up Alexander the Great not just that Alexander might conquer the known world of the time, but so that he could spread the Greek language and Greek learning hither, thither, and yon. After all, God knew that the New Testament was to be written in Greek, and he wanted literate people the world over to be able to read it at once for the salvation of their souls. God also knew that early Christian theology, in its formative period, would be developed in the Greek language using the categories of Greek thought, so, of course, God had to see to it, didn't he? that Greek became the lingua franca of the ancient world. So, you see, Rhadamanthus, through Israel as God's pedagogue and through the Greeks as the teachers of the language of the gospel, God very carefully laid the foundation for Jesus' arrival. Isn't that inspiring?" In later years Hypatia often made the same points to Romulus and Remus, and it pleased her no end that they generally wagged their tails enthusiastically whenever she put the same rhetorical question to them.

Rad learned from a dozen or more of the pious professors at the University of Kentucky, including two in the chemistry department, that advancing science and enlightened religion (i.e., liberal Christianity) were

428

marching triumphantly together into the future. Although that thought cheered him, he felt no need to act on it and, as a matter of fact, became tepid in his religious beliefs and irregular in church attendance. Still and all, he remained congenial to the faith of his fathers and laid no straw in the path of advancing religion. At Michigan his graduate studies in logic, the theory of knowledge, and the philosophy of science took him, for the most part, far afield from religion, leaving him to view it, with increasing indifference, as a matter of personal faith alone. Nevertheless, his indifference remained on the warm side, and he continued to befriend the faithful, feeling little or no animosity to their faith systems.

This attitude followed him to Algonquin. An agnostic insofar as he cared to think about God at all and a non-churchgoer, Rad remained, nevertheless, respectful of religion and understanding of believers, especially of the kind of young believers who peopled Algonquin State University. After all, religion was a good thing, beneficial to the believer and useful to society. Moreover, in its enlightened form it was still marching triumphantly into the future with advancing science. "So, what the hell?" Rad would sometimes muse aloud, "if religion makes you happy, if it makes you feel warm and safe and good all over, go ahead and believe it." That was, very largely, the view he was upholding when Adrian came to Algonquin. Now there was one who saw things very differently! Like the Roman historian, Tacitus, Adrian took Christianity to be a pernicious superstition. He saw it as fraudulent historically, disreputable philosophically, and unsupportable scientifically. He thought it scrambled people's brains, obscured their vision, and prompted them to act, even when doing what was right, for the wrong reasons. Rad is increasingly afraid that truth is on Adrian's side, and that, going against his grain, hurts.

But Rad cannot forget the People's Temple and the grisly culmination thereof at Jonestown, Guyana, November 18, 1978. He still shudders at the thought of the mass murder of children followed by suicide excessive beyond belief—men and women, boys and girls, and babies, all dead by the disgrace of purple poison or other lethal agents, and for what? For what? The ignorance, the credulity, the lamb-like stupidity of those who did Jim Jones's bidding still nauseate him and make him in his weaker moments (or is it in his baser moments?) contemptuous of human weakness. Like most people of moderate behavior and tolerance, Rad simply cannot come to grips with the enormity of Jonestown. If Adrian had lived, he too would have been sickened and repelled, but Rad feels sure that he would not have been surprised. He would have seen it as an instance of religion only slightly on the marginal side, only slightly more berserk than usual. He would probably have said something like, "People have been murdering their minds all along for religion, so what's so unusual about a few killing their bodies as well? And like good parents, of course, they wanted to share their religion with their children." Adrian had mentioned several times in Rad's presence that religion had something to do with human unity and coalescence around dominance-submission hierarchies, that for the most part religion was a form of monarchy.

429

"But that's an empirical matter, not a philosophical one," Adrian had said, then added, "Thought alone won't get to the bottom of it, and damn it! I don't know how to design the research strategy to prove my point about the dominance-submission business." Remembering those words, still intrigued by them, Rad has sometimes tried out the basic idea they contain on some of his more trusted friends and colleagues by observing that Jonestown simply shows how superbly the subjects of King Jim carried out their monarch's bidding—perfect authority and perfect faith wedded triumphantly. With very close friends in dark moments, Rad sometimes asks, too softly to be overheard, "What difference does it make if it's God or King Jesus or the Pope or Jim Jones calling the shots?"

As Rad lounges on his rocky ledge, gazing into the crystalline pool, purple against the granite where the water emerges from the mountain, he often reflects on the unexpected problem that burst upon him (not to mention others) shortly after his election to the Algonquin City School Board in 1975. That unexpected problem also calls Adrian to mind and makes him seem to have been a prophet. At the second biweekly meeting of the board that Rad had attended in his new official capacity, a half-dozen concerned parents appeared saying that it was only fair that the public schools offer what they called the Christian alternative to the godless religion of secular humanism that was being taught in the public schools throughout the country.

In response to their contention, he said, "I know I'm new on the board, but my children have gone through the public school system in this town, so I know a thing or two about it, and I must say I've never heard of the 'godless religion of secular humanism,' so-called, being taught here."

"Oh, but it most definitely is, I can assure you," one of the concerned parents announced, looking very grave and speaking portentously.

"Yes," said a second parent, "and it's part of a nationwide conspiracy."

"A conspiracy you say? Who are the parties to this conspiracy? pray tell," said Rad in disbelief.

"Why, state boards of education, the federal government and its various funding agencies, and, of course, those humanists themselves," said the first concerned parent.

"They're simply taking over public education and brainwashing our children," said a third concerned parent.

Assuring his colleagues on the board that he really did know his place as the most junior of members and that he did not intend to hog the floor, Rad persisted nevertheless, asking, "Just how is all this happening, if indeed it is happening?"

"Well, through teaching the satanically inspired doctrines of Charles Darwin, of course," the second concerned parent declared, then hissed, "you know, evolution and that sort of thing."

A fourth concerned parent, who had kept her peace until then, all but shouted, "Why, that evolution stuff is in *everything* these days; it isn't just in the life sciences and such as that, but it's in the social sciences—why, they even mention it in chemistry—and in that part of the basic science book that talks about stars and the solar system. They even say *stars* evolved. What won't they drag in next?"

At that point, other members of the board began to find their tongues, and the remaining two concerned parents, silent until then, also found theirs. In the verbal fray that followed, some astonishing things were said, so astonishing that Rad felt like pinching himself to be sure he wasn't having a nightmare. It seems that from the moment God created the world, or maybe it wasn't until the moment, shortly thereafter, when Eve sank her rebellious teeth into the forbidden fruit, but from very early on anyway, entropy became a universal fact. What entropy did, supposedly, was to deny sufficient energy for evolutionary processes to occur. So, there couldn't be any evolution toward higher or more organized and complex states of matter, the implication being that God must have created each species of living thing on one or other of the six days of creation just as Genesis says he did, and not more than 10,000 years ago either.

At that point, a board member who was an amateur archeologist piped up, saying, "But we have carbon-14 dating that goes back beyond 10,000 years ago and the . . . the potassium-argon technique that dates some hominid fossils at well over a million years . . ."

"Those are all the snares, deceits, and delusions of Satan," said the first concerned parent, breaking in abrasively.

"Yes," chimed in the sixth, "because none of those so-called dating techniques works farther back than about 10,000 years ago."

"How on earth can you say such a thing?" asked the board member, fearing for her sanity.

"Because the Noachian flood, which according to the Bible couldn't have happened farther back than that, caused a world-wide catastrophe, that's how," said the sixth concerned parent.

"Even if there was such a thing as Noah's flood, which seems most dubious," Rad said, "I don't see what you're getting at."

"Well," said the sixth concerned parent, really warming to his topic, "science and all these dating procedures are based on uniformitarianism, on the idea that physical processes like we have today took place at the same rates in the past. But catastrophism teaches just the opposite. It teaches that the Noachian flood caused a radical discontinuity in physical processes so that no dating techniques based on the speed of today's processes can be used for dating anything that happened before the flood, and the Bible teaches that that took place about 10,000 years ago, shortly after the creation of the universe itself. So all this talk about fossils older than that is just malarkey and not true science at all."

Before the night was over, the six concerned parents, who finally identified themselves as scientific creationists, pointed out that they were being big about the whole thing, very democratic and all, because they didn't want to take over the whole curriculum of the public schools; they just wanted

431

equal time for the Christian alternative to the godless humanism being taught whenever and wherever it was being taught. They also pointed out, with the slightest hint of a threat, that a statewide referendum was being readied (via the necessary petitions) to require equal time for scientific creationism in public education and that a bill had already been pre-filed in the state, by a sympathetic legislator, requiring voluntary prayer in the public schools.

As Rad trudged home that night, feeling himself to be in never-never land, he kept mulling over what he had heard, i.e., that the teaching of evolution is religious and that the teaching of creationism, as the Bible has it, is scientific. "Curiouser and curiouser," he said aloud as he let himself into the kitchen door of his darkened home. Some of the events that followed the board meeting that night were ironic in the extreme. How Adrian would have raged, but how he would have loved it all!

The three-world creationists of the Holy Nation yield to none in their hatred of the so-called godless religion of secular humanism, and their noses are as keen as any noses in sniffing out nonexistent conspiracies between secular humanists and the various governmental establishments relative to public education. The three-world creationists also want the impact of evolution minimized, neutralized, and eventually abolished in the public schools, and they too are in favor of required voluntary prayer in those same schools. But, and it is a huge "but," they detest all other creationists including the so-called scientific creationists, because it is three-world creationism that is *really* scientific, not the heresy being peddled by any and all other biblical creationists. In Algonquin, the Reverend Gregory T. Stovall, Manly's latter-day successor at the Church of the Chosen, launched a frenetic attack on all creationists who tried to show that the water that fell on the earth, helping to create Noah's flood, came from a so-called vapor canopy in the sky. "Search Genesis," he thundered in sermons, tracts, letters to newspapers, and in debates, "and see if you can find that the water that fell in God's great judgment upon sinful men in the days of Noah came down from clouds or other atmospheric sources. No, it came through openings in the firmament (Genesis 7:11), apertures at the top of the sky under the great ocean of waters above the sky in the days of the first heaven and the first earth, and it gushed up through the earth from the great deep upon which the first earth rested. These bedeviled people who call themselves 'scientific creationists' do not take God's word literally; they do not take it seriously; they try to compromise it with modern godless science to suit themselves, to tickle their own heretical ears. And they're not satisfied to mouth their heresies in their churches; no, they want to push those heresies down the throats of innocent children in the public schools. If these perverters of God's word really want to be scientific, let them first repent the error of their ways and then accept three-world creationism, which is not only true to God's teaching in the Holy Bible but is absolutely scientific, as has been shown repeatedly. Ah, if these perverse people claiming to speak for God but actually doing Satan's nefarious work would only recognize that our present earth is the second earth, our present heaven the second heaven, then they could join us in a truly effective, God-inspired, Holy Ghost-led crusade against the 'godless religion of secular humanism' that is infesting our land, infecting our children, and leading them to eternal perdition."

And, so, the battle was joined. Yes, indeed, how Adrian would have relished seeing the three-world creationists giving the scientific creationists a dose of their own disagreeable medicine! The battle, of course, was not limited to Algonquin but began to afflict (and still does) the entire country. Apart from the black humor of the dogmatist-eat-dogmatist battle, the affliction in question does not afford much benefit to the secular humanist nor to any others who want to keep science as pure as possible and science instruction as free as possible from being perverted and politicized. It doesn't matter much whether the three-world creationists of the Holy Nation win or the scientific creationists (of whatever denomination) win; in either case the public schools will be held hostage to faith, dogmatism, and ideology. If, in the name of democracy or of elemental fairness, a religious alternative must be taught in public education to anything or everything of a scientific nature that is just too, too disagreeable to the majority's taste, then there is no end to the compromises that have to be made, and nothing to prevent America's public school instruction from becoming the laughingstock of the civilized world. If cosmic and biological evolution are to be compromised today, Rad wonders, then why not heliocentricity tomorrow? Why not put our little planet in the center of the universe where the church once thought and taught it to be? Since the Bible clearly presupposes a flat and stationary earth, why not deny the earth's sphericity in the name of biblical literalism? Since in the New Testament and in original Christian teaching alike, it is demons that cause sickness as well as sin, why not do away with the notion (no doubt a deceit of the secular humanists) that it is microorganisms, bacteria and viruses, that cause many, if not all, diseases? Away with public health and preventive medicine and back to faith healing, the laying on of hands, and anointing with oil! Pondering all these things, Rad wonders darkly where it will end, or if it can end.

He is now sure, but most reluctantly, that Jonestown is not the end of it. He is also sure that the attacks of the scientific creationists on the teaching of cosmic and biological evolution in the public schools are not the end of it, nor is the asinine counterattack of the three-world creationists on all other creationists the end of it. Rad now recognizes, most reluctantly, that multiple irrationalities are welling up out of bedrock America as surely as water is gushing from the rock in his favorite glen on Mintonac Mountain. But, at least as bad as the bubbling absurdities of sectarian religion, as bad as the mouthings of the so-called moral majority (how reminiscent of Lenin, of his gall and his Bolsheviks!), as bad as the ignorant rantings and ravings of the media's many evangelists is the dreadful fact that the youth of the eighties in the United States make up the gibbering generation: kids who, by and large, cannot read, write, speak, and think at all well, kids who cannot send or receive clear, cogent messages, kids with scrambled brains. What easy prey they are! Moreover, the students Rad encounters day by day are scientifically illiterate in the main, innocents abroad in a world they know not, a world suffused with clever but ignorant persuaders in hot pursuit of their minds and souls. Rad is more than horrified; he is despondent at the magnitude of the disaster. How, he wonders, could it have happened, and what, beyond restoring literacy, is to be done about it?

At the very least, he does not see an easy retirement ahead of him. On the contrary, it looks as though he must grapple with the very thing he would most of all like to forget and simply leave alone—*religion!* Horror of horrors, it looks as though he must fight as he has never fought before, lugging the armaments of philosophy to the aid of embattled science and near-sighted scientists who don't know what is happening to them. Yes, he decides, the weapons of analysis, of logic, must all be dragged down from the empyrean clouds where they usually repose to the grimy, gritty earth where religious con men, zealots, and lunatics are afoot, where delusions multiply and abound, and where the hard-built structures of human knowledge are being eaten away by the acid rains of religion. It is not a battle he relishes—as Adrian did— and it is one, he knows, that can be fatal. That is, after all, what happened to Adrian. He was caught up in a faith fight and fell victim to credulity, to credulity rampant, to credulity rampant on a field of red.

Manly was not simply set free from the penitentiary at Bartauk (after only three and a half years), nor was he given early parole for exemplary behavior; no, he simply went stark raving mad and was transferred in accordance with state regulations to the hospital for the criminally insane at Mandan Springs.

Questions regarding his sanity were, of course, raised almost immediately after his arrest and quick admission that he had indeed executed Adrian DeWulf—but righteously. In an oblique way, the Handmaiden and the Five had dealt with the question by maintaining that Satan had entered into Manly John Plumwell, that he was, therefore, no longer one of the Holy Nation. His attorney also raised the question, even suggesting that Manly's plea should be "not guilty by reason of insanity," but Manly would have none of that. His stout insistence that he was sane, his lucidity (exhibited by his continued articulateness), and the consistency of the fairy tale of faith in which he lived convinced all and sundry that he knew what he had done and that he was competent to assist in his trial for the murder of Adrian DeWulf.

Although he felt no guilt over killing Adrian but continued to feel that he had done that which was right in the sight of the Lord, Rad's ploy (which Manly took seriously) had pierced him to the very marrow of his bones. How awful it was that he had not stoned the apostate as God would have had him do it! His bungling, innocent though it had been, together with the bad name of arrest and trial, would, he knew, be an offense against his flock. Some who were weak in faith, who were not yet ready to take the solid food of the gospel, might stumble and fall because of him, might forever miss the chance for salvation, not because he had done wrong in striking down the evil of blasphemy, not because he had sinned in offering himself as a ransom for a beloved friend, but because his bungling, brought on by haste, had given the devil a new occasion on which to work his wiles on the weak. Let the Handmaiden and the Holy Nation reject him if they would, he would not reject them, nor would he ever cease being a royal priest. These and similar thoughts consumed him throughout his trial.

Manly had not been incarcerated long before the Catholic, Protestant, and Jewish chaplains at Bartauk became aware of a new and potent rival. Manly, it seems, was the same old Manly: if sane, as sane as ever, if mad, no madder than before. In season and out, he preached the gospel of three-world creationism insistently, urgently, reproving, rebuking, and exhorting inmates and prison personnel alike, and, last but not least, undercutting Bartauk's institutional chaplains with slashing attacks on their manifold heresies. Impervious to their early requests to cease and desist and to their later demands that he knock it off, adamant even in the warden's face, he persisted, like any true soldier of the cross. Not even the fights that developed because of his zeal nor the beatings he received at the hands of other inmates daunted him. Indeed, these merely made him feel more like St. Paul than ever and magnified his boasting. In the end, there was nothing to do but to transfer him to a facility more appropriate to his case than was Bartauk.

When Manly arrived at Mandan Springs, he supposed the hospital compound to be his new parish; its denizens, employees and inmates alike, to be his new flock. Perhaps it was the Handmaiden's doing; no, it must be her doing, he decided, else he would not have arrived at that place constrained and compelled by the Great Commission to preach Christ and him crucified to the folk there. Manly's new parish, however, proved to be desperately daunting, a flock made up exclusively of black sheep, it seemed. He was conspicuously unsuccessful in rescuing the warden, who was Catholic, from popery. He also failed miserably to preach JEsus as the TRUE MESSIAH, foretold in Hebrew prophecy, to the chief psychiatrist, who was an agnostic of Jewish extraction. Whenever Manly raised the issue of religion with him, the psychiatrist would say that he knew nothing about it and would move onto some other topic. Manly had never before required potential converts to know anything about religion. It was enough that he, Manly, knew all that was necessary about the one true religion. But his potential convert would, maddeningly, change the subject every time Manly brought it up and did so with no hint of bad conscience or of need for salvation. Nor was Manly any more successful in dislodging his Mormon handlers from their Mormonism, in enticing his Adventist nurses from their Adventism, in delivering his various counselors from their whateverism. As for his peers, although he did not recognize them as such, what a gaggle of misfits and malcontents he found them to be! Some were so vacant that he could not plant the words of eternal life in them at all; indeed, they often seemed so despairing of the present that eternity held no allure for them whatsoever. Others merely gibbered at him, proof positive that Satan had beaten him to this place and clouded their minds. But, worst of all, some were even more zealous than he in the propagation of faith and much more intimidating.

One of the blackest of the black sheep among whom he had been called to dwell was a Black Muslim, once named Rote Jim Gillian but renamed Muhammad Ali Hasan, a former wrestler who had killed two perfidious prostitutes by systematically breaking them to pieces. He had also disemboweled a lady friend. With all the delicacy and grace of a pile driver, this powerful proselytizer of Blacks and the bane of Christian Whites kept thundering out thickly, "La ilaha illa Allah: Muhammad rasul Allah," without benefit of translation. Upon hearing Manly's brave confession of faith in God the Father, God the Son, and God the Holy Ghost, Muhammad Ali Hasan accused him menacingly of polytheism, of believing in three gods. This was followed by what sounded to Manly vaguely like Scripture:

> Surely, they are disbelievers who say, "Lo, Allah is one of three." For, there is no God but the One. If disbelievers do not stop from saying this, a painful doom shall befall them.

"The Holy Qur'an, chapter 5, entitled 'The Table Spread,' verse number 73," yelled Muhammad Ali Hasan, tensing his muscles ominously. After that he accused Manly of the deceitful belief that God had begotten a son of the Virgin Mary:

> Anybody who says that the Beneficent One has begotten a son utters a loathsome falsehood at which the very heavens are all but torn asunder, the earth rent, and the mountains pulverized to dust. Oh, that a person should dare ascribe a son to the Beneficent, when it is not appropriate that he should beget one!

"The Holy Qur'an, chapter 19, entitled 'Mary,' verses 89 through 92," yelled Muhammad Ali Hasan, his voice rising to concert pitch. That was followed by the dire prediction that Manly would have to eat the hideous fruit of the terrible tree called Ez-Zakhoum if he did not mend his ways:

> Behold the tree of Ez-Zakhoum, food for evil doers, like molten copper seething in their bellies as boiling water bubbles ("taste this," it shall be said); take him, propel him into the depths of Hell, then pour upon his head, drenching it, the torments of seething water.

"The Holy Qur'an, chapter 44, entitled 'Smoke,' verses 43 through 48," Muhammad Ali Hasan yelled yet again, trying to browbeat Manly. And, so it went, with various permutations, year after year.

Just as the hunter is not usually, if ever, pleased to become the hunted,

436

so the quoter of Scripture is not usually, if ever, pleased to become the one against whom it is quoted. Manly was dumbfounded, utterly speechless, no suitable passages of God's word ever coming to mind, but he could not have been heard over the booming and aggrieved voice of his assailant in any case. It was all he could do to hold his ground against that willful heathen who kept calling him (him of all people!) an infidel and an idolater. Moreover, Muhammad Ali Hasan threatened repeatedly to break Manly up in much the same way as he had disposed of the two perfidious prostitutes. Thus daunted, intimidated, and balked at every turn, a change began to come over Manly. His former brethren in the Holy Nation could never have predicted nor understood the change in question, but those who are wise in the ways of religion will not be altogether surprised at what happened.

Manly now writes mountains of short letters, secretly he thinks, addressed simply to THE GOVERNMENT or sometimes to THE SOVEREIGN POWER, Washington, D. C. The content of these letters remains much the same and reveals a preoccupation with miscegenation. He writes as follows:

Greetings:
I, Manly J. (for John) Plumwell, am duty bound to report to THE GOVERNMENT that Blacks are marrying Indians in our parts, and even one Chinese.

Esteemed SOVEREIGN,
I, Manly J. Plumwell, am obligated to inform you that snakes are cohabiting with turtles around here. Offensive though even a rare case of this kind would be, it has now become common. I am alarmed. Please send help at once.

Hail to the GOVERNING POWER:
Manly J. Plumwell believes it his duty to report to the GOVERNING POWER that rats and squirrels are, all too often, locked in carnal embraces here at Mandan Springs. Please send instructions. The persons who are in charge here may be in collusion in this matter.

Between outbursts of epistolary activity, Manly spends a lot of time preparing to receive sovereigns. Most often the sovereign is political rather than religious, judging from Manly's chatter. But sometimes a five-star general seems to be expected or perhaps a Sea Lord, to use a British term. Beyond the ordinary "divinity that doth hedge a king," the long-awaited sovereign does not seem to be a messiah in the usual religious sense. Those who monitor Manly's state of mind find this peculiar. When the arrival of the sovereign is imminent, he pays especial attention to his attire, tries to polish his shoes, practices saluting, and may be inferred to inspect invisible guards of honor. Manly is very deferential on these occasions and appears to aspire to nothing higher than being the best of conceivable underlings, a running dog of monarchy. He even makes awkward attempts at what looks like genuflecting, something he never did ritually as a soldier of the cross.

When he is not reporting blatant acts of miscegenation to THE SOVER-EIGN POWER or making ready for manifestations of that sovereignty, Manly launches into spirited harangues in which he appears to be justifying himself for something or other—anything, really, except for his actual short-comings. Indeed, he is so dependable in this particular that he is paraded before students from criminology classes at Algonquin who make an annual pilgrimage to Mandan Springs to study various sorts of criminally insane people. Before putting their prize exhibit of this sort on display, the warden, or the chief psychiatrist, will say something like: "Now, students, watch the next inmate brought before you. When asked any question about which he might feel defensive, he will launch into a kind of sales pitch, will promote himself in some way or other." Then Manly is led in. He is pasty-faced, thin, and ragtag in appearance. He sits down and eyes the students a bit furtively until the warden or the psychiatrist says, "And why are you here, sir, could you tell these visitors that?" Then Manly, as though on cue, rises, looks animated, halfway seems to sense a congregation before him, reaches out for an invisible lectern, and launches into a spirited narration that makes it seem that he saw a painful duty to come to Mandan Springs, left a prosperous career with many attractive options behind, and responded to a great need to help others, a need which he has dealt with so well that it no longer exists as a problem. He remains on, it seems, for other pressing reasons, but these are no more clearly delineated than is the nature of his former attractive work in the outside world. He never mentions his relatively recent discoveries in the various areas of miscegenation and never lets on to these annual visitors that he expects THE SOVEREIGN to arrive at any moment at Mandan Springs. These are his secrets for the time being; perhaps he will reveal them to an unsuspecting but grateful world in his own good time.

It is quite likely that Manly does not know that he is in a state hospital for the criminally insane, nor why he, of all people, is there. He never speaks of Adrian, even in anger, never yearns for Claire, as far as anyone can tell, and never adverts to his life at Algonquin in service of the Holy Nation. He remembers his grandmother and the Handmaiden only sporadically. God and Jesus are of interest to him only to the extent that they have some part to play in the general fact of sovereignty. His life in the ministry seems to be forgotten. For Manly, each day is like every other day, and each day will afford him time aplenty, until his days are over, in which to serve sovereignty, in which to report miscegenation, and in which to justify himself over and again for everything except the real mistakes of his life. While still very young, he murdered his own mind so as to enjoy the salvation of certitude. He aspired to serve a sovereign who would permit him to superimpose his own powerful will upon others while appearing to be a mere servant. In striking down the one who disbelieved in his gracious sovereign, and said so spiritedly, Manly was no more than a Myrmidon.

The remains of Adrian DeWulf lie in a wind-swept cemetery on the outskirts of Valentine, in the sand hills of Nebraska. No one visits his grave. Only the alumni office at Columbia thinks him still alive. The headstone that marks his desolate grave is small, the least expensive permanent marker his parents could find. From an early time in his life onward, Adrian had a sense of destiny, believing that he would do something really significant with his life, thinking that his name would live after him.

Claire Sumner, Ph.D., now lives in San Jose, California. She is a clinical psychologist, humanistic in orientation. She specializes in marriage counseling, in the treatment of sexual dysfunctions, and in community mental health. Now and again, she badly needs a dose of her own medicine, but that is hard to get down, partly because her one and only husband will swallow none of it. Although she practices under her maiden name, she has been married for seventeen years and has two teen-age children. At best, her marriage is only average as are her relationships with her children. By today's standards this means that she suffers a good deal of misery, episodically at least, and sometimes enduring distress.

When she is feeling down, really down, when her self-esteem is scuttled, when she faces a prolonged struggle to recover her zest and sense of worthiness, she sometimes goes to a certain shelf in her office and takes down a small book, a secret book, which she confesses never to have read. It is Plato's *Symposium*. Adrian once told her that it was the greatest work on love ever written. She remembers how enthusiastic, how uncharacteristically mystical, he would become when talking about it and how he hoped that one day she would come to love it even as he did. But in the early years after his death, she could not find the heart to look at it, and it was never required reading at any point in her psychology curriculum. Although she still says, if asked, that she must read it someday, she doubts secretly that she will ever do so. Perhaps she does not need to.

When she turns to the book she opens only its front cover. She does this in order to read and reread the inscription he wrote thereon, and that is enough. It says:

> To Claire, the one who, lovely of form but lovelier still of spirit, let me, through her precious Being, participate in the Beautiful and caused me to cherish her more for the Person she is than to love her for anything she has done or will ever do.
>
> Adrian

Tears no longer flood her eyes when she reads the inscription. Quite the contrary, a smile plays upon her lips as, in loving recollection, she draws nourishment from those words whose inspiration she does not know. They call to mind how confident of self and robust of spirit she used to be when he would tell her over and again that except for growing up, except for maturing, he hoped that she would never change but would always be as she had been when first they had loved. Bolstered by these words and heartened by these memories, the self she likes to think of as her real self flourishes and emerges from the doldrums to confront life anew. In so doing, she confers on him his highest immortality.

Adrian died too soon to be deathless in any other way. He ceased to be before he had begotten any great thought, before he had solved any philosophical riddle, before he had made any significant contribution, before he had built any enduring monument. Yet because of him there is a woman, still of queenly carriage, who realizes a part of his potential in addition to the potential he had discerned in her and had only begun to nurture when his life ended.

It is not that she learned only what he taught, that she recapitulates only his knowledge, duplicates only his thoughts, or parrots only his maxims. She never was a mere receptacle for his overflowing funnel, nor is she his clone nor his child, yet because their paths crossed for a time and merged for a moment, because he taught with Platonic eros, because they intended, if only briefly, to confront the world together so long as life should last, she came to see the world differently, to think about it, to act within it, to expect of it, and to hope for it in ways that might otherwise have eluded her, to her detriment, she firmly believes. His carnality begot no child upon her, yet the seed of his courage is within her. His mocking assaults on pious fraud and cant purchased her freedom, a freedom she defends fiercely and, whenever possible, invites others to seize and have for themselves.

His eyes no longer see, but because they saw for a season with glittering intensity, she believes herself able to penetrate superficialities, to see through banalities, to discern deep structures that had been opaque to naive girlhood and, but for him, might have remained indiscernible to womanly maturity. He was tough-minded, and courageous, and insensitive, but neither cynical nor despairing. All in all, he was for Claire a raging contagion. That contagion is, to be sure, diminished nowadays, its virulence attenuated, but it lives on; and in ways more loving and more effective than any he could ever have expressed or devised, she also seeks out those who are susceptible to intelligence, even as she had been susceptible (though hardly aware of it) when Adrian came to Algonquin.